You will make a spectacle of yourself, even if you succeed, Morning Song's inner voice warned and, briefly, she hesitated. But only briefly. Within seconds, she was striding forward, heedless of her nakedness and of the curious glances she was reaping. When her bare toes were within inches of the hearth, she crouched low, then launched herself across the heat-gorged embers contained by the ring of red-hot stones.

It was an act of desperation, and one that might well have ended in disaster or, at the very least, ignominy. Yet it did not. Morning Song released her pent breath and unflexed her knees to land neatly on the balls of her feet, directly in front of a clearly astonished Cloud Racer.

She was incapable of speech. Mutely she held out her hands to him. Mutely he grasped them and allowed her to pull him erect. Nor did he speak as he freed himself long enough to strip down to his own breechclout. Then his hands were clasping hers once more and, incredibly, he was following her into the undulating line of men and maidens already Shaking the Bush with uninhibited vigor.

Also by Kate Cameron
Published by Ballantine Books:

AS IF THEY WERE GODS

ORENDA

A Novel of the Iroquois Nation

Kate Cameron

BALLANTINE BOOKS · NEW YORK

Copyright © 1991 by Kate Cameron

All rights reserved under International and Pan-American Copyright Conventions. Published in the United States of America by Ballantine Books, a division of Random House, Inc., New York, and simultaneously in Canada by Random House of Canada Limited, Toronto.

Library of Congress Catalog Card Number: 91-92192

ISBN 0-345-35690-X

Manufactured in the United States of America

First Edition: December 1991

For Chuck, Rich, and Mary Ann

Whatever paths you choose, may you always learn from where you've been, take pleasure in where you are, and walk with confidence into the future.

Preface

I have tried, within the confines of this novel, to present a true picture of those seventeenth-century Native Americans whose blood ties them to the tribes known collectively as Iroquois. Because I wanted to incorporate customs and traditions peculiar to more than one of the Five Nations, I have refrained from naming the inhabitants of Morning Song's village Seneca, Mohawk, Cayuga, Onondaga, or Oneida; they are, quite simply, People of the Longhouse.

Where I have used original Iroquois legends, I have done my best to be faithful to them. And while I tried hard not to misinterpret in any area, I do confess to simplifying the histories of wars, treaties, and other landmark events of the period; I did not want a complexity of facts to dominate a work of fiction or, possibly, to confuse the reader.

The considerable research I undertook before writing the first word of *Orenda* left me with enormous admiration for the Iroquois people. Washington Irving said, "It has been the lot of the unfortunate aborigines of America, in the early periods of colonization . . . [that] their characters have been traduced by bigoted and interested writers." In many instances, this happened with the Iroquois; in others, they were romanticized to a ridiculous degree. I have attempted, by focusing on a single small village, to show the Iroquois *as people*, to address their strengths without ignoring their weaknesses, to foster an awareness of how much the Europeans might have learned from them had they restrained their own urge to conquer and subjugate, and to steal land that was by right the Indians'. (In the beginning, the ten-million-acre Iroquois Territory extended from Montreal southward and included all of upper New York State.)

It is fairly common knowledge that the union of the New World's colonies and, subsequently, the Constitution that made it binding, owed much to precedents set by the remarkable Iroquois Confederation, an alliance entered into about 1570 that—in necessarily diminished form—exists to this day. Yet our ancestors made little effort to understand those they labeled savages. If they had, they might have benefited further by adopting their ideas: on child-rearing, on the political power of women, on reverence for the land, on the importance of a personal code of honor, and on the courtesy and generosity that spread beyond neighbor and clan to embrace the stranger who came among them.

The rewards for all of us could have been great if the early settlers had been wise enough to walk for a time in the moccasins of the Iroquois.

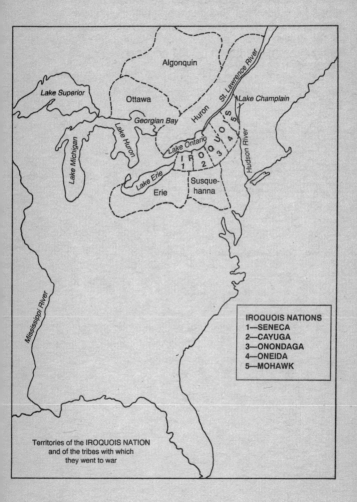

IROQUOIS NATIONS
1—SENECA
2—CAYUGA
3—ONONDAGA
4—ONEIDA
5—MOHAWK

Territories of the IROQUOIS NATION
and of the tribes with which
they went to war

The Clans in This Story

It will help the reader if he or she is made aware that the Iroquois society was a matriarchy. A man moved to his wife's lodge when they married, but he never became a member of her clan. Children, on the other hand, always belonged to their mothers' clans, never to their fathers'. Each longhouse was occupied by a single clan and by the husbands of the women of that family. Please note below that I have listed husbands with their birth clans, but added in parentheses the names of the longhouses they married into.

The longhouses of Morning Song's village at start of story (1642):

TURTLE CLAN:
Teller Of Legends, Matron (b. 1600) (widowed)
  Hearth Tender (b. 1616)
  Bountiful Harvest (b. 1619) (m. Covers His Eyes, SNIPE)
    Pumpkin Blossom (b. 1637)
    Day Greeter (b. 1641)
  Summer Maize (b. 1620, d. 1642) (m. Pierre Entite)
    Morning Song (b. 1637)
  Otter Swimming (b. 1632)
Se-A-Wi, Sachem (b. 1597) (m. into PLOVER lodge)

DEER CLAN:
Dancing Water, Matron (b. 1589) village's Chief Matron (widowed)
  Rain Singing (b. 1619) (m. Trail Marker, BEAR)
    Cloud Racer (b. 1634)
    Fox Running (b. 1635)
    Small Brown Sparrow (b. 1638)
Fierce Eagle, War Leader (b. 1615) (widowed)

WOLF CLAN:
Weeping Sky, Matron (b. 1613) (m. Far Seer, PLOVER)
  Woodpecker Drumming (b. 1633)
  Sun Descending (b. 1635)
Spear Thrower (b. 1609) (m. into SNIPE lodge)

PLOVER CLAN:
Sweet Maple, Matron (b. 1603) (m. Se-A-Wi, TURTLE)
  Tree Reaching Up, her niece (b. 1629)
  Deer Caller, her nephew (b. 1631)
    Hill Climber, her grandson (b. 1634)
Far Seer (b. 1612) (m. into WOLF lodge)

PIGEONHAWK CLAN:
Owl Crying, Matron (b. 1601) (m. Puma Walking Soft, BEAR)
  Stag Leaping (b. 1633)
Follows the Signs (b. 1593) (m. into BEAR lodge)

BEAR CLAN:
Lake On Fire, Matron (b. 1593) (m. Follows The Signs, PIGEON-HAWK)
    Hawk Hunting, her grandson (b. 1631)
  Trail Marker, her nephew (b. 1609) (m. into DEER lodge)
Puma Walking Soft (b. 1598) (m. into PIGEONHAWK lodge)

BEAVER CLAN:
Snow Comes Early, Matron (b. 1607) (widowed)
  Meadow Brook, her granddaughter (b. 1636)
Three Feathers (b. 1602) (widowed)

SNIPE CLAN:
Gray Squirrel, Matron (b. 1609) (m. Spear Thrower, WOLF)
Loon Laughing (b. 1615) (widowed)
  Bear In The Sky (b. 1634)
Covers His Eyes (b. 1616) (m. into TURTLE lodge)
Long Canoe (b. 1610) (m. into BEAR lodge)

SONG OF PRAISE

Every seed that sends down roots
and puts out leaves to greet the sun
honors its orenda.

Every fish that swims upstream
or keeps to shallows near the shore
honors its orenda.

Every bird that spreads its wings
and rides the currents of the air
honors its orenda.

Every beast the forest knows
that bears its young in lair or den
honors its orenda.

The people of the Iroquois,
walking proud upon the earth,
honor their orenda.

Now we praise the Maker of Life
who from his own orenda
made blade of grass and mighty oak,
creatures wearing gills & fins,
feathered beings that can fly,
fox and deer and wolf and mouse,
and all the Longhouse People.
To each he gave a spirit-self:
                    orenda.

Chapter 1

The laughter frightened her the most. The sound was alien to her ears, and the continual babble of voices puzzled her too. The old woman's voice was as dark and strong as the eyes flanking her beak of a nose; the other women's voices were higher and lighter, and difficult to tell apart. Shrill chatter from the children offered contrast, especially to the rumbling of the men. Unlike the women, whose words gushed like rain, the men's low-pitched utterings were doled out in careful measure. Many days passed before the interweaving of all these voices formed patterns Morning Song could recognize as conversation.

It took her longer to identify and separate the people who lived in the longhouse with a turtle carved over the entrance. It was hard enough to grasp that these strangers were somehow family, harder still that here was where Morning Song belonged. Her mother had said so, and she never doubted that Summer Maize spoke the truth.

She wished that her mother might have told her more before her fever-bright eyes dulled and the flesh melted from a body already painfully thin. But she had not, and now she never would. Morning Song had understood only too well the chant of sorrowing that signaled Summer Maize's dying.

Had there been but one bewilderment for the child to cope with—the complex plaiting of voice-spun fibers, or the awesome death ceremony—the child's awareness might have expanded to absorb the unfamiliar. Acceptance—even of her mother's death—would have stretched her fledgling emotions and awarded them new dimension. But terror spawned by confusion had seized control of her world.

In desperation, she curled in upon herself and wove silence like a protective cocoon securely around her.

Bountiful Harvest tipped the winnowing basket over the pot that hung above the fire and directed a stream of meal into boiling water. The sifted corn cleft the steam and penetrated the heaving surface.

"It may be that the spirit of my sister's child rejects the language of the Longhouse People," she said, wielding a worn paddle expertly. "I have heard that such rebelliousness often deprives the offender of the power to hear and speak."

Ten-year-old Otter Swimming tossed chunks of bear meat into the hominy and turned to their mother. The smile that generally lit Otter's features had retreated before a frown that drew together her crow-feather brows. "But Morning Song *can hear*, at least," she protested. "When He-No spoke in his thunder voice last night, she woke at his first bellow. I felt her trembling."

Callused fingers tested the huckleberries drying in the basket near the hearth before Teller Of Legends responded. "My granddaughter hears as well as you or I," she confirmed. Compassion softened the jet of her tilted eyes as she glanced toward the bed Morning Song shared with her youngest mother-aunt. The tiny girl huddled in the far corner of it, as though fearing to take more space than she should. "And it is my feeling that she can also speak. If she could not, Summer Maize would have told us."

Her firstborn daughter nodded agreement and leaned closer to the fire she had been feeding. Its glow painted the flesh hugging the prominent bones of Hearth Tender's narrow face. "Hers is not an arrogant spirit, but a troubled one," she put in quietly.

Bountiful Harvest knocked the stirrer against the rim of the pot and regarded her older sister with exasperation. "You would have us believe that anyone who misbehaves does so because his spirit is troubled," she pointed out. "I respect you as a Keeper Of The Faith, Hearth Tender, but surely there are those who act wrongly out of willfulness. Or from a wish to annoy."

Otter's outraged squeal brought three dark heads swiveling around, and she looked an apology to her mother before she loosed the words hovering on her lips. "You cannot mean you think Morning Song is being willful!" she said fiercely, and Teller Of Legends's long mouth quirked as she marked how this daughter sprang to the little one's defense. She had been hoping that Otter Swimming's instinctive love for the child would help to heal that troubled spirit Hearth Tender had spoken of; here was proof that it might have grown strong enough to do so.

Bountiful Harvest came to sit in the circle formed by her mother and sisters. Her face—the most beautiful of the four whose similarity revealed their kinship—was flushed from the heat, and the flawless copper of her complexion was heightened along her elegant cheekbones. Her sable-fringed almond eyes met her mother's briefly before they traveled to young Otter's face. "You are like the she-wolf whose cub has been threatened," she said soothingly. "Of course I meant no such thing. But even you must admit that this child is different from other children."

"Her years in the north were not happy ones, and she has lost her mother," Otter began, then fell silent as Bountiful Harvest shook her head sadly.

"What of the way she holds fast to you when we bathe each morning? My Pumpkin Blossom, and others even younger, beg to linger until the sun is high. Yet the daughter of Summer Maize coils around you like a timid snake whenever you approach the river."

"The river they lived beside may have been icebound in all seasons," the young girl offered weakly, but even she could not imagine such a possibility. Nor could she deny that Morning Song's small hands clutched at her whenever Otter carried her into the shallows. At first she had welcomed the way the child burrowed her silky head between breasts just beginning to bud. She would fold her arms around the frightened girl and whisper comforting words to her. But the river that girded two sides of their village was ordinarily a lazy one, its sun-sparkled water slow-moving and friendly. Leaves drifted on its serene surface, and tiny fish darted back and forth among them. There was nothing here to cause terror, nothing at all.

"Her spirit is troubled," Hearth Tender, her brooding gaze fixed on the flames, insisted. "If she would only speak, and tell me what she dreams of, I might be able to send away the demon that plagues her."

Teller Of Legends sighed and looked again at the child on Otter's bed. She had not moved in all the time they had been discussing her. She would sit up and eat when a bowl was put into her hands, and she would walk outside to relieve herself without waiting until Otter, bent on the same mission, was ready to do so. But she remained indifferent to her clan kin. Not even the coaxing of Pumpkin Blossom—who, like Morning Song, had been born five summers ago—won so much as a flicker from those tobacco-brown eyes.

"If only Summer Maize had told us more about their life in the Frenchman's cabin," she murmured. "We know so little beyond the fact that this taker of pelts called Pee-Yare On-Tee-Tay was cruel to my daughter because she could not give him the sons he hungered for."

"My sister felt shame for having turned her back on our clan to follow after such a man," Bountiful Harvest said. "And rightly."

Her mother's voice was mildly reproving. "It has happened before, that a maiden has chosen unwisely. And shall again."

Bountiful Harvest tossed her head and her mouth set itself in an unbecoming line. The bold warrior she had taken for a husband later proved himself a coward, but she fought to walk tall despite that enduring embarrassment. She looked to where Day Greeter, her second daughter, slept in a hammock suspended over her parents' bed. Girl-children were prized by the Longhouse People, but it was a man-child Bountiful Harvest longed for now. Someone to step into the moccasins of her mother's brother when they became empty. And Se-A-Wi was no longer young; if the village's next Sachem was to be of Teller Of Legends' lineage, Bountiful Harvest must make haste to conceive a son.

"We cannot even be certain that Morning Song is truly Summer Maize's daughter," she said suddenly. "My sister's womb might have been cursed. Morning Song may well be an Algonquin babe that she adopted."

"No Eater Of Trees would permit one of their children to be raised by People of the Longhouse," Teller Of Legends replied. "There is no treaty of peace between our tribe and theirs."

"The child could have been abandoned," Bountiful Harvest persisted. "It is no secret that the Algonquin are savages. Or perhaps she was the sole survivor of one of our raids. She resembles none of us who are supposedly her kin."

There was a small silence. It was true that Morning Song, with her birdlike arms and legs, could not be described as sturdy; that her skin was more bronze than copper, and her nose noticeably shorter than was common. Her eyes, set farther apart than most, were not at all heavy-lidded. And the delicate brows above them lacked even a promise of the winglike majesty that marked the faces they were accustomed to.

"Her hair forms an arrowhead above her nose, just as ours does," Otter Swimming ventured at last, "even if it is finer-spun. And if ever she learns to smile, I think we will see that she has a look of our mother in her face."

Teller Of Legends patted the clenched hand resting in the lap of Morning Song's self-appointed defender. "You must allow for the part of her that is *Onondio*," she told Bountiful Harvest. "We have never before seen what happens when the blood of a white man is blended with ours. And Summer Maize herself was not so solidly built as some." She held out one firm-muscled arm and eyed it ruefully. "My mother claimed I must have sprung from an acorn, to be everywhere shaped to imitate the oak."

She waited until the chuckles of the others applauded her jest before releasing her own smile. That smile relaxed her deeply incised mouth and told Otter that words she had spoken on impulse might eventually be seen as prophetic: Grandmother and granddaughter did indeed share that most enviable of features—a mouth made for laughter. And it would not be the fault of Otter Swimming if Morning Song did not soon learn to laugh and prove her right.

The little girl peeked through her lashes as Covers His Eyes shambled into the longhouse and seated himself beside Bountiful Harvest's hearth. As usual he said nothing, but only grunted when his wife ladled hominy into his bowl and pushed it at him. She said nothing, either. Morning Song suspected that this might be a relief to the only man in the village whose home was the Turtle Lodge. Other men were in and out, of course. Some were warriors, with smooth skin glistening on both sides of the narrow ruffs of hair that arced from crown to nape. Those men seemed always to be planning a hunt or a raid into Huron Territory, or trading boasts about one just ended. Morning Song had become aware that each hoped Teller Of Legends might choose to weave his exploits into one of her stories. But Se-A-Wi, her grandmother's brother, came most often to the longhouse. Unlike the rest, this quiet-spoken man with the kindly eyes never alarmed her. His concern for his people was carved like a benevolent mask upon a weather-roughened face; not even his jutting nose made it threatening. The coarse hair that straggled to his shoulders was streaked with gray, yet he walked so tall and stood so straight that Morning Song never doubted he had once been a warrior.

Covers His Eyes had been one, too, although what name the man had answered to when Bountiful Harvest took him as mate, Morning Song did not know. But she had overheard enough to learn how he had earned the name he wore now. He'd been with a hunting band tracking deer when they had stumbled upon an ill-tempered bear. His comrades promptly brought up lances to attack. Covers His Eyes had fumbled his weapon, and dropped it just as the bear rose on its hind legs and let out a ferocious growl. He'd made no attempt to retrieve his lance, but had clapped both hands over his eyes and huddled, shivering, in the considerable shadow of the enraged animal. The others had distracted the bear and slain it, saving his life.

Morning Song understood, in her child's way, that his display of cowardice had been his undoing. But those who sit still and listen are privy to much that others miss. She had come to realize that the biting comment poured on his head by Bountiful Harvest had done more than his own craven spirit had to demoralize Covers His Eyes. From time to time, she felt sorry for him.

"Morning Song."

The greeting came from Otter Swimming, the one who never failed to comfort her if she woke in the night, the one whose smile held more warmth than the sun Otter saluted each morning as *our older brother*. Behind her lurked Pumpkin Blossom, staring curiously at her cousin out of eyes as intriguingly slanted as her mother's were.

Otter plopped down on the floor beside the bed, pulled Pumpkin Blossom down beside her, and tossed into the air a clutch of straws she'd cut from the tassel stems of harvested corn. "We are going to play a game," she announced as the straws fell into an untidy heap. She turned to Pumpkin Blossom. "The rules are to pick up one at a time, but you may do so again and again so long as you never make a second straw move when you grab. As soon as this happens, it will be my turn to pick up. And after that"—she grinned and looked straight into Morning Song's closed face—"it will be Morning Song's turn."

Ignoring the lack of response, Otter Swimming signed to Pumpkin Blossom to begin, then watched the child's hesitant fingers reach out and close around the tip of the nearest straw. When she'd pulled it clear, Pumpkin Blossom looked smugly at her mother-aunt.

Otter was unperturbed. "That is only one," she said, "and little reason to feel triumph."

But when a second straw, and then a third, was successfully retrieved, Otter Swimming put on a scowl. "You are supposed to leave some for Morning Song and me to pick up!" she grumbled, but both little girls knew that her annoyance was assumed. Although Morning Song made no sound, nor even stirred, Pumpkin Blossom crowed delightedly—and sent two adjacent straws rolling when, still gurgling, she reached out to claim a fourth.

Otter approached her turn with concentration, selecting each straw only after conducting a hilarious conversation with herself as to which would be least likely to unsettle the others. By the time she had gathered up two of them, Pumpkin Blossom's face was contorted with mirth. And she shrieked with joy when Otter Swimming's next snatch cost her the turn.

The older girl rolled her dark eyes in Morning Song's direction. "It is for you to try now," she said easily, and leaned back.

Morning Song's fingers twitched, and she looked down at her hand with an expression of disbelief as her right arm guided it slowly, slowly over the edge of the bedstead, held it poised above the dwindling pile of straws, lowered it gradually to a place where a single straw lay temptingly alone. In a twinkling, two eager fingers had plucked it up.

"That is only one," Otter said quickly, just as she had to Pumpkin Blossom. And if there was something different in her tone this time, an ecstasy yearning to reveal itself yet not quite daring to, the others did not notice.

Morning Song uncurled her legs and slid to the floor between aunt and cousin. For a moment, she seemed startled to find herself there. Then she spied a second straw that lay in an exposed position, and all else fled her mind. She reached for it, and for another one as soon as she saw that she'd earned the right to do so. It was not until the cache at her side numbered seven that a too-abrupt move made it Pumpkin Blossom's turn once more.

Because Otter Swimming continued to complain, loudly, that her hands were no match for her nieces' smaller ones, Morning Song did not realize until Pumpkin Blossom had been declared victor that the drone of voices around them had ceased. And thanks to Teller Of Legends, who led extravagant praise of Pumpkin Blossom, the gaping spectators did not discomfort the child and reverse the progress Otter had made.

Otter had failed to make her niece laugh aloud. But Morning Song, when she slipped back onto their bed, did not pull up her legs and wrap her thin arms around them. And when she looked over at her aunt, her eyes were no longer the flat brown of a tobacco leaf; they were the color of rain-soaked bark flecked with the gold of a reemerging sun.

Bountiful Harvest's toothache brought the Company of Faces to the Turtle lodge next day. She'd awakened in the night with such pain in her lower jaw that she would have cried out had she not remembered in time that Teller Of Legends would never display such weakness. Otter Swimming, whose elation over Morning Song had made her own sleep fitful, heard the sufferer whispering to Hearth Tender about the obscenely swollen face that had haunted her dreams earlier that night.

It was just as likely, Otter thought uncharitably, that the ache was caused by the way Bountiful Harvest's jaw had dropped when she'd seen Morning Song playing snatch-stick. Otter was given occasionally to unkind feelings toward this sister of hers and, though she chided herself for them, she considered that they were justified. Small though she'd been in the years before Summer Maize—her favorite sister—went away, Otter remembered how Bountiful Harvest had more than once slyly used her sharp tongue to make the gentle Summer Maize weep.

Whatever the reason for Bountiful Harvest's suffering, Otter Swimming was glad that Hearth Tender had recommended summoning the False Faces. She had promptly volunteered to make the parched-corn pudding that, along with the finest leaves from Covers His Eyes's tobacco patch, would be presented to the Healers at the close of the ceremony. It stood ready now, and the inviting aroma rising through the smoke hole was surely responsible for the staccato muttering and eerie shrilling that marked the creeping approach of the society. And Otter's heart was made doubly glad when she realized that the excitement these sounds never failed to arouse in her was being shared by Morning Song. Features that had refused to be moved by emotion were suddenly and wonderfully animated. The scrape of rattles against the entrance post rounded her eyes and reddened her cheeks until her expression was twin to the one worn by Pumpkin Blossom. Otter Swimming grinned as she made a place for herself between the two five-year-olds.

Three times the rasping noise came, punctuated by rhythmic grunts and moans that set both little girls to shivering. Then the door was flung open, and in they came. So grotesque were their masks that it seemed there must be a host of them. But once Otter and her nieces were able to wrest their gaze from the Faces—from the wickedly skewed noses, the gaping mouths, the slitted and staring eyes, the protruding cheeks and brows—and focus instead on the buckskin-clad legs, they saw that the entire company numbered only six.

They made a circle around Bountiful Harvest, who stood respectfully by the center hearth as they began to dance, and their shuffling feet kept to the circumference they sketched on the hard-packed earth of the floor. Five of the company pointed at Bountiful Harvest with rattles fashioned from the carapaces of turtles (a good omen for the clan that honored the creature, Otter thought happily) and shook them fiercely to frighten away the spirit afflicting her. The sixth bent and, scooping a handful of glowing embers from the low-burning fire, blew ashes upon the person they had come here to cure.

Otter Swimming saw her sister blink rapidly as stinging sparks flared briefly upon her nose and chin. But that she stoically refused to flinch brought a murmur of admiration from the assembled witnesses.

Then, with an impressive eruption of growls and a final flourish of rattles, it was over. The masked Healers inclined their heads toward Bountiful Harvest, turned and bowed also to Teller Of Legends, and accepted the gifts of pudding and tobacco that were pressed, with thanks, into six outstretched hands.

Teller Of Legends looked down the length of her lodge and savored the sense of well-being that its orderliness and balance invariably spawned in her. Before her lay the central row of circular hearths, each precisely eight paces from the ones before and after it. Log-built beds lined the walls; shelves ran straight and true above them, tanned hides separated one set from another. Her gaze lingered at each of the lodge's four corners, their angles softened by clusters of casks containing parched corn, chunked maple sugar, dried squashes, and smoked meat and fish. Her family would not go hungry during the winter to come, however harsh the white season might be this year.

She smiled to see how personal possessions hinted at the characters of those who owned them. Hearth Tender, truly an ascetic now, needed less than half a shelf for hers. Carefree Otter Swimming let her jumble of garments and ornaments share space with eating utensils and snowshoes, so that her shelf, now that she kept Morning Song's bowl and tunics and moccasins there also, seemed on the verge of overflowing. Teller Of Legends's own shelf, on the opposite side of the main hearth, was the repository of all that she held dear, including the single arrow with frayed vane feathers that had belonged to the warrior-husband whose love and companionship she missed to this day.

The hearth nearest the entrance was Bountiful Harvest's. Her shelves were scrupulously neat, occupied only by folded garments and the supple skins from which others would be sewn. On her wall space hung bundles of ash splints, digging sticks, hoes, moccasins and snowshoes, Day Greeter's hammock, Pumpkin Blossom's cornhusk doll, and the bow and war club Cover His Eyes was forbidden to ever again take down. Teller Of Legends sighed. A sorry affair that had been, and surely a blow to her prideful daughter.

If only there were not five perpetually cold hearths, five sets of empty bunks and shelves! Hearth Tender's decision to live without a mate accounted for one of these, and Summer Maize's departure and subsequent death for another. Otter would wed eventually, Teller Of Legends was certain, and then three circles of flame would brighten the Turtle lodge. But not until her granddaughters had grown to womanhood would Teller Of Legends's longhouse be home to the sizable family she had always yearned for.

Three granddaughters so far. It was indeed a blessing to know that future Matrons were assured and that her lineage would continue uninterrupted. Day Greeter was a placid babe and would likely grow into a placid woman. Pumpkin Blossom imitated her efficient mother in all things, as Bountiful Harvest was determined that she should. And the daughter of Summer Maize . . .

Teller Of Legends sighed again. How could she—how could anyone—truly know what sort of girl Morning Song was, so long as she continued to remain silent? Her eyes, her expression, betrayed an intelligent interest now in what went on around her, and for that Otter Swimming deserved credit. But thoughts were accurately revealed only in speech (and sometimes not even then, Teller Of Legends reminded herself), and still the child would not be persuaded to talk. Not even by Otter, whom she adored.

It was time, the Matron of the Turtle lodge decided, to test a certain idea of her own.

To shake Morning Song awake while it was still dark and not disturb Otter Swimming also was no simple matter. The child was confused at first and reluctant to be lifted from her bed. Teller Of Legends, no stranger to the moods of children, offered her a chunk of maple sugar to sweeten her disposition, then stooped to whisper into the ear she freed from a tangle of hair.

"We are going to walk a little in the woods beyond the palisade. We shall watch the sun lift his face as we go, and I shall tell you a story that only you and our brother the sun will be able to hear."

Morning Song could not resist that inducement. She pulled on her wrinkled tunic, then tugged at her grandmother's hand.

In silence they left the longhouse and crossed the open ground where representatives of the village clans regularly sat in council. They unbarred the wide gate set into the circular pale fence that, at this point, gave onto the planting fields, and moved onward in single file. Teller Of Legends, who knew this trail nearly as well as she did the interior of her lodge, led the way through the darkness. By the time they approached the spot where the trail veered northward to the lake-hugging hills, the black had begun to fade from the sky, and Teller Of Legends picked up her pace. They must reach the forest before it brightened with the promise of dawn.

Morning Song, fully alert now, looked around eagerly when they came to a narrow path winding between shadowy maples and ghost-white birches. Low-growing shrubs, frothy ferns, and velvety mosses graciously permitted the pair to tread on them, but the little girl could distinguish neither color nor leaf shape at so early an hour. And, oh, it was quiet. The world was cloaked in a hush she thought she would feel if she stretched out her hands. Yet she made no such move. A waiting in the stillness infected her with a peculiar excitement, and she brimmed with instinctive respect for it.

Teller Of Legends looked down at her granddaughter and smiled. She understood what the child was experiencing; it was the same for her each time she walked here before the day had been roused from sleep. She turned to her right and led the way to the heap of tumbled, lichen-cushioned boulders she had been seeking. They had lain thus for a very long time, these rocks, perhaps since the Great World Turtle first consented to harbor Sky Woman, grandmother of the Longhouse People. And since they had absorbed the heat of yesterday's sun, they would be comfortable to sit upon.

She did nothing to break the wonderful waiting silence, but only gestured to Morning Song to scramble up and seat herself. Teller Of Legends eased down beside her, and that sense of anticipation heightened until the pine-scented air pulsed with it. Morning Song looked up at her grandmother with huge, questioning eyes. Teller Of Legends merely smiled, and signed to her to listen.

In the east, a slender band of rose-pink outlined the peaks of faraway mountains, widened, and draped itself upon the crests of drumlin and hill. But night had no intention of surrendering the lowland woods to intrusion until it must, and Morning Song and Teller Of Legends remained wrapped in deep shadow. Yet the tallest trees, those that held their leaf-crowned heads high above their brothers, did not go in ignorance of what was happening. Nor did the birds who roosted in them from dusk till dawn.

From their throats the music came, an achingly sweet anthem that lifted to the sky, then poured in a silver stream over, around, and into the soul of Teller Of Legends's granddaughter. The fluting hymns of warbler, finch, and white-throated sparrow met and merged and swelled, paid homage to the dew-washed morning, and helped a child to understand that the pattern of life is meant to be richly embroidered with countless beginnings.

When the splendid chorus had spun itself into a shimmering echo, Teller Of Legends spoke at last. "It was at dawn that you were born," she said quietly. "The name Summer Maize gave you describes what she heard when first she held you in her arms, only moments after your orenda—the spirit that called your life into being—separated itself from hers. Now you have heard what she heard then. It is your own birth song we have been listening to."

The little girl's face was flushed with joy, and her brown eyes were wide with amazement.

Teller Of Legends nodded. "You are grateful, I know," she went on, "that you may listen to it again and again, whenever you wish, through all the years of your life. And it seems to me that a child who has been blessed with such a name ought not hide her voice away as though it were some miserly squirrel's hoarded acorns. So"—she squeezed the slim hand lying next to her larger one—"if you truly wish to hear that story I promised you, then you must ask me to tell it to you."

Morning Song stared at her. Did her grandmother think she had *chosen* not to speak? Could she believe—did all of the clan, even Otter, believe—that Morning Song did not *want* to speak? Tears seeped into her eyes, and she raised a fist to scrub them away.

Suddenly a bird scarcely bigger than that fist flew across from a seedling maple and perched upon the thorny bush that grew beside the boulders. Four yellow blotches, like splashes of dye, marked its head and rump and breast. Was this one of the dawn singers, she wondered, come in search of praise? As if to answer her silent question, it cocked a shiny eye at her, then chirped so merry a greeting that Morning Song—before she knew it—responded to its brash approach with a spontaneous trill of laughter.

It mattered not at all that the little bird promptly flew away. Grandmother and granddaughter were too engrossed in each other to notice.

Morning Song swallowed hard, pushed her tongue against the roof of her mouth, swallowed a second time. Then:

"I would like to hear your story, Grandmother," she said.

Chapter 2

Teller Of Legends was pleased to have so many of the villagers respond to her invitation; or perhaps they were responding to the sparkling eyes and eager smile of Morning Song, who had raced from longhouse to longhouse to announce that her grandmother meant to offer a story. Between last summer and this, Morning Song's spirit had unfolded like the petals of a blossom. Not even Bountiful Harvest doubted now that she was Summer Maize's daughter. The smile she presented more and more was the one Summer Maize had worn as a girl; the smile that Otter Swimming maintained was Teller Of Legends' as well. Although Morning Song's memory refused to be sent back beyond the day she had arrived here with her dying mother, in every other respect she was just as she should be. And Hearth Tender had said that forcing the child's spirit to journey further into the past might harm her. Teller Of Legends had no wish to test the wisdom of her eldest daughter.

She let her eyes roam over her audience. Se-A-Wi was here, of course; the Sachem never missed one of his sister's stories. Nor, in his youth, had he been shy of regaling her with his own adventures so that she might use them to color her histories. His buxom wife, Sweet Maple of the Plover clan, stood beside him, her moon-shaped face glowing like the sunset. Teller of Legends' oldest friend became as excited as the children at moments like these. Sweet Maple's brother, Far Seer, had followed his young son and daughter out of the Wolf lodge and, having directed Woodpecker Drumming and Sun Descending to the inner circle, was speaking with Se-A-Wi. He was probably complaining again of their fellow councilman, Follows The Signs, who had been pressing for increased trading with the *Onondio*. Far Seer, already uneasy about their dealings with the French, would be advising caution. And Teller Of Legends was inclined to agree with him.

However, such matters must not intrude upon this hour, as the faces of the little ones reminded her. She smiled down at them and lifted her hand to ask silence of the grownups who stood behind them. "Since we shall soon be celebrating our first harvest of the season," she said, "I thought I would repeat for you one of the corn legends."

There were murmurs of approval from the older people, grins upon the faces of the children.

Teller Of Legends's voice altered subtly as she began to pronounce words spoken for the first time centuries before. "It is said that long ago there lived a handsome young man whose home was on a hill, a hill tall enough to thrust its nose into the sky. Indeed, it sniffed so often at the sky that the clouds threatened to tickle it and make it sneeze."

The young ones looked at one another and giggled, as she had planned, and she waited until they quieted before she went on. "I have told you the man was handsome, and he was. He stood straight as a pine tree, and held his head high with the pride of an ancient race. His brow was unmarked by frown wrinkles, and his strong mouth curved upwards to show his pleasant nature. He was fond of wearing, over a shirt and leggins of yellow-dyed buckskin, long, flowing robes that were as green as the grass on his solitary hill. And around his head he wore a warrior's band decorated with plumy tassels instead of feathers."

She had settled now into a familiar chanting rhythm, and Morning Song, squeezed between Pumpkin Blossom and big-eyed Sun Descending from the Wolf longhouse, wriggled happily and let a satisfied gurgle escape her parted lips. When a hand came from behind to grip her thin shoulder and urge her to be still, she did not need to turn in order to recognize it as Bountiful Harvest's. Briefly the child's lower lip protruded. Was this mother-aunt too old to be affected by the spell-casting lilt of her own mother's voice? Morning Song was certain Otter Swimming was not. And it surely had been Sweet Maple, *elderly* Sweet Maple, whose audible "*aah!*" had floated from the rear of the crowd to blend with the sound Morning Song had made.

But such thoughts lasted only as long as the pause Teller Of Legends allowed herself before taking up the tale once more.

"Now this handsome young man should have been a happy young man as well. Songbirds called him from his sleep each morning; rain puddled at his feet when he wished to bathe; the sun smiled on him whenever he craved light and warmth. Yet he did not know happiness. Can you guess why?"

She paused a second time, but even those who knew the story would not spoil it for the others by answering her question.

"He was not happy because he was a lonely young man. He had no mother, no sisters, no aunts. So I am sure you will understand that he wished most earnestly to marry. What man can long survive without a woman to care for him?"

The women murmured now, and their concert of appreciation fell sweetly on the ears of a vindicated Morning Song.

"The young man was wise enough to turn to the Maker Of Life for help in finding a mate. He planted his feet firmly on the top of his hill and offered up this chant: 'Say it, say it; someone I will marry. Say it, say it; someone I will marry.' And the words soared up and up until they reached the ears of his ancestors, who carried them tenderly to the Maker Of Life."

Teller Of Legends peered into the deepening twilight and sensed rather than saw the rapt faces turned to hers. "When he had sung these words for several days," she continued, "there came to him a fair maiden dressed in a moss-colored mantle decorated with bell-shaped ornaments of gold. 'I have come to marry you,' she said softly, and smiled. Her smile was lovely, and the young man was tempted. But wisdom warned that this woman was not for him.''

Someone made a soft sound of disappointment, so Teller Of Legends did not delay the progression of her tale. " 'I thank you,' the young man told her, 'but you would wander far from home, and run over the ground so swiftly I could not hope to keep you by my side.' The rejected pumpkin maiden bowed her head and crept away, and the man resumed his chanting: 'Say it, say it; someone I will marry,' he sang, and soon a second beautiful maiden came to his lonely hill. This one was tall as well as fair, and her green tunic was sewn all over with clusters of graceful blooms. And this time wisdom whispered that here was a woman the young man might safely love, one who would be true to him and never think to go astray. So he held out his arms to her and she went joyfully into his embrace. Which is why, to this day, in the fields of the Longhouse People two plants are inseparable: The cornstalk bean twines still around her lover.''

Teller Of Legends stood up and stretched out her own arms to welcome the children who raced one another to be first to give her thanks for such a fine tale. Far Seer and Follows The Signs, despite their disagreements during this morning's council, went together to close the palisade gate. The matrons, gossiping of this or that, drifted forward to urge the children to their beds.

Morning Song watched as Sun Descending and Woodpecker Drumming, Cloud Racer, Small Brown Sparrow, and Fox Running turned reluctant feet toward the two lodges built to the north of hers. How fortunate *she* was to live in the longhouse of Teller Of Legends. She saw Pumpkin Blossom leading her little sister in their mother's wake and wondered if her cousin recognized their mutual good fortune. Somehow she doubted it. It seemed to her that Pumpkin Blossom would rather be helping her mother with the endless tasks of the women than listening to one of their grandmother's stories. Bountiful Harvest believed that Morning Song should show a like interest in baking bread and weaving mats. But so long as Teller Of Legends wove words into stories, the weaving of mats—and all the rest—could wait.

Hearth Tender pondered her sister's question, although she had heard in Bountiful Harvest's tone nothing that might reasonably be called questioning. Was she merely observing propriety by consulting with a Faithkeeper? "Then you have not been plagued since by the toothache?"

"It is as though it had never been," the younger woman responded. "But the dream I had that same night has come again and again."

"Then it is possible that the spirits wish you to become a member of the Company of Faces," Hearth Tender said. "You know that Snow Comes Early is Mistress of the Healers?"

"I have just come from the Beaver lodge," Bountiful Harvest said importantly. "Snow Comes Early says she will be happy to welcome into the company one who is bound to bring credit to it." Her voice throbbed with self-satisfaction, her smile was radiant.

In the next instant that smile fled. Covers His Eyes, weary of sitting among the old men in the compound, was shuffling into the longhouse. Hearth Tender, poised to warn that a Healer who fattens on praise risks offending the spirits, withheld the caution: Living in the shadow of her husband's shame, Bountiful Harvest needed to have her own worth acknowledged. "Will you require help with your mask?" she asked gently. "Perhaps Se-A-Wi . . ."

Bountiful Harvest shook her head vigorously. "I am as capable of wielding a blade as any man," she said shortly.

As she strode away, she heard Hearth Tender sigh. Nor had she missed the pity in Hearth Tender's expression when Covers His Eyes made his untimely entrance. Bountiful Harvest's mouth tightened. How dare her sister—who had never had a husband of her own—feel sorry for her! She seized the blade lying ready on her shelf and, without sparing word or glance for the man who watched her with lackluster eyes, marched out the door and made for the woods, where the poplar she had already chosen waited for her.

To mark its surface with the shape of the face she'd seen in her dreams was easy, but to peel away the bark and make the gouges that would become eyes and a mouth was not. Only deep cuts could achieve the grotesquely swollen forehead, cheeks, and jowls she was determined to create, and a rough outline of the features must be carved upon a living tree. It would be late in the day before she'd be able to remove the section of the trunk to the longhouse for the rest of the work, but at least she had begun her mask before the sun was high. That would allow her to paint it red rather than black. And she wanted a red mask.

She would make sure she finished it in time to be initiated into the society before the Green Corn Festival. Then her mother would watch with pride, and her sisters envy her, as Bountiful Harvest performed the traditional dance of the Healers.

Chance only had taken Morning Song to the forest that same morning. When Pumpkin Blossom produced a new deerhide ball,

Morning Song had been as quick as the other girls to agree to a game of kickball. She'd felt confident that, with this replacement for the husk-leaking sphere they'd used in the past, she would finally score at least once and earn the cheers of her companions. But by the time the contest ended, Morning Song had not needed telling that her own clumsiness, and not the condition of the ball, was the reason her efforts had always been greeted with scorn.

She'd muttered something about an errand she'd forgotten to attend to and, escaping to the woods, had sheltered under this old evergreen to lick her wounds and try to make sense out of her embarrassing awkwardness. What was it that tangled her legs and skewed her aim every time she attempted to play kickball? And why did no one else have this problem?

The appearance of Bountiful Harvest and her attack on a nearby tree had put an end to Morning Song's self-questioning. Now, some hours later, when the girl had at last identified a pair of deep gouges as eyes and the slash beneath as a sneering mouth, she wondered if she dare risk moving away. For it had occurred to her that Bountiful Harvest might not be pleased to know she was being observed.

Yet Morning Song was no longer so comfortable as she'd been in the beginning. A sizable pebble was pressing against her achingly full bladder, and inquisitive ants had begun to wander up and down her left leg. Perhaps if she slithered backward slowly and carefully . . .

Unfortunately Bountiful Harvest paused to admire her handiwork just as Morning Song's foot came in contact with an acorn. The tiny plop the nut made when it bumped against an exposed root might have been ignored by one whose hearing was not so keen as Bountiful Harvest's. Immediately she wheeled around. Her eyes— every bit as sharp as her ears—searched the fir tree's sagging boughs and pounced upon the frozen figure of Morning Song.

"You!" she exclaimed, her gaze prodding the girl erect as swiftly as any spear thrust could have done.

"I—I am sorry, Bountiful Harvest," Morning Song began, with as much genuine contrition as apprehension.

Bountiful Harvest raised the hand that held the blade. "Sorry!" she spat. "You shall be more than sorry, to have deliberately hidden yourself in order to spy on that which is both sacred and secret."

"I meant no harm," Morning Song mumbled, cautiously retreating a step as her aunt moved toward her. "I did not know that what you were doing was something I should not see."

To her relief, the rigid arm lowered and the knife was dropped almost casually onto a heap of brown needles. "I won't tell anyone," she added hurriedly, backing farther away as she made the vow.

But a single long stride brought Bountiful Harvest to where she stood and a pair of suddenly clawlike hands reached out and seized the girl by the upper arm.

Morning Song looked down at them and, for one terrifying moment, they were not the slender fingers of her aunt that dented her flesh, but hands broader and blunter, hands covered nearly to the fingertips in coarse, dark hair, hands determined to probe deep enough to bruise the fragile bones beneath the girl's vulnerable flesh.

Morning Song blinked, and the sound-stifling fog vanished as suddenly as it had come; the angry words spilling from Bountiful Harvest's mouth were recognizable once more.

"No other child in the village would think to do so dishonorable a thing," she was saying now. "Only Morning Song. Which surprises me not at all." She slackened her grip abruptly, and the girl nearly tumbled to the ground. "We shall go at once and see whether Teller Of Legends is able to find words to defend you, as she has so often done before," she finished grimly. "Even Otter will be appalled when I tell her the awful thing you have done."

She continued to berate the child all during their rapid walk back to the longhouse, yet Morning Song was grateful that she did. Her aunt's relentless tongue kept her from dwelling upon an experience that had left her drenched in the icy sweat of soul-deep fear.

Sweet Maple, plump hands folded in her ample lap, beamed upon Teller Of Legends as her friend sorted through the stack of garments Otter Swimming had gathered up from the various shelves in the longhouse.

"Bountiful Harvest has sewn new garments for all of her family to wear to the Festival," the Matron of the Turtle lodge remarked without surprise. She handed them back to her youngest daughter and indicated that they should be returned to their proper places.

"Even the dress for little Day Greeter was prettily decorated," Sweet Maple said. "You have taught your daughters well, Teller Of Legends."

Her companion smiled. "Those intricate patterns are of her own devising. When have you ever known my fingers to be so clever, Sweet Maple?"

The smile dimmed as she unfolded the garment her oldest daughter meant to wear at the Green Corn Ceremony. It was soft from many wearings, faded from numerous washings, and neatly darned here and there. Hearth Tender's concentration on the spiritual had blinded her to defects that certain others in the village would surely notice. Well, she would have something new for the occasion. There was time enough for Teller Of Legends's untalented fingers to do some plain sewing.

"I have already decided to make new tunics for Morning Song and me," Otter said hastily as her mother turned her attention to the crumpled and none-too-clean dresses belonging to the pair. "With fringed hems," she improvised rashly, "to match the fringe on the moccasins I will sew also. Tree Reaching Up has said she will help me with them." She looked pleadingly at Sweet Maple, who was mother-aunt to Otter's particular friend.

"So she has told me," that obliging soul confirmed. "You are planning to begin them this day, I believe."

Otter Swimming grinned. It was only right that Sweet Maple should demand as much in return for her assistance. In any event, she could hardly put off what her own words had pledged her to do.

Teller Of Legends, happy to pretend ignorance of the intrigue, handed over the unworthy tunics without comment and waved her irrepressible daughter on her way. Otter took up her stitching gear and, with a flourish, a generous length of pale doeskin as she left.

Sweet Maple smiled more broadly and settled herself for an intimate chat. It was a tribute to her amiability that she was able to continue to smile when, before the two had exchanged more than a dozen words, another visitor came into the lodge.

"Greetings to you, Lake On Fire," Teller Of Legends said courteously, and Sweet Maple echoed the sentiment as her round eyes marveled at the newcomer's attire.

Lake On Fire was undisturbed by the scrutiny. Indeed, she pranced this way and that to display the brilliantly colored tunic of manufactured fabric that hugged the angles of a body that was long a stranger to the suppleness of youth.

"Follows The Signs took the material in trade from the white men who came last to our village," she announced smugly. "The beads, as well." Her hands, age-creased at the knuckles, caressed a string of multihued baubles looped twice around her scrawny neck. Lake On Fire had been a beauty in her day, fully as much a one as Bountiful Harvest was considered to be now, and refused to allow that the years had robbed her of this precious gift. "When the *Onondio* come again, he has promised to ask for more of these beads. Then I can decorate my moccasins, and my winter leggins."

"No rainbow has ever dressed the sky in colors brighter than these," Sweet Maple managed, fingering the proffered beads.

Teller Of Legends frowned slightly. "They are returning soon, the white men?"

Lake On Fire nodded. "So says my husband. Of course, he does not understand the words they speak—peculiar is their talk, he tells me, much like the honking of geese—but Trail Marker knows their tongue, and he has said that they will be back during the red season."

"I am not certain we are wise to permit them to come so often," Teller Of Legends said quietly. "When we traded with the Dutch only, we traveled to where they live. I was more at ease then. And I wonder that we dare trust any Frenchman when we know it is the French who encourage the Algonquin and Huron to refuse to make peace treaties with our nation."

Sweet Maple made a sympathetic sound. It was natural that Teller Of Legends should be mistrustful of all French-speaking *Onondio*. Indian allies of the French had slain the husband she had loved so much. And it had not been a war band Tall Pine was with, but a few comrades who shared his enthusiasm for fishing the colder waters to the northwest.

Lake On Fire, however, was aghast. "How can we survive, now, without the things they bring to us? Even you, Teller Of Legends, use your metal pots more often than your clay ones. And the knives! Would you return to scraping hides with sharpened bone and knapped rock?"

"Those things were available from the Dutch also," Teller Of Legends reminded her.

"But they refused to give us guns," Lake On Fire said triumphantly. "Which the French do not. And Follows The Signs says the day will come when a war party without guns shall be named no war party at all."

"I am surprised that he sets so much value on the white man's weapons. I have heard that in the time a gun is being readied for firing, a good bowman may loose six arrows! And it was a gun—treacherously used by a Frenchman—that claimed the life of Follows the Signs's father at the Place-Where-The-Waters-Meet."

"That was long ago," Lake On Fire retorted. "It does no good to dwell in the past, Teller Of Legends."

"It serves us well to learn from it—" her friend began, only to break off as Bountiful Harvest stormed into the lodge, propelling Morning Song before her. The little girl's face was not so easily read as her aunt's, but there was certainly misery in it.

Lake On Fire seized the opportunity to leave the Turtle long-house. Follows The Signs must he told what Teller Of Legends had said about the traders, since her opinions were frequently shared by Se-A-Wi. Sweet Maple, disinterested in politics and so close a friend that she was regarded by all as family, remained to discover the reason for Bountiful Harvest's anger.

"This granddaughter of yours is slow to learn what is proper behavior among the Longhouse People," the young woman proclaimed, glaring down at Morning Song. Belatedly she acknowledged Sweet Maple's presence with a curt nod.

Teller Of Legends let her eyes travel between her daughter and the downcast girl who stood before her. "Perhaps you will tell me enough that I may judge for myself?" she said mildly.

"Is there another child in our village—or in any of the five tribes of the Iroquois nation—who would deliberately spy on someone who has gone into the forest to carve a false face?" Bountiful Harvest demanded. "There is not! Most learn before they leave their cradleboards that this is ceremony. How can the spirit from my dream guide my hand if someone is watching?"

It was not anger alone, her mother realized, that caused Bountiful Harvest's eyes to narrow and her hands to clench. She truly feared that her niece's presence had weakened the spiritual communion vital to the making of her mask. She focused on her granddaughter. "You know that it was wrong of you to do as you did?" she asked.

"I do now," Morning Song whispered. "But"—her drooping shoulders straightened and much of her distress lifted as she decided to defend herself—"I did not, in the beginning. And it was *me* who was there first, Grandmother. Truly."

"Is this so?" Teller Of Legends asked Bountiful Harvest.

"That is what she told me," the young woman confirmed grudgingly. "Yet if it is true, she did not reveal herself to me, but only hid away so that she might watch what I did."

"I did not know what you were about," Morning Song flared, then dropped her eyes before her grandmother's warning glance. "I still do not understand what it was, or why it must be secret," she finished more moderately.

Sweet Maple's soft heart compelled her to interfere in a matter that ought to have been the sole concern of the Turtle clan. "I believe this child," she said. "Bountiful Harvest should remember that Morning Song was prevented by circumstance from absorbing our tribal mysteries while she was little more than a babe."

Bountiful Harvest's mouth quivered as respect forced her to swallow the words that would tell Se-A-Wi's woman that she had a clan

of her own and should confine her opinions within it. Teller Of
Legends's thoughts paralleled those of her friend, but she nodded
approval of her daughter's hard-won restraint. "I believe you have
learned from all of this," she said to her granddaughter, "that we
are careful not to be curious about one another, that it is never right
to secretly watch a person who believes herself alone."

Morning Song nodded—and did not ask, as she longed to, why
her aunt had been carving such a hideous face upon the trunk of
that tree. How did a girl come to know anything, if she must not
be curious? she wondered bleakly.

Teller Of Legends, suspecting what might be troubling her,
smiled. "One day soon," she promised, "I will tell you the story
of the Stone Giants. Listen well when I do, and most of your questions will be answered." Her smile broadened. "It is perfectly
proper," she added, "to be curious about a legend." She paused,
tried to make her expression stern. "Meanwhile, I think you should
apologize to Bountiful Harvest."

Thus prompted, Morning Song made her apology. And Bountiful Harvest—with reasonably good grace—accepted it.

Preparing for the Green Corn Ceremony was nearly as exciting
as the Festival itself. Men hovered over their tobacco patches, waiting for the perfect moment to pluck those leaves that would be
burned during the thanksgiving prayer. Women and girls harvested
and prepared beans and corn for the succotash. Boys, dispatched
to bring in kindling for the ceremonial fire, were advised to shun
the branches of the chestnut tree because its wood tended to fill the
air with biting sparks.

Morning Song, her hands sore from stripping beanstalks of their
bounty, looked yearningly after Cloud Racer and Fox Running and
their friends as they pushed an empty sledge along the path to the
woods. Their jesting and boasting, their boisterous laughter, the
yapping of the dogs that ran alongside, made her wish she could go
with them. Surely gathering firewood was more fun than cooking.

Pumpkin Blossom looked across at her cousin. "You *are* slow,"
she commented, tipping her own basket to show its rapid filling.
"And you know the beans must be boiled for a very long time
before the corn can go into the pot."

Morning Song—who had known no such thing, nor even cared—
sighed. "Why is it always the boys who gather the wood, while the
girls stay behind to work with the women?"

Pumpkin Blossom was shocked. "How else can we learn to do
the things we shall have to do when we are grown?"

"I am in no rush to learn them," Morning Song muttered, snapping a bean with unnecessary ferocity.

"No warrior shall be interested in being your husband, if you do not," her cousin rejoined, then smiled as her mother came to check on their progress.

Bountiful Harvest beamed upon her daughter's heaping basket, frowned at Morning Song's. "Day Greeter could have done better," she said caustically, gesturing toward the tiny girl who waddled after her.

Morning Song bent to her task once more. Bountiful Harvest had not truly forgiven her, she realized, for that day in the forest. Now she was not sorry to see her go on her way to visit the Beaver lodge, as she'd been doing more and more often of late. Somehow the girl's reluctant fingers grew clumsier still when this mother-aunt stood over her!

When Teller Of Legends came out of the longhouse, however, Morning Song had no such problem. Indeed, her small hands became almost deft when her grandmother sat down and announced that she would give them a story to speed their work.

"I have no need of a tale to make me work faster," Pumpkin Blossom said quickly. "But I should like to hear one anyway," she allowed, reaching for another laden stalk with hands that showed a grace inherited from her mother.

Morning Song looked up shyly. "Can it be the legend of the Stone Giants that you tell us?" she asked.

Her grandmother nodded, pleased. The child had not forgotten. It was, after all, only her early years that eluded her. "That seems appropriate, on a day so clear that the hills all around seem nearer than they are," she replied. "The legend is about the forming of these very hills." She gestured for the girls to go on with their chore. "In days long ago, there lived in this country a race of fearsome Stone Giants. The arrows of the Longhouse People could not penetrate their flesh; the sharpest spears could not so much as dent it."

Morning Song discovered that she had denuded a beanstalk without being aware of it, and picked up another.

"They were eaters of men, those ogres known as Stone Giants," Teller Of Legends went on. "They preyed on the People of the Longhouse just as the owl preys on the mouse, or the wolf on the fawn. But while the Maker Of Life meant for the owl and the wolf to be predators, in the same way that he intended our warriors to be hunters of woodland beasts, he had planned no such thing for

the Stone Giants. And he saw that if these monsters were to be
stopped he would have to take a hand in their destruction.

"So The Maker Of Life arranged for Te-Ha-Wro-Gah—He Who
Holds Up The Heavens—to disguise himself as one of the Stone
Giants and go among them. Once he had gained their trust, Te-Ha-
Wro-Gah persuaded them that he should lead them in their war
against mankind. 'We shall have the greatest feast ever, once we
have won the battle,' he told them. And the Giants licked their
stone lips and growled deep in their granite throats, to think of
gorging themselves on the tender flesh of so many Longhouse People.''

The cousins looked at one another and shuddered.

"Well, he was tricking them, of course. But they did not know
that; like boulders, the Giants' heads were too dense to permit
sensible thought. So the Upholder Of The Heavens called them
together and pointed to a mountain upon which the People of the
Longhouse had built a stockade. 'You see the hills that stretch between us and that mountain,' he told them. 'There are caves in
them where you must hide yourselves until first light tomorrow,
when I will send you a signal from the top of that mountain.'

"The Stone Giants readily agreed, and lumbered away to find
caves big enough to conceal them. As they went, they reminded
one another of the grand celebration feast they would have.''

Morning Song and Pumpkin Blossom fixed their eyes on Teller
Of Legends's face. Surely this time the ogres would be prevented
from filling their monstrous bellies with human flesh!

"Hundreds of flinty eyes watched as Te-Ha-Wro-Gah began his
trek to the base of the mountain. But it was a remarkably long way
that he had to travel, and even Stone Giants get sleepy. By the time
night had wrapped the world in darkness, huge jaws were creaking
and cracking with yawns they could not contain. And since they'd
been told that the signal for attack would be a shout loud enough
to split the sky, one by one those Giants closed their eyes and
slept.''

Teller Of Legends looked into the solemn faces of her granddaughters, and lowered her voice to a whisper. "This, of course,
the Upholder Of The Heavens had foreseen. He promptly changed
back into his own shape—which was a wonderful relief; it is difficult to walk fast when you are as heavy-footed as a Stone Giant—
and went like the wind up the side of that mountain. When he'd
arrived at the top of it, he reached down his hands and grasped the
edges of the land below him, and shook it just as I might shake a
robe some careless child has let trail in the dirt. Why, it was as if

earthquake and thunderstorm were doing battle to see which was the stronger! And when the land had settled back into place, all of its hills had shifted, so that each occupied a spot different from the one it had sat on before.''

Morning Song tugged at her grandmother's hem. "What happened to the Stone Giants?" she asked breathlessly.

Teller Of Legends put an arm around each of the girls. "It is said that they were trapped in their hiding places, and crushed to death,'' she declared. She waited until they had begun to smile to have a story end so happily. Then she made her expression doleful. "All but one, that is,'' she added. And made as if to rise.

Four hands pulled at her skirt, and two anxious faces pleaded with her not to leave them perplexed. She made a great show of considering the matter, then allowed herself to be persuaded to sit down again.

"It seems that a single Stone Giant—the *ugliest* one, at that—managed somehow to escape,'' she said. "And because he had done so, he came to believe himself more powerful than the Upholder Of The Heavens. From a snapping turtle's shell, he fashioned an enormous rattle. Then, naming himself master of the world, he went about shaking it to frighten all the beasts of the earth, and made a fearful sound with his mouth that scared them even more. While doing these terrible things, he contrived also to populate the world with the demons who strike mankind with illnesses.''

Pumpkin Blossom and Morning Song sighed in mournful unison.

"The Maker Of Life was furious with him, and went himself to challenge him to a contest of strength. 'Let us see which of us can command that mountain to move,' he told the Stone Giant. Well, the Giant tried, and, by concentrating all his power, was able at last to shift it. But only a little. The Maker Of Life merely looked at him, then lifted his hand. On the instant, that Giant felt a rush of air behind him and was struck right in his stony buttocks by the mountain, which had skimmed over the land with the smoothness of a duck gliding through calm water. 'We know now who is master here,' the Maker Of Life said sternly. 'It is surely not old Twisted Face.' And as punishment, he made the gruesome Stone Giant enter the dream of one of the Longhouse People and reveal to him that, to banish disease, the People must carve masks as hideous as the Giant's own face. When they wear these, and perform certain sacred ceremonies, they are able to drive away the spirits of disease that the last of the Stone Giants caused to be born.''

"The False Faces!" Pumpkin Blossom cried.

Teller Of Legends nodded, and watched awareness dawn in the face of her other granddaughter. When Morning Song said nothing, but only smiled, the old woman nodded a second time.

Understanding, unfettered by words, flowed between them.

Chapter 3

⟸ ⟹

Otter Swimming coaxed Morning Song into the shallows and dribbled summer-warm water from her cupped hands over the stiffened back and tensed shoulders of the girl's thin body. "Our brother the sun smiles on us today," she said, inclining her head toward the east. "Do you think he is as eager as we are to have the Green Corn Ceremony begin?"

Morning Song made a strangled sound that her mother-aunt took as an affirmative.

"We must remember to honor him when we offer thanks for the good spirits who watch over us," Otter said, turning her attention to Morning Song's long hair. Taking care not to let water splash in the girl's screwed-up eyes, she wet it thoroughly, then separated the dripping strands with her fingers. "Your hair shines like the fur of my namesake," she teased. "Perhaps we should call you Little Otter instead of Morning Song."

Her niece managed a small smile, which relief widened as the older girl led her back to the riverbank. "I think I must keep the name my mother gave me," she said seriously as she trotted by Otter Swimming's side and let the sun's increasing warmth shrink the droplets that clung to her pale flesh.

Otter reached out and hugged her. "And so you shall, for it is a beautiful one," she declared, and hurried her into the longhouse.

Since the Sachem belonged to the Turtle clan, that family was always host on such occasions. A huge kettle of succotash steamed over the rear hearth, and Bountiful Harvest was urging her mother and Se-A-Wi to try a little and see if it was not the best she'd ever cooked. Pumpkin Blossom, clad in her new tunic, was helping her little sister into hers. Hearth Tender, respectable if not resplendent in the simple dress Teller Of Legends had sewn for her, had just returned from carrying formal summons to the Festival throughout the village. Even Covers His Eyes was taking part in the preparations; having set the backless dance bench in position, he was neatly bundling his fresh-picked tobacco leaves.

The latecomers slipped hastily into their own new clothes; it would disgrace both Sachem and Matron if everyone was not ready to welcome those appointed to light the new-laid kindling in the center hearth.

The families from the other longhouses—Deer, Wolf, Plover, Pigeonhawk, Beaver, and Snipe—arrived hard on the heels of the Fire Starters, and boisterous greetings burgeoned into confusing banter. Hearth Tender needed to sign twice before the congregation would move to the seats lining the two long walls of the lodge.

At last she stood by the ceremonial fire, lifted a sober face to the smokehole above it, and began to offer thanks to their Creator, and to those kindly spirits who animated beasts, birds, trees, and the myriad countenances of the natural world. Such passion was in her normally quiet voice that Morning Song looked twice to be certain it was her mother-aunt who chanted this stirring litany. Then the child's nostrils quivered as tobacco was sprinkled on the hearth, and she turned her bemused gaze in that direction as Hearth Tender—in more familiar tones—began to list the dances to be presented on the first day of the four-day festival.

"Maker of Life," Hearth Tender finished, her face and voice lifting once more, "the council here assembled—the elders, the strong warriors, the women, and the children—unite their voices of thanksgiving to thee."

Music erupted then, drums and rattles setting the pace for songs passed down, generation after generation, among the Longhouse People. Morning Song, embarrassed that she did not yet know the songs well, kept her mouth tight shut and let her feet alone respond to the rhythm.

Suddenly Small Brown Sparrow, who sat next to her, clutched at her arm. Here came the proud warriors of the Eagle society! Morning Song stared at the man leading the procession. Like his comrades, he wore an intricately embroidered breechclout and leggins, and carried in his left hand an angled rod with four eagle feathers attached to it. Similar feathers adorned the snug-fitting skin cap he wore, and a bright red spot had been painted on each of his lean cheeks. It was several moments before she recognized him as Fierce Eagle, uncle to the excited girl who had drawn her attention to him, and so brave a warrior that he had been named a Pine Tree Chief. The Deer clan was justifiably proud of their kinsman, and Morning

Song smiled as Small Brown Sparrow bounced up and down in her exuberance.

And, oh, how vigorously the warriors stomped as they danced! Soon their faces gleamed with sweat, and heavy breathing swelled their naked chests. Those who chanted the ritual song were perspiring, too, for they paused only when one of the dancers signed that he wished to speak. Then Small Brown Sparrow and Morning Song would poke one another and giggle, for each panting warrior took care to be outrageously complimentary to his own clan and mildly derisive of all others. The boasting was sincere enough, but even the children understood that the gibes were offered in fun and were not meant to humble or enrage those who listened.

Other dances followed in such rapid succession that Morning Song, had she not been a little prepared for it, might have flinched at the sight of a chillingly familiar mask during the performance of the False Face Society. And the speeches! It seemed that everyone had something to be grateful for, and most were inclined to speak on until their words became a drone in Morning Song's ears.

Finally however—when the aroma of simmering succotash had set more than one belly to rumbling—Hearth Tender, with a sympathetic smile, sent everybody out into the compound for the games.

The young men, anxious to flex their muscles, persuaded their fellow warriors to grueling tests of strength and agility. The women and children shouted encouragement, and the men, although pretending indifference, were not unhappy to display their prowess—especially to those maidens whose compliments were sweeter to their ears than the songs they had sung or listened to within the lodge.

Morning Song was too excited and too hungry to stay with Small Brown Sparrow and mock the extravagant wagering that attended the peach pit game. She drifted from group to group until she overheard Se-A-Wi being challenged by several braves many years his junior.

"Surely you have not forgotten how to toss a spear," Far Seer was saying. "You, who were village champion for so long, and who taught each of us to do so!"

"My arm aches still," Fierce Eagle put in, "when it remembers how you refused to end a lesson until I had three times running hit the target you'd set for me!"

Their former tutor looked from one to another of their glistening faces, then nodded slowly. "You think to avenge yourselves for what I demanded of you in those days," he said, accepting the lance Far Seer was tempting him with. "Are you confident enough, I wonder, to award me the choice portion from your next kill if I win?''

A chorus of guffaws was quickly stifled as the instigators of this uneven contest nodded in unison. Hadn't Se-A-Wi himself taught them that only rigorous practice nurtures skill? And everyone knew that hunting and raiding were but memories to the Sachem now.

Se-A-Wi hefted the spear and squinted along its length. Then he signed to young Cloud Racer, who stood at the far end of the compound, to set spinning the small hoop that was the target.

Morning Song's heart was a drumbeat in her narrow chest as she watched Teller Of Legends's brother draw back a ropy arm and release the lance he held. Her eyes followed its arcing flight, and she held her breath as it approached the mark. When the weapon passed cleanly through the center of the revolving hoop to pierce a log in the palisade beyond, she let out such a shriek that Teller Of Legends, standing quietly beside her, laughed aloud.

''I suspected that they would regret challenging him,'' she said, with satisfaction. ''Se-A-Wi's eye is as keen as ever, and he has found ways to keep it so.''

Morning Song smiled up at her as her heart resumed a more normal rhythm. ''He should have been asked to take part in the Eagle dance,'' she said.

It was Teller Of Legends's turn to smile. ''Warriors rarely lose their command of the spear, so long as their vision does not blur. But only the young have the endurance to dance so strenuously. Which is as it should be; the old are granted wisdom to compensate for their creaking bones. Or''—she chuckled—''*some* of them are!''

Morning Song followed her grandmother's mirth-bright gaze to where it rested upon a huddle of female figures, among them Lake On Fire. In honor of the Festival, the old woman had draped neck, wrists, and ankles with strands of beads and tangles of shells and animal teeth. Her slash-sleeved tunic and voluminous skirt were sewn from fabric boasting a pattern of purple, red, and yellow checks. The colors had seemed garish enough in the dimness of the Turtle lodge; here in the sunlight they jarred upon the eye like an eldritch screech upon a tender ear.

''How can she be such a fool?'' Bountiful Harvest, coming up behind them, had also spotted Lake On Fire. ''She is a crone, and ought to know better.''

Teller Of Legends laughed. ''Never believe that only the young lack sense,'' she advised. She patted Morning Song's gleaming head. ''The contrary is often true. And Lake On Fire harms no one by pretending she is little older than a maiden.''

"No maid dresses as she does," Bountiful Harvest said scornfully. "Not even the dull-witted would do so."

The older woman sighed. Would this daughter of hers, who ex-
celled in so many ways, never learn charity? She turned her head,
saw that the swollen sun was allowing its own weight to drag it
behind the farthest hill. "It is time we were bringing out your
delicious succotash," she said, sending praise to chase the contempt from Bountiful Harvest's eyes. "Go and call the other children," Teller Of Legends urged Morning Song, "and tell them to
fetch their spoons and bowls." Then, beckoning to a pair of matrons who stood gossiping nearby, she hurried them along with her
to help Bountiful Harvest lift the heavy kettle and carry it into the
compound.

Morning Song was not the only one who found it hard to be
patient while the men found their places and conveyed their readiness to be served. The tantalizing smell of the food that the women
were ladling out taunted everyone's appetite. Only Hearth Tender's
brief, high-pitched prayer, which was repeated by a chorus of voices
chiming a lower note, held spoons at bay.

While the reverent shout still echoed around them, the children
dug into their bowls and crammed succotash into their mouths until
cheeks bulged all around the inner circle.

Sweet Maple, passing through their ring to sit with the other
matrons, looked down, smiled, and paused with her hand resting
on Hill Climber's head. "You would be wise to avoid being
greedy," she warned her grandson, then let her twinkling eyes
touch on each of the others. "And your friends, also. Remember
that Long Nose comes in the night to those who are gluttons and
sends them terrible dreams!"

Morning Song swallowed an enormous mouthful as she watched
Sweet Maple move away. "Who is Long Nose?" she asked curiously.

Pumpkin Blossom paused with a slab of cornbread halfway to
her mouth and sighed audibly. It was a sound her mother was much
given to and seemed to her to suit the situation. "There are times,"
she said to no one in particular, "when I wonder if my cousin
knows anything at all!" She nodded toward the tree where her baby
sister slept contentedly, strapped securely to the cradleboard she
was fast outgrowing. "Even Day Greeter probably knows that Long
Nose is a demon who loves to make boys and girls wake screaming
from their dreams."

Morning Song scooped another healthy portion from her bowl.

"I shall not worry then," she said when she had gulped it down. "Since I never dream, Long Nose will not be able to plague me. No matter how much I eat."

There was an uneasy silence, during which spoons were suspended in midair or left protruding from half-empty bowls. Heads swiveled, and an assortment of eyes fixed on Morning Song's placid face.

Small Brown Sparrow said it first: "But Morning Song, dreams come to everyone!"

"They come more often to some than to others, however." This from her brother Cloud Racer. "Perhaps you dream only rarely, Morning Song?"

The girl licked cornbread crumbs from her fingers, shrugged, and looked at the boy whose recent rapid growth made him sit taller than Woodpecker Drumming and Stag Leaping, both of whom were a year older than he was. "I do not dream at all. Ever," she replied.

Pumpkin Blossom turned to Meadow Brook of the Beaver clan. "Do dreams come to you?" she demanded.

The girl nodded slowly, and Pumpkin Blossom continued around the circle, putting the same question to each of her companions. Then she looked across at her cousin. "Only you sleep without dreaming," she told her. "This is not natural, Morning Song."

Eight-year-old Sun Descending, eldest of the girl-children, reached across Small Brown Sparrow and patted Morning Song's angled knee. "It is possible that you do not remember you have dreamed," she said.

Several of the children nodded solemn assent. "I'm sure that must have happened to me," Hill Climber said. He looked down into a bowl scraped clean, and grinned. "Perhaps I should hope it happens again tonight," he added. "I should prefer not to recall a visit from Long Nose, if he decides I have eaten more than I should!"

His droll expression set his peers to laughing, and they were glad to be diverted from something they could not understand.

Morning Song, crawling eventually into her bed, wasted no thought on a matter she did not see as important. Long before Otter Swimming stretched out beside her, Morning Song had tumbled, with a blissful sigh, into feather-soft—and dreamless—sleep.

Ever since her introduction to the dawn chorus of the songbirds, Morning Song had cherished the forest. When she stood surrounded by ancient trees, brushed her fingertips lightly over delicate fern and long-headed reed mace, inhaled the resinous scent that was the gift of the evergreens, she knew a sense of belonging that had nothing to do with clan or tribe. It puzzled her at times.

"It is the *orenda* of the forest calling to you," her grandmother explained one morning as she led the villagers in search of ripe blueberries. "*Orenda* is the spirit that exists in everything shaped by the Maker Of Life—" She nodded her thanks as the girl skipped ahead to hold back the branch of a thorny bush. "—even in Morning Song and Teller Of Legends." She gestured toward an acorn-laden oak. "That tree and its cousins are alive, just as birds and animals and people are alive. Which is why we acknowledge them as kin. You are deeply sensitive to this kinship, I think."

"Is it because I was born in the forest, that I feel so comfortable here?" Morning Song asked after a moment.

"Most of us emerge from our mothers' wombs in such a place, since this is our birthing custom. Perhaps Summer Maize made a habit of walking among the trees while she carried you within her belly."

After nearly three years, Morning Song's memories of her mother were vague. But as Teller Of Legends spoke of her, the girl found herself able to visualize her eyes, her loving smile, the grace with which her mother had moved on feet silent as a wary doe's. And she was all at once certain that those feet had often taken Summer Maize into the woods, to let the *orenda* of the forest reach out for the spirit of the babe that nestled beneath her heart.

Teller Of Legends had kept silent in the face of Morning Song's contemplations. Now she grunted suddenly and turned to wave forward the women and children who straggled behind. Lining the curving banks of a glistening stream were the shrubs they had come here to find, their tangled branches boasting a wealth of clustered berries. Grins plumped the cheeks of the basket-toting women.

Although the younger girls carried single baskets, Otter and Tree Reaching Up—both grown tall over the past summer and, at thirteen, children no longer—were allowed to have a pair suspended on straps over their shoulders, as the matrons did. Otter's burden did not hold her back; she leaped ahead of the rest, her hands lifted to receive the bounty of the nearest bush. Morning Song raced after her, piping a wordless counterpoint to the chant her mother-aunt began as she plucked the ripened fruit with greedy fingers. Soon all of the women and children had taken up Otter's song, and the musky autumn air swelled with the sound of their voices. Sunshine, stained red by the canopy of leaves it filtered through, dappled their upturned faces. Juice from burst berries purpled their fingers and ringed the mouths of those who could not resist tasting as they worked. On the other side of the man-high bushes, the water in the stream made music of its own as it trickled over boulders. An acrobatic breeze set dry leaves rustling on the branches of birch and elm.

Morning Song sighed delightedly. There had never been a day so beautiful, so throbbing with life, as this one. At Otter's request, she sped away to gather sumac leaves to cover her mother-aunt's brimming front basket, then helped her to swing it behind and bring the second one forward for filling.

"I am going to wade into the stream and gather the rest from the far side of the bushes," Otter decided, and flashed a mischievous smile at Morning Song. "Will you come with me?"

The girl shook her head. "I must go and empty my own basket," she said hastily. "See? It is filled nearly to the top."

Otter Swimming did not try to change her mind. She contented herself with waving her hand as she ducked beneath an overhanging branch, slid down the muddy bank it had concealed, and splashed happily into the water.

Morning Song, on her way to a larger container set near the path, smiled when she saw that Pumpkin Blossom was laboring still to fill her own basket for the first time. She allowed herself to strut just a little; rare indeed were the occasions when she bested her cousin.

She was unwise in looking aside, in trusting her contrary feet to keep to the path unaided. From beneath a drift of fallen leaves, a branch protruded—a bit of deadwood no thicker than Morning Song's wrist. It managed somehow to thrust itself across the toes of the girl's right foot. Morning Song stumbled, fought to disengage her pinioned toes, and went sprawling to the ground.

It was true that she was unhurt, true that many of the berries which poured in a gray-blue flood from her flying basket somehow descended into the very container she'd been making for. And no one—not even Bountiful Harvest, though she moved her head slowly from side to side—scolded Morning Song for her clumsiness. Most of those who witnessed her fall merely laughed indulgently before returning to their berry picking. But Morning Song did not miss an exchange of remarks between Pumpkin Blossom and Meadow Brook. And the children's laughter was uncomfortably like the sort that always attended her attempts to play kickball.

She struggled to her feet, retrieved her basket, and returned to her harvesting. But the day no longer seemed so beautiful.

Before winter's fingers had picked apart autumn's sleepy haze, the white men came again to the village.

Small Brown Sparrow had told Morning Song they were coming. "My father speaks the language of the *Onondio*," she said importantly, "so he will oversee the trading. And Cloud Racer will be there, too, this time. Trail Marker has even taught my brother to say *welcome*, and a word or two besides, in the tongue of the Frenchmen."

"Shall we be allowed to watch?" Morning Song wondered aloud. The children had been forbidden to leave the lodges when the *Onondio* had come before, but she yearned to see the sort of fabrics Lake On Fire fancied spread out in colorful array, with miniature mountains of sparkling beads heaped alongside.

Small Brown Sparrow shrugged. "I did not ask. But Cloud Racer is not yet a man, and if *he* may be with our father . . ." Her black eyes glinted, and her long mouth quirked at the corners.

"They will be here today?"

Small Brown Sparrow bobbed her head.

"Then why not go outside now and sit near the gate?" Morning Song asked. "If we are busy with a quiet game, perhaps no one will notice us."

The plan was good, except for the place she'd suggested. Follows The Signs, watching for the visitors, shooed them from the entrance and turned his back only when they had settled themselves between the Plover and Pigeonhawk longhouses.

"Well, we can see the compound from here, at least," Small Brown Sparrow sighed. "Which is better than nothing, I suppose."

"If any of the other children come around," Morning Song said worriedly, "someone will hear, and we will be chased away from this spot, too."

Small Brown Sparrow brightened. "We don't have to worry about the boys," she announced. "Fox Running said they were going into the woods with their slings and snares."

"And Pumpkin Blossom went with Meadow Brook to help Sun Descending plait baskets." Morning Song's voice betrayed her distaste for such a chore. Still, she was glad that Pumpkin Blossom would have no chance to see her cousin lurking near the compound on a trading day.

Suddenly she tossed up the straws she had brought along. "Your father and brother are coming," she hissed to Small Brown Sparrow, "and so is Se-A-Wi. Start playing, in case they look this way."

Small Brown Sparrow bent over the scattered straws and began to pick up those that lay by themselves. "If our Sachem is already here, we won't have long to wait," she murmured. She reached for a fourth straw, then jerked back her hand, and swiveled her head in the direction of the gateway. "Here come the *Onondio*," she said excitedly. "See, Morning Song! Follows The Signs is going out to meet them."

Morning Song, although supposedly intent on watching her friend, had been casting sidelong glances at the men gathering in the compound. She, too, had seen Follows The Signs put on a ritual courtliness and pass between the posts that stood like sentinels at the entrance to their village.

Now he was returning, and on either side of him walked a sallow-fleshed man clad in deerskin garments, which even from this distance Morning Song judged to be less than spotless. The trader on Follows The Signs's right was a fleshy man with brawny arms so short Morning Song doubted his hands would meet should he try to fold them upon his belly. His legs, too, were stunted, and his balding head was uncommonly small. Unless you looked closely, his bearlike torso was all that you saw.

If the other trader had not been so strikingly different, the gaping girls might have concluded that all *Onondio* resembled walking barrels. But this man, who towered over the first, seemed made entirely of angles. His long face wore a pointed nose. His mouth owned a triangular sharpness that whiskers the color of dirty snow could not conceal. The tips of his ears, peeking between strands of yellow-white hair, were pointed; and the bones of shoulder, elbow, and wrist threatened to pierce the fabric of his shirt. It hung on his lanky frame like a length of hide tossed upon a beanstalk.

Small Brown Sparrow tore her gaze from them, and her brow wrinkled. "Before, I heard my father say their names," she said slowly. "One is called Bree-And and the other"—she squeezed her eyes shut in an effort to remember—"is—is . . . Lah-Val! But," she added, dropping her voice in response to a warning look from her friend, "I do not know which one is which."

Morning Song cared little how the *Onondio* were called. Her attention had been snared by a straggling line of men. Bent beneath the weight of wooden crates and bulging sacks, they were coming up behind Follows The Signs and the two traders. "They are Indian!" she exclaimed. "Look, Small Brown Sparrow. They are our own people that these white men use as slaves!

Small Brown Sparrow paid scant attention. "They are not Iroquois," she said indifferently. "They are probably captives taken by some tribe that made a treaty with the French."

The procession had come all the way into the compound while the girls were talking. Now Small Brown Sparrow and Morning Song came cautiously to their feet and shrank back against the logs of the Plover longhouse. The traders stepped forward to greet Trail Marker and Se-A-Wi, the burly man's mouth stretching wide as he boomed out words indistinguishable to the girls. His companion merely lifted a hand, palm outward, and nodded his hairy head in response to the welcome offered by the Sachem and interpreted by Trail Marker.

"I wish we were close enough to hear," Small Brown Sparrow fretted.

But Morning Song cherished no such ambition. She found herself all at once in the grip of an emotion made more urgent by its senselessness. As the strangers seated themselves beside Trail Marker and signaled the bearers to lay down their burdens, she began to experience the sort of discomfort brought on by the intrusion of a cold draft into a cozy longhouse. Yet the air was still, so still that even the sparse blades of grass around Morning Song's feet showed not the slightest inclination to bend.

But the shivery sensation grew stronger. Morning Song, perplexed and more than a little frightened now, bit down on her lower lip. She pressed closer to the rough wall, seeking support for arms and legs she suddenly dared not trust. It did no good. Fear, a fear that knew no source, that could not be vanquished by reason, washed over her in frigid waves and all her senses screamed at her: Run! Run! Run!

Small Brown Sparrow, eyes and mouth round with astonishment, looked on as Morning Song uttered a choked cry, flung herself away from the wall, and bolted like a deer that has been panicked by a band of stalking hunters.

Morning Song did not stop running until she had hurtled into the Turtle longhouse and thrown herself into Teller Of Legends's arms.

Chapter 4

❧ ❦

Morning Song was unable to explain what had frightened her that day, but her grandmother had cuddled and comforted her, and Otter tried to make her smile by admitting to an old fear of her own.

"When I was your age, and woke in the night to find the fire dimmed by ash, I would whimper like a fox pup whose mother has been slain," she said. "I knew that the dark held nothing that was not there in daylight, but I was afraid anyway."

Although Morning Song had appreciated their efforts to console her, she could never accept, as the others seemed to, Hearth Tender's suggestion that some malevolent spirit had instigated her headlong flight. And when frost-whitened nights began to mark the trail into winter, prompting the family to concentrate on the work that was always done during the white season, she was glad to have reason to put the episode behind her.

For the women, this was the time for spinning and weaving, for splitting and hollowing out gourds, for the making or repairing of baskets and pottery and clothing. Morning Song had been impatient with such tasks in the past, but this year it soothed her to sit with the others and keep her hands busy.

On an afternoon when the north wind moaned around the lodge and made the flames on the hearth leap and squat then leap again, she was scraping hair from a rabbit pelt. She meant, with Otter's help, to fashion it into a bag to hold her cornhusk doll, six painted beads Lake on Fire had given her, and certain other small treasures. Pumpkin Blossom sat next to her, weaving a mat out of husks. Hearth Tender and Bountiful Harvest—having agreed that the clan's frayed burden straps must be replaced—were rolling fibers of slippery elm between palm and thigh.

Otter Swimming, strangely restless of late, had been helping her mother shape corn cakes to bake in the ashes of the rear hearth. Now she set the last one cautiously on the hot stone and walked to

37

the front of the longhouse. She twitched aside the sturdy entrance hide, peered out, then let the hide fall into place once more.

Hearth Tender looked at Teller of Legends and smiled. "It would seem the hunters have not returned as yet. Or at least that Deer Caller has not."

Morning Song, blade poised in midair, looked up, puzzled.

Teller of Legends was shaking her head and laughing silently. "I cannot accustom myself to calling him that," she said, taking a seat beside her eldest daughter and reaching for the buckskin leggins she'd been sewing earlier. "To me, he is still the small boy known as Muskrat Sitting Up."

Otter, returning to the warmer part of the lodge, overheard. "He has earned the right to be named Deer Caller," she said indignantly. "You know that he has, for we all saw with our own eyes the stag he brought home with him. And he has not been *small* for a long, long time!"

Morning Song was surprised that Otter would speak so to Teller of Legends and Hearth Tender, but the Matron of the Turtle clan showed no concern. "He has proven himself a man," she conceded blandly. "But you must allow an old woman like me a little time to adjust to such changes."

Otter grinned. "You and my sister laid a snare for me, and I walked into it," she said ruefully, then crossed to where her young nieces sat. "You are your mother's daughter in truth," she said to Pumpkin Blossom as she examined the tightness of her braiding. And you," she went on, turning to Morning Song, "are doing a fine job also. By tomorrow, that rabbitskin will be ready for stitching." She spotted the colored beads that Morning Song had put into a shallow basket along with her doll, several dried catkins, a snail's abandoned shell, and her clutch of snatch-straws. "We can make your bag pretty by using these to decorate it, if you like," she suggested.

Morning Song let her gaze travel to the pattern Otter was making on the floor with Lake On Fire's baubles, but did not think to stay the movement of her hands. "Oh, yes," she began. Then, "Ouch!" she yelped, and looked down to see red welling from the thumb that had wandered into the path of her scraping blade. She raised her hand and looked with dismay at the crimson drops spattering the rabbitskin.

"It will wash out," Otter assured her, at the same time jumping up and hurrying into the far corner of the longhouse. She returned with a bit of sticky spiderweb and wound it around Morning Song's thumb. "The bleeding will soon stop," she told her. "The cut is shallow."

"It does not even hurt," Morning Song said staunchly, and Otter patted her head.

"You're a brave girl—" she said approvingly, but was interrupted by Pumpkin Blossom whose tilted eyes were studying the rusty blotches marking the hide Morning Song had been denuding of fur.

"Why, your blood is red, Morning Song," she exclaimed. "Truly red. How can that be?"

Morning Song looked at her. "No redder than yours would be, had you stuck yourself with that needle," she said. "Or Otter's, or Hearth Tender's. Or—or anyone's!"

"I know that mine is red," her cousin said sharply. "And Otter's and Hearth Tender's, as well. But how can yours be? Surely the sallow-skin who was your father passed on to you some of his white blood?"

The drone of conversation, which had resumed when the women realized Morning Song's injury was a minor one, ceased abruptly. Morning Song looked from one to the other of the faces turned toward hers: at Otter, whose smile had vanished; at Hearth Tender, whose impassive features revealed nothing of her thoughts; at Bountiful Harvest, who wore an expression of watchfulness; and at her grandmother, who regarded her soberly, then slowly nodded her graying head.

"It is so, Morning Song," Teller of Legends said quietly. "Although"—her glance, suddenly flint-hard, went briefly to Bountiful Harvest—"*I* had hoped to be the one to tell you this, and at a time of my choosing."

Bountiful Harvest had not missed her mother's disapproval. "When Pumpkin Blossom asked recently why Morning Song's skin was so much lighter than hers, I told her the reason." Her tone was half defiant, half complacent. "It is the Iroquois way, to answer the questions of children honestly" she added virtuously.

"It would have been a kindness to let me know you had spoken to her of this," Teller of Legends said heavily. She rose and came to stand beside her stunned granddaughter. "I will not deny what Pumpkin Blossom has told you," she said gravely, "but it is of no importance, Morning Song. Any child born to a woman of the Longhouse People is considered by us to be Iroquois. This is the law. Even someone from another tribe altogether is seen as Iroquois from the moment of his adoption." She hunkered down until her gaze captured and held the stricken girl's. "You . . . are . . . Iroquois," she repeated, spacing the words for emphasis, "and a member of the Turtle clan. I hope you will always be proud that you are, for it would grieve me if ever the daughter of my daughter should feel otherwise about her family.''

Yet the shock and pain did not recede from Morning Song's brown eyes. Despite the love in her grandmother's voice, the touch of hands whose knotted veins did not diminish their gentleness, the girl's body, gone rigid with instinctive denial of what Pumpkin Blossom had said, did not relax. Instead, it arched like a bow drawn too swiftly, and before Teller of Legends realized what was happening, Morning Song had torn herself from the poor woman's tender grasp and streaked from the longhouse.

Memory screamed that she had done all this before, and the thought careened through her mind as she sped across the compound, through gates left ajar in anticipation of the hunting party's return, and along the path leading to the forest. Had it been an omen, her urge to flee from she-knew-not-what on the day the *Onondio* came? Now she ran away from the lodge, rather than toward it, but that was of small account. What she felt, inside, was the same: that if she ran fast enough, hard enough, long enough, she might somehow escape the inescapable.

This was what spurred her on, kept her knees pumping and her feet skimming over frost-hardened ground long past the point where every breath she drew seared throat and lungs like a fiery brand. And when she could run no more—when her chest was heaving and her legs were flailing and tears triggered by the icy wind were scoring her cheeks—she did not break stride but simply crumpled to the earth, with the muscles in her aching legs still tensed to carry her on.

Oblivion visited her then, cushioning her against the cold, and poulticing her fevered mind. The respite was brief, however. Once her erratic breathing had climaxed and begun its descent to evenness, Morning Song rolled over and clambered to her feet. Her dull eyes ranged over the starveling trees that surrounded her, the mush of decaying leaves that blanketed their feet, and focused at last on three squat firs that huddled like a trio of old warriors reminiscing around the fire. Recognition of the place she had come to sparked an ordering of her thoughts, and her face was pensive as she began reluctantly to retrace her steps. Common sense told her she could not long endure the onslaught of the freezing wind; she must return to her lodge with as much haste as her spent muscles permitted.

But . . . How should she approach those who waited for her there? Now that she knew herself for a half-breed, now that all of them were aware that she knew, how could things ever be the same?

She flung out her hands and lifted her eyes to the pallid sky. She ought to have guessed—and long before, she thought miserably. How often, and in how many ways, had she been shown that she was *different*! Even her appearance betrayed it. She pulled forward a strand of hair. It was midnight-dark, yes. But where other children's hair was firm-textured, hers was finespun; tendrils of it were forever escaping the imprisonment of braids to curl upon her forehead, against her traitorously pale cheeks, at the nape of her skinny neck. Which was another sign. Most of her playmates owned a sturdiness that spoke of strength to come; Morning Song was reed-thin from top to toe. The single arrow in a clutch of husky war lances, she was—and now she knew she always would be.

And her snail-slow mastering of skills that others learned so easily . . . The gracelessness that the naturally agile made mock of . . . These as well, she decided, must be charged to the part of her that was *Onondio*.

Sallow-skin. It was an ugly epithet, but one that she must accept applied to her. Running away had done nothing to change that.

She began moving rapidly along the path pointing back to the village, but soon slowed her pace. Despite the numbed fingers and toes that begged her to seek warmth, there was more thinking to be done, and she must make time for it. The day the traders came . . . It was foolish to think some sort of premonition had tied wings to the heels of a girl who had never been granted even ordinary dreams. So what had caused her fear that afternoon?

She shut her eyes and called up images of the two *Onondio*: One had been bulky and round, and had bared crooked teeth in what was meant to be a smile; the other had been angular and gaunt, with straggly white hair growing out of his scalp and obscuring much of his face.

She trembled as she pictured the pair, and knew that they *had*, somehow, been responsible for her terror. Had their spirits, sensing a kinship with Morning Song's, reached out to hers, taunted hers with a recognition she did not share?

She sighed. Hearth Tender might know if this could be; Morning Song did not. Besides, thinking of the *Onondio* had given rise to another puzzle: Morning Song's father had been a white man, as the traders were, yet nothing about them had been familiar to her. He might have been as different from the two as they were from each other, she supposed. But why was it she did not know how he had looked, this man who had sired her, with whom she must have spent the first five years of her life? Her memories of her mother might be hazy, but Morning Song had not forgotten her. Why was it she had no memory at all of her father?

She sighed again. What did it matter? Like everything else, these mysteries were simply things she would have to learn to cope with. If at the moment she could not quite see *how*, nonetheless she knew that she must, and furthermore that she would.

No step-by-step progression led her to this decision; she reached it by leaping across a chasm she dared not peer down into. And by making the jump, Morning Song thrust the better part of her childhood behind her.

The girl who slipped into the Turtle longhouse some minutes later was considerably older than the one whose anguish had driven her from it.

Eventually the Turtle clan came to realize that Morning Song had no desire to speak of what she had learned about herself. Teller of Legends contented herself with hugging her granddaughter more often than usual. Hearth Tender, because troubled spirits were her province, vainly pressed Morning Song to consult with her. Bountiful Harvest, smarting still from her mother's disapproval, treated the child with unusual gentleness for a time. Pumpkin Blossom, as she had been taught to do since infancy, followed her mother's example. Covers His Eyes—long disposed to ignoring most of what went on around him—had only a vague idea of what the women were concerned about, and did not care to learn more.

Otter chose to be direct. She asked Morning Song to join her in a stroll through the woods, and they had barely set out when Otter declared: "You are the daughter of my sister, and I love you dearly. I always have, and I always shall. If you try to deny full kinship with me merely because your father was *Onondio*, I will be hurt beyond healing."

Morning Song could not help but smile at the vehemence in her mother-aunt's voice. "I would never do that," she said.

"You must never forget, either, that you *are* Iroquois," Otter went on after a moment. "What Teller of Legends said is true, Morning Song."

If her niece had reservations about that, she did not admit to them. "Have we much further to go," she asked instead, "before we find the animal hidden in a tree that you said you would show me?"

Otter shaded her eyes against the dazzle of sun on snow and peered ahead. "We are nearly there," she said, pointing to an ash tree whose neatly paired branches were furred with white.

Morning Song ran ahead and studied it from all sides. "I do not see him, Otter," she called. "If an animal has hidden himself in this tree, he has done a fine job of it."

Otter Swimming's irregular features lit with anticipation. "If I find him," she challenged, "will you promise to play kickball with the other girls next time there is a game?"

Morning Song gawked at her. How did Otter know that she had been avoiding the games? "I am too clumsy," she muttered. "The others do not want me to play."

"How can you improve, except with practice?" Otter asked sternly. "And I am not asking you to become another Meadow Brook, you know. I only want to see you having fun with your friends." She tipped up the girl's face and smiled down into it. "You *do* want me to share the secret of the hidden animal with you?"

It was impossible to refuse Otter anything when she looked so! "Yes," said Morning Song.

"Then you will give your promise to do what I asked?"

Morning Song had looked hard at the leafless ash and seen nothing. Perhaps not all trees had animals in them, and surely any agreement made would relate to this tree only? "I do," she declared stoutly.

Otter Swimming marched over to the tree, towing Morning Song after her. She searched the lowest branch, then turned her attention to the one just above. "Aha!" she said suddenly, and rested a blunt finger on a twig projecting forlornly from it. "See, Morning Song! Here, beneath the sleeping buds of next year's leaves, is the creature I said I would show you." She pulled down the branch until it was at the younger girl's level, then traced the outline of a tiny face.

Morning Song followed the movements of Otter's finger, and gasped in amazement. Despite its smallness, it was the head of a deer, complete with tiny velvet-wrapped antlers, that she was looking at!

"In truth, it is only the scar left by a leaf that fell during the red season," Otter explained as she allowed the branch to spring back into place. "On an elm tree, the faces often seem to be winking at you, and the aspen's are usually heart-shaped and have ridiculously flat noses."

"It is strange, that the leaves that fall should leave behind such marks," Morning Song said.

"Perhaps what is peeking out at us is the spirit that gives life to the tree," Otter Swimming said comfortably. She caught Morning

Song's hand and swung it as they continued their walk. "You have not forgotten what you promised?" she added after a moment.

Morning Song shook her head. "I have not," she sighed. "When the girls play kickball again, I will join them."

Several days later an obliging sun had melted much of the snow, and Morning Song followed Pumpkin Blossom to the spot where chattering girls were assembling. A number of adults were also in the compound to bid farewell to Se-A-Wi. He was setting off to meet the Sachem from a nearby village who, like him, owned a seat on the Great Council of the Iroquois. They were among the delegates who would be traveling east and north to talk with representatives of the French *Onondio*, and with chiefs of the Algonquin and Huron tribes.

"The Indian allies of the French have had their scheming thwarted," Teller of Legends had told her family. "Although they had pledged to buy the pelts our hunters trapped or traded for, the Huron and Algonquin went to other tribes for furs to sell to the French. And traveled down one of our own rivers with them heaped in their long canoes! But the Iroquois warriors outsmarted them. They blockaded the river, and now our enemies have been forced to ask us to set conditions for a new peace treaty. If they agree to our terms, then the Iroquois will be dealing directly with the French chiefs, as once we did with the Dutch. Which is as it should be."

There had been no real enthusiasm in her voice. Teller of Legends understood that, these days, the prosperity of her people depended upon profitable trade agreements with the white men. Nor did she need reminding that the Iroquois must be guaranteed the right to roam farther afield in search of beaver, which were virtually gone from their own territories; after all, there could be no trading unless each side had something the other wanted or needed. Nonetheless Teller Of Legends had little faith in the integrity of the French, and mistrusted even more those Indian tribes who boasted of being under French protection.

As she watched her brother depart, she took care that her expression should reveal none of her misgivings. She was shrewd enough to know that some of those misgivings had been born on the day she learned of her husband's death, and it was not wise to allow emotion to influence judgment. Yet when the Sachem, resplendent in antler headdress and fur robe, had nodded gravely to his well-wishers and gone on his way, a shadow fell across her broad face that owed nothing to the positioning of sun and cloud.

Morning Song, going with dragging feet to fulfill her promise to Otter, saw it, and wondered at it.

Only briefly, however. Once the grownups had returned to their lodges and the boys had swarmed after Se-A-Wi to escort him to the outskirts of the neighboring village, the girls started choosing sides for the kickball game. Morning Song was unsurprised when she was the last to be selected, and she did not know whether to be glad or sorry that she was named to her cousin's team.

Still, it cheered her that everyone appeared to be in high spirits. Laughter made the crisp air ring when the ball was put into play, and perhaps it was a good omen that Pumpkin Blossom's team scored first.

Morning Song, assigned to block the opposition, began to trust that all might go well. Despite her slenderness, she was reasonably good at defensive play; it was not in her to give way merely because someone was bigger and stronger than she was. She became flushed with excitement as she dashed about trying to prevent the fleet-footed Meadow Brook from getting near the ball. But excitement became chagrin when the ball landed right beside them and a feint by the older girl put Morning Song off-balance and sent her sprawling. She could only watch helplessly as Meadow Brook's expert kick won a point for her team.

No one made too much of the incident; Morning Song heard only the groans that any fault, by any player, would have prompted. Encouraged, she picked herself up and returned to the play.

As the game wore on, though, the lightheartedness of the players was succeeded by a grim determination to win. The ball scarcely touched down before a foot was there to send it soaring. Still, the score continued even, and each point her team earned saw Morning Song shouting as lustily as her comrades. Grinning, she allowed herself to think that Otter, *dear* Otter, had been right: To join wholeheartedly in the game was all that had been needed to learn how to play it properly.

Confidence inspired by this thought sent Morning Song racing for the ball next time it descended. She drew back her right leg, prepared to bring it forward with all the strength she possessed. It would be the winning point that she scored, she realized gleefully, and already she pictured the ball spinning up and up and up as the whole of Pumpkin Blossom's team chanted her praises.

She ought to have known better. The snow dissolved by the sun had dribbled into the crusty topsoil. The pounding of a score of feet had helped to mix it in. And moisture of any sort, thoroughly blended with soil, produces just one thing: mud.

Morning Song had leaned toward the ball while she made ready to kick. Now, as her right leg began its forward thrust, her torso tilted sharply in the opposite direction. Her left foot shifted slightly to keep her steady, and pressed itself tighter against the ground.

But the ground betrayed her; it had gone soft and slick and yielding. Morning Song and her visions of glory were brought abruptly down to earth.

She heard the sound of running feet, a solid *smack*, a chorus of joyful shrieks, as someone from Meadow Brook's team seized the opportunity and kicked the goal that gave them the victory.

Morning Song struggled to her feet. When she shook the hair out of her eyes and turned to her teammates, she read in their grimy faces disappointment, resentment, and no little disgust.

She met their stares with an apologetic smile. It earned her instant rebuff. The mocking laughter, the rush to label her *Bumble Cub* or *Blind Mole*, which in times past had so tormented her, would have been easier to endure. Anger rose in her then; anyone might have slipped and fallen, and been forgiven once the usual jeering comments had been made. Anyone but Morning Song. They had *expected* her clumsiness to cost them the game.

She drew herself up tall, stuck out her chin, and returned glare for glare. Then she swung around, keeping her spine rigid and her head high, and walked away with measured tread. Hurt she might be, and doubtless would be again. But from this day, no one would ever see that she was.

To avoid the girls—who would, in any event, be bent on avoiding her—and also because the forest, even in winter, was her favorite place still, Morning Song took to trailing after the boys when they went to trap small game or to sharpen the skills they would need to become warriors. Some tried to send her home when they found her tagging along, but most only laughed to discover her watching as they practiced with the bows their uncles had made for them.

"Let her stay," Hill Climber said amiably. "Warriors must accustom themselves to being admired by maidens." He puffed out his chest and strutted a bit.

"She is scarcely a maiden," Fox Running protested. "She is only nine years old."

"And *you* are scarcely a warrior," his brother said mildly as he nocked an arrow and aimed at the tip of the tall pine some distance away. Cloud Racer's arrow flew straight and true, and Stag Leaping of the Pigeonhawk clan hooted derisively.

"That was a poor target to choose, Cloud Racer. Now you have lost an arrow."

The son of Trail Marker and Rain Singing made no reply, but strode to the place where the evergreen stood and, with remarkable economy of motion, hoisted himself into it. Keeping close to the slender trunk, he climbed higher and higher, bracing himself occasionally against its swaying, until the arrow was within his reach.

When he had descended and returned to the others, he looked at Stag Leaping. "Only a sorry warrior cannot retrieve the arrows he has loosed," he said quietly. Then he turned to Fox Running, who was tugging at his arm.

"Woodpecker Drumming has found a deer's spoor!" his brother said excitedly. "We mean to follow it, Cloud Racer."

Cloud Racer raised his eyebrows. "*All* of you?" he asked. "If the beast is anywhere around, it will surely arrange to be far from here when so many feet set the ground to shaking."

"We have learned to walk as hunters should," Fox Running persisted. "And you must come with us, Cloud Racer. Will you miss a chance to bring down your first deer?"

Woodpecker Drumming, coming to join them, laughed. "I expect it is far from here already. The trace is not recent, Cloud Racer."

The eagerness of the younger boys decided the issue, however. And, naturally, Morning Song followed when they went. But when the boy directly ahead of her spun around in response to her stepping carelessly upon a dry twig, she froze and lowered her eyes. Even though he only grinned and shook his head at her, she hung back when he resumed his tracking. In a moment, misery was her only companion.

"I understand that you walk like a heavy-footed sallow-skin."

Morning Song jumped, for the words spoken by Cloud Racer—who had left his friends and come back to where she stood—stung with the ferocity of a hundred bees. Yet there was no malice in his dark face, and his alert eyes did not castigate her.

"I have seen how often you visit the woods," he went on. "Why not learn to walk properly, so that the animals who live here are not disturbed by your coming?"

"I should like to watch them without their knowing," Morning Song found herself admitting.

He nodded. "It is only a matter of learning to keep your weight on your toes and to put one foot before the other," he said. And demonstrated what he meant.

Morning Song, brow furrowed in concentration, watched, and,

when he signed for her to do so, attempted to imitate his noiseless tread.

"You will need to practice," he told her gravely when he had observed her efforts. "But you can teach yourself to move quietly even when walking on dry leaves."

Then he was gone, as swiftly and as silently as he had come, leaving an astounded Morning Song with her heartfelt gratitude unexpressed.

Chapter 5

Just when they had begun to think winter would continue to mete out its snow in miserly portions, the villagers awakened to a shivery, silvery dawn. When they scanned a sky glutted with bruise-dark clouds, they nodded sagely at one another. Their world would be heaped with white before this day ended.

Morning Song welcomed the heavy fall; this snow was the sort that clung nicely when rolled into glistening balls. As soon as the sun reappeared, she approached the other girls and suggested a hurling competition. They were startled; Morning Song had not joined in their play for weeks and weeks. And never had she initiated a game.

"We should form two teams, or even three," Morning Song said with deliberate casualness, "since some of us are bound to score high and others, low."

Meadow Brook, whose expertise extended to double-ball and shinny, grinned. "Why not first test us one by one," she proposed, "to learn who our high scorers are?" She exchanged glances with Pumpkin Blossom, and grinned again.

It was a message clearly sent, and as clearly received: *Then we may all watch while the clumsy one makes another exhibition of herself!*

Morning Song merely shrugged and made no protest when the players lined up and she was shunted to the rear. Nor did she show dismay when the javelin hoop they'd chosen for a target was placed a challenging distance from the throwers.

It was agreed that each girl in turn would hurl snowballs until one failed to penetrate the hoop they'd suspended from an upended drying rack. Meadow Brook, who had assumed control of the game, signed to Small Brown Sparrow to throw first. Morning Song's friend narrowed her eyes and loosed the snowball that had been numbing her fingers. Everyone cheered when it passed through the hoop and buried itself in a convenient drift. Her next two tosses were as good; but her fourth ball veered to the right and struck lightly against the outer rim of the hoop.

"Everyone else will do better than that," she said cheerfully, and began making snowballs for those whose keener aim depleted their supplies in a hurry.

She was kept busy. But by the time Morning Song's turn came, no player had accumulated more points than Meadow Brook and Sun Descending. Each had managed thirteen perfect throws.

"We will be competing against each other in a moment," Meadow Brook told the older girl, her eyes shining with the light of battle. "Shall we wager a pair of moccasins on the outcome?"

"So long as they are new made!" Sun Descending shot back. "I do not want your castoffs, Meadow Brook."

The pair always enjoyed challenging each other in this fashion, and they went on with their lively banter until a peculiar hush fell upon their friends. They swung around then to see Morning Song catch a snowball tossed by Small Brown Sparrow and resume a surprisingly professional hurling stance.

"She has thrown eleven times and not missed once." Pumpkin Blossom's shrillness registered her disbelief.

"*Morning Song* has?" Meadow Brook's own astonishment was expressed in a whisper. She was used to excelling, and did not hesitate to congratulate herself when she did so. But she was as readily admiring of anyone who could do as well as she, or better. Now she gestured to Pumpkin Blossom to be still, and gave her attention to a girl she had never thought might warrant admiration.

Pumpkin Blossom stifled a gasp as yet another white sphere found the precise center of the dangling target. "Twelve!" she breathed.

Despite the cold, Morning Song's bronze flesh wore a sheen of perspiration. I must not exult too soon, she warned herself, but her heart was pounding hard enough to bruise her chest. She hefted a new ball and made herself wait until her breathing steadied before raising her arm and sighting along the invisible line that led to the hoop.

When she was ready, she let fly, then closed her eyes. But she knew by Small Brown Sparrow's joyful squeal that the toss had

been true. She had matched the score set by Meadow Brook and
Sun Descending!

Could she take the lead and win the game? To calm herself before
making the attempt, she thought of the village boys. If she triumphed now, she would owe the victory to them. Their attitude
toward their tagalong had graduated from exasperated indifference
to a gruff kindness, and some had gone so far as to instruct her in
some small skill or another. Their help had brought her to where
she stood now: surrounded by companions whose silent encouragement patched up any holes in Morning Song's self-confidence.

Her last snowball sailed through the hoop, and a shower of praise
warmed her to the tips of her frozen toes. But memory of the kickball game that had ended with her reaping silent scorn from these
same girls rankled still.

Because it did, she only smiled coolly to acknowledge their tribute. Then she turned without haste and walked away.

Her companions gaped after her. That she would do so strange
a thing left them offended, perplexed, and more convinced than
ever that Morning Song was a most peculiar girl, one who had no
sense whatsoever of what was fitting.

Morning Song decided that she would share her moment of glory
with one person only: Otter Swimming. She found her mother-aunt
watching the young men who had gathered behind the longhouses
for a game of snowsnake. A smooth-barked log had been dragged
through the snow, leaving a shallow trench behind it, and a score
of hands and feet had tamped down the sides and bottom of the
trench until the snow was hard-packed. The younger boys, eager
to assist their heroes, were sprinkling water in the trench to make
it slick.

The warriors clutched flexible sticks as long as lances. Those
tapered rods, Morning Song knew, were the snakes, lovingly carved
by those who had waited all year for just such a snow as this.

She moved close to Otter as the contest got under way. "I have
something to tell you," she began.

"Later!" Otter Swimming hissed, and did not even look at her.

She must have wagered on the game, Morning Song thought,
and prepared to contain herself until it ended. Se-A-Wi was acting
as referee, she saw. That ought to mean there would be no disputes
when the winner was finally named; but considering how heated
this sort of competition generally became, it probably did not!

Fierce Eagle, having stroked his snake with a fresh application
of the oil that the players called *medicine*, grasped it firmly in his

right hand and balanced it with his left. He stooped, holding the snake horizontal to the trench, then leaped forward and threw it with admirable force and accuracy.

Se-A-Wi handed a marker to Cloud Racer and sent him to flag Fierce Eagle's goal by thrusting it into the ridge of snow running parallel to the trench.

Long Canoe, his square-shaped face expressionless, put all of his hulking strength behind the cast it was his turn to make. When his snake skidded only half the length of the depression before glancing off one side, he endured stoically the barrage of insults that made mock of so sorry a performance.

Morning Song was near enough to Otter to be alerted when her mother-aunt suddenly tensed. She glanced at her, saw that her eyes sparkled more brilliantly than the untrampled snow heaped against the palisade, and looked to see what had animated her to such a degree.

Deer Caller, lately come to the status of warrior, was approaching the trench with his own round-headed snake. This young man was short-statured compared to many of his fellows, and stockily built; but he wore a face-crinkling grin that did not falter even when he studied the great distance he must send his snake if he hoped to best Fierce Eagle.

Morning Song counted it to his credit that he did not let himself be distracted by the hectoring of his comrades as he prepared to launch his snake. But she hardly thought it deserving of Otter's quick-drawn breath and tight-clasped hands. Then, in the instant before he bent from the waist, she saw Deer Caller's eyes seek out Otter Swimming, saw the look that flashed between them, and was so stunned by it that she could not have said, later, whether Deer Caller's attempt earned him the respect or the censure of the other players. She never doubted, however, that—so far as Otter was concerned—Deer Caller was, and would be, champion of them all.

By the time spring spread a medley of greens across the land, it no longer seemed strange that Deer Caller had come to live in the Turtle lodge. To have a hunter providing them with meat was an excellent thing, although only Bountiful Harvest—because she took joy in humiliating Covers His Eyes—was given to emphasizing this. She was greatly swollen with her third child, which Morning Song felt should make her show more kindness to her mate. It seemed instead to have honed her temper.

It had been difficult at first for Morning Song to accept that she was no longer the sole focus of Otter Swimming's attention. It wasn't that Otter had moved her belongings to a hearth closer to the rear of the longhouse, leaving Morning Song in lonely possession of the bed they had shared; this had been inevitable, and only required getting used to. But the shyness that enveloped the younger girl whenever Otter and Deer Caller were together in their part of the lodge filled her with discomfort and confusion. She and Otter had been so close, always; now she would have no one to share secrets with, no one with whom she might speak freely, as the other girls did with one another.

"Girls grow into maidens, and maidens into wives," Teller Of Legends told her. She watched Bountiful Harvest heave herself from her bed and cross ponderously to the hearth. "And wives become mothers," she added. "This is as it should be, Morning Song. I think you know that Otter does not love you less because she has taken a husband." Her eyes twinkled. "It will not be long, you know, before you will see the boys around you somewhat differently than you do now. As Pumpkin Blossom will, also."

Morning Song was jolted out of her misery. She liked most of the boys, and admired a number of them. She certainly found them, on the whole, more agreeable to be with than the girls, and she realized how fortunate she was to have been permitted cautious entry to their brotherhood. Why, Hill Climber had allowed her to try out his bow once, and Cloud Racer—until, on the way home from his Vision Quest, he had single-handedly brought down a bear—continued to monitor the way that Morning Song walked. But to feel toward any boy as Otter felt toward Deer Caller . . .

"It will be a long time before that happens," she said firmly.

Her grandmother laughed. "Well, we shall see," was all she said before hunkering down to help Morning Song examine seed corn for mold.

Rainfall was reluctant to bless the planting they were preparing for, and even the short-lived showers ceased as the green season surrendered to the yellow. The drought was a worrisome thing, and became more so when worms destroyed the corn that had managed to grow despite being moisture-starved. The Faithkeepers met to ponder the reason for their plight, and burned tobacco to implore the help of He-No The Thunderer. When their efforts brought no response from him, the prudent villagers began to husband what food they had left in bin and barrel, and portions at mealtime were meticulously measured out.

"It can be strengthening, to eat sparingly," the matrons advised those children too small to understand why their bowls were so shallowly filled. "Look at our warriors. See how greatly they value sinew and muscle? They recognize that it is weakening to be burdened with too many layers of flesh, and are wise enough to eat mostly meat and fish.''

Those, at least, were plentiful still, and the young men—thanks to the treaty the Iroquois Sachems had negotiated with the French—were able to make up hunting and fishing parties more often than they used to. Some of the women and children also fished in the rivers and streams that flowed, sluggishly now, near the village. They brought home the starchy roots of cattails to cook as well.

"Whatever happens, we will not be driven to eating the inner bark of trees, as the Algonquin have been known to do,'' they assured one another. But their eyes did not display the confidence that they forced into their voices.

Teller of Legends compensated the youngsters for meagerness of diet by providing them with an abundance of food for thought. She joined them after their mealtime, and entertained them with stories. Over the years Morning Song had become quite familiar with these stories, and it did not take her long to see how her grandmother was skillfully weaving humor into legends that had been largely devoid of it in previous tellings. Laughter could do nothing to fill an empty belly, but it helped Teller of Legends's audience to forget about their hunger.

"In the past, evil beings preyed upon the Longhouse People,'' she told them one afternoon. "And there was one so horrible to look upon that even warriors trembled to hear its name spoken. It is the grotesque Flying Head that I speak of. It had no neck, this head, although it was taller by far than the tallest of men; indeed it had no body of any sort, not even arms or legs. And it was ugly beyond your imagining. It wore a ferocious scowl, and from the side its nose resembled a range of sharp-peaked mountains. Its snarling mouth was fitted with fangs to make it easy for the Flying Head to devour its prey. And it hunted all living things, this monster, including people.''

"How was it able to fly?'' Sun Descending put the question everyone was poised to ask.

"The Flying Head was covered all over with scaly hide,'' Teller of Legends said, "which was in turn covered with matted hair. And from its hairy cheeks grew huge wings much like a buzzard's, and very powerful they were. The Flying Head had only to flap them and he soared high into the sky, to ride the wind until he spied a tasty morsel below. And that morsel''—she looked into the faces of the children, shook her head sadly—"was often a boy or girl whose greediness had made him plump as a porcupine.'' Her mournful expression made the children giggle. "And in those days, there were many who indulged their appetites in a shameful fashion. I am sorry to tell you this, but the Flying Head was able to eat frequently, and well.

"Finally the Longhouse People decided to hide from the Flying Head, and so they posted sentries to alert them to its coming. But a young matron who had recently borne her first child had no wish to see her son grow up learning to be a coward. When next word came that the Flying Head had been sighted, she said to herself: *Someone must take a stand against this monster. It might as well be me.*"

The girls in her audience smiled smugly—and cast disparaging glances at the boys.

"Well, she thought and she thought and—as usually happens when a person takes the time to think—an idea came to her. Everyone knew the Flying Head loved to eat, and was given to gulping down his food. It could not be bothered with taking small bites, or chewing thoroughly. Which *you*, of course, always do."

She waited for chuckles, chortles, and a few shamefaced looks to have their moment, then picked up her tale once more. "What this clever young woman did was build up her fire until it was blazing. Then she took large stones and threw them into the heart of the fire. She arranged a number of smaller stones closer to the edge of the fire, and turned them with a forked stick until they glowed red on all sides.

"When she was satisfied that everything was ready, she took her sleeping child to a bed in the back of the longhouse, where darkness would conceal him. Then she went to the front and fastened back the entrance hide.

"By the time the Flying Head—which was quite out of temper because it had found the village, so far, to be empty—peeked into the young woman's home, she was sitting again by her hearth. Without turning around, she took up her forked stick and, lifting one of the smaller red-hot rocks, pretended to put it into her mouth. (In truth, she passed it behind her and dropped it into the shadows.) Next, she rubbed her belly, and smacked her lips, and exclaimed, 'Ah, how delicious! Who has ever feasted on meat so tender and juicy as this?'

"Now the monster knew that cooked meat tastes better than raw. Although it had meant to make a meal of the Iroquois woman, it saw in the middle of the hearth what must be well-baked haunches of whatever animal had provided the flesh for the woman's meal.

"Quicker than I can tell it, that greedy Flying Head thrust its hideous face deep into the lodge, spread open its massive jaws, and swallowed without chewing a dozen fire-crimsoned boulders!

"This was its undoing, of course. It screamed—and that sound sent the roof of the young woman's longhouse high into the sky—and flapped its great wings. Still screaming, it soared into the night and went, hissing billows of steam, over mountain, river, and forest until the moment came when its voice dried up from the searing heat. The rocks, you see, had absorbed so much of the young woman's fire that the Flying Head burned up, from the inside out. Nothing was left of it but ash."

Stag Leaping, who had made a show of seating himself apart from the younger children and whose posture throughout had been intended to convey that he was not *truly* listening, gave a snort of derision. "If the Flying Head were still around, *I* would not be afraid to deal with it. No young woman is half so brave as I am!"

But everyone knew that Stag Leaping had been much put out ever since Cloud Racer, a year younger than he, had been invited to sit with the warriors. No one responded to his pointless boast.

As if the drought were not enough to make the people of Morning Song's village go about with grave faces, word came that the treaty with the French and their Indian allies had been broken. The *Onondio* were once again encouraging the Huron to bring pelts through Iroquois country without making recompense to the Longhouse People. If the Iroquois were not to appear fools, they must go to war.

The men began their preparations. Weapons were taken down and examined, tales of past expeditions were revived and shared with those who had been too young to take part in them. And wives and mothers postponed routine chores in order to make or refurbish the headdresses with free-spinning, upright feathers that only warriors were entitled to wear.

Then came the ritual fasting, for every man wanted to condition himself against the hardships he would be exposed to in the weeks ahead. And there were, inevitably, omens to be deciphered and dreams to be interpreted.

Spear Thrower of the Wolf clan came one morning to the Turtle lodge and awarded Teller Of Legends the greeting courtesy demanded of him. But his eyes were fixed on Hearth Tender, who sat beside her mother's hearth.

"I have been visited by a dream," he told her, squatting on the other side of the fire. The glow of it played upon his oddly foreshortened nose and stubby chin, giving them greater prominence than they possessed. "I wish you to tell me its meaning."

He fumbled in his bag and took out a brace of fresh-killed geese, less fat than these migrating birds had been in seasons past but welcome nonetheless. He fidgeted as Hearth Tender nodded approval of his offering and passed the birds along to Bountiful Harvest.

"Tell me your dream," Hearth Tender urged as her sister carried the birds outside for plucking. "Perhaps I may find a message in it."

"When I sleep," Spear Thrower began slowly, "I find myself setting out on a long journey. Alone. Somehow I know that ahead of me are mountains I must climb, and rivers I must cross, and I am filled with dismay. I look down to see that there is an axe in my hand, the kind of axe used for felling trees. And I understand that it is a forest I am traveling to." He paused, and drummed his fingers upon his angled knee.

Hearth Tender signed for him to go on.

"I set out on a long and unmarked trail, and wild beasts growl at my heels as I go. But I come at last to a place where trees grow tall and close together. I know at once that I am meant to cut down some of them, but I do not know which ones." He swallowed twice, and his voice when he spoke again had a rasp in it. "Then the axe flies from my hand and, by itself, begins to hack at the nearest tree. This is an ancient tree, one that lightning has struck a time or two. Suddenly it swerves and attacks instead a knee-tall sapling. I cry out and try to grab the handle of the axe. I beg it to stop, to let the young tree finish its growing."

Spear Thrower trembled with the remembering, and fell silent.

"Is there more?" Hearth Tender prompted.

He shook his head. "But I have been visited by this same dream three times. I need to know the meaning of it."

Hearth Tender closed her eyes and her dark lashes made half-moons of shade on her coppery cheeks. At length she sighed and looked again at the troubled warrior. "You have been sent a warning of danger lurking," she said slowly, "which will reveal itself when you go to war. The axe that needs no hand to guide it symbolizes Death, which hovers during any battle to seize the unwary." The ghost of a smile relieved the soberness of her expression. "The trees you saw in your vision are but a reminder, I think, of what the Longhouse People believe: that it is better to be broken like a young oak in the hurricane than wait for rot to set in and eat up the the heart. Sometimes we forget that those youthful warriors who are slain in battle have at least escaped the infirmities old age brings."

She smiled again, reassuringly. "The spirit that sent your dream directs you to be alert during battle, and to be ready to go to the aid of a young comrade who might need your help. It warns you as well to mix courage with caution while you seek glory."

When Spear Thrower had gone on his way, Morning Song, who had been shamelessly eavesdropping, looked at her oldest mother-aunt. She stood in awe of Hearth Tender, for this was a woman as much at home in the world of the spirits as in the visible world. That distinction made her seem as strong as the elements, even though ritual fasting had stripped most of the flesh from her prominent bones. She was like an arrow fashioned from green wood, Morning Song thought suddenly. Hearth Tender would never break under pressure, but only bend. "You did not tell him," she ventured hesitantly, "that he would return safe from battle."

Hearth Tender considered before replying. "His dream did not reveal that, one way or the other," she said. "Also, it was not fear of dying that made him come to me. Spear Thrower is not as young as he was, Morning Song. He knows that his days as a warrior must end soon, and watches for a sign to tell him when he should put aside his lance and devote all his time to serving on the village council. It will not be easy for him to give up the challenging life of a warrior; it may be he will see himself as less than a man when he does. But it would be just as threatening to his manhood to invite humiliation by continuing along a path he is no longer meant to walk."

"But you think that he should go with the war band this time?"

"His dream indicated this."

"And his woman, Gray Squirrel . . . She may expect him to return with the others?" Morning Song could not have said why she was being persistent to the point of impertinence, but an unease she did not understand drove her to it.

Hearth Tender smiled at her niece. "Even she would not ask this of me," she chided gently. "Yet I will tell you that I think she may."

Morning Song let her gaze probe the depths of Hearth Tender's dark eyes and was content that she predicted truly. But she felt vaguely dissatisfied still.

Otter Swimming, although she took pains not to show it, was desolate that Deer Caller would be leaving with Fierce Eagle's band. "I will not let myself fear for him," she told Morning Song. "He is a fine warrior and shall come home to chant a victory song. But I will be so lonely without him."

Morning Song took a moment to sort out her feelings. She was elated that Otter had spoken so openly to her; women whose men went off to battle expected one another to admit to nothing but pride that their husbands followed a trail that might lead to glory. And while she, too, would be sorry to have Deer Caller go away— he had been kind to Morning Song, had even given her his old bow when he made himself a new one—she could not help but be glad she would be having her favorite mother-aunt all to herself once more.

She bent and bestowed a casual pat on the head of a spotted bitch whose teats were swollen from the tugging of a litter ready for weaning. "Perhaps he will not be away long," she offered consolingly. "Small Brown Sparrow tells me that her uncle expects to surprise the Huron with this raid. If they are unprepared, surely they will be defeated quickly."

Otter brightened a little. "If that is so, then you are looking at one woman who will not be shy in singing the praises of Fierce Eagle as war leader!" She looked through the open gate, to where brown stubble marked fields that ought to have been green with autumn crops. "I hope they will remember to seize the Hurons' store of corn and beans, once the fighting is over," she sighed. "Otherwise we shall not be able to make a proper feast for their homecoming."

The war party was assembling near the post into which Fierce Eagle had flung his hatchet, and around which he had led his comrades in a dance miming the prowess they would soon display in combat. Their oiled bodies glistened in the sunlight, their faces had been blackened with a blend of charcoal and bear grease. War clubs, wicked-looking knives, and sharp axes dangled from their belts, and Morning Song was as admiring of their ferocious appearance as the rest of the villagers were. Everyone had turned out to urge the war band to bring honor upon themselves and their kin, even Dancing Water, the ancient who was grandmother to Cloud Racer and Fox Running and Small Brown Sparrow. Dancing Water leaned on the arm of her daughter, Rain Singing, but those who stood near enough to study her shriveled face chuckled to see how a pert young maiden peeked now and then from behind eyes sunk deep in corrugations of age-darkened flesh. One clawlike hand clutched the trail rations she'd insisted on presenting to her son.

"Where is he?" she demanded now. "Where is Fierce Eagle?"

She blinked lashless eyes and craned her head this way and that, muttering irritably all the while.

"There is a crowd around him," Rain Singing replied. "You must remember that he is leading this expedition. Many are eager to wish him success in battle."

"He has no need of well-wishers," the old woman said tartly. "My son is the strongest of the strong and the bravest of the brave. He is a Pine Tree Chief, after all. Tell them that, Rain Singing. At once!"

"Everyone knows, and praises him for it," her daughter said soothingly, and was relieved to see her brother working his way through the press of people. Their mother was not above using her seniority as an excuse for saying the sort of thing young folk were forbidden to say, and once begun she would not be hushed.

Morning Song and Otter, their own progress hindered by the throng, smiled to hear Fierce Eagle, come at last to bid his mother good-bye, being berated for his tardiness. "Were her tongue a whip, it would flay him," Otter whispered. "I am glad Teller Of Legends is not like that!"

"She could never—" Morning Song began, then stiffened. The group around the post had shifted, revealing someone she had not expected to see there. "Surely Cloud Racer is not old enough to be going with Fierce Eagle's band!" she exclaimed.

"When he killed that bear, he proved himself a man," Otter reminded her. "But on this expedition, he will serve only as scout and messenger, I imagine. This is usually the way of it when manhood is achieved before a boy's full growth is."

But her tone was detached. Deer Caller—on the watch for his wife—had come to smile his slow smile and say a last farewell. Otter gave him a pouch bulging with the mixture of dried corn flour and maple sugar that would sustain him during the march.

Morning Song, spotting her grandmother and Day Greeter standing a little distance away, left the young couple to such privacy as might be snatched in the midst of pandemonium. But as she approached Teller Of Legends, she saw Covers His Eyes shouldering his own way toward the Matron, and it was he who reached her first. He put a hand on her arm and spoke with some urgency, if the expression on his fleshy face meant anything. Morning Song quickened her pace.

"Bountiful Harvest's babe is about to be born," her grandmother informed her matter-of-factly. "She has gone into the forest, and Covers His Eyes worries that the war band, when it sets out, may stumble upon her."

"That would be dreadful," Morning Song said. "Can you stop them, Teller Of Legends?"

"I could not, nor would," her grandmother said placidly. "There are places we women know of where no man—not even a warrior drunk with battle lust—would think to go. Bountiful Harvest will give birth undisturbed. But you and I should find Pumpkin Blossom and Hearth Tender and return to the lodge. We women must be there to welcome my daughter when she returns, and rejoice in the child she brings with her. And I want to be sure nothing has been overlooked in the part of the longhouse that shall be theirs alone for a time. Although," she added, as she urged Morning Song ahead of her, "knowing Bountiful Harvest as I do, I am certain she has made everything ready."

So it was that, of the Turtle clan, only Se-A-Wi and Otter were watching when Fierce Eagle led his comrades through the palisade's gate and into the woods. Those who had gone into the lodge to feed the fire and set to boil a pot of anemic gruel knew when they left, however. The rattle and boom of voices high-pitched and low was all at once stilled. Only intermittent murmurs reached their ears, and the occasional squeal of a child reluctant to have the excitement over with.

"May their arrows fly straight and their lances strike true," Hearth Tender said softly. As her mother nodded solemnly, Otter Swimming came into the longhouse, looking around without expression. She did not ask why her mother and sister and nieces sat together in an attitude of anticipation but went, leaden-footed, to the bed that she and Deer Caller had made their own.

Teller Of Legends followed her with her gaze. "For women," she said heavily, "there is no glory in war."

In that moment, Morning Song understood what had bothered her while Spear Thrower was consulting with Hearth Tender, and what had prompted her question about Gray Squirrel. To wait and to worry, to have no way of knowing whether the end of a war would be cause for mourning or rejoicing, must demand more of a woman than the fiercest fighting required of a man. Yet should a dream visit a woman on the eve of battle, she was left to puzzle out the meaning of it unaided; the concern of the Faithkeepers was all for the warriors themselves. As was the praisegiving when they came home from war.

Although Morning Song had been taught otherwise, she was coming to suspect that to have been born a woman was not entirely a thing to be thankful for.

Chapter 6

❦ ❧

Morning Song grasped the string of Deer Caller's old bow. With her right arm at shoulder level, she drew it back until her ear responded to the *thrum* of it. Frowning with concentration, she sighted over the arrow's tip to a spot just below the lopsided circle she'd drawn on a bronze-leafed elm. Then she relaxed the fingers of her right hand and let the string roll off them. Just as Hill Climber had shown her how to do.

The arrow she had labored to make sped on its way with commendable swiftness. That it fell short of the mark, short even of the tree, was disappointing. But the boys, in the days before they'd mastered their bows, had done no better than this at the start.

Frazzled and faded leaves crunched under Morning Song's moccasins as she went to retrieve her arrow. She paused in a patch of sunlight and lifted her gaze to distant peaks framed by molting trees. Fierce Eagle's band would be coming from the north. When they came.

She sighed. A disquiet thick as autumn mist had come to shroud the village and invade the longhouses. In their innocent play, the smaller children laughed and shouted still, but those old enough to reckon the passage of time were inclined to talk only when necessary. Even Teller Of Legends was unnaturally quiet these days, unless Otter was nearby. For her, they all tried to find cheering words.

Morning Song notched her arrow a second time, aimed, and released it. Her own mood lightened considerably when, with a satisfying thud, its head pierced the bole of the elm and sent chips of bark scattering. She smiled. It had struck above and to the right of the ring she'd drawn with charcoal, but close enough to it to be encouraging. And she had the rest of the morning to practice in. She'd watched the boys go downriver in their canoes (and shuddered as the clumsy craft rocked crazily before the rambunctious youngsters settled themselves), so there was no chance they might come across her. Instinct warned that although her sometimes hi-

61

larious attempts to imitate them met with indulgent grins, the boys
might be less than amused by her trying *seriously* to develop a
hunter-warrior's skill.

A long-eared hare, its fur a mottled red and brown, poked his
twitching nose out of a mass of wood sorrel just as Morning Song
loosed her arrow for the third time. The rush of it sent the frightened creature bounding across the clearing. "You are safe from
me," she called after it, and laughed. She had yet to hit even a
stationary target. The rabbit, whose coat would soon transform to
winter white, had nothing to fear from such a novice. Someday,
however . . .

She laughed again, and resumed the practice that would speed
the coming of that day.

Morning Song returned to the compound in time for the daily
meal. When she had received her portion, she went out into the
sunshine and found a place in the children's circle. The boys were
still absent, which did not surprise her. Doubtless they had snared
several bushy-tailed squirrels and were roasting them on the spot.
They'd have the rodents' caches of nuts to eat as well, she thought
enviously.

She grimaced into her bowl of watery stew and spooned some
into her mouth. If the rain, which had fallen three times since the
moon began to wane, settled into this reassuring pattern, a late
crop might be forthcoming and they would have better food and
more of it.

"I knew that my mother's child would be a boy this time."
Pumpkin Blossom smiled smugly as she spoke. "I knew it four
days before he was born."

Morning Song choked on the single piece of meat she'd found in
her bowl.

"Did a dream tell you?" Sun Descending asked seriously, and
Morning Song, having dealt successfully with the stringy meat,
looked at her with astonishment.

Pumpkin Blossom nodded. "I saw him *grown*," she proclaimed.
"He wore a warrior's helmet, and he was very tall. But I knew at
once who he was. *And* I knew he would be called Fish Jumping."

Morning Song accepted that Pumpkin Blossom had seen a warrior while she slept. She'd heard tales of dream images stranger
than this. But she could not have put a name to him before his birth.
Bountiful Harvest had not given him his name until she'd heard a
splashing sound and looked up to see a fish leap out of the stream
she had washed her newborn baby in. Besides . . . "How is it you

did not see him as Sachem?'' she challenged. ''Your mother, when she carried him into the longhouse, said at once that her son will walk one day in Se-A-Wi's moccasins.''

Pumpkin Blossom tossed her head. ''He shall be a warrior before he becomes Sachem,'' she replied airily.

''You are fortunate that your dream was so easy to understand,'' Meadow Brook said. ''The dream that visited me last night did nothing but confuse me.''

''Tell us your dream,'' several voices urged.

The tall girl grinned. ''Are you Faithkeepers, that you can interpret it?'' she quipped. Then she shrugged. ''I will tell it to you anyway,'' she decided. ''There is a meadow that spreads itself before me, and it is filled with flowers. Birds are singing, and the sky is blue as the wing of a jay. Then, suddenly, the meadow is gone, and in its place is a pond. No birds sing now, and overhead are clouds so dark that the water in the pond is gray and cold-looking.'' She scraped the dregs of stew from her bowl and licked her spoon. ''That is all. My dream ended there.''

''Your name is Meadow Brook,'' Small Brown Sparrow said slowly. ''Perhaps this explains why there was a brook in your dream.''

''It was a pond, not a brook, that I saw.''

''Why not ask Puma Walking Soft?'' Pumpkin Blossom suggested. ''He is Keeper Of The Faith for your clan and the Bear clan.''

''I will wait and see if the same dream comes again, I think,'' Meadow Brook replied. Puma Walking Soft, a stern-faced man who scorned idle chatter, was not easy to approach.

''Woodpecker Drumming says he often dreams of wrestling a bear,'' Sun Descending said. ''I told my brother he had better hurry and grow big. If his dream is one that prophesies, the bear will win the match. Even a half-grown cub is stronger than he is now.'' She giggled. ''I think the dream came to him because Bear In The Sky, who is younger than he is, beat him when they wrestled together. Woodpecker Drumming will not be happy until he can force Bear In The Sky to the ground in return.''

''I wonder why the dreams that come to boys always have to do with fighting,'' Small Brown Sparrow mused.

''Would you expect the spirits to send them visions of seedtime and harvest?'' Meadow Brook said scornfully. ''Such matters will never concern them. They need to know whether they will have strength to call upon when they need it, and if they will bring honor to themselves by overcoming their enemies. With women, it is different. My mother still talks of the dream that told her my father would not be coming home from the hunting expedition he went on when I was a babe. She saw a huge eagle swoop down and seize him, and carry him to its nest high on a mountain. When clouds wrapped themselves like blankets around the mountain's peak, she knew that death had come to my father.''

Morning Song shivered. Surely it was better to be denied dreams altogether than to suffer those that brought misery beforetime. Yet it was not pleasant to sit with fettered tongue and envy the other girls as they compared nights made colorful by this vision or that. Her silence set her apart from them, and there was enough about her already to do that.

''I cannot tell you the number of times I have seen pumpkins when I dream,'' Small Brown Sparrow was saying now. ''Large ones and small, green ones and orange. Sometimes there are many, and sometimes only one. I asked Rain Singing about it, and my mother said that a pumpkin, because it bears a lake within itself, may be taken as a sign that I will someday journey over water.''

''Have the pumpkins you've seen ever worn faces?''

There was a startled silence; then all heads turned toward Morning Song, who did not let her own gaze wander from Small Brown Sparrow. ''They have come so to me,'' she went on solemnly, ''and it is strange indeed to see a pumpkin—or maybe it is a squash— with eyes that stare at you and a mouth that moves as though it were speaking.''

''You told us before that dreams do not visit you,'' Pumpkin Blossom said accusingly.

Her cousin ignored her. It was enough that everyone else seemed eager for her to continue. ''Occasionally this pumpkin face appears almost comical,'' she elaborated. ''But''—she lowered her voice to a hoarse whisper—''there are times when its expression is threatening indeed. Even its color changes then, taking on the red of sunset. Its mouth snarls, and its eyes narrow, like this''—she squinted and scowled dramatically—''so that I am filled with dread.'' She sighed. ''No doubt it is as well that I cannot understand the words its crooked mouth is shaping.''

''Have you *never* made them out?'' Small Brown Sparrow's voice was hushed, and she looked upon her friend with awe. Surely no one had ever been sent a more intriguing dream.

Morning Song shook her head and flicked tendrils of unruly hair from her thin cheeks. ''Never,'' she replied. ''Although I am almost certain that it speaks my name, this pumpkin face. What else it may say''—she contrived a shudder—''I do not wish to know.''

"Such a dream needs to be shared with a Keeper Of The Faith," Meadow Brook said, and the genuine concern in her tone almost unsettled Morning Song. "You must speak of it to Hearth Tender, for its message is surely not one to be taken lightly."

Morning Song thought furiously. "It has been a month since last I saw the pumpkin face," she parried, "and it was smiling then. So I will wait, as you have decided to do, before trying to have my dream interpreted."

Her friends—and all at once they seemed very much her friends—nodded understandingly.

"Only promise me," Meadow Brook said urgently, as they made ready to return to their respective lodges, "that if you see the terrible pumpkin face even once more you will go directly to Hearth Tender."

Morning Song agreed without hesitation. Old pumpkin face had served its purpose, and there should be no need to bring it back.

Bountiful Harvest removed from the wall the lance and bow that belonged to Covers His Eyes. With deft fingers, she tied them on top of the neat bundle she had made of his spare shirt, his leggins, moccasins, breechclouts, and robe.

Covers His Eyes watched her with a consternation that lent character to his lumpish face. "You cannot do this," he began.

Bountiful Harvest swung on him. "I *can*. From the day you showed yourself the coward that you are, I have waited for this moment." She checked his bowl and spoon for cleanliness, and set them on top of a folded blanket. "No one can say I have not been a proper wife to you, despite the shame you brought on the both of us. I have kept your clothes clean and mended, fed you well"—she eyed with disgust the girth of him, only slightly diminished by the sparse rations the drought had forced upon them all—"and borne you three children to prove I have not shunned to share your bed. But you have at last given me my son. It is the only good thing you have done for me, and I had almost begun to think you so unmanly that it could never happen."

Teller Of Legends watched with hooded eyes and told herself she must not interfere. She looked toward the door of the lodge as Morning Song and Pumpkin Blossom came in, and signed to them to come to her hearth. She wished they might have stayed in the compound until this distasteful scene was over, but Pumpkin Blossom, at least, must learn the truth of it sooner or later.

"You will shame me further, if you send me away," Covers His Eyes protested, and some remnant of the fighting spirit he had thought lost returned to him. "I will *not* go back to my family's longhouse, Bountiful Harvest."

"Then go elsewhere," she responded indifferently. "But go you shall. You know I am within my rights. It is my decision, and mine alone, whether we continue to live together. And"—she added a sweat-darkened headband to the things she was deciding were his— "I say that we shall not." She glanced down, her almond eyes approving her generosity, then gestured to the tidy heap on the floor. "Take what you own, and leave my lodge, Covers His Eyes. From this moment, you are no longer my husband."

His tenuous courage deserted him. "Bountiful Harvest," he said wretchedly, "would you deprive our children of their father?"

Morning Song, understanding at last what was happening, looked sympathetically at her cousin. But approval shone in Pumpkin Blossom's eyes as she watched her mother bend gracefully, scoop up Covers His Eyes's belongings, and walk with purposeful stride to the entrance. One foot lifted and kicked aside the hide that hung over it, and in the next instant all that Covers His Eyes owned, save for what he wore, lay tumbled in the dust outside.

She turned back to him then. "Must you also be thrust out?"

Teller Of Legends winced, and Morning Song groped for her hand.

Covers His Eyes hunched his shoulders and shuffled to the door. He sent a last pleading glance toward Bountiful Harvest, then passed into the compound.

They heard him grunt as he stooped to collect his scattered belongings. Then the sound of his footsteps faded into nothingness as he made his dejected way in the direction of the lodge that wore the Snipe totem.

There was little likelihood that his kin would rejoice to see him.

As dusk settled on the hills beyond the palisade that evening, an owl punctured the hush of predark with insistent questioning, and a brown mouse crept from its burrow to investigate fields new-turned and optimistically seeded. Night foragers are conditioned to be wary, and the mouse was disconcerted by an uncommon stir and bustle within the timbered enclosure where longhouses sat courteously apart from one another. Radiance from a generously stoked fire reached out to flicker upon an array of precocious sprouts, and this increased the trembling creature's apprehension; its hope of feeding depended upon the concealment offered by the friendly dark.

Those who thronged the compound spared no thought for a

mouse's distress. Cloud Racer, true to his name, had sprinted into the village just as the day's sun began a lazy descent into the west. Its incandescence had applied glaze to the perspiration that sheathed his near-nakedness, yet Rain Singing saw that it failed to plumb the depths of eyes seemingly a denser black than they'd been when he'd left with Fierce Eagle's war band. She made no mention of this; it would not be fitting, and Cloud Racer would not thank her for doing so. In any event, he was home, and unhurt.

She fetched him a dipper of water, smiled as he gulped it down, waited without impatience to hear his news.

"We return victorious," he said simply when his thirst had been slaked. "All of us," he added, looking around at the people who had been pouring out of the lodges since his shouted *"Ho!"* had told them that he was coming and that the news he brought was good.

Otter Swimming, clinging to Morning Song's hand, squeezed it hard, then set it free. Such radiance flooded into her face that the jealous sun promptly dived behind the hill he'd been perched on. "Deer Caller!" she breathed, and grinned so hugely that Morning Song, fleetingly, felt close kinship with her brother the sun.

"We had expected you to return sooner," Se-A-Wi told him. "Was the Huron Village not so unprepared as Fierce Eagle had trusted it would be?"

Cloud Racer turned to the Sachem, and the smile Otter's joy had won from him faded. "According to Fierce Eagle, that battle was not worthy of the name," he replied. "Most of their warriors were away. Even our small band outnumbered those who tried to defend the village." His eyes darkened further, and Morning Song wondered if a young man who had never before gone to war would label any battle *unworthy of the name*. "When we had gone from there," he continued, "we met bands from three other Iroquois villages. They suggested we join forces and carry the fight deeper into Huron territory. Which we did."

"Successfully?" This from Puma Walking Soft, ever a man of few words.

Cloud Racer nodded. "We attacked their settlements as we came upon them, until word of our raiding flew ahead of us. Then many of the Huron deserted their villages before we reached them."

Otter was unable to contain herself longer. "When will the rest of the war party be arriving?" she called.

"They should be here between nightfall and the high of the moon," Cloud Racer said.

With that, even the detail-hungry former warriors were willing to leave the weary young man in peace so that a celebration could be speedily arranged.

The boys were sent to gather wood for the fire, and every girl but the tiniest was pressed into service to help make the meal. The women, professing faith in their latest planting, nearly emptied their stores of dried beans and corn and squash, and strips of wrinkled venison were set to soak and soften. In every lodge pots were swung over hearths; the succotash would cook faster in them than in the huge communal kettles used on feast days.

"It cannot be as tasty as the kind that simmers from sunrise to sunset," Bountiful Harvest lamented, but Teller Of Legends only laughed.

"To men who have been fending off starvation with wetted meal for more than seven weeks, it will smell and taste better than anything they have eaten since childhood."

We will all appreciate it, Morning Song thought, her own mouth watering.

"Has anyone heard whether they shall be bringing captives with them?" Sweet Maple had left the stirring of her succotash to Tree Reaching Up. A chance to sit idle and chat with friends was what any sort of celebration meant to her, and now she made herself comfortable. Smiling, she invited Day Greeter to guess which of her plump hands held the lump of maple sugar she had brought along for her, then fussed over little Fish Jumping when Pumpkin Blossom had taken him from his cradleboard.

"I did not hear Cloud Racer mention it," Teller Of Legends said. "But he had little time to say much before we abandoned him to organize the feast."

"Which I am as ready for as our warriors will be," Sweet Maple said fervently, and Morning Song smiled. Se-A-Wi's wife looked across to where Bountiful Harvest was chopping lengths of venison into bite-sized chunks. "I see that Covers His Eyes has returned to Gray Squirrel's lodge," she said quietly. "The shame of it will steal warmth from the hearth she and her sister have lit to welcome home Long Canoe and Spear Thrower."

Teller Of Legends sighed. "I have pity for Gray Squirrel and Loon Laughing. I hope you will tell them for me that Covers His Eyes's leaving here was none of my doing."

Sweet Maple nodded. "I am sure they know that," she said serenely. "As I do. You have too much sense, old friend, to condone something that may bring discredit on your family."

Teller Of Legends's voice tightened. "If my daughter had sent him away when first his fellows declared him unfit to be hunter and warrior, I would have sanctioned his dismissal. But to heap further disgrace on him and his clan so long afterward . . .'' She shook her head.

Sweet Maple allowed tact to dictate a change of subject. Her gaze followed Morning Song as the girl darted to the entrance for the third time in as many minutes. ''To wait is hard on children,'' she said. ''On all of us, for that matter. I will be glad to see for myself that my brother Far Seer is unhurt. And it is not only Otter who will rejoice to have my sister's son safe home.'' She chuckled, and heaved herself to her feet. ''But our warriors will be here soon if Cloud Racer reckoned right, and doubtless each will have his own exciting tale to tell us.''

Teller Of Legends laughed as Pumpkin Blossom joined her cousin to peer out into the night. ''The children are more eager for food than they are for warriors' tales,'' she said. And was herself tactful enough not to add that she knew perfectly well her visitor felt much the same.

When the war band, preceded by a cacophony of jubilant whoops, strutted at last into the firelit compound, they found nothing to complain of in the exuberance of their welcome. Wives and mothers and sisters embraced them; the older men slapped their backs and beamed upon them; the children, shrill with excitement, exclaimed over the blood-encrusted scalps that the braves waved like banners, and jeered at the two prisoners who stumbled along in their midst. And the scented steam that rose like signal smoke from the cooking pots set them to whooping all over again.

Morning Song and Pumpkin Blossom helped with the ladling out of Bountiful Harvest's succotash, for Teller Of Legends had insisted that Otter must sit at her husband's side and be served when he was. ''It is not only those who go off to war who should be honored,'' she said quietly to Hearth Tender.

In the hullabaloo, no one even noticed. And Deer Caller, whose free arm encircled his woman's waist throughout their meal, heartily approved this departure from custom.

When she was able finally to fill her own bowl and sit down, Morning Song discovered that the only spot available to her allowed her full view of the two prisoners. They were the first Huron she had ever seen, and it disappointed her that they looked remarkably like Iroquois. So much so, that she wondered how a warrior recognized friend from foe when battle was raging. Perhaps the way the Huron dressed for war, or the shape of their helmets or weapons, identified them. But stripped to the skin, as these men were, there was nothing to distinguish them save a sullen defiance. They were shackled securely to upright posts, but the bonds confining their hands had been cut, and Morning Song saw that food had been brought to them.

Fox Running, having twice refilled his bowl and believing it prudent to remove himself from under his mother's gaze, squeezed herself between Morning Song and a stack of pelts that had been part of the war band's plunder. "Why do we feed our enemies?" Morning Song asked him.

Fox Running grinned, succotash dribbling from the corners of his mouth. "So they can strengthen themselves for what is coming," he mumbled. He swallowed and met her puzzled frown with a less garbled explanation. "They are to be tortured, once the feasting is done."

Morning Song's spoon clattered into her bowl and sank slowly into the congealing remains of her meal. "They are not to be ransomed?" The words came out in a horrified squeak, and to hide her discomposure she sent her fingers fishing for a spoon that all at once she had no use for.

Fox Running was too excited to pay heed to her traitorous voice or studied fumbling. "Not that pair," he said happily. "Fierce Eagle left their fate to the Matrons, and they have decided on torture." He sprang to his feet and looked over the heads of those who sat closer to the center of the compound. "Far Seer and Spear Thrower are wetting down a pile of deadwood," he told her. "When it is set around the posts the Huron are bound to, we will have some proper entertainment."

Entertainment? "And we will all be expected to watch?" she asked faintly.

It was his turn to frown. "Watch? I suppose you may, if you wish. But you'll find that tame, compared to having a part in it." He grinned again. "I borrowed an old kettle from my mother's hearth," he confided. "I will fill it with red-hot embers, and climb upon Hill Climber's shoulders, and dump those embers over the prisoners' heads. They will think it is raining fire!" He made as if to dash away, then squatted down and frowned a second time. "I had forgotten about the speeches," he said gloomily. "But it is only right that we should hear those first. Probably they will be shorter than usual; the warriors will not want the victory fire to burn out before the torturing begins."

Morning Song was grateful for any delay. She was aware that captured enemies were often tortured, but these were the first prisoners brought to the village since she'd come to live here. Now she recalled what she'd heard about the ritual of torture and was suddenly certain that she did not care to witness such a thing. She knew better than to say this to Fox Running, but she began to hope that the warriors would speak on and on, and give her time to prepare herself for what was coming.

The war leader, of course, stood first to boast of what he and his men had accomplished. "We have shed rivers of Huron blood, yet lost mere drops of our own," he was saying, and satisfaction swelled his resonant voice. "With the stealth of foxes we approached the Huron villages; like lions, we fell upon those who thought to drive us off; and as swiftly as birds did we disappear once we had carved our clan totems on nearby trees and left a tally of those slain." The firelight emphasized the angles of his lean face. "The few who escaped us raced ahead and warned their tribesmen to abandon their settlements and seek shelter with their *French protectors*!"

He flung out the last two words as though they tasted vile, and several of the elders spat upon the ground to demonstrate fellow feeling. Those who did so were remembering a man called Cham-Plain. As newfledged warriors, they had been among those summoned to parley with the Huron and Algonquin at a place called Ticonderoga—*Where The Waters Meet*. Unaccountably it had been the French sallow-skin who had stepped forward to greet the Iroquois delegation. And, instead of the peace talk the war leaders had been led to expect, Cham-Plain chose instead to speak with the first thunderstick the Iroquois had ever seen. When he had three times made it roar, two chiefs of the Longhouse People were dead and a third lay dying. Time was not long enough to blot out such treachery. The unrest that had previously existed between the northern tribes and the five Iroquois nations had been as the sport of boys compared to the enmity that had so often pitted them one against the other since that day at Ticonderoga.

Fierce Eagle's eyes were brooding now. "For all the length of my memory, the Huron—those we rightly call Crooked Tongues— have been sworn enemies of the Longhouse People. During the year that marked my first decade as a warrior, they captured and burned more than a hundred of our people." His mouth set harshly. "I was proud to be one of those who avenged our slaughtered brothers, and that was neither my first nor my last encounter with the Crooked Tongues. Yet each time we brought them to their knees—and we did this time and time again—the French *Onondio* raised them up and told them to ignore the pacts of peace we had insisted they make with our nations. It is my hope that, finally, the Huron have learned that they can never gain from dishonoring such treaties, that to challenge the Iroquois leads only to the shame of defeat.'' He paused, waited until the passions aroused by his words were spent, then moved on to the part of his speech that would win smiles from his listeners.

''All of the men who marched with me are to be praised,'' he declared, and his teeth flashed in his dark face. ''But I have reason to be especially thankful to the son of my sister. My life would have been forfeit during our first raid if Cloud Racer had not been so quick with his bow!'' He pointed to the palisade gates. ''The firstborn son of Rain Singing left this village to act as scout for us. He has returned to it a blooded warrior.'' He continued to smile as cries of acclaim were directed at his nephew, who seemed uncertain how to receive them. Which prompted considerable laughter from the onlookers.

Morning Song did not laugh. Nor did she marvel to hear that Cloud Racer's swift arrow had found its mark. He had always practiced longer and harder than any of his companions, whatever the skill to be mastered.

When Fierce Eagle insisted, Cloud Racer stood to acknowledge the tribute, then spoke briefly but feelingly about the courage and daring of every man in the war party. He was taller than his uncle, the girl saw, which she wouldn't have guessed him to be; Fierce Eagle's erectness of bearing gave him an illusion of great height. But all at once it seemed that it might be true, what his crone of a grandmother was fond of saying: that Cloud Racer had been sired by the spirit of the cornstalk, which keeps its toes dug deep in the nurturing earth and at the same time strives mightily to touch the sun.

The other warriors, called up in turn, knew better what was expected of them, and the round of speeches became a contest to see whose boasting might provoke from the audience the most uninhibited responses. The cooling night air rang with shouts and quivered with ululations as the villagers vied with one another to shower praise on kith and kin.

''Did you hear what Fierce Eagle said about my brother?'' Small Brown Sparrow had found the friend she wanted most to share her elation with.

Morning Song, who had jumped up to applaud Deer Caller, grinned at her. ''You must be very proud.''

The smaller girl nodded vigorously. ''This is a grand celebration,'' she signed contentedly. ''We will remember it for a long, long time.'' She went up on tiptoe to see more clearly, and clutched at Morning Song's arm. "Fierce Eagle is standing again," she exclaimed. "This must be the end of the speeches."

Morning Song made no comment, but only looked to the fire, which, faithfully replenished by those who sat nearest it, burned brightly still.

"I remind you that the Huron warriors we bested were crafty and tenacious fighters, and that the Iroquois honor such qualities even in their enemies." Fierce Eagle nodded toward the pair of captives, who regarded him with calculated impassiveness. "Those we brought home with us are deserving of your respect, and we shall give them every opportunity to prove that to you." He signed to Spear Thrower and Far Seer, and the two hefted bundles of dripping fagots, strode to the posts the Huron were trussed to, and arranged the sticks in a slant-sided ring at the foot of each. To Long Canoe went the privilege of setting alight wood that would burn listlessly but steadily. As he stepped forward with the torch, the villagers came hard on his heels to make a loose circle around the rough-barked stanchions. Their hands clutched sticks or knives or dampened rawhide thongs, and they displayed these to one another with anticipatory chuckles and grins. Lake On Fire, clad in another of her ludicrous costumes, brandished a lance with a broken shaft; Puma Walking Soft's scarred old war hatchet swung loose in his right hand; Fox Running and Hill Climber carried between them a dented kettle heaped with coals filched from the victory pyre.

"Oh! I have left behind my mother's old digging stick," Small Brown Sparrow exclaimed, and ran off to retrieve it.

Morning Song shrank back into the shadows. Yet her eyes insisted upon scanning familiar faces, faces now contorted almost beyond recognition. Her ears rang with the gibes and insults directed at the helpless Huron braves. And as the sluggish flames sent up isolated flares, the first whiff of slow-roasting human flesh invaded her nostrils and stuck in her throat.

She never knew who first leaped forward to gouge a collop of flesh from the thigh of the prisoner closest to her, but from the shape and size of the hand wielding the blade she knew it was either a child or a young woman.

It was then that the Huron warriors lifted their heads and began a chant that mocked their torturers and called upon them to behold a fearlessness and stamina no long-nosed Iroquois could ever hope to match.

In that moment Morning Song panicked, and fled to the sanctuary of her beloved forest.

Chapter 7

❦ ❦

Morning Song looked back and counted; the rounded earth Pumpkin Blossom was puncturing with her digging stick was the seventh planting hill in this row. She poked earth-stained fingers into her pouch of squash and bean seeds. They were smaller and flatter than the seed corn in her basket, and tried to glue themselves to moist flesh. Her cousin waited impatiently while Morning Song struggled to isolate just enough for this mound.

"Everyone is ahead of us," Pumpkin Blossom said as the two knelt and smoothed soil over the seeds. "My mother will not be happy if we finish last again today."

Morning Song said nothing. Since early spring the two girls had worked regularly in the fields. First the communal lands had been tilled and planted; now the women had moved on to seed the plots assigned to the individual clans.

"You are near to becoming maidens," Teller Of Legends had told her granddaughters, "and old enough to help with the crop-tending." She turned to Morning Song. "Bountiful Harvest has offered to instruct you along with Pumpkin Blossom, since the two of you are of an age." She hugged the girls to her, one on either side. "It will not be all work," she promised almost gaily. "There are rituals to be learned as well, and you will begin to understand what a fine thing it is to be female when you are fortunate enough to be born Iroquois."

Pumpkin Blossom's pretty face lit with an answering smile; she had been looking forward to this. But Morning Song's face revealed only dismay; *she* was not convinced that it was always a fine thing to be a woman. And to spend endless hours under Bountiful Harvest's critical eye, while she showed Morning Song the *proper* way to make pots and weave baskets . . . !

Teller Of Legends gave Pumpkin Blossom a final squeeze and sent her off to soothe a squalling Fish Jumping. "I know you wanted Otter to be your teacher," she told Morning Song quietly. "But tradition says that only a matron who has borne children may train the maidens-to-be."

The hollow sound of sorrow was in her voice, and Morning Song chided herself for showing her disappointment. Bountiful Harvest—who had despised her husband—had been able to bear him three children; but the seasons had stitched themselves into nearly two years, and Otter—whose love for Deer Caller made a radiance in her still—had been sent none at all.

"Perhaps I could wait until Small Brown Sparrow is ready?" she suggested hopefully. "Rain Singing likes me, Grandmother. If you were to ask, I am sure she would not object to teaching me when she teaches her daughter."

Teller Of Legends came as close to looking scandalized as was possible for her. "Indeed not! Surely you know that a girl must be led into womanhood by a woman of her own clan?" Her expression gentled. "In truth, you could not have a better teacher than Bountiful Harvest. You will be glad one day that you have learned from the best." She smiled down into Morning Song's unhappy brown eyes. "I am certain you will make me proud of you, child," she added softly.

Morning Song, with a sigh, had promised to do her best. To have given free rein to a rebelliousness she'd lately come to recognize in herself would have gained her nothing, and she knew it.

On days like this, that rebelliousness was strong. As she pressed seed into the earth, a breeze sweetened by honeysuckle and hobblebush made her wish she were in the forest, spying on the raccoons she'd discovered during the green season, or the she-wolf she'd tracked to its den. The boys who used to be her companions, and who were *boys* no longer, spent most of their time in the forest; hunter-warriors, she reflected bitterly, need never concern themselves with planting beans and corn.

Pumpkin Blossom snatched the pouch of seed from Morning Song's hand and thrust the digging stick at her. "Except for old Lake On Fire and Sweet Maple, who are gossiping at the end of their row, we are the only ones not at the river," she said crossly. "You make the mounds and let me sow the rest of the seed, or everybody will be back in the lodges before we can join them."

Morning Song, bending to heap up the damp earth, saw nothing to complain of in that. For her, the most unpleasant part of the planting ritual was the bathing that came after it. Bountiful Harvest and Pumpkin Blossom made a point of noticing how Morning Song kept to the shallows. Her cousin's superior attitude she could cope with, but Morning Song was hard put not to shrivel in the face of her mother-aunt's contempt. The other girls, aware of her discomfort, always giggled behind their hands, shattering the sense of belonging that rewarded Morning Song for her stint in the fields. Well, she had concocted a medicine to remedy this, and now was a good time to test it again.

She straightened up. "I have had another dream," she said, and her cousin's ill-humor vanished.

"Was there a monster in this one?" she asked, her long-lashed eyes shining with excitement.

Morning Song nodded, then stooped and punched a circle of holes in the mound she'd just made. They were hardly evenly spaced, but Pumpkin Blossom dropped seeds into them anyway. "If I can persuade my mother to let us sit in the compound with our looms, will you tell me about it?" she asked.

Her cousin made herself frown a little. "Meadow Brook and Sun Descending and the rest will not be happy if I tell my dream only to you."

"They probably have work to finish, too," Pumpkin Blossom said. "They can bring it with them and join us."

"That is a splendid idea," Morning Song said warmly, and helped tamp down the soil on the end hill of their row.

The last of the day's light blushed as it touched the kettle in which Otter Swimming was boiling sumac stalks. It glided across the floor and fell upon Bountiful Harvest, who was busy cleaning her small son. Fish Jumping had taken it into his head to investigate the cinders that had blown beyond the guardian stones of her hearth.

"Morning Song should have swept those up this morning, before we went to the fields," she said. "I did not think it necessary to tell her twice, but I see that I should have." With a dried corn cob, she scraped a layer of ash from Fish Jumping's rump. The tiny boy's eyes blinked rapidly as she scrubbed at his tender flesh, but he did not cry out.

Bountiful Harvest's children learn young to oblige their mother, Teller Of Legends mused. "Morning chores are often overlooked, or hastily done, during the planting season," she said.

"It is more than haste that leads Morning Song to skimp her work," Bountiful Harvest replied. "She simply has no desire to learn how to do it properly." She hugged her son, and set him to play with an old wooden ladle and a battered kettle. "And her attitude is strange in other ways, too. When I told the girls the things they must and must not do when their monthly bleeding begins, she plagued me with questions. I spent an entire afternoon explaining why she must not go near our Sachem, or approach any of our hunters and fishermen during this time. She just would not accept that her bleeding could dilute the strength of the men, saw no reason that the smell of it should scare off the game animals we need for food. Why, when I said that she must not even eat the flesh of those animals while she is bleeding, she came close to scowling at me! And when she heard that she is forbidden to touch her own body with her hands while the blood is flowing, well, she named this rule *nonsense*."

Otter laughed as she tossed pulverized galium root into the pot, seized a stick, and pushed in after it the length of hide from which she meant to sew a shirt for Deer Caller. He would look handsome in a red shirt, she thought, and a tender smile made her gnomish face beautiful for a moment. "I can recall when I became a maid," she said, "and wondered about such things. You may have forgotten, Bountiful Harvest, but we run about so freely while we are children that it is not easy to suddenly have to face all the restrictions that come with growing up."

"That may be true for a few girls," Bountiful Harvest said, "although I did not find it so. Nor does my daughter seem to. But wait until you hear Morning Song's response to my discussion of marriage and mating." She turned back to Teller Of Legends to gauge her reaction to what she had been bursting to divulge. "She insists that no man shall ever treat her in such a fashion, that she will choose to be maiden until she dies rather than submit to what she calls *prodding and poking!*"

Teller Of Legends managed not to smile. "Doubtless she is only saying what many girls her age think but dare not put into words," she said mildly. "Time, and love when it comes to her, will teach her otherwise, Bountiful Harvest."

Otter suspected that her sister's description of the union of man and woman had been delivered in the same dry tone she had used to describe the plaiting of ash splints. There would have been no mention made of the joyful affair it could be, and should be. She went to her niece's shelf and found the tunic Bountiful Harvest had overseen the painstaking sewing of. Carrying it to her bubbling pot, she let it sink into the dye. Morning Song would be delighted to find her plain garment transformed to scarlet, and she would look remarkably well in it, too.

"I hope you are right," Bountiful Harvest was saying earnestly to their mother. "But if you are impatient for great-grandchildren, you had better look to Pumpkin Blossom, not to Morning Song." Knowing that her mother yearned to see the advent of another generation, she was content to make these her final words on the subject. "I did not see Rain Singing in the fields," she said after a moment. "Is she ailing? Should the False Faces call on her?"

"It is her mother who ails," Teller Of Legends said heavily. "And I am afraid the Company of Faces can do nothing to help. Dancing Water has been feeble since the white season, and no longer has the strength even to sit up. Small Brown Sparrow came to me as we were leaving the river to say that her grandmother is preparing to chant her death song and wishes me to visit with her before she begins it." She rose as she spoke, and made ready to go on her sad errand.

Bountiful Harvest watched her mother pass out of the lodge and wondered who would be elected to take Dancing Water's place as Chief Matron. It seemed to her that the choice was obvious.

Morning Song, having surrendered her botched weaving to Pumpkin Blossom, smoothed the white fur of a pup who came nosing around the circle the girls had made on the north side of the compound. "It was stranger than any dream yet sent to me, this latest one," she told her friends, and thrilled to see them lean toward her. "I found myself standing in a forest greenly dark and shrouded in silence. No small creatures rustled the underbrush. The wings of no bird stirred the air. There was not even a breeze to set the leaves to whispering; they hung from branch and twig like lifeless things."

She fondled the ears of the pup, and he nestled against her with a contented sigh. "I wanted to run, to flee from so dismal a place. But my feet refused to move from the spot they stood on."

Meadow Brook held her hands poised over the moccasin she'd been lacing. "Was it fear that kept you from running?"

Morning Song considered. "I was afraid, yes. But it seemed that something held me fixed to the ground. I kept staring at my feet; they did not look as they should, somehow. Yet it was not until I looked up that I saw something even more peculiar."

She paused long enough for her listeners to speculate on what this *something* might have been. "Then," she said, pitching her voice low, "then I saw how the trees wore faces, and how their limbs were beckoning and gesturing just as the arms of people do. A frightful moaning spilled out of their bark-ringed mouths—and they began to sway back and forth, back and forth. The tree creatures were as anxious as I was to move. But, like me, they could not."

"Did they threaten you?" This from Sun Descending, who had abandoned the porcupine quills she was meant to be sorting.

"No. They appeared to be pleading with me, to be asking my help. But there was no shape to the moaning sounds they made; I could not guess what it was they wanted. Besides, I was no more able than they were to move, if you'll recall."

The pup had gone peacefully to sleep, and she rested her hand in the silky ruff that circled his neck. "Suddenly I sensed the stirring of a wind," she went on. "It was just a breeze at first, yet when it touched the back of my neck, I shivered. And the trees . . . Their leaves quivered, and I knew they felt the same eerie chill that I did.

"They were moaning louder, too, and the wind freshened to add its voice to their sorrowful song. But the wind did not sound sad. Indeed, the stronger it blew, the more triumph there was in its chanting. It beat against my back like a hard-fisted warrior pounding at a closed village gate. Only my firm-planted feet kept me from toppling over."

Pumpkin Blossom drew in her breath with a hiss. "What a mercy you did not!" she exclaimed.

Morning Song nodded. "The trees were not so fortunate, however," she said dolefully. "Their branches-become-arms bent before the wind. Their leaves showed white when they were whipped by it. And when its strength increased again, leaf after leaf loosed its grip and was blown away. Soon the trees stood naked, as they do in the white season.

"Next their flailing limbs were attacked. The air was alive with snapping and crackling noises as the wind sent tangles of branches soaring into the blackest sky I have ever seen."

"Had night come to your forest?" Sun Descending asked.

"I doubt it was anything natural," Morning Song replied, "that darkened the sky in my dream."

An uneasy murmur ran around the circle.

"In spite of the darkness, I could still make out the faces on those limbless trees. Their agony was plain to see. And when the wind blew so fiercely that I was forced to wrap my arms around myself to escape a little of its buffeting, I finally understood. I was witnessing the death throes of all those trees. It was *death* they had hoped I might save them from. For now the merciless wind was plucking them up and flinging them about as though they were lances thrown by a warrior-giant gone berserk. Even the stout grandfather trees could not withstand its power. They were yanked from the ground and hurled after their weaker fellows.

"The moaning stopped then—and all I looked upon were gaping holes with jagged bits of roots protruding from them. The forest—that whole host of trees—was gone."

"And the wind: Did it stop also?" Meadow Brook prodded.

Morning Song looked at her. "It did not," she said. "Its howling intensified, as though the destruction it had wrought had only whetted its appetite. And when I looked down at myself, I knew why." She savored a breathless silence. "Where I had thought to see my feet," she intoned, "I saw only exposed roots; the legs I believed I stood on, and the body I had wrapped my arms around, had fused to form an enormous trunk; and my arms had become twisted branches ending in a mass of splintered twigs.

"I had been transformed into the ancient one, the oldest tree in the forest, the tree that has stood for countless ages and weathered storm after storm after storm."

"And this one?" Pumpkin Blossom asked urgently. "Did you survive this one?"

"I do not know," her cousin said mournfully. "Just as I felt that monstrous wind creature gather itself for its final assault, my dream deserted me. Unless it comes again, I shall never be able to answer your question, Pumpkin Blossom."

"Morning Song."

The girl's head swiveled. Teller Of Legends was standing behind her. How long had she been there? Nothing in her face hinted that it had been more than a moment or two, and her eyes were neither fired with anger nor flat with disapproval. "Did you want me, Grandmother?"

Teller Of Legends inclined her head. "Yes. In the lodge." And, smiling upon the girls who'd begun to chatter excitedly, she turned and walked sedately in the direction of the longhouse.

Pumpkin Blossom and the others, puzzling over their friend's dream, paid no heed when Morning Song scrambled up and followed obediently after her.

The small white dog stood, too, and shook himself. Then he sniffed the ground and took up the rear in that miniature procession. But though he whined a time or two, the girl whose scent was strong in his nostrils did not turn around even once.

Only her grandmother and Bountiful Harvest were in the lodge when Morning Song came in. The girl approached Teller Of Legends's hearth, seated herself, and slowly raised her eyes to her grandmother's face. There was a sternness in it now, and Morning Song was hard put not to drop her head. The old woman was pleased when she refused to be cowed, but took care that her approval did not show.

"That was a spellbinding tale you were entertaining your friends with," she said.

Morning Song made no reply beyond a slight hunching of her thin shoulders.

"I did not hear the whole of it, unfortunately," Teller Of Legends continued. "But I heard enough to understand that . . . it was a dream you were describing?"

The inflection in her voice told Morning Song that response must be made. She nodded her head.

"Ah. Did it visit you recently, this dream?"

Morning Song hesitated. "There would be no sense in speaking of an *old* dream," she said carefully.

"New or old, it surely was a dream of exceptional length," Teller Of Legends said blandly. "I noticed you and the other girls sitting together when I was on my way to the Deer Longhouse. This was a visit"—her voice trembled, steadied itself—"I did not hurry to end. Yet when I left, you were speaking still to your companions. And having earned honestly the name I wear, I can recognize a circle of enthralled listeners when I see one. Which made me curious enough to eavesdrop a little."

"Perhaps I talked overlong," Morning Song said. "But is it wrong, Grandmother, to tell a dream to your friends?"

Teller Of Legends eyed her quizzically, and Morning Song felt her face grow warm. "It is not," she said quietly. "Nor is it wrong to tell them a story. What *is* wrong, Morning Song, is to confuse the two." She reached out and touched the girl's tight-clasped hands. "Was it a dream that you described to them?"

"No," Morning Song said in a small voice.

"And was this the first time you have let them think that some tale was, in fact, a dream?"

Did no possibility escape Teller Of Legends's attention? her granddaughter wondered miserably. She shook her head.

"Why have you been so ready to deceive them, child? Surely you must know that this is not the way friends should be treated."

"But they do not want to be my friends, otherwise," Morning Song whispered. "You must know, Grandmother, how often they have mocked me when we were playing this game or that. And you have seen how I am slower than all the others when we help the women with their work." Her voice rose, quickened. "It is always *my* bread that burns black in the fire, and *my* basket that turns out loose-woven and lopsided. The clay pot I made cracked the first time I filled it with water. And the rope I braided not only bulged with knots, it gave way when I tried to bind up a load of kindling with it! You may be sure I have been teased about all of these things, and made to feel stupid and awkward.'' She swallowed hard to slow the spate of words gushing from her mouth. She had not intended to say so much, or to have it sound so like whining.

"I can ignore the teasing,'' she said more moderately. "Most of it. But when the others began to talk from time to time about the dreams that came to them when they slept, and I realized that even in so ordinary a thing as this I was not as they are''—she unclasped her hands and flung them wide—"I could not bear it, Grandmother! So I pretended that I, too, am visited by dreams. And all at once they stopped treating me as though I was a hawk in a heron's nest.''

Teller Of Legends looked down at her granddaughter, into eyes shimmering with resolutely unshed tears, and wished she might leave off her questioning and simply comfort the child. But it was too soon for that. "So you have gone on describing dreams that are not dreams, and inviting the admiration that your friends never before offered you.''

Morning Song bowed her head. "Yes,'' she said.

The old woman's heart weighed heavy in her chest. If only she had been alert to Morning Song's distress over being slower to learn than others were! If only she had taken the time to discover how much a misfit the girl believed herself to be. How much wretchedness might have been spared her, had someone older and wiser only taken a hand! And what was to be done now? That there was reason—in the girl's own mind, compelling reason—for behaving as she had, did not excuse Morning Song's wrongdoing. "You must understand,'' she said gently, "that letting your friends believe you were describing dream images to them was presenting falsehood as truth. It is not our way to speak falsely, Morning Song, about anything. And among friends, it is particularly shameful to do so. For all your need to be accepted and admired—which I understand— this must *never* happen again.''

She allowed a moment for the warning to be absorbed. Then: "This awkwardness you speak of will not plague you forever, Morning Song. It is simply a thing that many girls before you—and boys, as well—have suffered while they were growing up. No one knows why some are afflicted and others are not. It may be that spirits more mischievous than malevolent single out certain children and play tricks on them to test their patience. But you may trust me when I say that the grace that eludes you now will come to you in time. As it has to so many others.''

Morning Song managed to look hopeful and doubtful at one and the same time. "How can you be so certain of this, Teller of Legends?" she asked, and her words were more plea than question.

Her grandmother smiled. "Because I was one of those whose hands wore five thumbs and whose feet seemed designed solely to make her stumble," she said drily. "But when I was not much older than you are now, Morning Song, I awoke one morning to find that I was able at last to control my contrary hands and feet, and make them do as *I* wished rather than as *they* did."

Hope dominated now; doubt was reduced to a mere pucker between the eyes. Teller Of Legends was not sorry to see it demoted, for there was more that she must say, and it was imperative that Morning Song pay greater heed to her final words than to all that had gone before.

"Morning Song, I am going to ask you to make me a promise," she said, spacing her words to mark their significance. "Never let yourself be tempted to trifle with things of the spirit, such as dreams. Not for any reason whatsoever. You only invite trouble into your life by doing so, and this is not something I would wish for you, or for anyone I care for."

The girl's eyes were huge as she nodded solemn agreement. Plainly she had not thought of her pretending as interfering in matters of the spirit, and was suitably awed to learn that it had been.

"Do you suppose I may already have angered the spirits, Grandmother?" she asked anxiously.

The Matron chuckled. "I suspect that the spirits recognize innocence when they encounter it, Morning Song," she said comfortably, then resumed her sober expression. "But they know that you have been warned now, so you will not have innocence to protect you another time, my dear."

"I understand," the girl said, "and I am sorry, Teller Of Legends, to have caused you distress by behaving so badly."

It was a formal response, one that every child learned early. But Morning Song's gravity told her grandmother the girl meant what she said.

"It is behind us now," the old woman replied, and chuckled again. "Since it is, I have a confession of my own to make. Great though my distress was when I realized what you were doing, I was unable to keep myself from swelling with pride as I listened to you." She rose and pulled her granddaughter up beside her, smoothed her unruly hair. "You are a fine storyteller, Morning Song," she said, "and this is a skill most would be willing to trade all of their lesser skills for. Remember that next time you become impatient with some lack you perceive in yourself, and be content.''

Bountiful Harvest, proud of the forbearance she'd shown by keeping silent, turned to her mother as soon as her niece had left the longhouse. ''Do you understand how trying it is for me to be training that one?'' she asked, and congratulated herself on sounding calm and reasonable when she was, inside, burning with resentment. ''She is right when she claims she is different, but she must be made to see that her own contrariness makes her so.''

Teller Of Legends raised her broad-palmed hands and pushed silver-streaked hair back from her temples. Her gesture was born of weariness; this had been a disturbing day, and therefore an exhausting one. ''A thorn-strewn path stretches between childhood and womanhood,'' she sighed. ''I wish there were some way to make it easier for all those who travel it.''

''That is why the girls have guides to counsel them,'' Bountiful Harvest said. ''I have done what I could for Morning Song, Mother, but she continues unwilling to help herself. And''—she hesitated, choosing her words with care—''I am afraid you may have made my task the harder by chastening her so lightly.''

''She was unaware that dreams, like all other things of the spirit, are sacred,'' Teller Of Legends said. ''Now that she knows, she will not make the same mistake again.''

Bountiful Harvest compressed her lips. ''We shall see,'' she said. ''What worries me is that she knew full well she was lying to the other girls.'' She was risking her mother's displeasure by offering criticism, but it would be unforgivably weak of Bountiful Harvest to say nothing when so much needed to be said. ''The Longhouse People despise a liar. Such a person is shunned by his own clan and by the tribe as a whole. Yet you prescribed no punishment of any sort for Morning Song. This is not right, Teller Of Legends.''

''It is also our custom to chastise children gently. And Morning Song—although she will be a maiden soon enough—is a child still. Also''—a smile relaxed the deep creases around the older woman's wide mouth—''a story is not quite the same thing as deliberate falsehood.''

''To deceive others, to let Pumpkin Blossom and the rest think she was relating dreams to them, is not a falsehood?''

Teller Of Legends's smile faded, and age reclaimed her. ''I believe I coped fairly with that,'' she said tartly. ''The important thing was to show my granddaughter how she had strayed from the trail laid down for us by our ancestors. Which I have done.''

Bountiful Harvest's hands clenched. ''I think—'' she began. But what she thought remained unspoken. A muffled wailing and keening arose in that moment, and neither woman doubted what had prompted it.

''Dancing Water's death chant is ended,'' Teller Of Legends said quietly.

And the two, their differences forgotten, went in haste to console their friends of the Deer clan.

Chapter 8

Morning Song got down on her belly and wriggled through the horizontal cleft that led into a shallow cave. She'd discovered it when her misdirected lance buried itself in bushes thorny enough to advise caution in retrieving her weapon. A meticulous separating of the brush had revealed the cave's entrance, and curiosity had urged her to investigate further. She'd been grateful ever since that it had.

Its smallness enchanted her; this was the perfect place to shelter from a rainstorm, an ideal place to come when she wanted to be alone with her thoughts. And it served as a cache for her bow and arrows, and her lance and hatchet. Concealing these treasures here and there in the forest had cost her many an anxious moment. It was good to have them now where they were safe from the prying eyes of roving warriors-to-be.

The whimpering she'd been ignoring was succeeded by a single imperative bark, and she laughed aloud. ''Come in then,'' she called. ''You know the way, White Shadow.''

There was a scrabbling of paws against rock and then a smooth tongue was licking her outstretched hand. He was no longer as chubby and round as he'd been on the day she had found him waiting for her outside of the Turtle lodge; his legs had lengthened and slimmed until they resembled those of a yearling deer. But his determination to follow in Morning Song's footsteps had only increased as he'd grown bigger. That he was rarely farther from her than her own sun-sketched shadow accounted for the name she'd bestowed upon him.

In the beginning, his persistent trailing of her created a problem or two. Although he'd understood that he was not allowed within the longhouse, White Shadow had assumed that he might go everywhere else with Morning Song. Most of the time, he'd scarcely been noticed; there were always dogs running around the compound, nosing along the path to the woods, or loping between the rows of maturing plants in the fields. When he'd lain at her feet during the death ceremony for Dancing Water, however, only the solemnity of the occasion had kept those who saw him from shooing him away. Yet the dog had preserved a respectful quiet while Hearth Tender led the chant promising that grief's dark clouds would not forever blot out the sun. It seemed, Morning Song thought afterward, as if the pup had sensed that this was a ceremony of mourning and was offering solace in the only way he knew how. Since that day, the bond between them had been unseverable.

"You are my friend, Shadow," she said to him now, scratching between ears that could not seem to decide whether to lift perkily or droop. "My one true friend."

And so she thought him. He did not look askance when she accidentally tipped a bowl of hulled corn into the fire. He did not go about telling everyone that Morning Song had no regard for the truth, as Pumpkin Blossom did when her mother informed her that Morning Song's *dreams* had not been dreams at all. And he never turned his back on her, as the other girls had done when they'd heard how she had abused their trust; even Small Brown Sparrow— always quick to forgive before—had lent herself briefly to the ostracism of Morning Song. Best of all, though, was the pup's delight whenever the two could sneak away to the forest. To that end, Morning Song had begun to apply herself zealously to the tasks set for her by her mother-aunt, the faster to finish them and escape the compound. Not that Bountiful Harvest withheld criticism if Morning Song failed to meet her exacting standards; but her censure stung less these days, as did the continuing coolness of the other girls. So long as she had White Shadow, and the woods to wander in, Morning Song was happy.

She groped in her pouch for a slab of berry-studded leaf bread, and shared it with her friend. His tail thumped the cave's floor as he gulped it down.

"What should we do, between now and sunset?" she mused. "Practice with the lance? With my bow? Fling the hatchet and see if I can give proper snap to my throw this time? Or shall we let the breeze lead us on a long walk and perhaps come to a place we've never seen before?''

White Shadow thumped his tail again, and she hugged him to her. "You would prefer the walk, I see," she said, laughing. "Well, this is a splendid day for it.''

She persuaded him ahead of her out of the cave, then both stood and turned their faces into a lazy wind. Shadow lifted his tapered nose, sniffed, and bounded away, stopping after a few paces to look back at her. Satisfied that she was following, he stretched his long legs once more until he was far enough ahead to have the leisure to investigate the scent decorating a clump of bracken.

Morning Song did not hurry to catch up. His need to pursue the trace left by weasel or fox had been born in him, and he never neglected to rejoin her as soon as he'd finished his run. Panting and grinning, he'd emerge from the underbrush expecting to be praised as a mighty hunter, even though he had never, to her knowledge, made a kill. Morning Song invariably obliged him by patting his silky head and crooning her admiration. She would do so this time. Meanwhile, she was content to stroll idly, to permit the dancing breeze to tickle her nose and urge her on. It was deliciously warm, yet the season of the blackfly was past. Those nasty stinging insects had taken themselves to wherever they went after their yearly visit to the forest, and man and beast were grateful to be rid of them.

She skirted a cedar swamp and set out along an ill-defined path that imitated the meandering of a fern-bordered brook. The feet of shrew and mole had pitted the damp earth around the greenery, and squirrels scampered along the contorted limbs of a lightning-struck beech. In the patch of sky visible between twin conclaves of fir trees, a broad-winged hawk circled and complained, and nearer to hand a flycatcher piped his distinctive triple-note call. All in all, thought Morning Song, this was a day to gladden the heart.

Because it was, she managed to smile pleasantly when she turned away from the twisting brook and found herself face-to-face with Stag Leaping. The son of Owl Crying and Puma Walking Soft, although he'd grown into a powerfully built young man with handsome black eyes, was no more attractive to Morning Song now than he'd been as a boastful boy.

"So this is where you come," he said, "when you disappear from the village.''

She started. He was mostly with the hunter-warriors now. Why had he known or cared where Morning Song was, at any time?

He threw back his head and laughed. "You surely realize that the matrons consider it their duty to monitor the comings and goings of those about to become maidens. I have heard my mother and Lake On Fire discussing you. None of the other girls vanish from time to time, Morning Song, and it is a mystery to them why you do."

Of all the ways in which he might have said this, Stag Leaping had chosen the worst. Morning Song's eyes flashed and her fine-arched brows made a straight line above them. "There is no reason I should not walk in the forest when my work is done. And what I do is no concern of yours, Stag Leaping!"

He did not bridle in response to her anger, but only smiled and rested his right hand casually on her shoulder. "Your secret is secure with me, Morning Song," he said softly, and squeezed her shoulder as if for emphasis. "I shall say nothing of where I found you, not even to Owl Crying."

She could not bring herself to thank him. "It would make no difference, in any event," she countered. "I am doing nothing that is forbidden."

His fingers pleated the neck edge of her tunic. "This red . . . it becomes you, Morning Song. It makes your eyes brighter"—his free hand lifted, settled lightly on her other shoulder—"and makes a man wish to discover if your flesh might be as smooth as it looks."

His left hand slid from her shoulder and began to trace the skin exposed by the slash that enabled her to slip the garment over her head.

She felt as though slugs were inching their slimy way down her chest. With a shudder, she brought up both hands and pushed at him. But the breadth of him spoke truly of his strength; he caught her hands, imprisoned them in one of his, and sent his blunt fingers exploring further.

"Stop that!" she said fiercely, twisting and arching her back.

He merely tugged at one side of the slit until he had worked the tunic over her left shoulder and angled it snugly against her upper arm. Now the gentle rise of one budding breast was uncovered, and his fingers tiptoed across her chest and caressed it. "You are indeed very nearly a woman," he murmured, and let the palm of his sweaty hand press hard against the nipple—a spot that had been uncommonly tender of late. Morning Song jumped, and began to struggle more frantically than before.

"Leave me alone!" she said through clenched teeth, and tried vainly to kick him.

"Be at ease, Morning Song," he said, his voice thickening. "I do not mean to hurt you, only to show you some of the pleasures maidenhood will allow you to enjoy.'' He drew back a little, looked down into her stormy face. ''We played naked together as children, have you forgotten? And were encouraged to look and to touch much as I am doing now.''

''This is not the same,'' she gasped as he pulled her to him, held her locked against him.

He laughed. ''That is what I have been saying,'' he whispered hoarsely. ''Then, it was but play, and led nowhere. Now . . . there are delights in store for you, Morning Song.''

If only I had brought my knife from the cave! she thought desperately, writhing and thrashing in the circle of his sinewy arms. ''I will speak of this to Teller Of Legends, and to your mother,'' she cried.

He laughed again, scornfully this time. ''And I will tell them that you invited my attentions, that this is why you go alone so often to the forest. We would not be the first man and maid to meet here. Only those who have taken a mate are bound by the law to restrain themselves.''

He thrust himself against her, his hands gripping her slender hips and holding them fast as he mimed the invasion he was determined to make. Terror mounted in her then, was brought to a boil by revulsion, and erupted from her mouth in a single piercing scream.

He paid no heed; in truth, the sound inflamed him. One hand moved to fumble at the ties that held his breechclout in place.

As he stepped back from her long enough to let it drop to the ground, there came a crashing from the thicket behind him. In the next moment, a savage snarl cocooned in a blur of white signaled the attack launched by a half-grown dog who, in the way of his kind, rejoiced to have his loyalty put to the test. Nor did that mighty hunter miss his mark this time. Fangs sharp and gleaming sank deep into the bared buttocks of Stag Leaping, sank deep and clamped down hard.

This time it was Stag Leaping who screamed, as he swung about, astonished, and flailed his arms in a futile effort to dislodge the beast that seemed bent on making a meal of the fleshiest part of him. Blood poured down the backs of the warrior's legs and stained the muzzle of White Shadow, who growled in his throat and tightened his jaws. The dog's red-brown eyes slid sideways to fix on Morning Song, but she, stunned into silence, stood as though transformed into oak.

Stag Leaping moaned. It was a sound any other warrior would have died before making, and the girl's lingering horror was displaced by utter contempt. She found she could move again, and did.

"I *might* be able to persuade him to let go," she said slowly, thoughtfully, walking twice around man and stubbornly clinging dog.

"Do so!" he snapped. She raised her eyebrows. White Shadow growled again, and Stag Leaping went rigid. "Only call off this misbegotten cur," he begged, "and demand what ransom you will, Morning Song."

The whine in his voice filled her with loathing, and suddenly she wanted nothing more than to turn away from this sniveling excuse for a man and put the ugly incident behind her. "White Shadow," she said firmly. "Let go." She had no idea whether the dog would respond. But when he had looked to her once more, he permitted himself a final rasping growl, then slowly unclenched his jaws. His hackles remained erect, however, as he retreated reluctantly from the man whose scent marked him permanently: *enemy*. Not even when he used a clump of grass to wipe blood from his muzzle did Shadow's narrowed eyes cease to watch Stag Leaping.

The warrior's own eyes were no less wary. "What sort of animal is that," he said spitefully, "who is not brave enough to *face* a man when he attacks him?"

Morning Song rested her hand on Shadow's head. "He stands no taller than your knee," she said harshly. "But had your face been available to him, I am certain he would have jumped high enough to fasten his teeth in your *nose*. Would you have liked that better, Stag Leaping?"

Reminded of his wound, the young man felt gingerly at his torn buttock and winced.

"Sit in the brook until the bleeding stops," Morning Song suggested unfeelingly. "How to explain the scar, even when you have long since healed, is a problem you will have to resolve for yourself. As for the ransom you promised me, it is this: You must pledge never again to stalk me when I leave the village. Also, if we pass each other in the compound, or happen to be in the same lodge, you are not to look at me, let alone speak. Abide by this, and I do not care how you account for the tooth marks in your rump, Stag Leaping. Otherwise . . ." She felt certain her message was clear.

"If ever you speak of this day, for any reason," he blustered, "both you and your flea-ridden mutt will suffer for it!"

But Morning Song, with stalwart White Shadow at her side, felt gloriously invincible. "Do not even think of crossing me again," she said arrogantly, and spun on her heel, snapping her fingers to summon the dog after her.

During the red season, the *Onondio* traders made another circuit through Iroquois Territory. Se-A-Wi and Trail Marker prepared to welcome them courteously; these men, who had somehow fallen into the habit of traveling together, had only a tenuous link with the Frenchmen who had earned the enmity of the Longhouse People. And the goods they carried from village to village had come to be viewed as necessities rather than luxuries.

Follows The Signs hoped they would bring guns as well, when they came this time. "With certain of the pledge-breaking Huron at war again with two of our nations, we dare not be unprepared," he said. "And now that our old enemies, the Algonquin, are taking in those Crooked Tongues who escape the Iroquois' reprisals, who is to say what might happen next, or where, or when. The day will come, I feel certain, when guns will mean the difference between victory and defeat for all warriors, everywhere."

The Sachem had deferred to the war leader on the matter, and since Fierce Eagle had not argued the point, Trail Marker decided he would bargain for some of the white man's weapons. He had only a sparse accumulation of beaver pelts to offer in exchange, but there were lynx and fox in abundance, and four magnificent bear-skins besides.

As it happened, Laval and Briand arrived empty-handed. Once the ceremony of greeting had been observed, Gaspard Laval combed out his beard with bony fingers and shrugged. "What I carried with me, it was gone in a day. You tell me what you need, Trail Marker. I bring it to you in the spring."

Burly Briand eyed the pile of fox furs greedily. Yet he, too, had taken advantage—yes, in his case *advantage* was definitely the word, he thought smugly—of the merchandise-hunger of the redskins farther east. He would have been a fool not to, and Henri Briand did not count himself that! But he had other business to attend to, this trip.

He jerked his thumb in the direction of the hills. "The head man of the village beyond the lake, he has said I may build me a cabin between his settlement and this one." He bared his teeth in a smile that did not extend past his lips. "My home in the north, it burned down. My woman"—he turned up the palms of his leathery hands—"she was careless with a lantern. I warn her and warn her to watch what she does, but—*mon Dieu!*—she does not listen, her." His oversized teeth revealed themselves a second time, and he nodded to Trail Marker and Follows The Signs, to Se-A-Wi and—

perfunctorily—toward Cloud Racer. The Frenchman could not be bothered to acknowledge one of so little consequence, and the young warrior's habit of wrapping his thoughts in silence was annoying to a man who hid his behind a shield of verbosity.

Laval, angling his knees to sit in the Indian fashion that, over the years, had come to feel natural to him, wondered why Briand did not deposit his wife in Quebec. For a surety, the man had no more use for women than Laval did. Which was little, save to satisfy certain elemental needs from time to time.

Trail Marker looked to the Sachem and translated the trader's words. Follows The Signs tilted his head to receive them also. Cloud Racer, who had no difficulty even with colloquialisms these days, merely studied Briand's face as though it were a mask deserving of penetration.

Se-A-Wi considered the matter. The chief of the next village was not only Sweet Maple's brother but a man Se-A-Wi respected for his good sense. Since he had approved the *Onondio*'s request, Se-A-Wi would appear less hospitable than his wife's kinsman if he did not. That would invite shame. Momentarily he wished it was Lah-Val who had asked; the taciturn man was more to Se-A-Wi's liking than the one who always smiled. "He would not be trapping or hunting on our land?" he said to Trail Marker.

Trail Marker turned back to Henri Briand and put the question to him.

"Me, I make my living trading," Briand boomed, stretching his lips automatically. "I may shoot a rabbit, yes, or net a fish or two. But only enough for my woman to cook for me."

While Trail Marker was interpreting this, Morning Song, bent beneath a basket of fresh-picked corn, slipped into the compound. She had been last in the fields this harvest day, and had lingered there to throw a stick for White Shadow to chase. Not until an intriguing scent lured him from their play had she headed home.

She had known the traders were expected; Small Brown Sparrow always made sure that everyone knew. But she hadn't known precisely when, and it took her unawares to find them right in front of the Turtle longhouse. She veered sharply to avoid them, and, as she did, Henri Briand became impatient for an answer.

"Tell your chief," he ordered Trail Marker, "how it will be good to have a trader living in his dooryard. If he wants hatchets, I get him hatchets, me. Sharper than any other trader has, yes! If his woman wants a new kettle, or some shiny beads, he may send a runner to my new cabin. So long as he has pelts to barter, like those otter skins there, we will be able to deal, him and me!"

Morning Song froze. She was unsurprised that this particular voice reached her ears; she remembered that the barrel-shaped trader was inclined to bellow like a moose in rut. But that she knew before Trail Marker began translating what the man was saying—that sounds which should have been as unintelligible as the barking of a fox separated themselves into recognizable words—struck her with the force of a lightning bolt.

If shoulder straps had not secured her basket, the corn would have tumbled to the ground. It was *not* possible that Morning Song could know each word the trader spoke in the moment it left his mouth! Perspiration beaded her forehead, the muscles in her legs tensed, and her feet made ready to take her back to the fields, to the forest. . . .

In the next instant she blessed the heavy load that prevented her flight. She had had enough of running away, and to bolt like a frightened rabbit would attract notice and invite questions, questions she lacked answers for. Until she had them, until she understood why an alien tongue should be familiar to her and why hearing it spoken shrieked *danger*, no one—not even Teller Of Legends—must know what she had discovered this day.

As she stumbled along the path leading to the rear entrance of the lodge, the girl scrubbed at her cheeks with both hands to reanimate features that felt locked in ice. Her face must not reveal her shock and confusion. But until four feet padded in her wake and a sleek, white body curled affectionately around her legs, she was too distraught to manage even the semblance of a smile.

"What were you chasing?" she asked her truant dog. And was relieved that no hint of strain showed in her voice.

Shadow trotted beside her until she rounded the corner of the longhouse, then flopped against its sun-warmed western wall. He would not whine when she left him, but his eyes told her how unfair it was that always he must wait outside for her.

Although his reappearance had banished all but shreds of her panic, it was a pensive Morning Song who finally entered the lodge and slipped the brimming basket from her aching back.

"You have come just in time," Otter Swimming called, beckoning to her niece. "We have been persuading Teller Of Legends to give us a story. Come and sit by me, and we'll listen to it together."

The Matron of the Turtle lodge gave no sign that a rhythmic thumping against the rear wall betrayed the presence of Morning Song's faithful companion. But the girl saw the laughter in the old woman's eyes, and guessed correctly what legend the sound would suggest.

"There was a time," her grandmother began, "when the beasts who walk on four legs sat with the Iroquois around a single council fire. Because they did, the Longhouse People learned from the beaver how to fish and how to build lodges the rain cannot enter, from the bear and the wolf how to follow a trail, from the raccoon how to climb trees, and from the dog how to stand sentry for many suns without wearying. In those days, every creature—even man— was able to understand the others when they spoke, for this was how the Maker Of Life had planned it.

"But some of the animals could not bring themselves to trust the furless ones who walked on two legs. The beaver worried that the Longhouse People would invade the rivers he'd marked for himself; the bear and the wolf feared the Iroquois hunters might seek their pelts; and the fox—who had taught them cunning—felt threatened because they'd mastered his teachings so well. One by one, the forest creatures disappeared from the great council fire, until only the dog sat with the Indians."

Morning Song and Otter exchanged grins.

"Fear is not easily laid to rest, however. Soon the four-legged animals were meeting around their own council fire. Wolf vowed that he would feel safe only if the beasts banded together and killed all the Longhouse People. Bear preferred to challenge the Iroquois to open war; big and strong as he was, he was certain he would prove the victor. Beaver suggested they wait until the white season and then destroy all the lodges; creatures without fur cannot survive without shelter, he reminded the rest. Fox held out for treachery; he would show the other animals how to be crafty enough to pretend friendship with the Iroquois and at the same time cheat and steal from them.

"Dog, who had sat silent while the others argued, looked around the circle. 'Our brothers, the Iroquois, fed me when snow was deep on the ground,' he said. 'I will not repay them by turning against them now. And I shall warn them if the rest of you continue to plot their destruction.'

"Well, it is said that all of his fellows turned on poor Dog then. Wolf accused him of cowardice, and Beaver said he'd been made foolish by the praise lavished on him by the maidens. 'He remembers nothing but the soft caresses of Indian girls upon his head,' he said contemptuously."

Morning Song smiled. She'd forgotten what a charming story

this was; or perhaps she was listening with new ears since Shadow had come into her life.

Teller Of Legends reached out and lifted young Day Greeter onto her lap. "Can you think what cross old Bear might have said?" she asked her, and the little girl shook her head.

" 'For a meager crust of maize cake,' he growled, 'one too hard for the teeth of the red man to crush, you are willing to surrender all claim to the rights held sacred by your kind down through the ages.'

"But Dog was undaunted, and only repeated his threat to warn the Iroquois that the animals meant to go to war with them. Suddenly the Maker Of Life appeared in their midst, and told them that his plan for all creatures to live in peace together must be abandoned. Because the animals were conspiring, he would dissolve the common language that they shared with one another and with man. From now on, they would be unable to communicate as equals. And since the Longhouse People had been so foully plotted against, the Maker Of Life decreed that, from this day, they should be the hunters and the beasts the hunted.

"Dog—although he'd attended this shameful council—had nonetheless proven his loyalty to the Iroquois. So, although he, too, would no longer be able to speak with them, he would retain his understanding of man's language and continue to serve as his friend and protector. 'Even after death,' the Maker Of Life proclaimed, 'you, Dog, shall be with the Indian still.' "

Morning Song sighed contentedly as she rose with the others to thank Teller Of Legends for her story. Only later did she realize that her grandmother's tale had described something more than the inherent loyalty of dogs. The Maker Of Life's decision to deny the animals a common language applied also to the separate families of man. So why had Morning Song—who knew only Iroquois—been allowed to understand the *Onondio* when he spoke? And she made herself confront what she had been refusing to recognize: Only a thinning of the mists veiling the memories of her earliest childhood could possibly account for such a thing.

She did not sleep as quickly, or as peacefully, as she had hoped she might.

Year after year, Morning Song had watched her village prepare for the Midwinter Festival. The Medicine societies rehearsed their elaborate dances; robes were trimmed with cornhusk braids for the Big Heads to wear when they stirred the cold ashes of the Old Year's fires and kindled fresh blazes for the new; thanksgiving chants were perfected by the Faithkeepers; and strips of hide were dyed bright colors to decorate the pole from which the sacrificial white dog would be suspended until the fifth day of the Festival.

This year was no different, and Morning Song was caught up in all the excitement. Afterward, she wondered that she could have been so blind. Of all the whelps the village's bitches had produced during the last twelve months, one pup only wore fur the color of snow.

"Grandmother, they cannot, they *must* not, do this!"

Teller Of Legends looked into the stricken face of her grand-daughter. "Morning Song, White Shadow shall feel nothing. He will be soothed and pleasured when Puma Walking Soft caresses him before he is strangled. The old man's hands are as strong as ever; he will not permit the dog to suffer in his last moments. Why, he is probably petting and praising him right now. You know that the dog selected for sacrifice is always pampered during the weeks before the Festival."

"But he will *die*! And—and his body will be *burnt*!"

The old woman sighed. She understood her granddaughter's an-guish, knew anguish herself because she could do nothing to relieve Morning Song's. "This is how we offer thanks to the Maker Of Life," she said gently, "and ask his protection in the year ahead. You know this, Morning Song, for the same ritual is performed every Midwinter."

"But I did not know they would choose White Shadow! I cannot let him be killed, Grandmother. He is my friend, and I *will not* let this happen to him!"

"You can do nothing to prevent it," Teller Of Legends said more strongly. "To accept what cannot be changed is an important part of growing up, Morning Song. If you cannot rejoice when the ritual sends your dog's spirit soaring to meet the Maker Of Life, then you must simply stand tall and endure." She leaned forward and made herself speak sternly, for it was not misery alone that was narrow-ing Morning Song's brown eyes, but rebelliousness as well. "Life often demands that we hold fast and endure. You will be glad one day that you learned how to do so while you were still young."

Morning Song sprang to her feet. "I hoped you might help me," she said tightly, "but I see that is not possible." She squared her thin shoulders and the ghost of a smile flitted across her child-woman's face. "I suspect growing up also means learning to help yourself, rather than depending on others." She inclined her head. "Thank you, Grandmother, for listening to me. And I promise I will not shame you when the rite of sacrifice is held this year."

Then she was gone, marching out of the longhouse on rigid legs and giving no word of greeting to Hearth Tender, who was just entering.

Pumpkin Blossom was easily persuaded that the two girls should visit Meadow Brook that evening. Ever since she and her cousin had experienced their first monthly bleeding within a day of each other, she had felt friendlier toward Morning Song. They'd been confined together in the longhouse, in a separate area much like the one Bountiful Harvest had occupied following the birth of Fish Jumping, and although Pumpkin Blossom would not admit as much to her mother, her menstruation had caused such cramping that the girl had been driven to wonder if she might be dying. In desperation, she had confided her fears to Morning Song.

"I do not believe this sort of thing causes death," Morning Song told her seriously. "It's possible your fear is making the pain worse, Pumpkin Blossom. That, and not being allowed to eat meat. It is hard to keep up your strength on vegetables alone!" She'd swallowed the last of the soup Bountiful Harvest had brought to them and grimaced. "I wish your mother had at least let a bit of venison dangle in the broth while it was cooking," she grumbled.

The look on her face made Pumpkin Blossom giggle, and her spontaneous laughter eased the muscles that fear had twisted. Cautiously she straightened her back. "The pain is not so bad now," she said, surprised.

Morning Song—feeling obscurely guilty because she was suffering so little—thought it might be a good idea to continue to divert her companion. "I will tell you a story to make the time pass more quickly," she said.

She launched promptly into an amusing one that proved effective medicine, and Pumpkin Blossom, even when her cramping was hardly enough to be felt, had asked for others during the remainder of their confinement. That had pleased Morning Song. And the agreeable murmur of their two voices, the clarity of their shared laughter, had drifted from the screened-off corner and brought smiles to the face of the woman who was their grandmother.

Now, as they neared the Beaver lodge, Morning Song was aware that she was about to jeopardize the compatibility that had been born between her and her cousin. "I am going to leave you here," she said, breaking stride, "and let you go alone to see Meadow Brook. There is something—something important—I must attend to."

Pumpkin Blossom's face clouded. "This was your intention from the start," she guessed shrewdly. "Morning Song, you know it can be dangerous to wander at night. And it will be counted as much my fault as yours if we separate."

"It is early still, even if it is dark," Morning Song pointed out. "And I will join you and Meadow Brook before the moon is a hand's span above the horizon. We'll return together to our long-house, and neither of us shall be faulted for behaving foolishly."

Pumpkin Blossom stamped her foot. It was a childish gesture, but nothing else would express so well the anger and frustration she felt. "You never change, Morning Song, do you? I should go back at once and tell my mother what you propose to do. Of course," she added bitterly, "I do not know what that is. But it is surely something no one else would even think of doing."

It took considerable time for Morning Song to coax her cousin into better humor, and even longer to persuade her to do as Morning Song had asked.

"But I will not quickly forgive you for this," Pumpkin Blossom fumed. "Nor will I let myself be shamed if you end by disgracing yourself. I shall simply insist that you sneaked away when I was not looking." And she made truth of her proclamation by turning her back on her cousin.

Pumpkin Blossom has not changed much either, Morning Song reflected as she darted away. Then she put aside all thought of her and crept toward the south side of the compound. It irked her to move slowly—there was so little time in which to do all that she had to—but to be heard or seen would mean an end to all her scheming. And the ground was brittle with frost; the grass that lingered here and there crackled when she inadvertently trod upon it.

Only extraordinary caution brought her undetected to her destination. There, against the palisade wall opposite Owl Crying's longhouse, was the cage Puma Walking Soft had built. Built to pen the white dog who, catching the scent of the one who approached, whined softly, pleadingly.

"Hush, Shadow," she whispered, and fumbled at the knotted rawhide that held the front panel closed. She had only touch to guide her, for the moon had not yet risen, but after what seemed an eternity the last knot yielded, and she was able to let an ecstatic White Shadow slip out of his prison.

She threw her arms around his neck, let him lick her chin, her nose. Then she stood and walked as swiftly as she dared toward the gate in the palisade's wall. The dog followed, making less noise with his four feet than she did with two, Morning Song realized ruefully.

It was easier than she'd expected to unbar that huge gate, but the operation was not entirely soundless. Blood throbbed in her neck and she cast anxious glances over her shoulder as she pulled it ajar and urged Shadow out of the compound. She stooped to pick up a long braid of rope she'd hidden under a bush nearby, then set her feet on the path leading to the forest.

"You must stay in our cave until I come for you," Morning Song said earnestly. "I know you will not understand my shutting you up after I've just set you free, but I have left you a bowl of water and meaty bones to chew on." She hugged him again, then signed to him to remain where he was while she wriggled back through the narrow slit. It cost her more time to work a heavy boulder into place, but she knew she must block the entrance in case White Shadow had not grasped what she'd told him. Then Morning Song tucked her knife and her hatchet into her belt and moved on to the next stage of her mission.

Grandmother Moon had made her appearance in the sky dome, and tonight her full face smiled on the earth. For now, that was to Morning Song's benefit; the way she must go was virtually unmarked, and even pale light was better than none at all.

Her heart bumped against her ribs when she passed near the pit snare she'd dug during the afternoon. One false step here, and its own maker would fall into it. Certainly she had concealed it well; the anger that had given her the energy to dig a hole of sufficient depth in frost-hard soil had not spent itself quickly. Enough fury-fueled strength remained to let her chop down a score of branches and lay them in a lattice pattern across the pit, and to strew a natural-looking layer of underbrush on top of that. Ignoring the scrapes and scratches inflicted by raspberry cane and thistle, she avoided the path until she was certain the snare was behind her.

The trickiest part of her plan was upon her, and she prayed that the *orenda* of the forest, which had always been in harmony with her own, would guide and support her now. She slowed her pace, concentrated on putting one moccasined foot precisely in front of the other, tried to make of herself a thing as insubstantial as mist. What little breeze there was came from the right direction; no trace of her scent would precede her.

She drew from her pouch one of the blades of grass she'd secreted there. She hoped that the hardy grass that defied winter's cold would, when she cupped it in her hand and blew upon it, produce the same sound that was easily coaxed from the tender grass of spring. And she could only trust that, if it did, the she-wolf whose den lay just ahead would mistake it for the cry of a fawn and be tempted to come after it. The wolf had a half-grown pup to feed—one with fur the color of ashes. Surely she would be unable to resist?

Morning Song hoped the wolf would not pause to wonder how a deer so young could be wandering the forest this late in the year. At least she had no mate to wonder also about this and perhaps warn the female off; Morning Song had never seen a male around, even though she'd been spying on this den for months. She had mourned when the gray pup's littermates sickened and died, and been glad when the single survivor grew into the sleek and frisky creature he was now. It had been in her mind to continue watching over him, but the fate the Faithkeepers had decreed for White Shadow dictated otherwise. In the past, a fox or wolf with a light-colored coat had served as Midwinter sacrifice when there'd been no white dog about the village. If Morning Song had her way—and she meant to!—that would happen this year, too.

Her noiseless tread had brought her to the copse of saplings she'd noted while the sun still illuminated the forest. Two strides carried her into the heart of it, where she stole a moment to wipe suddenly perspiring hands on the hem of her tunic. Then she lifted the spear of grass, straightened and positioned it, and raised her hands to her mouth.

Her first attempt produced no sound at all. But when she'd inhaled more vigorously, the rush of expelled breath against the angled blade of grass sent a tremulous bleat into the silent night. She blew against it again, and was herself almost convinced that a lost fawn was crying for its mother.

The forest and its creatures were nearly as familiar to Morning Song as the village and its clans. She knew full well that the she-wolf—if she rose to the bait—would scarcely come blundering through the thicket to locate the source of that cry. So, when she had made the grass whistle a third time, Morning Song sidled from the birch grove and retreated to a second spot she'd marked for her use, a bit of mossy ground to one side of the oak beneath which she'd dug the pit snare.

Her warm breath had wilted the grass she'd been blowing on. She took out a fresh spear and sent another trio of plaintive cries into the quiet night. Then she made herself as immobile as the tree she could not see around and waited.

There was not so much as a whisper of sound to tell her that the wolf, her hunting instincts aroused, had abandoned the security of her den to stalk a helpless fawn. Perhaps she had been sleeping so deeply she had failed to hear the bogus cries. Perhaps she was by nature too wary to be deceived by them. Perhaps—

There came a confusion of thrashing and crashing, quickly followed by a dull but dramatic thud. Morning Song sagged against the trunk of the oak. Dare she go and look? She'd taken care to use sturdy branches so that the weight of some small creature—skunk or raccoon, for instance—could not dislodge them. But a larger animal might have been prowling this night—cougar or white-tailed deer or shortsighted moose—and fallen into her trap.

On tiptoe, she went as close as was sensible to the rim of the pit. And a shaggy, yellow-eyed she-wolf glared up at her.

The beast snarled and gathered herself to leap, and Morning Song drew back hurriedly, even though she was certain the cavity was not roomy enough to allow the animal to escape in that way. Not yet. But wolves were intelligent; soon the bitch would be putting her powerful paws to work widening the bottom of the pit. When she'd given herself sufficient space to hunker down, she would spring to freedom.

Morning Song took no steps to stop her. If she must deprive the she-wolf of her only cub, she would grant her life and a chance to produce other litters. But she hoped—most fervently—that the time the enraged beast spent in maneuvering would permit Morning Song to erect the springpole snare and then to capture and spirit away the younger wolf.

Taking up her coil of rope, she turned her mind and her feet in the direction of the unsuspecting pup's lair.

Chapter 9

Grandmother Moon's face was all at once veiled with cloud, and Morning Song had to grope her way along the nebulous trail. Only by sliding her feet slowly, first one and then the other, could she identify obstacles in her path. How, then, was she to locate the slender sapling she'd planned to use for her springpole? Or see to lay her noose in front of the den?

Doggedly she continued on and let instinct lead her to where she trusted that the young wolf lay sleeping. Then she prepared to wait. What was it Teller Of Legends had said about *holding fast*? This she must do; and never mind that, while she did, a furious she-wolf might be contriving her escape and following the scent the girl had strewn behind her, might even now be silently baring wicked teeth and hunching herself to attack.

The hairs on the nape of Morning Song's neck tickled as she strained her ears for movements in the brush that would warn her to run. As if running—in the dark—from a creature so swift and surefooted could serve any purpose whatsoever! Nonetheless, she checked her breathing and listened.

How long she stood there, with every muscle in her body poised for futile flight, she would never be able to say. But the moments limped by as she visualized herself mauled by a vengeful wolf until her flesh hung in bloody tatters, heard an explosive *crunch!* as her ankle or wrist was caught in the vise of slavering jaws.

So absorbed was she that the gradual silvering of the needles on a nearby spruce did not catch her attention. Only when the last of the cloud deserted the moon did she realize there was light to guide her once more. And when she saw that the sapling she'd been seeking was within arm's reach, she shook off her horrendous fancies and went to work.

The sapling bent to the pressure she brought to bear on it, and she wrapped its narrow tip with the center section of her rope. One trailing end she secured temporarily by winding it twice around the trunk at the base of the little tree; the other—the section she'd formed into a noose—she drew out cautiously, placing the loop at the entrance to the wolf den.

She crouched, and stretched her ears until she made out a soft snuffling from inside. Reassured that her prey had not eluded her, she smiled, but the smile was short-lived. As she straightened and backed away, a problem she had not foreseen confronted her: How could she coax the wolf awake and out into the night? Was he old enough for the cry of a fawn to bring him running? Her brows met in a frown of vexation. Was she to lose all she'd gained thus far, lose White Shadow himself, because she'd been careless in her calculations?

A long stick poked into the lair might prod the pup awake, but Morning Song could not be simultaneously at the den's entrance and at the far end of her rope. And even half-grown wolves come equipped with teeth and claws and the will to use them.

Precious time raced by as she mentally proposed and rejected idea after idea. In the end, she saw that she had no choice but to try the grass whistle again. She followed her rope to the arched sapling, unwound the end she'd fixed to its trunk—and discovered she needed two hands to keep it taut. Which left her with none to hold the blade of grass.

A single attenuated howl rose to shiver the silence. It sounded beautiful to Morning Song; that frustrated howl meant the bitch was in the pit snare still. She gripped the rope tighter and glued her eyes to the barely perceptible entrance to the den. Unless all that she'd learned about the habits of woodland creatures was in error, Mother Wolf had solved Morning Song's problem for her.

The patch of blackness she stared at was cleft by a smudge of gray. Morning Song opened her hands, let the rope snap out of them, and the sapling sprang upright. The wolf cub, having stepped unwittingly into a circle of rope, found himself hauled into midair by his bound front legs.

Morning Song seized her blade and chopped the remainder of the braided rope into shorter lengths. She knotted the first piece around the dangling hind legs of the whimpering cub, then whipped her hatchet from her belt and began to hack at the base of the sapling. Nor did she pause, except for breath, until it was split far enough for the weight of the young wolf to carry it to the ground.

It had been easy to secure the cub's rear legs; to tie up his muzzle posed a problem. He was yelping now, and threshing about despite his leg restraints; moonlight gilded baleful eyes, gleamed on fangs nearly as long and sharp as his mother's. Morning Song's fingers shaping a second noose, were less than steady.

The she-wolf howled again, venting her rage and doubtless sending a message of warning that her cub would receive too late. Morning Song stood astride the squirming young wolf, felt his shuddering response to the bitch's call, and tried frantically to bind his snapping jaws. Sweat oozed from her every pore, dripped into her eyes, and made her hands slippery.

This would never do. She pulled herself erect, dashed the sweat from her face with her hands, wiped her hands on her tunic. To truss a struggling beast was not something hunters-to-be were usually taught, so Morning Song had no precedent to follow. Yet she needed to subdue, not slay; to deliver a dead wolf—no matter how pale his fur—would accomplish nothing. The sacrificial animal must be alive and healthy at the start of the Midwinter Festival.

The pup was panting shallowly now, she saw. Was he wearying, or merely calling up new reserves of strength?

She had heard warriors boast of lifting an enemy's scalp before dealing the deathblow. Little boys loved such tales, and begged to have their uncles teach them their methods. Morning Song had watched more than one demonstration on how to restrain a struggling foe while removing his scalp. Would a similar strategy serve her purposes now?

From the direction of the pit snare came another howl, this time one more determined than frustrated. It spurred her to action. She dropped, positioning one knee on either side of the wolf's prone body. Then she thrust the fingers of her left hand deep into the fur that circled his neck and, clutching the hide at the base of his skull, yanked his head up and back. His jaws sprang open in protest, but the pup could not turn his head, and the loop of rope Morning Song held in her right hand was wide enough to fit over his gaping muzzle. A firm jerk on it then and the knot slid into place, forcing the jaws closed and keeping them that way.

Breathing heavily, she clambered to her feet. Save for lashing the wolf to the felled sapling and hauling him back to the village, it was done. She looked down at the animal; twitching and trembling was all he could manage now. Suddenly she knelt again and scratched gently between his defeat-flattened ears.

"I'm sorry," she said softly. "You are a handsome animal, and a brave one. I ask your forgiveness, and hope you will understand that I do this only because I must."

Then she went to fetch the last of her rope.

As Morning Song emerged from the thinning trees on the edge of the forest, she put aside her notion of quietly penning the wolf cub in the cage Puma Walking Soft had built. The palisade gate stood wide, and so many shadowy figures milled about in the compound that everyone in the village must be going without sleep this night. *Pumpkin Blossom!* she thought bitterly.

She jutted out her small chin and once more hoisted the splintered end of the sapling onto her bruised and blistered shoulder. It had been a grueling walk, and the young wolf had grown heavier with every dragging step. But the end was in sight, and if she must enter the village beneath the accusing stares of all who lived there, so be it. She was at least returning in triumph. And White Shadow was safe in the cave.

No one offered her greeting as she marched into the compound. Indeed, she heard no sound at all except for her own plodding footsteps and the scrape of the carrying pole.

She looked around and saw Puma Walking Soft standing between Se-A-Wi and Teller Of Legends, and turned in his direction. When she was near enough, she bowed her head respectfully, then raised it and surveyed him with as much composure as she could muster. "I have brought you a magnificent beast to sacrifice at Midwinter," she said clearly.

The entrance hide was drawn back on the Pigeonhawk longhouse, and the blaze on its front hearth lit the Faithkeeper's face. It deepened the grooves that descended from either side of his broad nose to frame an unrelenting slash of a mouth. When that mouth remained obstinately shut, Morning Song fumbled for something further to say. "The wolf's fur, as you see, is the color of ash," she pointed out, "and he is young and healthy. The spirit of such a beast cannot help but please the Maker Of Life."

"Are you a Keeper Of The Faith," the man rasped, "that you can know this?"

Morning Song swallowed hard. "You know I am not," she said. "But everyone knows only a perfect animal may be offered in sacrifice. This one has no blemish. And it will not be the first time a wild creature is used in the ritual, rather than a d—dog." In spite of her resolve to speak calmly, desperation was beginning to lace her voice.

"We had a dog to sacrifice this year," Puma Walking Soft said sternly. "You will tell us what has become of him."

Morning Song clenched her hands and said nothing.

"She has set him free!" a voice shrilled. Pumpkin Blossom's. "That is why she left me, when I was not looking: to free the white dog."

"Perhaps she was visited by a dream telling her to." This, quietly, from Hearth Tender.

Morning Song wished she could encourage this explanation. No one would fault her for obeying a spirit! But her grandmother's lecture on the importance of truth remained vivid to this day. She shook her head. "There was no dream," she said.

"Then tell us where we may find the white dog," Puma Walking Soft commanded.

"There is no need." The words were couched in an exultant shout, and Morning Song, stomach churning with apprehension, swung round with the rest to watch Stag Leaping strut across the compound and dump a trussed White Shadow at Puma Walking Soft's feet. "I have brought back our Midwinter sacrifice," he said.

Morning Song knew at once how he had managed this: He had used the same strategy she'd used with the wolf pup. Shadow, catching his scent, would have charged out of the cave as soon as the boulder was rolled away from its mouth. Nor did she wonder how Stag Leaping had known where White Shadow was: He'd heard

Morning Song, or spotted her, when she'd helped her dog to escape. Despite the pledge he'd given not so long ago, he had followed them.

A babble of talking had swelled while these thoughts raced through Morning Song's head. Most of it, she noted bitterly, was as admiring of Stag Leaping as it was deprecating of herself. Her aching shoulders slumped, and tears stung her eyes as she went down on her knees beside the cruelly bound White Shadow, began to fondle his ears and comfort him with caresses and whispered endearments.

"It seems to me there is a decision to be made here." Teller Of Legends did not raise her voice; since she had been chosen Chief Matron of the village, no word of hers went unheeded. She moved forward a pace so that she stood by herself, and her dignity was reflected in the straightness of her broad back, the uncompromising line of her jaw, the way her eyes probed the faces turned toward her. "It is true that we must have an animal to sacrifice at Midwinter. It is equally true"—she let a certain dryness creep into her voice—"that we have no need for *two*."

Someone laughed, and Teller Of Legends nodded approvingly. She enjoyed having her jests appreciated. Still, this was a serious matter and she kept her expression solemn. "Since it is a ritual of sacrifice we are concerned with, I believe it only fair to consider how Morning Song—in order to save a dog she has become attached to—showed herself willing to sacrifice even her own life in an attempt to preserve his." Her black eyes swept the circle of villagers again and lingered on the faces of the Matrons who would be jointly making the decision she had mentioned. "Even a young wolf is savage when cornered. And wolves ordinarily live in families, as the Longhouse People do; I suspect my granddaughter had to deal with a mature wolf also."

Morning Song, scarcely daring to believe that her grandmother was coming to her defense, could only nod her confirmation when Teller Of Legends looked down at her.

"Yet Stag Leaping must be praised for his daring. The dog was certain to resist recapture, and any dog can be as ferocious as a wild beast if he feels threatened. So I think we must ask ourselves two questions: Who was exposed to the greater danger, and how compelling was the reason for risking so much? The answers we arrive at will determine whether the dog or the wolf should be our sacrificial animal this year. And"—the gaze turned on Morning Song had no pity in it this time—"I give you my promise that my granddaughter will offer thanks to each of you, whatever decision we come to.''

Slowly Morning Song came to her feet. ''Teller Of Legends speaks truly,'' she said faintly. ''What she has promised, I shall do.''

She watched as seven women, each one Chief Matron of her lodge, came forward to cluster around Teller Of Legends. Sweet Maple, though her round face was troubled, smiled encouragingly at Morning Song, and jolly Rain Singing, who had a fondness for all young people, sought Morning Song's eyes and twinkled at her. Diminutive Owl Crying was clearly bursting to boast of her son's valor and cleverness, and Lake On Fire—who was sister to Puma Walking Soft and aunt to Stag Leaping—would be an enthusiastic ally of Owl Crying. What Gray Squirrel, Weeping Sky, or Snow Comes Early might say, she could not guess; the former might still feel resentment toward the Turtle clan over Bountiful Harvest's rejection of Covers His Eyes. As for Teller Of Legends herself . . . she had intervened in her granddaughter's behalf, but she prided herself on impartiality. She would listen to each Matron in turn and her own decision would reflect a meticulous weighing of the opinions presented to her.

Morning Song sighed and averted her gaze from the deliberating women. She let it roam instead over the coalitions of villagers who waited with her for the Matrons to be done with their discussion. Her cousin, she saw, stood with the other maidens. Now and again they looked in Morning Song's direction, then whispered behind their hands. Only Small Brown Sparrow kept herself apart from them, and she emphasized her support by grinning when she felt Morning Song's eyes upon her. Otter Swimming, when her niece looked to where she and Deer Caller were standing beside Hearth Tender, smiled also. Behind the three, however, were Bountiful Harvest and certain of the younger matrons. A flutter of nuthatches, they were, snatching at morsels of gossip gleaned from tales of Morning Song's past misdemeanors! The men, both elders and warriors, were inclined to exhibit indifference to the whole affair. Except for Cloud Racer. He, like Small Brown Sparrow, stood aloof from his fellows and returned Morning Song's brief glance with a speculative one; then he turned his head to look with equal thoughtfulness at Stag Leaping. *That* one, Morning Song could not bring herself to look at for even a moment; she would be sorely tempted to fly at him if she did.

A flurry of movement told her that the waiting was over. With mounting trepidation, Morning Song made a half turn to face the Matrons.

"We have made our judgment," Teller Of Legends said. "We offer sincere gratitude to the warrior Stag Leaping for his prompt and proper response when he discovered that our sacrificial dog was missing. He is to be commended for setting out alone after an animal that might well have turned on him, and praised for bringing the dog back to us."

Morning Song's knees began to shake. No! she thought. No! How can I stand here and listen while White Shadow is condemned to death? But she would not run away, and could not shut out her grandmother's measured speech.

"Morning Song," Teller Of Legends went on, "must be told that her abduction of the animal selected by the Faithkeepers for sacrifice violates both law and tradition, and brings dishonor to herself and to her clan. It is only because she is newly come to the status of maiden that she will not be shunned for doing what she did."

There was a roaring in Morning Song's ears now, and she scored the palms of her hands with her fingernails in an effort to keep herself from swaying to the tempo of it.

"To her credit, however, are the courage and determination she displayed tonight. These are qualities the Iroquois admire above all others, and it is good to know that one so young owns them." Teller Of Legends looked at last toward her granddaughter. "What matters is that she learn to use them wisely, rather than foolishly or impetuously. In the hope that she will be persuaded to the importance of this, we recommend that she be rewarded for her bravery and strength of will, and reprimanded but forgiven for her wrongdoing. The wolf will be sacrificed this Midwinter."

Morning Song blinked rapidly, and her grandmother's face swam into focus. *Had* she said what Morning Song thought she'd said? Was it possible that the Matrons had voted to let White Shadow live? Were both Morning Song and her dog to be spared after all?

It seemed that they were. It seemed also, if the mutters arising among the onlookers were any guide, that many were less than pleased with the verdict.

But Morning Song took no time to fret over that. Her blade was in her hand once more, and she was severing the rawhide thongs that the odious Stag Leaping had used to bind White Shadow. Until the dog was on his own feet and prancing in circles around hers, she could not bring herself to attend to anything else.

Puma Walking Soft was eyeing the wolf cub dubiously. "How

am I to groom and pet such a beast as that?" he demanded of no one in particular.

"Perhaps that part of the ritual may be simulated?" Teller Of Legends suggested mildly. "And he can be bound then, as he is now, in any event."

The man nodded curtly. "That is so," he admitted. "Still, I cannot keep him trussed for all the days between, even though it is my responsibility to tend him until the Ceremony."

From the corner of her eye, Morning Song saw Stag Leaping's mouth twist as he swallowed the bitter seeds of defeat. His revenge on her had been thwarted—but that was not enough to satisfy Morning Song.

She turned to Puma Walking Soft, making her expression courteous and concerned. "It is no simple task that confronts you," she told him sympathetically, and took gleeful advantage of a lull in nearby conversations to claim a small counterrevenge. "No doubt Stag Leaping, stalwart warrior that he is, will be glad to help his father carry out so challenging a commission."

She smiled sweetly at the startled Faithkeeper, then turned away. She would find Small Brown Sparrow and thank her for her loyalty before seeking out the clan Matrons and expressing more formal gratitude to them. As she had promised to do.

Teller Of Legends, watching her go, reflected that there was nothing of repentance in her proud-set head and confident stride. And in his wagging tail, even the white dog who trotted behind her managed to instill jauntiness.

She shook her own proud head and sighed.

Morning Song was disconcerted to find that Bountiful Harvest, rather than referring frequently and scathingly to her niece's escapade, did not mention it at all. Indeed, she concentrated solely on Teller Of Legends, engaging her in soft-voiced conversation and pressing upon her extra servings of her favorite foods. She acted, a puzzled Morning Song thought, as though Teller Of Legends were recovering from a sickness.

Pumpkin Blossom, too, became markedly solicitous of their grandmother. Her avoidance of Morning Song, however, was likely due to her reluctance to face her cousin's anger. It was plain that Pumpkin Blossom had raised the alarm shortly after Morning Song left the village that night, even though she'd given her word to wait at Meadow Brook's lodge.

Only gradually did Morning Song come to realize that both Bountiful Harvest and her daughter were subjecting her to the shunning she might well have received from the whole village. Despite the generosity shown by the Council of Matrons, Bountiful Harvest and Pumpkin Blossom believed that Morning Song's actions had brought dishonor to the Turtle clan, and they meant her to know that they did.

Awakened to this unpalatable truth, Morning Song became sensitive to the fact that Hearth Tender's sorrowful gaze rested often upon her niece. Then she began to suspect uncommon reserve in Deer Caller; he no longer found the leisure to chat with her, or cared to invite her admiration of the new arrows he was making. And shy Day Greeter, from whom Morning Song had always managed to coax a smile and a few hesitant words, now made no response at all when Morning Song spoke to her.

Only Otter Swimming and Teller Of Legends treated her the same. But because she had patently lost esteem in the eyes of the rest of her family, this was little consolation to Morning Song. Guilt, an emotion new to her, darkened her days and disrupted her nights.

Finally, as they went to bathe on a morning crackling with cold, she unburdened herself to Otter. "I would give much if that dreadful night had never been," she said wretchedly. A damp nose pressed against the back of her knee, and she glanced down to smile briefly at Shadow. "Except for the fact that I was able to save White Shadow from being slain," she added. "I cannot regret that, Otter. And will not."

Otter Swimming shortened her loose-jointed stride, and Morning Song followed suit. "All of us feel that way," she replied bluntly. "Both about that night and"—she put out a hand to pat the dog who had insinuated his lean body between them—"about Shadow. He is a beautiful animal, Morning Song, and feels great loyalty toward you. I had never realized it was possible for so strong a bond to be forged between beast and human."

"We are friends," Morning Song said simply, then brought the conversation back to the problem that plagued her. "But I am sorry, truly sorry, that what I did has brought distress into our lodge, Otter. I wish everything might be as it was before. I would welcome Bountiful Harvest's sharpest criticisms, her silence pains me so."

Otter's lips quivered, but her expression remained sober. "We cannot undo what has been done, Morning Song," she said, "but only make the best of what is."

"I do not know how!"

"You are no longer a child," Otter said slowly. "You know as well as anyone that I, too, was fond of going my own way when I was younger. Yet when I became a maid, and then Deer Caller's wife, I made certain to abide by what I knew was right, by what was expected of an Iroquois woman. I owe that to my clan, and to my husband.''

Morning Song sighed. "If we had been born boys, we would not have to follow so many rules."

Otter's face lengthened. "You are wrong," she said. "Hunters and warriors have as many rules to guide them and as many traditions to uphold as we do. They are different ones, but they are rules nonetheless." She paused, then asked what she was longing to know. "Since we are speaking of hunters, there is something both Teller Of Legends and I have been wondering about: How did you learn to stalk a wolf to its den—or to set the snare that took the young wolf captive? And how did you deal with the adult wolf my mother guessed was there also?''

They reached the river and found themselves a spot to bathe in the icy shallows. It was not easy to speak through chattering teeth, but Morning Song told her mother-aunt enough about her adventure with the wolves to satisfy her curiosity. The rest—her trailing after the boys during her early youth, her solitary practice of the skills they had demonstrated to her—waited until they'd wrapped robes around themselves and were returning to the longhouse.

"You see," she finished earnestly, "although they laughed at my clumsiness, just as the girls did, their laughter was not so unkind. I imagine they thought my awkwardness could be laid entirely to the fact that I *was* a girl, and named themselves generous for putting up with me. But the truth of it is"—she looked squarely at Otter— "I am better at tracking and hunting than I will ever be at the skills Bountiful Harvest tried so hard to teach me."

Otter shook her dripping head. "Morning Song, we have no one but Deer Caller to bring meat to our lodge. And it is true that, excellent provider though he is, a family as big as ours does need more than one hunter. But to have a maiden become so unnatural a thing— It is against all tradition, Morning Song. And you must now show the utmost respect for our customs. That is the only way you can hope to restore honor to our longhouse, and to yourself." She patted her niece's arm, and banished her own soberness with a grin. "Just bear in mind," she added, her voice resuming its native buoyancy, "that we shall have two more hunters coming to us when you and Pumpkin Blossom marry!"

These words, instead of comforting, only gave Morning Song something else to worry about.

Small Brown Sparrow tossed aside a dehaired cougar hide, plucked another from the pile beside her. "Both my brothers will be going with our uncle to fight the Erie," she told Morning Song, and her eyes gleamed with pride.

Morning Song caught the free end of the hide and helped her friend work it back and forth across the stake anchored in the ground between them. "I am certain all three will bring honor to your clan," she said courteously.

Honor was not a word she used lightly these days, and she took care to guard her tongue against less than courteous responses. Restraint was not truly needful when she spoke with Small Brown Sparrow, of course. But it would not do to become lax in her campaign to model herself upon the village's most admirable matrons. Weeping Sky had recently expressed approval of a winnowing basket Morning Song had made, and even Bountiful Harvest found little to complain of lately. As for the maidens—well, she was one of them now, in every respect. Only White Shadow, because her campaign to win back the goodwill of the villagers meant cutting short the hours she spent roaming the forest, was displeased with the new Morning Song.

She flung the bald cougar skin onto a steadily growing pile, sat back on her heels, and looked around her. The blades wielded by Bountiful Harvest, Otter, and Tree Reaching Up flashed in the sun as the trio skinned a buck and hacked its flesh into manageable portions. Sun Descending and Meadow Brook were helping their mothers fasten a deerhide to one of the rectangular drying frames that had been set up around the compound, and Sweet Maple and Rain Singing were using scrapers on one already stretched. Even Day Greeter had a job to do: her round face was a study in concentration as she made a skin-softening compound from a glutinous mess of animal brains.

This was where she belonged, Morning Song thought as she leaned forward to grasp her end of another hide. And during the many moon cycles leading to this sun-bright yellow season, she had been granted the acceptance she had fought so hard to earn. So why did contentment continue to elude her?

She could not answer the question, however often she tried. So she focused instead on the buzz of conversation going on around her.

"The Erie were fools to give sanctuary to the Huron who fled the north," Weeping Sky was saying. "They should have known the Longhouse People would respond to such treachery with war! And many of our young men, who were children when last we sent out a war band, stand ready now to march with Fierce Eagle." She preened herself a little. "Woodpecker Drumming and his friends are eager for a chance to prove themselves." Her lugubrious expression was habitual, as her name suggested, and did not betray her eagerness for her son to be one of those who returned robed in glory.

Sweet Maple sighed. "It is time for some of the older warriors, who have already proven themselves in a score of battles, to yield their places to the younger ones." Her usually cheerful face lacked a smile and her eyes registered disquiet. "I wish that my brother . . ." She looked across at Rain Singing, who was Keeper Of The Faith for the Plover clan as well as for her own. "Has Far Seer told you his dream yet?"

The Matron of the Deer lodge nodded. "He has. But, like most dreams, it can be interpreted in several ways. And he will not accept the one that recommends his staying behind when the war party leaves."

Weeping Sky bristled. "Do you expect him to stay home when our son goes to war for the first time? Far Seer will not miss the chance to see Woodpecker Drumming win praise for his valor!" Pride burned in her small eyes.

"*My* son's father has never seen him fight, nor ever will," Owl Crying countered. "Puma Walking Soft hung up his war lance years ago. Nonetheless, Stag Leaping is a warrior *your* son could learn from!" Her spirited reaction to Weeping Sky's statement surprised none of those listening, but would have astounded her only son. She had doted on him from the day of his birth, but she took pains to conceal that truth from him; indeed, she nagged at him mercilessly on the slightest pretext.

Gray Squirrel and her sister Loon Laughing, arranging slabs of meat over the fire, traded glances that said they would not be left out of a conversation that promised to generate more heat than the blaze they were tending. "Bear In The Sky will win most of the glory when our warriors go raiding this time," Gray Squirrel pronounced decisively. She was an authoritative woman; even the thrust of her enormous bosom was peremptory. She paused for effect. "My nephew received a sign during his Vision Quest that told him he may one day find himself elected war leader."

"This is so," Bear In The Sky's mother confirmed in little more than a whisper. Although much like her older sister physically, she was so far from domineering as to appear almost insipid. "And he has since been visited by dreams that have confirmed it." She beamed upon Owl Crying and Weeping Sky. "Your sons shall do well, also, I am sure," she added.

Her sister made as if to speak further, but was distracted by Otter Swimming, who had brought another basket of venison to be smoked. Otter's face was as shuttered as her mouth was; she had no son to boast of, or daughter either, and it seemed more and more probable that she never would have. To her, this talk of war meant only that Deer Caller would be leaving her again, and Otter would be left alone to wait and worry and fear the worst.

Small Brown Sparrow's smile wore the unmistakable stamp of smugness. "Not one of our new warriors will be able to surpass Cloud Racer and Fox Running," she murmured to Morning Song. "Whatever anyone might think!"

Morning Song made no reply. This discussion was one she would take no part in lest her own feelings on the subject mark her anew as a misfit. In truth, she'd paid small heed to the boasting that invariably peppered the matrons' talk of war and warriors. But what Gray Squirrel and Loon Laughing had said about Bear In The Sky's Vision Quest loomed large in her mind. The Vision Quest provided direction for boys on the threshold of manhood. Surely, before their quests, many of them were as uncertain of their way as girls adapting to womanhood were? The solitude, fasting, and meditation of the Quest gave purpose to their lives and ordained their futures.

She had yet to hear of a single boy who was not granted a vision during that time. Surely it was possible that even a girl who was denied ordinary dreams might be visited by a spirit if she scrupulously observed the rules surrounding this common ritual?

And Morning Song was one girl who would not shrink from the rigors involved. Not if there was a chance that her ambivalence could be resolved and her mystifying discontent erased, merely by going on a Vision Quest of her own.

Chapter 10

If days were for eating, Morning Song told herself, this one would be especially savory. She plunged through an explosion of goldenrod and made for the trees on the far side of the meadow. It was a succotash day, all yellow and green and bubbling in the pot.

In truth, every season offered distinctive delicacies. Days in spring were like slices of tender squash, crunchy and delicately delicious. Autumn? Spirals of roast pumpkin and a haunch of venison dripping juices into the fire.

She pictured a clear, crisp winter day. Scooped-up snow, she decided, with the heated sap of the maple poured over it; teeth-numbing, yet wondrously sweet.

Suddenly she laughed. How ridiculous to be thinking of food when she was preparing to fast! Resolutely she turned her thoughts in a different direction.

Only Small Brown Sparrow knew that Morning Song meant to be away for four days, and even she did not know her destination. She would be able to forestall anxiety on the part of Teller Of Legends, though, when Morning Song did not return that night.

The younger girl's eyes had rounded with awe. "A Vision Quest! Oh, Morning Song. No maiden, in all the long history of our tribe, has ever thought to go on one before."

"I cannot think why," Morning Song retorted. "It seems to me we have as much need as boys do to discover the paths we are meant to follow."

Her friend shrugged. "Who wants to go without food just to learn that we will become wives and mothers and see to the nurturing of our families? As Iroquois women have always done."

"Perhaps they have never done anything else because they failed to invite the spirits to direct their feet elsewhere," Morning Song suggested.

Small Brown Sparrow looked as pensive as her natural ebullience allowed. "You may be right. At least you have the courage to find out if what you think is so." She picked up the burden strap Morning Song had tossed on her bunk, coiled it neatly, and set it alongside the older girl's knife and hatchet. "How wonderful it must be, to dare to be different!"

Morning Song, reaching for the dipper on her shelf, had paused with one hand outstretched and stared at her. Was this the reason Small Brown Sparrow had often sided with her friend when others mocked or shunned her? Because she admired the very thing Morning Song deplored in herself? "It is not such a fine thing, to be different," she said slowly.

"Perhaps not. But to be unique is to be noticed and remembered," Small Brown Sparrow said with uncommon shrewdness. "I see this happening with my brother Cloud Racer. His name is spoken in villages he has never visited because he questions what most younger warriors take for granted. Everyone seems to know that he asked our uncle why we should go to war against the Cat People when one of our own western tribes has also taken in the wandering Huron.'' She shook her head. ''Fierce Eagle was not pleased to have his judgment called to account, and by one so young. Fox Running would never do such a thing; he wants only to go to war and prove himself. Yet even when he does, it will be a long time before his name is recognized by warriors from other villages.''

''I am surprised to hear that Cloud Racer speaks so freely, about anything,'' Morning Song said, sliding her feet into moccasins. ''I never thought him the kind to spill out his thoughts as though they were corn hulls.''

''Usually he hoards them instead,'' Small Brown Sparrow agreed. ''Which is another way in which he differs from the rest.'' She giggled. ''I find that most hunter-warriors rejoice to talk on and on. Especially to girls old enough for marrying.''

Morning Song looked sharply at her friend. Was there something in the way she'd said this last that hinted at a secret she was bursting to share? Surely not. Why, it was less than a year since she had been named a maiden! ''You will watch over White Shadow while I am gone?'' she asked, dismissing the foolish notion.

''I will tell him every day that you will be returning soon,'' Small Brown Sparrow promised. ''And if there are any bones in our cooking pot, he shall have them.''

She had followed Morning Song into the compound then, and had been moved to hug the dejected dog when Morning Song walked away from the both of them without once looking back.

Shadow would miss her dreadfully, Morning Song thought now, but a Vision Quest must be a solitary undertaking, and comfortless.

She slowed her pace as she passed into the hush of the forest, and begged the spirits that peopled this ancient place to approve what Morning Song was doing. If one of them appeared during her quest and offered to be her guide throughout the remainder of her life, this would certainly be in keeping with what Teller Of Legends had said about her granddaughter's *orenda*.

Even with the sun's glare diffused by tiers of leafy branches, it was hot enough for the persistent drone of insects to have a listlessness about it. Well, it might be cooler after sunset; already the nights had been crisping around the edges occasionally, and soon the days would beget breezes hinting of the red season to come. Morning Song walked on, her arms swinging loosely at her sides, her feet moving confidently along a trail they had followed often. Blossoms pink and white and yellow drooped along its borders, their delicate scents lost in the headier aroma of the wood honeysuckle that grew farther on. No birds sang on this drowsy afternoon, but a flash of ruby red alerted Morning Song to the presence of a hummingbird as she neared the honeysuckle bush.

It was a feast for all the senses, to walk through the woods on such a day, and every one of hers relished it. Even though the sun's rays were nearly horizontal before she came upon the isolated rise that would be her home during her Vision Quest, she did not feel tired. And since she had taken care to eat heartily of the midday meal, she was not hungry, either.

She dipped water from the curving river that embraced the hill on the north and east and drank deep. Then she climbed the gentle slope, sent up a prayer to any spirits who might be hovering nearby, and sought out a grassy spot to serve as her bed.

Morning Song's Vision Quest had begun.

The eerie splendor of a loon's cry awakened her just before dawn, and she lay shivering in the morning damp while she listened to the weird *a-haha-hoo*. A symphony of yodels arose as more of the long-necked birds settled on the river to feed.

They might eat; Morning Song could not. She sat up and looked around. Coral streaked the sky, but the shadows on her side of the hill did not lift until the birdsong her name described had gifted the world with its beauty. When it ended, she stretched and yawned, and made ready to greet the day with prayer.

Rubbing sleep from her eyes, she stumbled up the hill and looked out over the river. She had already discovered that words sent in this direction repeated themselves, and hadn't Hearth Tender once said that echoes proved prayers were being borne aloft by spirit messengers? Morning Song meant to take advantage of any help available to her.

"Send a spirit, a bold spirit, to guide me," she chanted. "Alone, the daughter of Summer Maize is nothing, and moves through the days without purpose. Only show me the way to go, and my feet will never stray from the path that you mark for them."

Three times she spoke her plea, and heard the echoes register the urgency in her voice. Then she lowered her beseeching arms, bowed her head, and waited.

Nothing happened. Not so much as a whisper came to her, nor even the conviction that she was, somehow, no longer alone.

Well, she would not be discouraged. If Vision Quests spanned four days, there must be good reason for it. She left the brow of the hill, went to the river, and drank her fill before stripping off her tunic and dipping up water to splash over herself. She could not immerse herself here; narrow the river might be, but it was not without force and there were no shallows adjacent to its banks.

Because a swollen sun was soaring into the sky dome, she tossed her tunic over a bush and let heat-infused light dry her flesh while she collected boulders to make a hearth. In her pouch nestled a handful of tobacco leaves she had appropriated from Deer Caller's patch, and three more picked from the rectangle alongside the Plover longhouse. She'd persuaded herself that Se-A-Wi, if he knew, would not mind. And burning tobacco planted by a Sachem ought to guarantee that the smoke would ascend high enough to carry Morning Song's entreaties to the Maker Of Life himself.

She spent the morning hauling the boulders up the slope, setting them in a circle, and accumulating a store of deadwood and kindling. It was hard not to linger among the trees when she tended to this last chore; sparrows invited her to gossip with them, and a pair of chipmunks played hide-and-peep among the leaves of a hickory tree. She reminded herself sternly that she had not come here to be entertained, and crossed the ends of the burden strap over the brittle branches and rotting logs she had found.

The cloying warmth of midday dictated a small blaze, but Morning Song fed it regularly so that it would send up an uninterrupted tendril of smoke. She shredded one of her tobacco leaves and added it sparingly to the flames, all the while murmuring endless variations of her dawn prayer. Yet the sun heeled toward its vanishing point, and still nothing happened to advise Morning Song that her words were being received and understood.

When twilight announced that the reign of night was imminent, she built up her fire and prayed once more, loudly and passionately. And once more was left unacknowledged.

She stretched out beside the hearth, and silence wrapped itself around her. *Tomorrow*, she thought as she closed her eyes, *tomorrow I must try harder!*

It was not a loon's haunting call that roused Morning Song on the second day of her quest, but a griping in her belly. She'd known her fasting must lead eventually to this, but had not expected it so soon. She would embrace the pain; it might serve to unbar the gate between this world and the spirit world.

She drank and bathed, and coaxed her smoldering fire into a blaze, then sent another series of prayers into a purple-tinged dawn that betokened storm. No matter; if He-No spoke this day, she would appeal directly to him for help!

The threat of wind-driven rain did not daunt her, and the idea of enlisting the aid of The Thunderer excited her, so she delighted when the clouds heaped themselves atop one another to form slate-gray pillars. And when the first roar came, the command to hurl iridescent lances between cloud and cloud and to the earth beneath, she rejoiced to scream her needs, her desperation, into the turbulent sky.

Lightning spears zigzagged spectacularly as the wind's teeth tore huge chunks from swollen clouds. And the rain sheeted down, descending in torrents that pounded savagely against the hill and drowned her fire on the instant. She lifted her face to it, let it beat against her until she felt herself merge with the tumult, felt the blood pulse through her veins to reciprocate the rhythm of the throbbing tempest. She ceased to speak; to open her mouth would permit needle-sharp rain to invade it. But she continued to stretch imploring hands to the sky, to the bruised and pendulous clouds and to the invisible Thunderer whose instruments they were.

There came a shaft of lighting so vivid that its afterimage remained when the bolt had been extinguished. A violent *crack!* from beyond the river told her the weapon had found a mark, and that others might also. Yet the girl on the hill did not flee her vantage point, did not even flinch. This battle was being waged for her sake; she had nothing to fear! With arms still outstretched, Morning Song stood tall until the final lance had been tossed, the downpour had lost its sting, and He-No's resounding shouts subsided to a querulous grumble.

Her body was aquiver from the battering she had subjected it to, but she made herself trudge through a sea of mud, tugged boulders from her hearth so the water filling it could run out, retrieved scattered twigs and branches and laid them across a tangle of brush to let the late-blooming sun dry them. She scarcely noticed the hunger gnawing at her belly; the euphoria promoted by the storm was as effective as the False Faces for dispelling pain.

The sun's rays strengthened until the hill steamed. They sucked moisture from Morning Song's tunic, from her dripping plaits, from her squelching moccasins. Before day's end, she was able to kindle a fresh fire and see the smoke from it curl into a sky so clear and blue it might have been newly made. And the sunset . . . Never in her life had she seen one to rival it! The western horizon blazed with crimson and gold, vibrated with a radiance that hurt the eyes, was stained with color so intense that traces lingered long after the sun itself had taken its splendor into the spirit world.

The prayers she sent up then wore wings fashioned from elation. Confident that they would be heard and answered, Morning Song prepared herself for sleep, and for the dream that would surely visit her this night.

She opened her eyes to an opalescent dawn and the realization that there had been no dream. Even the cascade of birdsong that greeted this third day of her Vision Quest did not console her, and lethargy as well as hunger-spawned weakness made her movements sluggish. When she had drunk and bathed and breathed life into her fire, she sat beside it with her head resting on her knees, listening to the rumbling in her belly and asking herself why no spirit cared to come to her. Was she doing something wrong? Was there a ritual she knew nothing about that ought to be performed? She reviewed the chants of the Faithkeepers, those songs that marked festival and ceremony, but her mind as well as her body was lethargic and she had difficulty recalling the precise forms of the chants. If only it was not such a vast company of spirit helpers that Keepers Of The Faith appealed to!

She had nearly given up on the exercise when she recalled how often the spirits of ancestors were invoked in these rites. And she thought of the mother who had borne her and loved her, and who had gone too soon to walk among those spirits.

She lifted her head and let a languid breeze cool her face, then drew more shredded leaves from her pouch. Today, all of her pleas would be directed to Summer Maize, whose concern for her troubled daughter must be great indeed.

She crouched over her hearth and smiled as the fragrance of burning tobacco rose around her. Then she stood and began to pray. Her impassioned words were well defined at first, but, as the morning wore on, her throat began to rasp and hoarseness blunted them. The sun rode high, and heat shimmered around her. Perhaps a dipper of water to drink, and another splashed upon her burning cheeks, was what she needed.

Yet when she was about to drink, she called herself sharply to task. So far, Summer Maize had been as deaf to her petitions as He-No had been the day before. Could this be because Morning Song had not suffered enough? She'd heard of warriors-to-be who whipped themselves with nettles to show their willingness to endure pain. Morning Song lacked the strength now to manage that, but there were other ways in which she might prove herself worthy.

She tipped up her gourd and let the water trickle to the ground. From this moment, thirst as well as hunger would be her companion on this quest. Surely this was an appropriate way to convince the spirits of her sincerity?

She went on with her supplications, and each one intensified her craving for water. As the afternoon progressed, she found herself continually licking her lips and fancied she could feel them reddening. Whenever a breeze feathered the air she turned her face into it, hoping against hope that it would be moisture-laden. It never was.

Her prayers became shorter and shorter, and she spoke in a monotone. Yet she persevered. The stubbornness she'd regretted at times came to her rescue now; it kept her on her feet when she yearned to sit, let her go on begging the help of Summer Maize even though the sounds she produced were suggestive of a bullfrog's croaking.

When the sun descended that day, she spared not a glance for the fiery beauty that marked its setting.

Morning Song knew before she opened her eyes that the fourth day of her quest might demand more of her than she was able to give. She had slept overlong, and it was with reluctance that she built up her fire and added heat to an already sun-seared morning. The prayer that accompanied the tobacco she tossed upon the flames was couched in a mumble.

She abandoned the crest of the hill, half slid down its northern slope, and flung herself to the ground beneath a scraggly maple whose stunted arms offered meager shade. Morning Song began to fear that, like the legendary Flying Head, she might be burning to ash from the inside out.

Shame engulfed her as she accepted that thirst was an agony she could not cope with. Not while the air hung around her in smothering folds and merely to breathe called for heroic effort. Without water, she would die.

And what of the day's cycle of prayers? She had meant to climb back to her Place Of Echoes and chant unceasingly until darkness muffled her words and rendered them ineffectual. It was her last chance to accomplish what she'd come here to do, and she must not let a reckless vow steal it from her.

She picked up her gourd dipper and rose unsteadily from the patch of grass that lay in the rapidly diminishing shadow of the wind-warped maple. Her vision blurred, and a sound like angry hornets erupted inside her head. Drawing a ragged breath, she waited

for dancing circles of color to settle, for the dissonant buzz to be
muted, then started for the riverbank. She might be an old, old
woman, she thought, so slowly did she walk, so slumped her narrow shoulders. Had she, after all, robbed herself of the strength
she needed to endure this ultimate day of her quest? Surely a long,
cool drink of water would restore some of it, and never mind that
the liquid would slosh in her empty belly and bring on the painful
griping once more.

When she reached the ledge overhanging the river, she sank to
her knees. Any water she dipped from this spot would be muddy,
for the storm two days earlier had churned its bed. And she knew
that the placid-seeming surface belied an underlying current rambunctious enough to terrify a girl who looked upon any swift-
running water with trepidation. Well, she would use caution. And
this would not be the first time she had drunk water that was less
than clear! At least it would be *wet*.

The sun was approaching its zenith. It reached down and used
her bent head for a drum as she leaned forward gingerly, extended
her hand, and prepared to scoop up the liquid she was craving. Her
own face, drawn and pinched, looked back at her. Her hair, firmly
plaited at the start of her quest, hung limp as two somnolent snakes
over her breasts. It wasn't a pretty sight, her self-image, but for
some reason it fascinated her. The hand gripping the gourd hesitated as though loath to unsettle the girl who stared up at it.

Morning Song arranged her blistered lips in a tentative smile;
the girl in the river returned it. She frowned, and was rewarded
with a grimace. The ruffled-edge reflection of the yellow sun had
perched atop the dark hair of the girl that was Morning Song. It
was an ornament of startling brilliance, and she gazed at it, entranced. Then she gasped (as her image did also) as it animated
itself and slowly rolled away.

The astonished girl shifted position, looked up to see the sun—
the real sun—clinging securely to its midday resting place. She
looked down again into her own puzzled face. To the left of it,
the sun-image twinkled over the surface of the water, leaning to the
west and blushing around the rim as a westering sun often will.
Another peek upwards advised her that the sun in the sky was
slothful still, and disinclined to move.

The flesh on her arms puckered; she shivered. But as much as
she yearned to turn away from what logic refuted, her eyes were
drawn once more to that red-rimmed water-sun. As if to imitate
one of the hoops boys use for lance practice, it picked up speed

and rolled farther and farther from the mirrored features that wore Morning Song's bewilderment like a distorting mask.

But, no! Those were not Morning Song's features, nor even a convolution of them. Surely it was a beaver—sharp-toothed and small-eyed—who peered at her from beneath the surface of a river beginning to wrinkle with agitation? The girl shook her head bemusedly, looked away, looked back . . . into the face of a wolf, unmistakably a wolf, despite the ominous heaving of water gradually becoming storm-gray. It was a wolf, lean-jawed and with ears laid back, a wavering replica of the furious she-wolf whose pup Morning Song had stolen on a winter's night.

Yet this image, too, surrendered its place, between one wave and the next, to a bird of some sort. Wren? Plover? It was impossible to identify without seeing its body plumage, its size. And its name became irrelevant, for the fitful water dissolved it, thrust up at her a snarling panther . . . a stout and stolid bear . . . a timorous doe. . . .

The deer's wide-eyed, pricked-ear terror was contagious, and infected the girl who huddled on the bank. For now the whole river seethed with a commotion begat by that bizarre parade of beasts whose proper home was the forest. Morning Song could not draw back, could not command so much as a single muscle for all that she willed herself to move. She was compelled to watch the roiling level of the river swell and rise and clutch at its verge, and yank out jagged clumps of grass-crowned soil. She felt it reaching for her as well, sensed its eagerness to seize her arms, her legs, and pull her down, down, down to that awful place so many furred and feathered creatures had somehow been lured to. And above the threatening hiss of the hungry river there were other sounds, animal voices that, as in the long-ago days when the world was made, spoke the language of the Iroquois. All of them—limited though they were by growl, twitter, roar, squeal—repeated over and over again a single despairing phrase: "No, no. It is too soon, too soon!"

Morning Song, despite the horror that wrenched at her gut, the sweat of fear that glistened on her brow and trickled between her breasts, was mesmerized by this improbable chorus. She knew as surely as if Teller Of Legends were detailing a story that the animals freed from the river's depths had taken up lances and spears and gone in pursuit of the truant, river-born sun; that they were trying frantically to pierce that crimson hoop and abort its journey into the west. Into the west where death awaited it.

Morning Song moaned, a moan that lifted itself to become a wail, a keening. The dipper deserted her nerveless fingers and dropped into water that all at once was grudgingly still and confined within its rightful bounds. It shattered whatever image may have been rising to join its fellows, and the ripples spread in ever-widening circles until they had snared the errant river-sun and hauled it, too, back to its proper place.

A breeze murmured along the embankment, brushed against Morning Song's cheek, flicked at a strand of perspiration-soaked hair. She opened the eyes she'd squeezed shut against the impossible, the unbelievable, and echoed the breeze's sigh. A blue heron, indifferent to Morning Song's presence and to the incredible things that had been happening to her, was standing not twenty paces away with its aristocratic, black-crested head snuggled between hunched shoulders.

How can he sleep? the girl wondered hysterically. Then a small laugh escaped her quivering mouth. The huge bird shook himself irritably, unfolded its great wings, and one jaundiced eye glared at her before he took to the sky. His was an action so familiar, so ordinary, that the sight of him soaring upwards, long legs stretched out straight behind him, calmed the erratic pounding of Morning Song's heart, restored to her use limbs that had been leached of all sensation, returned her finally to a world where all was as it should be.

She sat back on her heels, lifted trembling hands to sweep dank wisps of hair from her cheeks, turned slightly so that the sun's dazzle would not torture eyes that had been tormented enough this day.

What had it meant, this vision of hers? What message had it brought to guide Morning Song along the unmarked trail that led into the future? And who had sent it? Had it been her mother? He-No The Thunderer? A spirit who rode the winds, or a spirit whose natural home was the mountains, or the forest? Or—she shuddered—one who frequented the lakes and rivers that were born in the high peaks and hurtled down to come to rest in the lowlands? Had it been a malicious spirit, rather than a benevolent one? The essence of her vision could scarcely be called benign, she thought. Yet some of the dreams brought to Hearth Tender for interpretation had seemed cloaked in menace before her mother-aunt made sense of them.

And what did Morning Song know of the visions others experienced when they quested for them? Nothing at all! Which led her to believe that *any* such manifestation might be overwhelming, might assault the senses and confuse the mind, and carry within it the seeds of terror. There might even be purpose to this, she decided. A gentle, unassuming vision would do little to impress, could never involve both body and soul in a ferment of sensation, would lack the intensity to etch itself deeply, painfully, into memory. The one that had come to Morning Song would be with her forever; of that much she was certain.

It seemed an inconsequential bit of knowledge to have gleaned from so portentous a vision, but, for the moment, it was all she had. The incongruity of it—when she had longed so passionately, pleaded so wholeheartedly, for an all-clarifying vision to come to her—prompted her to smile, and the expansion of her cracked lips warned her that she'd not yet dealt with her awful thirst.

Her gourd . . . She frowned, recalled that it had fallen into the river. Not yet trusting her legs to support her, she crawled to the water's edge and made herself peer into it to locate the dipper she'd lost. Only her own face looked back at her now, but she hadn't the least desire to study it this time.

She glanced to the side, saw the gourd bobbing invitingly against the bank. A maple leaf, sap-drained and shed before its appointed time, had pasted itself to the smooth, striped roundness, and she reached out, snatched up dipper and leaf together. When her parched throat and swollen tongue had been soothed by the water the gourd's hollow held, she peeled the maple leaf from the bowl and began to crumple it.

All at once she stayed the motion, laid the wet red leaf on her outstretched palm, and fitted each of its five veined sections to one of her fingers. Was it possible that this leaf was a symbol of whatever spirit guide had sent her perplexing vision? She'd heard that quite common things—odd-shaped stones, twigs, shells—were often treasured afterward by boys who had made Vision Quests. Still . . . Did Morning Song honestly want a memento of her experience? Surely the indelible memory of it would be more than enough for her to cope with.

Instantly she rebuked herself. Hadn't she already deduced that visions were meant to be disquieting? And why endure so much only to take nothing home with her? Would any boy among the Iroquois be so foolish, so—so cowardly as to reject a reminder of his quest?

Fumbling open the leather pouch that hung around her neck, she tucked the damp leaf, tight-rolled, into it. It was time to go home.

Chapter 11

＊━ ━＊

In the end, Morning Song decided to wait until the next day before returning to the village. Until she had eaten and rested, it would be folly to attempt the trek. Just to strip fruit from a nearby raspberry bush and cram her pouch with hickory and hazel nuts left her feeling dizzy. And when her empty stomach rebelled the first time she sent food into it, she knew she had made the right decision. She dared not eat again until evening, and was mightily relieved to have a handful of well-chewed berries stay down.

A good night's sleep restored her, and let her enjoy a satisfying meal of more sweet berries and the meat from her assortment of nuts. With her hunger appeased, she lifted her face to the morning sun and let a pleasurable excitement steal over her. She, who had lived fourteen summers without once attracting the spirits who sent dreams, had been granted a vision! Never mind its frightening aspects, its lack of clear meaning; it had been a vision in truth and a powerful one. When Hearth Tender had helped her to understand it, Morning Song would know what the future held and be advised of the path she should follow into it.

She fairly danced to the top of the grass-cloaked hill and kindled a fire on her hearth. "Maker Of Life," she chanted, tossing the last of her tobacco on the flames, "master of all things visible and invisible, master of all spirits whether good or evil: Command the good spirits to favor your child, and the evil ones to keep their distance, and accept the gratitude this smoke carries to you." She drew breath, then paid special homage to He-No The Thunderer and to the spirit of Summer Maize. She offered praise to her brother the sun, Grandmother Moon, the World Turtle, the old man who ruled the West Wind, and the Three Sisters—Maize, Beans, and Squash—who had from the beginning been the prime nurturers of the Longhouse People. She sang of her joy, and of her desire to learn what her vision meant.

When she was done, when she could not think of a single word to add to her prayer, she doused her fire, dismantled her hearth, and turned her feet toward home.

Morning Song had been away four whole days; she returned bursting with the wonder of her experience. Yet she might have left the village on something as ordinary as a berry-picking expedition. Family and friends did not rush to welcome her, and they responded to her momentous news with only courteous head bobbings and abstracted words.

White Shadow alone made a celebration of her return. His mournful eyes had been fixed on the palisade's gateway, and he leaped to his feet the moment she entered the compound. When he had hurtled across the ground between them, he skidded to a stop, jumped up, and washed her face with his tongue. It was plain that he had missed her greatly, and rejoiced to have her home.

Within the lodge, there was no particular rejoicing. Even Teller Of Legends, once she'd greeted Morning Song warmly, was clearly more eager to talk than to listen to her granddaughter's news. "We have had a busy time of it while you were away, and a disturbing one. The Thunderer sent a mighty storm on the morning Fierce Eagle's band was leaving, and our Faithkeepers were hard put to agree whether this boded good or ill for our warriors."

So this was the reason Otter had been so preoccupied that she had not lingered in the longhouse to hear Morning Song's tale; Deer Caller would have gone with them, of course. "But it was not to our warriors that He-No spoke," Morning Song said excitedly. "It was for me that he caused the sky to rage and the earth to tremble. Because I was on a Vision Quest."

Teller Of Legends looked faintly troubled. "I can see why you wish to believe that," she said quietly. "But our Keepers Of The Faith announced finally that He-No was showing his strength to assure us that he watches still over the Longhouse People. They know more of such things than we do, my dear."

Momentarily Morning Song was crestfallen. Then she reminded herself that, even if this were so, *someone* had arranged a vision for her. "But truly, Grandmother," she said earnestly, "I was visited by a spirit, a powerful spirit, while I was on my quest. And I need to tell my vision to Hearth Tender."

Teller Of Legends inclined her head. "This is understandable, Morning Song, but you will have to wait a little, I'm afraid. So many of our warriors were visited by dreams prior to their going that Hearth Tender and the other Faithkeepers exhausted themselves trying to decipher them all. She has gone off by herself, to meditate and calm her spirit. She will be pleased to counsel you when she returns, I am certain.'' She looked up at a signal from Bountiful Harvest, and came to her feet. ''Our food is ready to be served.'' She smiled down at her granddaughter. ''I expect that you are more than ready to have a proper meal,'' she said.

In the end, Morning Song sought out Small Brown Sparrow and confessed her bewilderment. ''Bountiful Harvest spoke no word to me, not even a disapproving one. And Pumpkin Blossom was so busy talking about marriage, of all things, that she heard nothing of what I was trying to say to her,'' she finished bleakly.

''Everyone is as happy as I am to know that you were sent a vision,'' her friend said. ''But you must realize that most of us are visited regularly by dreams. And a vision is only a dream sent by the spirits when you are awake rather than asleep.''

Morning Song was certain no night dream had ever been as intense as her vision, but did not press the issue. ''No one even seems surprised that I went on such a quest,'' she said.

Small Brown Sparrow grinned. ''They had four days to shape their thinking to the idea of it,'' she pointed out. ''And why should they have been surprised when they learned where you'd gone? You make a habit of doing what others do not, Morning Song. Besides, we have all had other matters to think about; the time you chose to be away was an eventful one here at home. My mother was kept from her sleep one night, because so many warriors brought dreams for her to examine.'' With the toe of one moccasin, she scraped a half-moon in the dirt. ''Even Hill Climber came to her,'' she volunteered.

Morning Song did not ask why her friend had singled out that particular young man. ''I hope Hearth Tender returns soon to our lodge,'' she said. ''Oh, Small Brown Sparrow, I am so anxious to know what I am meant to be, and do!''

''Truly, Morning Song,'' the younger girl said, somewhat irritated that the conversational trail she had blazed was being ignored, ''you are probably meant to be wife and mother, just as all maids are.'' She turned her head as a bevy of matrons herded laughing children into the compound, looked back into her friend's sad face, and was moved to sympathy. ''But it's possible you are destined to be more,'' she said kindly. ''A Faithkeeper, perhaps. Hearth Tender will advise you, once you have told her your vision. Meanwhile''— she grinned again—''you have come back at just the right moment, Morning Song! Because the children were so helpful when we went nut gathering yesterday, the matrons promised to reward them with a treat. We are to spend the afternoon playing games with them, and Teller Of Legends has said she will give us a tale or two afterward.''

Since Morning Song could do nothing to speed Hearth Tender's coming, she told herself she might as well help amuse the children. And she supposed she should feel fortunate to have returned when she did. On any other day, someone would have thrust a hoe into her hand!

Infected by the headiness that comes with being the center of attention, the children permitted no one to hold back. The older matrons, they said, might sit and fashion new dolls for the girls and cornhusk war clubs for the boys, but the younger matrons, with the maidens, were commanded to active participation. They ran endless races, tossed balls hither and yon, played numerous and creative variations of tag-me, until a sunbeam-studded curtain of dust was raised in the compound. The little ones shrieked with laughter when they outran their panting competition, and made innocent mock of old Lake On Fire. Once the cornhusk clubs had been distributed, she declared—with a properly menacing growl—that she was a bear the boy's must try to bring down. Watching her stomp about in her saffron-yellow tunic, with her inevitable beads clacking and jangling whenever she turned upon a juvenile attacker, set the grownups to laughing as merrily as the children were.

Pumpkin Blossom produced scraps of doeskin and persuaded Otter Swimming, Day Greeter, and Sun Descending to help her make clothes for the dolls the little girls were clutching as they watched the village's future hunter-warriors.

"There is no reason they should not have clubs, too, if they want them," Morning Song said, refastening the moccasin she had shed during the last relay race.

"War clubs are not for girls," Pumpkin Blossom said scornfully, smoothing the corn-silk hair of the doll she was dressing. "They are happier mothering these new dolls than they could be chasing after the Matron of the Bear longhouse."

Morning Song, who had thought Otter might come to her support, was surprised when it was Meadow Brook, strolling up to peer over Pumpkin Blossom's shoulder, who sided with her. "Perhaps playing warriors does not interest them," she said easily, "but I know something that will." She balanced on one broad palm the ball she had rescued from a game of throw and catch, and looked into the faces of the girls who made a circle around Pumpkin Blossom and her needle-wielding assistants. "I will show you all how to play kickball," she announced.

"And I will help," Morning Song found herself saying when no one responded to Meadow Brook's offer. "Even though some of you beginners will probably kick farther than I can even now," she added, giving an exaggerated sigh.

The children giggled. Where they had hesitated to accept a challenge from an athlete of Meadow Brook's status, now they clamored to play. Soon they had abandoned their dolls to Pumpkin Blossom's care and were devoting themselves to a game that, despite Meadow Brook's talent for organization, turned out to be more spirited than structured.

"It was fun, though," Meadow Brook said when short, chubby legs had begun to falter. "And they should be as ready as the boys to sit quietly, so perhaps we may all have a chance to rest now."

"Lake On Fire will certainly appreciate a chance to sit down," Morning Song said, watching her limp to where the older matrons had gathered in the shade cast by the Turtle longhouse.

"She is not the only one!" Meadow Brook said fervently. "I will also be grateful for a chance to sit and listen to one of your grandmother's stories."

And the two young women laughed together as they went to find places in the group forming around Teller Of Legends.

"Since this afternoon is dedicated to the little ones," the smiling Matron said when everyone had settled themselves, "I am going to speak of folk who never grow beyond the size of the smallest child, however long they live." She beamed into the faces upturned to hers. "Long ago there was a boy who took his bow and arrows and went out hunting. Soon he brought down two plump squirrels, but since he knew they would not be enough to feed the large family that lived in his longhouse, he decided to hunt some more. In a little while he came to a deep ravine. Growing out of it was a tree so tall that its crown was on a level with his eyes, and on one of its topmost branches sat a squirrel fatter than any he had ever seen.

"He nocked an arrow and was about to release it when he heard a sound coming from the bottom of the ravine. He thought at first that he was hearing the chittering of the squirrel's brothers, but the boy's curiosity was strong and he wanted to see for himself if this was so."

One venturesome lad looked at his mother and grinned. He would do the same!

"Well, the Iroquois boy crept to the edge of that gorge and peered into its rock-filled bottom. You can imagine his surprise when he saw below him a pair of men who surely stood no higher than his waist! They were hunters, those little men; they were drawing miniature bows and trying to send tiny arrows far enough to reach the squirrel the boy had been aiming at. But although they tried again and again, they could not shoot high enough.

"The boy felt sorry for them. He eased back from the ledge, took up his own bow, and sent an arrow into the unsuspecting squirrel. The creature tumbled down to where the dwarflike hunters stood, and their shouts of surprise lured the Iroquois boy back to the ravine's edge. But he was not so quiet this time, and the little men looked up and saw him there. They had been struggling to pull the boy's arrow from the squirrel's rump, and understood now where the gigantic thing had come from. When they had spoken together, they signed to the boy to join them in the ravine.

" 'We have need of your help,' they called in unison, their voices so thin that the boy had to strain his ears to make out their words.

"He scrambled down the sloping sides of the gorge and, quicker than it takes to tell, he was standing alongside the two little men. It felt strange to be looking down on people older than he was, so he was glad to bend and yank his arrow from the squirrel's body.

"The little men thanked him. 'It has been a long while since our people have eaten meat,' one of them told him, and the Iroquois boy promptly gave the pair the squirrels he had slain earlier."

Morning Song felt a damp nose intrude itself between her elbow and her side, and smiled down at White Shadow.

"The two small men were impressed, and said that their tribe would be proud to make a pact of friendship with the tribe that had produced such a fine lad. 'We are called Pygmies,' they explained, and invited him to come and meet their family. Their home was a cave farther along the ravine, and inside waited a little old man and a little old woman, father and mother to the hunters. The woman, who was pounding corn with a pestle no bigger than the Iroquois boy's thumb, insisted that he eat a bowl of corn soup. The bowl was so small that the boy knew its contents would scarcely wet his tongue, but his mother had taught him that it does not do to refuse hospitality when it is offered. Oddly enough, once he'd raised the bowl to his mouth, he found that he could eat and eat of the flavorful soup and still the miniature bowl remained filled to the brim. This, he thought, was a marvelous thing.

"His hosts read his amazement in his face and told him that Pygmies are the Great Little People, and that they live in three confederated tribes: the Stone-Throwers, who dwell along streams and under waterfalls and are strong enough to hurl boulders about and uproot trees; the Plant-Tenders, who wake the flowers in the green season and in summer turn the fruit so that all sides receive nurturing sunlight; and the Guardians, who stand sentry at entrances to the netherworld to prevent a herd of bad-tempered white buffalo from breaking out and wreaking havoc upon the earth.

"The little old woman was Chief Matron of the Guardian tribe and summoned all the Pygmies to a three-day feast honoring the Iroquois boy. Sacred tobacco was burned, and then the fire was put out and everyone sat in darkness to sing ritual songs. The hunters taught the boy a number of these songs, and told him to remember them always."

Some of the children were heavy-lidded now, and Teller Of Legends lowered her voice. "When it was time for him to go home, his new friends told the boy to perform the ritual he had learned whenever his tribe wished to communicate with theirs. The Pygmies would hear the drum beating, and come to feast with the Longhouse People. He was not to worry if he did not see them there; the Great Little People put on invisibility as easily as an Iroquois warrior puts on a breechclout.

"They gave him a round, white stone as a hunting charm, then made a request: Whenever his people heard the Pygmies drum or sing, they should go to the gulch from which the sound arose and throw tobacco down to their allies. It would please the Pygmies even more, they said, if the young people of the Iroquois would make bundles of their fingernail parings and throw those down also; for the larger beasts, whom the Great Little People feared, would catch the scent of humans and run away.

"The boy thanked the hunters and their family for their hospitality, promised to do what they asked, then climbed out of the ravine, and made his way home. But when he arrived, he saw that no one in his tribe was the same age as he'd been when the boy had left the village. And he realized that every day he'd spent with the Pygmies had been equal to a year in the lives of his own people.

"This was another thing to marvel at, and he included it when he told of his adventure. And since that time, the Iroquois have never failed to give feasts for the Great Little People who are their invisible friends."

Mothers and aunts and grandmothers gathered up their sleepy young and smiled gratefully at the storyteller. Morning Song's own smile faded as she watched them disperse, and her eyes were somber as she came to her feet. How she longed for Hearth Tender to return and put an end to her disquiet!

"No one can truly interpret a vision save the person to whom it was sent." Hearth Tender's soft words fell harshly on Morning Song's ears.

"I have no understanding of it, none at all!" she whispered. She stared into her mother-aunt's gaunt face, saw the smudges weariness had painted beneath her dark eyes, and grieved to thrust yet another burden upon her.

Hearth Tender read her expression and smiled. "To whom would you come, if not to me?" she asked gently. "I do not say that I find no message in the vision you describe," she went on, "but I want you to know that what I see may not be the only interpretation of it. Visions are like the nuts we eat, Morning Song. Useless shell surrounds the meat, and even Keepers Of The Faith may mistake a sliver of shell for the nut meat that lies in the heart."

It was midmorning, and Morning Song and her aunt had the longhouse to themselves. The clan's Faithkeeper had slipped into the lodge just after dawn and gone promptly to sleep. The rest of the family busied themselves with outside work, and it was only after Morning Song had gone three times to look in on Hearth Tender that she found her awake. "Will you tell me at least what you *think* my vision may mean?" she asked her now.

Hearth Tender nodded slowly. "The faces of forest creatures were imposed upon a reflection of your own, and this suggests masks to me," she said. "You know that the Company of Faces wears masks. Perhaps the spirit who sent your vision is directing you to them." She hesitated. "You are young," she said frankly, "to be a Healer. And that river-sun you spoke of"—she turned up her palms—"I cannot think what it might mean."

"But you do feel that I am meant to become a Healer?" Morning Song asked after a moment.

"Certain things you told me indicate this," her aunt said. "Still, visions often guard their messages almost jealously. It may be a long time before you understand the whole of it."

"Then how can it help me to find my way through life?" the girl cried passionately. "I need to see the path clearly, Hearth Tender. This is why I went on my quest."

Hearth Tender ached to be of more help. "It is possible that dreams will be sent to decipher what remains unclear," she told her. "Meanwhile, perhaps your youth will not count against you if you show yourself sincere in wanting to become a Healer. A sense of purpose is what you most need, Morning Song, and you might find it in the Company of Faces."

Morning Song opened her mouth, closed it without voicing her reluctance to approach the leader of that group. And during the small silence born of her hesitation, memory nudged her. When she looked again at Hearth Tender, her eyes were glowing. "But the Pygmy society is also a company of Healers," she said. "And yesterday Teller Of Legends gave us a tale about the Pygmies. Surely that was more than coincidence? Some of the creatures in my vision—the beaver, the bear, the bird that might have been a wren—are associated with the Pygmy society." She was growing elated now. "It seems to me that I am meant to join that society, Hearth Tender, and not the False Faces."

Her mother-aunt lifted a hand to stem the flood of eager words. "Morning Song, you must take care that you do not mistake your own impulses for spiritual prompting. What you say about the animals is true, but in the beginning you said you could not identify the bird that rose from the river. If it was not in truth a wren, then only two of the six animal faces you saw point toward the Pygmy society. You need stronger indication than that, I think, to arrive at such a conclusion."

The light went out of Morning Song's eyes. Hearth Tender's counsel was respected throughout the village; it must be respected by her own niece.

She stood up. "I thank you," she said politely, "for listening to me." Then, craving confirmation of the only hopeful thing her mother-aunt had said to her: "Is it certain that dreams shall visit me now?"

Hearth Tender smiled again. "When we deal with the spirits, nothing is certain," she said wryly. "But it is likely that they shall."

Her smile was replaced by a look of concern as she watched her niece pass out of the longhouse. Morning Song's vision had been embroidered with a wealth of symbols. Of those Hearth Tender had been able to recognize, not all had been good.

Morning Song found Bountiful Harvest at her loom, working one of her intricate designs. The girl had no trouble identifying the brown earth and the crops growing greenly upon it. Or the Snow-hairs lifting elegant peaks into the sky her mother-aunt was deftly weaving in blue. "That is beautiful," she exclaimed, and Bountiful Harvest swiveled to look at her. "I wish I owned such a talent."

"To do this sort of thing takes more practice than you would be willing to demand of yourself," Bountiful Harvest said, her tone less acid than usual; she was not loathe to be admired.

Morning Song sat down across from her. "You are probably right," she admitted, and put on a cautious smile. "I have been a trial to you at times, I know."

Her aunt was plainly taken aback. "This is so," she said swiftly. But her voice had softened further, and Morning Song let herself relax a little.

"I have been speaking with Hearth Tender," she said when she had watched Bountiful Harvest's sky give birth to a fluffy white cloud. "About my vision." Tension was creeping into her throat and she swallowed twice to combat it. "She believes that it may have been sent to persuade me to join the Company of Faces."

Bountiful Harvest turned her full attention on the daughter of Summer Maize. "You are here because I am their leader."

Morning Song nodded, waited in silence as her aunt's eyes searched her face.

"I do not doubt that my sister communes with the spirits," the older woman said at last. "It was Hearth Tender's reading of a dream of mine that led me into the company." Her eyes probed further, were suddenly granite-hard. "My doubts, Morning Song, are solely with the vision you described to her. You have always been imaginative. We both know that there was a time when you delighted in speaking of dreams that were not dreams at all, but only stories you had devised. Lies, Morning Song, is what those were." She leaned forward and her gaze was sharp as the awl used to puncture the toughest of hides. "How can I know that this vision of yours is not just another . . . story? Where is proof that you were granted a genuine vision while you were away from our village?"

Morning Song bit back a stinging retort. Her right hand reached for the pouch dangling from the thong around her neck, then dropped back into her lap. How could so ordinary a thing as a maple leaf, even one prematurely fallen, convince Bountiful Harvest that she spoke the truth? She would never be convinced of that, no matter what Morning Song might say or do, because she had no wish to be convinced. And all at once Morning Song knew that, vision or no, she wanted nothing whatsoever to do with the False Face society, or with this prideful and antagonistic woman who liked Morning Song no better than Morning Song liked her!

"My vision was real," she said tightly. "But you would not believe that it was even had you been there and witnessed it yourself." She sprang to her feet, looked with burgeoning arrogance into Bountiful Harvest's astonished face. "I am old enough now not to be disturbed by what you think, so think what you will. And be advised that I have reconsidered seeking entry into the False Face society. It is not the place for me, nor ever will be."

She spun on her heel and stalked away, rejoicing to have left her aunt speechless.

Yet she was seething still, inside, when she came upon her grandmother as the old woman was leaving the Plover lodge. "I think it a pity," Morning Song said abruptly, falling into step beside her, "that Bountiful Harvest inherited none of her mother's gentleness and wisdom."

Teller Of Legends marked the rigid back, the imperious jut of chin that spoke loudly of her granddaughter's anger. "Indeed," she murmured. "I suppose the pair of you have finally crossed lances openly?"

Morning Song's narrowed eyes slid sideways. "You cannot mean that you expected this to happen?"

"It has been inevitable," she said. "Two people so much alike cannot fail to clash eventually. Only the difference in your ages has postponed the confrontation until now."

"I am not," Morning Song said forcefully, "anything like my mother-aunt."

Teller Of Legends turned to face her granddaughter. "Pride is no stranger to either of you, and a need to prove her worth drives Bountiful Harvest just as it does you. And the both of you"—she smiled—"have wills of iron."

Morning Song was flabbergasted. She was far removed from pride, and would give much to possess the strength Teller Of Legends was blithely crediting to her. She would not deny that she felt a need to prove herself, but surely no one as dauntingly efficient as Bountiful Harvest could ever feel unworthy.

Her grandmother patted her arm. "The likeness is there," she said comfortably. "I have been aware of it for some time. But it is nothing to fret about. And is it so surprising that you and your mother-aunt should share some of the same qualities? You are of the same blood, Morning Song."

Morning Song sighed. "I cannot agree with you, Teller Of Legends, nor does it make me happy to be compared with Bountiful Harvest. But, at the moment, other things worry me more."

"Your vision, perhaps?"

Morning Song bobbed her head.

"Hearth Tender told me that she talked with you. And I suppose you went straight to Bountiful Harvest to ask about joining the False Faces?" Reading confirmation in Morning Song's face, her grandmother chuckled. "I take it you will not be joining."

"I will not," Morning Song said. "I no longer care to," she added loftily. Then her set mouth trembled and she turned toward the unruffled woman who stood at her side. "Teller Of Legends, what do the spirits want of me? Why must I go on my way undirected? Why didn't the spirit that sent my vision make the message clear? How long shall I have to wait before I can understand it, and be guided by it?''

Teller Of Legends steered her granddaughter in the direction of their longhouse. "So many questions, Morning Song, and all at once, too. I realize that the experience you had during your quest was overwhelming. I know you wonder why the rest of us are not as concerned about it as you quite naturally are. But we have learned that revelations from the spirit world are never heaped upon a single platter and served all at once." She sought for words to enhance the metaphor she had impulsively chosen. "You have seen people whose shameful gluttony is betrayed by their swollen bellies?''

Morning Song thought of Covers His Eyes, whose fleshiness had matured into a disgusting obesity since his expulsion by Bountiful Harvest. She nodded.

"Would you have your spirit beome similarly distorted from being fed too much too quickly?" Teller Of Legends smiled again. "Have patience, my dear, and do not waste time agonizing over what cannot, and should not, be hurried."

Morning Song stepped back to allow her grandmother to pass ahead of her into the lodge. What she had said made sense, but, oh, it had answered not even one of the questions Morning Song had put to her!

Would anyone, or anything, ever be able to do so?

Chapter 12

＊ ⇒

The only light in the crowded longhouse came from ash-furred embers on the rear hearth. To hear the sound of breathing, an occasional soft cough, a rustle as someone sought a more agreeable position, yet to have her companions unidentified, bordered on the eerie. Well, Rain Singing she was sure of, Morning Song amended silently. The leader of the Pygmy society, and the only person to know who the other members were, was seated next to her. Small Brown Sparrow's mother had been quick to agree that Morning Song's vision foretold her initiation into the Pygmy society.

"You have only to learn the songs attached to our ritual," she'd said, "and you will be admitted to our ceremonies." She'd chuckled and leaned closer. "There are a remarkable number of them," she'd confided. "But the granddaughter of a woman who has committed to memory all the legends of our people should not find this beyond her talents."

Morning Song's confrontation with Bountiful Harvest had seemed to condemn the younger woman to her former directionless existence. But when her temper cooled, and reason returned to her, Morning Song had gradually come to see the episode in a new light. Couldn't it have been some ploy of the spirits, a sign that she must retrace her steps and try another path? Hearth Tender had not ruled out the Pygmy society when she'd spoken of Morning Song becoming a Healer; she'd said only that her niece must be cautious, and wait for stronger indications before seeking a place in that fellowship.

The longer Morning Song considered, the more confident she became that she was, indeed, being prodded again toward the Pygmies, and Rain Singing's enthusiastic reception of her had provided all the verification she'd needed.

Now she listened to the rhythm of horn rattle and water drum, took up the chant Rain Singing had begun, and told herself she must not try to put names to her companions by the sounds of their voices. To do so would offend the Pygmies who, cloaked in their customary invisibility, had come to the Deer longhouse to take part in this ceremony. She focused instead on the enchanted animals being honored with this cycle of songs: the Blue Panther, who was the herald of death; the Great Horned Serpent; White Beaver; Great Naked Bear. These, and a variety of others, were as much members of this group as Morning Song was, and far superior to her—and even to Rain Singing—in rank.

As the chanting came to an end, she exulted to feel kinship with such powerful spirits. Her link with the supernatural, forged during her Vision Quest, fit snugly into the powerful chain that bound the mortal world to its spiritual counterpart.

She felt Rain Singing stir and rise, listened to the shuffle of her feet as she made her way to the fire. The dark-thickened air moved sluggishly as every head turned toward the hearth and all ears prepared to receive her words:

We now commence to thank the Maker Of Life,
We are thankful that we who have assembled here are
    all well.

We are thankful for the world and all that is upon
  it for our benefit . . .

Morning Song felt gratitude enlarge her heart. It was indeed a
splendid thing, this world her people inhabited, and in this moment
no one appreciated it more than Morning Song!

A familiar aroma sweetened the shadows as tobacco began to
smolder. "Now the smoke rises!" Rain Singing sang. "Receive
you this incense, you who run in the darkness."

Otter Swimming had confessed once that, as a child, she'd been
frightened of the dark. How foolish of her, Morning Song thought;
the dark was friend and comforter. Her brow puckered. Otter was
not so open with her these days. In truth, she seemed oblivious of
everyone and everything, was content to occupy herself with solitary tasks and solitary musings. . . .

Morning Song started guiltily, sent her wandering mind back to
Rain Singing:

You, the Pygmies, love tobacco and we remember
  this;
So also should you remember us.
Now the drum receives tobacco.
And the rattle also.
It is our belief that we have said all,
So now we hope that you will help us.
Now these are the words spoken before you all,
You who are gathered here tonight.
So now it is done.

There was a small silence, mute endorsement of Rain Singing's prayer. Then, without haste, the members of the Pygmy
society—visible and invisible—slipped quietly out of the Deer
longhouse.

Morning Song kept her eyes cast down as she went, lest she
recognize any of her fellows. Only a child lets curiosity rule her,
she reminded herself sternly.

But it took prodigious determination to keep her gaze fixed firmly
on her own two feet.

Teller Of Legends looked up, and welcome warmed her eyes as
her brother entered the lodge. "You have been neglecting us, Se-
A-Wi," she teased gently. "I had thought, with our warriors gone,
that you might visit us more often."

The care-sharpened ridges of his face softened as he hunkered down beside her, but his pouched eyes remained somber. "There are matters that demand my attention, even with so many of our councilors away," he told her. "And news has come to me that I wish heartily had reached my ears before Fierce Eagle left."

Bountiful Harvest had been scraping into a bowl the blackened kernels from a parched corncob. Now she covered them with boiling water and set the bowl upon her hearth.

Teller Of Legends watched approvingly. "My daughter is preparing a drink for you," she said to Se-A-Wi. "While it cooks, tell me what disturbs you."

"The Cat People are said to be dipping their arrowheads in venom," he said bluntly.

Teller Of Legends closed her eyes briefly. It was as well that Otter was not present to hear this. "You are certain?"

The Sachem shrugged. "Who can say? Follows The Signs asked me to dispatch a runner to the cabin of the Frenchman, to remind him of the guns we have been promised when next he and Lah-Val come to trade. It was Bree-And who sent the message about the Erie, when he understood we had gone to war against them."

"How can he know what the Cat People do?"

"Traders go everywhere, Teller Of Legends. Bree-And probably deals with the Erie nation just as he does with the Iroquois." His tone was bitter but resigned. The actions of independent traders could not be controlled by treaty, as dealings between tribes usually were.

"He might have warned us sooner," his sister said tartly. "It is our land that he lives on. Is the *Onondio* a stranger to loyalty?"

"He did not know we have declared the Cat People our enemies," the Sachem pointed out, accepting with a grunt of pleasure the steaming bowl Bountiful Harvest brought to him. "Fierce Eagle makes the utmost of secrecy whenever he plans a raid. It is one reason he is so praiseworthy a war leader."

Teller Of Legends nodded. "Yet you cannot help wishing that our warriors might already have the guns the trader promised us."

"If they are as good as he says they are, yes." Se-A-Wi sipped at his parched corn coffee. "Bree-And sent back a message to say we shall have them soon. We can only hope," he went on, lowering his voice, "that they do not arrive too late for some."

"Such a hope is futile," Teller Of Legends said heavily. "Even if the weapons are delivered tomorrow, how can we get them to Fierce Eagle in time? Perhaps this is why our warriors were sent so many troublesome dreams before they left. The Faithkeepers were careful not to promote alarm, but it was clear that the omens were not entirely favorable.'' She laid a hand on his knee as Morning Song and Pumpkin Blossom came in, allowed herself a moment to contemplate the pair. The lissome yet robust daughter of Bountiful Harvest had inherited her mother's elegant beauty, and fairly glowed with awareness of her good fortune. The daughter of Summer Maize, taller and slimmer than her cousin, lacked Pumpkin Blossom's womanly curves. Her face was more arresting than beautiful. A fine arch of brow shadowed eyes seeming darker than they were, owing to her inward-looking nature. Her delicate nose and the sensitive mouth that was so expressive of her moods were countered by a small but uncompromising chin. Her features, Teller Of Legends decided, might have been drawn with a bit of charcoal that had been knapped to an extravagant degree.

She turned once more to her brother. ''It will be wise to say nothing more now,'' she murmured. ''It is not only sons and brothers and husbands who are with Fierce Eagle, but all of those young men—some still untried—whose safe return will mean much to the maidens ready for marriage. If we lose too many of these . . .'' She forebore to extend the prediction.

The creases framing Se-A-Wi's bony nose and age-thinned mouth deepened. ''It shall be those yet unborn, whose faces should be coming from beneath the ground, that are sacrificed,'' he finished for her, and got to his feet.

Teller Of Legends watched him go, and rearranged her expression so the fear that iced her belly did not reflect in her face. She looked to Bountiful Harvest and shook her head slightly, was relieved when her daughter nodded soberly. She would say nothing, either. It was enough that the two of them must be burdened with additional worry while the days until the war party returned crawled by like a parade of indolent tortoises.

Pumpkin Blossom drew her cousin to the shelf on which her possessions were neatly stacked. ''I want you to see the design decorating the sleeping robe I have been working on,'' she said, taking it down and spreading it across her bunk.

Dutifully Morning Song admired the way she had worked the day sun in red, the sky dome in blue, and the night sun in yellow, repeating the motif along all four edges of the robe. ''You must delight in using your needle, Pumpkin Blossom, to go to so much trouble to embroider a coverlet. A plain one would keep you just as warm.''

Pumpkin Blossom bestowed upon her one of those mysterious

smiles she had lately begun wearing. "This is no ordinary sleeping robe, Morning Song," she said. "I made it to cover my marriage bed."

Morning Song regarded her with undisguised astonishment. "You are *seriously* considering marriage?"

Her cousin's slanted eyes glistened. "I mean to choose my husband before one of the other maidens thinks to have him," she declared. "You should do the same, Morning Song. The best will be spoken for first, you know."

Morning Song laughed. "Not every young woman is so eager for marriage."

Pumpkin Blossom's smile this time was annoyingly indulgent. "Meadow Brook and Bear In The Sky mean to wed as soon as our warriors have come home," she responded. "And although she has said nothing to me, I feel that Small Brown Sparrow will soon be baking bridal cakes, too."

Morning Song was aghast. "She is too young to take a husband," she protested. "You must be wrong, Pumpkin Blossom."

Pumpkin Blossom refolded her robe, taking care to follow its original creases. "If you doubt me, ask her," she said serenely. "Those of us who were girls together shall all take husbands during the next season or two. It is time that we did, Morning Song. And if you hold back from it, you will end up a spinster, like Hearth Tender and Tree Reaching Up."

The coolness in her voice said that she would not be surprised if Morning Song elected to walk a path others would shy away from, but Morning Song was unperturbed. "I imagine I shall recognize when and if I am meant to marry," she said airily. "My spirit guide can be depended upon to advise me about something so important."

"Well, I trust he will not be a laggard, if you would have children before you are a grayhair!" Pumpkin Blossom rejoined, and went to help her mother at the cooking fire.

Morning Song glanced toward Bountiful Harvest's hearth, judged that her help would not be required for so simple a meal, and was content not to offer it. She slipped outside and breathed deep of the smoke-free air, stooped to fondle her tail-wagging dog, and spied Otter Swimming making for the planting fields. Impulsively she hailed her and, when her mother-aunt responded, hurried to join her. White Shadow loped by his mistress's side, then bounded ahead to greet Otter in his own exuberant fashion.

"If you are going to gather the last of the pumpkins and squashes,

I will fetch a basket and go with you," Morning Song said when she'd reached them.

Otter displayed empty hands. "I was only going to walk a little," she confessed, "but I'd be glad of your company."

Morning Song's spirits lifted. Otter seemed suddenly more like herself, and she was pleased to accept her invitation. "It is nice to find someone besides me who considers it worthwhile to walk aimlessly and enjoy the day," she told her. "So many women leave their lodges only when there is work to be done outside. And then they are too busy to appreciate the warmth of the sun or the sweetness of the air or the music the songbirds make for us."

Otter grinned and pointed her feet along the track that led to the river. "The water sings, too, on so brisk a day as this," she observed. "As does the wind when it whistles through the dry cornstalks."

Morning Song eyed her closely. Otter was not generally given to flights of fancy. "You are joyful today," she said. "Have you heard that the warriors will be home soon?"

Otter's shining eyes clouded, and Morning Song regretted that she'd asked the question. "There has been no news of them yet," Otter replied somberly. Then brightness reclaimed her. "But surely they will be here before much longer, and Deer Caller shall have a homecoming more wonderful than any he has had before." She stopped walking and the face she turned toward her niece was stunning in its radiance. "Morning Song, we are to have a child. At last! And he will be as thrilled as I am when he hears."

Morning Song threw her arms around her mother-aunt and squealed with happiness. "As I am, too!" she proclaimed. "Oh, Otter."

Shadow leaped and capered to show his readiness to share in their rejoicing but was, for once, ignored even by his mistress. "I had intended to let no one know until I'd told Deer Caller," Otter Swimming admitted, "but I am not sorry to have told you. It has been so hard to keep such grand news to myself."

"This is why you have been so quiet and so solitary these past weeks," Morning Song said as they resumed their walk. "I had begun to think the Otter I'd always known had changed shape and become someone entirely different."

"Doubtless Teller Of Legends feels the same," Otter said ruefully. "I shall tell her also, I think, when we return to the village. But no one else."

Morning Song nodded. "And I will not tell anyone," she vowed. They ambled along in companionable silence until the river, its usually placid surface pleated by the wind's probing fingers, stretched before them. Morning Song kept her distance from its banks, and Otter Swimming knew better than to urge her closer.

"Pumpkin Blossom is thinking of taking a husband," the younger woman said abruptly, "and so is Meadow Brook. My cousin insists that Small Brown Sparrow is, too, but I doubt she would be so foolish."

Otter laughed. "I was no older than the daughter of Rain Singing when I asked Deer Caller to come and live in the Turtle longhouse."

Morning Song sighed. "Perhaps Pumpkin Blossom is right, then," she said morosely. "She may be right also when she says I will be the only one not to marry before the next yellow season comes."

"No young man appeals to you?"

"Not even the idea of marriage appeals to me," Morning Song said firmly.

Otter laughed again, more softly this time, and pointed to the river. One of her namesakes, wet fur outlining his flat head, was swimming against the current. "I told you when you were a child that you should have been called Little Otter," she said to her niece, "and perhaps I was right. Like that stubborn fellow there, you prefer to go your own way even when the going is difficult."

They watched as the animal fought to cross the river at an impossible angle, and Morning Song found herself silently cheering him on. When he succeeded in reaching the far side, she grinned. "Difficult, perhaps, but not impossible," she said smugly.

Otter Swimming conceded this.

"Yet will he find fatter and tastier fish there, than would have been available to him downriver?" she asked mischievously.

That was a question Morning Song had no answer for.

The guns Se-A-Wi had been expecting—those that would be of no use to the war band already in Erie country—were brought to the village seven days later. Trail Marker, Puma Walking Soft, Follows The Signs, and Se-A-Wi gathered around a hastily lit fire to welcome the traders and examine the weapons before exchanging precious furs for them. When Henri Briand, impatience larding his voice, had ordered the bearers to set down the guns, he waved one thick-fingered hand toward them and addressed himself to Trail Marker.

"Me, I would not offer to my friends, to people I now also call neighbors, the sorry weapons some traders might bring with them.

But these are the finest guns this side of the *Océan Atlantique*,'' he boasted. Seizing one by the barrel, he thrust the butt of it into Trail Marker's hands. "Feel how smooth the wood," he commanded, "and how weighty. See: Here is the touchhole"—he jabbed at the vent that would carry fire to the charge—"and here is what is named the pan. And I have brought along the powder you will need to fill it, and the shot as well."

He beamed as Trail Marker hefted the arquebus, peered into its barrel, and passed it over to Se-A-Wi. The Sachem eyed the weapon dubiously; it would be awkward to carry and, he strongly suspected, equally clumsy to use. Still, he was old, and set in his ways. Without revealing his skepticism, he passed the gun on to Puma Walking Soft and Follows The Signs.

The burly trader grinned more broadly as the latter took it up and expressed his elation to be holding something wondrously new and therefore surely superior. "Tell him I shall make him a gift of that one," Briand told Trail Marker, and spread his hands to make light of his generosity. His grin faltered, however, when he saw Trail Marker frowning over a similar gun he had lifted from the stack.

"You are certain our warriors will be able to aim these as easily as they aim an arrow?" he asked the trader.

"When they have learned how," Briand said confidently, "they shall throw away their bows, your brave warriors!"

Gaspard Laval had sat in silence, with his watchful eyes traveling from face to face; now he spoke. "The warriors, they are intelligent as well as brave," he said, squashing a beetle that was investigating his ankle. "They will keep their bows, I think."

Trail Marker's gaze sharpened as he turned to him. "What is wrong with the guns?" he asked quickly.

"The guns, they are fine weapons," Briand shouted. "The best! *Sacré bleu*, have I not said this? Laval means only that the men shall not wish to squander powder and shot when they hunt. That is all." He directed a poisonous look at his fellow trader, who deflected the glare with a shrug of his scrawny shoulders. Briand looked back at Trail Marker. "Now we decide how many of these so-beautiful guns you will barter for," he told him. "I cannot let you have all of them, me. Other villages wait for lightning sticks, and Henri Briand is an honorable man who delivers what he promises."

But Trail Marker would not be hurried. He turned and spoke to his companions, his hands gesturing as he outlined his sudden misgivings.

Briand understood little of what he privately termed their gabble, but he was clever enough to deduce that only Follows The Signs still wished to have the guns. He clambered to his feet, rounded on Laval, and stood over him menacingly. "What is the matter, you?" he shouted. "Why do you make trouble for me, your compatriot? These savages cannot get guns better than the ones I have brought to them."

Laval unfolded himself and stood also. "I have been trading in this village a long time," he said tightly. "Trail Marker and the old chief, they are good people. It may be useful for their braves to own guns, yes. But I will not permit you to tell them that these guns will make better weapons than the bows and lances they have already."

The corpulent trader's face reddened. "Who was it went to Quebec for the guns, eh? I ask you to buy them for me while you are there, and you say no, there are no decent weapons to be had. Me, I knew better. Now you interfere because all the profit will be mine. You think the savages will offer pelts for your pots and knives and hoes when I show them guns? They will not." His hairy hands formed big-knuckled fists. "I tell you, Laval, to close your mouth. Or me, I will do this for you!"

Gaspard Laval had arranged his life so that he had as little traffic with his fellow man as possible. Mistrust had set in early when, newly come from France, Laval had seized on trading as the way to make his fortune. The merchants he'd been forced to rely on for goods the redskins would swap valuable furs for had looked upon a rawboned peasant, marked him as ignorant, and proceeded to cheat him. Gaspard Laval was of peasant stock, but stupid he was not. He learned to pit one merchant against another until outrageous charges had been reduced to merely exorbitant; and his experience of fraud and deceit had made of him that rare thing, a scrupulously honest trader.

He did not boast of it. Nor did he think of it now, when the grudging admiration he had come to feel for the Longhouse People moved him to put aside his detachment from the human race. He sensed in the Iroquois the same directness and lack of pretense that had contributed to making Gaspard Laval a stranger among his own kind.

"You tell them how much time it takes to load and fire those old matchlocks," he said harshly. "How, sometimes, they do not fire at all! Me, I say nothing . . . unless you say nothing."

"These weapons work as well as those that other tribes own," Briand blustered. "*This*, I tell them. But no more than this."

His companion's narrowed eyes became slits. "One of us," he said, "shall speak truth here. All the truth, Briand."

The veins in Briand's corded neck throbbed as he unleashed a spate of invective, gutter language Trail Marker did not comprehend. His rasping voice became a caterwaul as his rage erupted in curse after colorful curse, and in every lodge entrance hides were pulled back as those inside peered out at the bellowing man.

In the Turtle longhouse, Teller Of Legends and her daughters and grandchildren crowded together, drew breath in unison as the barrel-shaped trader raised a meaty fist and shook it warningly in the face of the second *Onondio*. The Chief Matron murmured admiringly when Laval did not retreat, or even flinch. She was watching still when Briand's temper truly exploded, when he bombarded his bearded companion with spittle as well as vulgarities, and brandished both fists as he described the blows he was bent on delivering.

One member of the Turtle clan ceased to watch then. The blood drained from Morning Song's face and she lifted a trembling hand, clamped it over her mouth to muffle the scream vibrating in her throat. She swayed, steadied herself, backed away from the others, and stumbled to her bed.

Only when she curled herself into a tight little ball and began to whimper did the others realize she was no longer standing with them in the entrance to the longhouse.

Teller Of Legends wasted no time sending the rest of her family elsewhere. Not even Hearth Tender was permitted to stay behind. Then she lifted her granddaughter and propped her against her own ample bosom. Her strong arm supported the young woman and her callused hands patted her back gently as she spoke to her in the singsong voice of a mother soothing a tiny child. "I am here, Morning Song. Your grandmother is here. You are safe. My arms and my love keep you safe."

She brushed tendrils of hair from Morning Song's damp brow and looked anxiously upon eyes that remained resolutely closed; upon a face still as death. "Morning Song, nothing can defeat you if you will not let it." She held the girl tighter. "Feel my strength flow into you," she chanted. "Feel it pass between my flesh and yours; feel it being absorbed into your blood, your bone."

Morning Song's eyelids flickered, and Teller Of Legends allowed her tensed muscles cautious respite. "Your blood is warming now as the strength I am lending you blends with it, and it travels more easily beneath your skin. You imagine that you stand in a circle of yellow sunshine on a cold winter's day, that our brother the sun looks down on you and smiles and smiles until even your toes are no longer frozen, until it is his own splendid glow that you wear.''

The young woman stirred. Her eyes opened . . . closed . . . opened once more to meet the face near to hers with a glazed stare. Her grandmother continued to croon, but the syllables she shaped now were wordless, rhythmic encouragement.

The veil lifted from Morning Song's eyes, and recognition flooded into them. ''Grandmother,'' she said faintly, and struggled to sit up.

Teller Of Legends made no move to stop her. To put on dignity was strengthening. ''We shall sit quietly for a time, you and I,'' she said, straightening her own back.

She held one of Morning Song's hands, squeezed it now and then as she waited for her granddaughter to regain her composure. The altercation between the two *Onondio* must have ended, for no raucous shouts, no hurled imprecations, now assaulted the ears of the pair who sat on in silence.

''Teller Of Legends, I cannot think what demon drove me to act so childishly.'' Morning Song's voice faltered as her grandmother returned her attention to her. ''When I heard the trader, the round-bellied one, roar so loudly, and when I saw him making ready to strike his friend, then . . . it happened.'' She shook her head as though to dispel the image. ''He said such awful things, Grandmother,'' she whispered brokenly.

Teller Of Legends fought to keep her own composure. ''You understood his words?''

''Enough of them to understand his meaning,'' she said. ''I had not told you,'' she added bleakly, ''but when last they came, those traders, I discovered that the language they speak is familiar to me.'' She raised questioning eyes to her grandmother's face. ''I realized then that the white man who fathered me must also have been a Frenchman.''

Teller Of Legends nodded slowly. ''He was.''

Morning Star hesitated. ''Grandmother, when the *Onondio* began to shake his hairy fist, to threaten the other trader with harm, I knew that—somehow—I had seen this happen before. I think it must have been when I was very small, when I was still with my mother and that—that man. Do you know if this might be so?''

The old woman clenched her own hands, then spread them flat on her buckskin-covered knees. She had known that the day would come when she must confront old and distressing memories—had known it, and dreaded it. "Yes," she said. "It is your childhood that you are recalling."

"My father was cruel to my mother." The statement was made flatly, as though it was incontestable.

"As your mother did, I met the man who would become your father when he came to our village offering to buy furs," Teller Of Legends said after a moment. "In those days, you see, everyone would go into the compound when a trader came. It is our custom to offer hospitality to a stranger, and a white man was a curiosity none could resist. He was a handsome man, Morning Song, and Summer Maize was impressed because he looked so often in her direction. She had grown up in the shadow of an exceptionally pretty older sister, you understand, and although she was lovely in her own way, Summer Maize was unhappy that so many of our warriors saw only Bountiful Harvest when the sisters were together. Pee-Yare On-Tee-Tay—for this was the trader's name—saw in her what our young men had overlooked, I suppose, and when eventually he asked her to go away with him, she was easily persuaded to do so." She smiled a little. "All women desire to be admired and wanted. I never blamed my daughter for leaving us, only grieved to lose her."

"But he cannot have loved my mother, if he was cruel to her!" Morning Song cried.

"Perhaps he did, in the beginning, and then changed. This has been known to happen, Morning Song. And when Summer Maize came home at last, bringing you with her, she told us little before she died. Her husband had expected her to bear him many sons and was angry when she failed to. He had hoped to become a man of some importance, to establish what he called a *trading empire* in the north, and without boy-children that could not be. Beyond this we learned nothing, for she would not speak further of the man she had fled from."

"She ran away because he struck her so often," Morning Song said in a small voice. "I am certain of it, Grandmother."

Teller Of Legend would not deny what she, who had seen the scars, the bruises, herself believed.

"Was it because he beat her that my mother died before her time?" The young woman's question was formed of separate beads strung on a thong pulled taut by anguish.

"I think that very likely, Morning Song. I wish I could tell you it was not, but I refuse to lie to you now that you have remembered so much."

Morning Song stood up and began to pace. "Grandmother, I had come to accept that both white blood and red went into the making of me. But, Teller Of Legends, Iroquois men do not abuse their wives! And I am daughter to a man who delighted in doing that. It is a terrible thing, to have such hatred for the man who fathered me, for a man whose face I could not recognize if he walked into our longhouse now. And it is more terrible still to wonder if there does not lie hidden in me that same urge to hurt, to destroy, as he possessed. I do not know if I can endure the thought of this, Grandmother. Yet I have no choice, do I?'' She did not look toward the old woman as she flung out the bitter words, but her bowed head and slumped shoulders testified to her agony.

"Morning Song, choice is precisely what you do have,'' Teller Of Legends responded sternly. "We are more than just the residue of those who happen to be our parents. The sort of people we ultimately become depends far more on the choices we make as we walk through life. Those responsible for our being born cannot dictate the turnings our feet shall make, the destinations we shall seek. Only we can do so, and the spirits who guide us.''

Morning Song turned slowly and managed a fleeting smile. "I will trust that your words are wrapped in wisdom, as they usually are,'' she said wearily, "for there is no hope for me otherwise. But I must ask you never again to speak of the *Onondio* who sired me. From this moment, I mean to pretend that he never existed, that I am a daughter of the Longhouse People and no other. And how I wish''—a sob thickened her voice—"it could be true!''

She swallowed the tears that welled in her throat, then squared her shoulders, and set her chin. "If the traders come another time,'' she said evenly, "I will go into the forest until they have gone. Never again shall I chance looking upon sallow-skins. For what one of them did to my mother, I assign guilt to all of them. I will despise the *Onondio* through all the years that are granted to me, and any children that are sent me shall be taught to hate them also.''

Teller Of Legends refrained from saying that rashly made vows generally prove impossible to keep. For now, she much preferred seeing her granddaughter's eyes flashing with anger than made frighteningly dull with half-remembered horror. Anger, too, could be a begetter of strength.

Chapter 13

＝ ⇒

When Fierce Eagle and his warriors returned this time, no runner raced ahead to proclaim their coming.

The day had been blustery from the start; clouds like quarrelsome gray foxes nipped at a cowering sun and held its warmth at bay. To the young women digging a new storage pit behind the longhouses the chill-laden wind was welcome.

"But it does not yet reach below ground level," Meadow Brook said as she climbed out of a rapidly deepening trench. She dashed moisture from her forehead, transferred a drop to the tip of her tongue, and grinned. "This feels like sweat, and it tastes salty like sweat," she said. "And when it dripped into my eyes, it stung like sweat!"

Teller Of Legends, sitting with Sweet Maple, Owl Crying, and Lake On Fire, smiled. "It is healthy to sweat when you labor hard. As all of you have been doing."

The maidens were working turn and turn about, according to their size. "The smallest should go first," the Matron of the Turtle clan had told them. She looked with exaggerated concern at Small Brown Sparrow. "It would sadden me to have to tell Rain Singing that her daughter was swallowed up by a hole deeper than she was tall."

Small Brown Sparrow had laughed with the rest. "That would sadden me, too," she'd retorted, "but at least I would not go hungry. Not once corn and pumpkins had been put in the pit with me!"

As she applied the point of a spade to the spot Teller Of Legends had marked, White Shadow came up behind her. And when her initial thrust managed to dislodge only a thin layer of the crusty topsoil, the dog nudged her aside and put his front paws to work with enthusiasm. Soon waves of dirt were flowing from beneath his angled body—and falling like brown rain upon the moccasins of a grinning Small Brown Sparrow.

"That mutt will be digging foot-snaring holes all over the compound now,'' Owl Crying said waspishly. ''Just as he did when he was a pup.''

''He shall not,'' White Shadow's mistress stated confidently. ''He has learned since then what he must and must not do.'' She watched him scramble out of the sizable hole he'd made and rejoiced when Small Brown Sparrow and the other maidens praised him for the fine start he'd given them.

The work had gone quickly after that, helped along by more good-natured banter. They would vie with another, the girls decided, to see who could complete her stint the fastest. The supervising matrons promised to name the winner at the end.

Now it was Morning Song's turn, and she grabbed the dirt-encrusted handle of the spade Meadow Brook held out to her. To shape the floor of the pit was the hardest part, and she could scarcely hope to match the speed of her companions. There was a time when that would have distressed her, but today she only looked across at her grandmother, rolled her eyes, and smiled.

Teller of Legends returned the smile and rejoiced that her grand-daughter seemed to have recovered well from the ordeal sparked by the traders' visit. ''Perhaps you should carry White Shadow down with you,'' she called merrily, ''and let him finish what he began!''

Morning Song laughed and shook her head, then poised herself to leap into the man-high, rectangular hole. Suddenly a shrill of female voices from the front of the compound made her abort her jump and rush to join the others as they swarmed in that direction.

''Our warriors' canoes have rounded the bend in the river.'' Bountiful Harvest, hurrying toward her mother, raised her voice to be heard above the din. Rigid control was all that kept her face from betraying her apprehension. ''They are not singing,'' she added flatly. ''And some of them do not sit erect, but lie unmoving in the bottoms of the canoes.''

Teller Of Legends absorbed the ominous news with a control equal to her daughter's. She lifted one hand to still the clamor of the anxious women and children. ''Save your keening until we see if this is called for,'' she told them. ''It may be that the men lying in the canoes are only wounded. If so, they will need our help, not our tears.'' She looked around her, was satisfied that they understood. ''We shall go to meet them,'' she finished quietly, and led the way out of the compound.

Otter Swimming strode between her mother and Morning Song. ''I know you yearn to run,'' Teller Of Legends said gently. ''But we women must not dishonor our warriors by surrendering to panic.''

Otter made no reply. Her expression was grim, and Morning Song ached for her. She had planned so splendid a homecoming for her husband. Deer Caller is unharmed: he will leap from one of the canoes and come to you and embrace you, Morning Song longed to say. But she dared not.

Even Teller Of Legends—who had fallen back to speak softly with Se-A-Wi—quickened her pace as they left the planting fields and turned toward the riverbank. They could see men hauling canoes out of the water, but from this distance none could be identified. Save for the ruffs of hair marking the shaven scalps of the older warriors and the loose braids signaling the younger ones, they were simply a collection of muscular backs and sinewy arms and legs. For a moment—for a single, cowardly moment—this was how Morning Song wished they might be always. She could see the litters now, at least six of them, and she dreaded to discover who occupied them.

Sweet Maple broke the eerie silence that had fallen upon the villagers. With a sharp cry—''Aiee!''—she broke into a shambling run, then fell to her knees between two of the litters. A young warrior—Hill Climber—sprinted to where his grandmother squatted, watched helplessly as her moon-round face swiveled from one supine figure to the other. And Otter's echo of Sweet Maple's cry, her rush to join the Matron of the Plover lodge, destroyed the remnants of Morning Song's hope. The two women knelt beside Far Seer and Deer Caller.

Within seconds a stricken Weeping Sky hurtled forward to add her grieving to theirs, but that was something Morning Song did not see. She had shut her eyes to blot out Otter's anguished face—and did not open them again until all at once the timbre of her aunt's voice altered.

One of those litter-bound figures had moved his hand. Otter had clasped it, and was holding it against her cheek as tears spilled from her eyes and splashed upon Deer Caller's naked chest.

There was lamenting enough to shiver the night that followed; besides Far Seer, four others had lost their lives in the land of the Erie. But the Death Ceremony, and the comfort it would eventually bring to the bereaved, was postponed. Five captives had been brought home and their fate left to the wives and mothers of the slain. Nobody was surprised when the vote was for torture, and death.

The Turtle clan was aware of the decision, but all of its attention was for the injured warrior who was husband to a tight-lipped Otter Swimming.

"His sight was stolen from him on the second day of battle," she'd said brokenly as Cloud Racer and his brother carried Deer Caller's litter to the longhouse. Her face had been shiny with tears then; now it was dry and set as she coaxed him to eat the stew Bountiful Harvest had ladled from her pot. When liquid from the spoon Otter held to his mouth dribbled over Deer Caller's chin, Teller Of Legends signed for the rest to look away.

"It is difficult enough for the two of them even without Otter, at least, knowing we are watching," she said. She raised her face to a curl of woodsmoke drifting in from the compound. "It is time we were going outside, in any event," she went on. "We shall leave my daughter and her husband to themselves."

"For now, only Deer Caller shall stay here," Otter said as she returned the bowl to her sister's hearth. She nodded her thanks. "He is ready to sleep, and I"—she compressed her lips—"must have a hand in what is coming."

They waited in silence as she went to pick up her skinning knife, then let her precede them out of the longhouse. "My daughter will rest easier, afterward," Teller Of Legends murmured to Morning Song.

Bountiful Harvest, white-knuckled fingers wrapped around the handle of her longest and sharpest awl, nodded. "As I shall," she snapped, "when I have taken revenge on the Cat People for depriving us of our only hunter."

Teller Of Legends saw the mixture of shock and disgust that flitted across Morning Song's face. "It may seem that her grievance pales alongside Otter's," she said in a low voice, "but it is a valid one nonetheless. It distressed Bountiful Harvest more than any of us, I think, that we were for so long dependent upon others for meat. As we shall be again." Her moderate tone took on a harshness it seldom assumed. "The prisoners Fierce Eagle and his band brought home will find themselves wishing they had not been given this chance to test their courage before they die."

For the first time, Morning Song realized that her hands alone were empty. All the others—her own kinfolk, the young and old of every clan—carried devices for inflicting pain on the Erie warriors. She was not without a weapon of sorts, however; since the day Stag Leaping had accosted her in the forest, she'd worn a sheathed blade strapped to her thigh.

Slowly, reluctantly, her hand went to her knife and lifted it from its leather casing. Think of Deer Caller, of poor Otter, she told herself. Bear in mind that tomorrow we must prepare to mourn Far Seer and the others whose lives were so fiendishly wrested from them. For Fierce Eagle had lifted his resonant voice as their dead were brought back to the village and told how only one of the Cat People's arrows had found a mark that proved instantly fatal. The other warriors, struck in shoulder or hip or knee, had survived the wounding only to succumb to a virulent fever that the arrows' poisoned tips sent raging through them. They had gone to their deaths screaming; the demons unleashed by the venom prevented them from chanting their death songs and dying with dignity.

They burned up, from the inside out. The phrase shaped itself suddenly in Morning Song's head and she wondered vaguely where she had heard it before. But now the villagers had begun to threaten the Erie, to promise a brutalizing that would leave them choking on their own unsung death songs. Acrid smoke frittered the night air, spiraled upwards to invade the mouths and noses of the defiant captives. The smoke thickened as a flood of men and women and children fanned out. They formed circles that fast became undulating ellipses surging around the stanchions the prisoners were lashed to. Morning Song, swept along by the tide, found herself next to Otter Swimming. She looked away from the hate-distorted mask that was Otter's face, and met the bold stare of the Erie warrior they were circling. His coppery flesh glistened, for the fire at the base of the post burned hot. Yet a knotting of the tendons in his bound legs was his sole response to flames that lapped intermittently at his bare feet, his ankles. His eyes bored into Morning Song's, and so scornful was his gaze that she knew he suspected this woman had no stomach for torturing him, that she hesitated to raise the hand holding her gleaming blade.

But if he were Onondio . . . if this were a man dedicated from birth to violence, a man who worshipped cruelty for its own sake . . . She gasped; it was as though the words had been spoken aloud, so ringing were they. She flung back her head, returned the mocking stare this warrior of the Cat People challenged her with. She let her imagination drain his skin of color, transform the Indian into the sallow-skin he must become for Morning Song to do what was expected of her.

When Otter stooped, seized a smoldering fagot, and rammed it into the warrior's left eye, Morning Song did not wince but only echoed her mother-aunt's jubilant howl. Her own hand tightened on the haft of her knife. She brought it up, gloried in the tensing of her muscles, and vented soul-deep rage in a harrowing screech as she ran the point of it deep into the prisoner's side.

She had drawn first blood. A mighty roar went up from the circle to praise her, a score of eager hands reached out to hack, to burn, to bruise, to mutilate the prisoner she had stabbed. In their frenzy, her people jostled one another as they maneuvered for position. Each blow delivered must avenge their silent dead and exact retribution for a man condemned to walk forevermore in darkness.

They would not permit the Erie warrior to die quickly. Those who swung clubs aimed for the ribs, for elbows and knees; narrow scrolls of skin were peeled from arms, from legs; lances penetrated the meatiness of shoulder or buttocks. But their victim ceased his singing only to name his tormentors cowards and fools, to declare that nothing they did to him could destroy his pride or undermine his valor. And those who eyed greedily the genitals they meant to lop off, the nostrils they would cram with cinders, the fingers they planned to amputate one by one, answered his boasting with offers to bring him food if he hungered and water when he thirsted, so long as he continued to earn their respect by entertaining them in this fashion.

Morning Song was deaf and blind now to all of it. Her eyes were riveted on the blood that gushed from the slash her knife had made. Red it was, darkly red, the smell of it more potent than the woodsmoke, than the stench of charred human flesh. It dribbled down the warrior's flank, crimsoned the crevices in his loins, painted a thin scarlet snake on his inner thigh.

How could she have forgotten that human blood was so red, that it owed nothing to the color of the skin or to the breed of the person who shed it? Blood was blood, no matter whose veins it leaked from. Life itself splashed to the ground it spilled on.

She looked down at her knife, at the accusing crimson that tainted its blade, and shuddered. The shout that had burst from her throat when she'd made the thrust had left rawness in its wake, and the bile that suddenly churned her belly bubbled up like liquid fire.

It could not be contained, and she knew it. She elbowed her way through the clamor, the chaos, careless of any who might mark her going, and commanded her legs to take her away from this place, to carry her far from the bloodred evidence of her own bestiality.

She had barely exited the compound before that searing liquid fire became vomit. While tears salted her cheeks, she retched and retched and retched until long after her stomach was empty.

Teller Of Legends went often to the Plover longhouse as lackluster days stretched into ash-colored weeks. "If I thought it could benefit Otter and Deer Caller," she told Morning Song, looking to where her daughter sat with her sightless husband, "I would stay here. But I am powerless to make acceptance of this easy for them." She took up a basket containing fresh leaf bread and cubes of the maple sugar her oldest friend was so fond of. "Sweet Maple has lost so many over the years," she said, shaking her head. "First her sisters—twins, and the mothers of Tree Reaching Up and Deer Caller. They died so young that Sweet Maple raised their children. Then her daughter, the only child sent to her, did not survive Hill Climber's birth; him, she has raised as well. Now her brother, too, can be with her only in spirit. And her nephew"—she looked again toward the rear hearth, sighed—"well, Sweet Maple suffers the same as we do for what has happened to him. She looks at the weapons that were Far Seer's and ought to be Deer Caller's inheritance, and wonders what to do with them." Teller Of Legends shook her head again, and her heavy braids thudded against her wrinkled cheeks. "It is harder when natural order is disrupted."

"She is old; how will she bear this latest sorrow, on top of all the rest?" Morning Song asked. "She has always seemed as carefree as a child who has known only contentment. We will all be sorry to have her change."

Teller Of Legends flung a robe around her shoulders, for the morning air was plaited with cold. "She will not change," she assured her granddaughter. "Sweet Maple has learned that the tree that bends in the wind survives the gale. She will devote herself to living rather than waste herself in regretting. But she has need of friends to talk with, people who understand that her smile is hard won and who know that laughter can be medicine for a grieving heart."

Bountiful Harvest, making ready to take the family wash to the river, paused beside them. "She is strong, the Matron of the Plover clan," she said, "as Otter must learn to be. My sister should be grateful that her husband is alive, instead of mourning because his vision was destroyed. At least he returned a hero; he will be treated with respect even though"—she settled her basket more firmly, frowned down into it—"his hunting days have ended."

"They need time," Morning Song protested, "to accustom themselves to Deer Caller's being blind. Otter offers him comfort, which is surely all that anyone can do for him for now."

Bountiful Harvest looked at her niece. "Comforting is for infants," she told her. "If Otter Swimming wraps her husband in an excess of comfort, he shall become as much a child as the one in her womb.''

She followed her mother out of the longhouse without waiting for a response. That was as well. However much Morning Song and Bountiful Harvest continued to irritate one another—and probably they always would—Morning Song was forced to concede that there was truth in what she'd just said.

She turned a troubled face toward the pair who sat by Otter's hearth. Her mother-aunt was idle—a thing unusual in this longhouse, as in any other—for her hands were holding her husband's while she murmured consolingly to him. Except for mealtimes, when she spoon-fed him as though he were the child Bountiful Harvest had described, this was how she'd been occupying herself since the day the war party came home.

Impulsively Morning Song went over to them. ''Otter,'' she said, with studied urgency, ''there is a barrel of fish waiting to be laid out for drying, and I am afraid the day's sunlight will fade before I can fill the rack. But if you would help, the two of us could have it done by midmorning.''

Astonishment rearranged Otter's features. ''Morning Song, you know I cannot leave Deer Caller.''

''I am not near death, Otter, or even ill,'' her husband said, freeing one hand and patting hers. ''The bump on the back of my head has disappeared, and taken the pain with it.'' A grin—a genuine one, Morning Song thought—lit his broad face. ''And I am unlikely to run away while you are gone!''

Otter Swimming stared at him, struggling to cope with his jesting about a matter so serious, and Morning Song made good use of her stunned silence. ''You are perfectly aware, Deer Caller, that I hate handling dead fish,'' she said, summoning from somewhere a genuine-sounding laugh. ''Ordinarily you would be mocking me for my squeamishness. Which leads me to think you are encouraging Otter to help me so you will have the freedom to do just that!''

He brought himself to his feet before his wife could spring up to support him, and his grin widened. That he swung his head from side to side and ended pointing his face to the right of where she stood made Morning Song feel like weeping. Instead—and even though he could not see it—she returned his grin. ''If you should be gone when we get back,'' she teased, ''I shall have White Shadow pick up your scent. You would soon be found, Deer Caller!''

He shuffled the few paces to his bunk, grunted with satisfaction when his knees came up against its wooden frame, made a half turn, and lowered himself onto it. "I might as well stay here then," he replied, settling himself comfortably. And smiled once more.

Morning Song made the most of opportunity and urged Otter outside while she was still bemused. She chattered animatedly to keep her mother-aunt from dwelling on the fact that they had abandoned Deer Caller to a midnight-dark the brightest of fires could not relieve. "It was Hearth Tender who persuaded the early risers to go with her to the river to catch all these fish," she said as they began to wrestle slimy creatures out of the barrel and onto the drying frame. "They went before dawn because Hearth Tender said that it invigorates both body and mind to stand ankle deep in icy water." She shuddered dramatically.

Otter's worried face smoothed a little. "I know of someone who would not be persuaded to go, even were the water midsummer warm," she said.

"Which is why it falls to me to prepare the fish for drying," Morning Song said. "I thank you for helping me, Otter, for it is true that I detest both the smell and the feel of fish."

"If they were forest creatures, you would love them," her mother-aunt said, "stink or no." And she was smiling!

Morning Song sniffed at her fingers and wrinkled her nose. "I doubt that," she retorted, and delighted to see Otter smile a second time. "Deer Caller seems in good spirits," she ventured then.

Otter's face tightened. "It was for your sake only, I'm afraid, that he pretended to be," she said. She reached for another fish, let it dangle limp as her dark eyes welled with tears. "Oh, Morning Song, what is to become of him? To never again send an arrow soaring, or watch the plants grow tall in his tobacco patch. Or paddle a canoe into the sunrise, or join in the warriors' dances during our ceremonies. To never *once* be able to look upon the face of our child!" She choked on the last word, and Morning Song ran to hug her, to take the glassy-eyed smelt from her unresisting fingers and thump it back into the barrel.

"Otter," she said earnestly, "Deer Caller is blind, yes; and it is true that he shall never see your child. But he will be able to put out his hands and touch him; his ears shall be filled with his baby's cries and laughter and, one day, his words. Otter, he is alive, to hold his son or daughter once it has been born. If he'd been struck by one of those poisoned arrows Fierce Eagle told us about, he would have died without even knowing that he was to be a father. And died horribly, too. Now"—her voice rang with passion—"you need never watch him leave with another war party and have to wait and wonder if he shall come home again."

Otter's head was bowed; her niece could not read her expression. She was silent for so long that Morning Song began to wish she had followed Teller Of Legends's example and let Otter and Deer Caller deal privately with the woes that beset them. Was Otter angry that Morning Song had dared to say what she had? Or hurt because the younger woman was too insensitive to offer the solace she had every right to expect from her?

But there was neither anger nor sorrow in Otter's face when she looked up at last. Instead, a ghost of her old teasing grin trembled on her lips. "I can recall a time when I spoke bluntly to you when no one else would," she said. "You think to return the favor, I see." She pressed the hand Morning Song had rested on her shoulder. "You are right in what you say, and I feel shame that I needed to be reminded of these things. I suppose I, too, have been blind in a way, not to have seen them for myself."

"It is hard to see clearly when you are suffering," Morning Song said softly. "And I think you may be suffering even more than Deer Caller, Otter."

Otter shook her head vigorously. "No. Never think that. He is frightened, Morning Song, dreadfully frightened. He is a young man, and doomed to spend all the years left to him sitting with the elders, or drowsing in the sun, while his friends hunt bear and stag. It is a dismal path that stretches in front of him, Morning Song."

"He has always seemed the sort of man," Morning Song said slowly, "who thrives on challenge. I cannot see him spending what remains of his life drowsing in the sun, Otter."

Otter laughed suddenly. "Nor can I," she said, with surprise. "Perhaps I have been wrong to coddle him so much. Even now, he did not need my help to walk from our hearth to the bed, did he?" She leaned over the barrel once more, started tossing fish onto the rack. "I begin to think he has allowed me to hover over him only because he is too kind to send me away. I mean to ask him if that is so, and if it is"—she groped for the last of the smelt—"then tomorrow he must manage his meal without my help if he wants to eat!"

Her words were brave, and resolutely optimistic. But Morning Song knew that she was apprehensive still about what the future held for the husband she loved so much.

It seemed to Morning Song that the maidens chattered of nothing but men and marriage once Bear In The Sky moved his belongings into the Beaver longhouse, as Pumpkin Blossom had foretold. Small Brown Sparrow no longer kept secret her admiration for Hill

Climber. "He is slender and tall," she sighed, "and yet so strong. Why, he can wrestle anyone but Cloud Racer to the ground. And not even breathe heavily afterward!"

"*Both* of your brothers proved worthy opponents," Sun Descending said quickly. "If Fox Running had not stumbled, he would have won his match with Hill Climber." She flushed as everyone turned toward her, and bent hastily over the winter leggins she was stitching.

Meadow Brook—enjoying her new status as matron but more at ease still with the young women she had grown up with—chuckled. "You have just proved what I'd suspected, Sun Descending. Now we all know it is Fox Running you are interested in!"

Pumpkin Blossom finished her gratifying inspection of the boots she'd made for her little brother's fast-growing feet. The warrior she had marked as hers had apparently failed to attract any of her companions. They were fools, she thought, to settle for less than the best, but at least she would have no competition. "I am looking forward to the Midwinter Ceremony this year," she offered slyly.

"To the Naked Dance, you mean," Meadow Brook said, amused. "Well, I could not wait so long. Nor"—she smiled smugly—"did Bear In The Sky want to."

"It does seem dreadfully far away," Small Brown Sparrow said, looking toward the trees beyond the palisade as though willing them to shed the last of their leaves and make way for the white season.

Morning Song, who owned no patience with coyness and had no interest in this talk of marrying, was too restless to sit and listen further. She drifted away, trailed by the faithful White Shadow, and eyed the westering sun. There was enough of the day left to walk in the forest if she did not wander too far.

She crunched through heaps of fallen leaves to release the wonderful musk of autumn, but then failed to give the rising scent the attention it deserved. This was her thinking place, and there were matters she needed to ponder.

Both Deer Caller and Otter seemed happier now that Otter let him do what he could for himself. He'd begun to insist that he could handle such simple tasks as pounding corn into meal, and would not allow his awkwardness with mortar and pestle to be blamed on his blindness. "My big hands are to blame," he'd said ruefully. "My own fingers get in my way. But give me time, and I shall be as fine a cook as Bountiful Harvest!"

It was his nature to invite laughter, Morning Song reflected, and they were glad to oblige him. Yet she doubted—as did Otter, she was sure—that Deer Caller would be satisfied to occupy himself

forever with women's work. When it no longer proved a challenge
to him . . . well, that was a problem to be faced when it came.

But the scarcity of meat remained an ongoing problem. Morning
Song named it tactless that Bountiful Harvest mentioned it so often,
but it was true that what they had left of Deer Caller's last kill would
soon be gone. And a steady diet of unseasoned vegetables would
do little to tempt appetites.

White Shadow interrupted her thoughts with a bark. Morning
Song glanced up, and laughed; they had come to her cave, and she
had not even noticed. "It has been awhile since we've been here,"
she agreed, ruffling the silky fur between Shadow's ears. "Shall
we go inside, you and I?"

The slithered through the narrow cleft, blinked in the gloom of
the interior. Nothing had been disturbed, Morning Song saw when
her vision had sharpened. There were her lance, her bow, the clutch
of arrows.

She raised up so suddenly that she bumped her head on the cave's
low roof, but she was too excited even to rub the sore spot.
"Shadow," she said, "there is no need for the Turtle clan to depend
upon the generosity of others for meat, and no need for Deer Caller
to have his helplessness constantly recalled to him this way! I can
shoot an arrow as straight as any man in the village, and I am quick
with my lance, too."

She seized her bow and arrows, and pushed them ahead of her
out of the cave. Then she spoke sternly to her dog. "Shadow, if
you wish to come with me while I hunt, you must be help and not
hindrance. Walk at my heels—and do not bark, whatever you see
or scent."

He wagged his tail, and his alert brown eyes seemed to promise
that he understood; but in the end she spent some time rehearsing
him in the art of staying one pace behind her before she dared set
out in search of game.

A rabbit was the first animal she tried for, and she had Shadow
to thank for the opportunity. He darted suddenly from the path and
flushed one of the long-eared, heavy-rumped animals out of the
scraggly brush that bordered it. Morning Song—unprepared for
such active assistance—was slow to respond, and the rabbit scuttled
to safety before she had properly nocked an arrow.

"From now on, I'll keep one at the ready," she told her proud
dog.

Their next available prey, a squirrel, obligingly announced himself by his chittering. But he scurried along the branch when he
saw her raise her bow, and her arrow went wide of the mark. "It

is more difficult than I'd thought, to hit something that moves so fast," she muttered, and resolved to aim ahead of her quarry when she shot again.

By the time the sun's face was half hidden by the distant mountains, Morning Song had succeeded in missing a second squirrel, a lumbering porcupine, a muskrat, and two plump quail raised by her companion. Her disappointment was great, but she would not be daunted.

"I have learned to hit any target I set for myself," she said stoutly. "With practice, I shall learn to shoot just as true when my target wears fur or feathers and cannot be counted on to be still."

Confidence, as if somehow made twin to White Shadow, walked with her all the way home.

Chapter 14

A thin gray spiral rose from the Plover clan's cooking fire and merged with the autumn haze that seeped languidly into the longhouse. "When I saw a pumpkin moon last night, I knew warm weather would visit us once more," Sweet Maple said. "It is good, to have summer return like this."

Se-A-Wi was not as sanguine as his wife. "The hunters tell me that the bark has thickened where trees are exposed to the north. And squirrels set their nests lower than usual during the last green season."

Teller Of Legends nodded soberly. The grass in the meadow had been uncommonly green during the summer, too. "When the cold returns, it will be harsh," she agreed. "I am grateful that the men are rested from the fighting and ready to hunt again. A bitter winter always means the disappearance of most of the animals whose flesh we eat." She looked to Sweet Maple. "Your grandson will use your brother's bow when he hunts?"

Her friend nodded serenely; it no longer hurt to speak of Far Seer. It had troubled her, though, that his weapons could not be passed on to Deer Caller, as the laws of inheritance dictated. She'd hesitated to raise the question of their disposition with her nephew;

his blindness brought with it enough other concerns to be dealt with. "It was kind of you to speak to Otter Swimming. Deer Caller's suggestion that I give Far Seer's possessions to Hill Climber pleased my grandson. Both of us are grateful to Deer Caller, and to you and your daughter also."

Teller Of Legends smiled to acknowledge an appreciation she knew was heartfelt.

"I can no longer hunt, or go to war," Deer Caller had said bluntly, "which means that I may outlive my nephew. And with him carrying the weapons my uncle once used, the spirit of Far Seer will be persuaded to accompany any war band leaving our village."

She sighed. A bitter winter, should all the signs be right, would at least make war and raiding impractical. For this the Turtle clan's Matron was thankful. The women could be free for a while of their greatest worry.

"Hill Climber can become familiar with Far Seer's bow while he hunts, which is good," Se-A-Wi commented. "No man should take into battle a weapon that has not come to feel like an extension of his arm." The Sachem's eyes were brooding, and his sister wondered if he was remembering the days when he had gone to war. But his next words were on another matter.

"Young Cloud Racer put a question to Fierce Eagle that has lodged itself in my mind," he said. "Would our foray into Erie country have ended so disastrously if the other nations of the Iroquois had sent war bands to join with ours? In the old days, he said—and his words were truth—no tribe went to war without the sanction of the Confederation." Se-A-Wi's mouth relaxed as he chuckled. "At first, Fierce Eagle was upset; he supposed the boy was questioning his wisdom. But when Cloud Racer explained further—which was surprising; *that* one never uses two words where one will serve—he realized no insult was meant. The lad was merely asking why the Iroquois League no longer exercises much control over our Five Nations."

His gnarled fingers caressed the bowl of his pipe. "Fierce Eagle did not know what to tell him, nor do I. But we cannot deny what Cloud Racer sees for himself: It is commonplace now for one tribe to take to the warpath without consulting or advising the others. I have even heard of Iroquois going against Iroquois, when warriors make raids upon neighboring villages. Doubtless these reports are exaggerated by youths hungering for glory. Still, it is contrary to the laws laid down by our Confederation's founders."

"Why do we ignore these laws?" his sister asked quietly.

Se-A-Wi shrugged. "It began before our time, this wandering from the path our ancestors pledged to follow. Perhaps it was because each of the Five Nations grew larger. Perhaps it happened because there will always be differences between one tribe and another, League or no, and some may have seemed impossible to settle. Bad decisions might have been made in the Great Council, even quite innocently; then resentment would have kept some Sachems from bringing other matters to the Confederation for resolution. Who can say?" He reached for a bit of kindling to light his pipe. "You had better ask young Cloud Racer. He is a thinker, that one, as well as a fine warrior, and this is a matter he has apparently given much thought to."

"It is also possible," Teller Of Legends replied astringently, "that our Councilors have simply suspended their vigilance over the years." She was more disturbed than her brother by the issue Cloud Racer had raised, and meant him to know that she was. If ancient laws were suffering erosion, then tradition—which Teller Of Legends deemed as staunch a supporter of the Iroquois as the sister crops of corn, beans, and maize—would soon be sapped of strength. And the effect of such a thing on the People of the Longhouse would prove infinitely more ruinous than any war against the Erie ever could!

Se-A-Wi puffed until the tobacco glowed, took his pipe from his mouth. "When the League was formed," he reminded her patiently, "the Iroquois did not even know that the *Onondio* existed. Now, we have the Frenchman at our back, the Dutch at our feet, and the Englishman beginning to press against our side. In the beginning, trade was uncomplicated; one tribe exchanged goods with another, who exchanged goods with a more distant one, until all of us owned whatever was needed, and were satisfied. Now the white man pits one nation against another, one tribe against another, even one village against another, so that his profit may increase." He tapped out his pipe against a hearthstone. "*Profit* was a word we did not know, before the Europeans came. Now there are villages that must depend upon profit from trading merely to survive! We deal with what is, Teller Of Legends, and not with what was. The old ways did nothing to prepare us for the problems we face today."

"But do all Five Nations cooperate in solving these new problems?" his sister demanded. "Or do tribal leaders mostly make decisions as the need arises, without first meeting in the Great Council?"

Se-A-Wi unfolded his legs and stood up. "We do not meet in

Confederation as frequently as we should," he conceded. "Nor do
we always discuss soon enough the things that affect all of us. The
trader Bree-And's insistence that the Iroquois need guns was never
debated, I know. As a result, some villages have been persuaded
to their usefulness; some—like ours—have not. Yet we should be
in agreement, one way or the other. These are subjects I will introduce at our next Great Council, Teller Of Legends. You have my
promise."

Sweet Maple watched her husband leave the lodge. "Where
would they be, without women to guide them?" she murmured
affectionately, then settled herself for more entertaining conversation. She was glad it was Teller Of Legends and not Sweet Maple
who was Chief Matron of the village. To have to monitor the actions
of the Councilors was a responsibility she would be ill-suited for.
"Did you know," she said, leaning toward her friend and beaming,
"that the daughter of Rain Singing wants my grandson for her
husband?"

Teller Of Legends made concerted effort to focus her mind on
her friend's idle chatter. "Do they mean to marry soon?" she asked
politely.

"Not until after Midwinter," Sweet Maple said. "But that is not
so long, is it? And what of your oldest granddaughters? Are either
of them discussing marriage?"

"According to Bountiful Harvest, Pumpkin Blossom is eager for
it," Teller Of Legends replied absently.

"And Morning Song? Will she wed when her cousin does?"

Teller Of Legends's whole attention was suddenly fixed on the
subject Sweet Maple had introduced. "She seems to have no interest in taking a husband as yet," she said slowly. "Which is one of
the reasons I have put off telling her about the arrangements her
mother made for her. I was not happy about them from the start;
indeed, I tried hard to persuade Summer Maize there was no need
for her to do such a thing."

Sweet Maple nodded soberly. "I know, too, that you agreed
in the end because you could not bear to see your dying daughter
made distraught. You did as any mother would do in like circumstances."

"And now I must speak with my granddaughter and see that
Summer Maize's wishes are carried out," her companion said
heavily. "How I felt about the matter then, how I feel now, is
unimportant. But I confess, old friend, that the talk I will soon be
having with Morning Song is not one I am looking forward to."

The sun was a soft golden disc, the air shimmered and hovered visibly on the horizon. "Today, I shall make a kill," Morning Song vowed. White Shadow dutifully wagged his tail. "On such a glorious day," his mistress continued, "my *orenda* will be stronger than ever. It will summon all the spirits of the forest to direct my arrows."

Her confident grin faltered as she spoke of her *orenda*. It had been so long since her Vision Quest, yet not a single spirit had ever visited her in dreams. Why she should be shunned was a mystery Morning Song tried not to dwell on, but she could not forget that the spirit who spawned her vision seemed to want no further communion with her.

"It is unfair as well as perplexing," she informed her dog, who only wagged his tail again. She plodded disconsolately through a drift of rust-colored leaves. Could the fault be in her? she wondered. Perhaps she did not know how to open herself to a dream.

She halted abruptly, and Shadow barreled into her. "There are other ways in which the spirits may communicate with us," she murmured, patting her confused companion. "The day that the war band returned . . ." Her fine-drawn brows met in a frown. When the ritual of torture began, and she had feared that, once again, she might dishonor herself and her clan by cringing from it . . . what of the voice that told her how to overcome her aversion, that instructed her to lift her knife and bury it haft deep in the flesh of the Erie captive?

That voice could only have belonged to her spirit guide! Who but a spirit could prod Morning Song to an act she would never have committed otherwise?

Yet to think about that day recalled the red, red blood that had gushed from the wound she'd made, the blood she fancied she could still see traces of on the blade she'd vigorously cleaned. She tensed the muscles of her stomach to thwart an onset of nausea.

"I will think of something else," she told herself firmly. But spirits, she discovered, are not so lightly brushed aside. The tree she stood near chose that moment to give up one of its few remaining leaves, and it fluttered down in front of Morning Song's face. There was no wind; it wafted on the merest breath of autumn air, and her hand reached out and arrested its leisurely descent.

It was, of course, a maple leaf, in shape and color identical to the one she kept in her pouch. As she had done with the original, she spread it upon her palm, traced its scalloped edges with a contemplative forefinger, silently begged it to reveal the message it surely carried. But like the crimson leaf the spirit had given her during her Vision Quest, the one she held now remained mute.

She tilted her hand, let it slip from her open palm and resume its lazy journey to the ground. It had been a reminder only of the leaf she already possessed, a way of chiding her because she had not divined what that spirit-gift had been intended to convey.

Shadow whined pleadingly, and she made herself walk on. But her thoughts spiraled backward as she went, backward in time until they'd fixed on the final day of her quest and summoned up images of the river that had wound below the hill, the girl peering down into it, the aberrant sun, those animals that had freed themselves from a watery prison.

Joy garlanded her soul with rainbows as one part of her vision became clear as morning dew. They had been *game* animals that erupted from the river that day—deer and panther and beaver and wolf. Which must mean that her spirit guide had foreseen a time when the Turtle clan would have no man able to provide flesh for the cooking pot. It had been a precursory sanctioning of Morning Song's hunting, that vision of hers!

The revelation removed from Morning Song's path an obstacle she'd scarcely realized was there. She had never been quite comfortable defying tradition, and her disquiet—though she'd refused to acknowledge it to herself—had surely kept her from bringing down the prey she came into the forest to track.

She slowed her pace, and the single thick braid she'd lately taken to wearing ceased to bounce against her narrow back. White Shadow, familiar with the ritual of the stalk and delighted to be moving deeper into the woods, prepared himself to warn his mistress should he pick up a scent she'd want to know about.

Morning Song's tread was as nearly soundless as her dog's; she held her bow in one hand, gripped a new-fletched arrow in the other. Her eyes examined the ground she walked on, the tangled yellow thicket on either side, the trees whose virtually leafless branches afforded little concealment to creatures fond of climbing. Her ears made ready to remark the snapping of the frailest twig, the stealthiest rustle in the brush, the softest of footfalls on the mulch-cushioned ground.

But her dog's tensing and the flaring of his sensitive nostrils first alerted her. She went down on one knee beside him, brushed tattered leaves and brown pine needles from a patch of earth. Shadow lowered himself to his haunches and kept a watchful silence as she studied the pawprint pressed into a bit of damp soil.

A lynx, and a sizeable one, had walked here recently. She came erect slowly, let her gaze roam the area to her right, search bedraggled bushes, trace the limbs forking from the trunks of skeletal trees. Suddenly she stiffened, retreated a step so that a young spruce stood between her and a wide-spreading oak whose shriveled leaves would cling stubbornly until new growth supplanted them. On one of its lower branches, stretched to invite the kiss of the warmth-giving sun, lay the spotted gray cat she was looking for. The eyes in his whiskered face were slits; the languorous length of him testified to the fact that he slept.

A tidal wave of gratitude almost diluted the coldness of purpose Morning Song needed to make the kill. And this was a kill the spirits had led her to! She inhaled cautiously, mutely begged forgiveness of the beast's *orenda* for what hers required, and nocked the arrow she'd been clutching. Then she raised her bow and moved warily away from the evergreen. She drew back the arrow, sighted, and prepared to shoot.

With a snarl, the lynx was on his feet and staring at her. She had made no noise; instinct alone had warned him of danger. In the next heartbeat he would leap to the ground and vanish!

Morning Song slackened her tight-curved fingers, sent her arrow flying. Would it be quick enough? Had her aim been true?

It was no leap that took the huge cat to the ground, but a dead-weight fall. The lynx's slanted eyes had glazed before Morning Song could fight her way through thorny vines and pull the feathered death-dealer from his neck. She knelt beside her first kill and marveled at the size of him. His fur was long and silky, too. She would be taking home to her family more than just food; so fine a pelt as this would allow them to barter for other things they needed as well.

Pride as much as determination enabled her to sling the heavy cat across her shoulders and, with Shadow prancing excitedly ahead of her, tramp back to the village without once pausing to rest.

"I suppose it was witless to expect you might change merely because you have grown up, Morning Song," Bountiful Harvest sniffed. "You shall be either laughed at or scorned, when the rest of the village hears. I begin to think you relish being the subject of gossip."

Fish Jumping, curious as any four-year-old, reached down a stubby finger to prod the lynx's tufted ear. Pumpkin Blossom yanked him back. "Truly, Morning Song," she said in a tone of genuine grievance, "no warrior will want to come as husband to this lodge! It would demean him to live where there is a maiden who does not know the difference between man's work and woman's. Do you think to go raiding next?"

Ordinarily Day Greeter rather admired Morning Song's courage, although she knew better than to say so. But because she would be a maid herself before many more seasons passed, her round face betrayed alarm at her sister's words.

"I know it is not a woman's place to hunt," Morning Song said, herself more than a little exasperated. "But you, Bountiful Harvest, have been fretting about having a dependable source of meat, and this is not a problem that will solve itself. I was only—"

"Oh, Morning Song! How could you have been so uncaring?" The anguished cry came from Otter Swimming, and the younger woman flinched. "You took no thought for how Deer Caller would feel when you decided to do this; you stand here now and speak words that must pierce his heart as he hears them."

Deer Caller murmured something Morning Song could not make out, and his wife returned hurriedly to his side. But her reproach lingered on the air and stung more fiercely than any criticism Bountiful Harvest could unleash.

Morning Song swung around to look at her grandmother. "And you, Teller Of Legends? Will you, too, censure me for trying to help my family?"

Hearth Tender, sitting in the shadows beyond her mother's hearth, replied to this. "I may not be wholly surprised by your actions, Morning Song," she said mildly. "But I am astonished that you would speak to your grandmother so discourteously."

Morning Song bowed her head. "I am sorry," she said wearily, and for the first time noticed the ache in her shoulders. The lynx's carcass had been more of a burden than she'd realized. "I only want *somebody* to understand that I mean no disrespect to anyone, that I did not intend to cause hurt to anyone, or to invite anyone's anger." She crossed to where Hearth Tender sat, crouched before her. "And the vision that came to me during my quest," she said rapidly, "I have come to see a little of what it meant." She described the flash of insight she'd had, and waited for the Faithkeeper to nod, to agree that Morning Song had been directed by her spirit guide to hunt.

But she did not. "I have told you," she said heavily, "that only the person to whom it was sent can properly interpret a vision. I said also that one ought not shape conclusions rashly. And never, never should we attempt to alter a vision to make it say what we would like it to say. It is possible that the animal faces you saw represented the forest creatures marked by the Maker Of Life as prey for our people. But whether it meant also that you are to hunt them is something I do not know." Her eyes were somber; she brimmed with sympathy for her niece, yet could not compromise truth as she perceived it.

"I know nothing of hunting," Teller Of Legends mused aloud. "Still, I imagine it is not easy to bring down an animal as fleet as a lynx." Hope stirred briefly in Morning Song. "However," the old woman went on, "we all know that the Turtle clan will not starve so long as our fields continue fertile." She inclined her head toward Bountiful Harvest. "You expressed concern, and more than once, because we might lack sufficient meat to flavor your excellent stews. Now you seem more concerned about gossipers than about a scarcity of animal flesh. Either might be named a problem, but neither is cause for distress."

She shifted her gaze to Pumpkin Blossom, studied the perfect cast of features that earned her the right to be called beautiful. "No maid as lovely as you need fear that any warrior will hesitate to accept an offer of marriage, even if your cousin will not confine herself to what you label *woman's work*. And you may rest content that no young man shall ever regard Morning Song as either comrade or competitor."

Day Greeter giggled, and Bountiful Harvest frowned.

Teller Of Legends stole a moment to flash a smile at her youngest granddaughter. If the rest had also taken her byway into levity, they might be ready to see that this situation was less than calamitous. "You are all aware that it is against custom to forbid anyone to do what he or she sincerely believes he must, particularly when it may be that some form of spirit guidance encourages him."

Bountiful Harvest frowned again, more darkly. "How are we showing proper respect for custom if, at every turn, we approve those who are headstrong enough, or selfish enough, to flout it? And what will become of the Longhouse People when custom is no longer respected?"

"I have always respected custom," her mother said blandly, "and always shall. I do not slight it now. What I find disturbing—and I know this disturbs Morning Song as well—is that she failed to consider how Deer Caller might be affected by her actions."

There was a small silence. Then Deer Caller stood up and nodded in the direction of Teller Of Legends's voice. "I can never hunt again," he said quietly. "I have accepted this, so how can it dishonor me if someone else brings meat to the lodge? Indeed, I am grateful that you let me stay here with my wife, when the custom you mentioned permits you to send me away now that I can no longer provide you with meat or serve as a warrior." He spread his hands. "It is not my place to say whether Morning Song should hunt or not. But"—his mouth twitched at the corners—"I long to know what weapon she used to bring down that lynx!"

Now there was a chorus of laughter, and it fell pleasantly on Teller Of Legends's ears. Deer Caller was important to this clan, blind or no, and she hoped he understood that.

"It was your old bow that I used," Morning Song said, surprise embroidering her voice. "But the arrows you once gave me I have had to replace."

"You made the new ones yourself?" Deer Caller's interest sharpened.

"I did. They are not nearly so fine as the ones I had from you, however."

"May I see one?"

There was another silence, more prolonged and more uncomfortable. Then, without speaking, Morning Song selected one of the arrows she had tossed on her bunk and put it into his hands.

His fingers measured the length of it, investigated the flint tip gingerly, traced the fletching at its opposite end. "Luck as much as skill was with you today, Morning Song," he said gravely. "You have done well shaping your arrows, but you need to learn more about balance."

Otter Swimming rose abruptly and went to stand before Morning Song. "I should not have spoken to you as I did," she said. "It was I who was thoughtless, and not you. I hope you will forgive me, Morning Song."

In response, Morning Song hugged her. "You need not ask forgiveness for worrying about your husband, Otter. And it was thoughtless of me not to be concerned for his feelings." They both looked to where Deer Caller, who had resumed his seat, was trying the strength of the arrow he held and testing how securely the point was attached to it. "He is a remarkable man, Otter," she finished softly.

"As I have known from the beginning," her mother-aunt said. "It bothers him still that he cannot in some way provide for us, and I suspect it always will. But he does not let this make him bitter."

"It seems to me," Bountiful Harvest said firmly, "that we have forgotten what is at stake here. If my niece means to go on bringing shame on us by pretending to be a man, then I should at least expect her to prepare us for each new outrage she plans—before the entire village hears of it."

Teller Of Legends sighed. "Morning Song will do as she feels she must. But she is advised to be circumspect, and to remember that no lodge needs an *over*abundance of meat. In any event, most of her time will be taken up by the chores that all of us share in; that is her primary obligation to the family.'' She looked about her. "There is work that we ought to be doing right now, if I am not mistaken,'' she added pointedly.

No one needed telling a second time. Otter and Morning Song, still chatting amiably, took up the robes that required airing and went out together. Hearth Tender asked Day Greeter's help with the winnowing basket she was making. And young Fish Jumping sidled over to Deer Caller's bunk to beg another tale about some raid he'd been on, and to be assured that one day the son of Bountiful Harvest would be recognized as a fearless warrior.

Only Bountiful Harvest did not immediately return to the task she'd been absorbed in. "Always, Morning Song is allowed to go her own way,'' she said to her mother, and it was sorrow rather than anger that ruled her face. "Teller Of Legends, it is not easy for me to say this, but you are inclined to favor her, just as you once did her mother.''

This, Teller Of Legends had not been expecting, and the shock of it fettered her tongue.

"It is true,'' Bountiful Harvest persisted, reading accurately the disbelief in her mother's eyes. "When we were young, it was Summer Maize you demanded the least of, Summer Maize you indulged. She enjoyed your affection and approval even when they were not deserved. And now you have turned the same benevolence upon her daughter. I know that must distress and bewilder my daughters, for all that they have said nothing about it.''

These charges were couched in a moderate tone that only emphasized the passion behind them. "Bountiful Harvest,'' her mother said carefully, "I had no idea that you thought this of me. And I cannot think what I might have said or done to make you doubt that I loved you as much as I loved your sister. I have always loved all of my daughters, just as I love all of my grandchildren. A mother's affection, or a grandmother's, expands as her family grows. It embraces everyone. Surely with three children of your own you have come to know this.''

"I did not question your love for me,'' Bountiful Harvest said, "and I do not question that you love the grandchildren I have given you. But you certainly show it differently, Teller Of Legends. I remember how often you would praise Summer Maize when she had mastered one small skill or another, the way you took the time to cuddle her when she failed in what she tried to do. You found reasons to excuse her whenever that happened. Just as you find excuses for Morning Song when—usually through her own misguided efforts—something goes wrong for her.''

"Has it never occurred to you," Teller Of Legends said softly, "that Summer Maize suffered because she never ceased comparing herself with the older sister she thought perfect in every way?''

"That makes no sense," Bountiful Harvest said impatiently. "There is no one who is perfect, Mother.''

Teller Of Legends smiled sadly. "I did not call you perfect, Bountiful Harvest, but only said that Summer Maize thought you were. And I could never have persuaded her otherwise. So I made much of her accomplishments and tried to console her whenever she felt she had fallen short of the daunting example you constantly set for her. It was not always easy to make her see that she was as special in her way as you were in yours, and no doubt I did take more time with her while trying to.'' She chuckled. "I even attempted to point out your faults, but your sister stubbornly refused to acknowledge that any existed!''

Bountiful Harvest was momentarily diverted. "I never thought of my sister as stubborn," she exclaimed. "I did not see her as strong enough to be willful.''

"Which means that your image of her was as distorted as hers was of you," her mother said dryly. "In her own fashion, Summer Maize was as obstinate as my other daughters are.''

"And as you have always been," Bountiful Harvest declared, and smiled. The smile faded quickly, to Teller Of Legends' regret. "And I suppose stubbornness causes Morning Song to act without regard for other people's feelings or opinions. This is behavior that ought to be discouraged, however, whatever its cause.''

"It is hardly surprising that Morning Song possesses a quality all of us own, to some degree," the Matron of the Turtle clan said. "Her brand of stubbornness, if not its direction, is much like yours, Bountiful Harvest; like you, she will not be easily discouraged from any course she sets out on. And this is not the only way she resembles you.''

Bountiful Harvest's horrified expression was twin to the one Morning Song had worn on the day Teller Of Legends said a similar thing to her. The old woman hid a smile. "Like you, she secretly yearns to be praised when she has succeeded in something most women would not even think to attempt. Morning Song was hurt when we did not applaud her skill as a hunter, but rather than say that she was, she took refuge in anger. What neither of you realizes is that the rest of us have come to accept that both of you are capable of the extraordinary. It seems to us that you cannot help but know that you are; to offer you praise would be as purposeless as pouring green dye upon the grass of midsummer.''

"But I would never go beyond the bounds of what is proper,'' Bountiful Harvest said fiercely. "Never!"

Teller Of Legends laughed. "In this, the two of you *are* different. But you shall always go as far as you might within those limits, Bountiful Harvest. And as you are clever, often you go far indeed.''

Her daughter digested this quietly, and the process was aided by an inner glow of satisfaction. At long last, Teller Of Legends had paid tribute to Bountiful Harvest's achievements, had even named them *extraordinary*. To extend the compliment to include Morning Song was shortsighted of her. But that young woman, if unrestrained, would one day disillusion even her doting grandmother. "I fail to see how my niece and I are at all alike, then,'' she said at last. "And I still feel that she will bring disgrace on herself, and on us, if she persists in hunting wild beasts.''

"These excursions will end when she and Pumpkin Blossom wed,'' her mother said lightly. "Which, in the natural order of things, will be soon. This is why I saw so little cause for concern when my granddaughter brought home that lynx you and I should be attending to.''

"Morning Song herself should be skinning and gutting it,'' Bountiful Harvest pronounced grimly, but there was no real rancor behind her words. What Teller Of Legends had said was true: When the Turtle lodge had welcomed new hunter-warriors, Morning Song would cease this foolishness. Until then, they would simply have to endure.

Her mother, however, had been reminded of something that had been weighing heavily on her mind: It was time for her to have that talk with Morning Song. In truth, she thought guiltily, it was *past* time that she did.

Before Teller of Legends found her opportunity, it was evening, an evening so serenely lavender-gray that she was glad of a reason to be outside. "The ground is comfortably warm still,'' she observed, seating herself beside her granddaughter.

"By the time Grandmother Moon shows her face, we shall be shivering,'' Morning Song predicted.

"We will not be out here as long as that,'' Teller Of Legends replied. "I only want to talk with you a little.''

Morning Song sighed. Now she would be treated to the gentle condemnation she had known was coming. She appreciated that

Teller Of Legends had not chided her in front of the others, and would tell her so, after her grandmother had finished speaking.

"When a girl of the Longhouse People passes into womanhood," her grandmother began, "certain things are expected of her. She begins to work as hard as any matron. She learns to take pride in this work, and she gladly assumes new responsibilities."

Morning Song listened courteously.

"Her greatest responsibility," the old woman said, turning her head to be sure she had her granddaughter's undivided attention, "to both herself and her family, is to marry and bear children who shall one day bring honor to the clan."

Morning Song was quick to swallow an involuntary exclamation. Her astonishment was so great, however, that it revealed itself in an almost comical disarrangement of her features.

Teller Of Legends chuckled. "I shall not ask what you had thought I would discuss," she told her, "since I can guess. Some traditions may be bent a trifle without anyone coming to harm, I suppose. But what I am speaking of now is not one of them, Morning Song." She was serious again, and her granddaughter decided not to say what she was moved to say. Not yet. "You know, of course, that your cousin plans to marry, even if she has not revealed which of our warriors she has chosen."

Except to her mother, Morning Song thought. Pumpkin Blossom would make no decision that was not sanctioned by Bountiful Harvest.

"Am I right in thinking you have not yet made a choice?" Teller Of Legends asked, and there was in her voice an urgency Morning Song could see no reason for.

"I have not," she said emphatically.

Her grandmother's sigh was one of relief. She had assumed as much, from all the signs, but it was good to have it confirmed. "Then I need not fret that I've delayed a little about telling you something you had a right to know when first you became a maid. I could not bring myself to do so then because it was plain to everyone that you were not exactly elated to find yourself on the threshold of womanhood."

Despite the curiosity Teller Of Legends's words had aroused in her, Morning Song grinned. That was certainly true!

Her grandmother permitted herself an answering grin; then she sobered. "We can no longer close our eyes to the fact that you *are* a young woman, however. And a young woman of marriageable age. So I will tell you now that your mother, before she died, was understandably concerned for your future. She regretted her years

with the Frenchman, I think—and all the more so because, by staying with him, she deprived you of the kind of childhood you were
entitled to. She was determined to do what she could to make
certain you would never again be cheated of your birthright. Summer Maize would not let herself die until she had assured you a
place with us, a secure place for both the child you were then, and
for the woman you would become."

Morning Song was perplexed. "Surely you had already showed
her that you welcomed me, and would be willing to care for me,
Teller Of Legends."

The old woman nodded. "Nor did she need telling, so far as this
went. It was Morning Song the woman she worried most about."
She paused briefly, drew impassiveness round her like a cloak; what
was done, was done, and perhaps it was all for the best. "Possibly
she feared that you might make the same mistake she had made in
choosing a husband. I do not know. But to ensure that this could
never happen, and that you would remain always in this village,
Summer Maize invoked an ancient custom, one that has fallen into
disuse over the years. She made a marriage treaty for you, even
though you were scarcely five summers old."

Morning Song's pulses began to race; perspiration beaded her
forehead. "With whom was this treaty made, Grandmother?" she
asked faintly.

"With the Chief Matron of the Pigeonhawk lodge," Teller Of
Legends said evenly. "She and Owl Crying agreed that, when you
had grown, you would wed Owl Crying's son. You are promised to
Stag Leaping, Morning Song, and he is pledged to you."

Chapter 15

⟸ ⟹

"No," Morning Song said. "No, Grandmother. You cannot
mean that you expect me to take Stag Leaping for my husband."
Her throat had constricted as though her clenched hands had
wrapped themselves around it, and her voice was a rasp.

Teller Of Legends was grateful for the thickening dusk. "Your
mother had only your happiness in mind, Morning Song," she said.

"She wanted to be sure that, one day, her daughter would be raising children of her own in the Turtle longhouse."

"But I will never leave here," the young woman cried. "You know that, Teller Of Legends. And the spirit of Summer Maize must know it, too. It is not necessary for me to marry to prove that I will live forever in our lodge."

"A promise made on your behalf must be honored as though you had shaped the vow with your own lips, Morning Song," the old woman said. "And, as I have said, it is your duty as an Iroquois woman to marry and bear children."

"Hearth Tender has never wed," Morning Song pointed out. "Nor has Otter's friend, Tree Reaching Up."

"My oldest daughter was aware even as a girl that she was meant to divide her time between this world and the spirit world. Because of that, she felt it would be unfair of her to take a husband. As for Tree Reaching Up, she had planned to marry, but the warrior she chose was slain during a raid on a Huron village. Grief kept her from asking someone else, and when she recovered from it, all our warriors had been spoken for." She shrugged philosophically. "Such things happen, and can only be endured. But rare indeed is the woman who never marries, Morning Song. And you are not destined to be one of them."

"Grandmother," Morning Song said desperately, "if I must take a husband—eventually—then I must. But I cannot marry Stag Leaping!"

Teller Of Legends smiled; the girl had taken a step forward from saying that she *never* wished to marry. "Morning Song, I know you have resented the son of Owl Crying ever since he nearly thwarted your scheme to save White Shadow from being sacrificed. But you are old enough now to understand that he had both the right and the duty to do what he did. To continue to feel antagonism over it does you no credit. According to Fierce Eagle, Stag Leaping has acquitted himself honorably in battle. He is a well-favored man, and carries himself with pride. These are things Summer Maize could not have predicted, so you may consider yourself fortunate that it is not a timid rabbit of a man with a squint that you are promised to!"

Teller Of Legends would not treat this matter so lightly if she knew about the time Stag Leaping had tried to force himself on Morning Song! Yet the young woman could not bring herself to speak of this. Not now. Her grandmother would ask why she'd said nothing before and—should the tale be repeated within the longhouse—Bountiful Harvest would insist that if Morning Song did not actually lie she was at least exaggerating the incident.

She shuddered with the remembering. Stag Leaping's fingers on her exposed breasts had filled her with revulsion; his bruising embrace was a prison she would never willingly return to; and what he had been meaning to do to her—before Shadow changed his mind for him—was a thing Morning Song would never, ever, allow!

Briefly she recalled Bountiful Harvest describing the coupling that is necessary to produce children. Morning Song had been appalled that this was so like the seasonal rutting of beasts. To suffer such degradation from a hot-eyed, rough-handed Stag Leaping was—was unthinkable! "Grandmother," she said, "there must be a way the treaty can be put aside. If you were to suggest this to Owl Crying, surely she would not object? She has always disapproved of me, as you know. Well"—she turned up her hands—"many of the clan Matrons have, at one time or another; but Owl Crying more often than most, I think. And all the women know that she dotes on her son; she will want the best of the maidens for Stag Leaping, Grandmother. And I am far from that. Why, she probably hopes that you have forgotten all about the marriage treaty, and will be glad to do the same."

Teller Of Legends looked into the indistinct oval that was her granddaughter's face. The girl had never taken kindly to any form of coercion, had always guarded fiercely her right to choose. Still, however unpleasant the walk would be for her, she must in this instance be led firmly along the path to acceptance. "Morning Song, Owl Crying is an honorable woman; she will never renege on a contract she agreed to. What you propose is that we insult both the Pigeonhawk clan and the spirit of my daughter. I will have no part in doing this, and Owl Crying will not. Nor shall you." She lifted herself from ground that was rapidly absorbing the night's chill. "I am afraid you must accustom yourself to the idea of marrying, my dear. And prepare to bake bride cakes to be delivered to Stag Leaping's mother."

The next day's sun had not yet risen when—without her bow this time, for she was too troubled to concentrate on hunting—Morning Song slipped away from the lodge and made for the woods. A sleepy Shadow tagged along, pausing twice to stretch and yawn before he shook himself fully awake.

The early mists thinned as they trudged along, and by the time they reached the forest only isolated strands remained to writhe around a tree trunk here, cocoon a trailing bit of shrubbery there.

The stillness was absolute, and they took pains not to disrupt it, to leave the severing of this remnant of night to the songbirds whose province it was.

For once, though, Morning Song scarcely noticed the splendid chorale. "I must find a way," she muttered, heedless of the shower of melody that fell around her. "But what I do must not distress my grandmother, or give Owl Crying cause for grievance, or allow anyone to think I lack respect for what is right and proper."

Shadow stopped to nose at a woolly caterpillar humping over a fallen leaf. His mistress tramped on. "Teller Of Legends knows I am reluctant, but she is determined to abide by my mother's wishes." Sun-glow seeped around the distant hills and trickled over the translucent leaves that clung stubbornly to birch and oak; Morning Song was blind to it. "She shall tell the others about the marriage treaty, and they will be delighted." She kicked savagely at a half-buried log, and a covey of agitated beetles abandoned it. "If I do not want to listen overlong to their comments and advice—for Bountiful Harvest can be depended upon to offer me *that*—then I must act soon. Only . . . I cannot think what to do!"

She lifted her face and a finger of sunshine caressed it. It shall be another warm day, she thought vaguely. How I wish I were free to enjoy it.

But she was not. She skirted a marshy spot carpeted with drowned moss, avoided a scattering of boulders that ringed a gentle rise spotted with chubby firs. On impulse, she turned back and climbed to the top of the mound and found a drift of spongy needles to sit on. Her dog followed her up, collapsed beside her, and rested his head in her lap.

"It is too lovely a day to spend wrestling with problems I cannot solve," she sighed, stroking him absently. The slight eminence she was perched on allowed her to glimpse, between the trees, a lavender haze edging the muted blue of the sky. Birds winged lazily overhead, or twittered contentedly as they scratched for grubs, and intermittent rustlings betrayed the furry creatures that followed their own twisting trails through the brush.

When rustle and twitter ceased abruptly, Morning Song stayed the hand that had been scratching behind Shadow's suddenly peaked ears. Together they watched a white-tailed deer materialize below them. It was a stag, and dressed already in his bluish-gray winter coat. He picked his way delicately along the path, setting his black hoofs precisely and swiveling his antler-crowned head as his probing nose tested the breeze.

What he was seeking, he apparently found; for he was there one

moment and gone the next, bounding lightly between the trees that
edged the path. Morning Song released her pent-up breath and
shook her head at a dog trembling with excitement and anxious to
be on the stalk. "I have no weapons," she reminded him. "And
if I had, I am not certain I would go after him." She soothed him
with stroking. "There are other deer in the forest, Shadow," she
explained, "and it is their mating season now. Surely a doe waits
somewhere for a stag as handsome as our visitor was."

She was talking nonsense, she knew. And perhaps, had she been
carrying her bow, Morning Song would not have surrendered to
fancy. Nonetheless, doing so permitted her to resume her roaming
with a lighter heart. It did not banish her problems, but it distanced
them until they no longer loomed so threateningly.

It was past midmorning when she sought a stream to drink from,
and the sparkling water both refreshed her and reminded her that it
was almost mealtime. "Perhaps I shall think of a way out of my
predicament as we walk home," she said to a dripping-muzzled
Shadow, and let him lope ahead of her. Instinct would lead him
back by a more direct route than Morning Song might choose, and
there seemed no sense in dallying. If the *orenda* present in the forest
decided to commune with her and give Morning Song the answers
she needed, it could do so as easily while she was striding along as
it could while she merely ambled.

Shadow's sudden sharp bark alerted her to the fact that they were
no longer alone. Immediately her thoughts returned to Stag Leaping, and she steeled herself to find him waiting on the far side of
the oak she was approaching. While she maneuvered over roots
that coiled around the tree's foot like a nest of petrified snakes, she
felt anger fire her blood. To think that he would dare follow her
again, deliberately accost her again, after what had happened the
first time! Well, he would learn not to do so a third time, she
promised herself grimly. It mattered not at all that Summer Maize
had rashly pledged her daughter to the man whose outstretched arm
she could see now, whose long fingers held a bit of corn cake that
a hungry dog was leaping to claim.

She halted, dumbstruck, and felt her rage evaporate. It was not
Stag Leaping who grunted approval as Shadow jumped high enough
to reach his hand, who dropped the corn cake into the animal's
eager mouth, and bent to rub his wedge-shaped head. "Cloud
Racer," she gasped.

He turned and nodded courteously. "I thought you must be
nearby," he said. "You and your dog are seldom far apart."

She looked at Shadow. Hopeful of being fed again, he was gam-

boling around Cloud Racer's buckskin-clad legs. "He seems happy
to desert me for a taste of corn cake, however," she remarked. And
chuckled inwardly to think that, were it Stag Leaping the dog had
come upon, his tidbit would probably have been another chunk of
that warrior's flesh.

Cloud Racer smiled, and for an instant his habitually sober expression lightened, and she saw in the tall firm-muscled man the
reed-slim boy he'd been—the boy who had once taken the time to
convince a disheartened little girl that most liabilities could be overcome with patience and persistence. He had changed considerably
since those days. Both his face and his body had broadened and
toughened, and hair dark and heavy as a brooding sky was worn
plaited now to show his status in the tribe. An authority in his face
said that here was a man it might be better not to cross, but she
noticed now that his deep-cleft mouth was not without a certain
gentleness.

She became aware that she was staring, which was rude indeed,
and that he'd made no response to her quip about White Shadow.
Well, there had been no real need to respond, and she'd heard that
Cloud Racer seldom spoke without purpose. That made conversation between the chance-met a bit difficult. "I am on my way
home," she said, dropping her eyes. She signed to White Shadow
to fall in behind her and felt absurdly proud when he obeyed.

"As I am," he informed her, and—somewhat arrogantly, she
thought—took the lead in their small procession. "You are a child
of the forest still, I see," he observed after they had walked in
silence for a time. He tossed the words over his shoulder, for his
whole attention was on monitoring their going.

Should I acknowledge the comment? Morning Song wondered.
She doubted that he would, had she been the one to make it. Yet
she found herself wanting to confess her love for the forest to someone she suspected would understand it. "I find it peaceful here,"
she said to his brawny back. "If I am worried about something,
the vastness of the woods makes me see that what disturbed me is
of small account. When I am sad, its beauty counters my sorrow.
There are times—" she hesitated, then plunged boldly on; it was
easier to describe feelings when there were no eyes examining
her face "—times when I yearn to break the bonds of law and
custom. I had no part in making these rules! But when I come to
the forest, I see that there are rules here, too. The trees must surrender their leaves in the red season, whether they will or no. The
weasel that devours the mouse knows that he, in turn, may make a
meal for a bear. New plants cannot grow unless the old ones give

up their seeds. It calms me to recognize that all of this"—she flung out her arms in a sweeping gesture he could not see—"flourishes only because of laws set by the Maker Of Life. I think—" She choked back the rest of the sentence, all at once mortified to be battering the ears of this oh-so-quiet man with a speech worthy of Teller Of Legends when she embarked on an extravagant monologue. She wondered miserably why Cloud Racer was not lengthening his stride in order to flee the rattle of her voice.

"I, too, come here to think," he said suddenly.

She ceased her self-castigation on the instant. "You think a great deal," she blurted out (for this was another thing people said of him).

"Perhaps."

"Do you have questions that sometimes seem unanswerable?" she asked.

"Everyone does. Or should."

A curious elation bubbled in her then. She had never imagined that anyone—and surely not the phlegmatic Cloud Racer—could experience the same uncertainties as she did. "Then you do not think me strange for wandering alone in the forest when I can?"

He turned to face her. "There is nothing unnatural in it," he said firmly.

Now her elation came to a boil. Had she found at last someone she might talk with, and take no care to guard her tongue? Someone to whom she might say things she had never dared say to anyone else, and not be laughed at or scorned? If so, there was much more she wanted to tell Cloud Racer, and a great deal she would like to ask him.

But they had reached the outskirts of the forest, and she knew before he lifted a hand in casual salute that she would have no opportunity to speak further. Not today. She watched him stride along the path leading to the palisade, and told herself that there would be other times when Cloud Racer and Morning Song walked together in the woods. The prospect was pleasing.

It wasn't until she herself had reached the compound that she remembered how she had failed to find a solution to the problem of Stag Leaping and the marriage treaty. Which effectively neutralized any lingering elation.

Animated discussion of her arranged marriage greeted Morning Song's arrival in the longhouse.

"You might have told me the truth," Pumpkin Blossom said

reproachfully, "instead of pretending you had no interest in taking a husband."

Teller Of Legends met Morning Song's startled glance with a smile meant to be conspiratorial. So her grandmother had let them believe that Morning Song had always been aware of her mother's plans for her. It was easy to see why: Any protest Morning Song made now would be dealt with lightly if not impatiently by the rest of her clan. She turned to her cousin. "I spend little time thinking about marriage, let alone speaking of it," she said shortly.

"I will show you the best way to make bride cakes," Bountiful Harvest offered, a generous smile masking her enormous relief. Once her niece had wed, there would be no more making a spectacle of herself by taking up a man's weapons and going hunting!

"You shall be more content, Morning Song," Hearth Tender said over her sister's shoulder, "when you have a husband and children to devote yourself to. Had I known before of this treaty Summer Maize made with Owl Crying, I might have been better able to advise you when you brought your vision to me. The spirits, you see, are never without thorough knowledge of the person they send messages to; they know her as she was and as she shall be, not only as the person she is in the present. That you were already betrothed naturally affected the message they sent."

Morning Song thought that unlikely, particularly since the marriage would never take place, but she forbore to say so. Hearth Tender meant well; they all did, she supposed. And, one and all, they sincerely assumed that marriage was what Morning Song needed to arouse in her a passion for propriety. Even Otter beamed upon her when the rest had turned their attention to the chowder Bountiful Harvest was ladling out. But what set aglow a face pregnancy had rounded and softened had nothing to do with treaties or marrying. "Look, Morning Song," she said excitedly, and thrust two arrows into her hands. "Deer Caller made these! He asked me to give him the short lengths of wood he recalled leaving beneath our bunk, and to take down the flints and feathers from our shelf. I could not think what he meant to do at first, and when I understood I was afraid to encourage him. Being Deer Caller, he went ahead anyway. He sat up most of the night over the first arrow he made, and discarded several before he was satisfied with what he'd done." She laughed. "He showed it to no one—not even to me—until he had carved another and fitted both with points, and fletched them. But see what splendid arrows they are!"

Her eyes sparkled as her niece obediently inspected them. Despite Morning Song's immersion in her own troubles, she was sincerely impressed by arrows as fine as any she'd ever seen. "They are indeed splendid," she told Otter and, taking her by the arm, went to offer praise to a master craftsman.

"Deer Caller, when I look at these, it makes me want to take the arrows I made for myself and hide them away. And to think you went without sleep to work on them. You must have been eager to prove that you could do what you wanted to do."

He smiled. "I was. And I have discovered that the one advantage to being blind is that I have no need to wait for light in order to work." He shook his head as she began to lay the arrows on his lap. "Keep them," he said. "I made them for you. Even though"—his smile ripened into a grin—"what I have been hearing tells me you shall have little need of them now."

For a few moments she had been distracted, had even let herself be infected by Otter's joy. But the jest served to darken her world once more. "I thank you," she managed, and managed as well a strained smile for a puzzled Otter Swimming. Then, clutching the arrows she had no intention of letting go to waste, she went to her bed and perched on the edge of it.

If a blind man could teach his fingers to see for him, then a young woman whose every sense was intact ought to be able to knead the clay of circumstance until she had reshaped it to her advantage. The only question was, how?

She still lacked an answer when the day ended, and was for once less than delighted to hear Teller Of Legends announce that she wished to rehearse a story she meant to tell at Midwinter. "It is one I have not told in a long time," she explained, her pouched eyes somber. "Too long, perhaps. I must be certain I have the whole of it neatly arranged here"—she tapped her forehead—"before I offer it to the village during the Ceremony."

She interlaced her blunt-tipped fingers and regarded her family. "Before my grandmother's grandmother's time, the people who would become the Iroquois preyed upon one another as though they were beasts rather than men. Because such barbarism distressed Te-Ha-Wro-Gah, the Upholder Of The Heavens, he turned himself into a mortal man and went among the people to teach them how to live in peace. And, just as importantly, to give them laws and precepts to guide them in the future."

Fish Jumping yawned. He had hoped for a tale of courageous warriors, of enemies met and conquered, an *exciting* story!

"The Upholder Of The Heavens," his grandmother went on, "who wore the name of Hiawatha while he was a man, knew that first he must win the people's trust. So he said to them: 'If you will follow me along the path from the sunrising to the sunsetting, I will show you land more beautiful than any you have ever imagined. It is land no man has yet seen, and you shall have custody over it.'

"They flocked to follow him then, and marveled at the way he easily cleared obstructions from streams and rivers so that much of their journey could be by water. They made good use of the canoes he had shown them how to build and to paddle." She paused and gazed into the fire; and the fire gazed back, reddening her skin and filling the crevices of her face with shadow. "When they had reached the banks of a magnificent river, Hiawatha—who was also Te-Ha-Wro-Gah—separated certain families from the others, gave them corn, beans, squash, tobacco, and dogs to help them when they went in search of game." She looked to Morning Song, smiled. "And to be companions to them, also," she added. " 'You shall be known as the Mohawk,' he told them. And from that day, they were.

"The rest set out again, although some looked back enviously and wished they might have been made Mohawk also. But when they arrived at a fertile valley surrounded by lush forest, they changed their minds. Hiawatha commanded another group to make this place home, gave them all that was necessary for them to prosper, and named them Oneida. So they are called to this day."

Morning Song wished she might have been the first person to step among trees no one had ever leaned against, or climbed into, or marked blazes on. Had the one to do so appreciated the privilege that was his? Or hers? Surely even among the ancients there had been a girl like Morning Song.

"When the rest had gone on and come upon a mountain so tall that clouds wreathed its crest and eagles built nests upon its crags, Hiawatha stopped again. 'You shall be the Onondaga,' he told the families he singled out, 'and you are to build your villages at the foot of this mountain.' And he gave them, too, the gifts they would need to make the most of life.

"The shores of an enormous and sparkling lake were given to a tribe he named Cayuga. And the last of his followers he brought to a smaller lake, one which spread itself in the shadow of a mountain, and told them to build lodges nearby. 'You shall be the Seneca nation,' he said, 'and Keepers of the Western Door in the same way as the Mohawk are Keepers of the Eastern Door. For the whole of the territory we have just crossed is to be looked upon as a single longhouse, and all those who dwell within it are to be regarded as clan kin.'

Teller Of Legends looked around her. If she could not impress her own family with this tale, she could never hope for it to be absorbed and remembered by the the entire village. And it was vital that everyone understand that it was history, more than legend, that she described for them.

She cleared her throat and resumed her tale. "The Upholder Of The Heavens continued in his guise as Hiawatha, for during the journey he had come to love a beautiful maiden. She returned his affection, and asked him to make his home in her family's new-built lodge. In time, she presented him with a daughter, Mni-Ha-Ha, who surpassed even her mother in beauty and womanly accomplishments. Hiawatha adored his daughter as much as he did his wife.

"He never neglected his mission, however. Traveling in a magic canoe, which floated above waters and meadows as though fitted with wings, he went frequently from nation to nation, preaching peace and harmony and urging the people to keep all things in balance. A chieftain named Dekanawida was both friend and disciple to Hiawatha, and went with him on these expeditions. I must confess that not all were supporters, however. Another chieftain, Wa-Tha-To-Tar-Ho, was devoted to war and tried to influence the Longhouse People against Hiawatha. Still, it is the law of the universe that happiness alternates with sorrow, life with death, harmony with discord; and Hiawatha was not surprised that this should be.

"Nonetheless, Wa-Tha-To-Tar-Ho's actions made it difficult for Hiawatha and Dekanawida to teach those who regarded war and dissension as natural things that peace would benefit them more. 'To persuade them to this,' Hiawatha said to Dekanawida, 'we must make them believe that what we are telling them is only something that has been in their minds from the start. When they are convinced it is their own idea, then they shall desire peace above anything. For this is the nature of man.' "

Fish Jumping was asleep, Teller Of Legends saw. But the others were showing more interest than they had earlier. As they should. They, too, lived in a time when war and dissension had become commonplace, and it surprised them to learn that this was not the way it was meant to be. War was necessary upon occasion; who could deny it? And there would always be hot-blooded young warriors eager for raiding; this, too, was the nature of man. But the people must understand that the ancients had laid down rules to promote harmony and peace and order. They had never sanctioned fighting without just purpose.

"Hiawatha summoned together all the nations he had formed. It was in the territory of the Onondaga that they gathered, and four days later a white canoe bearing Hiawatha and his beautiful daughter came gliding through the mists. The pair stepped ashore, and Hiawatha greeted the Sachems and elders who hurried forward to bid him welcome."

Suddenly Teller Of Legends wished she had asked her brother to be here for this story. It would do him no harm to hear it twice told, she thought. But it was too late for that. "As Hiawatha prepared to speak," she went on, "there came a noise like the rushing of a mighty river in full spate. All heads lifted—for the noise had come from the sky—and all eyes widened as a bird a hundred times larger than the largest of eagles flew out of the clouds. The beating of its wings was louder than He-No's fiercest thunderclap, and the people screamed and cowered as it dipped lower and lower.

"Hiawatha and his daughter did not move. As the mysterious bird hovered just above the ground, the Upholder Of The Heavens laid his hand on Mni-Ha-Ha's dark head. She looked up at him and said quietly, 'Farewell, my father,' then calmly went and seated herself between the huge wings of that awesome bird. When she had settled herself, it spiraled up and up and up until it had flown beyond the clouds and into the great blue vault of the sky.

"When it had vanished, Hiawatha's grief brought him to the ground, where he covered himself with a panther-skin robe to show that he mourned the daughter who had been taken from him. For three days he huddled in silence, while the people wondered among themselves if perhaps he had offered his only child as a sacrifice. They told one another that, if so, then he had done it for them; Hiawatha loved the Longhouse People just as he had loved Mni-Ha-Ha.

"There were those, of course, who claimed afterward that the bird had been an illusion, that young Mni-Ha-Ha had been slain by her father's enemy, Wa-Tha-To-Tar-Ho. But others insisted that this was not possible; Hiawatha—who believed in living what he taught—had already made an ally of the chieftain who had been against him at the start.

"In any event, when his mourning was done, Hiawatha asked the Great Council to meet. 'Listen well, my people,' he said to them, 'for my time among you is nearing an end and these shall be my last instructions to you.' Then he said solemnly that he recognized how the wise leaders among them deplored the conflict that misguided chieftains tried to promote between tribe and tribe and even between village and village. He reminded them of how he had brought them into this country and shaped strong nations out of an unruly band of wanderers. 'You must reunite now, and act as one,' he told them, 'and never again forget that I have made you brothers. You must have one fire, one pipe, one war club.' "

Oh, why had she not thought to have Se-A-Wi here! Teller Of Legends fumed silently. He above all needed to listen to this. "He sprinkled on the fire sacred tobacco—the same tobacco he had given them seeds for and taught them how to grow—so that its sweet smoke enveloped them as he spoke again: 'Your tribes must be like the five fingers of a warrior's hand, impossible to separate. Unite as one, and your enemies shall recoil before you.' Then he told them to retire and take counsel among themselves, and begged them to let his words sink deep into their hearts and minds."

The Matron of the Turtle clan paused again, this time to let the words she had repeated sink into the minds and hearts of her family.

"On the next morning," she said softly when she could be certain they would remember, "the Sachems of Mohawk, Oneida, Onondaga, Cayuga, and Seneca tribes came to Hiawatha and vowed that they would, from this day, be as one nation. Hiawatha rejoiced to hear this and let them see his pride in them and his love for them. He gathered up the white feathers left by the mystery bird that had borne away his daughter and gave the plumes to the leaders of the assembled tribes. 'By these feathers,' he said, 'you shall be known as the Ako-No-Shu-Ne, the Iroquois.' Thus was the mighty League of the Iroquois born, and thus did Hiawatha earn for himself the name Great Unifier. And the Five Nations held sway undisturbed over all the land between the great sea of the East and the great river of the West, the territory they were to think of always as their Longhouse."

The fire had burned almost to ash; Teller Of Legends picked up a stick and poked at it until it revived enough to bathe all of their faces with flickering light. "The last advice Hiawatha gave to the tribal leaders was this: 'Friends and brothers, choose the wisest women in your tribes to be the future clan mothers and peacemakers. Let them turn any strife arising among you into friendship. When there are disputes, let your Sachems go to these women for advice.'

"Then he bade them farewell and stepped into his canoe. As he did, they heard a sound that put them in mind of the forest at dawn, a blend of breeze-caressed leaves and silvery birdsong. And the canoe Hiawatha sat in lifted from the surface of the lake and rose slowly, slowly, into the sky, bearing the Great Unifier toward the same place his daughter had been carried to. Where this is we cannot know, for he never returned to the People of the Longhouse. But it is certain that the teachings of Hiawatha live on.'' She looked around her, her black eyes compelling them to mark her last words. ''And they always must,'' she finished softly. ''They always must.''

Chapter 16

⊷ ⊶

Two days later, Morning Song asked Bountiful Harvest to teach her to make bride cakes.

''You are wise not to wait,'' Hearth Tender said with a smile. ''Owl Crying may feel slighted if they are not delivered soon.''

''As Stag Leaping will,'' Pumpkin Blossom declared. ''Although I think it sad that you will not be able to surprise him, Morning Song. He should have to wait with the rest, to learn which maiden has chosen him.'' Her brow wrinkled. ''It might make a man complacent,'' she said, ''to know beforetime.''

Morning Song did not respond to either of them, except with an abstracted smile. She ought to have known her grandmother would speak with the Matron of the Pigeonhawk longhouse! And apparently Teller Of Legends had been right when she'd insisted that its Matron would abide by a pledge made years before. But it hurt regardless, to have her grandmother so stubbornly out of sympathy with Morning Song's opposition to this marriage. To any marriage, at least for now. With a sigh, she turned her attention to what Bountiful Harvest was saying.

''Bride cakes are simply cornbread shaped in a certain way and wrapped in cornhusks for cooking.'' Her mother-aunt was positioning a pot of water over the fire as she spoke. ''The secret is to remove them from the boiling water the moment they float to the top.''

She droned on as she signed to Morning Song to sift meal into a bowl, but her niece scarcely heard her. She was busy reviewing a plan that would let her evade marriage without bringing dishonor to her family. The tale of Hiawatha had provided her inspiration, but Teller Of Legends need never know that.

''Wet your hands with cold water,'' Bountiful Harvest said, and

Morning Song thrust her hands into the dipper. "Now, shape the dough into twenty-four rounds of equal size,"

"It is a messy job," Otter Swimming said, coming to peer over Morning Song's shoulder. "I can remember when I made the wedding bread for Sweet Maple."

"Forming snowballs is easier," her niece said as chunks of moistened meal plopped back into the bowl set between her angled knees. But eventually she produced a series of lopsided spheres that bountiful Harvest named passable, and aunt and niece, working together, wrapped them in cornhusks.

"Now tie them in pairs," Bountiful Harvest directed, pointing to the lengths of husk that dangled from each ball, and Morning Song needed only three tries to join the first two. Which, in the circumstances, she deemed admirable, for apprehension stirred now that she had come this far. What if her scheme failed?

"Your bride cakes will be ready before the sun is halfway down the western sky," Bountiful Harvest said as she lowered the last of the husk-sheathed double globes into the pot.

Morning Song scrambled to her feet. Succeed or fail, it was time to get on with her intrigue. "I shall be back by then," she promised, and was so anxious to be gone that she almost forgot to thank her for her help.

It should not be hard, Morning Song thought grimly, to locate Stag Leaping. He'd have learned about the marriage contract by now, and would be lurking not far from the Turtle longhouse.

He was. She'd scarely been in the compound long enough for Shadow to materialize beside her before the warrior made his approach. The dog lowered his head and grumbled when Stag Leaping, this time, did not veer from their path, and Morning Song laid a warning hand on Shadow's arched back. "Be still," she said firmly, and felt his puzzlement as he relaxed his threatening stance.

Morning Song reminded herself that Hiawatha had persuaded all the Longhouse People that what he wished for them was precisely what they wanted for themselves. She had to convince only a single warrior that what she wanted, he wanted also.

Stag Leaping strutted before her like a grouse in mating season, and refused to flinch when Shadow planted himself directly in front of his mistress. "It is good that this cur of yours is not allowed into the lodge," he told her strongly. "It would be annoying to have to wrestle him away whenever I'm of a mind to embrace you, Morning Song."

She longed to retort that it was a match he would lose, but dared not. *Remember the plan,* she reminded herself sternly. "You are willing to marry me then?" she asked, injecting a note of wonder into her voice.

He gave her a slow and meaningful—horribly meaningful—smile. "I have always known you were the woman for me," he said, "even before you were grown. Surely"—his eyes burned into hers— "you have not forgotten?"

She almost recoiled, but instead veiled her eyes as if modesty ruled her demeanor. "No, I have not . . . forgotten. But"—she raised her lids, gazed into his face—"I would have thought you too prideful to let yourself be bound by a treaty made by our mothers when we were merely children."

"And so I should have been," he blustered, "had the terms not suited me. But it is *you* I was promised to"—he put out a hand, caressed the warm flesh of her arm despite Shadow's immediate stiffening—"and this suits me, Morning Song."

She gritted her teeth and warned herself that she must endure the repugnant touch. Must do more than that, in truth. Slowly she lifted her free hand, placed it over his. "Then I am glad that the bride cakes are already cooking," she murmured, and made valiant effort to imitate the expression Otter wore when she looked at Deer Caller. "For I, too, am pleased with what our mothers arranged for us."

Exultation flamed in Stag Leaping's face now, as well as desire. "You shall see how eagerly they are received, and how soon afterward Owl Crying delivers cakes she has made to the Turtle longhouse," he said thickly, his fingers kneading her upper arm.

Morning Song knew that he imagined he fondled more than her arm, and the realization sickened her. "It is a pity," she managed— and managed as well to sound as if she meant it—"that certain maidens in our village will have to be disappointed."

Puzzlement displaced some of the lust in his eyes. "Disappointed?"

She nodded. "We talk among ourselves," she said, trying to ignore his urgent fingers. "Several have confessed to being attracted by you, Stag Leaping, and they would have competed for your attentions come Midwinter."

She withdrew her own hand as his dropped abruptly. He *was* interested in what she told him. And never mind that she'd yet to hear even one maid mention his name. There was surely someone who would not be averse to having Stag Leaping as husband.

"I wonder that my mother knows nothing about it," he muttered. "She seldom misses anything that is said, or even hinted at."

"We maidens know that to be true of all matrons," Morning Song declared, trying a trill of laughter. "So we keep secret anything we are not ready to have gossiped about." Her laughter sounded false to her own ears, but Stag Leaping did not seem to find it so. "I should never admit to this," she went on confidingly, "but one of the maidens who yearns for you would make a better wife than I ever could. She is a better cook; she is prettier, and inclined to be docile. Which no one has ever said of *me*! She would look up to you, Stag Leaping, in more ways than one, for she is not so unnaturally tall as I am, either."

It was true that Morning Song's eyes were nearly on a level with Stag Leaping's; she hoped he would deduce from this obvious truth that the rest of what she'd said was true also.

He grinned, and for a moment she thought he did believe her, that he would demand to know the name of this admiring and admirable maid. "Not only am I distressingly tall," she continued eagerly, "but even my own family complains that I am contrary and stubborn. I doubt," she finished rashly, "that I could ever be a proper wife to any man, and it is certain that the bold Stag Leaping deserves better."

He laughed and, scorning White Shadow, stepped closer and clutched at her arms in a way that reminded her of the afternoon he had accosted her in the forest. "Your contrariness and stubbornness excite me, Morning Song," he said in a voice rough with passion. His eyes burned hotter and his mouth grew slack. "The prospect of taming you delights me. And I promise that you will revel in every moment of that taming, Morning Song, fully as much as I will."

With a jerk, she pulled away from him. So much for Hiawatha's shrewdness, she thought angrily. Well, she had more weapons than gentle persuasion to use against this loathsome man!

"I have tried," she said tightly, "to suggest that you look elsewhere for a wife. You should have taken that advice. You are a fool, Stag Leaping, to continue to want me when"—she flung the last words in his face—"I do not want you! I never have. I never shall."

His grin did not falter; her passionate speech only fueled his desire for her. "But we are promised to each other, Morning Song," he said softly. "And when I have bedded you, you will not be sorry that we were."

Her eyes became slits. "Oh but you will, Stag Leaping," she said in a voice shafted with steel. "If Owl Crying accepts the bread Teller Of Legends delivers to your longhouse, if your mother sends her own cakes to ours, and you with them, then I make you a solemn vow: I shall bring my knife to our marriage bed, Stag Leaping. And I will use it on the both of us before I permit you to lay a hand on me!''

"You would not dare," he began, then fell silent as he looked into a face so resolute it might have been sculpted from stone.

This time it was he who stepped back, and Morning Song rejoiced to know that—as she had suspected—he was not so brave as he pretended to be, as even Fierce Eagle believed him to be. In battle, he doubtless took strength from having his comrades around him. But when he stood alone, as he did now, he surrendered substance; he shrank from the prick of mere words, just as rumor said happened when his sharp-tongued mother berated him. ''Will you chance that I do not mean what I say?'' she asked with menacing quiet. And when Shadow—alert to every mood of his mistress—growled this time, she did not tell him to be still.

Stag Leaping struggled against his diminishment, stretched himself so that he might, for once, look down on her. His eyes flicked from her set face to the dog whose hackles were visibly lifting, and back again. ''It does not become a warrior to listen to such nonsense,'' he said, folding swagger around him as though it were a ceremonial robe. ''Particularly since I know you only think to arouse me further with your childish pretense of fierceness.'' He bared his teeth in a smile meant to taunt and disconcert her. ''Whether it has or no,'' he concluded, turning on his heel as he spoke, ''is a thing I will leave you to worry about.''

His laughter as he strode away sounded suspiciously hollow to Morning Song, but that might be only because she wanted it to, because she needed desperately to feel sure that she had succeeded in frightening him off. In the moment that he retreated from her, she'd felt secure that she had. Now she simply did not know.

She found it difficult to behave naturally on returning to the longhouse, but her impatience for the bread to be done brought amused smiles to the faces of Teller Of Legends and Bountiful Harvest. Morning Song, peering into the bubbling pot, knew how quickly those smiles would fade if she revealed the true cause of her restlessness.

At last the loaves surfaced. Bountiful Harvest lifted them out, let the water drain off, and slid them into the basket Teller Of Legends was holding. ''They are as near perfect as can be,'' she said to her niece. ''Owl Crying will find no fault with these.''

''Nor with you, Morning Song, in whose name I shall present them,'' her grandmother said roguishly.

Morning Song's tenuous grip on composure slipped further, but she peeked into the basket and made the admiring noises expected of her. "You are taking them now, before they have cooled?" she asked as Teller Of Legends started toward the entrance.

"They shall have cooled enough, by the time Owl Crying has accepted them and exclaimed over them," Teller Of Legends said, mistaking her alarm for the anxiety any marriage-minded girl might be experiencing. And went on her way.

"Truly, Morning Song," Bountiful Harvest scolded, picking up the tunic she'd been sewing on, "anyone might think that your marriage to Stag Leaping was not already arranged, and that you feared he might reject you."

Morning Song—after flashing her mother-aunt an apologetic smile—departed the longhouse before some inadvertent look or gesture betrayed her true feelings.

She wasn't fool enough to expect that the spirits of the forest would reveal to her Stag Leaping's decision. They would keep their own counsel, she thought sadly, as they seemed determined to do where this girl was concerned. Nonetheless, it was to the forest that she and White Shadow went; she could not bear to remain in the lodge, or to seek out the other maidens, who would be sitting and chatting over their assorted tasks. If word had spread as quickly as it generally did, they were doubtless discussing the marriage of Morning Song and Stag Leaping!

Her tension subsided as she walked familiar paths and tossed a length of deadwood for Shadow to chase and fetch back to her. She'd done everything she could; to torture herself with wondering how it would end was senseless. If worse came to worst, and Stag Leaping showed himself determined to have her, perhaps she might leave the village, make a home of sorts for herself and Shadow in the forest. There was always her cave!

Care retreated a pace as she laughed aloud. The cave had seemed small when she was young and White Shadow a pup. Now that both were grown, they were forced to huddle together, and Morning Song to keep her head hunched between her shoulders, when they occupied it at the same time. No; confining quarters were out of the question for two who shared such love of freedom.

She laughed again when Shadow—as if to prove her conclusions—put nose to the ground, snuffled a time or two, and abandoned their game to follow a scent he'd discovered.

"You are joyful today."

Morning Song looked up to see Cloud Racer perched on the

protruding wedge of a boulder that, in some century long past, had lodged itself between a pair of trees. "If I sound so, then the forest is to be thanked," she said. What good could come from confessing the misery that lay beneath her laughter?

"It is owed thanks from me as well," he said, "for the stillness that persuaded me to rest here." He folded his arms and leaned into the bow of the tree nearest him. "I have come from the home of the trader Bree-And."

Morning Song nodded. The log-walled structure that Henri Briand had built to house his wife and himself was not far from here, but Morning Song carefully avoided that part of the forest. If the man had battered his visitor with the thunder-boom of his perpetual ranting, she could understand why Cloud Racer craved quiet now. "You have seen his woman, then?"

It was Cloud Racer's turn to nod. "I met her first when their home was new built. I had been hunting with Hill Climber and Woodpecker Drumming. They were curious to see it."

Morning Song was curious, too. "What manner of woman would choose such a lout for a husband?"

Cloud Racer considered. "She is small, smaller than my sister, and scrawny as a fledgling bird. She was frightened to see us there, I think."

There was room for another person on the projection of rock Cloud Racer had claimed, but Morning Song would not climb up uninvited. The lowest limb of the maple she stood beside was on much the same level, however, so she hoisted herself onto that. "Perhaps she had never seen an Iroquois warrior before," she said, settling herself comfortably and letting her legs swing free.

The son of Rain Singing permitted his mouth to lift at the corners. "I can remember a time when you thought climbing a tree was a skill you could not master," he observed. "You may be right," he went on, returning to his description of Briand's wife, "but I think it is the nature of the woman to be easily alarmed. She did not let that keep her from being kind; she offered us bread."

Kind she may have been; or fearful of angering three Iroquois braves by failing to offer them hospitality. And Cloud Racer, who would never respect someone who cringed and cowered, had probably seemed the most threatening of the three. "If Hill Climber has not changed," she said, smiling reminiscently, "then I expect that he, at least, was delighted to be fed."

"He was," Cloud Racer confirmed, and turning his face into a slanting column of sunlight, he closed his eyes against the glare and let his flesh absorb the unseasonable warmth of it.

Morning Song had been savoring their conversation, had been pleased that he seemed as much at ease with her as, amazingly, she was with him. She had no intention of letting him drift into one of his silences now. "Did Trail Marker send you to Bree-And?"

Cloud Racer jerked upright as though she had stretched out a hand and prodded him in the ribs. "He did," he said, provoked into recalling a mission he'd had little enthusiasm for. "Fierce Eagle asked him to arrange for new knives and axes—long-bladed knives and battleaxes—to be delivered to our village. It seems"—his mouth twisted briefly—"that my uncle and the war leaders from several other villages plan to begin new raids against the Erie when the green season comes again."

His voice was without expression, but his face hinted that he disapproved of the idea. Morning Song thought that strange; she had heard that Cloud Racer's warrior skills were praised even by enemy warriors. "You are not eager to go raiding again?" she asked, puzzled.

"I shall go," he said shortly. "But I had hoped that our Sachem, who usually encourages arbitration whenever disputes arise among our own warriors or between our village and another, might urge Fierce Eagle to appeal first to the Great Council. Then all the tribal leaders could decide together if and when we should follow the path of war into Erie country."

Morning Song was dimly aware that Fierce Eagle, as a Pine Tree Chief, had the right to address the Councilors of the League. Yet why did Cloud Racer think he should speak with them about something so ordinary? Well, she would ask; how else could she find out?

She had no need to. Cloud Racer, despite his reputation for brusqueness, did not need urging when the subject was one he'd given prolonged and, in this case, painful thought to. "One of the reasons the League was formed," he said, "was so the Five Nations would always wield a single war club. I cannot understand why so many choose to forget that—or how they can forget that Hiawatha taught our ancestors to choose peace instead of war. Those were words he wasted breath speaking, I think."

Morning Song's eyes widened with sudden comprehension. "I know of Hiawatha," she said. "Teller Of Legends spoke of him, and of the way he helped us become the People of the Longhouse. She, too, said that he counseled peace before war in most instances. Although she said also," she added honestly, "that the Iroquois are much given to fighting, even among themselves."

"So it would seem," Cloud Racer said, and his black eyes

brooded beneath their heavy lids. "Did your grandmother tell of Dekanawida, and the Tree of Great Peace?"

Morning Song frowned. "Of Dekanawida, yes. But I do not recall that she mentioned a tree."

"It was an evergreen, a spruce, that grew tall enough to touch the clouds," Cloud Racer explained, and his dark face took on a glow it seldom wore. "Its purpose was to remind us of the Great Peace that was the dream of Hiawatha and Dekanawida. Its five strong roots symbolized our nations, and an eagle roosted in its topmost branches to watch for enemies who might threaten that peace. Only when the eagle cried were we to go to war, and always the nations would fight as one." He paused, and the inner fire that had been blazing in his eyes, that had lit his whole face, was abruptly extinguished. "I do not believe the Erie pose a threat to our people," he finished, then clamped shut his mouth as though ashamed of having talked so long. Or with such feeling.

Morning Song was sorry to see the glow fade, more sorry to recognize what his clenched jaw signaled. "If they do not, then we ought not go to war against them," she prompted gently.

But it did no good. Even before Cloud Racer jumped down from the rock, she knew that his excursion into eloquence was at an end. The next time they met he might even be curt, because he had surely spent more words this afternoon than he usually did from new moon to full.

Now, his farewell was silent, merely a nod and a lift of the hand. Yet when he had gone on his way, what he'd said lingered in Morning Song's mind. His voice had been charged with emotion when he'd spoken of Hiawatha and Dekanawida, as though the words had been trembling on his lips for a long, long time.

Why he had chosen her ears to pour them into, she did not know. Perhaps he had done so only because he felt confident that Morning Song would listen, where others might not. Perhaps—and she smiled as she deserted her own perch, for the thought exhilarated her—perhaps Cloud Racer had trusted that Morning Song would not only listen, but understand.

When dusk spread itself over the forest, absorbing Morning Song's exhilaration along with the last of the sunlight, she summoned White Shadow and returned reluctantly to the village. The greeting she murmured as she entered the longhouse was courteously acknowledged, but the faces that turned toward her were not wearing the contented smiles they had worn earlier in the day.

Hope fluttered in her heart, but she kept her voice carefully expressionless. "Has Owl Crying visited yet?" she asked.

Her grandmother shook her head slowly, and Morning Song saw concern in her eyes.

Bountiful Harvest was briskly optimistic. "She had cakes of her own to make," she said. "That takes time, Morning Song. As you know."

But not so long as this! her niece thought exultantly.

Pumpkin Blossom's expression was solemn. "Oh, Morning Song, what shall you do if she does not come?" she whispered.

"I will accept that she has rejected the cakes Teller Of Legends took to her," she said, shrugging her shoulders.

"How will you bear it?" her cousin mourned.

"Your grieving is premature," their grandmother said sternly. "If Owl Crying disavows a treaty she herself made, then the shame shall be hers, and not Morning Song's." But it was evident that a spirit unaccustomed to stooping was beginning to feel the press of mortification.

"It may be Stag Leaping who refuses me," Morning Song said hastily. Teller Of Legends' pride was great and must not suffer erosion on her account. "Until recently, he had no notion of what had been arranged for us, just as I did not."

"Oh, but that would be far worse." Pumpkin Blossom exclaimed. "To be spurned by the warrior she has chosen is the most dreadful thing that could happen to a maiden!"

"I have said that neither of us chose the other," Morning Song reminded her sharply. "Our mothers did this."

Suspicion began to reshape Teller Of Legends's features, and her granddaughter softened her tone. "I shall be disappointed," she made herself add, "but I will find the strength to bear it, I suppose."

"There are other warriors worthy of your choosing," Otter Swimming called encouragingly, and her teeth flashed in the shadows that were gathered around the bed she and Deer Caller sat on. "Besides, as my sister said, there is time yet for Owl Crying to come."

Morning Song seized the opportunity to avoid her grandmother's speculative stare and to divert conversation. "And what is Deer Caller working on now?" she asked as she lowered herself to the floor in front of Otter's bunk.

He laid aside his blade and held out the tall piece of hickory he'd begun to carve. "Arrows I can make; but they are useless without a bow to launch them," he said simply.

She ran her fingertips over the end he'd been narrowing, sliver by patient sliver, and murmured appreciatively. "Deer Caller, I believe your touch guides you more truly than your eyes ever did."

"That may be because I am forced to work slowly, and because I am able to keep in my head the image of what I am making."

Otter grinned, and had it not been for the present unwieldiness of her body, Morning Song might have imagined that it was a young girl whose eyes twinkled at her. "I borrowed the arrows Deer Caller made for you, and showed them to Fierce Eagle," she confided. "When he recovered from his astonishment—you would have been delighted to see his expression, Morning Song—he came back here with me and asked Deer Caller if he would agree to furnish weapons for any warriors who might need them!"

He is planning for the spring, for the raids he means to make against the Erie, Morning Song told herself. And even though Cloud Racer was unhappy about that, she was grateful, for Deer Caller's sake, that the war leader had not been dissuaded by whatever arguments his nephew had used with him. "I do not need to ask if he said yes," she said, laughing.

"I told him I would be willing to try," Deer Caller corrected her. But he was laughing, too, and there was confidence in the sound; and Otter's faith in him radiated from her like brightness from the summer sun. Deer Caller felt it, for he put out one hand and touched the face that was turned to his.

Morning Song was aware of a tightening in her chest, and knew it for envy. Her aversion to marriage might vanish if she could find someone who would love her as greatly as Deer Caller loved Otter, someone she could love in return as unreservedly as Otter loved the man she had chosen.

She pulled her knees up to her chin, linked her hands upon them, and let her thoughts meander as they would. They followed a pleasant path, and she scarcely noticed when Hearth Tender slipped into the lodge and began a low-voiced discussion with Teller Of Legends. Indeed, it was only after her grandmother had twice called her name that she came—reluctantly—out of her reverie.

"Hearth Tender passed the Pigeonhawk lodge on her way home," the old woman said heavily. "The cakes I delivered to Owl Crying are sitting on the ground outside. I would not have thought it possible, but it seems she has refused them."

"Grandmother," Morning Song said urgently, "do not sorrow for me. And, please, do not feel anger toward Owl Crying. I am certain it was Stag Leaping who rejected me. I have heard"—she was not lying, for she had certainly heard her own words as she'd uttered them—"that there is another maid who wishes to have him for a husband. He cannot be blamed if he returns her affection. And you have known all along that I own no love for Stag Leaping."

"You realize that you must go and retrieve the bread?" Hearth Tender asked quietly.

Morning Song nodded, and a mischievous glint danced in the depths of her brown eyes. "If I make no more sound than a mouse come to steal corn from our fields, perhaps no one shall know of my mission save the clans concerned, Grandmother. It is night, after all. There is not likely to be anyone in the compound to see me."

"The matrons will all be talking of it tomorrow," Bountiful Harvest said swiftly. "Never doubt for a moment that they will know about it, Morning Song. Once again—thanks to you—the Turtle clan shall provide the village with something to gossip about."

"The maidens may gossip," Pumpkin Blossom said, "at least a little. But mostly they will be sad that you have been so cruelly rebuffed, Morning Song."

Morning Song suspected that all of them—her cousin as much as the others, no doubt—would enjoy commiserating with her, and silently vowed that she would give them no opportunity to. She stood up. "I will not postpone what must be done," she said. "Do I bring the cakes back here, Grandmother?"

Teller Of Legends nodded. "We will build up the fire and burn them," she said. "Or bury them. Anything, so long as we do not eat them."

Otter Swimming chuckled. "In ancient times, bride cakes were allowed to harden, then used to pelt the matron who had disdained them. Would you like to throw yours at Owl Crying, Morning Song? I would be happy to help you."

Grateful as she was to have Otter relieve a gloom she saw no need for, Morning Song refused the offer. "I think the sooner those cakes are disposed of, the better," she added, and went out to make good her words.

The night air was cool, but Morning Song found it refreshing after the fire-fed stuffiness of the longhouse. Shadow, whose favorite sleeping place was at the corner of the lodge, uncurled himself and trotted at his mistress's side as she walked without haste toward the southern section of the compound.

The basket of wedding bread was there, just outside the entrance to the Pigeonhawk lodge. There was enough moonlight for Morning Song to see that not even the topmost rounds had been un-wrapped, proof that Stag Leaping had been quick to tell Owl Crying he did not want Morning Song for a wife.

She grinned and picked up the basket, carried it toward home. She was trailed now by a motley collection of dogs. That surprised her not at all; doubtless they had been sniffing around the basket ever since Owl Crying set it out.

The cakes should be buried or burned, her grandmother had said, but Morning Song—released at last from her fear that she might end married to a man she despised—was in a whimsical mood. Why should something that had taken considerable effort to make go entirely to waste? A more sensible means of disposal literally begged to be employed.

She set down the basket, unpeeled the blanched husks from the first pair of rounds, and began breaking the bread into pieces. Shadow, ears perked and eyes gleaming, wagged his whip of a tail in anticipation.

She tossed a good-sized chunk to him, then scattered the rest among his companions—and was suddenly grateful that she had so much left to distribute. The message that here was food had some-how been signaled to every dog in the village, and they converged on her from all sides, whining pleadingly or yapping demandingly according to their dispositions. One old dog, eyes bleared and one drooping ear half bitten off in some long-ago fight, snapped futilely to the right, to the left, as younger and stronger animals shouldered him out of the way.

"You shall not go without," Morning Song told him, and pushed her way through a surge of furry bodies to honor her vow. She crouched and held out a thick slab, warned off a pair of would-be thieves, and waited while he snatched and chewed and swallowed; she even lingered to let his tongue blot up the crumbs that adhered to her palm.

"Can it be that you are no longer satisfied with only one dog?"

The tone was amused, the voice unmistakably Cloud Racer's. Morning Song straightened and looked to where he stood in the shadows behind her. "Rain Singing sent me to discover what had aroused the dogs," he explained.

Morning Song broke the last pair of bride cakes, tossed the pieces to the canine horde, and sighed. "I suppose you will have to tell her what I am doing," she said.

"You do not wish my mother to know that you are, for some reason, giving them food?"

Morning Song hesitated, then spread her crumb-smeared hands.

The village would know all the rest; they might as well know this! "That I was giving them the bride cakes I had made, and that Owl Crying refused," she said. "Or that Stag Leaping would not allow her to keep."

He did not respond, and she jutted out her chin. "Do not feel sorry for me," she snapped; for she could not abide that, not from someone who had seemed able to make some sense of the complexity that was Morning Song. She shoved irritably at the fawning mongrels who would not accept that the feast was at an end, looked back toward Cloud Racer, and started. Had the moon's pale gleaming touched briefly on a mouth shaped into a smile? "Nor laugh at me," she added truculently.

"I do not laugh. As a warrior, I know that cunning may often succeed where strength can not."

She hoisted the empty basket, rested it on one shoulder. "I am not certain what you mean by that," she said cautiously. But she knew, suddenly and surely, that Cloud Racer understood that the opposition to the marriage arranged by Summer Maize and Owl Crying had come from Morning Song herself. Yet there was no way he could have known, she thought confusedly.

"It does not matter." The shadows shivered as he began to move away. "I will let Rain Singing think that a fox was unwise enough to sneak into the compound," he told her over his shoulder.

Then the deeper shadows swallowed him up, and Morning Song, still confused, was left to stare at nothing.

Chapter 17

⊨ ⟹

Morning Song had been foolish to think Stag Leaping might be content with rejecting her offer of marriage and telling everyone who would listen that he had. He was bound that she should suffer as much humiliation as he could contrive to heap upon her.

"He goes about saying that only a desperate man would choose to marry someone who is less than a woman," Pumpkin Blossom informed her cousin, her slanted eyes glittering with a blend of sympathy and excitement. "He says that you lack the qualities a proper wife should have, and that you can never hope to be soft and round enough to warm Stag Leaping's bed."

"Owl Crying's remarks are worse," Bountiful Harvest put in, anger directing a violent stirring of her succotash. "She insists you would rather sleep with that dog of yours than with a man." She raked her niece with accusing eyes. "She adds that this is just as well, because she doubts there is a warrior anywhere who would willingly come to your hearth."

"I do not see why you blame me for what Stag Leaping and his mother say," Morning Song began hotly, but Hearth Tender intervened.

"You misunderstand my sister's wrath, Morning Song. It is aimed at those who would listen and repeat what is said, not at you. It is not pleasant for her—for any of us—when friends suddenly stop talking as we approach them."

Morning Song knew what she meant. Whenever she walked through the compound these days, knots of matrons or maidens put their heads together and murmured, or giggled, or merely fell silent while their eyes examined her as though she were a stranger.

Otter advised her how to deal with that. "Raise your eyebrows just a little"—her dark brows separated, lifted—"and smile so"— she let her lips part slightly—"and focus just beyond them, as though you do not realize they are there."

"What purpose will that serve?" Morning Song demanded.

Otter's calculated mystique vanished as she grinned. "They will wonder why you are not casting down your eyes and slinking away, as those who are embarrassed are expected to do. And they shall eventually conclude that you know something they do not. Matron and maid, they will be more interested in discovering what it is than in chewing the stale bread of yesterday's gossip."

"What would you know about such things?" Morning Song asked. "You have never been gossiped about, Otter."

"True. But I am a watcher of people, and have found that a woman who puts on the expression I showed you never fails to baffle others. Surely you have noticed it on Pumpkin Blossom. That smile first visited her face the day she decided to keep secret the name of the warrior she means to marry—and I think she practices it before she goes to sleep each night. You must do the same, Morning Song."

Morning Song laughed then, and promised to do as Otter suggested. Yet dissembling did not come naturally to her; look how abysmal the results when she'd tried it with Stag Leaping! She found it easier by far to return the speculative glances of the gossipers with a challenging stare. They invariably responded by averting their own eyes and beginning to talk of something—or someone—else.

Teller Of Legends approved this course. "You have learned that nothing quells rattling tongues so effectively as indifference," she told Morning Song one day. "When I saw Owl Crying at the river this morning, I made sure that everyone there heard me tell her how I hoped Stag Leaping would be chosen by the maid he wished to be husband to." She chuckled, and Morning Song rejoiced to see that her mirth was genuine, that both her pride and her equanimity had survived the Pigeonhawk clan's rejection of her granddaughter. "I hinted, too, that your interests, as well as his, lie elsewhere." Her shrewd eyes rested on Morning Song's delicate features. "As I suspect they do."

Morning Song was taken aback. "Grandmother, there is no one I wish to marry!" she protested.

The creases at the corners of Teller Of Legends's mouth bowed to make room for her smile. "When you said this before, on the night I told you that you were pledged to Stag Leaping, I believed you," she said. "But there has been a look about you of late that tells me this is no longer so."

For the first time in her life, the young woman questioned her grandmother's shrewdness. "Teller Of Legends, I have no wish to marry anyone," she repeated firmly. "If you think otherwise, then you will be disappointed."

Yet what her grandmother had said lingered at the back of her thoughts, just as the scent of musk lingers on a trail long after an animal has gone from it.

Because a keen-edged breeze warned that warm weather was preparing to forsake them, Morning Song took her bow and the arrows Deer Caller had made for her, and spent the rest of the day in the forest. Once winter invaded the woods, once ponds glazed and ice sheathed the trees, even the beasts who did not hibernate or travel south would be safe from those who ordinarily stalked them.

"Fingers rigid with cold fumble on the bowstring and cannot loose arrows quickly enough," she told White Shadow. He merely wagged his tail the harder. Now was what mattered to him; tomorrow could be dealt with when it came.

They took less-traveled paths this day, almost imperceptible tracks that wound eventually into the heart of the woods, and Morning Song noted how thoroughly brown had encroached upon her world.

What foliage had not been shed was dull and listless, although traces of green still haunted the occasional cluster of fern. Only the resinous pines and spruces and firs sported a greenness nothing would bleach. Yet the sun reached out and spread a shimmering veneer over the blue of the sky-dome, reached down and let warmth and brightness spill upon the land. The lively breeze made the evergreens sigh and yearn toward one another like lovers hungry to embrace. It rippled Shadow's fur, and freed strands of dark hair from the plait that hung down Morning Song's back. And when her sharp eyes discovered that badger and muskrat and some variety of cat frequented the part of the forest they'd come to, she named herself content.

Content surrendered without protest to excitement when she came upon a single two-toed print betraying the passage of a running buck. She signed for Shadow to drop back, and painstakingly examined the area all around. She found another print in the brush, and a pair of them on a strip of soft earth where some smaller animal had been grubbing. These were fresh made, and proved that she was downwind of the deer, but she must take care to approach him from the side rather than from front or rear. Morning Song did not mean to let carelessness cheat her of this prize!

She scanned the terrain and deliberated. Like any sensible creature, a deer unaware of danger would take the easiest route to his destination. She closed her eyes, called up a broader picture of this section of the forest. Just over the next rise, a stream threaded a tree-ringed glade; probably the stag she followed was heading for a watering spot on it.

She picked up her pace, and was thankful that any leaves she trod on were limp and decaying, silent underfoot. When she came to the hillock, she crept around it, then slid between pale birches whose slender trunks threatened her with exposure. She breathed more easily when she positioned herself behind the ampler girth of a towering oak. Her probing eyes fixed on a series of indentations, and she grinned: Only the hoofs of a deer could have made them, and recently.

If Morning Song was patient enough, and skillful enough, the buck's lazy progression to the watering place would be his undoing. She began to drift from tree to tree, her eyes constantly sweeping the ground ahead. And always she pressed forward, always kept as her goal the pewter sheen of the rivulet whose low verges offered easy access to any animal that thirsted.

When the trees thinned, she dropped flat and inched from bush to scraggly bush, from tussock to grassy tussock, keeping her face turned to the ground. Then a rhythmic splashing sound gave her pause and invited her to raise her head and peer through a skeletal thicket.

There stood the same stag she and Shadow had glimpsed during rutting season, or one who was twin to him. Branching antlers stretched halfway across the narrow stream he drank from, and his blue-gray coat seemed to absorb and retain the light that angled into the tiny glade. Morning Song, transfixed by the sight, wondered uneasily if the unnatural glow the creature wore might not render him invincible.

Fancifulness gave way before a resurrection of flint-hard resolve, and she slithered toward a denuded willow that marked the place where the river's banks began to heighten. Its profusion of drooping boughs provided cover of sorts, and she was nicely situated for the shot she was determined to make.

She rose to all fours, then to her knees, and slipped an arrow from her quiver before cautiously unfolding the rest of herself. The stag was drinking still, but so daintily now that Morning Song knew she had no time to lose. She raised her bow, drew back on the string, squinted along the shaft, and launched at her elegant prey the elegant arrow a blind man had made.

Morning Song had aimed for the deer's graceful neck. From his neck her arrow protruded when the buck crumpled to the ground; from his neck blood flowed out to redden the water his magnificent head rested in.

Twice the wounded creature fought to come to his feet, to reclaim the dignity that was his birthright. Twice his slender legs refused to support his weight, bowed, and sent him crashing down again. By the time Morning Song had ducked beneath the flimsy canopy of the willow's branches and run to where he lay, death had released his courageous spirit. The ritual words of apology and gratitude that she spoke were directed into the sky after it, but this brief communion with the stag's *orenda* went beyond the traditional. It conveyed awe that Morning Song—so little experienced in the tracking of big game—had been permitted to make this kill, and sent up thanks that the deer had been spared the agony of a lingering death.

Then she sat back on her heels and beamed upon enough venison to feed her family throughout the white season ahead. She was beaming still when a crunching of brittle twigs on the far side of the stream made her look up. It would be Shadow, of course, freed from the obligation to keep a discreet distance while Morning Song closed on her quarry.

But it was not Shadow who splashed through the shallow stream and came to join her. It was Cloud Racer, and his face was thunder-dark. "I had been stalking that stag," he said tightly.

The excitement of the chase and the glory of its climax had filled Morning Song with elation. Here was someone with whom she might share her joy, who would truly understand her pride. "And what a grand stag he is!" she told him, grinning broadly. "I cannot believe that I brought him down with a single arrow!" She spread her arms to measure the length of the carcass, and waited for Cloud Racer to acknowledge the magnitude of her accomplishment.

"It is the custom," he said instead, "for a hunter to let it be known when he means to go on the stalk. And to ask first whether others had planned to be in the part of the forest he is making for."

Morning Song's exhilaration fled before the accusation in his voice. "You did not ask that of me," she countered.

"It is not the custom," he retorted, "to ask among the *women*."

She surged to her feet, put her hands on her hips, and faced him squarely. "Then I think it should *become* the custom," she told him, "if this sort of thing is not to happen again." As soon as the words were out, she was sorry. How would she have reacted if Cloud Racer had loosed his arrow before she'd released hers? She would have been just as upset, if not more so! "I know how you must feel," she added quickly. But he was not interested in sympathy.

"It is permissible for women to trap small game or birds. But for a woman to take up a man's weapons and hunt with them is contrary to nature," he informed her.

Morning Song's sympathy dissolved. "Should a woman's skill with the bow be as great as a man's, or greater, then for her *not* to hunt would be contrary to *her* nature," she flashed back.

His black eyes smoldered. "I see that I should have paid more heed to those who hinted that you must be a man in woman's dress," he said. "You bring shame on an honorable clan, Morning Song."

"I bring food to a family that no longer has a hunter in their lodge," she said fiercely. "No shame should be attached to me for it."

"Surely you knew the other hunters would willingly share with the Turtle clan?"

"The Turtle clan need not be in debt to anyone while I can provide for us," she pointed out with a superior smile. How dare Cloud Racer overlook what she had proven herself capable of? As a boy, he'd instructed and encouraged an awkward misfit of a girl;

grown, he had seemed to understand how, even today, Morning Song needed to stray occasionally from the path that tradition had marked for her feet. What had happened to him? She narrowed her eyes. "I think you rant so because you are accustomed to excelling whenever hunter-warriors compete. To be bested at all would wound your vanity. To be bested by a woman—as you have been this day, Cloud Racer—is more than you can bear."

He shook his head slowly, disbelievingly. "In all the years you have roamed this forest," he demanded, "have you discovered even one vixen who would be a he-fox, one hen-turkey who has tied to her breast the bristle feathers of a cock, a single doe who walks as though antlers grow upon her head?"

He neither expected nor wanted an answer to his question. His eyes studied her face for a moment, moved to the carcass sprawled at her feet. "You will need help hauling that back to the village," he said abruptly, and reached for the blade hanging at his waist.

And she, no doubt, would be made to walk several paces behind as they went, so that all who witnessed their approach would assume that the beast slung from the carrying pole had been Cloud Racer's kill. "I slew the stag; I shall take him home," she told him sharply. "I have no need of help, Cloud Racer."

She whipped out her own knife, went down on her knees beside the inert buck, and had already ripped open his belly by the time the man she had thought her friend wheeled around and left the glade. She did not look up when she heard him go.

Even gutting the deer and removing the hoofs and antlers did not reduce the carcass to a weight Morning Song could drag back to the village alone. Much though she yearned to flaunt the awesome size of her kill, she dismembered the beast and carved it into manageable portions. She lashed them onto a triangular sledge she improvised, but then found it difficult indeed to hack out a path wide enough to accommodate the load. By the time she was halfway home, burning hands and complaining muscles warned that she must make different arrangements, or she would not arrive at the village before full dark further complicated matters.

The cave, she thought wearily. I will leave some of the meat in the cave.

This meant veering from a trail that would take her directly home; but she was too exhausted to repel any predatory beast that might, even now, be sniffing at the blood that dripped from haunch and shoulder and spotted the ground behind the sledge. And it was both unfair and unwise to rely on White Shadow to do so.

She trudged on until she reached her hideaway, then fumbled with the knots securing her precious cargo. Leaving on the sledge only the choicest portions, she plodded to the cave's narrow entrance, stooped down, and thrust the rest of the meat up against its rear wall. She struggled to her feet again, piled deadwood in front of the cave, then sawed a many-twigged branch from a nearby tree and swept the area bordering the cave, once, twice, three times.

Before she went back to the sledge, she summoned the dog who was guarding it and told him he must stand sentry by the cave instead. "Let the animals who hunt make their own kills," she said. "I shall trust you to keep safe what is mine."

His eyes pleaded with her, but he went dutifully, if reluctantly, to his vigil.

"You shall have the liver, when all of the meat has been brought to the lodge," she promised him, then grasped the rope and began hauling home her diminished load. The only thing that kept her stumbling feet moving steadily along the path pointing out of the forest was the sight of the stag's wide-spreading antlers tied firmly atop the rough-cut slabs of flesh. No one who saw the splendid crown would doubt that Morning Song's kill had been one even a seasoned hunter might boast of.

Despite the envious Cloud Racer's censure, she was fully aware of the praise owing to her.

This time, praise was not withheld. Disapprove though they did of Morning Song's adopting a hunter's guise, most of the villagers were moved to exclaim when they saw what she had brought home. And when she impulsively presented the stag's heart and part of the haunch to Se-A-Wi—who, as Sachem, was more accustomed to giving freely of what he had to those who lacked—she earned their respect also. Hill Climber, whose own hunting skills kept the Plover lodge supplied with meat, was disgruntled when his grandmother lauded Morning Song for being so thoughtful, and the other hunter-warriors were no less annoyed to have a woman invading their territory. But several of the younger lads were quick to volunteer when the tactful Se-A-Wi suggested that the strongest of them go with Morning Song to bring back the rest of the meat.

Once it had been brought to her lodge, the meat was received gladly. If Bountiful Harvest rolled her eyes to remind everyone that her niece was once again holding them up to ridicule, she nonetheless pounced greedily upon the pile of venison.

Teller Of Legends, when Morning Song blurted out the tale of Cloud Racer's jealousy and his unwarranted criticism, seemed more interested in studying her granddaughter's indignant face than in the venison her three daughters were efficiently dealing with. "If you choose to pit your skills against those of a man, Morning Song," she said mildly, "then you can scarcely hope for him to be pleased when he discovers that you are extraordinarily proficient. Particularly when it costs him a stag he has been stalking."

"But I did not *know* that he was," Morning Song repeated, eyeing with distaste the blood-spattered tunic she had just shed; it would mean a trip to the river to remove those stains, and her dislike for the river was as strong as ever. "There was no way I could know. And had it been his arrow that brought down the buck I was aiming at, I would have praised his marksmanship despite my disappointment. Cloud Racer should have been generous enough to speak favorably of mine."

"Men save their admiration for true women," Pumpkin Blossom declared. "As any maid but you would have long since learned." Her tilted eyes expressed sorrow over Morning Song's ignorance.

Day Greeter was aghast. "What if all of the warriors scorn you, Morning Song? How shall you ever persuade one of them to be your husband?"

"She shall not," her mother called stridently. "Unless she shows herself willing to be done with her waywardness, no warrior worthy of the name will have her." She wondered fleetingly if she should encourage Pumpkin Blossom to speak now to the man she had chosen. Teller Of Legends would never allow Pumpkin Blossom's husband to suffer loss of status; she would forbid Morning Song to hunt once he had come to live with them. Still, Midwinter was not far off, and the sky this evening foretold weather cold enough to put a virtual end to all hunting. . . .

Deer Caller let their conversation direct him to where they stood. "Even among the proud Iroquois," he volunteered, "there ought to be a warrior who realizes that there is no lessening of his own status merely because a woman has learned how to hunt." He held out toward Morning Song the antlers he had been examining. "It must have been a magnificent buck," he told her. "Which doubtless aggravated Cloud Racer the more. And for all that you say otherwise, Morning Song, I think you would have been as furious as he was if Cloud Racer had slain the deer before you could. With any two hunters who chanced to cross each other, the same thing would have happened."

"From any other hunter, I would have *expected* anger," Morning Song conceded. "But I had thought Cloud Racer less . . ." She groped for a word, and did not find it. "Or more—more . . ." Her voice trailed off.

Rather than responding, Deer Caller merely nodded and grinned as he turned away, increasing Morning Song's confusion. And his seeming to understand something she did not caused her to drop her knife twice when, obedient to Bountiful Harvest's command, she went to help cut up the venison she'd brought home.

For some weeks afterward, new-come winter's mood was vengeful enough to dissuade anyone from roaming the forest. Even the snow that replaced a vanguard of stinging sleet did not swirl gently out of the leaden sky, but pelted down violently until everything it fell upon had been sealed in vaults of smothering white.

When at last the wind was spent, the snow-silence was as awesome in its lack of sound as the gales had been in their shrieking abundance of it. And the cold stretched out invisible fingers to probe the elm-bark sheathed walls of the longhouses, find gaps in their gabled roofs, sidle over and under and around the heavy hides that blocked their entrances. Only roaring fires could keep them at bay, and the families of the village huddled close to their hearths and drank endless cups of parched-corn coffee.

Gradually they armored themselves mentally against the discomfort, convinced themselves that vigorous stamping would restore feeling to numbed feet and that a brisk rubbing was enough to uncramp frozen fingers. Then they took down bundles of ash splints, unrolled lengths of softened hide, separated dried husks according to their suitability for braiding or shredding, and engrossed themselves in the variety of tasks they had reserved for this season. Morning Song did her share of the basketweaving, began to sew the tunic Teller Of Legends insisted she make for Midwinter, and abandoned either job on the instant whenever Deer Caller asked her help in smoothing the long shafts to which he would be attaching spear points. She felt honored that he allowed her to work with him, but worried that Otter—who usually assisted her husband— had become so restless that she could no longer do so for more than a brief span of time.

"There is no need to fret," her mother-aunt said lightly. "It is only that my time is near, Morning Song." She patted her enormous belly and grinned. "My babe pokes and kicks in his eagerness to be born, so I walk about until he is tired enough to sleep. Which neither of us does very often!" The smudges beneath her eyes attested to that, yet they did not detract from her patent joy.

"Meanwhile, I am grateful that you are willing to help Deer Caller, for he has promised Fierce Eagle a score of lances by spring."

"I am happy to," Morning Song assured her. "Indeed, helping Deer Caller gives me reason to abandon work I would prefer to postpone for now. Rubbing grit into the shafts is no hardship, not even for someone whose hands"—she stared ruefully at them—"have suddenly become contrary when I ask them to do anything else."

"No doubt the cold has stiffened them," Otter said. "Just as it interferes with your wandering, Morning Song."

Her niece only nodded, and did not admit that something other than the freezing weather was to blame for both her recurring clumsiness and her avoidance of the forest. In truth, she enjoyed walking in the woods when her breath puffed into miniature clouds, loved the snow-sparkled evergreens, and was fascinated by the clustered icicles that made mystical things of barren trees. To break the crust of untrodden snow with every step she took delighted her, and no amount of shivering lessened her appreciation of the dazzle that winter brought to the woods. No, it was not the cold—however bitter—that made her hesitant to go there now. She was not entirely certain what held her back, just as she did not know what made her fumble the most ordinary task; but she knew it was not the cold.

Both she and Otter turned as a flurry of icy air announced that the Turtle Clan had visitors, and both hurried forward with the rest to greet Rain Singing and Small Brown Sparrow.

"I praise the winter for giving us more time to be with our friends," the Matron of the Deer lodge said. She twinkled at all of them, went to sit beside Teller Of Legends, and made a merry show of threading her needle in order to hem the robe she had brought with her. Everyone knew she had no intention of setting a single stitch unless she did so absentmindedly, but a woman so consistently cheerful would never be criticized for occasional idleness.

Her daughter, on the other hand, let her fingers fly as fast as her tongue while she sat with Otter and Morning Song and Bountiful Harvest's two daughters. "I must have these finished for the Festival," she explained, displaying moccasins whose narrowness announced that they would be worn on her own small feet. Her wide mouth shaped itself into a gladsome smile. "I had thought Midwinter would never come, yet now it shall be here before we know it."

Morning Song picked up the stuff that would, in time, become her tunic for the Festival, and wielded her needle in fits and starts. Rain Singing would not be faulted for only pretending to work, but

Bountiful Harvest would surely pounce if Morning Song did nothing. "I suppose your brothers have been practicing the dances they will take part in?" she asked, bending over the bleached hide.

Small Brown Sparrow laughed. "Fox Running certainly is! It will be his first time to dance, and he means to collect compliments from the maidens. As for Cloud Racer"—she shrugged—"lately he has been as short-tempered as a bear prodded out of its winter's sleep. We are none of us sorry when he decides to go off on one of his lonely walks. Although why he would tramp through the forest in weather like this is something I shall never understand."

"Morning Song shows better sense this year," Otter observed, smiling affectionately at her niece. Then she frowned, sighed, and stood up. "I will be happy when this babe decides to be born," she said fervently, and began again to pace in ever-widening circles.

Small Brown Sparrow watched her for a moment, then turned to Pumpkin Blossom. "Do you realize that, by next Midwinter, one or both of us may be waiting for a child to be born?" she exclaimed.

Pumpkin Blossom nodded as she looked up from the bodice of the dress she was decorating, and allowed one of her secretive smiles to tremble on her lips.

Morning Song stabbed herself with her needle, scowled, tossed aside her sewing, and scrambled to her feet. "Deer Caller has need of me, I think," she mumbled, and made for the far end of the longhouse.

Her friends neither heard what she said nor remarked on her going. They had more exciting matters to concern themselves with.

But Teller Of Legends, who had been using one ear to eavesdrop while Rain Singing chattered into the other, watched her retreating granddaughter with speculative eyes. She nodded slowly and smiled a little; apparently she did so in agreement with something Rain Singing was saying.

Chapter 18

Before the next day's dawning had roused the village, Otter Swimming spoke briefly with her mother, said a reassuring word to her husband, and put on her snowshoes. She took a bundle from her shelf and went out of the fire-warmed lodge and into the cold, into a teeth-numbing cold she prayed would be tempered by the rising of her brother the sun.

Teller Of Legends hoped the same and said as much to Morning Song, who had been awakened by their low-pitched voices. "It is worrisome, to give birth during the white season. Shelter is hard to find, and an infant whose first tears are likely to freeze on his tiny cheeks must be hardy indeed to survive. The animals plan more wisely than we do, I think."

"Why must Otter be forbidden to give birth here?" Morning Song asked, suddenly fearful for her favorite mother-aunt. "Surely this would be more sensible, Grandmother, for any woman whose babe comes during the winter."

"From the beginning our women have gone into the forest to give birth," Teller Of Legends said. "The earth is our mother; it is fitting that we cling to her breast at such times and ask the help of benevolent spirits and the ghosts of our ancestors." She looked into her granddaughter's anxious eyes and smiled. "Otter shall be comforted by many who no longer inhabit this world, Morning Song, for there is this to be said of winter: The barriers between their world and ours are weakened then. Doubtless your own mother shall be with Otter Swimming today, and whisper encouragement to her."

She prodded the drowsing embers until they yawned, fed tongue tips of flame with kindling. "Will you take Deer Caller to his mother's lodge? My brother and Sweet Maple will keep him from brooding until the birthing is over and Otter and their child are safe home. And please," she added softly as Morning Song nodded agreement, "do not reveal that you worry also. In some ways, it is as hard for a man as it is for a woman when a babe comes. She, at least, has an active part in the proceeding."

Morning Song grinned dutifully; given the choice, she would rather be involved than condemned to the agony of waiting, whatever the situation. Yet Deer Caller need not hunt out a spot where evergreens grew close enough to provide a windbreak; his shaking hands would not have to spread a robe to squat upon, and his legs and buttocks would not be exposed to frost-sharp air; and never, ever, would he experience the body-wrenching pain unique to childbirth. Perhaps, she thought grimly, it was only right that a man should worry a little when a woman endured so much! Still, she liked and admired Deer Caller, so she did her best to divert him as they walked to Sweet Maple's lodge.

"I suppose you will put aside the weapons you are making, and begin to carve playthings for your child," she teased. "Although what Far Seer will say when he hears is beyond my imagining!"

Her jest was wasted. "Will Otter return by midday?" he asked. He tilted back his head, frowned. "Why is the sun so slow to show his face this morning?" He inhaled deeply. "We shall be having snow again, that is why. Morning Song, Otter must be home before it comes." He gripped her arm. "Promise that she will be," he said.

"If she is not," Morning Song said, moved by the anguish in his sightless eyes, "then I will go after her and bring her back to our lodge."

"Even if our babe has yet to come!" he said strongly. "Say it."

Morning Song hesitated. If the child still clung to her womb, Otter would refuse to return to the village. Yet Morning Song was as certain as Deer Caller that a fresh fall of snow would put at risk both laboring woman and new-come babe. "I will honor the vow, no matter the circumstances," she said rashly, then raised her voice to alert Sweet Maple to their arrival.

The Matron of the Plover lodge clapped her plump hands when she learned the reason for her nephew's visit. "Then the spirit who sent my dream last night spoke truly," she exclaimed. "Otter shall bring you a boy-child, Deer Caller. I am certain of it."

She hugged Morning Song. "You must tell your grandmother of my dream," she said, and began to dispense a wealth of confusing detail. Morning Song could not see how a vision of muskrats offering pond-lily roots to a turtle hatchling could possibly refer to Otter's babe, but she was happy to accept that dreams predict indirectly.

She watched Deer Caller settle himself between Hill Climber and Se-A-Wi while Tree Reaching Up fetched pipes and tobacco for all of them. "I will come again as soon as Otter returns from the forest," she told Sweet Maple then.

The older woman went with her to the entrance. She patted Morning Song's arm. "Do not be concerned for Deer Caller. The men will be trading stories of hunting and raiding, and you know how that sort of thing goes on and on and occupies all their thoughts." Her eyes lost their sparkle suddenly. "But I shall be waiting to hear, Morning Song, so please do not delay." She held aside the length of hide that a fretful wind was buffeting and looked up at the graying sky. "This is not a good time for a woman to be having a baby. May Otter's be quick to leave the womb, quicker than most firstborns care to be."

Sweet Maple's disquiet did nothing to ease Morning Song's, and her heart was kin to her plodding feet as she tramped through ankle-deep snow to the Turtle longhouse. Every hearth wore leaping flames now, in anticipation of Otter's homecoming. She warmed herself by Teller Of Legends's hearth and tried to smile. "Deer Caller has a tale-spinner on either side of him. He will have no room in his head for distressing thoughts," she announced. "And Sweet Maple says that a dream has told her Otter's child shall be a boy." Her smile wavered, vanished. How her mother-aunt must be craving the heat that her niece was so callously enjoying!

Hearth Tender saw the chagrin on her face, knew the reason that Morning Song stepped away from the fire. "My sister shall be befriended also," she said quietly. "No woman is truly alone when she gives birth, Morning Song. And refusing to warm yourself does nothing to send warmth to Otter. She will have arranged shelter for herself by now, in any event."

"But Deer Caller said that the air is scented with fresh snow. And the wind is beginning to blow from the north."

Bountiful Harvest sampled her corn pudding, added a pinch of maple sugar. "Otter Swimming is no fragile-stemmed blossom to wither in a cold wind," she said. "She will give birth as easily as I have always done, and take no more thought for the weather than I ever did."

"None of your children came during the white season," Morning Song said swiftly and not without anger.

"It is the spirits who decide when a woman is to conceive, and when she is to deliver," Hearth Tender reminded her. "They are with Otter now. You may depend on it."

"If you do not calm yourself, Morning Song, you will be as much an irritation as Deer Caller would have been," Bountiful Harvest snapped. "Either find a way to be busy or take yourself elsewhere until my sister returns."

Teller Of Legends signed to her granddaughter to come sit beside her. "We have garments we are working on, you and I. Let us put the waiting time to good use by finishing them."

Pumpkin Blossom and her sister took up their own sewing and came to sit with them, oblivious for once to their small brother's plea for a story or a game. "My dress for Midwinter is ready," Pumpkin Blossom said. "Now I am making leggins and a breech-clout for Fish Jumping to wear." She looked at him. "A *warrior's* breechclout," she said, and was satisfied to see her brother's disgruntlement disappear. "He will not pester us now," she said confidently, "and I shall play with him when I am done."

"There is no reason he should not have a story before then, however," her grandmother said.

Sturdy little Fish Jumping grinned, and plunked himself down in the center of the circle the needle-pliers had formed.

"Of late, there has been considerable talk about the weather," Teller Of Legends said, "so I shall speak of the spirit who is responsible for the seasons that rule our lives. He is kin to Earth Woman, this spirit, and one of the names he is known by is A-De-Ka-Gag-Waa."

"Who is Earth Woman?" Fish Jumping asked.

"Earth Woman was the daughter of Sky Woman, and her father was the Upholder Of The Heavens," his grandmother said. "The West Wind came to her when she was grown and left two children sleeping in her womb. Both were boy-children, just as you are. But one was very, very good, and the other—his twin—was evil beyond your imagining. It was because Earth Woman spent all her strength trying to beat the badness out of him that she died."

Fish Jumping gasped; he had never before heard of a child who was *beaten*, however disobedient he might have been.

Teller Of Legends smiled. "He was more than mischievous, this boy called Evil Spirit," she explained. "He brought wickedness and contention into the world before his twin brother—whom we know as the Maker Of Life—finally triumphed over him. But let us return to my story."

Her voice became a compelling chant as she described how Earth Mother persuaded A-De-Ka-Gag-Waa to make fertile the land of her people, the Iroquois. She told how, in turn, A-De-Ka-Gag-Waa had to convince He-No the Thunderer and Ga-Oh the Wind Giant that this was a fine idea. "He-No bellowed with outrage when he learned that he would be expected to curb his strength from time to time," Teller Of Legends said, "and Ga-Oh shrieked that he saw no reason to tame his powerful winds."

Fish Jumping's eyes grew huge as his grandmother inflated her own voice to show them how furiously those two argued with A-De-Ka-Gag-Waa; and he sighed with relief when she went on to say that Earth Mother got her wish in the end.

"A treaty was made, and is abided by to this day," she finished. "Conditions were set by He-No and Ga-Oh, of course, and not even Earth Mother expected her kinsman to leave his home in the south for more than half the year. This is why we have four seasons, and arrange our lives to suit them."

Morning Song had been darting glances at the smoke hole over the hearth. Now she touched her grandmother's arm and directed

ier eyes toward a pale gleam of sunlight illuminating the circle.
Teller of Legends, hunched over the fire throughout her story,
straightened so promptly that her granddaughter knew it was not
iunger for warmth that had slumped her shoulders, but anxiety over
ier youngest daughter.

Now, if only the sun continued to show his face, perhaps Otter's
ravail could be a little eased.

By the time they had eaten, even that anemic glow had faded.
High, feathery clouds streaked the dull sky, and denser clouds
formed a bruise-colored mass to prove the prediction Deer Caller
iad made. And the winds blew stronger, moaned around the cor-
iers of the lodges, and pummeled the helpless trees.

The snow descended lightly at first, spiraling down in huge flakes.
But the wind, disenchanted by so pallid a display, roiled the clouds
until the stuff spilled from them in a white cascade and mounded
wherever it found support for growth.

"Morning Song, you must secure the hide. No fire is powerful
enough to fight the cold you are inviting in." Bountiful Harvest's
one bore its customary tartness, but her niece suspected that worry,
this time, was responsible for it. Hearth Tender had gone to the far
end of the lodge, to meditate and to beg the help of every spirit she
could think to invoke. Day Greeter looked frightened, and Pumpkin Blossom was having difficulty putting the finishing touches on
Fish Jumping's breechclout.

Morning Song grieved for Teller Of Legends. She had made
courageous effort to appear serene and had tried to divert them with
her story. Now she sat in silence and in shadow, her head turned
away from the hearth so that none could see how the lines in her
face had been deepened by fear's chisel. But Morning Song did not
need to see them; the fear that emanated from her grandmother
nourished her own terrible apprehension.

She went to the wall over her bunk and lifted down her snowshoes, snatched her hooded robe from her shelf. "I am going to
find Otter," she said as she passed the rawhide thongs of one
webbed snow-walker around her heel. "I no longer care whether
it is *right*, or no," she added. "I am going."

She did not say that she was fulfilling a pledge she had made to
Deer Caller; she would have gone regardless, and she knew it.

"I shall go with you," Day Greeter said bravely, but Morning
Song shook her head. "I will travel faster," she said, flinging her
robe around her narrow shoulders, "if I am alone."

No one else said a word, but Morning Song felt their eyes on her as she clumped to the entrance and knew there was no disapproval in anyone's gaze, but only hope and encouragement. That knowledge made a warm tide to wash her out into a world thickly veiled by falling snow.

My feet will recognize the way, she said to herself, then halted as swirling white shaped itself into more substantial white and Shadow greeted her. "You shall guide me if I go astray," she murmured, stroking his wet fur. "We must make for the place where blueberries grow, I think. Otter—being Otter—shall have chosen to be near water when her babe comes. Particularly since the bushes nearby are thick enough to give shelter of a sort. Yes," she finished, striding forward as rapidly as her snowshoes permitted. "I am certain we shall find her there." And she would not let herself consider, for so much as a moment, what dire straits they might find her in.

To go from the village to where the woods began presented no problem; diminished visibility offered only a minor challenge. And once among the trees, the blinding snow met resistance from bole and branch, so that Morning Song occasionally glimpsed a grouping of birches, an isolated tall pine, an especially massive oak— signs that warned of a wrong turning or led her to the one she sought. Her dog plodded ahead, and she set her feet upon his pawprints. Snowflakes clustered on the dog's furry hide and coated his ears and muzzle. They glued themselves to Morning Song's eyebrows and lashes, tried to find purchase on her nose and chin, invaded the hood that encircled her head. Neither paid heed to them, save to shake or brush them away from time to time. Icy air seared Morning Song's nose and throat, the speed she demanded of herself took heavy toll of her leg muscles; but these were agonies she could and did ignore. Woman and dog pressed on, breasted the wind-driven snow as though it were of no more account than gentle spring rain, refused to recognize the numbing cold as an adversary.

Shadow was panting, and Morning Song gasping for breath as they skirted the tumbled boulders she had perched on while her grandmother introduced her to the dawn chorus that was her namesake. White-clad now, the boulders loomed like grotesque ghosts, but Morning Song smiled as they passed them. They reached the configuration of skeletal elm and maple that bordered the path to her cave, and veered in the opposite direction. Now the wind was at their backs, and breathing at least was made easier.

"Not much farther," Morning Song said between teeth she had clenched to deflect the knife-sharp air. Shadow trotted on, stepping as quickly as he could so that he would not sink belly deep into the fresh fall of snow. For all his care, that happened once or twice; then Morning Song waited while he scrambled onto the treacherous crust once more. She would not let herself show impatience toward so faithful a companion. Indeed, his determination heightened hers, helped her to lift her feet and put them down after her legs had begun to cramp in protest.

All the while, she kept her mind resolutely blank, would not think beyond the moment, did not dare to reflect on the woman who had been exposed to such perilous weather for hours. Only when they'd reached the narrow stream that eventually wound itself around the place of blueberries did she admit the ogre called fear to her thoughts again. And nothing could have stayed it then.

They followed the looping ribbon of ice, snapped their way through tangles of snow-rimmed branches to avoid a detour Morning Song could not take time for, and found themselves approaching their destination. Morning Song dashed snow from her eyelashes, squinted, and gazed despairingly upon a winter-sculpted distortion of the commonplace. She recognized nothing, could not even trust that this was the spot she'd been seeking, questioned whether they might have traveled too far, or not far enough. The ice-bound stream they'd followed . . . had it truly been the one that sang to the women whenever they gathered the plump berries a kindly sun had ripened for them?

She made herself examine more slowly the blue-shadowed drifts, a congregation of miniature mountains, the twig-studded humps that resembled monstrous porcupines. Suddenly her heart thudded against her ribs. That was no natural growth, that snow-heaped rectangle stretching between the tallest of those would-be mountains . . .

"She is here!" she shouted, and White Shadow leaped ahead of her, deposing majestic clumps of snow as he crashed through the brake directly before them.

His mistress plunged after him, widened the gap his hurtling body had made, did not even wince as vicious briers clawed her cheeks. Across the white-carpeted clearing she went, fuming at her slowness, keeping her eyes fixed upon the robe Otter had lashed to the sturdiest of the blueberry bushes. The snow that had accumulated on it caused it to sag in the middle, so that its outer edge met a ridge of snow the wind had shaped upon the ground. And beneath the coverlet, behind that flimsy barricade, must be Otter Swimming!

Morning Song's numbed fingers wrenched at the knots securing her snowshoes, worked them loose at last. She dropped to her knees, thrust her arms elbow deep into the snow, used her hands precisely as Shadow was already using his paws. They labored together to make an opening big enough to crawl through, to permit them to reach the woman who—surely, surely—waited within the shelter she had managed to contrive.

The dog broke through first, but Morning Song was right behind him, blinking to stimulate her vision as she met a gloom only a little less frightening than the awful silence that greeted her. "Otter?" she called, trepidation giving a querulous edge to her voice.

There was no response. But in the snowlight that filtered through the breach they had made, she saw near the drooping middle of the shelter a huddle of fur-lined robes. On hands and knees, she scrambled across the rucked-up robe that had been spread to make a floor, reached out, and rested a shaking hand on the tightly curled, fearfully still figure that was Otter Swimming.

Her mother-aunt did not stir, not even when Morning Song, the pulses in her neck throbbing like hard-beaten drums, cautiously peeled back a corner of the stuff Otter had wrapped herself in. The face revealed to her might also have been a winter sculpture; the eyelids did not flicker, the mouth did not quiver, the angles of that beloved face were rigid as stone. And the flesh—which looked not at all like flesh—was cold, so cold, to Morning Song's touch.

The younger woman yanked back her hood, laid her own cheek upon Otter's icy one, felt her tears trickle slowly between their pressed-together flesh. And heard a sigh so faint that she thought she'd imagined it until she saw a strand of her own hair shiver as Otter's feeble breath caressed it.

She sat up, her eyes glowing now despite her tears. Shadow whined softly, and she looked across at him. "She lives!" she cried. "Otter lives."

But she did not deceive herself. The life that persisted in her mother-aunt was fragile; it hovered on the edge of extinction and pleaded for rescue.

Otter must be taken back to the longhouse, and quickly. Morning Song fought back despair and berated herself for not anticipating that she would need help to carry Otter home. How foolish she'd been to brush aside Day Greeter's offer to come with her. Timid-natured though her cousin was, she was young and strong. Together, they might have been able . . .

But this was senseless, Morning Song could not change what was; she could only go on from the place that overconfidence and lack of foresight had led her to.

Shadow whined again, and began to nose at the heavy robe Otter was rolled in, and his mistress was rudely jerked from her paralyzing self-blame. *The baby!* Otter had come here to bear her child, and Morning Song had not even thought to look— She leaned forward, gently probed the cocoon of hide that surrounded her mother-aunt. But not until she burrowed beneath the final layer did she encounter the knobby bundle Otter had placed in the protective curve of her body. Morning Song stripped off her own robe, lifted the precious bundle from its nest, and snuggled it in the soft fur. A hint of movement, the mere shifting of tiny limbs perhaps, told her that Otter's babe had also survived, and a warming tide of thankfulness rushed through her. She took a moment to tuck Otter's coverlet tight around her, then put out a trembling hand, raised the flap that rested over the spot where the babe's head must be, and cried out in amazement. For she uncovered not one round-cheeked, blunt-nosed face, but two. Side by side they lay, the twins Otter had borne in the midst of a raging winter storm.

White Shadow had come to stand beside her. Now, before she could restrain him, he sniffed once at each tiny head, then put out his tongue and licked the forehead of the babe nearest him. The infant squirmed; yet it was his twin who let out the puny wail that, despite its thinness, clearly registered annoyance.

The lustiness absent from that cry was a warning, however. Morning Song hastily drew her robe around and over the pair. The babies, too, must be taken swiftly to the Turtle longhouse, or the life granted to them this day would be snatched back abruptly. That recognition forced upon Morning Song a decision she dreaded to make. The chances that she alone might somehow transport Otter Swimming to the village were slim. She was reasonably certain, though, that she could retrace her steps, and fairly quickly, if she carried only the two infants. But could she bring herself to desert the unconscious Otter, the cold-fleshed, shallow-breathing Otter? Everything in Morning Song rebelled against the thought of it. Yet were she awake and alert, Otter Swimming would not only agree that her children should be cared for first, she would insist upon it. And Morning Song was honor-bound to abide by the choice Otter herself would have made.

She bent and again rested her cheek upon her mother-aunt's, looked up to discover that Shadow had lain down beside Otter, had fitted himself against the incurving arch of her motionless body.

"You are doing what I cannot," Morning Song said brokenly. "Stay with her, Shadow, until I return. And keep her as warm as you can."

The dog thumped his tail to show that he understood; only his eyes followed when she tied on her snowshoes, scooped up the securely swathed babies, and—heedless of the assault that would be made on her own exposed flesh—crawled out of Otter's birthing place and began the trek home.

One of them must have been watching for her. Morning Song, although the snow had ceased to fall, was struggling against a wind that whipped violently across the compound when she heard a babble of voices and the hide covering was swept back from the entrance to her lodge.

"Have you found her?" The words, uttered with simultaneous urgency by Hearth Tender and Teller Of Legends, barely penetrated Morning Song's frozen ears; gasping for breath, she could do no more than bob her head in response. She looked to where Bountiful Harvest stood beside her hearth, a daughter on either side of her. "Please," she croaked, "take Otter's babies."

Why it was Bountiful Harvest she instinctively asked this of, she did not know. But she surrendered the precious bundle to her without a qualm, and was unsurprised when her mother-aunt—scorning to take the time to question her or to exclaim over the fact that Otter had delivered twins—carried the infants to the warmest spot in the lodge to unwrap and examine them.

"Otter?" Teller Of Legends's whisper was ragged with anxiety.

Morning Song tore off her sodden clothing, clutched round her the robe Hearth Tender rushed to supply. "She is alive," she said. "But someone must go back with me, and at once, to bring her home." She coughed, took a moment to fill her lungs with air that would not brand them. "We will need a litter," she finished hoarsely.

There were no more questions then, from anyone. Morning Song stood by the fire and pulled on dry garments, slid her feet into boots borrowed from Pumpkin Blossom. Hearth Tender snatched down two of the poles from which dried corn hung, letting the ears tumble into an untidy heap, and called Day Greeter to help her stretch a strip of tough hide between the poles and fasten it tight. Then still without wasting energy on words, the two put on their heaviest outer garments.

"It will take four of us," Morning Song said, turning to Teller Of Legends. "If you will help look after the babies, then either Bountiful Harvest or Pumpkin Blossom can go along, too."

Her grandmother reached for her snowshoes. "My newest grandchildren are in capable hands," she said, "as you knew they would be. My concern now is all for my daughter. I am going with you, Morning Song.''

The litter was rolled for carrying, and Morning Song, Teller Of Legends, Hearth Tender, and Day Greeter prepared to go out into a day that was both bitterly cold and near to dying. Pumpkin Blossom hurried after them to give two neatly folded bedrobes to her sister. ''You may need these to cover Otter Swimming,'' she said, then smiled as one of the babes her mother was holding began to cry fretfully. ''Tell Otter not to worry about her sons,'' she added. ''Bountiful Harvest says they are hungry, and what better sign to prove that all is well with them?''

''Deer Caller should be told about the babies,'' Morning Song said wearily. ''He will be frantic by now. Pumpkin Blossom, when your mother can spare you—''

''I will go and tell him,'' her cousin said swiftly. ''And say that you have gone now to bring Otter home.''

''We will have her here as soon as possible,'' Morning Song said, her voice suddenly iron-hard. Then she turned aside, lowered her head to minimize the wind's battering, and began to lead the way to where Otter Swimming waited.

She had been careful to say nothing of Otter's condition, but her companions guessed at what it must be and no one complained at the grueling pace she set, no one fell behind during a journey that was arduous, indeed, for people unaccustomed to walking so rapidly even in the kinder seasons.

As dark day prepared to surrender to darker night, the howling wind lost some of its power. Now it only circled and nipped at them, instead of biting like a maddened wolf. ''I shall be able to find the way home,'' Morning Song called over her shoulder during a lull. ''And it will not be long before we come to where Otter is.'' She gestured to a snow-laden spruce. ''The stream we follow to her shelter is just beyond that tree.''

They stretched their legs to the limit then, and all were wheezing when they came to Otter Swimming's frail refuge. Shadow barked once at the sound of his mistress's voice telling the others to remove their cumbersome snowshoes. But when the four pushed beneath the sagging hide, he had not moved from his place beside the woman they had come to take home.

It was her mother who discovered that the spirit of Otter Swimming remained with her still, for she quelled Morning Song with a look when her granddaughter attempted to reach Otter first. ''The blood moves slowly through her veins,'' Teller Of Legends said, ''but I promise you that it does move. We have come in time.'' Her voice creaked, as though she had all at once grown impossibly ancient, and Morning Song thought grimly that—even bearing the stretcher—they must make as much haste returning as they had coming, or her grandmother might fall prey to one of the demons who afflicted the vulnerable with sickness. If only three pairs of hands served to balance a litter . . .

Shadow barked again, louder this time. He looked an apology at his mistress and leaped up, ran to the fresh gap they had made in the snow that met the overhang of the hide roof, and sent a series of friendly yips into the gathering night. He quieted and moved back only when a dark head thrust its way through the opening; but not until a pair of broad shoulders had worked their way after it did the stunned women recognize the man Shadow had instantly identified.

"Cloud Racer?" Morning Song's expression was an odd mixture of bewilderment, relief, and something that only Teller Of Legends—despite her fears for her prostrate daughter—silently put name to.

The warrior hauled the rest of himself inside, folded into the crouch the close quarters demanded, and took in the situation with a glance. "The child has come?"

Morning Song nodded. "Children. Otter is mother to twin boys. I have already taken them to the longhouse. Now"—she looked a plea at him—"the four of us have brought a litter to carry Otter Swimming home."

"It will be faster if I carry her," he said briefly.

Morning Song, who had only hoped he might take one end of the litter and spare Teller Of Legends, turned to her grandmother.

"Take her, and as swiftly as you can," the old woman said. "May the spirits aid your going, Cloud Racer."

He had backed out of the shelter before she'd finished speaking, was directing them to ease the blanketed Otter onto his outstretched arms.

By the time the women had emerged, Cloud Racer—accompanied by the dog who had deserted Morning Song to lope beside him— had gently lifted Otter Swimming and was moving smoothly but rapidly along the trail leading back to the village.

Chapter 19

⇔ ⇒

Rain Singing's face wore an alien somberness as she listened to Morning Song.

"Five days!" the young woman cried. "Five days, and Otter has neither moved nor spoken. Not even Deer Caller can awaken her. And she is deaf to the cries of her babies."

"The False Faces have visited?"

"On the day after Cloud Racer carried her home. And Hearth Tender burned sacred tobacco and chanted prayers, and Teller Of Legends and Bountiful Harvest gave her an elderberry concoction to prevent fever and made a brew from shadbush twigs to try to stop the bleeding."

"I have heard that the shadbush medicine was not effective," Rain Singing said softly. "I understand that nothing helped until you filled Deer Caller's tobacco bag with snow and placed it between Otter's thighs. Your spirit guide must be wise in the ways of healing, Morning Song."

Momentarily surprise diluted Morning Song's anguish. Her spirit guide? She had credited common sense for reminding her that Otter had bled little before they'd brought her back to the warmth of the longhouse. And once she'd suggested that cold might stanch that life-leaching flow, once the poultice of snow had slowed the flood to a trickle, she'd given no more thought to where the idea had come from. Perhaps Rain Singing spoke truly . . . "I shall offer thanks to the spirit, and soon," she said hastily. "But Rain Singing, even though Otter's bedrobe is no longer saturated with blood, she remains beyond our reach. Which is why the Pygmy society must perform a ritual for her."

The Matron of the Deer lodge nodded. "And so we shall. Ask Teller Of Legends to take her family to visit Sweet Maple. You, of course, will stay in your lodge with Otter. Then the society will come, and we shall do what we can." She took one of Morning Song's white-knuckled fists between her rough hands and coaxed it to unclench. "We must have faith that we will succeed," she

227

said. "Let tension drain from you, Morning Song, so that the spirit of healing can take its place."

Morning Song did her utmost to heed this advice, but it was not easy to relax when she sat alone beside Otter's bed in the dark and silent lodge. If the Pygmy ceremony failed, too, must the Turtle clan simply wait for Otter Swimming's labored breathing to cease altogether?

"Oh, Otter," she murmured, clasping her mother-aunt's limp fingers, "do not leave us. Deer Caller will be lost without you. And your sons . . . they need their mother. Bountiful Harvest tends them admirably; why, she has taken greased gut from the bear Deer Caller killed last spring and fastened a bird's quill to it so that your babies have something to suckle. But butternut liquor is sad substitute for the milk that swells your breasts, Otter! And the songs Teller Of Legends sings cannot replace a mother's crooning. In the ears of an infant, perhaps—but not in the heart of him." She bent and rested her cheek on Otter's dark head. "And I miss you, too," she sighed. "Of late, there is much about myself that puzzles me. Yet if I could speak with you, I think—"

She broke off as the entrance hide was pushed aside to permit a line of shadowy figures to file in. In a moment, Morning Song found herself on the perimeter of the circle they'd formed to include Otter and her.

She closed her eyes, tried to rid her mind of all that troubled it, imagined herself a blossom opening to receive the kiss of the rain, the caress of the sun. Those who sat with her would likewise be sending up purified thoughts to merge with the goodwill of the Pygmies who, unseen and unheard, had traveled on the wind to be with them.

Rain Singing, when the time was right, walked to the hearth and sprinkled tobacco upon it. She chanted:

Now the smoke rises,
receive you this incense
you who run in the darkness . . .
When first you knew that men-beings were
   on earth
you said, "They are our grandchildren."
You promised to be one of the forces for
   men-beings' help,
for thereby you would receive offerings of
   tobacco . . .

Her rhythmic voice, echoed by drum and rattle, set everyone to swaying back and forth, back and forth, until the darkness moved in charged waves around them.

You are the wanderers of the mountains;
you have promised to hear us whenever the
*   drum sounds . . .*
Now all of you receive tobacco . . .

Aromatic smoke spiraled upwards as the offering was made in Otter Swimming's name.

. . . let this awful illness cease . . .
henceforth give good fortune,
for she has fulfilled her duty
and given you tobacco.

Voices lifted then, and the lodge was filled with poignant song. Morning Song kept her eyes tight-shut as she begged the spirits of their ancestors to come to the aid of her beloved aunt. As the music soared, she told herself that surely they would respond and lend their power to the magic of the Pygmies; they would work with that invisible host to guide the spirit of Otter Swimming back to the world of the living.

It was Deer Caller, sightless Deer Caller, who first noticed the change in Otter. Afterward, he could never say how he had recognized that her sleep was suddenly not so unnatural. But when he'd called hoarsely to Teller Of Legends, and she went to lean over her daughter, the face she raised to her watching family glowed with hope renewed.

"She seems to breathe now without pain," she said joyfully. "See how her chest rises and falls as easily as yours or mine does when we sleep."

It was true, their eyes told them. And as they watched further, Otter shifted a little, as if trying to arrange herself more comfortably.

"I think we might turn her on her side," the practical Bountiful Harvest decided when faces that had been carefully devoid of expression relaxed to accommodate smiles.

Morning Song, helping her, did so with hands that trembled. She had been coiled tightly, inside; and tighter still since the Pygmy society's ritual had not instantly spawned the miracle she'd prayed for. She leaned against Otter Swimming's bedstead and wondered if she dared trust her limbs to support her.

"Now we shall have a meal," Bountiful Harvest announced, and Morning Song almost laughed aloud. Of course she was unsteady! Food was a thing no one had taken thought for, save to prepare what they must for the twins and for young Fish Jumping.

When their bellies had been filled by the soup Pumpkin Blossom ladled out, when they had reassured themselves that Otter Swimming's sleep was the sort that would promote healing, they took up the tasks they'd only pretended to be busy with until this moment. "We must let everyone in the village know that Otter will recover," Teller Of Legends said, thrusting her needle into the hem of a new robe she was making for Otter Swimming.

"They have been anxious for her, and for us," Hearth Tender agreed.

"I will carry the message to the Deer longhouse."

Morning Song and Pumpkin Blossom, having spoken in unison, gaped at one another. "I should like Rain Singing to know that the ceremony she arranged was successful," Morning Song was quick to explain. "I suppose it does not matter which of us . . ."

"The Pygmy society may have helped," Bountiful Harvest said sharply, interrupting her, "but I am certain that Otter's healing began on the morning the False Faces danced for her. True healing begins deep within, where the spirit dwells; there are seldom outward signs in the beginning."

"I expect that both medicine societies are to be thanked," Hearth Tender said placatingly. "Their members should be praised, and invited to rejoice with us."

Pumpkin Blossom rose and retreated quietly from the group seated around the hearth. She flung a robe over her shoulders and, just as quietly, slipped out of the longhouse.

Bountiful Harvest, weaving hickory splints to make a new hominy sifter, was uninterested in Hearth Tender's opinion. "What disturbs me," she said forcefully, "is that none of this was necessary. Had my niece owned the good sense to take someone with her when she went to search, my sister might have been brought back soon enough to be spared the worst of her illness."

Morning Song bristled. She should have known that once the danger was over Bountiful Harvest would revert to her disagreeable self. "I did not hear you offer to come, when I said I was going."

"*I* offered," Day Greeter said softly, then wished that she had not; her cousin's set features said that she, too, remembered, and had already reproached herself for not taking Day Greeter along.

Teller Of Legends looked around her and sighed. "It seems a pity," she observed, "that only in times of crisis is animosity forbidden entry to this lodge."

Her deliberate avoidance of specific address was more potent warning to daughter and granddaughter than the words themselves, and they bent hastily to their work. The Chief Matron of the Turtle clan returned to hers, and a small smile twitched the corners of her mouth. Dissension between these two was less than pleasant, but it felt rather good to have her world familiar again.

Otter's recovery was slow, but each day brought signs by which her family might judge its progress. She stirred often, murmured from time to time, swallowed more and more of the broth the women took it in turn to offer her. And they laughed to see her grimace whenever they dosed her with a strength-restorer distilled from pine needles and bark. Yet no one was surprised when, in the moment that her murmurs took on identifiable shape, the first words Otter spoke were the two that formed her husband's name. The twins were asleep on the double cradleboard their father had carved for them, and Teller Of Legends briskly but quietly shooed the other women ahead of her into the compound.

"Find someone to visit, or walk to the river," she told them. "We must allow Otter and Deer Caller time to be alone, now that she is wholly awake."

It did not take them long to scatter, Hearth Tender to have a word with Puma Walking Soft, Bountiful Harvest to call on Snow Comes Early, and Pumpkin Blossom and her sister to join a crowd cheering the warriors engaged in a hotly contested game of snowsnake.

"You do not wish to go with your cousins?" Teller Of Legends asked Morning Song.

"I would prefer to walk," the younger woman said, fending off a white dog whose boisterous welcome threatened to knock her of her feet.

"You will not mind if I go with you? I know you delight in being alone, and you've had scant opportunity for it of late."

"I'd be pleased if you will come with me," her granddaughter said. "You and I have not walked together since I was a child, I think."

"On the day that you first spoke," Teller Of Legends confirmed. "So it seems fitting, does it not, that we should do so on the day Otter Swimming breaks a fearfully long silence?"

They set out for the forest, through snow so thick-crusted that their boots did not sink into the softer stuff beneath. The sky was winter-pale, but the sun was a heartening sight.

They did not make for the tumbled boulders that had been their destination on a morning long ago. It was the dramatic green of a balsam grove that drew them this time, and both sniffed appreciatively as they neared it. "Is there a legend that explains why these trees keep their color when all the world is drab?" Morning Song wondered aloud.

Her grandmother chuckled. "If there is not, I suppose I can invent one," she said comfortably.

Morning Song swung to face her. "Invent one? Teller Of Legends, I have always believed that your tales were handed down by the ancients, that you repeat them word for word, just as they were spoken in the first instance!"

"Of many, that is true. Although I add to them when circumstance calls for it, or leave out parts that might have lost meaning over the years." The old woman's face was elfin in its mischievousness. "But other stories, I devise to suit my listeners. Why not? Even the oldest of legends was created by someone, at some time in the past. And those that come from me, if they are worthy, if there is truth in them, may someday be repeated by others and eventually be absorbed into the rich store of legend that is our heritage."

Morning Song scooped up a handful of snow, rounded it, and tossed it at the evergreen farthest from where they stood. "I cannot decide whether I am disappointed or intrigued by what I am learning," she admitted. "But I understand now why you never fail to produce a story appropriate to the occasion."

"Some occasions require a more direct approach, however," Teller Of Legends, never one to bypass advantage, said swiftly.

Her granddaughter bruised the tip of a branch, reveled in the pungency of the scent she released. "And what do you do then?" she asked.

"At such times, I prefer to speak plainly," the old woman replied. "As I mean to do now."

Morning Song turned and met the obsidian eyes that regarded her intently. "You wish to say something important to me?"

"I do. And I ask you to listen to all of it and not waste my time and yours by delivering protests without substance."

Morning Song tried to keep wariness from showing itself; and it would be discourteous—and futile—to dissent. She inclined her head submissively.

"I have learned," Teller Of Legends went on, "who it is Pumpkin Blossom means to marry. Had you eyes for anyone other than Otter on the day her babies were born, you would have discovered this also.''

Morning Song thought wryly that her grandmother, even in the midst of chaos, somehow registered all that went on around her. She fixed her mind firmly on this phenomenon, because memory had begun to nudge her, to compel her to recognize what it must have been that Teller Of Legends noticed that day. And it was a thing she was not ready to deal with.

No option was offered her. ''It is Cloud Racer that she hopes to have for a husband,'' the Matron of the Turtle clan said flatly. ''Pumpkin Blossom has decided—or perhaps her mother has persuaded her—that our family should share in the glory he has won for himself since he became a warrior.'' She gestured to Morning Song to resume walking, for the wind was freshening. ''I do not choose my words carelessly when I say this,'' she continued. ''I have been watching, and I see no sign that Pumpkin Blossom feels love for Cloud Racer. Complacency that she will have what she deems the best, certainly; pride that she shall restore to us the honor her father cheated us of; and, most assuredly, pleasure that Bountiful Harvest sanctions her choice. But her face does not soften when she speaks his name. I read in her eyes no unexpressed longing for Cloud Racer, the man, for all that she may desire Cloud Racer the warrior; if I saw even a hint of it, I would not interfere.''

Morning Song kept her own eyes resolutely on the footprints they had made on their outward journey, and her grandmother smiled.

''The only face that reveals a yearning for Rain Singing's son,'' she finished softly, ''is yours, Morning Song.''

Her granddaughter opened her mouth, shut it again when Teller Of Legends lifted one hand to remind her of the condition she'd set. ''Do not deny what both of us know is true,'' she said. ''And do not be so stubborn—for that is a failing of yours, Morning Song—as to reject the advice I am going to give you. Pumpkin Blossom has made it no secret that she intends to wait until Midwinter before she speaks to the man she wishes to wed, so we know that no marriage contract has been discussed by my daughter and Rain Singing. And though it may be frowned upon for an Iroquois woman to hunt game''—the twinkle that crept into her eyes was reflected in her voice—''the stalking of the man she wants for a mate is both permitted and encouraged by our people.''

A prolonged silence suggested that Teller Of Legends had, for the moment, said all that she cared to. And it invited a response

Morning Song was finding it difficult to frame. "He thinks me unwomanly," she muttered finally.

Teller Of Legends did not need to ask who *he* was. "You had wounded his pride, and he retaliated," she countered. "It is my belief that Cloud Racer sees a woman—and an admirable one— whenever he looks at you. You need only convince him that you are as desirable as you are admirable. And I tell you frankly that I would rejoice to see the pair of you marry, to know that your separate strengths have been joined. For you and Cloud Racer, there will come a time when your spirits as well as your bodies shall embrace. And an entirely new strength is granted to whose whose spirits find union, Morning Song. It is a strength that brings wisdom and understanding. A man has need of these qualities, but even more so does a woman—especially an Iroquois woman. We Matrons select the Sachems, and we alone withdraw the privilege of leadership should they prove unequal to it. That is rarely necessary, because it is the women who raise the children. And when a mother opens herself to wisdom, her son cannot help but grow into a praiseworthy man."

Her blunt-tipped fingers encircled her granddaughter's slender wrist. "Nor is it only her son that a woman influences, Morning Song. Her husband will also be courageous or cowardly, confident or uncertain, in response to her perception of him."

Sadness tinged Teller Of Legends's voice as she said that, and Morning Song understood that her grandmother believed Bountiful Harvest partially responsible for Covers His Eyes's failings. But this was of little account at the moment. "If I must marry," she said hesitantly, "I suppose I would rather take Cloud Racer as husband than one of the other warriors."

Teller Of Legends received the grudging confession with aplomb. "Then you must consider how best to go about it," she declared, and shortened her stride to allow time for rigorous counseling before they reached the village.

The Ceremony of Midwinter would come with the next full moon, and Morning Song must be prepared for it.

The Chief Matron of the Turtle clan smiled inwardly to see how her family seethed with excitement when the new year arrived. Oh, most of them pretended that they felt no more than ordinary elation. Indeed, only Otter Swimming made free with her exhilaration. The old woman looked to where her youngest daughter held one of her babes to breast while Deer Caller cuddled his sated and sleepy brother. How proud the new parents had been on the final day of

the old year, when the names Otter had chosen for the twins were
formally bestowed on them.

The old woman chuckled. *Bold Leader* and *Brave Companion:*
What imposing names for a pair of infants! Yet her daughter had
put forth good reasons for selecting them.

"My first son whooped like a warrior when he came into the
world," she'd said. "And my second followed so swiftly on the
heels of his brother that I think they would have emerged side by
side had that been possible. And he howled, too, as loudly as my
firstborn; together they nearly drowned out the sound of the wind.
Bold and brave they were, my sons, else how could they have survived that dreadful day? I shall not call them otherwise."

She had not been deterred by Hearth Tender's quiet reminder that
those who share their mother's womb are generally destined to
become foretellers of the future. "Those who predict what-shall-
be must own as much courage as a man who seeks glory on the
warpath," she'd countered. "There shall certainly be times when
what they say will be less than welcome to those who hear it."

Bountiful Harvest and Pumpkin Blossom were talking softly together, as had come to be their habit, and Teller Of Legends told
herself that she'd been right to force upon Morning Song advice
the girl had not asked for. She had hoped that Bountiful Harvest's
daughter would choose a warrior she'd truly developed some fondness for, if not a soul-deep yearning. But eavesdropping had convinced the old woman that what passion lurked within Pumpkin
Blossom was as yet a tight-closed bud. And no woman should
marry until love's petals were moved to unfurl.

Day Greeter, her broad face solemn, was arranging Morning
Song's hair. Teller Of Legends was grateful that Morning Song had
put herself in her young cousin's hands. The tunic she'd sewn from
bleached doeskin was unadorned, as Morning Song's usually were;
left to her own devices, the girl would do nothing to call attention
to herself. But Day Greeter, exclaiming shyly over the shining hair
she'd unplaited, obviously meant to smooth the length of it with a
comb before girding the crown of Morning Song's head with a
beaded band. A necklace—also provided by Day Greeter—hung
around Morning Song's neck, and surely those bright blue beads
had been begged of Lake On Fire. Who else owned such baubles,
or would so generously lend them? The tail feathers of a jay hung
pendant-fashion between the gentle swells of Morning Song's
breasts, and Day Greeter had reserved the longest of the black-
barred blue feathers to attach to the front of the headband as a sign
that this young woman was unmarried.

As though in a village this small anyone went in ignorance of the fact! Teller Of Legends grinned and shook herself slightly. The five days just past, with their cycles of music and dancing, the prodigious feasting, the rituals of dream-renewal and sacrifice, the evening storytelling, had been as exhausting as they'd been satisfying. This celebration was what made the bleak white season endurable, but there was no denying that Teller Of Legends' weary bones were pleading for a long and uninterrupted sleep. Tomorrow, she reminded herself; I may rest tomorrow. Then, nothing would remain of this Midwinter Ceremony but the memory of it. And perhaps—her hooded eyes flicked once more in Morning Song's direction—a maid radiant with discovery and truly ready for marriage.

Had there ever been a Festival to equal this one? Morning Song wondered. The pounding of warriors' feet during this morning's Feather Dance, the ceaseless chanting that had rung in her ears throughout the afternoon, seemed to echo still—despite the clatter of peach pits into a wooden bowl, the patter of children's feet, and the amiable cautions their mothers shouted after them. It seemed incredible that a single longhouse could contain so much laughter, so many separate conversations.

Winter reigned outside, but the fires belched heat-swollen smoke, and every face she looked upon glistened with sweat. Morning Song was hotter than she need be; her unbound hair clung to shoulders and back like a waist-long cloak, and was nearly as heavy. If it would not grieve Day Greeter, she'd gather it up and braid it again. But it was difficult to be the age that Day Greeter was, to be maid but not fully woman; and she had taken such delight in her accomplishment that Morning Song would give her no cause to think that what she'd done was unappreciated.

She sighed. It was equally difficult—although Day Greeter had yet to learn this—to be maid-become-woman. Her glance skittered to the entrance and she was tempted to sidle after it, to ease her way out of heat-wrapped noise and let body and soul be soothed by cold, fresh air. Two obstacles stood in her path however: That air would be uncomfortably laced with frost, and what she wanted to escape from—other than the noise and the heat—she had already sworn to face.

She studied the jovial crowd, spied Small Brown Sparrow and Sun Descending, and wished that her face might be aglow as theirs were. They doubted neither themselves nor the partners they would claim when next the drums began to beat. For Morning Song, it was quite the opposite, and she thoroughly regretted the promise Teller Of Legends had extracted from her. Were it not for that pledge, she would be gone from here, would plunge into the frigid night and find a place to hide herself until dawn signaled the end of this Midwinter Festival.

"I can recall a granddaughter of mine saying that to run away solves nothing, and that she shall never more do so." Despite the smile that rounded her cheeks and abridged her chin, Teller of Legends's words were intended as a challenge. They also revealed her awareness of Morning Song's inclination to flee; but that in turn merely proved how much better armed she was than the granddaughter she was shrewdly provoking.

"I honor my promises, Grandmother," Morning Song said.

"Do you think you might be persuaded to do so while wearing a more cheerful expression?"

"I do not find it easy to look happy when I do not feel so," the young woman retorted. "I shall do as you told me I should—but whether Cloud Racer shows himself willing or no, Pumpkin Blossom shall never forgive me, nor shall Bountiful Harvest. This will not make life in our longhouse more pleasant, for any of us."

"And how pleasant will you find it if you have to spend the rest of your days watching your cousin and Cloud Racer share the same hearth, the same bed? Which, ill-matched though I am convinced they are, may well happen if you hold back tonight, Morning Song. As for Pumpkin Blossom, surely you agree that she will be more content if she waits for love to guide her into marriage?"

"What do I know of marriage?" Morning Song demanded. "Or of love?"

Teller Of Legends laughed. "You know enough of love to be ready to learn more," she said, "as I am able to recognize. You forget that I was not always old. There was a time—"

She cut short her reminiscence as one of the grotesquely costumed figures called *our uncles, the Big Heads* began to sprint around the lodge, the rattles in his raised fists calling the congregation's attention to the fact that space must be made for those who wished to dance. Laughing, the elders and matrons sought seats or ranged themselves against the walls and urged reluctant children to join them there.

"Ah," Teller Of Legends said. "The moment has come, Morning Song." She saw her granddaughter swallow nervously and ball her hands. "I shall sit beside you," she announced, "until the dance is under way." And she gripped Morning Song's elbow and propelled her into the circle forming around the central hearth.

Morning Song had no choice but to lower herself to the ground next to her grandmother; and it did not reassure her to look across the hearth and discover that she sat opposite the son of Rain Singing.

"Your spirit guide must have ordained the seating," Teller Of Legends whispered when she saw Morning Song avert her head.

"If so, then my spirit guide wears your face!"

But her grandmother merely laughed to see Morning Song so discomfited and, squinting through the smoke, concluded that Cloud Racer—for all that he was practiced in impassiveness—was likewise disconcerted to be facing Morning Song. Which, at this stage, was precisely as it should be.

It was late now, and most of the children had been induced to cuddle in the laps of mothers, aunts, and grandmothers. When the drums began the playfully erotic beat that signaled the dance known as Shaking the Bush, Pumpkin Blossom—who sat just beyond her mother on Teller Of Legends's other side—was the first maiden to rise and slither out of the beaded tunic she had labored over for so many weeks. Morning Song saw how the firelight was mirrored in her coppery flesh and knew that more eyes than hers were drawn to those proud-thrusting breasts, the provocative curve of buttock that an embroidered loincloth left exposed.

I cannot do it, she thought miserably. I cannot walk, nearly naked, as Pumpkin Blossom is doing, and not bow my head for the shame of it. Never mind that others are doing likewise, or that the matrons are smiling and nodding their approval. I simply cannot do it!

But Teller Of Legends had stretched out one callused hand and her fingers were nipping at Morning Song's upper arm. When the girl did not respond, she only pinched the harder until Morning Song raised her downcast face. Following her grandmother's stare, she saw that Pumpkin Blossom had reached the far end of the longhouse, was turning gracefully and purposefully toward the opposite side of the hearth . . . To where Cloud Racer sat with his comrades.

"You are a fool if you falter," the old woman hissed, and applied another sharp pinch to send Morning Song to her feet.

Apprehension made the young woman fumble with her tunic fastenings, and in the end she was forced to whip the garment up and off with unseemly haste in order to avoid further assault by Teller Of Legends' fingertips. By this time, Pumpkin Blossom was scarcely a dozen paces from Cloud Racer's position in the circle. Even if Morning Song ran, she would be unable to reach the spot before her cousin did. Unless . . .

The fire had consumed its latest offering of kindling and its sluggish flames lacked the energy to leap high. *You will make a spectacle of yourself, even if you succeed,* Morning Song's inner voice warned and, briefly, she hesitated. But only briefly. Within seconds, she was striding forward, heedless of her nakedness and of the curious glances she was reaping. When her bare toes were within inches of the hearth, she crouched low, then launched herself across the heat-gorged embers contained by the ring of red-hot stones.

It was an act of desperation, and one that might well have ended in disaster or, the very least, ignominy. Yet it did not. Morning Song released her pent-up breath and unflexed her knees to land neatly on the balls of her feet, directly in front of a clearly astonished Cloud Racer.

She was incapable of speech. Mutely she held out her hands to him. Mutely he grasped them and allowed her to pull him erect. Nor did he speak as he freed himself long enough to strip down to his own breechclout. Then his hands were clasping hers once more and, incredibly, he was following her into the undulating line of men and maidens already Shaking the Bush with uninhibited vigor.

Chapter 20

She could not look at him at first and was glad when, out of the corner of her eye, she saw that another couple had moved into place beside them to complete the circle of squares this dance required.

"You are a sly one!" Laughter made bubbles of the words and proved to Morning Song what the smallness of the maiden's feet had hinted at: Small Brown Sparrow and Hill Climber faced each other as Cloud Racer and Morning Song were doing, and were matching steps with them. Morning Song was able to relax a little as all four concentrated on stomping simultaneously with the right foot and then, in perfect unison, sliding the left one forward to meet it. "I never dreamed that you had your own plans for Midwinter." Small Brown Sparrow's remark was punctuated with pauses as she competed with the singing that accompanied drum and rattle; Morning Song hoped that Cloud Racer had not over-heard, would not be wrongly persuaded that she had long been scheming to snare him.

The beat altered subtly, signal for the circle to reverse its counter sunrise drift and allow the maidens to dance backward. Those who made the drums talk played faster, and Morning Song had to lift her head to maintain balance while her feet obeyed the drums' commands. Yet there was nothing to prevent her angling her face to the right, toward a Small Brown Sparrow whose breasts bobbed energetically each time she stamped her foot, and who seemed unconcerned that Hill Climber was eyeing them with the look of a man half starved. No, *unconcerned* did not express her attitude; her smile, the way she consciously drew back her shoulders, *invited* Hill Climber to stare, and to hunger for what he saw.

Morning Song looked away, and directly into Cloud Racer's dark, dark eyes. And saw in them something that, this time, made her unable to drop her own. He was not grinning absurdly, as Hill Climber was. Yet his lips, which had so often reminded her of the unyielding contours of sculpted stone, looked new-leaf soft this night, and tiny sparks of brilliance lurked in the depths of his compelling eyes. It was a trick of the firelight, a bemused Morning Song told herself. But even when Cloud Racer's back was to the hearth, the dazzle that lurked in the midnight black of his eyes did not fade into nothingness, did not even dim.

The dancers had reversed once more, and their section of the now-straggling ellipse had reached the shadowy end of the long-house. Here and there, the circumference of the unwieldy circle showed gaps where couples had taken advantage of the reversal to abandon their places and slip outside. Morning Song was aware of their leaving; each time the hanging over the rear entrance was swept back, eddies of cold air swirled around her ankles. She knew, too, why they went; on this one night of the year, man and maid were encouraged to yield to those urges that the throb of drum and the peculiar conditions of the dance aroused in them. She was not surprised when a giggling Small Brown Sparrow seized the willing hand of Hill Climber and hurried him away.

But it startled her considerably to have Cloud Racer move closer suddenly and touch her arm, to have him indicate the route the others had taken and silently suggest that they, too, have done with dancing.

When she nodded slowly, the miniature flickers of light that burned in his eyes ripened into full-fledged suns, so that Morning

Song felt bathed in warmth as he twined his fingers with hers and led her into the winter night.

He turned to the right as they emerged, toward the northern end of the compound. By the time the Deer lodge loomed ahead of them, Morning Song's bare feet were crusted with snow and the blood that had been coursing beneath her skin was beginning to move so sluggishly that her flesh once again felt the pricking of lance-sharp air.

Cloud Racer pushed aside the hide to permit them entry into his family's longhouse, then stiffened. A low laugh floated out on a wisp of wood smoke. Morning Song shrank back, but her instinctive protest was unnecessary. Others might be agreeable to sharing the temporary accommodations that seven vacant lodges traditionally offered on this night, but Cloud Racer was as bent on seclusion as Morning Song was.

The white moon's glimmer lacked the power to illuminate his face clearly, but she knew that Cloud Racer frowned, recognized when his frown was erased as an alternate plan occurred to him. He eased into the longhouse, returned to wrap round her a fur-lined robe.

"We shall be walking some distance," he said, thrusting a pair of boots into her hands before flinging a second robe over his own shoulders and stooping to shod his own feet.

Morning Song hoped they were not his sister's boots that Cloud Racer had brought out; she might as well try to tug on a child's footwear as Small Brown Sparrow's.

"They are old ones of my brother's," he said, straightening up. His response to a concern she had not voiced showed that he was as privy to Morning Song's thoughts as—a moment ago—she had been to his. That was unsettling. Despite the warmth of her borrowed garment, she shivered as she followed him to the front of the compound and out through the palisade's gate.

He set a demanding pace, and she wondered if eagerness prodded him to stretch his legs or if brisk walking was simply a natural reaction to the nose-numbing cold. Had he spoken at all, or turned his head to see that she was keeping up, she might have been brave enough to put the question to him. Yet Cloud Racer—being Cloud Racer—did neither, but only guided her swiftly and silently along a path unfamiliar to her. It brought them eventually to the range of hills that circled the lake beyond the forest's eastern perimeter.

"There is a cave here," he explained as he decapitated a mound of snow with a well-aimed kick.

Morning Song smiled to herself. Doubtless he had come across it on a day when he'd been fishing in the lake's waters, had stumbled upon it just as she'd stumbled upon hers. And it was likely that he visited it, as she did her cave, whenever he needed to be alone. She was smiling still when, heedful of his warning, she ducked her head and crouched low to pass into his sanctuary. "You cannot stand upright," he cautioned as they squatted side by side in the dark, "but the ceiling is high enough to sit comfortably.

This cavern was much deeper than hers, Morning Song deduced, for his words evoked a faint echo. She arranged herself into a sitting position, raised one hand to gauge the height of the roof. Only her fingertips touched it, and that only when she reached as high as she might.

Cloud Racer was feeling his way into the remote recesses of his cave. Alerted by the sounds he made when he'd fumbled his way back to the entrance, she was unsurprised when a shower of sparks and the crackle of new-lit kindling announced that heat and light would not be denied them on this Midwinter night.

But with the pushing back of the dark, shyness overwhelmed Morning Song. She was not, after all, ignorant of why they were here, nor had she forgotten the day she had told an astonished Bountiful Harvest that this girl would never, ever, willingly lend herself to beastlike grappling and groping.

She lowered her eyes, held herself rigid as Cloud Racer, satisfied with his small but healthy blaze, rejoined her. Only after several moments inched by did she relax her vigilance. Perhaps, she thought hopefully, he wanted only to talk with her, as he had when they'd met in the forest.

"I like your cave," she ventured, surveying rough-textured walls that narrowed and darkened as they retreated from the fire. Where she and Cloud Racer sat, the floor was relatively smooth and padded with a carpet of last year's discarded leaves. "Do you come here often?"

He nodded, a gesture her roaming eyes almost missed.

"I suppose these hills contain a number of caves," she mused aloud. "Teller Of Legends's story about the Stone Giants—do you remember that one?—says that they do. But I come so seldom to the lake that I have never seen any of them. Until tonight." Her smile thanked him for bringing her here, for showing her the one they occupied.

"There are many," he agreed.

"Are all of them as large as yours?"

He shook his dark head.

Morning Song, drawing up her knees and hugging them to her chest, wondered uneasily if he would prefer her not to talk, if one of the reasons he valued his cave was for the way it shut out sound. He certainly did not seem interested in this conversation she was struggling to promote. Yet to let herself be made uncomfortable by an imagined need of Cloud Racer's was foolish. He had chosen to bring her here; if he wished her to be still he was capable of saying so. He knew she understood how soothing silence could be; anyone did, who deliberately sought out the hush of the forest. But surely he realized that a silence such as the one they were trapped in now had nothing that was soothing in it! It was so swollen with the outpouring of their separate thoughts that she wanted to flail her arms and puncture the pregnant air with her fingers, to expose what it held to the light.

Yet at the same time she feared to release secrets that Cloud Racer as well as Morning Song would be free to examine. Certain thoughts were better left unshared. She shifted slightly and their two arms touched briefly before she drew back. Resolutely she ignored the hiss of indrawn breath—his? hers?—that threatened the swag-bellied silence. But she could not ignore the heat that had begun to sheathe her robe-wrapped flesh in prickly moisture. She looked to the fire; it burned no hotter than it had a moment ago. Was she only imagining that she sweltered?

Apparently not, for Cloud Racer had shrugged off his fur-lined wrap and let it puddle around him. She turned her head away. Why should he seem more naked now than he had during the dance in the longhouse? It made no sense that a single sidelong glance should reward her with a fascination of detail: the perfect symmetry of muscle that rippled beneath taut skin when he moved; the tapering of his lean body as it descended to the waist; the ridged masculine nipples, so dark against his ruddy flesh . . .

She raised one hand furtively and scrubbed at the moisture beading her upper lip, her forehead, and wished she dared fling off her own robe.

Unseen by her, Cloud Racer smiled. And it was his hands that lifted, that slipped the stuff from her shoulders and drew it away from the dewy globes that were her breasts, let its folds spread themselves upon the leaf-strewn floor. He gathered up the length of her hair then, rubbed it between his fingers, touched his nose to it, held it out so that it made a curtain between his face and the fire. "It is like the night sky in the yellow season," he murmured, "when there are so many stars that the darkness itself seems to

shine. And it is fragrant as a summer meadow when the breeze
crosses it.''

Morning Song's eyes widened. Had it truly been Cloud Racer—
he who claimed kinship of custom with the laconic Puma Walking
Soft—who had spoken those words? Her face reflected her won-
derment, and he settled her hair lightly upon her shoulders once
more, letting his hands linger on her soft flesh as he did.

She quivered beneath his touch, and those surface tremors sent
down roots, unbelievably deep roots, when his fingers responded to
the erratic fluttering of the pulses in her throat by tracing the delicate
bones beneath its hollow. When they slipped lower still, when they'd
discovered the twin rises ascending to peaks all at once achingly hard,
Morning Song gasped and covered his searching hands with hers.

He looked at her, gazed long into gold-flecked brown eyes that
revealed a fearfulness he had not expected of her. Without speaking, he turned his two hands palm outward and clasped her restraining ones. There was reassurance in his grip, and a promise
that she might safely put her trust in him. And she was tempted to
believe that she should, to wonder if her conception of the mating
ritual was not, after all, a false one. Morning Song was no Bountiful
Harvest, and Cloud Racer was not—in any respect—Covers His
Eyes. Certainly her mother-aunt had never harbored the fledgling
hunger that had begun to flutter somewhere inside of Morning Song,
and Cover His Eyes would have been incapable of animating something long confined within a shell of mistrust. Shyly she returned
the pressure of the hands that held hers, and that downy hatchling
matured on the instant and put on the boldness of a full-grown eagle.

Staring into the depths of Cloud Racer's unwavering black eyes,
Morning Song slid her hands up to his wrists, relished the resilience
of tendon, the unyielding bone that gave shape to them. She stroked
his forearms, investigated the smoothness of his inner elbow, probed
his sinewy upper arms with the heels of her hands, her fingertips.
And found herself clutching his powerful shoulders and drawing
him close, closer, closer yet, until she was embracing him, had
imprisoned between their two bodies the hands that cupped her
breasts. But it was not to distract him from his exploration that she
did so. When she looked up at him, the smile that trembled on her
mouth was more than invitation for him to go on, to teach her all
that she craved to know of love, of passion; it was very nearly a
command that he do so.

Cloud Racer exulted as he eased her back against the spread robe.
He bent his head to the breasts that arched to meet him, began to
tease with his tongue and then to suckle their distended nipples.

Morning Song made a sound deep in her throat and, as though of their own volition, her thighs parted to receive his hand. Slowly he caressed the silky-haired mound guarding the cleft between them. As he coaxed her to open herself fully to a phallus so engorged that its throbbing was nearly unbearable, her frantic breathing announced that she was ready to receive him. But Cloud Racer would not let himself hurry, would not chance failing to honor the vow he had silently given her.

Suddenly, *"Please!"* she cried; and seizing his shoulders a second time, she urged him to cover her flesh with his, to thrust into her the round-tipped spear of his manhood, to move upon her with a vigor she was ready and able and eager to match.

When the neglected fire dwindled to a scantling of lethargic embers, neither noticed. They had created between them a glorious substitute for the warmth it had provided, and would have no further need of it this night.

The villagers arose uncommonly late next day and were, for once, content to occupy themselves with random tasks. Among the matrons there was much visiting back and forth, and among the maidens many low-voiced confidences. The compound was rarely empty, for all that it was a dismal and blustery morning; an unending procession of maids and warriors hoped for accidental encounters with those they had come to know intimately during the night just past. Where understandings had been reached, of course, such meetings were not the happenstance affairs they seemed to be; and they sparked ribald comments from anyone old enough to recognize the truth of it. And the children—quick to ferret out opportunities for teasing even if they might not be wholly aware of the reason for it—delighted to laugh at those sisters and brothers whose posturing invited ridicule.

Morning Song took no part in the informal ritual. She had awakened first that morning, in a cave cold as the gray dawn that glimmered beyond Cloud Racer's improvised hearth. She'd spared no thought for the chill; cuddled against the warm length of her lover, she was happy to lie there and study his face. Sleeping, he appeared more like the boy she remembered than the strong-featured warrior he'd become. Perhaps that was because his tousled hair fell across one cheek and his lips were soft-edged and slightly parted. Recalling how those lips, keeping to the trail blazed by urgent hands, had aroused the woman hidden within Morning Song rekindled her desire. She'd stirred restlessly.

Cloud Racer had opened his eyes then, and she'd turned toward him, certain she would see in them a twin to her own yearning. But in that moment of awakening they registered shock, followed on the instant by consternation as he realized that morning had come while they slept. Those couples who'd used the abandoned lodges for their trysts would have long since returned to their own long-houses. He'd sat up, found the boots they'd discarded, and signed to her to hurry as he'd jerked his over his bare feet. She'd had no option but to obey, to wrap herself once more in the crumpled robe that had been their bed, and move rapidly in his wake as he left the cave and began to stride homeward.

He had at least smiled at her when they'd parted in the compound, and Morning Song had been clinging to the memory of that brief and enigmatic smile ever since. To that, and to her conviction that Cloud Racer had taken as much pleasure in their lovemaking as she had. But he had not *spoken* of love to her, not even once. And she knew that it was not unheard of for a man and woman to avail themselves of the license offered at Midwinter, yet never marry.

Her initial bewilderment transformed itself into a kind of ag-grieved depression, a condition that pride would not permit her to confess. Not even to Teller Of Legends, who had been awake when Morning Song returned and whose welcoming smile had widened at the sight of her disheveled granddaughter.

"It is a powerful man whose ardor can be sustained for an entire night," she'd said approvingly, "and your need for such a one is as strong as mine once was. You are surely thankful now, Morning Song, that I recognized this, even if you did not."

She'd grinned again, and elation lit her tired eyes when Morning Song smiled in response. But as the day matured, such smiles as the young woman managed grew more and more distracted. Doubts assembled and multiplied until a dense cloud of them surrounded her. She was isolated from the chatter of maids, from the boasts of warriors, from the jests of elders and matrons, and the jabber of chortling boys and girls.

In the end, and perhaps inevitably, it was Bountiful Harvest's voice that penetrated her fog, although her words were supposedly directed at Otter Swimming: "I hope it will not humiliate Morning Song that the warrior who rejected her has chosen to be husband to my Pumpkin Blossom."

Otter, who knew perfectly well that Morning Song was intended to overhear, lifted a squalling Bold Leader from the cradleboard and prepared to suckle him. His brother promptly signaled his own hunger, but that did not dismay her; next time, Brave Companion would be the first one fed. "I imagine that our niece has marriage plans of her own,'' she said pointedly. And was mildly exasperated when Morning Song, ignoring the opportunity she'd given her, said nothing.

Neither woman guessed that Bountiful Harvest's revelation had pierced Morning Song's shroud of bemusement with the sword of guilt. Pumpkin Blossom to marry Stag Leaping? No, it could not be! Never mind that her cousin had probably been hoping to spite Morning Song by choosing him as her partner in the Naked Dance; she wouldn't have done so if Morning Song had not claimed the man she'd been planning to have.

The drone of her aunts' conversation receded as the young woman wondered feverishly how to undo the harm she'd done. Pumpkin Blossom must be warned about the sort of person Stag Leaping truly was, yet she would never—in the circumstances—credit anything Morning Song said about him. She would charge criticism to jealousy, and be deaf to any mention of swagger disguised as courage, of poorly bridled animal lust, of overweening vanity. . . .

''My daughter had considered Cloud Racer, you know,'' Bountiful Harvest was saying, and—oddly—it was the lowering of her voice that recaptured Morning Song's attention. ''But it seemed to the both of us that a man who comes too soon to the status of warrior, and is too often praised by a war leader who is, after all, his own uncle, may be prone to arrogance. And an arrogant man does not make a good husband.''

Morning Song started. Had Teller Of Legends been wrong? Had Pumpkin Blossom, all along, meant to have Stag Leaping, and only Stag Leaping? Even Morning Song could not deny that the son of Owl Crying was well favored; and there was, in truth, no explaining the attraction between man and maid. Before Deer Caller had come to live in the Turtle lodge, Morning Song had regarded him as unexceptional; now she knew him for the fine and good-humored man Otter alone had recognized from the beginning.

''Shall Pumpkin Blossom be delivering bride cakes soon?'' Otter asked idly as she began to suckle her second son.

Bountiful Harvest laughed. ''Soon, but not immediately,'' she replied. ''My daughter is wise; to make a man wait for what he wants makes him appreciate it all the more.''

Otter Swimming, who had been impatient of delay once she'd decided on the husband she wanted, made no response to this. But the glance she sent in Morning Song's direction said plainly that she had little use and less respect for such conniving.

Morning Song agreed wholeheartedly. But that did nothing to resolve her own dilemma.

* * *

Two days later, she watched her cousin mold perfect rounds of cornmeal dough and wrap them in pairs. And she was, she realized sadly, envious of Pumpkin Blossom. Not for the reason that her aunt had predicted she would be, of course. What she envied was Pumpkin Blossom's serene assurance that Stag Leaping and Owl Crying would be anxiously awaiting the cakes she was making. This time, Morning Song thought wryly, Owl Crying had probably already cooked the bread that would be her gift to Teller Of Legends.

She felt her grandmother's eyes on her and sighed. Teller Of Legends had not asked why Morning Song wasn't following her cousin's example, but the question hung in the air between them as though it were one of the braided ears of corn that dangled from the rafters. Morning Song had tried her best to decide whether or not she should take bride cakes to the Deer longhouse. She'd told herself finally that her only recourse was to seek out Cloud Racer, that a single glance at his face would tell her whether she courted rebuff by doing so. But although she'd been haunting the compound, not once had she seen him. Other warriors, striving vainly to act as if walking aimlessly within the palisade was something they were accustomed to doing, had been conspicuous there. And it had not made her futile vigil easier to see how their eyes shone when the maidens they sought appeared. Indeed, it had reinforced her fear that Cloud Racer might be deliberately avoiding her.

Well, it could do no harm to try again. And anything would be better than to sit here watching Pumpkin Blossom while Teller Of Legends' unspoken question nagged at her with all the subtlety of a pesky fly on a summer's afternoon.

White Shadow bounded up when she stepped cautiously into the compound, and she was glad to encourage his attention. Playing with him gave her excuse for being where she was and might distract hovering matrons from speculating about Cloud Racer and her. It would not prevent that entirely, since none had missed seeing the pair go off together during the Naked Dance. But so long as the dog kept bringing her a stick to toss, Morning Song thought they might not realize how desperately she longed to see him.

She took up the piece of kindling Shadow had filched from some clan's wood stack and flung it high into the air. He ran, leaped, and caught it in his teeth before it could hit the ground, then grinned as he brought it back to her.

"You are a clever dog," she said absently, and his tail sketched semicircles in the frosty air. She hurled the stick again, watched him streak after it and retrieve it from a sad-looking heap of dingy snow. It was a pity, she thought, how quickly a fall of snow lost the pristine whiteness that gave it beauty, how soon sweetly curved drifts and mounds were deflated. Still, most things that she named beautiful were fleeting: dawn and sunset; the first delicate curl of leaf on a barren bush; puffballs of cloud against an iridescent sky; the tapering shadows of late afternoon; the passion that crimsoned the night when she and Cloud Racer came together . . .

Had she responded too fervently to his caresses? Had she, without realizing it, frightened or disgusted him with her eagerness to be loved? Was it conceivable that—

"I have been wondering," someone behind her said suddenly, "if White Shadow accompanied you and my brother the other night?" Morning Song swung around to see Small Brown Sparrow's merry eyes regarding the dog who'd dropped into the half-crouch that signaled his wish for their game to continue.

"He did not," she responded, drawing back her arm and sending the stick to the far end of the compound.

Small Brown Sparrow transferred her twinkling gaze to her friend. "It surprises me that he allowed you to go anywhere without him," she said.

Morning Song shrugged. "When the weather is cold, he often huddles with the other village dogs alongside the Bear lodge. They can be away from the wind there. And he would never have thought to watch for me at such an hour."

The daughter of Rain Singing stooped to persuade a panting Shadow to let her throw the stick this time. "I confess that I had been imagining Cloud Racer and White Shadow competing for your caresses," she said, giggling, then sobered as she saw that even this bit of foolery had not lightened Morning Song's tight-lipped face. "You are very serious today," she said slowly. "Were you"—she hesitated, but it was not in her nature to hold back—"disappointed on the last night of Midwinter, Morning Song? I would have expected my brother—"

"You must not think that!" her companion exclaimed before she could finish. If Small Brown Sparrow should attribute Morning Song's ill-humor to clumsiness on the part of her brother, she would likely tax him with it. Or, worse yet, *tease* him about it! "It is only that I am a bit tired still," she finished lamely.

Small Brown Sparrow's relief was patent, her merriment instantly restored. "And so I should have realized," she burbled. "It was after dawn when the pair of you sneaked home! Of course, I would not have known that if Hill Climber had not kept me so wonderfully occupied that I'd crawled into my own bed only a little

while before Cloud Racer came in.'' Her impish face softened.
''Hill Climber and I were meant for each other, as I'd thought we
would be. And I am happy indeed to have his weapons and snowshoes decorating the wall above my bunk.''

''You wasted no time delivering bride cakes to Sweet Maple,''
Morning Song observed, smiling in spite of herself to see her friend
so content.

''As soon as I could struggle out of bed that morning, I made
them for her,'' Small Brown Sparrow said, and giggled again. ''Hill
Climber had threatened to stand over me until I did, if they were
not at the Plover longhouse by midday.''

Now it was Small Brown Sparrow that Morning Song felt envy
for! Why, oh why, did matters proceed smoothly and naturally for
every maid but Morning Song? And what, she thought miserably,
was wrong with Cloud Racer, that he could not have said—one way
or the other—how he felt about her?

All at once, anger thrust past the dejection that had been plaguing
her. How dare he leave her unsure of his feelings? Who was he that
Morning Song should humble herself by standing hour after hour
in the compound hoping to have him walk by, praying that he would
come to her and favor her with a smile, a careless word or two?
''Where is your brother?'' she said. And so harshly that Small
Brown Sparrow gaped at her.

''When you did not send bride cakes to our mother, he took his
bow and said he was going hunting.'' She studied Morning Song's
blazing eyes. ''He has been away since the evening of the day
following Midwinter,'' she went on. ''And we have begun to wonder if he shall return to us at all, if you are not interested in having
him for a husband.''

The stick that Morning Song had been meaning to toss for her
patient dog dropped from nerveless fingers. ''You mean that he is
willing to marry me?'' she whispered.

Cloud Racer's sister laughed until tears brimmed in her eyes.
''*Willing?* Morning Song, I should not tell you this—and my brother
will never forgive me if you let him know that I have—but I believe
that he is more besotted over you than Hill Climber is over me.
And I promise you that I could not put it stronger than this if I tried
from now until next Midwinter.''

Chapter 21

❦ ➡

"Your lodge, Teller Of Legends," Sweet Maple said, "is not the quiet place it once was."

Lake On Fire fingered the beads decorating her dress and laughed. "Perhaps you spoke so often of wanting to see a new generation born that your granddaughters competed with one another to oblige you. If they go on doing so, this longhouse will soon need lengthening!"

Teller Of Legends beamed upon her friends. "To be crowded with family is not to be crowded at all," she told them. She scooped up Brave Companion, whose stubby fingers were tugging at the lacings of her moccasins, then reached for his brother. She had an ample lap, and was happy to have it occupied by Otter's sons.

Sweet Maple looked to the bunk Morning Song and Cloud Racer shared. The young woman was dusting her tiny son's buttocks with maize powder as she chatted with an attentive Day Greeter. "When Bountiful Harvest's second daughter takes a husband, you shall have six hearths burning," she said.

"I do not look for that to happen soon," Teller Of Legends said. "Day Greeter is shy, and will not be as quick to choose a husband as her sister was."

"No doubt she compares herself with Pumpkin Blossom," Lake On Fire remarked. "She is truly a beauty, that one. This can be disheartening to those not so well favored." She passed a bony hand over her thinning hair, smiled archly to remind her old friends that beside them sat the avowed beauty of their generation.

Teller Of Legends watched Pumpkin Blossom pick up the little girl who would doubtless be the beauty of the next generation. She sighed. "It is a pattern I have seen before," she murmured. "I must begin to spend more time with Day Greeter and try harder to persuade her of her own worth."

"She is a sensible girl," Sweet Maple said easily. "I am sure she realizes that it takes more than a pretty face to attract a good man. Beauty does not last the way a generous nature and a pleasant disposition do.''

Lake On Fire tossed her head. She'd been much given to the gesture in her younger days, when someone displeased her.

''Certainly what you say is true,'' Teller Of Legends said to Sweet Maple. ''And I hope you are right, that Day Greeter knows her worth.''

Otter's twins were beginning to squirm, and she set them down. ''Go if you will, but do not get into mischief,'' she warned, and the two waddled off as rapidly as their chubby legs permitted.

Sweet Maple chuckled. ''When they are a year older, and the two younger children are also walking around, your lodge will be livelier than ever. Visiting you then will teach me to appreciate the peace and quiet of my own longhouse.''

Seven-year-old Fish Jumping burst into the lodge and nearly tumbled over Otter's sons, who were hunkered down side by side to study a beetle their inquisitive eyes had spotted. Teller Of Legends laughed. ''Perhaps I shall beg to go home with you when that time comes,'' she told her. ''Pumpkin Blossom's second child will be here by then.'' She did not add that she thought Morning Song was also breeding again; they would find that out soon enough.

Lake On Fire tittered. ''It is obvious that your granddaughters wed hot-blooded warriors,'' she declared. ''Doubtless your longhouse is as busy a place at night as it is during the day.''

The Matron of the Turtle clan only smiled. It was not courteous to mark the sounds of lovemaking, but the inadvertent eavesdropper could scarcely ignore them altogether. How could anyone guess when or how often rhythmic thumpings and muted moans of pleasure might stir the night? Except when the sounds came from the bed near Pumpkin Blossom's hearth. The daughter of Bountiful Harvest seemed to measure out her passion as precisely as she measured out the food when it was her turn to cook. Still, so long as her husband was satisfied . . .

''I suppose Stag Leaping and Cloud Racer will be leaving with Fierce Eagle's war band?'' Sweet Maple asked suddenly.

Teller Of Legends nodded. ''Yes. And they may be away much longer than they were during their last raid against the Erie. Many bands of warriors, from many different villages, will be going against the Cat People this time. Cloud Racer tells us they have agreed to fight on until the enemy either flees or sues for peace.''

''Follows The Signs says this is no more than the Erie deserve,'' Lake On Fire said importantly. ''It was foolhardy of them to fire one of our western towns, and to begin attacking our hunting par-

ties. Long Canoe and my grandson were among the first to respond
to Fierce Eagle's summons.'' She nodded toward Otter Swimming's hearth, where Deer Caller sat smoothing a length of hickory
wood. ''Your daughter's husband made fine new weapons for them
to take with them.''

Sweet Maple, pleased to have her nephew praised, smiled. ''I
see that Pumpkin Blossom has her bread baking,'' she said then,
and turned to Lake On Fire. ''Which means that you and I should
go home and tend to our own hearths, I think.''

Lake On Fire stood up, shaking out her skirts with a practiced
twist of her hips. ''Shall we plan now,'' she asked as she prepared
to follow Sweet Maple out, ''for all of us to eat together during the
Green Corn Festival?''

With a smile, Teller Of Legends agreed, but the smile faded once
they'd gone on their way. The war party would head south three
days after the festival. For some men, this year's ceremony might
be the last they would ever take part in. Selfishly the Matron of the
Turtle lodge hoped that would not be true of the two warriors who
called her longhouse home.

It had been Morning Song's idea to slip away from the crowd
after the peach pit game got underway. ''No one will notice. Anyone not playing will be wagering on those who are,'' she'd told
Cloud Racer. ''And if Swift Arrow wakens—which is unlikely—
Day Greeter has promised to soothe him back to sleep.''

Once they'd reached Cloud Racer's cave, they had not wasted
time making a fire. A warm summer breeze drifted around them
as they lay together, as they let their love lead them along a path
both continued to glory in.

Cloud Racer, exhausted from the day's activities, slept soon afterward. But Morning Song had promised herself that she would
savor every moment of the time they had left before Cloud Racer
went to war. A bulbous moon rode placidly in a star-bleached sky
and streaked the face of Morning Song's sleeping husband with
silver. ''Grandmother Moon,'' she whispered, ''let your light cling
to him, let it protect him against all harm when he is away from
me.''

She never failed to implore every spirit she knew of to watch
over him, but no effort stayed her fear that one day Cloud Racer
would not return to her.

She had not yet told him of the babe that would be born in the
spring; now she decided she would not. He might never admit to
it, but if he knew of her pregnancy he would be concerned for her

while they were separated. And his mind must be undisturbed when he went against the Erie. Morning Song dared not rely on the spirits alone to ensure his safe return.

She smiled into the youthful face he wore when he slept, and found herself remembering her own youth and the quest she had gone on then. Suddenly she started. That wandering water-sun, which even Hearth Tender could make no sense of . . . why, that had been no more than a symbol of Morning Song herself, blundering from the path others trod because she went in ignorance of her appointed destination. Until Cloud Racer's love reached out and drew her back to the place where she belonged.

How wonderful to realize this at last! No longer would she harbor even the ghost of regret that she had surrendered her independence to became the sort of woman an Iroquois warrior deserves. It had been a sacrifice worth the making if, all along, her spirit guide had meant her to become what she was now: a matron worthy of respect. And if she was not yet worthy of praise, as the competent Pumpkin Blossom was, well, Cloud Racer at least did not seem to notice her deficiencies.

She looked again into his face, stretched out one hand, and trailed her fingers over his arch of brow, along one cheek. There was no response. She moved closer, close enough that her breasts flattened themselves against his naked chest. Her nipples hardened and the breath fluttered in her throat like a wild thing caught in a thicket.

He murmured, opened his eyes, and smiled. Then . . . he rolled lazily onto his back and his eyes closed as though the lids were weighted so heavily that keeping them raised was beyond him.

She pulled away and sat up, fuming. She had never denied *him*, ever. How often had she come out of the soundest of sleeps the moment she'd felt him touch her? And always she had responded, had turned to him eagerly and rejoiced in their lovemaking.

She was achingly aware that her desire, far from being dampened by his lack of cooperation, only burned the hotter. In the next instant, she threw herself across him, made furious use of lips and tongue to demand that he become conscious of her and of her need for him. She tugged at his sterile nipples, thrust her tongue into the partitioned maze of his navel, reached for the flaccid organ it was not beyond her talents to inflate. . . .

And found it not so subdued as she'd expected it to be. It pulsed within her hand, came rigidly erect as she began to stroke it.

She turned to find Cloud Racer's eyes wide open, to discover in them a yearning as great as the one that had driven her to act so impulsively.

Morning Song raised up, swung one leg over Cloud Racer's hips, braced herself with her hands, and lowered herself onto the tumescent shaft that waited for her. Cloud Racer reached out and grasped her wrists, began to move to the rhythm she set, eased away and thrust back until Morning Song's scream and his belly-deep groan echoed through the cave to signal the mutual climax they had been striving for.

She subsided upon him and felt the heaving of his chest lessen as the serenity that is the rightful aftermath of love stole over them. "You wanted me to do that," she said against his corded neck, and tasted the saltiness of his sweat. She flicked out her tongue to absorb another drop.

Laughter rumbled through him and he nodded.

She let herself relax completely. "I may do it again one day," she murmured; and as if to mock her assumption that a future existed for them, the imminence of his departure reasserted itself.

Cloud Racer was reminded also. He tightened his arms and lifted both himself and Morning Song until, still clinging together, they were sitting upright. "We must be returning to the village," he said quietly.

"I had hoped, when you told me of the new treaty between the Confederation and the French *Onondio*, that you would not be returning to the path of war." With an effort, she kept her voice even.

He gathered up his breechclout and the tunic she'd been so impatient to shed. "The Iroquois have more enemies than the French," he told her.

"We seem to be surrounded by them," she said bitterly, easing out of his lap to maneuver into her wrinkled garment.

"More than you know." He was groping for his moccasins. "Rumor says that the Painted People—the Ottawa—have arranged with the fugitive Huron to deliver furs to the place the French name Mon-Tre-Al. Which is contrary to everything the Frenchmen agreed to when they accepted our terms for peace. The Ottawa"—he grunted as he reached behind him for his headband—"must know we are concentrating our strength against the Cat People. Although I cannot think how they discovered that."

Morning Song, painfully aware that their time alone was coming to an end, began to feel irritated that Cloud Racer would speak at length only on such matters as war and treaties. Yet she could not bring herself to charge him with thoughtlessness, to tell him that it hurt when he did not use these last moments to say how sorely he would miss her, to tell her that he loved her. . . .

He tensed suddenly, and jerked back the hand that had been fumbling for his headband. Strands of web were wound around thumb and forefinger, and he shook his arm violently to dislodge them.

Morning Song laughed. "You have invaded a spider's long-house," she teased, grabbing his wrist and plucking the sticky fibers from his skin.

He swallowed audibly, and she looked up to see his mouth locked into a grimace. "What—" she began; but on the instant he resumed control of his features and shrugged his broad shoulders.

"I do not like spiders," he said, then urged her ahead of him out of the cave.

But Morning Song, falling into step behind him, knew that simple dislike could not account for Cloud Racer's reaction to the spider web. And she understood why, instead of making light of her morbid fear of fast-moving water, he had been so patient with her recently when she'd refused to travel downriver in a canoe.

Somehow, to know that he was prey to an aversion as compelling as her own made her love him all the more.

When the war party had been gone three weeks, the traders came to the village. This time Morning Song did not hurry away to walk into the forest. "It is different, now that I have a babe to care for," she told Teller Of Legends as she laid Swift Arrow in the hammock Cloud Racer had suspended over their bunk. "I will stay inside while they are here, however." Her mouth was a thin line, and her grandmother saw that the woman Morning Song nurtured in her heart the hatred that the girl Morning Song had planted there.

"We shall be busy enough sorting the late beans to give you reason for doing so," the old woman said mildly. "And there are squashes to prepare for drying. But many of our friends will find excuses to be in the compound this morning. The matrons cannot be blamed for wanting to choose their own pots and kettles and lengths of fabric." She chuckled. "Men are scarcely knowledge-able about such things." Her gnarled fingers picked through the purple and white beans Morning Song had heaped between them. "I often wonder about the woman who is wife to Bree-And," she went on. "I hear that she does not leave their cabin from one season to the next. It is a lonely life she leads, that woman." She frowned, shrugged. "Why the *Onondio* are given to living apart from their kin is one of the many things I do not understand about them."

"I neither know nor care why they do," Morning Song replied

tautly. "But I would like to know why we are allowing more and more sallow-skins to live in Iroquois territory."

"Their being here was approved by the Confederation," her grandmother told her, and sat back on her haunches. "They are Keepers of the white man's faith, these men. And"—her black eyes met Morning Song's rebellious brown ones—"the Longhouse People respect all Faithkeepers. The color of their skin is of no account."

"It is to me," Morning Song retorted. "And should be to others." She swatted behind her the heavy braid that had fallen across her shoulder. "Cloud Racer told me about a tribe in the north, the Painted People. While our war leaders were occupied with making plans to invade the Erie, they began selling furs to the French—furs the French chieftains had pledged to buy only from the Iroquois! He wondered how they knew we would be too busy elsewhere to put a stop to the unlawful trading, but I think we need not look beyond these late-come *Onondio* to learn the answer to that."

"Those who keep alive the faith of their people do not concern themselves with trade or treaties, Morning Song," her grandmother said reprovingly. "Can you imagine Hearth Tender doing such a thing, or Puma Walking Soft?" She saw the young woman's lips compress themselves and decided not to pursue the subject. "Your son sleeps," she said instead, sending a doting smile in the direction of the hammock.

Morning Song's expression softened as she laughed a little. "Only because he exhausted himself crawling from one end of the lodge to the other," she said ruefully. "He does not close his eyes merely because I say he should, the way Hidden Moon does for Pumpkin Blossom."

Teller Of Legends grinned. "Other women's children always seem better behaved than your own," she said. "But would you exchange your venturesome son for Pumpkin Blossom's docile daughter? You would not."

Morning Song acknowledged that truth with a smile. "I hope for a daughter of my own this time, though," she said after a moment.

"Only the spirit who arranged for you to conceive knows this," Teller Of Legends said. "But Hearth Tender feels confident that it will be."

From the compound came a burst of guffaws, a rattling of bombast. Morning Song shuddered. "That one is given to ridiculing our ways," she said.

"Bree-And?" Her grandmother, too, had put name to the voice.

Morning Song bobbed her head. "When the traders came during

the last green season, I was stretching pelts and could not set out at once for the forest. I heard him say to Lah-Val that the Iroquois are like children to believe that spirits dwell in trees and lakes and hills.'' She cast down her eyes. ''I prayed that one of those spirits would arrange for He-No The Thunderer to strike him with a lightning spear!''

Her grandmother sighed. ''Morning Song, it will be you who angers the spirits, by demanding such a terrible thing of them.''

''Grandmother, the *Onondio* are coarse and foul-tongued and evil-smelling! How dare they look down upon the Iroquois, who are none of these things? And why do we go on trading with a man who has nothing but contempt for us?''

''You would do better to ask this of Cloud Racer, or of his father,'' Teller Of Legends said cautiously, for she had never become wholly reconciled to the idea of white men coming at will to their village. ''In any event, I doubt if Bree-And was so careless as to let either of them overhear what you heard.''

''I told Cloud Racer,'' the young woman admitted. ''And was angry enough to remind him that it was one of the French breed who destroyed my mother. He said perhaps I misinterpreted what the Frenchman said and, even if I had not, I must realize that all men are not the same, *whatever their skin color*!'' She flung out her hands and scattered the beans she'd just finished sorting. ''You spoke similar words to me only moments ago, Teller Of Legends. And I shall never understand how either of you can truly believe what you say.''

Otter Swimming, who had watched Morning Song fret away the long months of winter, rejoiced to see the younger woman grin as she made a second gash in the venerable maple whose burgeoning juices traditionally proclaimed the arrival of the green season. This time, a healthy trickle of sap oozed out.

''It is time for our ceremony,'' Otter said, licking the fingers of the hand that had plugged the slash. ''Then we will have sweetening for our puddings, and sops for our little ones again.''

''And make sugar eggs for our men to take with them on hunting expeditions,'' added her niece, settling Swift Arrow more securely against her hip. She had let him walk to the forest, and White Shadow had loped in circles around him, alert for the moment when the boy would reach out and try to grab the dog's waving tail. His mother had known Swift Arrow would need carrying on the return trip; a one-year-old was not endowed with limitless energy. But Otter had left the twins with their father; she would transfer Swift

Arrow to her own strong arms if her niece showed signs of wearying.

Morning Song's grin faded. "If ever they return from the war, that is," she added bleakly.

"It should not be long now," her mother-aunt comforted. "You were premature to look for them during the winter. Even if they dealt swiftly with the Cat People, it would have been folly for them to return overland—through all that snow—when waiting for the thaw would let them use their canoes."

Morning Song shifted her son to her other hip, looked down ruefully at her protruding belly. "He did not even know we were to have another child, when he left."

Otter lifted the wriggling child from Morning Song's arms. "The same happened to me," she reminded her. "Deer Caller was away when Bold Leader and Brave Companion were growing in my womb." Recalling suddenly how he had returned from that war on a litter, she made haste to speak of something else. "If Hearth Tender offers thanksgiving to the maples in the morning, we can begin at once to drain and cook the sap." She sniffed the air. "Tomorrow will be another fine day, I think."

And so it was. The sun soared into a cloudless sky and warmed the cradleboards hanging from the lower limbs of one of the sturdier maples. "It is good to see the branches reddening," Morning Song said to Small Brown Sparrow, who was positioning her infant daughter between Swift Arrow and Hidden Moon. Her hand went to the pouch she wore around her neck and she thought of the leaf nestling within it, tattered cousin to those soon to be decorating these trees.

Small Brown Sparrow cooed like a dove until Bending Willow ceased to fret, then grinned at her friend. "Particularly since the coming of spring means you will deliver soon," she said. "You have grown round as a pumpkin with your second child, Morning Song."

"And clumsy, too," Morning Song said with a sigh. She looked at Pumpkin Blossom standing in the semicircle forming at the foot of the old maple. "My cousin's babe will be born a month before mine, yet there is nothing blundering about her movements."

Small Brown Sparrow steered her to a gap in the curving line. "Pumpkin Blossom has been remarkably graceful all her life," she said practically. "I think she was born that way."

Morning Song stumbled, righted herself. "No one can say that of me," she grumbled.

"You do well enough ordinarily." Small Brown Sparrow low-

ered her voice. The moment had come to offer thanks to the Maker
Of Life and express gratitude to the Pygmies who were the Plant
Tenders. But Morning Song, as she repeated the ritual prayer,
thought gloomily that no woman here lacked natural grace; from
Morning Song alone had this proof of Iroquois heritage been with-
held.

The babe in her womb moved restlessly, and she shifted her feet.
Everyone thought Morning Song and Pumpkin Blossom were fortunate to be breeding a second time while their firstborns were still
cradleboard-size, but Morning Song did not. When Cloud Racer
came back from Erie country, she would be so bloated and ugly
he'd have no desire to hold her, caress her, love her. . . .

She shook herself out of her melancholy and saw the others hanging bark tubs on sticks protruding from the gashes whitening the
maples. Snatching up a kettle, she humped it over to a new-lit fire
on the other side of the clearing. Swift Arrow's round eyes followed
her, and he babbled her name as she passed him. She smiled and
ruffled his dark hair. How she loved her son! She had savored every
moment of his womb-time, and thrilled to anticipate his birth. His
coming had completed the circle of Morning Song's identity, had
proclaimed her the woman-wife-mother she was proud to be.

She grunted as she stooped to balance the kettle on a ring of
boulders and felt momentary shame that her feeling for the child
she carried now should be different.

The day the war band returned was rife with omens. Pumpkin
Blossom, newly purified from childbearing, emerged from the low-
roofed sweathouse only moments before their canoes rounded the
bend in the river. Gray Squirrel had just confided a dreadful dream
to her sister, Loon Laughing. And Morning Song, throwing a robe
around her cousin's bare shoulders, was wondering whether she
ought to mention how she had seen a wayward star plunge from the
sky during the hour before dawn.

In the end, she kept silent about it, for it did not need a Faithkeeper to explain how the sweathouse must be made available to
the exhausted warriors, or to point out that poor Gray Squirrel must
prepare to mourn both her husband and her brother. And the falling
star had been a warning that Morning Song's reunion with Cloud
Racer would, as she had feared, be passionless.

It was natural that he should grieve for Spear Thrower and Long
Canoe. And his concern for Fierce Eagle, whose knees had been
shattered by an enemy war club, was understandable. But did either
of these explain the terse greeting he'd given the woman waiting for

him? No. The sight of her had been the reason for it. What man wants to embrace a wife whose swollen body makes her a travesty of the woman he'd left behind?

Later, she sat with the rest of her clan, ponderous belly resting on splayed legs, and listened to her husband address the villagers in his uncle's stead. He had words to spare for this, she thought resentfully; but she made no attempt to shut them out.

"Venom-tipped arrows fell around us as we built counter-palisades to scale the walls of the Erie towns," he told his rapt audience. "The Cat People fight like the puma they are called after. But"—he paused, let his eyes travel the circle of faces turned toward him—"they were, in the end, no match for us."

The victory fire lit the night, and Morning Song thought he had never looked so handsome, so desirable. Trail rations and the rigors of battle had fined his body, sharpened the angles of his face, emphasized his sinewy strength.

"I would share with you," he went on, looking respectfully toward the uncle who would never again be able to stand erect, "the chant our leader offered when the Erie sent to know by what power the Iroquois demanded their surrender." He lifted his head and half closed his heavy-lidded eyes. *"I am of the Five Nations,"* Fierce Eagle told them . . .

and I shall make supplication
to the Maker Of Life.
He has furnished this army.
My warriors shall be mighty
in the strength of their creator.
Between him and my song they are,
for it was he who gave the song,
this war song that I sing.

Then Cloud Racer bowed his head to signal the reverence in which he held his mother's brother, a man who had served magnificently as war leader, had earned the right to be named Pine Tree Chief, and who must now put aside his weapons forever.

A chorus of shouts went up to praise Fierce Eagle until, despite his pain, he managed to smile. When the clamor subsided, he looked around him and smiled a second time. "I give thanks to the son of my sister," he said formally, "and to all of you. But never think that one man alone—war leader or no—can win a battle. Every man who went with me is worthy of your praise. And all have stories to tell!"

Morning Song tried vainly to make herself more comfortable. Her advanced pregnancy would permit her to absent herself from the torture of prisoners, but she would be called discourteous were she to slip away before the warriors had been given a chance to speak. She arranged her face into an attentive expression and sighed as Stag Leaping was the first to stand up. That one could go on for hours, she thought irritably, and all of his boasting would be of himself. She stole a glance at Pumpkin Blossom, who held Painted Sky to her breast. She seemed fascinated by her husband's exaggerations. So did Bountiful Harvest.

Guiltily Morning Song swung her head around. As she looked up, Stag Leaping paused in his fulsome description of bloody hand-to-hand combat and met her indifferent stare. His face tightened as he stared back at her, and suddenly his eyes narrowed to direct at her a fury so intense that it pierced Morning Song's apathy with the force of a new-honed lance.

She lowered her gaze, pretended to be absorbed in the sight of Swift Arrow sprawled in Teller Of Legends' lap. Why had Stag Leaping reacted so strongly to her lack of enthusiasm for his extravagant chronicle? He would have been justified in frowning; but she'd done nothing to invite an anger potent enough to leave her feeling bruised and shaken. She clasped her hands until the knuckles paled, prayed that the speeches would soon be done.

Teller Of Legends cried *"Ho!"* with the rest when Stag Leaping ended his rambling tale, then prepared herself to listen to Hawk Hunting. This warrior was nearly as scornful of lengthy oration as Cloud Racer was. Even if his father were not one of those they would mourn tomorrow, he would merit her attention.

"Grandmother."

It was an urgent whisper, and the son of Long Canoe was forgotten on the instant. Teller Of Legends looked to her granddaughter, read accurately the signs of birth pains beginning, and sent back a mute promise to watch over Swift Arrow until his mother could return to him.

She marked Morning Song's efforts to leave unobtrusively and smiled to see so many eyes register her going. She hoped those who watched would never tell Morning Song how much she resembled an overweight duck in this moment!

As the old woman looked back toward the fire, she saw that two of the warriors had also focused on that waddling figure. It did not surprise her that Cloud Racer—concern briefly twisting his impassive features—gazed after his wife; but she was startled indeed to

see Stag Leaping grin almost mockingly as he watched Morning
Song's awkward progress to the palisade's gates.

Morning Song sat on a cornhusk mat and fumed to be confined.
Beyond the screens marking the perimeters of her prison, people
talked and laughed and ate heartily of the venison stew that the new
mother was forbidden even to taste.

Her son's familiar babble grew louder all at once, and this time
it was Otter Swimming who intercepted his march to Morning
Song's corner of the lodge. "Want Mama!" he wailed as she picked
him up, and Morning Song visualized him kicking and squirming
as Otter carried him back to the central hearth. He had been shown
his new sister, and told that Morning Song and the babe must stay
by themselves only until the moon was full again. But that had not
satisfied Swift Arrow. She smiled.

The smile vanished as a flurry of greetings said that the Matron
of the Pigeonhawk lodge had come again to visit. It was ridiculous
of the woman to think that bragging about her son to the matrons
would ensure his being named war leader, but Owl Crying was
tireless in her campaigning. She had even enlisted the help of
Pumpkin Blossom and Bountiful Harvest.

"The decision will be made today," she said now, "and I am
certain Stag Leaping shall be chosen. You spoke to the younger
matrons, Pumpkin Blossom?"

"I did," Morning Song's cousin said. But discontent frittered
her voice, had Morning Song strained her ears to learn the reason
for it. "It amazes me that so many insist that *their* husbands are
more deserving of the honor. Everyone knows how Fierce Eagle
himself praised Stag Leaping for his valor!"

Morning Song rolled her eyes. During a victory celebration,
Fierce Eagle made a point of praising, by name, every warrior.

"Some of the matrons wondered why Stag Leaping did not bring
home any captives." This from Bountiful Harvest, who spoke more
moderately now than when she'd urged her daughter to confront
Stag Leaping with this oversight. Pumpkin Blossom had done so at
the first opportunity, and Morning Song had winced to hear the
echo of Bountiful Harvest's stridency in her cousin's voice. Stag
Leaping had responded with bluster, which anyone could have predicted.

"When the battle fever is on my son, he does not concern himself
with taking *captives*!" Owl Crying said sharply. "Has anybody
implied that Stag Leaping did not lead the rest in the number of
Cat People *slain*?"

"Since each brave keeps his own tally, no one would be likely to." Teller Of Legends spoke so quietly that surely the others must realize—as Morning Song did—that she was weary of being subjected once again to a too-familiar dispute. It was a reminder, as well, that two warriors lived in her lodge, and it would ill-become its Matron to favor one above the other.

Red Bird opened her eyes and rounded her tiny mouth. Morning Song reached out and began to rock the hammock she'd improvised from an old winter cloak. Red Bird was given to fussing between feedings, something Swift Arrow had rarely done, and Morning Song did not want the conversation she was listening to drowned out by infant plaint.

"Has it been decided what is to become of the Erie maiden?" Otter Swimming, at least, was aware of Teller Of Legends' desire to talk of something else.

"She continues to serve any matron who summons her," Bountiful Harvest said. "She is said to be uncommonly strong, and a tireless worker, so there is no danger of her sitting idle."

"She is also said to be uncommonly beautiful," Pumpkin Blossom put in, "although this seems to me an exaggeration. Why, she is bigger-built than some of our warriors are; she would appear a giant among Pygmies were she permitted to sit with the matrons of our village."

"But she is sweetly proportioned," Otter countered reasonably, "and steps lightly when she walks. And I envy her the serenity I see in her face."

"Serenity is all very well," Owl Crying sniffed, "but I would be happier to find humility in her. She is as much a prize of war as the beaver pelts the men brought home. Yet there is nothing humble about the Erie maiden."

"Doubtless that is why some have taken to calling her Proud Woman," Teller Of Legends said. She chuckled. "Were I in her place, I would be honored to be so called."

"It was Cloud Racer who named her," Owl Crying said, and Morning Song slid closer to the reed screen. "She was his captive, and he seems to feel responsible for her still." She laughed. "I am grateful that my son did not let a pretty face make him forget who is enemy and who is friend! Of course, Stag Leaping is wed to you, Pumpkin Blossom; this helps him avoid the weakness of less fortunate men."

Pumpkin Blossom murmured her appreciation for the compliment. Morning Song, in her prison, seethed with rage. How dare the Matron of the Pigeonhawk lodge suggest that Cloud Racer was championing this woman? Captives, if they were young or female, were frequently adopted by some clan, or given thrall's status in a village. Cloud Racer had merely been showing sense by delivering to the matrons a maiden he recognized as strong enough to work for them.

And beautiful. Otter, straight-tongued Otter, had said that she was, and even the opinionated Owl Crying had not disputed the word. So Cloud Racer had been in the company of a beautiful woman while he'd traveled back from Erie country. No wonder he'd been repelled by the ugly and misshapen wife he came home to! And custom had kept Cloud Racer and Morning Song apart since then. Her eyes brimmed with frustrated tears. Teller Of Legends' precious tradition made Morning Song more a slave than the Erie maiden was. At least the girl was able to walk at will in the compound—walk *lightly*, she reminded herself bitterly—whenever she was not occupied with some task. *Morning Song* was prisoner as well as slave; Proud Woman was free to let her eyes seek out Cloud Racer, to smile at him shyly, or even enticingly, if no matron was watching.

But would Cloud Racer smile in response? Would he offer to this daughter of the enemy the slow-dawning smile Morning Song had trusted was reserved for her alone? Surely he would not. Surely he would turn away instead, if he did not actually scowl at the girl for thinking he might welcome her attentions?

She pounded her bent knees with impotent fists, and the sound woke Red Bird. Morning Song flipped back one side of the vestlike garment she wore, snatched up the crying babe, and thrust her against the breast she'd exposed. Yet she was not soothed by the tugging of a tiny mouth against the teat the babe quickly found. Her breasts ached for the weight of Cloud Racer's gleaming head and the urgency of Cloud Racer's passionate lips; this ritual of nourishment did nothing but stimulate her need for him.

The women were talking now of the recent planting, and wondering if the strawberries might not ripen early. Morning Song told herself to concentrate on their chatter and borrow a measure of calm from its ordinariness. She owed it to her babe to keep sweet the milk she needed, and disquiet was likely to curdle it. She bent her head over Red Bird's, and made herself croon a lullaby.

"It was to please Fierce Eagle that they voted as they did, and because they wanted to show sympathy for his suffering."

Stag Leaping's agitated words preceded him into the longhouse, yet even though his companion's reply was merely a grunt, Morning Song knew Cloud Racer was with him.

"The warriors have chosen a new leader?" Owl Crying was shrill with excitement, and Morning Song pictured the wiry woman jumping to her feet while her snapping eyes demanded an answer.

"Our new war leader is the son of Rain Singing," Stag Leaping said sullenly. Morning Song—who had expected nothing less—grinned, her ill-humor flown.

An uncomfortable silence followed that bald statement. Owl Crying was momentarily speechless, Morning Song gathered. Pumpkin Blossom and her mother would be trying to conceal their own disappointment. And no doubt Otter and Teller Of Legends were wondering how to simultaneously congratulate one man and condole with the other.

"This matron is pleased that a warrior who calls her longhouse home has been chosen," Teller Of Legends said at last—showing what might be achieved when shrewdness was wed to tact, Morning Song thought, amused.

In the next moment, Owl Crying rounded on her son. "You were a fool to expect to be chosen," she said scornfully. "You, who lacked the sense to bring back a single prisoner!"

"I brought home twice the number of scalps that Cloud Racer did," Stag Leaping protested strongly.

"Scalps!" his mother snorted. "Can *scalps* entertain us with chanting while fire consumes them? Can *scalps* dig holes to receive seeds, or hoe around plants when they grow, or lug pots of water from the river?"

"And there were not that many scalps tied to your spear." Now it was Pumpkin Blossom who was venting her displeasure. "You had no more than Hill Climber, and fewer than Hawk Hunting, if I counted correctly."

"You did not," he muttered.

"Hill Climber," Pumpkin Blossom said remorselessly, "brought back eleven, just as you did. Hawk Hunting had nine fastened to the shaft of his spear and five dangling from his belt."

Morning Song was tempted to call out that only the ignorant judge a man by the number of scalps or prisoners he claims. A war leader must be capable of planning, and of carrying out his plans; he must be someone who can recognize an enemy's weakness, and take advantage of it. He must be a man like Cloud Racer. . . .

But Owl Crying was ranting anew at Stag Leaping, naming him Flat Head and Turtle Anus, epithets so degrading that Morning Song was embarrassed for him. And he could not know that only moments ago the woman had been chanting his praises! Briefly the eavesdropper felt compassion for a man she detested. With such a mother, how could he be other than he was?

"It is a relief to me that one like you no longer lives in my longhouse," the Matron of the Pigeonhawk clan finished acidly, and took her departure.

"Only one man may be elected war leader," Otter Swimming said after a moment. "This has never meant that those not chosen are undeserving of respect."

"It does not mean, either, that the one chosen had hoped for the honor." Morning Song smiled proudly as her husband spoke, then frowned a little. Perhaps it was not merely a diplomacy equal to Teller Of Legends' that prompted him to make this statement; she would hate to see him burdened with a responsibility he had no eagerness for.

"We have been wondering, Cloud Racer," Bountiful Harvest said, and Morning Song tensed at the silkiness of her tone, "what is to become of the Erie woman you brought home."

Stag Leaping laughed unpleasantly. "The one you would not let me kill," he put in. "Even though she was carrying a man's weapon and fighting like a man. Until I rested the point of my lance against the back of her lovely neck."

"The Iroquois do not deliberately slay women," Cloud Racer said harshly.

"Most assuredly not, if they are as beautiful as the one you rescued," Bountiful Harvest purred. "But I ask you again, Cloud Racer, what is to become of this maid you call Proud Woman?"

"That is for the matrons to decide," he responded. "As for the name I gave her, it is hers by right. It was pride as much as courage that made her take up her dead father's spear."

"You admire her, then." This from Pumpkin Blossom, who never failed to follow where her mother led.

"Anyone who witnessed her valor must," he said shortly.

"Courage is always to be admired," Teller Of Legends remarked. "We shame ourselves when we do not praise it."

"To adopt a maiden possessed of both pride and courage can only bring honor to a clan," Cloud Racer said slowly. "Perhaps, Teller Of Legends, the Turtle clan—"

"No!" Morning Song shouted so loudly that the word bounced among the rafters and repeated itself over and over. "There are enough women living in this longhouse. Find another place for that *Proud Woman* of yours, Cloud Racer. I will not have her here!"

Chapter 22

❦ ➡

Red Bird's cradleboard bobbed against Morning Song's back as she led Swift Arrow through the forest, and White Shadow frolicked in miniature showers as he plowed through brush that a brief summer storm had drenched. They had stopped often along the way—to admire a butterfly drying its fragile wings; to examine the pellets left by a deer who'd made a meal of wood ferns; to watch a white-throated sparrow drink from a poplar's cupped leaves—for leisure was as rare these days as red kernels on a corncob, and they meant to make the most of what they had.

"We will let your sister walk, too, when we come to a clearing I know of," she told Swift Arrow. "And if the raspberries are ripe, you may pick some for her to eat."

"I bring berries to Red Bird," he said, grinning hugely. "And some for me to eat!"

"As we go," she went on, after she'd steered him away from a shrub whose sap was highly irritating, "perhaps we shall meet your father. He-No's roaring might have persuaded the hunters to return sooner than they'd planned."

Merely speaking of Cloud Racer brought a tender smile to her lips, brought so vividly to mind the night just past that the blood began to sing in her veins once more and her pulses to flutter anew with desire for him.

Shadow trotted up with a stick for Swift Arrow to throw. Once the dog would have chosen his mistress for his playmate, and for a moment Morning Song felt envy that he cavorted more often with her son these days. Then she smiled ruefully; why should a contented matron, mother of two fine children and wife to the village's war leader, regret the perfectly natural passing of her youth?

She stooped beneath branches of a moose maple to enter the clearing she'd been making for, and told herself that she would work twice as hard tomorrow to atone for today's truancy. For now, she would simply savor the freshness of rain-washed air, the softness of the grass she was lowering her daughter's cradleboard onto, the sweetness of birdsong, and the drone of nectar-seeking bees.

Little Red Bird looked around dubiously as her mother hung the empty cradleboard on a branch, and Morning Song laughed to see such an expression on a face that was a miniature version of her own. "It is a little damp," she told her daughter, "but you have never minded your feet being wet." Indeed, to be taken to the river each morning was something Red Bird had delighted in since infancy.

But apparently grass that glistened with moisture did not have the same appeal. Until Swift Arrow, plump raspberries spilling from his hands, came to share his bounty with her, Red Bird would not be persuaded to move from the spot she stood on. Her mother watched the fragile-built girl toddle cautiously around the small glade and wondered how a child made in Morning Song's image could be so unlike her in every other way. Red Bird had never crawled all over the longhouse, as Swift Arrow used to; the single time she had attempted it, she'd fretted over her dirty hands and knees until her mother wiped them clean. Teller Of Legends said afterward the child's aversion to dirt had prompted her to take her first steps so soon. But even then Red Bird did not wander far from her family's hearth. She was not venturesome, this daughter of hers; she would rather sit and cuddle her cornhusk doll or play solemnly with the bowl and spoon Pumpkin Blossom had given her. She was as docile as Pumpkin Blossom's own daughter was, for all that Morning Song allowed her as much freedom as she'd always given Swift Arrow.

A red-furred squirrel paused in midscamper halfway along the branch of the elm Morning Song sat beneath. His round ears pricked and his whiskers quivered as he held himself motionless. Then, in the blink of an eye, he had hidden himself among the glossy leaves of an adjacent limb. Morning Song tilted her head and, in a little while, heard the rumble of voices that the squirrel's sensitive ears had been quick to perceive. Beyond the spikiness of holly and thorn apple that walled the clearing on the east, the ground dipped and became a hemlock-studded bank descending to a brook. The sounds came from that direction, and Morning Song strained to identify a voice she'd been hoping to hear. But Swift Arrow recognized it first. He squealed excitedly, dashed to the tree that guarded the entrance to the glade, and called his father's name.

Morning Song, springing to her feet to welcome him, retreated instead when he appeared. Accompanying Cloud Racer, Stag Leaping, Hill Climber, and Hawk Hunting were *Onondio*—two brown-robed men who fixed curious eyes on Morning Song and the children she hastily summoned to her side.

Morning Song looked a plea to her husband: Only nod, and speak, and *leave*, she begged mutely, so that I may do the same.

But Cloud Racer smiled warmly at his family, then turned to the older of the strangers and spoke to him slowly in the language his father had encouraged him to learn. "This woman is wife to me," he told him, "and the little ones are my children."

The white-haired man with the stooped shoulders moved one arthritic hand in a gesture that meant nothing to Morning Song, inclined his head toward her, and beamed upon Swift Arrow and Red Bird. Then he spoke haltingly a phrase that, after a startled moment, she understood was intended to be a familiar Iroquois greeting. Confused, she bent her own head briefly, then looked again at her husband.

"Father Fo-Ret has been learning the language of the Longhouse People," he said gravely, and she alone saw the twinkle in the depths of his eyes. "He has come from the settlement of *Onondio* Faithkeepers with Brother Mont-Blanc." He gestured toward the second sallow-skin, and Morning Song—despite her fervent desire to escape—looked from one to the other of the white men. The frail Foret had skin pale as mother's milk, but the square frame of the second *Onondio* was overlaid with healthy flesh nearly as brown as the coarse garment that flared above his sandaled feet. Even his hairless head was the color of a hickory nut, and a pair of luxuriant brown mustaches drooped to meet a boldly jutting jaw. How was it possible that two so unlike could be brothers? Or was it father and son?

She shook her head bemusedly. What did it matter? All she wanted was to take Swift Arrow and Red Bird and go home. Now.

But the mustached man was striding across to where they stood. "You have told us we go to your village, and speak with your chief," he said to Cloud Racer. "Why do we break our journey?"

The older sallow-skin gently chided his impatient comrade; but Morning Song—although she was careful not to reveal that she understood everything they said—seized the opportunity and murmured to Cloud Racer that she would return to the village by a little-used path. And although Swift Arrow's face fell when his father took his companions back onto the well-marked trail, Morning Song was weak-kneed with relief to see the men, white and red, file out of the glade.

"I do not know why they have come," Morning Song repeated, "but it disturbs me that Se-A-Wi allows them to remain here." She laid Red Bird in her hammock and shooed Swift Arrow away to play near Otter's hearth.

"It is for five days only," Teller Of Legends said. "And you cannot expect my brother to refuse the request of a Faithkeeper, Morning Song."

"They are nothing like those who keep the faith for us. Do we accept that they are merely because they say so?"

Grandmother and granddaughter looked up as the entrance hide let in a shaft of sunlight—and a guest Pumpkin Blossom had clearly been expecting. Teller Of Legends saw Morning Song's face harden when she recognized Proud Woman, and sighed. If Morning Song would spend some time with the pleasant-natured maid Gray Squirrel had adopted, she might eventually feel as friendly toward her as others were coming to do. No one could ever replace the husband and brother the Matron of the Snipe longhouse had lost to the Erie, but Gray Squirrel delighted in her new daughter. Affection was growing between the two, and Teller Of Legends' heart was gladdened to see it. But Morning Song continued stubbornly aloof from the Erie maiden, and Teller Of Legends suspected that she would never be convinced that courtesy alone had prompted Cloud Racer to suggest that the girl be accepted into the Turtle clan. "I think we need not doubt what these Frenchmen tell us," she said, recapturing her granddaughter's attention. "Se-A-Wi tells me that those who came before the Great Council were dressed as they dress, and wore dangling from their belts the metal ornaments the *Onondio* call *crosses*. This is a symbol by which all of them may be identified."

"This may be so," Morning Song said. "Yet why are they visiting our villages to speak of the spirits who guide the white men? Even if the one called Father could make himself understood, how can such talk possibly interest our people?"

"It is *one* spirit that the *Onondio* prays to, rather than a host of them," the old woman said. "So my brother told me. And it seems that this spirit, called God, has directed his Faithkeepers to speak of him to the Iroquois. The Sachems would not stand in the way of men who respond so promptly to the bidding of a spirit; they gave permission for the *Onondio* to fulfill their mission. I doubt we shall benefit greatly from their coming, but these Faithkeepers—who are called *priests* by their own people—merely do as they are inspired to do, I suppose. As our own Faithkeepers do when they have been sent visions."

Morning Song was moved to smile. Teller Of Legends could be relied upon to nose out all there was to learn about virtually any subject. She was never satisfied with imprecise information, but made herself learn how people and places were properly called, then stored away her nuggets of knowledge until she had use for them.

In truth, her grandmother was far from content with the little she'd been able to find out about the palefaced Keepers Of The Faith. Only because she needed to learn more had she been pleased to see the two come to her village. She meant to watch what they did, listen to what people said of them, and speak with Cloud Racer when she had questions she wanted put to them.

As if summoned by her thoughts, the young man entered with the bundle of ash splints Morning Song had asked him to cut. Teller Of Legends saw her granddaughter's eyes narrow as her husband greeted Pumpkin Blossom's guest, saw them flick from Cloud Racer to Proud Woman and back again. The old woman thrust behind her the problem of the *Onondio* Faithkeepers—if problem it was—and took it upon herself to create a diversion.

"A fine summer evening is an excellent time for a story," she declared, coming to her feet and smiling at the enthusiasm her announcement generated. The children abandoned their game and ran to surround her, Bold Leader and Brave Companion begging to be allowed to select the story. Swift Arrow and Painted Sky vowed to sit quiet as hawk-threatened mice during her tale, and the little girls decided between themselves that Teller Of Legends's lap would hold the both of them. Even Fish Jumping scrambled to his feet and shouted *"Ho!"* before he remembered that a warrior-to-be did not betray excitement.

Proud Woman hurried away to the Snipe lodge, and by the time the Turtle clan made their way into the compound, others were congregating there. That much was no surprise, but Teller Of Legends was startled when she scanned the outer rim of the circle and discovered among the Councilors and warriors two brown-robed figures. Why had the *Onondio* come to hear a story when one of them, at least, would understand not a word of it?

She had no time to dwell on this, however; the children were clamoring for their tale. "There were once two brothers," she began, "who lived alone in the wilderness. The elder hunted game to feed the two of them, for the younger was neither big enough nor strong enough to handle a bow. Indeed, the only thing the little boy was, was curious. And this he was to a remarkable degree."

Swift Arrow nudged Brave Companion and grinned. It was Bold Leader who swiveled his dark head to return the grin, but that was the way twins were, and Swift Arrow did not consider it strange.

"One day," Teller Of Legends went on, "the younger brother realized that never, ever, had he seen the hunter eat anything. Does he have his meal at night, the boy wondered, when I am sleeping? And, being more inquisitive than a half-grown raccoon, he decided to stay awake and find out if that was so." She leaned forward so the children might see her peer at them from behind the screen of her lashes.

"He watched his brother," Teller Of Legends said when high-pitched giggles subsided, "and this is what he saw: When he thought the little boy asleep, the hunter took from hiding a whip and a dented old kettle. He filled the kettle with water, set it on the fire, and struck it with the whip. 'Grow larger, my kettle,' he chanted; and suddenly that kettle began to grow and grow, until it became as big around as the hearth. And when finally the hunter lifted it from the fire, he took up a spoon and made so satisfying a meal of whatever bubbled in it that he was constantly belching in order to make room in his belly for more.

"Need I tell you," she asked, looking around her, "that next morning the younger brother wasted not a moment taking kettle and whip from their hiding place? But when he examined the kettle, there was nothing in it but half of a chestnut! That puzzled him, but it intrigued him, too. So he filled the kettle with water, put it on the fire, and struck it with the rawhide whip. 'Grow larger,' he shouted, repeating the words his brother had said.

"And it did. That kettle grew larger, and larger, and larger still. And it was not until the sides of it pressed against the walls of their house that the boy ceased striking it and urging it to grow.

"By the time the hunter came home, his brother was sitting on the roof stirring the mush in the kettle with a stick he'd poked down through the smoke hole. 'I have made your dinner,' he called proudly. And waited to be praised."

That made sense to the children. Until Teller Of Legends—after a carefully timed paused—spoke again.

" 'You have killed me,' the hunter said sorrowfully, when he had shrunk the kettle by muttering a few sacred words. 'It was a magic chestnut my kettle held, and you have cooked it all away. I am not permitted to eat anything else, so now I must starve to death.' "

The children's mouths gaped, and their round eyes were huge.

"Well, the little boy, who loved his big brother, insisted that he would go and find more of the magic chestnuts. And when the dying hunter saw he meant it, he told him where to look for them: 'You must travel from sunrise to sunset to reach a river so fast-running that none but the bravest can ford it. On the opposite bank is a lodge, and near that a tree on which these nuts grow. A white heron stands vigil there whose voice is loud enough to summon six dreadful women from the lodge. Whenever anyone approaches the chestnut tree, they use their war clubs to slay the intruder. It is hopeless, what you are planning to do, Little Brother.' ''

The boys who were listening straightened their backs and squared their shoulders, anticipating Little Brother's response.

'' 'I am going, and I shall return with the nuts you need,' the boy said stubbornly; for he was—in addition to being curious—a child who owned courage. And go he did.

''The long march did not dismay him, and he suffered no more than a drenching when he crossed the perilous river that separated him from the chestnut tree. The first thing he spied when he'd beached his canoe was a bush bearing seeds much prized by herons. These he picked, and scattered them on the ground as he approached the tree. When the bird bent his head to gobble them up, the boy began snatching nuts from the tree's laden branches.

''Suddenly, however, the bird spotted him. He shrieked, and out of the lodge dashed six warrior-sized women, whooping and screaming as they came. As they rushed toward him the boy realized that, instead of clubs, their outstretched hands held fishing lines the sisters had been mending. Nonetheless, their awesome size was daunting, and the boy ran for the riverbank. He tumbled into his canoe just as the first of the sisters reached the river's edge, and began to paddle furiously.''

The children, silently cheering on the little boy, were thrusting their heads forward as though they were turtles struggling to exit their shells.

''One screeching woman tossed out her line—and in a heartbeat it had wound itself around Little Brother's neck. But he was discovering strength he'd never known he had. He put up his free hand and, with a sharp tug, broke it. And even though her sisters were equally skillful at throwing out fishing lines, the boy snapped each one as it snared him. In the end, the six women could only stand there screaming with rage while Little Brother began his journey home.''

''Did he reach the hunter in time?'' This from Bold Leader and Brave Companion in unison.

Teller Of Legends nodded. ''He did, and saved his life. But I think that what Little Brother learned about himself during his adventure was just as important as what he was able to do. When you have thought about it, I expect you will agree.''

The youngsters in the village had gradually become enthralled with the *Onondio* that Trail Marker told his son was a *Jesuit priest*.

"They are fascinated because many have never been so close to a white man before, and because this Fo-Ret seems to sincerely love children," Teller Of Legends said when Morning Song had once again forbidden her son and daughter to go with their friends and sit at the feet of the sallow-skin Faithkeeper. She chuckled. "He tries so hard to speak our tongue," she added, "this Father Fo-Ret. Yet what a tangle he makes of it!"

"He depends upon Cloud Racer and Trail Marker to teach him this word and that," Morning Song said, "and Cloud Racer insists there is no harm in him learning what he can. I think my husband hopes to persuade the Faithkeeper to take a message to the Frenchmen in Mon-Tre-Al. They have paid no heed so far when our delegations complain about them buying furs from the Painted People. This is a violation of the treaty they made with us, and Cloud Racer hopes it will not need our going to war to show them how wrong this is." She fell into a brooding silence. Her dislike and mistrust of the *Onondio* had not abated, but neither did she want to see Cloud Racer have reason to leave her again.

"It is peculiar that a war leader should make no secret of his liking for peace," Pumpkin Blossom said, tossing aside the skins she'd been sorting. If Stag Leaping did not bring home a bear or a moose from his next hunt, he would have no new winter cloak this year; and so she meant to tell him. "If my husband led the warriors, he would not be wasting time trying to patch broken treaties with *messages*. He would long since have thrown his hatchet into the war post, and our men would be preparing to let spears and arrows speak of the Iroquois' displeasure."

"Then why is Stag Leaping so often with the sallow-skin called Brother Mont-Blanc?" Morning Song asked sharply. Like the others, she knew now that Foret and Montblanc were not blood kin, that *Father* and *Brother* were merely titles of respect among their kind. "I have heard that they communicate with hand movements and with a few of the garbled Iroquois words Mont-Blanc learned from Father Fo-Ret." Small Brown Sparrow had told her this, and been convulsed with laughter as she described the waving of hands and fluttering of fingers she'd witnessed.

"Do you think only Cloud Racer is clever enough to study a language that makes it easier for us to deal with the traders?" Pumpkin Blossom said, bristling. "Stag Leaping is looking ahead to the day when he sits on the Village Council. He means to impress those who come to barter with us when that time comes.''

"He shows good sense,'' Bountiful Harvest said. ''Follows The Signs is an old man, and the future of an old man is measured in days, not years. When his death song has been sung, it will be Stag Leaping who speaks for the Pigeonhawk clan in matters of importance.''

"No more than seven years,'' Teller Of Legends said, ''separate Follows The Signs and your mother. I hope you do not feel, Bountiful Harvest, that I should begin to rehearse my death song?''

Bountiful Harvest, who was not close enough to see the mirthlight in her mother's eyes, shook her head forcefully. ''I would weep to hear it,'' she said quickly, ''did your years number a hundred.''

"That is good,'' Teller Of Legends said, permitting her amusement free rein. ''The chant would stick in my throat if I tried to sing it before I am ready to.'' She laughed aloud. ''And as all of you shall find, when your own years gather themselves into decades, *old* is never what you are, but always what you shall someday become.''

They threaded their laughter through hers, and even Morning Song forgot for a while the sallow-skins who were guests in their village.

Since Bountiful Harvest had no brothers, Deer Caller had asked Lake On Fire's grandson to be honorary uncle to Fish Jumping. Hawk Hunting and Deer Caller had trained together in their own youth, and it was already agreed between them that he would see to the warrior training of Bold Leader and Brave Companion when the twins were older.

"Hearth Tender may be right when she predicts that our sons will be more suited to be Keepers Of The Faith than warriors,'' he'd explained to Otter, ''but no boy should come to manhood without developing the skills that mark a man as such.''

Now, whenever the men were not away on a hunting or fishing expedition, Fish Jumping spent long hours practicing to become the Turtle clan's first warrior in almost two decades. Morning Song, watching him return to the lodge begrimed with mingled sweat and leaf mold, realized that it would not be many years before Otter's boys would come in looking the same. And her own Swift Arrow would follow closely in their footsteps.

She spoke of this to Cloud Racer. He—watching their son slyly encouraging the long-suffering White Shadow to chase his own tail—smiled. ''He will do well, when the time comes, for he is strong and quick-thinking even now. But he has years left to be a child in, Morning Song.''

"I suppose Hawk Hunting will teach him also, when he is ready,'' she went on thoughtfully. "I never took much heed of the man before Deer Caller arranged for him to train Fish Jumping, but I am impressed with what I have seen since.''

"He is a fine man,'' Cloud Racer confirmed, "although somewhat shy of women. But he shall not be Swift Arrow's mentor. Stag Leaping will teach him, as I will teach Painted Sky.''

Morning Song took pity on her panting dog and sent Swift Arrow to play with the other children. "You are not Pumpkin Blossom's brother,'' she said slowly, "and Stag Leaping is not mine.''

Cloud Racer nodded. "But you have no clan brother, and Pumpkin Blossom's will scarcely be experienced enough by then to train Painted Sky. And we are at least uncles of a sort to each other's sons.''

"It would please me,'' Morning Song said, "if you would train our son yourself.''

"That is not the way of the Longhouse People,'' Cloud Racer said quietly. Then, "Is there a reason you do not want Stag Leaping to teach him?''

There were many, but Morning Song hesitated to list them. Her first unhappy encounter with Stag Leaping had occurred long ago; to describe it now might cast doubt upon the reliability of her memory. Yet should Cloud Racer accept without question what she told him, he might well decide to challenge Stag Leaping, even so long afterward. She would not like to be responsible for such a thing, not when she knew full well that her own behavior, when she'd sought escape from the betrothal arranged by Summer Maize and Owl Crying, had been no more praiseworthy than Stag Leaping's. Since that year, since Pumpkin Blossom took Stag Leaping for her husband, Morning Song could complain of no specific insult. Cloud Racer would name her fanciful were she to speak of being uncomfortable when Stag Leaping was in the longhouse, of sensing him watching her when both were in the compound, of the peculiar rage that had emanated from him on the night the warriors celebrated their victory over the Erie. . . . "You are war leader,'' she said at last, "and I would have Swift Arrow learn from the best.''

"I have no skills that Stag Leaping does not own also,'' Cloud Racer said firmly. As she had known that he would.

"But,'' she began, then swallowed the remainder of her protest as Teller Of Legends' raised voice distracted her. She turned to see the Matron of the Turtle clan and Trail Marker approaching, and it was clear that Teller Of Legends was agitated about something. She did not even notice Cloud Racer and Morning Song, although she and her companion came to a stop within an arm's length of them.

"The children must not be told such things." Teller Of Legends's tone was imperious, her natural dignity so fueled by anger that she appeared to stand taller than she truly did.

"He meant no insult," Trail Marker said soothingly. "He was only trying to tell the little ones about this Je-Sus, who is son to the *Onondio*'s god, and was describing for them what he calls *miracles*. One of the children—Meadow Brook's oldest daughter—can decipher the man's odd shaping of Iroquois words. She said to her friends that Je-Sus was like the hunter in the tale about the two brothers, the one who could make a small kettle grow huge and brim with nourishing food."

"And this was when Fo-Ret said what he did?" The old woman shaded her eyes with one hand to moderate the sun's dazzle.

Trail Marker, unfailingly courteous, moved so that he stood between Teller Of Legends and the westering sun. "Yes. He said that it was false, what you told them, and that they must not believe there has ever been a magic kettle, or a tree bearing nuts so marvelous that half a one will feed a man."

"Yet he claims that his Je-Sus transformed a single slab of bread and one small fish into a meal big enough to satisfy more people than live in our village?"

Trail Marker shrugged. "Even the *Onondio* may have their legends," he said.

"But they may not mock ours!" Teller Of Legends snapped. "This is a thing I shall not permit. Faithkeepers or no, the *Onondio* must leave here, and at once. Who can measure the damage this man may already have done, by speaking as he did to our children?"

"None of them understood all of the white man's words, and most recognized so few that they will remember only what the daughter of Meadow Brook said." Trail Marker was aware that in Teller Of Legends' opinion he should have dispersed the Jesuit's youthful audience more promptly than he had. Although a man of considerable status in village and tribe, he now wore an expression much like that of a small boy whose elders saw cause to censure him.

Cloud Racer touched Morning Song's arm and signed that they should quietly withdraw. "My father will think I do not honor him,'' he said as they walked toward the fields, ''if we listen while your grandmother challenges his judgment.''

''Teller Of Legends was too upset to realize their conversation might be overheard,'' Morning Song said loyally.

Cloud Racer made no response; he knew that was so. Nor would Morning Song imply criticism of Cloud Racer's father by saying that she agreed wholeheartedly with her grandmother.

And she would not confess her relief that, finally, someone shared Morning Song's distrust of the *Onondio*.

Chapter 23

⇐ ⇒

''It shamed all of us,'' Stag Leaping said, ''to hear the war leader from this village persuading the leaders of other bands that we should abandon our attacks on the French fortresses!''

Morning Song made unnecessary clatter with the spoon she was using to stir the hominy. Half a year the men had been back, and Stag Leaping continued to gnaw at a bone of grievance he'd first pounced on when they'd been home only a few days.

''Which peckerwood succeeds in his hunt for food?'' Cloud Racer asked, careful not to let exasperation salt his voice this time. ''The one who blunts his beak on a hardwood tree, or the one that seeks grubs beneath the softer bark of a spruce?''

''You prattle of birds,'' Stag Leaping said scornfully. ''What have they to do with a war leader who accepts defeat too readily?''

The handle of Morning Song's spoon snapped in two as she rapped it against the rim of the kettle. Month after month—even during winter's deep snows—Cloud Racer and his fellows had besieged the high-walled strongholds of the *Onondio*, until Iroquois warriors lay heaped like windfall fruit upon the ground. One village, he'd told Morning Song bluntly, would see none of their young men return alive.

''I could have said, as many did, We are not cowards; we will fight on until every last man has been slain. They are noble words, but what would such a thing accomplish? Our reason for going to war was to convince the French that they must honor the trading treaties they made with us. We learned that we are ill-equipped to breach the walls they built around their larger settlements. One method failed; another must be tried."

"Blockading!" Stag Leaping spat. "Where is the glory in lying in wait for canoes bringing the Painted People to Mon-Tre-Al?"

"The canoes bring down the Long River not only the Ottawa warriors," Cloud Racer said, "but a wealth of furs also. If we can keep them from reaching the *Onondio*, we will be able to insist that the French abide by the trade agreements favoring our people. A nation is no longer measured solely by the strength and valor of its warriors, Stag Leaping; this counts for little if its people do not prosper. If we Iroquois cannot force the sallow-skins to honor their pledges, we will be brought to our knees just as though an enemy had risen up in our midst and destroyed us."

Morning Song, tossing the broken stirrer into the fire, wished bleakly that the Longhouse People need not be so dependent upon trade with the *Onondio*. But wishing has never altered what is, and it would not change things now.

"I once heard Fierce Eagle say that the hardest part of being war leader is to recognize when to attack and when to withdraw." Deer Caller's offering was made quietly. "The warrior who follows him is free to concentrate on the enemy he struggles to overcome, but the leader must never lose sight of the battle as a whole, or of the reason it is being fought. Had you stood in Cloud Racer's moccasins, Stag Leaping, you might have found yourself counseling retreat in order to devise a more promising strategy. Blockade served us well before, if you recall. And you will be exposed to as much danger—and have as great a chance for glory—when you intercept canoes bearing hostile Ottawa as when you meet a foe on land. More, perhaps. For the river will challenge you, too, and it can be a deadlier adversary than the fiercest of warriors."

Stag Leaping's blustering rebuttal was less than a mumble in Morning Song's ears; what roared in them was the crash of white water. What her lid-darkened eyes looked upon were thunderous foam-flecked waves, waves powerful enough to seize unwary warriors and fling them onto jagged rocks, to wash over them, surge into their gaping mouths and flared nostrils. . . .

Her eyes flew open. She willed herself to be calm, commanded her trembling legs to take her to her bunk. Only then did she permit the shudders she'd held at bay to ripple through her until she was driven to pull her bedrobe around her.

"Morning Song." She looked up to see Day Greeter standing over her. "What is wrong? Are you ill?"

Morning Song squared her slumped shoulders, shrugged off the robe. "It is nothing, only a slight dizziness. From standing near the hearth on so humid a day, perhaps."

Day Greeter, relieved, sat down beside her. "It is true that the heat swells the air and gives it enormous weight," she said, wiping perspiration from her broad forehead with one blunt-fingered hand. "Many would be complaining, I suspect, if they did not fear offending our brother the sun."

"I hope the spirits will not object if I say how much I long for He-No to regain his power," Morning Song said, charging her hallucination to the mind-clogging heat. This unnatural weather was affecting all of them, and what thunder they'd been sent was sullen and sluggish. The brief showers spawned by infrequent storms had only left earth and air steaming. She looked around the lodge, noted thankfully that the men had separated, Cloud Racer to examine the bow Deer Caller was working on and Stag Leaping to speak with his wife. "The hominy is ready," Morning Song said, and came to her feet. "I will go and call the children, but I do not know where Hearth Tender is. Did you see her go out?"

Day Greeter followed her into the compound. "She went with Sweet Maple to visit her Sachem brother," she said, smiling as a clatter of hungry youngsters raced into the longhouse. "They will be gone three days or more, for Sweet Maple will not leave her brother's village until she harvests a store of gossip to share with the matrons here."

Morning Song grinned. "May she not overlook a scrap of it!" she said fervently. "To listen to gossip we have not heard a dozen times before might help us forget the discomfort we are forbidden to speak of. Sweet Maple will win thanks from all of us if she is able to do that."

Apparently the *Onondio*'s god did not mind his children criticizing their world, or perhaps Laval and Briand were contemptuous of his wrath. In any event, the traders who arrived two days later took no pains to lower their voices as they cursed the heat that had made their journeying a misery.

"One thing only is good about it," Briand said when he had ceased his flow of colorful invective. "The blackfly, he does not like it so hot, either."

Because it was late afternoon, they sat in front of the Turtle longhouse to avail themselves of its shadow. Morning Song hated to have them there when the entrance hide must be fastened back to allow any stray breeze to enter; but, like the weather, this too must be endured. She bent her head over the gourd she was hollowing out and her hand was only a little less than steady. It helped that Teller Of Legends had refused to join those women whose fascination with the *Onondios'* wares had lured them outside.

"The demand for pelts," Laval said saying, "is not so great as it was, you understand." He combed his beard with tobacco-stained fingers and sent a sidelong glance toward Trail Marker.

"So long as the Ottawa keep Mon-Tre-Al well supplied, it shall not be otherwise for us." Cloud Racer said this, and Morning Song's ears pricked. He was more inclined to listen than speak during the trading, but he meant these men to know how the Iroquois felt about French abuse of the latest treaty.

"This does not mean we will not take your furs," Briand said hastily. "But"—Morning Song pictured him heaving his beefy shoulders in an eloquent shrug—"it shall take more of each kind to bring you the goods you need. Me, I wish it were not so. Yet when you see what I bring today, you will not mind this. I have the most sharp hatchets you ever see, knives that never lose their edge, blankets of wool elegant enough for a chief to wrap around him. And for your women"—there was an audible bustle as the matrons pressed closer to the men's circle—"fabrics whose colors never fade, awls and needles and pewter spoons, ribbons and beads . . ."

He rumbled on over the rattle and thump of merchandise being spread for display, and nearly drowned out Laval's reminder that, although furs were not so highly valued these days, pipestone and copper and obsidian continued to be. If the villagers had obtained any of these from the tribes to the west . . .

Morning Song deposited the gourd's seeds in a basket, began to snap the beans she had harvested earlier, and shut out as much as she could of a confusing babble that would go on until the bartering was completed. Ignoring it was easier to do when Teller Of Legends laid aside the winter robe she was sewing and came to help with the beans.

"Our vines produced a healthy crop," she commented, holding up a nubbly pod. "And the new corn is ripening well." *Despite the searing heat* was left unsaid; Morning Song understood that they should be grateful to have been spared a drought. She smiled agreement.

"Your son is so proud of the small bow Deer Caller made for him," Teller Of Legends said, chuckling. "I think he will be a fine warrior when he is grown."

"Just as his father is," Morning Song said.

They talked lately mostly of the children, for her grandmother never tired of imagining them as the men and women they would someday be. It came to her suddenly that Teller Of Legends did not expect to share the years beyond their childhood. The idea was sobering, and Morning Song was loath to entertain it.

"Your daughter refuses to be outdone by her cousin, whatever skill is being taught to them," Teller Of Legends was saying enthusiastically. "And she is a year younger than Hidden Moon."

"Red Bird was wise to choose Pumpkin Blossom, rather than her own mother, to pattern herself after," Morning Song said wryly.

Her grandmother's dark eyes twinkled. "She learns from you as well, as you will one day discover," she said cryptically, then began to paint a magnificent future for Otter's twins. By the time she had transformed those mischief-loving boys into Faithkeepers whose omen interpretation would be unfailingly accurate, relative quiet had descended upon the compound.

A glance showed Morning Song that the Council and all of the onlookers had dispersed. The trading was over, and only Se-A-Wi had remained behind while Laval and Briand made ready to leave. The Sachem's voice was seldom heard during the bartering, but even the Frenchmen were aware of the rapid signing Se-A-Wi and Trail Marker engaged in before any firm decisions were made.

Briand grunted as he hefted a sack of metal pots. "Me, I had thought to rid myself of more of these, until I saw the old one spread his hands," he muttered. He looked around the nearly empty compound. "I thought, too, that we would find Jesuits here."

"The chief clerks of the fur trade, they were sent away from this place," Laval said sourly.

Morning Song laid a hand on Teller Of Legends's arm, signed for silence.

Briand laughed. "It serves us well—*n'est ce pas?*—to have at least one village where we need not worry about competition from the good fathers!"

Laval's response to this sally was heated. "You think it amusing that these so-called holy men act as agents for the merchants in Montreal and Quebec while they baptize as many redskins as they can bring to conversion? It says to me that it is the same here as it is in the old country: priests flaunting velvet and jewels while they brand as sinners those who must steal to feed their starving children. Me, I spit on those who say how blessed are the poor yet keep busy fattening their own purses! And I am happy that the Chief Matron of this village would not permit the Jesuits who came here to stay."

"It was a woman who decided this?" Briand's rasp was incredulous. "These savages, they are even too ignorant to know that *le bon Dieu* made men to command, and women to obey." He hooted suddenly. "To obey, and to . . ."

The coarse phrase that followed *obey* was not one that Morning Song could decipher, but instinct told her Briand's meaning and fury sent her springing to her feet. Only Teller Of Legends' murmured caution kept her from catapulting out of the longhouse; the anger that glutted her soul had left no room for trepidation.

"Perhaps," Teller Of Legends suggested mildly, "you will tell me what was said that has upset you so much?"

Morning Song swung away from the sight of the odious traders ambling across the compound and told her grandmother what she had overhead. "I am not certain," she finished, "what Lah-Val means when he speaks of baptizing and conversion. But I *have* learned that I was right when I said the *Onondio* Faithkeepers told the French in Mon-Tre-Al when it would be safe for the Painted People to bring furs there."

"A rumor I have not wanted to believe says that the sallow-skin Faithkeepers have turned some of our people in other villages from the traditions of their ancestors. They have persuaded them to honor instead the white man's god and this son of his that they call Je-Sus. I think this is what Lah-Val referred to." Distress deepened the lines that bracketed Teller Of Legends's mouth. "This Je-Sus, because he was sired by a spirit and born of a virgin, is the one they talk of most. Yet how is his mother different from Earth Woman, who received the seed of the West Wind and brought forth the Maker Of Life and his evil twin?" She came heavily to her feet and began to pace. "The strength of any spirit increases according to how many offer him praise. If there truly are Longhouse People who forsake the spirits we have recognized since the beginning of time, then I am appalled. How have they come to this? How?"

"Perhaps what Lah-Val said referred to something else altogether," Morning Song ventured, for she grieved to see her grandmother so disquieted. "And once I have told Cloud Racer what I have learned this day, I think the *Onondio* who claim to be merely Keepers Of The Faith will soon be gone from Iroquois country."

Teller Of Legends nodded. "And I shall tell my brother," she said grimly. "He must take this information to the Great Council."

The Confederation's councilors had been reluctant to recognize the *Onondio* as a threat to the heart and heritage of the Five Nations. But they would surely be incensed when they knew that at least some of these sallow-skins represented the fur dealers in Mon-Tre-Al. They would not deal kindly with men who had been no better

than spies in Iroquois Territory, men who had conspired with the
French leaders to divert to the Ottawa trading rights promised to
the Iroquois.

"You were in the longhouse," Pumpkin Blossom said, "and
heard what Teller Of Legends and Morning Song told Cloud
Racer." She shaped a perfectly round loaf without taking her accusing eyes from her husband's face. "You should have gone at
once to Se-A-Wi and offered to lead a band against the *Onondio*."
She slapped another handful of moistened meal onto the flat stone
she knelt beside, held up a warning hand when Stag Leaping opened
his mouth to respond. "Over and over you have named Cloud Racer
unfit to be war leader because he held back from proposing another
assault upon the French. You made sure that everyone in the village
knew he lacked the nerve to fight again. But did you think to point
out that our warriors deserve a man—you—who would not hesitate
to fling his hatchet into the post? You did not."

"The Sachem would have refused to listen," Stag Leaping said,
scowling. "Like the rest of the elders, he has always favored the
son of Rain Singing."

"You could not be certain of that," Pumpkin Blossom retorted.
"And had you owned sense enough to win some of our warriors to
your cause before you approached him, Se-A-Wi would have been
forced to consider what you told him. Now it is too late. Cloud
Racer went to him, and it is Cloud Racer who has gone with him
to address the Great Council." She set the bread in the low fire and
stood up. "When you failed to do what any ambitious man would
have done, my mother said that you are coming to be as sorry a
man as my father was." She looked down on the disgruntled man
squatting near her hearth. "You delight in shouting your ability to
lead, Stag Leaping," she said bitterly, "but I think it is not in you
to be other than a follower. Boastful words cannot make a leader
out of someone whose deeds are not worthy of notice."

"You shall see," he began furiously, jumping up to face her
squarely. But what he meant her to see remained undescribed when
he realized that Bountiful Harvest and Hearth Tender had come
quietly into the lodge. His scowl deepened, and he awarded the
pair only the briefest of nods as he strode past them and took his
anger into the sultriness of the summer afternoon.

Pumpkin Blossom welcomed warmly the aunt she had not seen
in five days, then waited for her mother to comment on what she
had overheard. But Bountiful Harvest had neither praise nor criticism for her daughter.

"Make a bundle of my herbs and tonics," she told her instead, "and of the fever remedies in particular." She turned to her sister. "I will take my mask and rattle also," she said. "If the Company of Faces there should ask, I will join in the rituals they are surely performing regularly."

"Two of their company," Hearth Tender said gravely, "can no longer dance. They, too, suffer from the illness." Her bony face was drawn with concern. "I must tell you," she added, "that the False Faces have not been able to drive away any of the demons that brought this sickness to so many longhouses."

"Are you speaking of the village where Sweet Maple's brother is Sachem?" Pumpkin Blossom asked, adding a pot of maize flour and one of fresh-picked elderberries to the pack she was organizing.

Hearth Tender nodded, took a moment to smile in greeting as her mother, Otter, and Morning Song came in. "It is," she said. "Sweet Maple remained there, and I shall be returning as soon as your mother is ready to leave." She looked fondly toward Bountiful Harvest. "I knew she would be willing to come with me, and use her medicines to help those whose flesh is flame-hot to the touch."

"If you find you have need of still more help," Teller Of Legends said quietly, "send a message to say so. Our matrons who have young children cannot be spared, but there is nothing to keep me here if I can be of use elsewhere."

Hearth Tender shook her head. "You are to this village," she teased gently, "what the ridge pole is to the longhouse. And we know what happens to a roof when its support is taken away."

"You exaggerate," Teller Of Legends protested. But the compliment had pleased her, even though the wording of it reminded her that time brings decay to the stoutest of timbers. The shrewd builder is alert for signs of this, and makes ready a replacement— a task not to be approached lightly, or attended to in haste.

"I know you cannot share my bed tonight," Morning Song said, "since your war party will be leaving at dawn. But I shall be holding close the thought of you, as I will every night until you can be with me again."

"We cannot remain at home more than four days, once we have dealt with the Jesuit settlement," he cautioned. "That should not take long. Only threescore men are there, and many are elders. But when we have captured them, and sent word to the French that they may ransom the priests only by making a binding treaty with the Longhouse People, we must prepare to set out again, on the trail to the Long River. War parties from every Iroquois nation will be there before us. The blockade, like the ousting of the *Onondio* Faithkeepers, was sanctioned by the Confederation.''

"You must be proud that both your proposals were well received by the Councilors," Morning Song said, filling his pouch with maple sugar–laced meal.

"I am pleased that, from now on, no nation or village will go to war without the approval of the Confederation," he said soberly. Then his mouth quirked. "The assembled Sachems were astonished to learn that it was my wife who interpreted what the traders said to each other."

She did not respond for a moment; it discomforted her still that the language of the *Onondio* should be so familiar to her. "I hope they did not approve the raid solely because of what I heard," she said anxiously.

He stripped off his tunic; it was time for him to go to the sweathouse. "Councilors from other villages had become suspicious of the sallow-skin Faithkeepers and sent scouts into the territories north of the Great Lake," he told her. "These warriors confirmed what Lah-Val said to Bree-And."

When he had gone out, Morning Song joined her cousin, who was attaching a decorative strip of copper to the band of Stag Leaping's headdress. "Will the day ever come," she asked disconsolately, "when our husbands can be with us more often than they are away?"

Pumpkin Blossom looked up. "If it did, they would only sit around telling stories of battles already fought. As the old men do. And they would likely become fleshy and soft-muscled besides. Who would want such a man as that?"

"Hunting would keep them both busy and fit. And there are always games and contests."

Pumpkin Blossom surveyed her handiwork with a critical eye, found no fault in it. "To have them home more than they are would be burden, not boon," she said decisively. "Hunting and testing their skills could not possibly fill all of their time, yet I cannot see them working alongside the women in the fields."

Neither could Morning Song. They would be fools to spend their lives in a monotonous cycle of sowing and reaping when tradition did not demand it of them. She looked longingly at the bow gathering dust above her bunk, the sweetly shaped bow Deer Caller had fashioned for a younger and more venturesome Morning Song.

Pumpkin Blossom laid the headdress on her bunk. "There is corn waiting to be harvested," she said pointedly, and picked up her neatly woven baskets.

Behind her back Morning Song grimaced, then went resignedly to fetch hers.

Teller Of Legends stirred, opened her eyes to darkness, and wondered irritably why the old cannot sleep as soundly as the young. She turned her head toward the entrance; the rectangle was pewter gray. Almost dawn, then. But what had called her too early from her rest?

A moan trembled the heat-laden air, and she raised up on one elbow. From which bunk had the sound come? She narrowed her eyes and peered around her, studied each shadow-wrapped form until she found one that tossed uneasily. When the sound came again, and louder, she slid from her bed, went swiftly to the one that was Pumpkin Blossom's, and crouched beside it.

Should she wake the girl? She ducked her head as Pumpkin Blossom flung out an arm and whimpered, and this decided her. She spoke her name quietly but insistently. When she had said it twice, her granddaughter drew breath sharply and sat up.

"You were sent a dream so distressing that you cried out," Teller Of Legends said. "I thought it best to awaken you, and send away the vision."

Predawn light was filtering into the lodge now, and she could see that Pumpkin Blossom's face was arranged in anguished lines. "It was dreadful, Grandmother," the young woman cried hoarsely, and gripped the hand Teller Of Legends had rested on her drawn-up knees.

A flurry of movement told the Matron that now others, too, had been roused. "Since Hearth Tender is not here," she said soothingly to Pumpkin Blossom, "I hope you will permit me to listen to your dream. It may relieve you to speak of it." She looked over her shoulder, smiled reassuringly into three worried faces. "Otter and Morning Song and Day Greeter will listen, too. We are none of us Keepers Of The Faith, but we do at least own ears. And all of them are available to you."

Day Greeter melted into the gloom, returned with a dipper of water for her distraught sister. When she had sipped and swallowed, Pumpkin Blossom sought for words to explain what had frightened her so.

"There were vast fields of harvest-ready corn," she began haltingly, "and the sun beamed on them. In the center of these fields, which seemed to have no beginning and no end, there stood a stalk taller and greener than the rest, and it was hung all around with the plumpest ears I have ever seen.'' The eyes she lifted to her grandmother's were luminous with wonder. ''It was in my own field that this remarkable corn grew,'' she said, ''and my heart was filled with joy to see it.''

The children, sleepy-eyed and curious, were beginning to hover around Pumpkin Blossom's bunk. With quiet efficiency, Otter Swimming assigned her twins to take the younger children to the river and oversee their bathing. Morning Song knew that her own two were as delighted as their cousins by this early morning surprise. Swift Arrow would swim farther than ever he dared while his mother was at hand to monitor him, and Red Bird would not even pretend to keep to the shallows. She smiled as a familiar barking punctuated the children's shouts. White Shadow, although he spent most of his time now sleeping in the shade, loved the water as much as the youngsters did. And even if Bold Leader and Brave Companion relaxed their vigilance, Shadow would not. She turned her attention back to Pumpkin Blossom.

''I began to walk to where that splendid stalk grew,'' she was saying. ''Suddenly the sun's face darkened until only a murky light guided my footsteps.'' She shivered. ''It was as though I walked through the trailing skirts of a black cloud,'' she told them. ''Yet so long as I could still make out that giant cornstalk, I felt safe in going on.''

She paused to drink a second time from the dipper. ''There came a burst of thunder,'' she said tightly, ''so loud that I covered my ears with my hands. I began to run, to run as fast as I was able; I knew that if I did not somehow reach the cornstalk . . . a terrible thing would happen to it. And to me.'' She linked her hands together, and her knuckles gleamed white. ''Before I reached it,'' she said, staring straight in front of her, ''a single shaft of lightning was hurled to earth. It was sickle-shaped, that lightning, and''— she buried her head in her hands, and her voice was muffled—''with one stroke it toppled the tall-standing cornstalk. Then the rain came beating down, and pounded and pounded at the plant until the leaves rotted and the ears it had borne so proudly withered into nothingness.''

Those who stood around her looked at one another in silence. What solace could they offer in the face of such a dream? Morning Song, who had sometimes questioned whether her cousin worried about Stag Leaping even half as much as she herself did about Cloud Racer, felt shame that she had doubted. And they had been gone five days, their warriors; they might this moment be grappling with men who would be armed with death-dealing thunder-sticks. . . .

Pumpkin Blossom raised her head. "It was my mother, that noble corn plant," she said dully. "She will die, and I will not be able to prevent it."

Chapter 24

❦— ⟹

It was all that the village matrons talked of as they brought in the rest of the corn. "I grieve for your cousin," Small Brown Sparrow, straightening with a grunt, told Morning Song. She was growing big with her second child, and Morning Song noticed that her mother looked anxiously toward her from time to time. "It is a terrible thing, to be sent a vision that warns of death."

"When I heard her describe it," Morning Song said, "I was glad that dreams do not visit me."

Small Brown Sparrow's eyes widened in astonishment, narrowed again quickly as the sun's brilliance made them tear. "They have never come to you, despite the Vision Quest you were brave enough to go on?"

Morning Song shook her head and wished she had thought before she'd made the admission. "It is of small account, I suppose," she said. "Will you have a son or a daughter this time?" she asked, choosing a subject certain to distract her friend.

"Rain Singing thinks it will be a boy-child," Small Brown Sparrow told her, "but I feel it may be another girl. Either will be welcome, since I waited so long to conceive again." She looked speculatively at Morning Song, who laughed.

"No," she said. "I am not breeding, Small Brown Sparrow." She plopped three more tasseled ears into her basket. "Cloud Racer is scarcely home often enough for that."

"It is true that we see little of our husbands," Small Brown Sparrow agreed. "Still, I suspect the two of you make good use of opportunity when it offers. Just as Hill Climber and I do. Whether we make a baby or not, you must admit that trying to is fun." She grinned to see Morning Song's raised eyebrows. "Do you recall," she went on mischievously, "the days when you insisted you never, ever, wanted to marry?"

"I have learned one or two things since then," Morning Song said with mock solemnity, then let her face put on the wide smile she'd been suppressing. "I have had a fine teacher," she finished, "as you did also, I think!"

The daughter of Rain Singing rolled her eyes. "The best," she said fervently. Suddenly she went up on tiptoe and craned her neck to peer over the denuded stalks they'd left behind them. "They are back!" she shrieked. And, thrusting her half-filled basket atop the one her friend held, she began to hurry out of the field.

Morning Song did not need to look to know what had excited her so. Nor would she let herself be encumbered with two baskets of corn at such a moment. She set them down hastily, heedless of the ears that tumbled out, and sped after Small Brown Sparrow.

Only Cloud Racer's rigid jaw and drawn-together brows slowed her flying feet and made her cover the last few paces almost sedately. "What is wrong?" she asked when she had assured herself that he bore no visible wounds.

"The raid did not go as planned," he said shortly. And this was all he would tell her until he had urged her toward the village, until the warriors he led were so busy greeting their own wives and mothers that his words would be lost to them. "Where is Pumpkin Blossom? I did not see her come out of the fields with the rest of you."

Morning Song was confused by both the question and the bowstring tautness in his voice. "She offered to watch the children this morning. She was planning to take them to visit Owl Crying."

"I should not speak of this," he said, "until after I have reported the matter to the Village Council. But I feel strongly that you ought to hear about it first."

Morning Song trusted her feet to recognize turnings they had made countless times and fixed her eyes on his grim face. "I shall not repeat anything you say to me, unless you give me leave."

He smiled briefly. "I know that. So I will tell you what we found at the *Onondio* settlement. In the largest of their timber structures, there were signs that a boat of some sort had been hastily built. Other than that, there was nothing—and no one—there."

"How can this be?" she exclaimed.

"It appears"—the hand he had rested on her shoulder tightened—"that the sallow-skins were warned of our coming."

She shook her head. "I cannot believe that one of the tribal Sachems would talk carelessly of a raid they had sanctioned."

"It was not a Sachem's loose tongue that betrayed us," he said bitterly, "but one of our own warriors!"

Instinctively she turned her head, numbered the men who had followed Cloud Racer home, and understood suddenly what all of this had been leading to. When she swung round to meet his brooding gaze, her own eyes were eloquent with shock. "Stag Leaping?"

He inclined his head, steered her through the palisade gateway. "That is why you need to know now," he said, "for the news must be taken to Teller Of Legends. Your grandmother can explain matters to Pumpkin Blossom before your cousin learns that Stag Leaping did not come back with the rest of us. I would not have her think he has been slain."

"It would be better for Pumpkin Blossom if he had been," Morning Song said sadly. "You are certain it was Stag Leaping? Why would he do such a thing, Cloud Racer?"

"Why, I do not know. But he was missing from camp when we awoke after our first night on the trail. We thought at first he'd gone to relieve himself, but when he did not return we went to find him. Fox Jumping discovered the direction he'd taken, even though he had tried to leave his path unmarked. Only when we'd tracked him for some time did we realize he must have gone ahead of us to the Jesuit settlement. We stretched our legs then, of course, but he'd had the night and the early part of the day to outdistance us."

Her step faltered as they neared her longhouse. "I shall not enjoy watching my grandmother's face when she hears this," she said, "and I suppose I am a coward to be grateful that the Pigeonhawk lodge is at the far end of the compound, and that the children are probably chattering so loudly that neither Pumpkin Blossom nor Owl Crying has heard the war band return. For Owl Crying will also have to be told what has happened, Cloud Racer."

"Leave it to Teller Of Legends to say what must be said," he advised her, "to the both of them. It can only bring further hurt to Stag Leaping's wife and mother if the wife of the war leader tells them he is a traitor. They will suffer enough as it is." He pulled her to him, rested his cheek momentarily upon the fragrant darkness of her hair. "Would you like me to speak with Teller Of Legends?" he asked gently.

"No," she replied, managing a faint smile. "I will not shirk from doing what I must, Cloud Racer. I have never been so great a coward as *that*!"

But it was on stone-heavy feet that she made her way into the Turtle longhouse.

The Pumpkin Blossom who followed their grandmother home
from the Pigeonhawk lodge was a young woman Morning Song
scarcely recognized. No longer were her tilted eyes haunted by the
remnants of her awful dream; they were granite-centered and over-
bright, and her mouth was a resolute slash.

Day Greeter made a move to go to her, checked it abruptly when
Pumpkin Blossom halted in the entrance and sent a challenge ahead
of her. "I want no sympathy," she said harshly, "from any of you.
It would remind me that I am not just daughter to a coward, but
wife to a traitor as well." She went swiftly to the bunk she and Stag
Leaping had shared and stripped the robe from its mattress. "The
first of those disgraces," she went on, spreading it upon the floor,
"I can do nothing about." She took from her shelf a stack of
garments, from the wall above it worn moccasins and new-strung
snowshoes, from beneath the bunk a basket in which pipe and
pouched tobacco shared space with assorted headbands and sashes
and belts. Her movements were unhurried as she laid all of this in
the center of the robe, drew up the four corners, and knotted them
securely. "The second," she said, pulling herself erect, "it is within
my power to change."

Teller Of Legends shook her head at Otter, who had opened her
mouth to speak. It would do no good to interfere, and Pumpkin
Blossom would welcome advice no more than she would commis-
eration. Any more than her mother would have done on a similar
occasion. The circumstances of this one, however, were different;
Teller Of Legends approved the decision this woman had made.

Pumpkin Blossom beckoned to her brother. "I ask you, Fish
Jumping," she said, with a formality that commanded his compli-
ance, "to deliver to Owl Crying her son's possessions."

Fish Jumping, in some ways more boy than man still, was clearly
uncomfortable to be sent on such an errand. But Pumpkin Blossom
resembled Bountiful Harvest at her most imperious, and he knew
it was not for him to argue, but only to obey.

When he'd slung the pack over his shoulder and gone out, Pumpkin Blossom busied herself lighting her hearth. "I know now," she
said, "what my dream foretold: From this moment my husband
ceases to exist for me just as though he were dead." She brushed
her hands together briskly to dislodge the ash that clung to them
and, fleetingly, Morning Song permitted herself to suspect that
Pumpkin Blossom was happy to be husbandless so long as it had
not been the loss of her mother that her terrible dream foretold.

Yet it was not right, she thought, that everyone should simply
stare mutely at a woman who must be suffering in a way none of

them would ever fully understand. She abandoned her place in the semicircle they'd unconsciously formed and went to her cousin. "I am sorry," she said quietly, "that this misfortune has visited you. But I am filled with admiration for your calmness in the face of it."

Something flickered in Pumpkin Blossom's eyes, and Morning Song thought she swayed a little. In the next instant, however, she looked disdainfully at the hands Morning Song had impulsively held out. "I have said that I will not accept pity," she told her. "Stag Leaping's disgrace is none of mine. As for the man himself, I will not miss him. I have my children, and my pride; they are all that I have need of."

Morning Song backed away slowly and tried to rid herself of the feeling that, despite her brave words, there was one thing Pumpkin Blossom needed in addition to her pride and her children: If Bountiful Harvest did not soon come home and lend her daughter a quantity of her own enormous strength, the mask of self-reliance Pumpkin Blossom wore was apt to disintegrate. And what lay behind that mask was something Morning Song dreaded to see.

It was Cloud Racer who told Teller Of Legends about Gray Squirrel's sister. "Loon Laughing shivers, and her belly sends back what little she has been able to eat and drink," he said. "Proud Woman asked my mother to summon the Pygmy society to the Snipe longhouse. The False Faces have danced, but Loon Laughing is no better for their coming."

Teller Of Legends began lifting pots from her shelf. "I am not as knowledgeable as Bountiful Harvest about such things," she said, "but I know a remedy or two that may bring comfort to her." Her measured tones disguised her uneasiness. "Have you heard if anyone else is ill?"

Cloud Racer's eyes locked with hers; he knew what had prompted the question. "Only Loon Laughing," he said, then hesitated. "My father received a message from the trader Lah-Val, however," he added. "The runner told us we must not expect to see the traders again before the next green season. It seems that the demons who brought sickness to the next village have already visited others, and the *Onondio* will not travel in Iroquois territory until they have gone away altogether."

"If the sallow-skins do not recognize the spirits of the Longhouse People," Teller Of Legends said dryly, "it seems strange that they fear our demons!" She picked up her basket, smiled reassuringly at Cloud Racer, and at Morning Song who had come to stand by him. "Well, we shall survive without them until spring has come again. Even if Lake On Fire must remove the beads from an old dress in order to trim a new one to her satisfaction. Meanwhile, I shall call on Gray Squirrel. Perhaps Loon Laughing has only eaten something that angered her belly. I have a potion that will soothe it, if so.''

Morning Song looked at her husband as her grandmother left the lodge. "She suspects, as I think you do, that Loon Laughing's illness is the same as the one preying on the village where Sweet Maple's brother is Sachem.''

He nodded. "It is not unheard of,'' he said, his brow puckering, "for sickness to fly like a ravenous hawk from village to village. But it has never happened among the Iroquois.''

"I would not be surprised,'' she said, "if the *Onondio* were the cause of it.''

"How can sallow-skins influence spirits who are invisible even to us?'' Cloud Racer asked reasonably. He glanced around to be sure that Pumpkin Blossom, sitting with Hidden Moon and Red Bird, could not overhear. "I did not tell your grandmother the rest of Lah-Val's message,'' he said then. "He claims to have seen one of our warriors in Mon-Tre-Al. It can only be Stag Leaping, Morning Song. When we have reached the Long River, I will take a few men and go after him.''

Everything else fled her mind. "You cannot hope to capture him there,'' she protested. "Stag Leaping served the French by betraying your plans to the *Onondio* Faithkeepers, and they will protect him.''

He shrugged. "Perhaps not. No one respects a traitor, Morning Song. Not even those who benefit from his treachery.''

"That is true in the Indian nations, of course. But I doubt that the white men think as we do.''

"Whether they do or not, I would dishonor myself if I did not try to find Stag Leaping and make him pay for what he did.''

"And you will be leaving at once.'' It was not a question; she knew as well as he did that he must.

On the day following the war band's departure, Bountiful Harvest was brought home. She lay on a litter borne by the two sons of Sweet Maple's brother, and her fever-dulled eyes, sunken cheeks, and blister-studded flesh made her virtually unrecognizable. A stunned Pumpkin Blossom went down on her knees beside her and cried out to feel the heat that rose from that emaciated body, to feel the awful dryness of the hand she reached to clasp.

"Her sister asked us to bring her home," the taller of the men was saying to Teller Of Legends.

"My oldest daughter is not sick?"

The two men looked uncertainly at each other. "She says she is not," the one acting as spokesman said slowly. "These days, anyone able to stand claims to be well."

And he would not say more, beyond the fact that Sweet Maple refused to leave her dying brother even though he had tried to send her away.

Otter Swimming was sponging Bountiful Harvest's face with cool water while Pumpkin Blossom removed her mother's sweat-soaked garments. "The sores are little different from wounds," Otter told her niece. "Some of our slippery elm salve may be able to heal those which are festering."

Morning Song and Day Greeter had gone to the river for more water, and Teller Of Legends composed herself before crossing to her daughter's bunk. "You see how much attention is lavished on you," she said to her, "when you have been away from us too long. But do not expect it to continue, once we have made you well again."

Bountiful Harvest's cracked lips twitched, but what creased her thin cheeks was a shocking travesty of her lovely smile.

"You have given her water to drink?" Teller Of Legends murmured.

Otter looked up. "She could swallow only a drop or two."

Pumpkin Blossom, unfastening Bountiful Harvest's tunic, kept her head bent, but her hands shook as she exposed a body whose ribs could be counted, whose pelvic bones nearly pierced the skin covering them. And even here pustules were abundant.

Teller Of Legends turned as Morning Song and Day Greeter, bent beneath the weight of sloshing kettles, approached the bed. "It will not serve Bountiful Harvest," she said, "to have too many crowding around her. You will be of more help if you tend the children, and arrange with Rain Singing for them to have their meal in her longhouse."

Day Greeter shook her head. "Bountiful Harvest is my mother," she said with unaccustomed stubbornness. "My place is with her."

Morning Song laid a hand on Teller Of Legends' arm as Day Greeter went to kneel beside her sister. "She is right," she told her grandmother. "And I can care for the children myself." She looked at the frail figure stretched beneath three pairs of ministering hands, swallowed against the bile that rose in her throat. "Will she die?'' she whispered; and was appalled to have given voice to the thought.

"I do not know," Teller Of Legends said heavily. "We shall do all we can, the medicine societies will come"—she raised an eyebrow, and Morning Song bobbed her head; she would arrange for that, also—"but . . . I do not know."

"So the sickness has come to us." Bountiful Harvest moaned as the fever raged anew within her, and Morning Song's hands clenched. "Is there no way to stop it, no way we can hide from loathsome spirits that go where they will, and when they will, to sow the seeds of destruction?"

Suddenly it became unbearable, the sight of her mother-aunt lying helpless while disease, like some foul and greedy worm, crawled beneath her flesh and devoured her strength and beauty. "I must go to the children," she said abruptly, spinning on her heel.

Outside, she stood in the glare of the sun and berated herself, hated herself for being relieved that Teller Of Legends had sent her out of the lodge. The others did not seek excuse to turn away from that wasted body; they went without hesitation to soothe and comfort. Yet Morning Song—who had spent so much of her life at odds with the sick woman—had dreaded to think she might be expected to do likewise. Pumpkin Blossom, fastidious to a fault under ordinary circumstances, did not recoil from blisters that oozed yellow whenever she touched them; Day Greeter, timid Day Greeter, insisted upon remaining in a place that reeked already of death and decay. And it was their own mother who lay on that bunk! Only Morning Song had been overwhelmed with revulsion, a revulsion it had cost her dear to conceal for the brief time she'd been in the longhouse.

She looked around for the children and caught sight of Proud Woman walking toward the gateway. She would be fetching more water; Loon Laughing's blood was afire, just like Bountiful Harvest's. But was Proud Woman repelled when she looked upon the ravaged body of the woman she was helping to nurse? No, Morning Song thought wretchedly, she was not. Only a gutless woman would harbor such feelings.

Yet . . . wasn't it more than the fever-ridden hag her aunt had become that made her niece shrink from her? Wasn't she, in truth, pretending that what she refused to look upon did not exist? Despite their differences, their many differences, Morning Song had always respected, had even envied, Bountiful Harvest's extraordinary strength. If this vigorous woman could be felled by the demons, then no one—no one at all—was safe from them! Morning Song's shame lay in being afraid to confront that truth.

Swift Arrow had spotted his mother, was calling to his sister and cousins that their meal must be ready. She went to meet them, looked down into their bright faces, their sparkling eyes. And froze in their midst as she understood that even their small and sturdy bodies might be assaulted by poison-belching demons.

No! she shouted silently. *I will not have it!* All of her confusion and self-abasement was swept away by the tide of resolution that washed over her. How she would protect them, what armor she would devise to ward off what could not be seen or heard or touched, she did not know. But Morning Song meant to keep them safe, keep all of these children safe. Somehow.

The darkness, Morning Song thought, had a smothering quality about it; she felt the exhaustion of all those taking part in this healing ritual. She could not understand how Rain Singing, summoning the Great Horned Serpent and the Great Naked Bear, could do so without faltering. For it was her daughter and granddaughter—and the grandchild still unborn—that the society was singing for.

Morning Song choked on an intricate phrase and blinked tears from her eyes as she made herself resume the chant at the next beat of the water drum. Small Brown Sparrow. Kindhearted, merry-natured Small Brown Sparrow. And Bending Willow, whose smile was so like her mother's, whose unceasing chatter never failed to remind Morning Song of the girl Small Brown Sparrow had been. Small Brown Sparrow. Her friend, her good friend. At times, her only friend. Now she burned with fever—and the ominous lesions had begun to form on her body.

As they were beginning to on Otter's. Morning Song tightened her clasped hands until blood pounded in the tips of her fingers. She had insisted upon tending Otter, had refused to surrender—this time—to the urge to close her eyes to what she did not want to recognize. There had been no one to object; Pumpkin Blossom and Day Greeter, near collapse from watching over their mother, had been relieved by Teller Of Legends. And the distraught Deer Caller could do no more than sit by his wife and whisper heartening words, until Otter emerged long enough from delirium to order him to the Plover lodge.

"I can smell my own sickness," she had told Morning Song, her swollen tongue distorting her voice. "How much ranker it must seem to him, whose blindness sharpens all his other senses."

Morning Song, using a forefinger to introduce water, drop by
drop, into Otter's reluctant mouth, had shushed her. "Save your
strength to get well," she'd said, making herself smile. But Otter's
words had lingered in Morning Song's mind, had put down roots
and sprouted an idea. A foolish one, perhaps, but desperation will
seize upon even a straw to build with. Now, in the stench-laden,
occlusive dark of the Deer longhouse, she knew she would try
anything in order to honor the pledge she'd made to save the children.

"I do not know—how could anyone?—whether we can deceive
the demons who attack with sickness rather than spears," she said
to Teller Of Legends. "But surely you have noticed how the children skirt Bountiful Harvest's hearth, and Otter's? How they beg to
spend their time out-of-doors even when the heat of midday would
ordinarily drive them inside? Red Bird wrinkles her nose whenever
she walks the length of the lodge, and of late Swift Arrow and the
twins slip out by the rear to avoid passing the bunks where the sick
women are."

Teller Of Legends looked automatically—as was her habit these
days—to see if her granddaughter's eyes might be glazed with the
onset of fever. Despite the purplish shadows that lack of sleep ringed
them with, Morning Song's were clear. "I admit that this sickness
is odorous," she said then, "as festering wounds often are. Yet I
have never known anyone to develop an injury merely because he
smelled the pus seeping from a warrior's wound."

"But a wound is not the same as an illness," Morning Song
argued. "Wounds are inflicted by human hands, Grandmother. The
spirits who send sickness . . . surely it is at least possible that their
noses lead them to a longhouse where someone has already been
stricken? They came here when Bountiful Harvest had been brought
home and attacked Otter. Gray Squirrel, who has never known
illness of any sort, ails with the same disease that claimed the life
of her sister. And"—she hesitated, not entirely sure if she ought
name someone sick who had not yet taken to his bed—"I visited
the Deer lodge again this morning. Fierce Eagle was sitting outside
and, Grandmother, he did not recognize me although I was within
an arm's length of him. His eyes . . ." She shuddered.

So Morning Song was also sensitive to this sign that warned of
the blood's unnatural heating. It might even be that her perception
was keener than her grandmother's, and had sired the proposal she
was making. "There is enough sense in what you say," the old
woman said slowly, "to persuade me." She paused, considered.

"I will speak to Owl Crying," she decided. "She and Puma Walking Soft were in good health when last I saw them. If they move in with Lake On Fire—for there has been no illness in her lodge, either, as yet—then the Pigeonhawk longhouse can be set aside for the children."

"She will never agree," Morning Song said.

"There is no one," Teller Of Legends said gently, "who is all good or all bad. You have never seen that Owl Crying is a generous woman because you have never expected her to be one. She will not refuse, Morning Song. She may even offer to remain there to care for the little ones."

"I was thinking," Morning Song said, her eyes seeking out the slump-shouldered figure of her cousin, "that Pumpkin Blossom might do that. With Day Greeter's help."

But Morning Song will stay here to look after Otter, thought Teller Of Legends. At least she had not suggested that the clan's Matron should seek the supposed protection of a separate longhouse. "They will not want to leave their mother," she cautioned.

It was no time to flinch from what she saw as truth, Morning Song told herself. "If Pumpkin Blossom sees her mother die," she said starkly, "the spirit that sustains her own life may be shattered beyond repair. And they will go if Bountiful Harvest says they must. Will you ask her to, Grandmother?" For the indomitable Bountiful Harvest, even now, was capable of rational speech. She could not talk long, or loudly, but what words she managed continued to be coherent.

Teller Of Legends looked hard at Morning Song. "That is for you to do," she said. And she wondered if Morning Song would guess what lay behind her edict.

But the young woman merely bowed her head. "You wish to go at once to Owl Crying, of course," she said, accepting the mission without demur. "May we both be successful," she added, and made for Bountiful Harvest's bed.

Her mother-aunt's eyes were closed, and the transparency of her dark-lashed lids, indeed of all her flesh, gave Morning Song pause. Then her imagination presented a glimpse of Swift Arrow and Red Bird grown equally wan and wizened, and she leaned over the sick woman. "Bountiful Harvest," she said softly.

It was several moments before her eyes opened, and others limped by before they focused on Morning Song. Yet lackluster as they were, their alertness had not been entirely quenched. "I need your help," Morning Song said simply. "When you hear why, I believe you will give it."

Bountiful Harvest studied the face bent over hers. "Ask," she croaked.

I must not tire her, Morning Song told herself, and wasted no words describing her plan to isolate the village's children and her hope that Pumpkin Blossom and Day Greeter would go with them. "They will want to remain with you instead," she finished. "But it seems to me"—she caught her breath; dare she say it? And knew that she did; were their positions reversed, Bountiful Harvest would not skimp to be honest with Morning Song—"that you will have your last days made easier," she went on in a rush, "if you know your daughters can be spared this sickness. I honestly think they can, Bountiful Harvest, if they are sent away from here."

Bountiful Harvest's eyes closed again, and Morning Song thought miserably that she had, after all, been wrong to be so blunt.

"You . . . plan to stay?" The dark eyes had reopened, were probing her niece's.

"Yes," Morning Song said quietly; but her chin jutted out as though to defy anyone who might suggest otherwise.

Bountiful Harvest's colorless lips twitched. "My mother . . . was right." Her thin hand clutched the edge of the bunk, clung to it as though it represented life itself. "We have . . . a kinship of the . . . spirit, you . . . and I. Summon . . . my daughters . . . Morning Song."

Tears stung behind Morning Song's eyes. She fumbled for her mother-aunt's skeletal fingers and squeezed them with a tenderness she had never thought to feel for this woman, and that pitiful arrangement of brittle bones contrived to return the impulsive caress.

"It is because we are both inclined to be flint-edged," the younger woman whispered. "This is why we have so often grated against each other."

It was all she could say, without letting the tears spill out. Which she would never do while this courageous woman was watching.

Morning Song retreated a few paces to permit Bountiful Harvest a measure of privacy while she spoke with Pumpkin Blossom and Day Greeter. When her daughters realized what Bountiful Harvest was asking of them, the calm expressions they'd put on for her sake became riddled with consternation.

"I cannot leave you," Pumpkin Blossom said, aghast at the mere thought of it. "Nor will I separate Hidden Moon and Painted Sky from their grandmother merely because Morning Song says that I should." Weary and worn though she was, her eyes flashed angrily as she looked over her shoulder at her cousin. "No one but you would invent such nonsense,'' she said. ''Neither my children nor I will be parted from my mother!''

Day Greeter's somber gaze touched upon her sister, her mother, moved to meet Morning Song's. But she said nothing.

''Pumpkin Blossom.''

Bountiful Harvest's rasping whisper somehow achieved a familiar note of command, and Morning Song watched as Pumpkin Blossom was pressed back firmly into the mold of obedience she had long ago been fitted to. Despite her reluctance, she would go to the Pigeonhawk lodge with the children. And she would devote herself to caring for them, because this was what her mother expected of her.

Teller of Legends entered so quietly that the others were oblivious of her presence until she spoke to Morning Song. ''I see that your mother-aunt agreed to what you asked,'' she said.

''She has been . . . magnificent,'' Morning Song replied. ''Pumpkin Blossom has given her promise to leave here''—she looked up anxiously and Teller Of Legends signaled the success of her own mission—''and there is only Day Greeter left to be persuaded.''

But that was not to be. When Bountiful Harvest signed for her younger daughter to come nearer, Day Greeter shook her head and spread her broad hands in a gesture of appeal. ''Please,'' she begged. ''Do not ask this of me, Mother. I cannot say yes. Not even to please you.''

There was anguish in her voice and in her round face, and her grandmother—quicker than the rest to sense the truth of the matter—took a long stride forward. Even so, she was barely in time to catch Day Greeter before she crumpled to the floor.

Chapter 25

❖ ⟹

Morning Song asked herself how many times features could be reshaped by sorrow and resignation before the faces they belonged to became impossible to tell apart. Even the children, standing together in a bewildered group, owned a chilling likeness to one another these days. Behind them, Meadow Brook—who had moved into the Pigeonhawk longhouse to help care for them—was supporting a shivering Pumpkin Blossom. Where did Meadow Brook find the strength, when only five days ago it had been her mother and her uncle the villagers had sung the death chant for? And there had been Gray Squirrel to sing for before that. And Loon Laughing . . .

Where would it end? When every longhouse stood empty and only spirits walked in this village, their disembodied voices keening with the wind Ga-Oh would send when the white season came?

"Now we become reconciled as you start away," Puma Walking Soft intoned.

Morning Song, joining in a chant they no longer needed prompting in, stiffened. *She* was not reconciled to death, and never would be!

"You were once a woman in the flower of life, and now the bloom is withered away," she sang, and would not let herself be overcome by the fact that today those words honored Bountiful Harvest. She must not. There were those who had need of her still. Lake On Fire and Owl Crying had gone to the Turtle lodge so that Teller Of Legends and Morning Song could be here; but she and her grandmother would be returning to Otter Swimming and Day Greeter, to resume the bathing of flesh so hot that water was powerless to cool it, the smoothing of unguent on pus-engorged blisters.

"Looking after your family was a sacred duty, and you were faithful," Puma Walking Soft said, and Morning Song's voice blended with the others to repeat an accolade surely owing to Bountiful Harvest. There were fewer mourners than on the last occasion, of course—and none from the Deer lodge. Fierce Eagle and Trail Marker were seriously ill, and Small Brown Sparrow and her daughter . . . they were dying.

Morning Song blinked rapidly, concentrated on the prayer. No one was here from the Snipe longhouse, either, she realized when she had recovered a little. Its Matron and her sister had been the first to die, and Proud Woman was caring for Covers His Eyes. He frequently shouted, in his delirium, for the woman whose death chant stirred the sultry air.

Teller Of Legends's voice swelled, and Morning Song felt all at once humbled. The Matron of the Turtle clan was mourning her own daughter; a second daughter and a granddaughter lay ill in her lodge; no word had come from either Hearth Tender or Sweet Maple since the day Bountiful Harvest returned home; yet Teller Of Legends managed to move calmly through the morass of despair that strove to drag her down. Morning Song, feeling its tug, had lost her own footing more than once. And on days like this, she questioned whether she even wanted to resist its oddly seductive allure.

Yet if her grandmother owned the courage to reject the sanctuary desolation tempted her with, then Morning Song would shame both Teller Of Legends and herself if she did not do likewise.

"The children?" It was the first thing Otter asked, always, whenever she roused from her comalike sleep.

"They are well, all of them," Morning Song reassured her, trying to keep pity from her eyes as she looked into Otter's ravaged face. Her own mouth trembled as her mother-aunt declined the dribble of water Morning Song tried to coax between parched and swollen lips.

"No use." It was a halting whisper, yet it forced recognition of what both of them knew. "You will be mother," she said, after a silence pregnant with Morning Song's dismay, "to my sons?"

Morning Song swallowed hard, nodded. If Otter did not wish it, there must be no more pretense between them. "I will." She leaned closer. "Shall I fetch Deer Caller?" she asked quietly.

Otter moved her head slowly from side to side, attempted to speak again and could not. *She does not want him to see her like this.* As clearly as though Otter had succeeded in voicing it, the reason for her refusal leaped into Morning Song's mind. Had Otter forgotten that her husband was blind? Should Morning Song remind her? But it was not Otter Swimming who was confused; it was Morning Song, who was overlooking Deer Caller's habit of seeing with his fingertips what he could no longer see with his eyes. Otter knew he would be unable to recognize any part of her that he touched, and she loved him too much to allow that.

Morning Song smoothed lank hair from her aunt's sunken cheeks. "I will miss you through all the days of my life," she said brokenly—and was suddenly grateful that she and Otter were facing the truth together. She could never have uttered those words otherwise, and would have regretted forever that she hadn't. She bent and laid her cheek against Otter's burning forehead. As she had done on a different occasion, when winter's bone-chilling cold, not this unquenchable inner fire, had threatened Otter. If only the outcome this time might be as it had been then. . . .

But it could not. She stood up, summoned from somewhere a crooked smile, then went to tell her grandmother that the time had come to say farewell to Otter Swimming.

From that day, Teller Of Legends and Morning Song swore vengeance on the demons who dealt in death. Two they had lost to him; the third, they were determined to save. Their faces were grim as they tended Day Greeter in turns, persuaded her to drink more than she thought she could of water and broth, wrapped her in dripping robes when her fever raged, and snuggled her in dry ones when, alternately, she shivered. Her bed became their whole world, and neither would have taken the time to eat if Owl Crying—proving Teller Of Legends' assessment of her—had not brought food each day and goaded them until they ate enough to satisfy her.

Owl Crying served up news along with her tasteless soups and stews. She delivered it in a carefully dispassionate manner, since the news she brought was so seldom good. Still, some of the observations with which she sprinkled her dolorous recitals were as peppery as her cooking was bland.

"Covers His Eyes has died," she announced during one visit, "so I suppose we shall be expected to ignore what a poor excuse for a man he was in order to mourn him properly. The Erie maiden"—Proud Woman would never be anything but that to her, adoption notwithstanding—"was with him to the end, but went next day to help Rain Singing." She sniffed. "I suppose she thinks Lake On Fire and I are too old to be of much use; although how Rain Singing could have managed this long without us, I cannot imagine. I will be surprised if her granddaughter survives the night to come, and her daughter . . ." She shook her head, and Morning Song pushed away the bean soup.

"Fierce Eagle fights all his old battles over again when the fever fires his blood," she went on, picking up the half-empty bowl and placing it firmly before Morning Song once more. "And sores are appearing on Trail Marker now."

She scowled at Morning Song until the younger woman took up her spoon and made herself eat more. "Meadow Brook tells me the children are thriving, except for those who have lost a mother or father. And they are afflicted with sorrow only, and not illness, she says. Pumpkin Blossom is well, also, although Meadow Brook's youngest—who was listening to us; she has long ears, that one—tells me she weeps in the night. I cannot see how this helps her, and it must frighten the children. Nonetheless"—she shrugged—"it seems that Pumpkin Blossom is one of those who cannot contain her grief."

"She has had much to bear, of late," Teller Of Legends said, with more mildness than Morning Song could have achieved had she made the response.

When the Matron of the Pigeonhawk longhouse had gone, Morning Star told her grandmother, "I admit that Owl Crying is generous, in her way, but she is an irritating woman all the same!"

"It was a terrible blow to her, to have her son betray his clan and his tribe," Teller Of Legends reminded her. "Stag Leaping was the only one of her seven children who lived beyond infancy, and we all know how she doted on him."

"*He* never knew that she did."

"Which, if you think about it, makes the situation all the worse for Owl Crying," her grandmother said. "We who mourn our dead are perhaps more fortunate than she is, Morning Song. Sorrow is often easier to deal with than shame."

Had anyone other than Teller Of Legends claimed that, Morning Song—in the circumstances—would have argued that nothing could be more soul-battering than sorrow. But the Chief Matron knew more of sorrow than her granddaughter did. Her husband, the babes she had borne who had never drawn breath, three of her four daughters—all had gone ahead of her into the land beyond the sunset.

She looked to where Day Greeter lay sleeping, winced to see her toss fitfully, to see a face so like their grandmother's made haggard by sickness. "We must save Day Greeter," she said harshly. "We must."

"We may be helped by the fact that the child is so sturdy," Teller Of Legends said. And prayed that this was true.

Not child, but woman, Morning Song wanted to say. Yet to Teller Of Legends, those born of her daughters would forever be children, she supposed. "Day Greeter is built to resemble the oak," she said aloud. "Which is how you occasionally describe yourself, Grandmother."

The old woman smiled a little. "An oak is hard to fell," she observed. "And Day Greeter has youth in her favor besides."

But the same might be said of Small Brown Sparrow. And of her daughter, whose seventh summer this was. Morning Song jumped up. "I am going to boil some dried venison," she said. "Cloud Racer brought home a noble stag when the men last went deer hunting, and a broth made from it will strengthen Day Greeter."

That she must be able to swallow it, and to keep it down, in order to receive its strengthening was a problem she would not dwell on until the moment presented itself.

Proud Woman, not Owl Crying, came to the Turtle lodge next day. Teller Of Legends welcomed her pleasantly, and Morning Song—too numbed by sorrow, sleeplessness, and worry to remember how dismayed she'd been when Cloud Racer had praised his beautiful captive—echoed her grandmother's cordial greeting.

"Owl Crying and Lake On Fire are with Rain Singing today," Proud Woman explained as she ladled out a fine-smelling succotash. "She has need of old friends now," she went on, then looked directly at Morning Song. "Small Brown Sparrow and her little one," she said to her, "died in the night."

Morning Song dropped the spoon she had raised to her mouth and bowed her head. That she had known this must happen did not make acceptance easier.

"You will tell Rain Singing that we grieve with her," Teller Of Legends said, in tones so precisely measured that Morning Song realized how deeply her own agony was understood and shared. Poor Hill Climber's homecoming would be a painful one, she thought wretchedly. And Cloud Racer and Fox Running, when they came back from the north, must cope with the loss of the sister they had loved so dearly. . . .

"Fierce Eagle?" she whispered. "And Trail Marker?"

"There has been no change," Proud Woman replied, her movements deft as she poured parched-corn coffee for Teller Of Legends, "in either." She set down the lidded kettle. "You will want to be there," she said, "when the death chant is sung for Rain Singing's daughter and granddaughter. Weeping Sky has offered to stay in the Deer longhouse then; I will come here and watch over Day Greeter."

While Teller Of Legends was thanking her, Morning Song looked more closely at the bearer of this sad news. Proud Woman's elegantly molded face, her lithe, young body, seemed at first unaffected by strain or concern. And she had not let herself become neglectful of her person. Her glossy hair continued to be arranged in a smooth knot at her nape so as to give a regal tilt to her head. But her eyes were heavier-lidded than they had been, and the flesh surrounding them was darkly smudged. Well, she knew sorrow, too, for Teller Of Legends maintained that Proud Woman and her adoptive mother had been truly fond of each other. And she must be weary, as weary as Morning Song was, from ministering to those who were sick, to those who died despite all she could do for them. Certainly it was to Proud Woman's credit that she had remained in the village after Gray Squirrel died. She might have gone away instead, turned her back on this demon-infested place and rejoined what was left of her birth tribe. No one would have stopped her, or blamed her for doing so.

When Proud Woman made ready to leave, Morning Song walked with her to the entrance. "You will watch closely over Day Greeter?" she said urgently. "For Teller Of Legends' sake, she must survive this fever, Proud Woman. My grandmother is strong, but . . ."

"It is the same with Rain Singing," Proud Woman said, and although there was no censure in her voice, Morning Song felt chagrin that she had taken no thought before she spoke for the newly bereft Matron of the Deer longhouse. "You may trust me to do what I can for your cousin. I have no more liking for death than you do. Or for the suffering that accompanies it."

She ducked beneath the hide Morning Song had drawn back, and only by an adroit swerve avoided collision with the man who stood just outside. Se-A-Wi's somber gaze and firm-set mouth warned Morning Song that this visit to his sister was one he was reluctant to make.

Teller Of Legends moved slowly to meet him. As they exchanged searching glances, Morning Song saw for the first time how greatly they resembled each other; not so much in cast of feature, although the high-arched noses were very like, but in the way age had abraded from their faces all that was not bone-deep. What had been spared revealed the intrinsic man, the essential woman, and even a stranger would not be blind to their stoic acceptance of all that life had sent to them, or to the dignity of spirit which had evolved from this.

"I have heard," Se-A-Wi said, his voice reedier than Morning Song thought possible, "from the eldest son of Sweet Maple's brother."

Teller Of Legends did not speak; she did not move, or even blink.

"My wife and your daughter will be brought home in two days," he said, and inclined his graying head to respond to a question there was no need for her to put to him.

She took one of his gnarled hands, pressed it between hers. "When you are ready to return to the home of your childhood," she said after a moment, "there will be a place for you at my hearth."

He nodded again, and Morning Song understood that he was incapable of further speech. As her grandmother was also, for she let him walk away from her without even a word of good-bye.

But that might have been because Teller Of Legends, like Morning Song, had had enough of good-byes.

The children continued healthy, which fired Morning Song's determination that Day Greeter could and would recover. And her own reinforced resolve was all that she had to sustain her now, for Se-A-Wi's visit had brought about a change in Teller Of Legends. It was a subtle transformation. She went on fighting as hard as Morning Song did to outmaneuver Day Greeter's alternating fever and chills. She coaxed and cajoled and even threatened in order to make her swallow water and thin gruel. Yet she was not the same. A lassitude stole over her during the hours when their patient slept, a lassitude she made no attempt to throw off. She appeared somehow diminished—her breadth of shoulder was no longer so impressive; erectness had been subtracted from her bearing. And she was quiet. Too quiet. She spoke rarely, unless it was needful, and then too briefly.

But disturbing as this was, it was her reaction to Owl Crying's announcement of two more deaths that terrified Morning Song.

"Fierce Eagle last night, and Trail Marker this morning," Owl Crying said as she set slabs of cornbread alongside their bowls. She snapped out the words, as was her habit, but her voice lacked its usual sharpness. "And now Rain Singing herself needs caring for. No, no," she said hastily as Morning Song interrupted with an exclamation. "It is not the fever-sickness, but exhaustion. That, and more grief than ought to be sent all at once to any woman!"

Teller Of Legends broke off a bit of the bread, dunked it in her stew, and transferred it to her mouth. She chewed stolidly—and said nothing.

"We grieve for Rain Singing, and with her," Morning Song said into the silence. It discomforted her, to speak the words it was her grandmother's place to say.

Suddenly Teller Of Legends pushed away her half-eaten meal so violently that gravy surged out of her bowl. "How is it," she demanded of their visitor, "that I go on living? And you, Owl Crying? And Lake On Fire, who is older than we are. What makes these demons choose the young? It is wrong. It is wrong, wrong, wrong!" She stood up, flung out her hands, tipped back her head, and fixed her tortured eyes on the smoke hole. "I challenge you, demons!" she shouted. "Strike me, who prefers dying to watching others die. Give back to us those who owned youth, those from whom you have stolen the right to grow old. Take us instead, who have lived beyond our usefulness to anyone, even to ourselves!"

Morning Song leaped to her feet, ran to her, clutched at her shoulder. "Grandmother," she said, her fear a writhing serpent within her. "Grandmother, please! Do not do this."

Whether it was her touch or the pleading in her voice, Morning Song did not know. But one or both succeeded in bridling her grandmother's frenzy. Teller Of Legends let her arms fall to her sides, lowered her head until her chin rested on her chest, and sighed. "I am tired, Morning Song," she said pitifully. "That is all. I am tired." And she was docile as a child when the trembling young woman led her to her bed and helped her onto it.

"What did she mean by all of that?" Owl Crying demanded as she gathered up her pot and ladle and the remains of her cornbread. "Trail Marker was no youth. Sweet Maple was surely old, and Gray Squirrel and Loon Laughing were a long way from maidens. It is not only the young who have died."

"Like Rain Singing, Teller Of Legends has lost too many in too short a time," Morning Song said dully, seeing her out. "The worry, the grief, the fatigue that is born of hopelessness . . . they cannot help but mark any woman, Owl Crying." She rubbed at temples in which the pulses throbbed angrily. "And we none of us know when it will end. Or even *if* it will."

She watched Owl Crying go on her way, took a moment to fill her lungs with air a little less suffocating than it had been. Then she plodded back into the longhouse to resume her vigil beside Day Greeter's bunk.

She sat watching her sleeping cousin, now and then darting uneasy glances toward her grandmother. Would Teller Of Legends be herself again when she'd rested? Or would new cracks appear in a woman Morning Song had thought to be indestructible as the oak she compared herself to? On the afternoon Se-A-Wi had come with his terrible news, she had marveled at Teller Of Legends' fortitude. She had envied her, and at the same time been thankful that here was a fountain of strength from which Morning Song might drink whenever she needed to.

Where, now, would she find a source at which to replenish herself? If the heaping of tragedy upon tragedy had undermined even Teller Of Legends, what was left for Morning Song to brace herself against? Or aspire to?

All at once, and with a passion different from any she'd known before, Morning Song wanted Cloud Racer, wanted the security of his hard embrace, the evenness of his reassuring glance, the comforting sound of his breathing to banish loneliness from her nights. She closed her eyes and called up a picture of his strong-featured face. It soothed her, and let her thoughts travel paths infinitely more pleasant than the one they'd been stumbling along. . . . With a smile haunting her lips, Morning Song slept.

It was full dark when she awoke. Only the fire on the main hearth tempered the blackness, and even that was little more than a collection of sullen embers. Guilt over her negligence propelled her to her feet, and she noticed suddenly that the hearth was not the perfect circle it ought to be. One segment seemed strewn with pitch. As her sleep-fuddled brain tried to make sense of this, a series of rustling sounds marked a rejuvenation of the anemic fire; by the time a ring of small flames danced within the stones, Morning Song knew that Teller Of Legends had risen from her bed to tend it.

"I had hoped you might sleep longer."

Relief flooded through Morning Song at the sound of her grandmother's voice. It was as calm, as confident, as she'd hoped it would be. She started for the hearth, remembered with an even sharper pang of guilt that she'd named herself responsible for Day Greeter when she'd urged her grandmother to rest. And it had been midday when last she'd given her water and spread salve on the worst of her sores!

"Day Greeter rests easily." Cautious elation vibrated in Teller Of Legends' voice, and Morning Song found herself holding her breath. "Her skin is not so hot to the touch as it was this morning." She lowered her voice as Morning Song came nearer. "This may mean nothing, or everything," she added. "We can only wait and see. But your falling asleep did her no harm and"—she examined Morning Song by the light of the maturing fire—"may have done you good. As mine did me."

She sat down, gestured to her granddaughter to do likewise. "I frightened you," she said bluntly, "when Owl Crying was here."

Morning Song somewhat hesitantly confirmed this.

The old woman sighed. "I frightened myself," she admitted. "But I have thought about it, and I believe I know what moved me to behave so outrageously."

"It is not outrageous to be so saturated with pain and grief that a bursting point is reached," Morning Song said quickly.

"It is true that I have had too much of both," she agreed. "But I am no stranger to either of them. Indeed, they are a necessary part of life, for they balance the joy and contentment that are given to us in abundance."

"There has been no contentment for you of late, nor anything at all akin to joy."

"That, too, is true," her grandmother murmured, staring into the flames. "Yet it was not their lack that caused the problem. In the past, whenever I lost someone I cared for I made no attempt to hide my grief. As I've come to do lately. Also"—she raised her head, looked into Morning Song's attentive face—"do you recall our warriors' first battle against the Cat People? The one in which Deer Caller had his vision stolen from him and Sweet Maple's brother was slain?"

Morning Song nodded.

"Then you may also remember how frequently I visited the Plover lodge after our warriors came home. At first, I went to mourn with my old friend. Later"—she picked up a stick, poked idly at the fire—"it was to spend hours reminiscing with her. We spoke of Far Seer, the boy he'd been and the man he had become. Often, we laughed; in his youth, Far Seer was fond of playing pranks on his sister and her friends." Her wide mouth curved, even after all this time, to look back on those days.

"What we were doing, of course," she went on after a moment, "was keeping the memory of Far Seer from being drawn into the spirit world after him. Memories are the medicine a grieving heart needs, Morning Song. And I neglected, this time, to dose myself with them."

"It is true that we did not talk of my mother-aunts after they had . . . died," Morning Song said slowly. "I dared not mention them," she added, "for fear of distressing you."

Teller Of Legends smiled again.. "And I would not, because you did not," she said wryly. "You seemed to have no need of memory-medicine. Why, even after we sang the death chant for Otter Swimming—and you loved her above all others in the clan—your spirit did not break, or even bend. You simply turned all your energies to caring for Day Greeter. I told myself that if you, who are so young, can be so strong, then I would disgrace myself by confessing that my own strength required bolstering."

"Strong?" Amazement made Morning Song's voice shrill. She shot an anxious glance toward her cousin's bunk and continued in a whisper. "Grandmother, I have not felt less strong since I was a child! I have been beset by doubts, by fears, even by anger that so much tragedy has come to our longhouse. I have longed to let despair triumph over me, because it seemed a way to escape the horror. I have been everything but strong, Teller Of Legends."

"You said nothing of any of this."

Morning Song laughed, but the sound was soblike. "I dreaded to have a woman as strong as you know my awful weakness," she said.

Teller Of Legends shook her head. "We have been foolish, you and I. How much easier, and how much more sensible, to have been honest with each other.''

Her granddaughter moved closer, rested an arm across her shoulders. "Well, we have come to it now."

"Since we have," Teller Of Legends said, "this might be a good time to teach you something I seem to have neglected."

"You have taught this ignorant woman a great deal," Morning Song responded affectionately, "but there is much more I need to learn."

"The person who feels otherwise," Teller Of Legends said tartly, "is the one who truly goes in ignorance, Morning Song. But it is our talk about strength that concerns me now. I begin to feel that you give this word a meaning it was never meant to have, and that you do not know its proper meaning at all."

"I know that I find in you more strength than I shall ever own. I know that Bountiful Harvest was so strong that she would not die until she had divided her possessions between her daughters and said farewell to all of us." She paused; it astonished her still, and always would, that Bountiful Harvest had refused to loose her tenuous hold on life until she was ready to. "Otter"—she shaped the name timidly, repeated it; and saw again a face whose irregular features lent themselves perfectly to a drollness made for coaxing giggles from those who needed to laugh—"Otter showed enormous strength when she would not let me pretend she could survive her illness. Even Pumpkin Blossom—"

Teller Of Legends held up one hand. "Enough!" she said. "You have just proven me right, Morning Song. Oh, I agree that each of my daughters was strong in her own way, just as my granddaughters are. What you fail to see, however, is that enduring strength is no gift, but a thing that must be earned. It comes of forging ahead despite uncertainty, of stubbornly repudiating fear, of forcing yourself to rise above the weaknesses that are common to all of us. Strength is not an inborn fearlessness, my dear. Someone who has never been so frightened that he wants to run away and hide has no right to boast of being strong. Such a person has never been tested, and it is only through being tested again and again that real strength seeds itself and grows. Strength has grown tall in you, Morning Song; if you are blind to it, others are not."

"When you slept," Morning Song said deliberately, "I tortured myself with wondering whether you would ever again offer the support I have become accustomed to. Because I could not be sure that you would, I began to yearn for Cloud Racer . . . and consoled myself with thoughts of borrowing strength from him. There is nothing strong about a woman who shrinks from standing alone.''

"Do you think the grandmother you call strong was permanently weakened because of what happened earlier, when she was the one who could not stand without support? Do you think I have become a doddering old woman because I am taking comfort from talking with you like this?''

"You know I do not.''

"People have need of one another," Teller Of Legends said gently. "That has little to do with strength or weakness. It is in the nature of things that we depend upon others from time to time, and that they depend on us. Given a choice, few would insist upon standing alone. This is something we do only when we must. As for your desire to have Cloud Racer home with you''—she chuckled—''I should think you an unnatural woman if you felt otherwise!''

Morning Song laughed, easily this time. "I am not unnatural in that respect, I promise you.'' Then she sobered. "Grandmother, I want desperately to see him again, yet his homecoming will be so sad. Except for his mother—and Fox Running, who went north with him—all of his family is gone. And I am afraid to have him come home. The fever sickness . . . suppose it should strike at Cloud Racer? This I could not endure, no matter how much strength you imagine I have." It came to her all at once that she had not, this time, found herself agonizing over the possibility that Cloud Racer might be slain during the fighting. Perhaps something in her simply refused to deal with yet another torment; perhaps exposure to so much tragedy had thrown up a palisade that would not let her see beyond the immediate.

Teller Of Legends turned so that she was facing her squarely. "If that happens, you will endure it," she said sternly. "But it serves no good purpose to anticipate such a thing." She grunted as she uncurled her legs and prepared to rise. "I am too old to sit for so long in the same position," she sighed as Morning Song hurried to assist her, "which I know full well." She grinned. "It seems that neither of us is thinking clearly at the moment." She tilted her head toward the entrance. "And little wonder! A new day has come while the two of us were talking." She took a cautious step, nodded with satisfaction; the cramp was gone. "Yet I feel better because we did.''

"As I do,'' Morning Song said, leading the way to Day Greeter's bunk.

Opalescent light fell across the young woman's face, and Morning Song stretched out her hand to measure the heat radiating from that lesion-studded forehead. But before her fingers had gauged the progress of the fever, she aborted the motion and went down on her knees beside the bed.

"Grandmother," she said tightly, "there are two sores on her face that are no longer spitting pus. In truth"—she bent her head, studied them more closely—"scabs are beginning to grow over them!"

Teller Of Legends closed her eyes and welcomed hope back into her world.

Chapter 26

The first frost had silvered the late crops and gilded the birch leaves before the survivors dared believe that the Time of the Great Sickness was over. Then they were inspired to a frenzy of busyness: The matrons and maidens went in chattering groups to the river to scrub sweat-stained garments, gathered together to cut and sew new ones, looped back hides at both ends of every longhouse to let cleansing breezes sweep through. And the children, returned to their respective clans, clamored to have a part in the bustle.

"I am not certain," Morning Song said to Day Greeter when Red Bird and Hidden Moon had picked up their hoes and gone out with Pumpkin Blossom, "whether we are celebrating our deliverance, or devising a ritual to banish the sorrow that the Great Sickness sent into our lives." She heaped the outstretched arms of her son and Otter's twins with musty bedrobes, warned them to shake them vigorously before draping them over the drying racks. "It is good that the three of you are so strong," she told them solemnly. "I could never carry so many and still have the energy to shake them." She grinned as they strutted out, then turned back to her cousin. "Why not sit in the sun for a while?" she said. "It might hasten the rest of your healing, if you spent part of each day in the compound."

Day Greeter shook her head. "I am not ready yet for that, Morning Song," she said quietly.

Morning Song did not press the issue. The sores that had clustered on Day Greeter's flesh were gone now, but where they had been the skin was pitted; and her face wore most of the scars. Teller of Legends and Morning Song had seen her retreat from the hearth until shadows veiled her from chance visitors, watched her avert her face if anyone sought her out; and both were intent on showing her that people were not so easily repelled.

Yet to push too hard too soon would accomplish nothing. "I am glad to have the young ones back," Morning Song said now, using the tip of her blade to score a hide she'd marked with a tracing of Red Bird's foot. "Their laughter, even their shouting, makes a music we have been too long without."

Day Greeter nodded and began to lace the first moccasin Morning Song had cut. "As Teller Of Legends would say, 'We need the joy they bring into the lodge to balance the sorrow it has been filled with.' I am happy to see that Bold Leader and Brave Companion can laugh with the others. I was worried that they might be grieving still for Otter."

"Swift Arrow tells me their grief was enormous when they learned of her dying," Morning Song said soberly. Then she smiled. "When neither seemed able to sleep, he decided it might distract them, and comfort them, if he brought White Shadow into the lodge. He knew this would be difficult; if you'll recall, Fish Jumping had volunteered to watch over the women and children, and he had made his bed near the entrance."

"Since Swift Arrow is your son," Day Greeter returned, her own mouth lifting at the corners, "I expect that he managed to carry out his plan, nonetheless."

"He did. He waited until everyone else was asleep, then slipped outside with a chunk of meat he'd saved from his meal. Shadow has never been a dog to refuse a bit of venison. Swift Arrow lured him in through the rear, then encouraged him to lie down between Bold Leader and Brave Companion. He was swollen with pride, my son, when he announced that, only moments later, both the twins and the dog slept."

"Surely he did not allow Shadow to remain inside all night!" Day Greeter, absorbed in the chronicle, forgot to keep her head bent; Morning Song was careful to show no elation.

"He did. In the morning, the three were huddled together, still sleeping soundly, when Meadow Brook and Pumpkin Blossom and Fish Jumping awoke. Meadow Brook and your brother laughed to see them, Swift Arrow says, but your sister was less than entertained. And did not hesitate to let Swift Arrow know it."

"Pumpkin Blossom was right to be concerned," Day Greeter said loyally. "Dogs have never been permitted in the longhouses, Morning Song." Then she laughed aloud, something she had not done in so long that Morning Song had forgotten how warm a sound her laughter was. "But I confess that I would have enjoyed seeing my sister's expression when she found him there."

She was laughing still when Teller Of Legends, followed by Tree Reaching Up, came into the lodge.

"How is it," their grandmother demanded, her eyes taking on a twinkle Morning Song rejoiced to see, "that the pair of you may sit and jest while the rest of us work so hard that we have no time even to gossip?"

"We are not idle," Morning Song protested, displaying the moccasins they were making. But her protest was as much pretense as Teller Of Legends' criticism and was likewise for Day Greeter's benefit. And not even the appearance of Tree Reaching Up had prompted the younger woman to turn her head away.

"I have been saying to Teller Of Legends," their visitor remarked, settling herself comfortably on the floor, "that Deer Caller's recovery is nearly complete. In every respect. When Fish Jumping came to speak with him—as he does each morning—Deer Caller asked him to choose a length of hickory. He means to carve the warrior's bow he once promised for the son of Bountiful Harvest."

Day Greeter lowered her head, concentrated fiercely on the seam she was sewing. "Does he bear scars," she asked slowly, "from the fever-sickness?"

"He has scars both visible and invisible," Tree Reaching Up replied. This soft-spoken woman, who had kept to herself the fact of Deer Caller's illness so as not to further distress the Turtle clan, was conscious of Day Greeter's particular problem. "Yet they do not make my cousin less admirable than he was before."

Day Greeter looked up quickly, bent her head again, and said nothing.

"This will be my brother's first night in my lodge since he was a young warrior," Teller Of Legends said, wisely leaving her troubled granddaughter to ponder what Tree Reaching Up had said. "I think Se-A-Wi might welcome a story in honor of the occasion."

"Only if Deer Caller and I may come and listen to it also," Tree Reaching Up said quickly, and was unsurprised to be assured that they might.

* * *

"It occurred to me," Teller Of Legends said when the setting of the sun brought her family and their guests together, "that my tale should be one that glorifies the courage of the Longhouse People. At first, I planned to speak of a warrior whose prowess in battle has made him a legend among us. There are, as you know, many of those."

"The men of the Iroquois," Fish Jumping said, "are the bravest there are." He preened himself; when Deer Caller had finished his bow, Fish Jumping would be ready to be tested and named warrior.

His grandmother smiled. "But there are many kinds of courage, Fish Jumping. And I am going to pay homage to the kind of courage that any of us—warrior or no—may own."

Pumpkin Blossom looked to the children to reassure herself that they were not fidgeting. Habit alone made her do so; they had been warned to sit quietly, and would obey whether they felt her eyes on them or not. Still, to check on her children was a thing her mother had never failed to do. . . .

"A certain maiden possessed the brand of courage I speak of," Teller Of Legends was saying, "and her name was A-Li-Qui-Pi-So. She was young and lovely, but like the rest of her tribe she was unhappy. A fierce enemy had driven them from their village into the deep forest, where they had hidden themselves among huge rocks, in caves, and on desolate mountains. Their warriors were too few, you see, to vanquish the invaders. If the people wished to survive, there was nothing left for them but to hide."

Se-A-Wi, remembering this tale, looked approvingly at his sister; she had chosen wisely.

"A dream was sent to A-Li-Qui-Pi-So one night, and in the morning she asked to address the Council. 'I have been told how we might defeat our enemies and regain our village,' she said to them. 'Behind us stands a mountain whose slopes are covered with heavy boulders and sharp-edged rocks. If our warriors climb to the top of this mountain, and the invaders can be brought to its foot, then those who have forced us from our homes will be crushed and destroyed by a mighty avalanche.'

"The Sachems gazed perplexedly at one another, and at the slim, young maiden. 'Our warriors can easily climb the tall mountain,' they said at last. 'But how are we to arrange for the enemy war band to come and stand beneath them? They are wily, these enemies of ours, in addition to being better armed than we are. And there are many more of them than of us.'

" 'This was revealed to me by my vision,' she said. 'I am meant to lead the invaders there so that all of them may be slain.' "

"But how can the maiden save herself?" Hidden Moon asked anxiously, and Teller of Legends took her on her lap.

"I think you know what must happen to A-Li-Qui-Pi-So," she said quietly, "and she also knew. As I said before, there are many kinds of courage. And while A-Li-Qui-Pi-So may have lacked the sinew-strength that warriors possess, she had an abundance of heart-strength. The members of the Council saw this, and were awed by it. The chief came to her and hung round her neck strands of white and purple wampum. 'The Maker Of Life,' he said to her, 'has granted you both courage and wisdom. Your people will never forget the name of A-Li-Qui-Pi-So.'

"Next day, the maiden let herself be captured by enemy scouts and dragged back to her burned-out village. The leader of the war band told her that her life would be spared if she agreed to lead them to the rest of her people. 'If you refuse,' he said bluntly, 'you will be bound to a stake and tortured.' "

Morning Song shifted uncomfortably and hoped her grandmother's description of the torture would not be too explicit.

"The Sachem had been right when he named A-Li-Qui-Pi-So wise," Teller Of Legends said. Her eyes—which were still more sunken and dark-rimmed than Morning Song thought they should be—touched on each of the young faces upturned to hers. "The maiden knew better than to consent immediately. Even when two of the warriors lashed her to a tree stump, even when they grabbed flaming torches and singed her tender flesh, all that left her mouth was a song praising her people. When she had endured all that she could, however, she cried out suddenly, 'Stop! I will show you the way.' "

Day Greeter, whose compassion for the bereaved Deer Caller had led her to a place beside him in the circle, spoke softly. "Otter's love for others made her strong, just as A-Li-Qui-Pi-So's did." He turned and smiled at her. Day Greeter ducked her head, then lifted it as she realized that a man who cannot see is immune to ugliness.

"Darkness lay heavy around them," Teller Of Legends said, her voice quickening as she took them with her into that crucial night, "before they freed A-Li-Qui-Pi-So from the stump and tied her blistered hands behind her back. 'Do not betray us,' they snarled, 'or you will be the first to die.'

"They made no sound as they followed her into the forest, not even when they forded the streams that crossed their path. Finally they arrived at the base of the towering mountain, and A-Li-Qui-Pi-So urged them in a whisper to gather around her. 'My people are sleeping in a cave that opens into this mountain. A winding trail leads to it, and you must stay close to one another or you will lose your way.'

"They crowded closer, as she had known they would. And as they did, A-Li-Qui-Pi-So raised her head and uttered a piercing cry: 'The enemies are here. Destroy them!' "

The children gasped, and even the adults were moved to murmur among themselves.

"No one knew," Teller of Legends finished, "whether the war leader carried out his threat and drove the point of his spear into A-Li-Qui-Pi-So's back. For it was not only the invaders who were buried beneath the welter of rocks that thundered down the side of the mountain then; brave A-Li-Qui-Pi-So—who had willingly given her life to save her tribe—lay beneath them also."

Morning Song wondered, as she urged her children and Otter's to their beds, why her grandmother had elected to tell them a story whose ending had been sad. Surely they had known enough sadness of late. But when she had warned the boys that their wrestling match must wait until morning and convinced a giggling Red Bird that her conversation with Hidden Moon must be interrupted, she understood that none of them had been distressed by the tale. Indeed, the opposite was true. They'd learned how their ancestors had been visited by trouble and grief and sought for a way to overcome them. Just as the families in this small village had done, and were doing, and would continue to do.

And it was not impossible that among the children in this longhouse was one whose heart-strength might someday equal that of the ill-fated A-Li-Qui-Pi-So. For it followed that if adversity was not confined to a single time or place, then neither was courage.

The trees flaunted leaves of crimson and yellow. Huge orange pumpkins were heaped in the compound, and new-turned earth made the fields as richly brown as a beaver's pelt. The vividness of a scene that only autumn could paint met the eyes of Cloud Racer and his warriors on the day they came home.

They were nearly to the village before they were sighted. Then Fish Jumping's jubilant shout split the sky to announce that long-absent husbands and sons and brothers and uncles had returned at last.

This time, Morning Song did not race to meet her husband, but walked sedately between Teller Of Legends and Se-A-Wi. "I yearn to see him," she said to her grandmother, "but I am loath to tell him what I must."

"He will know a similar confusion," Teller Of Legends said.

"He will mourn for those who cannot be here to welcome him home, yet rejoice to be with you and his children once more."

Morning Song went up on tiptoe, craned her neck to see. "The children are with him already," she said, and anxiety puckered her brow. "I must get to him before they tell him something that should come only from me," she threw over her shoulder as she broke into a run.

Her worry had been for naught. When she reached the three, Swift Arrow was beaming because he'd been allowed to relieve his father of his bow and quiver, and Red Bird was concerned solely with the fact that now one of Cloud Racer's hands was free for her to clutch.

Morning Song, disheveled from her plunge through the milling throng and dreading to burden her husband with grief, stole a moment just to look at him. Then he spoke her name, and she went to him, heedless of the children who had to make way for her, of the clusters of people who stood around them, of everyone and everything except Cloud Racer.

He disentangled his fingers from Red Bird's grip, entrusted his war club, too, to Swift Arrow, and embraced her. "It is good to be home," he said against her hair. She drew back a little, searched his face with her brown eyes. "There is something you must know," she said haltingly, "that will darken the day for you." She signed for their children to return to the compound and, with her hands still resting on his broad shoulders and her eyes still looking into his, described the assault of the Great Sickness upon their village. "I weep for you," she finished simply. "Of your birth family, only your mother and your brother are left to you."

He had been silent throughout, and unmoving, although his eyes spoke of the pain that her words, carefully chosen though they were, brought to him. Now his mouth thinned and lengthened. "You are wrong," he said harshly. "The spirit of my brother walks also in the land of our ancestors. Fox Running was slain in the north. As was Hill Climber."

Morning Song could not speak; she only felt again the insulating numbness she had experienced so often during the summer just past. It was unfair, she thought dully, that the lengthy chronicle of their recently dead must be expanded to include two more names. She thought of Sun Descending, who had seen her mother recover from the fever-sickness. She had not, after all, been spared a reason to mourn, but merely had it postponed; Fox Running had been her husband.

Morning Song could not know that her weariness of spirit was reflected in her eyes or that her embrace had involuntarily slackened. To Cloud Racer, more battered by grief than he had ever been by an enemy's weapons, her apparent withdrawal from him was like a spear-thrust to the heart. It inflicted a wound that left him too weakened to try and make sense out of the unthinkable.

He moved so abruptly that her hands slipped from his shoulders, and when she reached for him again he stepped away from her. "I must be alone for a while," he muttered. Then he turned and set his course for the path leading into the woods.

Shock anchored Morning Song to the spot she stood on. She watched him stride away, and color faded from her world until everything she looked upon had been bleached to soulless gray.

"You must go after him, of course," Teller Of Legends said. "he has had most of the day to come to terms with what you told him, and will be craving comfort now. Who better than you to provide it?"

Morning Song remained uncertain. "Surely he will come back here when he is ready to? If I go to him, and he does not want me . . ."

Teller Of Legends eyed her sharply. "Did you think to tell Cloud Racer that the Turtle clan has also suffered loss? Does he know how devotedly you tended your mother-aunts and your cousin? Has he been told that it is thanks to Morning Song that so many children not only survived but were not even ill?"

"It did not seem sensible to tell him too much all at once," she said. "Naturally I spoke first of the Deer clan. When I would have said more, he was gone." She pushed back tendrils of hair from a face so finely honed that hollows emphasized its delicate bones. "And we do not know that confining the children to the Pigeonhawk lodge was what kept them safe. They might have escaped the demons' notice even if they had stayed in their own longhouses."

"I will never believe that." Pumpkin Blossom spoke with a firmness that, these days, rarely lent texture to her voice. "My gratitude is too great to be measured, Morning Song; I shall never forget how I might have lost Hidden Moon and Painted Sky along with my mother, were it not for you."

There was no mistaking her sincerity, and Morning Song mumbled her appreciation for praise she neither looked for nor considered to be warranted.

"Your spirit guide," Pumpkin Blossom went on, her slender hands less than steady as they cut strips from a smooth-skinned pumpkin, "is more faithful to you than mine has been to me. You know that I would have refused to listen to you if Bountiful Harvest had not favored your plan." She sighed. "I have begun to wonder whether my guide was not just an extension of the one who directed my mother's life. Now that she is . . . gone, the spirits seem to have deserted me."

"It may be," Teller Of Legends said, "that you sometimes confused the voice of your spirit guide with that of Bountiful Harvest. Spirits speak softly, Pumpkin Blossom, and you shall have to listen for what is fainter sometimes than a whisper. When you do, I expect you will hear it."

Morning Song would have liked to echo that reassurance; it saddened her to see Pumpkin Blossom shedding the confidence and self-command her mother had fostered in her. But the daughter of Summer Maize knew perfectly well that no spirit guide had suggested that the children be kept apart from the rest of the villagers: That had been nothing more than an idea born of desperation.

Besides, she had more pressing matters to concern herself with. She stood up, straightened her tunic, loosened and replaited her hair.

Teller of Legends' glance was approving. "You are going to him," she said.

Morning Song smiled slightly. "Your counsel is at least as reliable as any spirit's has ever been."

But she was not smiling when she slipped out of the lodge into the frost-begetting crispness of the autumn night.

She went straight to Cloud Racer's cave, and the glow cast by a small blaze within proved her instinct correct. She did not hurry to join him; his abandonment of her, although she accepted Teller Of Legends' explanation for it, had rankled. It still did. But hurt and anger paled beside her need to be with him, to comfort and be comforted in return. She crouched, and passed uninvited into Cloud Racer's refuge.

He looked up from where he was squatting by his fire, but said nothing. His hair was damp, and the grubby garments he had worn lay in a crumpled pile some distance from where he sat. He had bathed in the river then, and not long ago, either. This, surely, was a heartening sign?

Refusing to be deterred by a silence that was not uncommon in this man, Morning Song skirted the hearth and hunkered down beside him. "I could not wait longer for you to come to me," she said quietly.

He made no reply.

"It did not make me happy, to cause you pain," she said. "But I would not add to Rain Singing's distress by leaving it to her to tell you what happened while you were gone." She studied his profile, saw that only iron control kept his mouth from drooping at the corners. She did not miss the slight flaring of his nostrils, or the failure of the flames he looked into to soften the intensity of his brooding stare.

Still he said nothing, and now the palms of Morning Song's hands were pearled with sweat and her heart had taken on the weight of a stone. How could she give comfort to someone who would not bestir himself to receive it? And what of the comforting that was due Morning Song, who had suffered also? She moved a little away from him. "I ask your forgiveness," she said stiffly, "for intruding upon your sorrowing. I thought you might have the same need for consolation as I do. You were not the only one who lost family to the Great Sickness, Cloud Racer. I watched both Bountiful Harvest and Otter Swimming die. And your sister, Cloud Racer . . . She was friend to me; I loved her dearly and will never cease to miss her." Her voice rose, tightened. "You are grieving, yes. But you were at least spared the terrible helplessness that comes with seeing someone you love slowly dying, while death-bringing demons defy all the healing measures known to the Longhouse People."

Cloud Racer swiveled his head to look at her, and the tendons in his neck swelled. "I saw my brother struck down," he shouted. "Yet we were surrounded by so many—for the northern tribes have allied themselves against the Iroquois, Morning Song—that I could not get to him, could not stanch the blood that gushed from his chest—"

She flung herself forward, put her arms around him, and wept with him. Time suspended itself until the echoes of their separate lamentations faded. Then his arms encircled her waist, and he was crushing her to him so fiercely that she labored to draw breath. She did not protest; like him, she was driven by a desire to shut out pain and grief and be rid of the self-doubt and self-loathing that are the furtive companions of despair.

No robe cushioned Morning Song from the cave's hard floor this time, and Cloud Racer's grip on her shoulders was bruising, his thrusting into her frenetic.

When, sweating and panting, he collapsed upon her, she closed her eyes so that he might not see the disappointment in them. He must never know that the release granted to him had been withheld from her.

"Cloud Racer tells me that even the Algonquin—who were defeated by us before I was born—seek to take advantage of our circumstances," Morning Song told her grandmother and the visiting Deer Caller, raising her voice to be heard over the rain that battered the roof. "They are sending raiding parties against our more isolated villages. Some of those are poorly defended now, he says, since the warriors of the Longhouse People did not entirely escape the fever-sickness. Cloud Racer's band attempted to break their journey at several villages, only to be turned away by Sachems who could not extend hospitality because they were mourning their strongest and bravest."

"Those of us who live in villages far to the south need not fear being attacked by the Algonquin," Deer Caller said reassuringly. "But it is not good that word of what has happened in our territories should spread to tribes who are no friends of ours. Still, I suppose there was no way to stop it."

"The *Onondio*, who trade with all the tribes, were aware of it," Morning Song said. "You may be certain they did not keep the information to themselves."

Although the remark reflected Morning Song's hatred for those whose skins chanced to be white, Teller Of Legends agreed with her. "But surely the Iroquois remain strong enough to deal with sporadic raiding? And no tribe will rush into open battle with even one of the Five Nations on the strength of rumor alone, whatever its source."

"That is so," Deer Caller agreed. "If our warriors are fewer in number, that does not necessarily make us easy prey. Fierce Eagle always maintained that a single Iroquois was equal to three from any other tribe." He smiled, but Morning Song saw the muscles in his jaw twitch. How galling it must be for him, as able a man as ever except for his blindness, to recognize that he would be of no use to anyone if marauders *should* dare to come this far!

"We are threatened from the south also," Teller Of Legends said after a moment. "Se-A-Wi says our westernmost nation is besieging and being besieged by the Susquehanna."

Morning Song nodded. Cloud Racer had spoken of this, too, on the night she had gone to comfort him. Coupling with her had loosened his tongue. "Once again the Iroquois are dividing, and this will weaken us more seriously than what the sallow-skins call the plague has done," he had said of the war in the west. Indeed, this news had been his only reward for his trip north; attempts to barricade the Long River had failed, and of Stag Leaping there had been no sign, just hints that someone fitting his description had been asking for sanctuary among the enemies of the Longhouse People.

"At the next meeting of the Confederation's Great Council, a plan will be made to deal with all our enemies," Teller Of Legends said after a moment. But there was no real certainty in her voice. Death had claimed many tribal elders. In this village alone, the Councilors now were mostly inexperienced: Bear In The Sky; Cloud Racer (although she trusted the shrewdness and good judgment of that one); Woodpecker Drumming . . . She must ask her grand-daughter's husband his opinion of these young men. If he had reservations about one or more of them, well, she would go to the women, suggest changes. . . . She sighed. How could she have forgotten that many of the Chief Matrons were also newly raised to that status and untried? And it would be no different in other villages.

She'd speak with Cloud Racer anyway, she decided, and do what she could afterward. "Where is your husband, Morning Song?" she asked.

"He went out earlier," Morning Song said. "I did not think to ask where, or when he would be back."

Day Greeter called from the hearth where she was rotating the spit that held a haunch of fresh venison. "I heard him say to Se-A-Wi that he was going to the Deer longhouse."

Morning Song was unsurprised. Cloud Racer had been spending considerable time with his mother, which was only right. He and Rain Singing had no clan-kin left, save each other, for Cloud Racer's children belonged to their mother's clan.

She turned as Swift Arrow—reeking of fish and dripping wet— came in, followed by the equally pungent sons of Otter Swimming. Bold Leader and Brave Companion went to sit on either side of their father and treat him to a tale of the morning's adventure, but Swift Arrow was more concerned with how soon their meal would be ready. "I could eat the whole of that roast," he said fervently, "all by myself." He offered his mother his engaging grin. "But I will be courteous instead, and leave enough for the rest of you. Shall I go and tell Se-A-Wi and my father it is time to eat?" he asked hopefully. "Now that the sun shines again, the Sachem is in the compound with Puma Walking Soft. And probably Cloud Racer is still with Rain Singing and Proud Woman. He was there when he went to the river, and I have not seen him come out."

"When you have scrubbed off some of the stench that clings to you," his mother said, determined not to reveal the unease his careless words had aroused in her, "then you may go and tell them that our meal shall be served soon. You will have to go to Meadow Brook's lodge afterward, and say the same to Pumpkin Blossom and Hidden Moon and your sister.''

When he had darted away, pausing only long enough to inhale appreciatively as he passed the cooking hearth, Morning Song turned to her grandmother. "It surprises me," she said casually, "that Proud Woman is more often in the Deer lodge than she is in hers.''

"She lives there now," Teller Of Legends replied calmly. "It seemed foolish that both she and Rain Singing should live alone. I do not know about Proud Woman, but for Cloud Racer's mother to meet silence on all sides is akin to an unarmed warrior suddenly finding himself surrounded by lance-bearing enemies. She is lost without someone to talk to, and Proud Woman is an attentive listener." She chuckled. "In time, Rain Singing will have entertained her with an abundance of gossip both old and new, for she never forgets a thing once she has heard it. And Proud Woman respects Rain Singing; she will listen patiently to all of it, even when it concerns people she has never met.''

Morning Song tossed aside her sewing. "Swift Arrow said that the rain has stopped," she said. "I believe I will enjoy our meal more if I walk a little first.''

She would not go near the Deer longhouse, she told herself as she stepped outside. But her contrary feet would have carried her there if she had not spied Sun Descending sitting in front of her lodge. Morning Song put on a cordial smile and greeted the widow of Fox Running as though she had come into the compound solely to visit with her.

"Your mother fares well?" she asked amiably. "And your sons?"

Sun Descending nodded. "And my brother, too," she said. "It is my husband only that cannot be named well, Morning Song. Unless, perhaps, we refer to his spirit. And his spirit, unfortunately, does not sit at my hearth.''

Her words were barbs, and the target of them ceased on the instant her stealthy surveillance of the Deer longhouse. She focused on Sun Descending's face, stiffened with shock when she saw how prolonged sorrowing had stolen every vestige of youth from it. "I wish his spirit could put on flesh and be with you once more," she said when she found herself able to speak. "I ache for you, and understand your bitterness. When Bountiful Harvest and Otter died—''

"Neither of them was your husband!" Sun Descending snapped, interrupting her. "It is different when it is a husband you have lost,

Morning Song. It is worse, far worse.'' She looked away, to where two solemn-faced boys were trudging toward them. ''They will be hungry,'' she said wearily, ''and I have nothing cooked for them.'' Without another word, she turned aside from Morning Song and disappeared into her lodge.

Morning Song, stunned and shaken, resumed the walk she had forgotten her reason for. She paced aimlessly as she wondered how she could help this friend of her childhood overcome her desolation. Weeping Sky, still frail from the fever she had survived, must be distraught to see her daughter like this, and must worry about the unnaturally subdued pair who were her grandsons.

The sound of Cloud Racer's voice cut short her speculations. She retreated to the far side of the Wolf longhouse and peeked around its corner. Proud Woman had escorted Cloud Racer to the door, and Morning Song eyed that slim and graceful figure, the smooth hair that capped her elegant head, with loathing. She heard the young woman laugh softly, saw Cloud Racer's mouth curve into a responding smile, and winced.

Then she dared watch no longer. Cloud Racer was taking his leave of Rain Singing's permanent guest—and why had he never mentioned that Proud Woman had been invited to share his mother's lodge?—and Morning Song would not risk his catching her skulking about!

She stumbled to the rear of the lodge, began a hasty crossing to the Turtle longhouse, and blundered into an ankle-deep puddle of rainwater. She looked down at her submerged moccasins, grimaced, and clenched her hands until the fingernails punctured her palms.

Too wretched even to step back, she lowered herself until her buttocks rested on the soggy ground, then peered between her angled knees at the image that swam among the ripples her invasion had created. It was not a sight to hearten her, not even when the water settled and presented a placid surface to the sky. What was revealed to her said plainer than words that Sun Descending was not alone in showing the ravages of grief and despair. They had taken their toll of Morning Song, too. Looking back at her was a face whose gauntness made it nearly unrecognizable.

She stifled a sob, then lifted both feet and plunged them again into the puddle, moved them this way and that until the image was blotted out by the mud she churned up.

The memory of it, however, was not to be so easily erased.

Chapter 27

❦ ❦

Teller Of Legends was grateful for the soft-edged summer breeze drifting into her lodge. The Maker Of Life, she reflected, could be gentle with his children when it was needful. He had chosen not to remind them of the last yellow season, when every sweltering hour had been further inflamed with sickness and sorrowing. He was countering bad with good, was restoring balance to their lives.

"Hidden Moon is unhappy," Pumpkin Blossom was saying to Morning Song, "because Red Bird is so much taller than she is."

Her cousin scooped chunked bear meat into a pot of bubbling broth. "In a year or two, she will see that it is no boon to tower over other maidens," she said absently, resuming her place among the women. "My daughter will be the one to fret then. As I once did."

"I am sure they will both come to see how pointless it is to be discontented with themselves," Day Greeter said placidly.

Teller Of Legends hid a smile. Day Greeter, after a long struggle, had come to regard herself—pitted face and all—as worthy of acceptance, and this was certainly another thing to be thankful for. *I am near to bursting with gratitude this day,* the old woman told herself, and this time could not contain her smile.

"A girl as pretty as Hidden Moon," Lake On Fire said, peering nearsightedly at her friend and trying to make sense of the quirking of her long mouth, "should not worry about so trifling a matter as height." Her beads, as vividly red and blue as the stitching on her skirt, jangled as she fingered them. Now that the traders came regularly again, she owned beads to match each of her costumes.

"Every one of us," Teller Of Legends said cheerfully, "has at some time wished to be what he or she is not. This does no harm, so long as we come eventually to like ourselves as we are." She beamed upon Day Greeter, and hoped that what she was beginning to suspect of her might also be true. . . .

Her expression sobered as Morning Song went to stir the stew. Why had this granddaughter of hers scraped her lovely hair back into a bulky knot at the back of her neck? Now her face appeared longer and thinner than it actually was. Had she decided that the thick plait she'd always worn was too youthful a style for a matron? Teller Of Legends lifted her hands to the braids that hung over her own shoulders, and knew that was absurd. Perhaps Morning Song had impulsively arranged her hair in this new way and Cloud Racer had admired it? Everyone knew that men were sometimes attracted by what any woman would instantly name unsuitable.

She shook herself out of her reverie. It was a sign of age, to let her mind wander from the conversation going on around her! "Have you spoken lately with Weeping Sky?" she asked their visitor.

Lake On Fire shook her head. "I went to the Wolf lodge before I came here, but Sun Descending turned me away." Her face clouded. "She said her mother was sleeping, but I think it was Sun Descending who did not want company."

"It is sad," Pumpkin Blossom said softly, "that she cannot have done with her grieving."

The others murmured agreement; everyone in the village had begun to worry about Sun Descending, especially since even Puma Walking Soft had failed to persuade her that to mourn for more than a year offends the spirits.

"Your friend walks in a shadow-land," Teller Of Legends said to Pumpkin Blossom. "Her feet cannot stray from this world, but she keeps her face turned to the world Fox Running's spirit has gone to. If nothing is done about it, or if what is done does not succeed, the time will come when she cannot return to the light even if she wants to." She shook her head sadly, then put on a welcoming smile as Red Bird, carrying a basket of freshly husked corn, came in.

Morning Song was prying charred stew from the bottom of her neglected pot when the girl crossed to their hearth. Red Bird shook her neat head when she saw blackened bits of meat rising to the surface. "Why not let me watch it for you," she said. "I can sit here while I strip the corn from the cobs."

"My daughter considers herself a better cook then her mother," Morning Song told Teller Of Legends when she'd handed over the spoon, "or at least a more careful one. And she is right. How someone like me managed to raise a proper little Iroquois maiden is a mystery, but it seems that I have." She nodded to Pumpkin Blossom. "It is thanks to you that she is so capable, of course. But I wish that, now and then, she would permit me to think that I do not suffer too much by comparison with you!" She smiled when the others laughed, although she had not spoken wholly in jest. She

bent and fumbled beneath her bunk. "White Shadow has earned
this," she said, taking out the bone she'd stashed there. "Swift
Arrow cannot seem to realize that the dog is growing old, and
Shadow wears himself out trying to act the puppy in order to please
him."

She found her old friend sprawled in the shade, his eyes following
the boys as they tossed blunted lances through a hoop. Swift Arrow
was as sharp-eyed and deft-handed as the best of his peers, his
proud mother saw. As he moved to take his turn spinning the hoop,
she recalled what Cloud Racer had said of him: "He walks with
his head thrust forward and his chin jutting out, as though he means
to achieve his destination at any cost," he'd told her. "As you do,
Morning Song." Yet what was appropriate in the someday-warrior
was unattractive in a settled matron, and Morning Song had wondered if Cloud Racer was not comparing her unfavorably with a
woman whose bearing was regally self-assured. She had taken pains
since to adjust her own gait, to hold herself straight as a spear, and
move with a stateliness alien to her. She hadn't been entirely successful; her unmonitored feet had tangled with a child's abandoned
ball one time, and she'd narrowly avoided stepping upon a snake's
triangular head on another. Still, she'd known since childhood that
nothing can be mastered without practice. One day she, too, would
earn her husband's unqualified admiration.

She sighed. When that day came, perhaps their lovemaking would
regain its spontaneity. She knew that she was partly to blame for
the unsatisfying ritual it had become. After the night she'd gone to
Cloud Racer's cave to comfort him . . . it had taken so long before
she could do more than pretend enthusiasm for his embraces, particularly since she'd needed almost two seasons to recover from a
soul-deep tiredness stemming from the Time of the Great Sickness.
Yet Cloud Racer, if he cared enough, should have sensed all this
and helped her to overcome her unwitting apathy.

What frightened her was the possibility that he no longer cared
enough. He did not go so frequently to his mother's lodge these
days, but this did little to put her doubts to rest. A man need not
be always in the company of a beautiful woman to remain entranced
by her. And Proud Woman was beautiful. Incredibly beautiful.

Shadow set one forepaw possessively upon the remains of his
bone and laid his head in Morning Song's lap. She stroked his pale
fur, scratched behind his ears, saw his eyes close contentedly. It
would not be such a dreadful thing to be a dog, she thought all at
once; then shook herself irritably. If she went on this way, Sun
Descending would have a companion in that shadow-land of hers.

For a moment, she let herself imagine that her husband, like Sun Descending's, had died, that there was no longer a Cloud Racer whose attention might have strayed to a woman younger and prettier than Morning Song. . . . With an exclamation she jumped to her feet, dumping Shadow's head unceremoniously onto the grass.

How dare she, even briefly, compare her self-spawned misery to Sun Descending's! How dare she wallow in a self-pity that, in truth, there was no sensible reason for? She patted her startled dog and made herself examine the foolish woman who had been withholding her love from the living, breathing, warm-blooded man who willingly shared her bed and her hearth. And all because of a baseless jealousy that would be inexcusable in a ten-year-old! *Cloud Racer* was not responsible for the constraint that had arisen between them; Morning Song was.

Well, amends must be made. First, she would return to her husband the woman he had known and loved from the start.

She laughed aloud, put up her hands, tugged at the hair she'd twisted behind her head, and laughed again as it fell like a soft cape around her. As for this nonsense of standing and walking as though a spear shaft were tied to her spine, it was over as of now.

Shadow barked once, and she looked down to see him studying her curiously. "Do not try to guess what I am about," she advised him, "for I do not know myself. I only know that I feel younger than I have in a long, long time, that I see beauty"—she spread her arms, twirled as though she were weightless—"wherever I look. I mean to give myself a chance to enjoy it, and let my *orenda* be refreshed by it." She snapped her fingers, and the dog's whip of a tail wagged furiously. "We will go to the forest, you and I," she told him, "as we used to. When we return, I will make my peace with my husband. And the night to come will see a rebirth of our love."

The boys' game had ended, and Swift Arrow ran to meet his mother as she strode across the compound. "I will go with you," he announced when he learned where she was heading.

Morning Song put out a hand and rumpled his black hair. "You will not," she said cheerfully. "I have a need," she explained when his face fell, "to be alone occasionally. I pretended that the need ended when my childhood did, but I see now that it did not."

"You are not alone if White Shadow goes with you," he said.

"White Shadow," she replied, "does not *talk*." She hugged him, smiled down into his eyes. "You may go with me next time," she promised. "Meanwhile, I will trust you to let Teller Of Legends know where I have gone. She will understand, I think."

She beckoned to the dog, who sent an apologetic look at Swift Arrow, then trotted after the human to whom he had first given his devotion. His memory of the girl she'd been had never faded; as the woman's stride lengthened, as she lifted her face to the summer sky, the years began to fall away from him as well. Before they reached the woods, both were loping along with almost youthful abandon.

She encouraged Shadow to take the lead as the trees thickened and the trail narrowed. "It matters little where we go," she told him, feasting her eyes on the lush growth bordering the path, the thick-leafed canopy arching above their heads. A miscellany of birds hopped along branches or soared from tree to tree. Like all creatures, they cherished these weeks that linked the end of the yellow season with the onset of the red.

A frog called hoarsely from the beaver swamp they were passing, and Morning Song paused to watch a striped-tail raccoon prick up his ears and move stealthily toward a possible dinner. Let him and his kind fill their bellies with unwary frogs; this was better than having them creep out of the forest to gorge themselves on the last of the village's corn.

White Shadow doubled back to see what was delaying her, and Morning Song laughed. "You are as happy to be here with me as I am to be here with you," she murmured as he nuzzled her hand.

They scrambled together to the crest of a rise whose slopes bristled with juniper and balsam, raced one another down its far side, stopped to drink from a stream burbling at its foot. Morning Song wiped her hand across her mouth and looked around. Huddled oaks smudged the horizon on their right, and she started toward them. Shadow bounded ahead; he knew that where there were oak trees there were squirrels.

Morning Song smiled indulgently after him, stepped in among the silvery birches on her left, and flung herself down in a patch of shade. When he'd chased every squirrel impertinent enough to flaunt a bushy tail at him, he'd come searching for her. Until he did, she would lie here and savor the peace that had come to visit her. . . .

She did not sleep, not exactly. But the balm she was applying to her spirit was effective, and she did not doubt, later, that she may have dozed.

The sound of moccasined feet padding over spongy ground made her open her eyes. She stayed where she was; she was too comfortable to want to move, and there was nothing in the sound to

alarm her. Many of the men had been taking advantage of this
glorious weather; these would be only a pair of hunters returning
to the village. But she sat up suddenly when they came close enough
for their voices to be distinguishable. The first voice to reach her
ears was familiar indeed.

". . . would be begging for capture to venture this far south,"
Cloud Racer was saying. "And the Algonquin warriors, whatever
else they may be, are not witless."

"I believe Follows The Signs is hopeful that they'll come here."
That was Hawk Hunting. "Like all old men, he yearns to be a
warrior again. If the Tree Eaters extend their raiding, he says he
stands ready to protect the village while we are not around."

A splashing sound told Morning Song that the two had knelt to
drink. Should she reveal herself? she wondered; then decided
against it. She had not maneuvered to overhear their conversation;
circumstance had arranged it, so she might as well enjoy herself.
Her mood was buoyant still, and she grinned to think how surprised
Cloud Racer would be to have her repeat, word for word, something
he had said only to Hawk Hunting. She'd confess then, of course,
and they would laugh together about it.

"Our village has rarely come under attack, and it seems unlikely
that the Algonquin will choose to venture this far now," Hawk
Hunting said more soberly, "which is all to the good. Too many of
our longhouses hold women only when we warriors are not there.
Your mother's, for one."

"But Rain Singing has Proud Woman with her now, and she is
no ordinary maiden," Cloud Racer said quickly.

Morning Song's grin vanished; the buoyancy went out of her.

"You were not near enough to see how she fought, on the day
we defeated the warriors defending her village," Cloud Racer went
on enthusiastically. "Proud Woman showed herself braver than
many of those trained to lance and bow, and I am glad I took her
captive. She has proven herself praiseworthy in every respect since
she was adopted into the Snipe clan."

"Lake On Fire has mentioned her kindness during the Great
Sickness," Hawk Hunting said after a moment. "After Gray Squirrel died, she went from lodge to lodge to care for the ill. She did
not wait to be asked, Lake On Fire says, but gave help generously
wherever it was needed."

"She is pleasing to look upon, also."

Morning Song flinched as if Cloud Racer's words had been blows.
But what he said next was lost in the shuffling of feet, the retrieval

of weapons and game bags, as the pair made ready to go on their way.

When they had moved beyond hearing distance, she stumbled to her feet and plodded in the direction her dog had taken. She could hardly believe that her ramble through the woods, begun with so light a heart, should have brought her to this; that so little time had elapsed between her naming her fears baseless and the awful realization that they were not. The truth had come from Cloud Racer's own mouth, and now Morning Song must face it squarely.

Yet, strangely, there was no return of the depression she'd been prey to when conjecture alone hinted at Cloud Racer's interest in the Erie maiden. Instead, she seethed with anger and was clench-jawed with resolution. "I will not," she said aloud as a panting White Shadow materialized at her side, "wring my hands and wallow in misery while some sly daughter of the Cat People lures away my husband. Proud Woman may have bested enemy warriors, but she will meet her match when she goes against Morning Song!"

The dog applauded her with a flourish of his tail.

"And I will waste no more time trying to become someone I am not, never could be, and do not want to be. No one has ever called me beautiful, or graceful, or said that I owned the courage of a seasoned warrior—but that did not prevent Cloud Racer from loving me in the beginning. If I was able to win him then, I can win him again. No matter what Proud Woman has to offer him."

White Shadow barked encouragement and matched his pace to hers as they plunged into the coolness of the oak grove.

"If an Iroquois warrior is worth three from any other tribe," she muttered, sending a chunk of deadwood flying with a savage kick, "then a woman of the Longhouse People is worth six from the Erie tribe! As both my husband and Proud Woman will soon be learning."

How she would teach them was still to be worked out, but she would find a way. When she had wanted to hunt, she had learned to send an arrow straight and true to its mark; when she had opposed the betrothal her mother arranged for her, she found a way out of it; when Teller Of Legends insisted Cloud Racer was the man for her, she had dared to snatch him from under the nose of her own cousin. She came to a halt, looked down at her faithful dog. "And when you were marked for sacrifice, Shadow, who rescued you?

"I never realized before," she went on, "that I have done so much merely because I would not let myself think that I couldn't."

Her mouth twisted wryly. "In stubbornness, if in nothing else, I believe I am more than equal to the Erie maiden."

And certain of her accomplishments had required forethought and detailed planning, so here was something else she was capable of. Proud Woman's beauty, the valor Cloud Racer credited her with, her willingness to serve others, even the fascinating aloofness the maiden cloaked herself in—what would they be worth against a strategy that took them into consideration? How could they prevail against an obstinate refusal to admit or accept defeat?

Her thoughts raced ahead of her as she left the oaks far behind. Neither Cloud Racer nor Proud Woman knew she had been awakened to the truth; that was also in Morning Song's favor. Had not Cloud Racer himself told her that the element of surprise often decrees whether a war band will be victors or vanquished?

She snapped a dry cane from the raspberry bushes that drooped over the trail, swung it idly as she continued with her scheming. White Shadow eyed the stick hopefully; would she toss it for him to fetch? When she did not, he sighed, but his mistress was too engrossed to notice his disappointment.

A few moments later, Morning Song echoed her dog's sigh. She seemed to be placing her husband in the enemy camp and this was distasteful to her. She brightened a little; she would name him neutral instead. And if that made him but a trophy for the conqueror to claim? Well, that was how it must be—for now. The Morning Song who had felled a great stag with a single arrow and outwitted an enraged she-wolf had not let doubt distract her; and the Morning Song whose preoccupation had brought her to an unfamiliar part of the forest was confident that, in the end, Cloud Racer would be wholly hers once more.

The breeze that was the harbinger of evening rustled the leaves of tree and shrub. When its cool fingers rippled Shadow's fur and Morning Song's unbound hair, the young woman became aware that they had come a remarkably long way from the village. "We will never reach home before full dark," she said ruefully as she urged Shadow around to begin their return journey. "But Swift Arrow has told my grandmother where we are, and even if we have not done so recently, it will not be the first time you and I have stayed away overlong."

She swatted at a deserted spiderweb with the stick she held, then set out so briskly that her dog was hard put to keep up with her. "You have grown fat and lazy since last we spent a day in the forest," she teased affectionately. "When I have restored peace and order to my hearth, we shall come here more often, I think. We have always been—''

What it was Morning Song and White Shadow had always been was left unsaid. All at once her companion stiffened and growled in his throat. Morning Song, startled, looked up—and met the unwinking stare of two tall men who were strangers to her. One carried a spear, the other a war club; and they stood elbow-to-elbow, blocking her path.

She could not speak. She rested her left hand on Shadow's erect hackles and prayed he would remember that this was the signal to stay quiet. And although she yearned to close her eyes and hope that when she looked a second time the men would be gone, she dared not let her steady gaze falter.

For these men that barred her way were not hunters from one of the other Iroquois villages. Their weapons, their headdresses, proclaimed them warriors; and what she saw in their faces, the ready-to-pounce tension of their oiled bodies, told her that it was not by right of birth that they walked in Iroquois territory.

Morning Song's eyes ached from being stretched so wide. Somewhere a bird called, spilling drops of music onto the trees, and brown pinecones danced among green needles as though responding to its rhythm. The shadows were lengthening and flattening as, beyond the forest, the sun dipped into the west. Morning Song, with her white dog rigid beside her, stood fast and wondered bleakly what was going to happen next. The possibilities were varied and none of them appealed.

At last one of the warriors moved, gestured toward Morning Song, and spoke to his comrade. She could not understand his words, but she glimpsed the symbols embroidered on his quiver and recognized them as birds and muskrats. She knew from hearsay what tribe saw the wind as a huge bird and believed that their race had been born from the union of a muskrat with their Spirit Ancestor. These men were Algonquin, and they had no intention of allowing her to pass unmolested.

Since she was a child, Morning Song had heard tales about the Algonquin. Terrible tales. That she was a woman would not move them to mercy. They would kill her, and rejoice to. The best she might hope for was that death would come quickly.

The men had begun to argue, using their hands for emphasis. Morning Song's eyes narrowed in speculation. If death was inevitable, and to die quickly desirable, then there must be something she could do to hasten it. All thoughts of Cloud Racer fled her mind; her children might never have been born; and Teller Of Legends and the rest of Morning Song's family became no more substantial than the dusk that was graying the world. Later, when she walked with the spirits, she would permit herself to think of them again and weep because she had left them so abruptly. In this moment, she could concentrate on nothing but her own end, and how she might bring it about swiftly, swiftly. . . .

The fingers of her right hand tightened around the stick she had broken from the berry bush. It could scarcely serve as a proper weapon. But it wore thorns, and the flexibility that denied it clout might possibly be turned to her advantage.

Shadow tensed as he felt her gathering herself for what she meant to do, and his brown eyes slanted toward her. Morning Song prayed that he would not betray her intentions to those she wanted ignorant of them until the very last moment.

He did not. And when she was ready, when she had inhaled deeply and told herself firmly that this was the best way, the only way, she brought up her arm and lashed out with the raspberry cane, using it like a whip to strike the face of the Algonquin warrior closest to her.

He grunted, raised one hand to his cheek as though unable to account for the stinging pain. But his companion—who carried the spear—swung on the instant to face Morning Song. And it was his arm that lifted this time, that raised the spear so the head of it pointed at the tight-lipped woman's breast. Morning Song closed her eyes as he drew back just enough to lunge forward and thrust its lethal tip home; closed her eyes and waited for the quick, clean death she had contrived for.

It did not come. Instead, there was a shout from behind her, followed at once by a hate-filled snarl from the dog at her side. Then there came a laugh, a laugh that iced the blood in her veins and puckered the flesh on the nape of her neck.

There was no need for her to open her eyes and turn around to identify the man who found this situation so amusing. Yet she did so and kept a restraining hand on Shadow all the while.

Stag Leaping, his eyes gleeful, swaggered towards her. Behind him walked two more Algonquin warriors.

If Morning Song's position had been perilous before, how much more so was it now! Yet she would not add to Stag Leaping's amusement by cowering before him. "I had heard," she said coldly, "that you ran to the enemy. It is something traitors do, I suppose."

Shadow, who had recognized the man before Morning Song

could, snarled again, and Stag Leaping came to a halt well before he reached her. "There are tribes," he said, flicking his eyes at the dog and scowling, "who recognize a man's worth, and reward it when his own people refuse to. A hero-song will be chanted for me when I go back to the northern country, Morning Song!"

She snorted. This braggart had never received anything but contempt from her; it was all she would offer him now.

He ignored the derision in the sound, strutted from one side to the other of the narrow trail without taking his eyes from her. At length he nodded, approving some conclusion he'd come to. "When I have been named war leader," he said, "I mean to take a wife. Unfortunately"—he ceased his pacing, let his gaze slowly travel the length of Morning Song—"I have yet to meet an Algonquin maid who tempts me. Oh, many have tried; but there are things I look for in a woman that all of them have lacked."

"Your *friends* will not be happy, to hear you insult their women."

He shrugged. "They know only a word or two of our tongue. I speak to you alone, Morning Song. For it occurs to me"—he stroked his chin contemplatively but his eyes were hot—"that a man adopted into a tribe might as well marry a woman who has also been received into it. And the Algonquin are shrewd; they will adopt a female captive who is strong and healthy."

The fingers she'd buried in Shadow's silky fur spasmed. The dog, advised of the new rage that surged through her, lowered his head and pleaded silently to be permitted to attack.

"If you think—"

He laughed again. "*You* must think, Morning Song. About what will become of you if you decline. I offer you life, a life that shall be forfeit otherwise. And I can promise you," he added when she made no response, "that the manner of your dying would be unpleasant." He barked several words to the watchful warriors. All four looked to Morning Song and chortled. One rubbed his hands together, and the rasping sound produced, taken together with a gesture Morning Song had no difficulty deciphering, sponsored hoots of laughter.

With an effort, she controlled a shiver. "I shall continue to refuse you," she said to the man who had counted on this byplay to persuade her, "so long as there is a single breath left in me." She did not shout, did not force defiance into her voice. Its unnatural flatness verified what she said.

Stag Leaping glowered. "Perhaps I should describe," he said, "what my friends and I do to those we take prisoner."

She regarded him stonily and resolved not to listen.

'There is a place we know of, on the edge of Iroquois Territory, where no one ever comes. When we are in the mood for sport we take our captives there and bind them to stakes. They will never fall down, these stakes. We dug steep-sided holes to contain the saplings we felled—healthy young saplings that resist burning—and surrounded their lower ends with close-packed boulders before we shoveled dirt back into the holes and tamped it down. The earth all around is blackened now, from the fires we lit to tickle the feet of our prisoners—and that is a pity because it will prevent you seeing the blood that has seeped into it—but the stakes stand ready to receive as many as we care to bring to them. One of them waits for you, Morning Song.''

Morning Song had been unable to shut out his words. "You seem to have forgotten," she said stoutly, "that we Iroquois are quite familiar with the ceremony of torture."

If she had thought to fetter his tongue, she was mistaken. "I do not speak of ritual," he spat. "We have no interest in testing the courage of those we torture, and still less in honoring them. We relish their screams and their cries for mercy. When they beg for death, we find it amusing. Nor do we hold with this foolishness of bringing food and drink when they weaken. It is no *ceremony* you will be taking part in, Morning Song, but a prolonged and painful dying." He grinned again, jerked his thumb toward the Algonquin. "Strong Arm is a master with the cudgel," he said. "He can break one bone, or two, or a dozen, by the amount of force he puts behind each blow. And he delivers his blows slowly, so that you see the club approaching arm or leg or shoulder and guess the exact spot it will land. Wolf In Winter prefers to work with sharpened splinters. He has devised a way to insert them under fingernails and toenails, and into the nostrils and the ears and the navel and the anus. And he, too, finds his work more satisfying when it is done without haste."

Morning Song swallowed, balled her hands so their unsteadiness would not be seen by the man who was taking such pleasure in this torture-before-torture. She cast her mind back to a confrontation she had had with a younger Stag Leaping. When it had been only the two of them, Morning Song had made short shrift of him. Doubtless he, too, remembered, and gloried to take revenge. Supported by four stalwarts who were brothers of the spirit if not the blood, he named himself invincible. His voice gradually took on the quality of a throbbing water drum. Every word he uttered was fondled before it was released; and those that did not prick fastened like leeches to Morning Song's soul.

"Thunder Roaring has a cache of lances—some long, some short—and a splendid array of knives," Stag Leaping was saying now. "He likes to cut, to see blood run out, but he is cautious. I have seen his blades go so deep that it seems the heart or lungs or spleen must surely be punctured. And if that happened too soon"— he spread his blunt-fingered hand—"the rest of us would be less than delighted with him. But Thunder Roaring is skillful; he always stops just short of killing." He looked approvingly at the man whose face Morning Song had struck with her makeshift whip. "We are grateful for his skill, and you will discover why we praise him for it.

"We have praise for Screaming Cat as well," he went on, gesturing toward the fourth man—who promptly folded his arms and scowled at Morning Song. "The fire must be burning steadily before you have the chance to appreciate him, however. It excites Screaming Cat to watch flesh shrivel and blister when heat is applied to it, and his touch is so sure that I have seen him trace symbols on back or chest or belly or buttocks with the tip of a flaming fagot." He frowned. "You are not big enough to permit him to produce his boldest designs, I'm afraid, but he will manage well enough. It may be he shall choose to work a pair of coiled serpents, one on each of your admirable breasts. I will put the suggestion to him, but it shall be for him to decide."

Morning Song had given up trying to escape the sound of that gloating voice, and was bent on foiling Stag Leaping's aim. How much more he would gloat, if he could make her suffer the torture twice over! They are only *words*, she told herself. Words cannot hurt, cannot smite or pierce or slash or burn. But when what he described became real—and she did not question that it would— how long could she endure the sight of her own blood gushing out, the stench of her own flesh charring, the unrelenting pain? Panic gnawed at her vitals and she fought to subdue it. *Words*, she told herself again; they are only *words*.

Stag Leaping was disgruntled that he had not won the response he'd been looking for. This woman had always taken joy in thwarting him, he remembered. He knew, vaguely, that it was one of the reasons she fascinated him. But his fellows—like him renegades from one of the raiding parties that had swept south during the last green season—were growing restless. They would not wait much longer for him to convince Morning Song that marriage to Stag Leaping was vastly preferable to being taken prisoner by his band. And when, by her own choice, she was his woman . . . His loins quickened at the thought, and lust seasoned his concluding arguments.

"You will be the first woman we have brought to our place of torture, you see," he said, his eyes gleaming, "and we shall vary our methods accordingly. The first fractures must be confined to your arms and legs, I think. Wolf In Winter will be advised to restrict himself similarly, at the start. Until the second day, your breasts and buttocks"—his lips glistened, appeared fuller than they had been—"must be only lightly carved; but since Thunder Roaring will be eager as the rest of us to make use of the first woman we have seen in several months, he will refrain from damaging those parts of you that are designed to pleasure a man. Or, in this instance, men."

He flicked out his tongue, ran it across his lower lip, then his upper one. "Afterward, of course, it shall make no difference. To us. To you? Well"—his laugh was harsh, ugly—"I can speak only for myself, of course. I plan to demonstrate to Screaming Cat how I have benefited from what he's been teaching me. Since you have borne two children, perhaps you will stretch easily enough to receive the smoldering fagot that I intend to put where my penis has lately been. Or"—he bared his teeth—"perhaps not."

Morning Song screamed. The arching sound, torn from unwilling lips, spiraled up and up; the evening air reverberated with it. And Shadow leaped.

The warriors who stood behind Morning Song closed in on her, seized her arms, and twisted them behind her back. Yet it was not at them that the white fury sprang. It was his mistress's old enemy, and his, that the dog went for with fangs exposed and eyes slitted with hate.

Stag Leaping threw up one arm to shield his face, flung out the other, and closed his fingers around the war club Thunder Roaring thrust into it.

White Shadow was in midflight when the awful blow fell, and the sickening thud that sent him plummeting to the ground was never to be erased from Morning Song's memory. Nor was the unspeakable thing that Stag Leaping did then. Wrapping both hands around the club, he raised it and brought it down, raised it and brought it down, until the narrow trail he stood on, the bushes that lined it, the lower branches of the trees on either side, were spattered with red-dyed tufts of pale fur, with chunks of raw and bloody flesh, with shards and slivers of bone. Like obscene, late-blooming flowers, they clung to leaf and twig.

And when the warriors who gripped her slender wrists shoved

ıer ahead of them toward the spot where their canoes were hidden, Morning Song was made to tread upon ground thickly carpeted with this same unholy growth.

Chapter 28

Whiplike vines bit cruelly into wrist and waist and ankle, and Morning Song's blistered fingers were unaware that the flaming splinters had long since disintegrated into ash. But worse than both of those was the stench emanating from her singed hair. Cloud Racer, whose economy of words was legend, had once made a song about Morning Song's hair. Every joy-bringing phrase of it returned to her now, and the tears she had refused to shed in response to pain were a boiling cataract behind her eyes.

She came close to letting them fall. Who would know? Her captors, wrapped in blankets against the night's chill, slept as only the unconscionable can. No one would witness Morning Song's surrender to despair, except forest creatures whose habit it was to roam at night.

But the stubbornness that had earlier forbidden her to cry did not relax its guard. So she concentrated instead on the animals who, after all, would have no weeping woman to fix their yellow eyes on. What—besides lynx and mouse and raccoon—might be walking soft among the trees this night? She closed her eyes and a parade of images offered themselves: beaver, wolf, deer, bear . . . all of the creatures who had visited her during her long-ago Vision Quest. For a moment, she let herself believe that they truly were out there in the darkness. Then she blinked, and they were gone. Which was a pity. Had she been able to conjure up living beasts, they might have rescued her, just as the beasts had rallied to save the life of a wounded warrior in one of Teller Of Legends's stories.

What foolishness, to think that such things really happened when imagination was the sole begetter of so many legends. She strained once more against bonds she knew would not give way, swallowed a scream as they tore into raw and bleeding flesh, and sought distraction from the pain by snatching back her scattered thoughts.

There had been another tale her grandmother had told, about a grotesque head. Like the animals of Morning Song's vision, there had been no body attached to it, and that was doubtless the reason memory called it up.

It had been a monstrous thing, this mythical head, with huge wings extending from its hairy cheeks, but in the end a young woman had bested it by means of a clever ruse. Something to do with persuading the Flying Head to swallow red-hot stones by pretending to do so herself . . .

Morning Song's bowed head lifted suddenly. Was it possible that even seemingly preposterous legends, like visions, had a cache of precious meat hidden deep in worthless shell?

One of the blanket-wrapped figures stirred, mumbled, and tossed aside his cover. Morning Song froze as she recognized Stag Leaping, but he spared no glance for her, only stumbled in the direction of the nearest tree. She heard him grunt, identified the hiss of urine as he relieved himself, watched him shuffling back to where his companions lay snoring. Hatred flooded into her and its acid seeped into her nostrils, her throat. Since she'd been a girl she'd loathed this man. Now . . . She struggled against nausea as she recalled his exultation when he'd swung a borrowed club to destroy the huddle of bloodied fur that was her beloved White Shadow. And she knew, suddenly and surely, that she must not only survive this ordeal, but escape what remained of it. To go unresisting to the slaughter, to meekly subject herself to the rape and torture that would only end with her dying, was to reward a monster for his barbarity. It was akin to chanting the praises of someone who was unworthy even of contempt.

Her eyes narrowed as they tracked his progress over the uneven ground. "Stag Leaping!" As soon as she whispered his name, she wondered why she'd been so reckless and what she would say if he responded. Well, it would come to her. It must!

She croaked his name twice more before he swung his head around; then he took so long to approach the sapling she was lashed to, and was so indifferent to the pebbles his unwary toes drove before him, that she feared one of the others might rouse before he reached her.

They did not. But when he was so close that Morning Song, had her hands been free, might have reached out and touched him, what to say continued to elude her. Finally, "Water!" she gasped. "I . . . must have . . . water."

He laughed unpleasantly. "No," he said, and began to turn away. "Wait," she called weakly, and to her relief he hesitated. When

ne saw him turn back, she lubricated her cracked lips with the tip
f her swollen tongue. "Stag Leaping," she choked, "if you will
t me drink, I will be your woman."

He came close enough this time for his unsavory breath to foul
ne air in front of her face. "I find it hard to accept," he said, "that
ou are agreeable now to what you scorned before we came here.
And if the mild torture you have endured so far has changed your
nind, I am no longer certain you are fit to be the wife of Stag
Leaping."

She made her tone placating, no simple thing when her parched
nroat scraped nuance from every word. The thirst she begged re-
pite from was real. "Had I been sure I would belong to you alone,"
ne faltered, "I would have agreed then. But I thought the others
vould insist . . ." She let her voice trail off. He had listened to her
isjointed explanation without interrupting; could this mean he be-
eved it?

"No man may share what is mine," he blustered. "Did you
nink me unable to defend you?"

She let herself sag against her bonds. "They are so many," she
ighed. "I was afraid you might have to watch the friend of your
hildhood, the maid you claimed once to love, rough-treated and
hamed." Although its shape was disguised, it was a challenge
renched in honey that she set before him. And Stag Leaping was
nough of an Iroquois still to take it up.

"I am leader of this raiding party," he said strongly, and so
oudly that once again Morning Song expected one of his compan-
ons to awaken. "The others follow in my footsteps. They go when
say go, and stop when I say stop. They would not dare lay hand
n you should I forbid it. They have learned to respect the power
f Stag Leaping, as his woman must also." He studied her drawn
ace, her pleading eyes. "She must earn his trust as well," he said,
"which you have not. I think that nothing but thirst makes you offer
ourself to me. That, and your dread of the sport my friends and I
vill have with you tomorrow."

She tensed. He was not entirely a fool, this one; she must use
aution. Yet she felt sure that his bold eyes burned now as they had
vhen he'd stripped her, and she doubted that the welts scarring her
vody would dilute his lust. Indeed, they would likely whet his ap-
vetite! If only it were not so dark, and the fire so low; she would
give much to be able to read his expression.

"If you bring me water," she said piteously, "I will prove what
say by lying with you this very night. And I promise you pleasures

that forcing yourself upon me would deny you. What joy can come from taking me in turn with your comrades, Stag Leaping?"

His laugh was grating, but it held a hint of excitement. "You say this only to persuade me to loose you. And I have said that I do not trust you."

She moaned and made herself droop again, wished that the ropes that held her upright might let her posture to better effect. "To what purpose?" she asked, raising her head with visible effort. "I am at your mercy, Stag Leaping, and know that I am."

Again he studied her in silence; then he laughed on a different note. "It pleases me to hear you beg, Morning Song," he said, and folded his arms. "Tell me more of these pleasures that will be mine if I do as you ask."

With scarcely a pause to think, she did. "My breasts shall be ripe melons for you to suck the nectar from," she said softly, "and you will believe it is a legend you are living. For the harder you suckle, the sweeter shall be the juice that spills from them. And when you are sated, you may lie back and let this grateful woman use her lips, her tongue, to taste the sweetness of your flesh, to coax your manhood to an awesome size."

On and on she went, and although the salacious imagery she teased him with, the verbal caresses, left the taste of vomit in her mouth, no brooding pigeon ever cooed so seductively. Even her need to drink, and drink deep, became of no account. She remembered the pretend-dreams she'd related to her friends in a different time, a different place; the talent was with her still. Teller Of Legends at her best, she thought grimly, had never made myth sound so plausible.

Her sultry murmur threatened to become a rasp, and the trembling of simulated arousal had almost depleted her resourcefulness when Stag Leaping yanked a knife from the sheath strapped to his thigh. Sweat beaded on Morning Song's upper lip; had he realized what she was trying to achieve? Would Morning Song end her life with extravagant promises of sexual delights still hovering on her deceitful lips? Well, she would at least be granted the swift end she had prayed for. And Stag Leaping and his fellows would be cheated of their entertainment.

His attack on the thongs that bound her left her weak as a newborn pup, but it was all to the good that she slumped into his arms when the last one parted. When he made as if to lower her to the ground and mount her there and then, however, she recovered herself.

"They will hear!" she said sharply, and the fear she expressed was not pretense.

Stag Leaping, panting in his eagerness and fully erect, saw the sense in her protest. He prodded her ahead of him to where close-growing shrubs made a barrier between the two and the Algonquin. Then, with escalating impatience, he attempted once more to shove her to the pebble-strewn ground.

She produced a convincing giggle. "First remove your tunic and breechclout," she whispered. "I am fond of flesh against flesh, Stag Leaping."

He made a strangled sound and his shaking hands scrabbled at the hem of his grease-stained garment.

"I will do it *for* you," she said, and seized the tunic's fringe with fingers that took no note of their painful blistering.

She tugged upwards, let her right arm drop as folds of deerskin briefly veiled his face. *Please,* she prayed, *let me find what I seek!*

And it was there. A rock, large and reassuringly sharp-edged, thrust itself into her groping hand. She raised it, poised it, put all the strength she could command into its descent. Stag Leaping exhaled with a satisfying *whoosh* and crumpled to the ground.

She hit him once more, to be safe, and a third time in honor of a white dog who surely watched from the world he had gone to and who would rejoice to be avenged. She cared not a whit if the blows killed Stag Leaping, did not even stoop to see if he was dead before she dragged his tunic the rest of the way over his lolling head and threw it over hers. It was far too large, and its smell disgusted her, but clothe herself she must. She had neither the time nor the energy to deal with the sense of vulnerability that nakedness imposes upon a woman.

She shot a glance at the inert form sprawled at her feet. Never again would Morning Song doubt that even the most absurd legends may yield kernels of wisdom to the careful gleaner. Then she spun on her heel and considered what to do next.

Escape! That was what all of this had been in aid of, and she must not delay for an instant. Stag Leaping might or might not be dead; his companions were not.

She made for the forest, and not until she found herself in a glade surrounded by sky-sweeping evergreens did she pause to study the stars above her head, and in particular the single star that remained fixed while all of its kin circled around it. It was to the south that she must go, and then to the west; she was certain of that. Terrified though she'd been during their journey, she had managed to mark that they had traveled east before they headed north.

When she left the glade, she kept the fixed star at her back. She was plodding now; the torments and tribulations of the day just past were taking their toll, and she stumbled often over nothing at all. Fear and stubborness were all that kept her moving; and when she spotted the river her captors had followed north, a sob of thankfulness rose like a bubble and burst from her lips. She knelt and drank, then splashed water over her face until she rid herself of the worst of her fatigue. Now she would simply follow this winding ribbon of water to where it straightened itself and sent out a tributary to the southwest. It was here that her abductors had left their canoes, and to come upon them would confirm that she was on course.

But before she reached the junction of the rivers, ears sensitive as a doe's were twitching in response to faint but unmistakable sounds of pursuit. Either Stag Leaping had regained consciousness, or his fellows had awakened, or both. It was no more than she had been expecting, but her chances of outdistancing the warriors were halved because they'd picked up her trail so soon. They had been refreshed and strengthened by slumber; Morning Song had not. Dare she hope at all to make good her blundering escape?

She knew what punishment awaited her if she failed to. She began to run, heedless of the noise she made, indifferent to her complaining muscles and the light-headedness that exhaustion plagued her with. Mercifully, numbness dropped like a shroud around her. The pounding of her bare feet was all that she heard, and the whine of her labored breathing. Instinct, not awareness, made her streaming eyes recognize the twin canoes when suddenly she came upon them. As she jerked to a trembling halt, she saw that she still carried in her hand the jagged rock that had felled Stag Leaping. Morning Song made herself wait until just enough strength returned to her; then she used the rock to slash the hull of one of the canoes.

She regarded the second with distrust even as she heaved it upright. The paddles lay beneath. She picked them up gingerly, flung all but one of them into the river, and steeled herself to make for the single exit open to her.

She drew a ragged breath and pushed the canoe into the river, leaped into it before it surged away from the bank. It rocked crazily, and she gripped its slender sides until it steadied. Then she seized the paddle and plunged it into the water.

She stifled a scream when one thrust carried her into the current, and her aching body clenched. Rock-ribbed she was, and when she attempted a second jab with the paddle, the canoe canted and she was drenched by the water that poured into it.

It was cold, that water; but that was not what set Morning Song's teeth to chattering and made her shiver violently. The elm-bark craft, lacking direction, began to drift shoreward, was blithely returning her to the place she was frantic to be away from. She yanked on the paddle; the canoe geed and hawed, tipped this way and that, and water flooded into it once more.

How can I guide this thing, she raged silently, when my slightest movement sets it listing? Yet I know that it can be done. If only I could figure out how . . .

Inclining her head cautiously, she stared down at her bent knees and frowned. Balance. It must be a question of balance. Perhaps if she centered herself more precisely?

With her lower lip caught between her teeth, she moved one knee warily, then made herself relax so that her body weight shifted in harmony with it. The canoe rocked; the water she'd already taken in sloshed disagreeably; but there was no fearful tilting this time, and no fresh influx of river water.

It occurred to her that the deliberate loosening of her bunched tendons might have contributed to the success of her maneuver. Although her vigilant ears warned that her pursuers were drawing closer with every second, Morning Song concentrated all her attention on slowing the beating of her heart. This was the only antidote to tension that she knew, and she prayed it would be effective now.

It was. As her breathing deepened and evened, she became once more mistress of herself. Fingers, toes, elbows, knees—all of her that had been frozen by fear and frustration—were leached of rigidity and answered to control.

She watched her fingers resettle themselves around the paddle, felt her body sway easily, naturally, as she dipped the blade. When a strong tug took her back into the west-flowing current, she wanted to shout for joy. And after a second thrust had borne her farther still from the shore, she let herself believe—a little—that Stag Leaping and his friends were well and truly cheated of their quarry.

Only then did she permit herself to recognize that water—the restlessly moving water she had ever dreaded and shunned—was acting as her savior; it would, *if* Morning Song could remain in command of this contrary canoe, eventually take her safely home.

She adjusted her bent knees so that neither bore undue weight, then squeezed her eyes shut and begged memory to assist her. The clumsy thrusts she'd been making would never take her where she needed to go, but time and again she'd watched the warriors setting off in these water-skimmers. Even young boys handled them easily, particularly when there were two to lift and dip the flat-bladed paddles. Still, one person alone was enough; warriors-to-be delighted to race across the river this way.

She took firm hold of the worn paddle, placing one hand atop the grip so that it would not slip when she reached forward to begin a stroke, and peered out over the dark water to decide whether to make the first one on her left or her right. The current was bearing her straight down the middle of the river. Surely it made no difference which way she began, so long as a second stroke was made on the opposite side?

There was one way to find out. She dug the blade into the water that flowed on her left and drew back on the paddle as though to sweep the water behind her. The canoe hove over slightly, and she stopped breathing until it righted itself.

Now on the right. Droplets of cold water sprayed her, merged with salt-flavored sweat as she brought the paddle over and initiated the balancing stroke. No. Her grip was wrong now. She groaned, rearranged her hands, dipped the blade—just moments before the elm-bark craft careened into the riverbank.

She must be quicker, then. And the stroking must be mastered here, where the water ran quiet. Sweat dripped into her eyes, her blistered fingers burned hotter than they had when the fire seared them, and her muscles pleaded for respite, yet she persevered. She scarcely noticed when the stars winked out, when the blackness that cloaked the world began to bleach. She was deaf to the sleepy twitterings of birds nesting in the trees on both sides of the river. Morning Song went on pitting her paddle against the strength of the current—on the right, on the left; on the right, on the left—until she happened upon a rhythm that gave her a degree of control.

But her breath was a clangor in her chest, and the pressure on her raw fingers an agony. While pink unrolled across the eastern horizon and fringed the ripples on her left, and the fully roused songbirds began their tribute to new-come day, she slumped upon her bruised and aching knees. She could not go on; she could not. This too was torment . . . torture. Tears scorched her eyes and blurred her vision.

Her brother the sun peeked shyly over the tallest hill, and warbler, grosbeak, finch, sparrow, and flycatcher went into a fervor of harmonious praise. Morning Song lifted her head, swung it slowly from side to side. The birds that sang so sweetly, that never failed to express their joy because light and warmth had been given back to them, could not know at dawn whether they would survive the bright day they were welcoming. Prey they were, to hawk and eagle, to arrows gone astray from the bows of would-be hunters. The fledglings they tended might tumble from the nest and be pounced upon by weasel or fox. Yet this did not mute their songs. And if broad-winged, taloned kin circled above their heads, they did not simply fold their wings and wait to be devoured! Like all creatures, they took what precautions they could to protect and preserve themselves, and trusted that they would be around to usher in the next day's dawning.

And what of White Shadow, who had died trying to protect Morning Song? Should she dishonor his memory by submitting to something he had given his life to save her from? Was this wretched woman to show herself less stalwart than bird or beast?

She flexed her fingers and cried out. The knotted muscles in shoulders and upper arms could and must be ignored. But her hands . . . somehow she must shield them. She looked around. The bank was low on either side and, if the brown tinge to the water spoke truly, was constructed more of soil than of granite. Trees and shrubs grew nearly to the river's edge and arched their leafy branches over it. But leaves, however broad, however cool their dew-glistening surfaces must be to the touch, would slip and slide if she tried to use them for padding. Moss would be better, but she dared not risk beaching her craft to find some. She had no notion how to land, and who could say how close her pursuers might be?

She glanced down at the filthy tunic she'd stolen from the man she'd outfoxed. Its hem was a separate strip, taken from a discarded garment, perhaps, and sewn onto a new. And if she had no knife, she did own something that could substitute for one.

She checked to be certain the lazy current still carried her forward, that she was not drifting too much to one side or the other, then yanked up the tunic and began tearing at the stitching with her teeth. The dirt-encrusted hide left a foul taste in her mouth, made her gag more than once, but in the end the strands parted and her mutilated fingers were able to rip them free the rest of the way.

As she wound the narrow length of hide around the paddle's grip and the upper section of its handle, she glanced frequently over her shoulder and stretched her ears for sounds of stealthy footfalls. She had lingered overlong in this part of the river; she must press on, take herself beyond the reach of Stag Leaping's band, and somehow make her way back to the village.

She crouched rather than knelt this time, and would do so until the river swung to the west, until—fed by scores of underground streams—it widened and quickened. Then, when she would need all the leverage she could muster, she'd go back on her knees. It had not taken much experience to teach her that. She must go as quickly as possible, but she must also conserve her strength for the rougher water ahead. The water that led to the rapids . . .

She tried to recall just where the downpouring of white water had forced her captors and their prisoner out of the canoes, how long they had carried the boats through the forest before they were able to launch them again. For Morning Song had no intention of letting herself be drawn into and over the terrifying frenzy of foam that roared between towering rocks and pounded upon a nightmarish array of sharp-toothed boulders. Just to think of it set her to trembling.

The sky was a vibrant blue now, the water—deeper than it had been—more gray than brown and streaked here and there with green. A family of crested ducks swam single file along the water's edge. Beyond them a moose, come to drink, shook his huge head and stared at the canoe that was making for his watering spot. Had Morning Song's situation been other than it was, she would have thrilled to the splendor of this summer day. But she could spare only the most fleeting of thoughts for anything save the lifting and plunging of the paddle that kept her moving steadily along the south-flowing river.

It expanded so gradually that she did not immediately recognize what was happening. Until she was forced to maneuver around an outcrop of shattered rock—an exercise that proved more daunting in the anticipation than in the accomplishing—she did not realize how such a projection at the start of her precipitate voyage would have barred her way. Then she noticed how the river's banks had moved back, how berry bush and bracken and holly had retreated to more than ten-paddle lengths from where she squatted in a canoe that despite its sturdy construction, seemed to her fearfully flimsy.

Yet it responded obediently when, some minutes later, she approached the bend which the sun's position confirmed marked the veering to the west. Here, isolated boulders thrust gleaming heads above the surface of water that frothed around them. Had she not been so intent on navigating the turn, Morning Song would have been filled with trepidation. Why it was that one of those boulders, lurking beneath the fretful water, did not catch her unawares, was a thing she never did understand. Perhaps the spirits who guarded the world's watery places decided among themselves that this woman of the Iroquois should be permitted to pass unharmed. Perhaps her safe passage was no more than happenstance. Whatever the reason, she was grateful for it, encouraged by it.

Which was as well. In this westward-pointing leg of the river, the current was not so predictable; new techniques needed to be learned. Morning Song, after an aggravation of false moves, discovered how to turn the paddle's blade until the flat of it was parallel to the canoe and then to stroke outward. That helped her to hold to a reasonably straight course, but she was drenched in sweat by the time she'd chanced upon the strategy. The vaster expanse of water surrounding her, the canoe's inclination to rock at the least provocation, revived and nurtured all her long-held fears. Now no amount of resolve could keep them at bay.

A kingfisher, perched on the limb of a tree lightning had toppled into the river, tossed a wriggling fish into the air and caught it in his long bill as it descended. Morning Song's attention was distracted by the glittering scales of the bird's prey, and she was suddenly reminded of her own gnawing hunger. She shook her head to clear it, swung the paddle from right to left to sustain a rhythm that had become automatic now, and frowned. The river she traveled possessed a voice, and she realized that its purling monotone had altered subtly while she'd been preoccupied. There was a depth to its throaty murmur which had not been there before.

She raised her eyes to the trees gliding by. They were passing into and out of her sight more rapidly than they had been, surely. That could only mean that the current was accelerating. She drew in her paddle; the canoe rushed on unaided.

The numbing lethargy which is the legacy of ordeal upon ordeal dissolved; Morning Song became alert as a wolf on the prowl. She shaded her eyes with one hand, peered downriver, and was stunned to find her view obstructed by squall-like clouds of spume. The white water that marked the beginning of the rapids! How had she come upon them so soon?

The thrust of the current answered her question. And she had no energy to waste upon speculation, in any event; all of her waning strength must be marshaled to take her swiftly to the shore.

She seized the paddle, plunged it into the water on her right, stroked once, twice, three times to persuade the canoe to turn about. It did—in a complete circle. And all the while the current bore it downriver. She tossed the hair out of her eyes, began the maneuver again, made herself wait after the first stroke until momentum swung the canoe to the left. A half stroke, a prompt feathering of the blade that was done purely by instinct, and she and her elmbark craft were pointed toward the nearest landfall. She began to paddle furiously—to the right, to the left; to the right, to the left—plunging the blade deep into the water each time, pulling back on it with every ounce of strength she owned. She was on her knees again, and the sinews bulged in her slender arms, her wrists cramped, and her abused fingers oozed drops of blood that mingled with the spray spawned by her vigorous paddling. Yet the shore, its shape continually changing, stayed as stubbornly beyond her reach as it had been at the start. She sat athwart the current, but she was still being borne downriver. Downriver, to where the rapids waited.

They waited for Morning Song. Having confronted this awful truth, she was all at once icy calm. She let the canoe swing back so that it faced squarely the challenge she was being forced to meet. The river's bass voice was a roar now, a roar that bounced from the sheer rock walls bordering the cascade and echoed in her ears like thunder. Directly ahead, gleaming lances of water shot high into the air, and Morning Song used her paddle to steer the canoe into the rift where the river's bore reigned supreme. Then she closed her eyes and abandoned herself to its whim.

Chapter 29

⟸ ⟹

She was a child's ball tossed into a hurricane, a spinning, slewing, weightless thing sucked into a maelstrom. All connection with time and space, with any sense of self, was obliterated. Her mangled fingers had grafted themselves to the sides of the canoe, yet no pain radiated from them, or from the rest of her bruised and battered body. She did not feel the sting as dripping strands of hair slapped viciously against her face. If her heart still beat, the throb of it was drowned in the pulsing of the cataract she was riding. Briefly, confusedly, she recognized the eerie serenity that comes with submitting to the inevitable, the unavoidable, the all-powerful.

Then she was plummeting downward, a bit of flotsam swept up by a giant's broom. Morning Song opened her mouth to scream, clamped it shut—the sound still locked in her throat—as the water that was over, under, everywhere around her, flooded into it.

A bone-rattling thump, a screech of rent timbers, and she was no longer falling. Her eyes snapped open, fought to adjust to a world of boiling mists, while her ears tried to muzzle the bellowing of the crazed river she had hoped would take her home. The canoe

at had brought her this far would take her no farther; hung up on
e jagged peak of a submerged boulder, broadside to the tyran-
cal current, it was pivoting with obscene slowness, indifferent to
e fate of the woman who clung to its splintered sides. In thrall to
e river whose master it had been, the wounded craft swung up
d back, up and back, as the water surged and receded. And the
oman who huddled in the bottom of it knew that her end had
me; the next upward swing of the pinioned canoe would both
ose and capsize it.

When it did, when Morning Song found herself flung into the
cing water and dragged along by triumphant waves, the voice of
e turbulent river was all at once transformed. It took on the timbre
a man's voice, gruff and guttural, a voice so forceful it shattered
e sluice gates remembrance cowered behind. With the dam of
ppression broached, a deluge of recollection was unleashed,
isting upon poor Morning Song the image of a face—a face that
the voice the river had evoked. Bearded it was, that face, and
e eyes beneath bushy dark brows a cold flint gray. And the mouth
. . it was cruel, cruel as the words that spilled from it: "A girl-
ild . . . she gives me nothing but a girl-child, this red-skinned
oman. Me, I need sons, strong sons, to work with me, to help
ild the empire Pierre Entite means to have!" His hairy hands
d been cruel, too, crueler even than his mouth or his eyes as they
stened on a bewildered child, as they hauled the daughter he
spised from the bed of his sick and frightened mother.

Memory brought back the smell of him then, an acrid smell,
asty, which intensified each time he opened his hurtful
outh. "I shall show her, me, that I am a man of my word. I say
her, If you do not give me a son—a live and healthy son!—by
inter's end, I take this girl-child you give all your love to and
spose of her."

The woman Morning Song was buffeted by brutal waves; jarring
otsteps had buffeted the little girl a brutal man slung over his back
he took her to a river, a river in full spate from the snow melting
the mountain that rose above it.

The four-year-old Morning Song had made no sound when the
arded man threw her down on the riverbank. She'd been told to
nothing that might anger him, and she would not shame her
other by disobeying. But when he picked her up again and thrust
r head and shoulders beneath the surface of the fast-running river,
stinct had made her cry out. And the water had rushed into her
ping mouth, invaded her nose, collected in her throat, beat against
r inner ear. . . .

Past and present merged, became one; a circle closed as an an cient unnamed terror, understood at last, imposed itself upon th now. Morning Song screamed, flailed her arms, strove mightily t escape the ravening swirl of water she emerged from memory t find herself in. The river retaliated, raked at her arms, her leg drew her down, down, down. She screamed again, thrashed in vain effort to free herself from its clutches, knew that she neve would, knew that the twisting, whirling, vengeful water was deter mined to claim the life it had once been cheated of.

She could fight no more. In a gesture of surrender, she expose her face to stiletto spray, and was granted asylum in the comfortin womb-dark of unconsciousness.

The man whose careful tracking had led him to the riverban stiffened, looked up, began to run to a point of land overhangin the whirlpool Morning Song spun in. He poised himself on th edge of the narrow spit, filled his lungs with air, then dove clean into the churning water far beneath. When he'd arrested his down ward plunge and reversed it, when he'd propelled himself to th surface, he knew a moment of terror because his searching eye found no trace of the woman he was determined to rescue. H shouted her name; the sound was stolen on the instant and absorbe into the maniacal laughter of the river that sought to keep her fro him. He swung his head this way and that, located the heaving ri of the eddy that was her prison, began to swim strongly, tirelessl as though he had not gone sleepless these last three nights, had n devoted the days between to searching for the woman whose spir had been calling ceaselessly to his.

The straining muscles in his arms and legs defied the curren and he plowed through every curling wave that aimed to thwa him. Farther and farther he went, something other than sight guid ing him now, until a final scissoring of his long legs brought hi to the spiraling water that was slowly swallowing the woman trappe in its coils.

He reached for one limp arm, had it torn from his fingers in th moment that flesh met flesh; commanded himself to wait until th inevitable circling brought her closer to where he treaded the per ilous water. He glimpsed her face as her orbiting body swung awa from him. The eyes were closed, the long-lashed lids resting again cheeks drained of color. The mouth—that soft-lipped, vulnerabl mouth—was slack and drooped at the corners. Fear coursed throug him. Was he too late? Had the spirit—surely as tired of fighting a the rest of Morning Song—gone out of her? Would he bring to shor

ith him only the deserted shell of the woman who was his wife,
e mother of his children?

He tensed, stretched out both hands, clamped them upon one
in wrist, used the eddy's own impetus to begin pulling Morning
ong free of it. By the time it was drawing her away again, he had
asped her shoulders. He heaved her toward him, and let his hands
ide quickly to her waist to give himself best purchase in this deadly
g-of-war.

He waited again. Never mind that the undertow was wrenching
him, as eager to gulp down two as one, and as capable of doing
. Cloud Racer held on grimly, studied the hypnotic wheeling of
e ruthless water, insisted that his legs ignore the pummeling of
e current and act as anchor. Now! He threw himself backward,
d Morning Song with him, struck out with one hand to pull them
owly, slowly, beyond the range of the vortex, through barricades
rown up by collaborating waves, to where the river—its awesome
ry finally spent—was content to let them pass without interfer-
ce.

Warmth. Sun-warmth. It was a caress, a benediction, a distilla-
on of hope resurrected.

Morning Song opened her eyes, winced as this most ordinary of
ovements set her temples to pounding. She took refuge again in
arkness, but it was no longer a silent darkness. A breeze
rummed; in response to its prompting, blades of grass whispered
concert and leaves chittered softly overhead. Somewhere in the
istance, an eagle screamed. Closer to hand, a mallard squawked
provingly. And all of these sounds played against the larger
und—muffled now, she realized vaguely—of crashing white wa-
r.

Then . . . there came another sound, one she had thought never,
ver, to hear again.

"Morning Song," Cloud Racer said quietly.

Heedless of pain, impervious to it, her eyes flew open once more,
idened, glistened with unshed tears as they beheld the man who
oke her name, blinked repeatedly until she could focus clearly,
ngrily, on his anxious face.

She made as if to move, to sit upright, and he laid one broad-
almed hand gently upon the shoulder nearest him and shook his
ark head. "It is too soon," he said.

But the warning sent out by every nerve, every muscle in her
ody, had already told her that. She tried to talk instead, to ask him
. . oh! so much; but her parched and aching throat managed only

a croak. Her expression registered her puzzlement; how could throat and mouth and lips be fever-dry when all of her had so recently been steeped in a terrifying abundance of water?

Cloud Racer smiled reassuringly. "You were as saturated within as without," he said. "I had to force the water from your chest and belly to make it possible for you to breathe." He continued to smile down at her, but his eyes were somber. She need never know how frantically he had worked over her, how he had almost despaired before water began to gush from her nose and mouth, how even then he'd feared she might never gag, and gasp, and—at long last—take in that first shuddering gulp of life-restoring air. . . .

"For some of your bruises," he added ruefully, "you have me to thank." Many of the others must be charged to the violent river, he knew. Those that could not be, however . . . well, he would learn the reason for them, and for fingers swollen and raw-fleshed, for lacerations only a sharp-bladed knife could have made, for strands of hair singed at the ends and others burned off at the scalp. His hands tightened involuntarily, and a rage greater than any battle fever was born in him. But he made himself go on smiling as he took up a greenish-brown turtle shell. "The creature's meat is cooking for our meal," he said, gesturing to where a small fire burned steadily beneath a greenwood spit, "but you will not be ready for such food before tomorrow. For now"—he fumbled in his pouch, lifted out a pinch of maple sugar–laced meal—"it is trail rations and water you must have."

She grimaced. She had had enough of water to last her a lifetime. Yet she knew he was right. Weakness, more than pain, immobilized her. And, impossible though it seemed, she *was* thirsty. She swallowed the drops of water he let slip between her lips, put out the tip of her tongue to accept the dab of meal, drank a second time from the turtle's shell.

"Now rest again," he commanded, lightly brushing the hair back from her brow with his long fingers. The throbbing in her temples was eased by his rhythmic stroking, and the gnawing in her belly by the burgeoning cornmeal. Very soon, Morning Song slept.

The dawn chorus of the songbirds awakened her next day, and she smiled the smile of one who has happened upon a delightful secret. For she knew why they sang, her feathered brothers and sisters; like her, they were grateful to be alive and able to greet this sparkling dawn. Cloud Racer's sleep-slowed breathing tickled her right ear, and she understood that they lay together beneath his cloak. He had roused her several times during the night and, ignoring her mumbled protests, insisted that she eat and drink a little each time. For that, too, she was thankful. The nourishment he'd pressed upon her contributed much to the sense of well-being that now warmed her to her toes. She stretched experimentally; aches there were, a multitude of them; but no real pain stabbed anywhere.

She sniffed, wrinkled her nose at the odor of charred meat. Cloud Racer had forgotten to remove the spitted chunks of turtle from over the fire. Well, other matters had concerned him more, she thought. And smiled again. When he offered it, she would eat as much as she could of the blackened meat. And tell him how delicious it was, too!

Her stirring, discreet though it had been, had called Cloud Racer from his slumbering. He raised up on one elbow, studied her intently, looked pleased. "You are stronger this day."

She nodded. "I am. Much stronger." The vigor of her voice proved what she said, and he reached out and embraced her gingerly. She turned slightly, smiled at him. "You may hold me tighter than that," she whispered. "I will not shatter, as yesterday I might have done."

But he only grinned at her and sprang to his feet. "We will not risk it. Yet," he amended when disappointment clouded her face. Surely she knew that he was as much in need of her embrace as she was of his, was as desperate for reaffirmation of love, of life itself, as Morning Song must be. "You have not," he told her with mock sternness, "tried to sit up, let alone stand."

"For what I was considering," she said, "neither is necessary." To have triumphed over death brought with it a heady sense of freedom, and she enjoyed startling him with her boldness.

"You are in truth the granddaughter of Teller Of Legends," he remarked after a moment.

It was Morning Song's turn to be surprised.

"Her words so often extend themselves over a long and winding path that you must follow closely to discover her destination," he explained, gazing in disbelief at the dried-out hunks of meat on his spit. "Then—when you least expect it—she forges ahead with such directness that you are unprepared for it."

"But I am always direct in what I say," she declared, lifting herself cautiously until she had managed to sit up. Her head swam for a moment, then cleared, and she looked at him smugly.

He handed her a bit of the unappetizing turtle meat. "You are not," he said calmly, hunkering down beside her and beginning to chew the piece he'd taken for himself. "For some time now, you have been quieter than usual, and smiled seldom. You have . . . removed yourself from me. Yet you never said why." He spat out the inedible part of his meat, swallowed the rest, and grimaced.

Morning Song covered her confusion by chewing more rapidly, although no amount of chewing could possibly soften the stringy stuff. She had been disinclined, the day before, to waste any thought on the reason she had ventured so far into the forest, and so made herself easy prey for Stag Leaping and the Algonquin renegades. Now the memory of what had triggered her flight resurfaced. He came after me, she told herself, and saved my life. Which must mean that he cares for me still, at least a little. But the old hurt, the old doubts, were not to be lightly dismissed. "You never asked about it," she said defensively, and none too audibly; she downed the tasteless meat and repeated the counterchallenge.

"I did not think it needed saying that there should be truth between us." He looked hard at her, decided she was sufficiently recovered to deal with the questions that had been circling endlessly in his head. "Shall we begin with your telling me how you, who have always shied away from anything but the shallows, came to be in the most dangerous part of this river? Why you are marked with wounds that not even the rapids could have dealt?" His mouth tightened. "And who inflicted them?"

This, he must be told. And for all that Morning Song dreaded to relive them, she knew that to speak of these things now might spare her being haunted by them later. She would, however, omit the reason she had gone so far into the woods in the first place.

She spoke haltingly at the start, then the phrases began to tumble from her lips, one upon the other, until she had built a firm foundation for the history she was narrating. Cloud Racer steeled himself against distracting her with any hint of his mounting fury as she told of the appearance of the four Algonquin warriors, of Stag Leaping's calculated threats, of the relish with which he had detailed what they meant to do with Morning Song.

"I screamed then," she went on, bowing her head. "I could not help myself, Cloud Racer." The face she raised to him pleaded to be forgiven for what she saw as cowardice, and he exclaimed sharply, opened his mouth to tell her not to be such a fool.

But her words were racing one another, for this was the part she had most dreaded coming to, the part she must not dally over lest she disgrace herself by weeping. "White Shadow"—her voice thickened—"sprang at him. And—and Stag Leaping—" She clamped her lips upon the sobs that begged to be released, let her head droop again, and her shoulders sag.

Cloud Racer, too, had difficulty speaking. "I found him," he said at last. "Found White Shadow, and wrapped him in my tunic, and marked the place where I buried him with heaped boulders."

She looked up, her expression piteous. "He was trying to protect me."

He nodded. "I knew that he must have died for your sake, and that you would not want him left for scavengers. I made sure that none shall ever reach him, Morning Song." He slid an arm around her, pulled her closer to him. He felt the tears she could no longer hold back trickle over his naked chest, and vowed silently that Stag Leaping would be begging to be killed, would be crawling on his belly like the snake that he was, before Cloud Racer would be moved to deliver the death blow.

A loon downriver laughed, and a host of his fellows echoed the sound. Morning Song scrubbed the tears from her eyes and sat up straighter. In a voice steadier than Cloud Racer would have expected, she picked up her abandoned tale and listed almost indifferently the instruments of torture her captors had used, the chillingly systematic way they had applied them. "My grieving for Shadow numbed me in the beginning," she said earnestly. "After that, I was so angry that I forgot to be frightened. And when the day ended, and they slept, I could think of nothing but escape." She faltered, eyed him uncertainly. "It does not matter how I managed this," she said in a hurry, "but only that I succeeded."

He had taken one of her hands, was staring at her fingers, at the leprous, bloated tips, at what was left of her ripped and jagged nails, at knuckles purpled and distended. They would heal, these hands. Eventually the swelling would dissipate, new skin would grow to shield that weeping flesh, new fingernails would form to replace those split and dislodged by the burning splinters forced beneath them. He wondered briefly if Morning Song realized how her immersion in the river might have diluted the worst of the infection. He thought not, but that was of no account. How they had arrived at so wretched a state, who was responsible for it, was of primary concern. "It matters," he said harshly. "I must hear all of it, Morning Song."

She sighed. "First, I will stand up," she said, "for I am anxious to know that I can." He rose when she did, held himself ready to support her should she need him; but he was wise enough to refrain from helping unless she showed signs of wanting him to. Once erect, she leaned against him momentarily, then pushed away, stood alone and unaided, lifted her face to the early sun. "Now I am certain that I truly did survive," she murmured happily, and the breath caught in his throat to see the joy that radiated from her.

Being on her feet made it easier to finish her story, and not only because she could pace back and forth—never mind that she stumbled a bit before she found her balance—and avoid her husband's gaze as she described the ruse she'd employed to persuade Stag Leaping to unfetter her. When, occassionally, she did flick her eyes in his direction, she could decipher nothing of the effect her words must be having, although his tight-set mouth relaxed slightly when she told him matter-of-factly of the rock she'd used to strike down her abductor and, later, to put one of the canoes out of commission. And she fancied she glimpsed a flash of amazement in the eyes that followed her pacing figure when she spoke of launching the undamaged craft and teaching herself to paddle it.

"And you came over the rapids in that canoe?" For all his resolve to keep his voice expressionless, incredulity crept into it.

That did not displease his wife. "I had no choice," she responded airily. But suddenly all of it came back to her—the menacing roar of the raging waters, the knife-sharp spray that had battered her, the assassin rocks that lay in wait for whatever the torrent sent down to them—and she covered her face with trembling hands.

Cloud Racer went to her, held her hard against him. "It is over. All over."

Slowly she lowered her hands. "More than you know is over," she said brokenly. "For I have learned why it is that I have always been terrified of fast-running water." And she shared with him what memory had revealed to her as she plummeted over the falls. "I know, too, why I did not drown, that day," she ended. "My mother, weak as she was from her illness—she had lost a child, I think—came after us." She paused, swallowed hard. "Summer Maize killed my father," she said flatly, "because he was trying to kill me. She saved my life, Cloud Racer, and until now I have never known that she did. I would not have thought her capable of slaying any man; I remember her as being mouse-quiet, and mild-natured as a woodland fawn."

"You were her daughter, and she loved you," he said quietly. "The meekest of creatures springs to the defense of its young." He led her to a fallen log that lay beside his improvised hearth. "You have been standing long enough," he said firmly. "Sit here and rest while I see if I can snare some muskrat or rabbit to roast. I doubt"—he smiled down at her—"whether either of us will ever care to make a meal of turtle meat again!"

She watched him retrieve his bow, his quiver, and stride away between the trees that encroached upon the riverbank. Then she turned her gaze to the river itself. It was placid here, its surface mirroring the blue sky and the immature clouds that were playing a lazy game of tag. "I can never be fond of you," she murmured to it, "as Otter used to be. And I shall never let myself be drawn again to any spot where your waters whiten and rush furiously down to a lower level. But the terror you used to inspire in me is gone. If I cannot honestly pledge devotion to you, I can at least offer you respect."

And she was content that her own *orenda* and that of the river had made a treaty of peace between them.

If Morning Song thought Cloud Racer's questioning was done, she was soon to know better. When she had overseen the cooking and serving of a hare and two plump river ducks, she moved to douse the fire with some of the drinking water he had fetched in his emptied quiver.

"Leave the embers glowing," he told her. "It will be easier to build up a blaze against the night's coolness."

"But surely we are going home now," she said, perplexed. "You have seen that I can stand, and walk. And since I now own moccasins of a sort"—she stuck out one foot for him to admire the clever use she'd made of another strip torn from Stag Leaping's tunic—"I see no reason not to set out at once."

"You would find yourself tiring before we had gone very far," he said. "Another sleep will strengthen you further, and let your injuries heal a little, besides. There is no need for haste, Morning Song."

"But our families will be worried. They have no way of knowing that you have rescued me, and that we are together, and safe."

He gnawed the last of the meat from the rabbit's hind leg, tossed the bone aside. "Teller Of Legends never doubted that I would find you and bring you back," he said. "She spoke so positively that everyone believed her." He did not tell her how his faith in her grandmother's prediction had been shaken when he came upon White Shadow's bludgeoned body.

She was silent for a moment. "You do not think," she said hesitantly, trying to keep apprehension from her voice, "that Stag Leaping and the Algonquin warriors are tracking me still?" This had been her worry since shortly after Cloud Racer had left her alone, but she hated to let him see how the possibility frightened her.

"No," he said decisively. "If they did not actually witness your going over the rapids, they have surely spotted the wreckage of their canoe. They will assume you to be dead, Morning Song. And Stag Leaping, if he survived the blows you struck with that rock, has more than one reason to avoid our village; he will know that I have been eager to claim revenge since the day he betrayed us." HIs eyes were as granite-hard as his words, and Morning Song's tentative fear gave way before a more assertive one.

"You will not go alone against the five of them, Cloud Racer!"

His gaze softened. "I do not lack courage, but I am not foolhardy, either. Many will want to go with me, when they hear what has happened." He came and sat beside her on the log. "Meanwhile, there is time enough for you to explain various matters you neglected to speak of this morning." He shifted so he could look directly into her face. "You knew, as all of us did, that Algonquin war parties have been raiding here and there throughout Iroquois country. Why did you wander so far on the day you were captured?"

"I had not realized how far I had gone," she said lamely, "until it was too late."

His eyebrows arched, but his insistent gaze did not release her. "Of anyone else, I might accept this. But you know these woods as well as I do, Morning Song. You could not have walked so great a distance unwittingly."

He would never believe, either, that she had forgotten the rumors about the Algonquin raids. She was cornered as effectively as a stag in a deer drive, and the hunter bent on bringing down the truth was her own husband. But unlike the stag who is pushed to exhaustion by such tactics, Morning Song did not mean to shiver and collapse, would not simply crouch here and permit Cloud Racer to berate her for what was—now that she was furiously considering it—his fault.

She threw back her slender shoulders and glared at him. "Because I owe you my life," she said stiffly, "I have decided to overlook the fact that you were responsible for my being in a place where I could be taken prisoner by the renegades."

Astonishment left him speechless, and she let reviving hurt and anger urge her on. "It is a dreadful thing for a woman to cope with, when her husband has come to care for someone else more than he does for her."

"You speak in riddles!" he exclaimed. "Or else you were injured more seriously than I thought." He made as if to reach for her, and she put up her hands, palms outward.

"I had almost come to think I was deceiving myself about this," she told him, and sorrowing briefly overlaid her anger. "Until I overheard you and Hawk Hunting talking together while you were returning to the village that day." Fury gained the upper hand. "Your words were whiplashes to me when you praised and praised the Erie maiden," she shouted, "and I knew then that any deception was not mine, but yours! 'Proud Woman is no ordinary maiden,'" she mimicked savagely. "'She is braver than many trained to lance and bow. She is praiseworthy in every respect, and pleasing to look upon'!" Morning Song clenched her outstretched hands as tightly as she was able to, beat upon her husband's naked chest. "Do you deny that you said these things? Do you?"

He lifted his own hands, caught her flailing fists, imprisoned them as tenderly as he would a pair of baby birds he meant to return to their nest. "I do not," he said quietly.

"You have admired her since the day you made her your captive," she accused, struggling to free herself.

"I have," he said calmly.

Morning Song abandoned her futile twisting and turning, shook her head wearily. "It is why I went so far, that day: So I could decide what to do about your preferring Proud Woman to me."

She did not resist when he laid her wounded hands in her lap and rested his own hands on her bowed shoulders. "Morning Song," he told her, "you are both right and wrong in what you think. Yes, I like and admire Proud Woman, as she deserves. You would admit her worth were you not so confused. But my praising her to Hawk Hunting was not a sign that I secretly desire her, or think her more admirable than my wife, my woman . . . my love."

She looked up at him. Never had Cloud Racer addressed her so before! And, oh, how often she had prayed that he would.

He knew what was in her mind. "I have never been one," he said slowly, "to say much about what is closest to my heart. It is hard for me to do so, even now. Yet I must make you understand that there is no woman anywhere I could love more than I do you, none that I recognize as more admirable."

"Then why did you speak so to Hawk Hunting? And why do you go so often to your mother's lodge now that Proud Woman is living there?"

"I spend every moment that I can with Rain Singing because we are all that is left of our family," he said soberly. "I thought you knew that, and approved."

She nodded. "I did. At first. But later, I began to think it was Proud Woman you went to visit, more than Rain Singing. And it is true that you delighted to sing her praises to Hawk Hunting, Cloud Racer.''

Surprisingly, he smiled. ''I had good reason to,'' he said. ''Proud Woman loves him, Morning Song. And Hawk Hunting, who has always been uncomfortable around women, would be fond of her it he allowed himself to be. When I knew how she felt—for Proud Woman trusts me, Morning Song, enough to tell me she would like to have Hawk Hunting for her husband—I suggested she wait until Midwinter and make him her partner in the Naked Dance.'' He grinned broadly. ''Surely I need not say why I suggested this particular solution to her problem?''

Morning Song, tension seeping out of her, smiled in return.

''Of course,'' he went on, ''I doubted that even Proud Woman would be so bold as to leap over a fire and confront Hawk Hunting, as a woman I know was brave enough to do to the man she had chosen.''

Morning Song relaxed completely, fitted herself into the waiting curve of his lean body. Was this truly Cloud Racer, *her* Cloud Racer, speaking at such length, and on such a subject? She suppressed a giggle.

''Proud Woman,'' he said, ''was aghast at the idea of exposing herself to his rejection.'' His eyes, glinting with laughter now, said that Proud Woman's reluctance to take his advice had cost her a little of his admiration. ''She would not approach Hawk Hunting unless she could be certain he wanted to be approached.''

''So that is why you spoke as you did, to stimulate his interest in her!'' Morning Song sighed blissfully. ''I have been stupid, Cloud Racer.''

''No,'' he said seriously. ''You are many things, Morning Song— unpredictable being the one that fascinates me the most—but never stupid. Except, perhaps, for failing to see yourself for the praiseworthy woman that you are.''

She surged against him then, and the arm he had around her tightened until her suddenly erect nipples made circles of heat against his chest. ''Love me,'' she said urgently, timing her words to the agitated throb of his heart. ''Love me now, Cloud Racer!''

''You are not strong enough yet for it,'' he said weakly. ''Morning Song, we should wait . . .''

But already she was standing; had, amazingly, pulled him up with her, was tugging him down to the green, green grass that spread an inviting carpet over the ground.

The tunic that had been Stag Leaping's was shed, and Cloud Racer's breechclout cast aside. And in the full and benevolent sight of their brother the sun, a pledge of true love was gently yet joyfully renewed.

Despite Teller Of Legends' complacent reminder of her prediction that Morning Song would return to them, her broad grin only partially erased a network of new worry lines from her face. Yet Morning Song felt good to know that she cared so much, and to see everyone looking happy to have her home again. Even Cloud Racer's unobtrusive departure with a carefully picked party of fellow warriors could not dilute the warmth of their welcome. She was confident he would overtake Stag Leaping, if he lived, and those he traveled with. Both White Shadow and Morning Song would be avenged.

Pumpkin Blossom fussed over her almost annoyingly. "Your poor, poor fingers," she exclaimed each time she applied salve to them. "And your hair!" she mourned, insisting upon combing it lest Morning Song's impatient tugging do even more damage to it.

Day Greeter contented herself with lending a hand wherever it was needed. "I will cook, and tend your crops," she told her cousin, "while you look after the children. Red Bird is no problem; she and Hidden Moon are mostly with Pumpkin Blossom. But Swift Arrow is as likely to get into mischief as not—as you know—and the twins have taken to spending hours in the woods each day. They play at being warriors, and take their game seriously indeed. You are better able than I am to track them down when it is time to eat."

"They will not make it easy for you," Deer Caller, visiting the Turtle lodge, said of his sons. "Brave Companion and Bold Leader delight in leading astray whoever goes searching for them. They pretend an enemy is stalking them, you see, and I understand that they have become skilled at concealing their trail."

"What one does not think of," Day Greeter confirmed, "the other does."

Morning Song, preoccupied, only smiled; two ten-year-olds, however crafty, would be no match for her. She returned to her grandmother's hearth, seated herself alongside the Matron of their clan. "It came again in the night," she said softly. "That dream about the red maple leaf."

The old woman nodded. "There was no more to it than before?"

"No." Morning Song frowned. "It means nothing, save to remind me of my Vision Quest. Were I full-blooded Iroquois, there would be some message in it, I suppose. But I am not, and there is not. I wonder now if the vision sent me during my quest was not

just a distorted memory of the day my father tried to drown me."
She spoke calmly; having told both Cloud Racer and Teller Of
Legends about the revelation the rapids had gifted her with, she
had come to terms with it. "I begin to think that memory substitutes
for visions in those cursed with the white man's blood. The *Onondio* are possessed of demons rather than spirit guides, perhaps, and
so are denied prophetic dreams."

"I would not name demon the spirit who is sending you dreams
about the maple leaf," her grandmother cautioned. "You must stop
blaming your lack of understanding on your mixed blood, Morning
Song. That only makes you bitter, and blocks recognition of what
the maple leaf represents." She attempted to settle herself more
comfortably; the way her joints were creaking these days, she did
not look forward to the winter. "Or perhaps not," she finished.
"The spirits are often inclined to be mystifying."

"That seems to me a sorry way to deliver a message," Morning
Song said gloomily. "Whether it is spirit or demon who visits me
in the night, he had better learn to do so more openly. I can only
ignore him, otherwise."

"Yet you do not," her grandmother pointed out. "Or you would
not be so quick to tell me each time you have this dream."

Morning Song grinned. "You are right, as always. To dream at
all, after so many years, intrigues me." She breathed in the fragrant
steam escaping from the pot Pumpkin Blossom was stirring. "It is
time I went in search of our wandering twins," she observed, getting to her feet. "Pumpkin Blossom is displeased whenever anyone
comes late to a meal she has cooked."

"My daughter named those two aptly," Teller Of Legends said,
smiling. "Bold and Brave they are, and venturesome with it."

They were also, Morning Song realized when she'd walked farther than usual without finding the pair, both swift- and sure-footed.
Her sharp eyes had soon picked out the path they'd taken, but it had
led her up hill and down dale and through a ferocity of thorny
bushes. She would not call out; they would refuse to answer, and
Morning Star was one who understood what they were about. She
knew they never went beyond the limits she had outlined for them.
Within these bounds, however, they might be anywhere. And the
sun was fast approaching its zenith.

She stopped walking when she'd breasted a familiar hillock,
turned slowly in a circle, and tried to filter out the commonplace
forest noises. It would be futile to listen for the boys' voices; Bold
Leader and Brave Companion had always been able to communi-

cate without speaking. But if she heard twigs snapping, or the muted
thud of a footfall . . .

There was nothing. The first lesson the sons of Otter Swimming
had learned was evidently the one Morning Song, in her own youth,
had found so difficult: the art of walking silently. She sat down,
clasped her hands lightly around her knees. The balm Pumpkin
Blossom had been treating her fingers with was remarkably effective. The tips and knuckles were nearly normal size once more,
and only a little tender to the touch.

Suddenly she swiveled her head to the right. Surely it had been
the sound of feet tramping through underbrush that she'd heard? It
came again, and louder. She leaped up, peered in that direction.
Two dedicated warriors-to-be would hardly be careless enough to
herald their approach; yet if it were not Otter's boys, then who was
it?

Her heart leaped into her throat as she recalled how Stag Leaping
and the Algonquin had materialized on another day, in another part
of the vast forest. Then reason came to her rescue; an enemy would
take even more care than the twins not to advertise his presence.
And the *Onondio* traders Morning Song still took pains to avoid
always approached the village from the opposite direction. Reassured, she descended the small hill and fixed her eyes on a pair of
fir trees whose soft-needled branches, on this windless day, were
beginning to quiver.

Two sturdy, black-haired figures pushed their way between them
and headed toward Morning Song. One carried a pair of ash bows,
and two quivers of arrows dangled down his back. The other was
limping, and badly, and a strip of white fabric was wound around
his left leg.

Morning Song fairly flew across the boggy stretch of ground that
separated her from Bold Leader and Brave Companion.

Chapter 30

Whenever the twins embarked upon a tale of their adventures, neither completed a sentence; he left it to his brother to do so. This made for a confusion that ordinarily brought laughter, but today no one was amused. The Turtle clan was concentrating on making sense of the dual recital.

"It was a deer—a huge stag—that we were stalking," Brave Companion said importantly. "We came across his spoor—"

"Near a clump of wood fern," his brother put in, seating himself near Morning Song so his knee could be examined. "We thought how surprised everyone would be if we brought down such a beast—"

"Before we are old enough to be named hunter-warriors," Brave Companion supplied. "We stayed on his trail while we were downwind of him, and then—"

"We began to circle so he would not catch our scent."

The other children were crowding around, the two girls huge-eyed, and Swift Arrow and Painted Sky exclaiming enviously at every other word.

"The arrows I made for you," Deer Caller said quietly, "are fletched and tipped for small game. They would have served you ill against anything bigger than a muskrat."

"We remembered," Bold Leader assured him. "Which is why we each picked up a heavy stone while we were circling. It seemed to us that—"

"We might startle the stag with our arrows, and then hurl the rocks at his head before he could think—"

"To run away!" his twin finished. "The stones were big enough, and heavy enough, to stun him, and you know that we never go into the forest—"

"Without our blades. And everyone knows that an animal will die if his throat is slashed. Which we meant to do, as soon as we had stunned him. Only, the boulder my brother was carrying—"

"Was heavy indeed," Bold Leader said mournfully, looking

370

down at the bloody knee Morning Song had uncovered. "When I was hurrying after Brave Companion, I stumbled because of its weight. I fell down and landed—"

"On a rock covered with leaf mold and pine needles." Brave Companion shook his head. "It was not a smooth rock, either. When he got up, a splinter of it was sticking in his leg, and blood was running down from the cut it made. He tried to go on in spite of that, but—"

"The stag had heard me drop my boulder. Then the woman came—"

"Out of the trees." Brave Companion watched as Day Greeter brought water for Morning Song to wash his brother's wound with. "*She* did that, too," he informed them. "The woman cleaned Bold Leader's wound after she pulled out the sliver of rock."

"Who was this woman?" Teller Of Legends asked him.

Naturally it was his twin who answered. "We did not know her. She is a sallow-skin, and talks like the traders. We could not understand what she said. She had to gesture and point to tell us how we were near the place where—"

"She lives. It is a small lodge that she has," Brave Companion told them solemnly, "with only one hearth."

"How do you know that?" Morning Song asked, moving aside to allow Pumpkin Blossom to smooth medicine on the injured leg.

"She took us there," Bold Leader said, striving manfully not to wince as Pumpkin Blossom dabbed at his torn flesh. "And when she had washed off the blood and dirt, and wrapped up my leg, she—"

"Gave us some flat, sweet bread to eat."

"Not truly bread, for it was small and crunchy. It tasted good, though. She gave us more of it when we left, but—"

"There was not much, and we ate all of it before we found Morning Song."

They glanced at each other, looked together toward Pumpkin Blossom's hearth. "So we are hungry still," they chorused hopefully.

"It was surely the wife of Bree-And that they met," Teller Of Legends said when Day Greeter had taken the boys to get the succotash she'd kept warm for them. "She must be a good woman, that one."

"It is hard to credit, that a good woman would take so loathsome a man for a husband," Morning Song said. "Yet I heard before— from Cloud Racer—that she is kind. He told me, too, that she is timid-natured."

"How could she be otherwise, living with such a one?" Teller Of Legends asked. "Her goodness should be rewarded, however. One of us must go and let her know we are grateful that she was willing to help Bold Leader."

Morning Song greeted this announcement with silence. Clearly she was the one to go. Otter had entrusted the twins to her, and no one else would be able to communicate with the trader's woman. Yet the thought of visiting an *Onondio*, even a timid-natured female, had no appeal for her.

"I will go with you." Morning Song's daughter was at her elbow. "Brave Companion has told me the way to the woman's lodge. It is not very far."

"I know where the trader lives," Morning Song said shortly, and sighed. Teller Of Legends' expression was neutral; like Red Bird, she believed Morning Song should take on the mission, but the decision rested with her granddaughter.

"If we are to go," she said resignedly, "then let us go now. We should take the woman a gift, I suppose."

"I will ask Pumpkin Blossom to fill a basket with some of the squash we harvested this morning," her daughter said, and went to help choose the finest of the fresh-picked vegetables.

A breeze, cool enough to be named vanguard of the frost-bearing season, made their walk pleasant. It was the sort of day, Morning Song reflected sadly, that Shadow would have exulted in.

"The squirrels are like Iroquois matrons," Red Bird said suddenly. "They work hard to gather acorns so their families will have food during the winter." Her dark eyes, wide-set like her mother's, sparkled as she watched one bushy-tailed rodent, cheeks bulging with nuts, skitter to his nest high in the tree's trunk.

Morning Song, brought out of her reverie, smiled at the girl. And realized all at once that this was the first time she and Red Bird had walked alone together in the woods. "It is likely," she observed, "that the women who were our ancestors learned their careful ways from watching creatures like the squirrels."

"They were wise to do so," Red Bird said. "And surely they delighted to be in the forest, where there is so much that is beautiful to see, and hear, and smell."

Morning Song eyed her curiously. "I never knew you were fond of the woods. You do not come here often, except for berry picking and nut gathering."

Red Bird shrugged. "I come with Swift Arrow, whenever he lets me. And sometimes with Day Greeter and Deer Caller."

Her mother stopped short. "Deer Caller walks in the forest?"

"Only along the path that leads to the hills near the lake. Day Greeter persuaded him to, the first time, and she asked me to walk on his other side so he would not wander from where the ground is smooth underfoot. Now he does not need anyone to guide him, but Day Greeter walks with him all the same, I think." She waited courteously for Morning Song to resume their journey. "I go along only if there is no work to be done in the lodge or the fields," she added primly.

This child was surely a matron in miniature, Morning Song decided. Red Bird would never be the truant her mother had been, even if she did own a similar liking for the fragrant stillness of the woodlands. "The home of the trader and his wife is just over the next ridge," she said, turning onto the narrow trail that would take them there.

The lodge was indeed small, Morning Song saw as they came upon it, and built low to the ground besides. She had hoped that Bree-And's woman would be outside, but there was no one working in the uneven square that contained the sallow-skins' crops, no one to be seen anywhere in the clearing around the log-built structure. She set her feet down firmly as she and her daughter moved closer, inviting a hard-packed stretch of earth to thump with each step. But the shadows that clustered beyond the rough-hewn entrance continued undisturbed.

"Do you think she is not here?" Red Bird whispered her question, and Morning Song was unsurprised. Something about this place inspired low voices and caution.

But this was nonsense! It was merely a tiny, indifferently built lodge, and nothing to be apprehensive about. Were the trader here, Morning Song might have reason for uneasiness; but his presence would never be a silent one. And if the woman was a sallow-skin—well, she was at least only a woman. Just as Morning Song was.

She strode forward, passed through the shadowy doorway, blinked to adjust her eyes to the dimness of the smoky, windowless room she found herself in.

"I think she is not here," Red Bird repeated, looking around her. "Which is—Oh!"

Morning Song spun on her heel. Sprawled on the dirt floor beside the hearth was a woman whose voluminous garment emphasized the boniness of her outflung arms and legs. Blue veins snaked beneath her fishbelly-white skin, and dreadful bruises further discolored thigh and forearm. More bruises marked the gaunt face that was partially veiled by a straggle of thin white hair.

Morning Song went down on her knees beside the unconscious woman. "She has been beaten, horribly beaten," she said tersely.

Red Bird moved close to her mother. "The Algonquin?" she breathed.

"I think we will find," Morning Song replied grimly, "that her husband did this to her."

Red Bird dropped her basket and somersaulting squashes brought flashes of sunshine yellow into the dreary cabin. "No man would beat his wife!" she said, aghast.

"Among the *Onondio*," her mother said, noting the puffed and purpling flesh that ringed one closed eye, "anything is possible." It was how my own father treated Summer Maize, she wanted to say; but could not bring herself to tell Red Bird how her heritage was tainted. In the child the white man's blood was diluted, and no more than a trickle would tarnish the veins of the babies Red Bird would eventually bear. She reached out, eased the woman's limbs into positions more natural to them, smoothed her disarranged garments over them.

Marie Briand's thin lips parted to release a pitiful moan. Her sparsely lashed lids fluttered, lifted. And terror leaped into her uninjured eye.

Morning Song sat back on her heels and thought frantically. She was able to decipher the language of this woman and her kind, but she had never tried speaking it. And the woman must be reassured before they could help her.

"We come as friends," she ventured, the unfamiliar syllables tangling her tongue. She shook her head, tried again. "We will not hurt you," she said, the words pronounced as precisely as she knew how. A flicker of recognition encouraged her. "We have come," she went on, ignoring the bewilderment on Red Bird's face, "to thank you for helping the boy we call Brave Leader."

Marie Briand's mouth shaped itself into a quivering *O*. Here was a redskin, an *Indian*, yet she spoke words borrowed from the French! What did this mean? Henri had said it again and again: All redskins are crafty devils. Did painted warriors lurk outside? Did they prepare to burst in, to seize Marie Briand and scalp her?

Her face reflected her fear, and Morning Song ached to dispel it. "We will not hurt you," she repeated, and signaled Red Bird to come forward and let herself be seen by the old woman.

Some of the rigidity went out of Marie Briand at the sight of the little girl. This Indian would never bring a child along unless, as she had struggled to say, she came as friend. How shameful that the two should find her like this! Her work-hardened hands scrabbled for purchase, she crooked her callused elbows. She must make herself sit up, try to stand . . .

She could not. Morning Song slid an arm beneath the woman's frail shoulders, lifted her gently, supported her until Red Bird had fetched a ramshackle wooden crate to prop her against.

The trader's wife closed her eyes, strained to recall what she'd understood of Morning Song's halting speech. "I do not need thanks, me," she said, but the slurred syllables were gibberish to Morning Song.

"Please, you must talk more slowly," she said.

Mme. Briand repeated her words, separately and distinctly, and Morning Song grasped her meaning this time. "Kindness must always be acknowledged," she said formally. Then the anger she had been suppressing surfaced. "We will do you a kindness in return," she added strongly. She gestured to the visible bruises, to the eye that was swollen shut. "It was your husband who beat you?"

Marie Briand averted her face, answer enough for the daughter of Summer Maize.

"We shall take you back to our village," she announced, "where you will be safe from him."

"No, no!" the old woman cried weakly. And tried to explain that she could not, would not, leave; that her husband expected to find her here when he returned.

But Morning Song was outlining the situation to Red Bird. "The woman can never survive another assault by that bully," she said. "We have no choice but to take her away."

Red Bird gave up trying to cope with the realization that her mother knew the sallow-skin's tongue and turned her attention to the practical. "Do you mean to take her home with us? She cannot walk so far, if at all."

"I will carry her," Morning Song said briefly. She laughed a little to see her daughter's reservations. "Look at her, Red Bird. She weighs no more than a good-sized basket of corn."

Both of them looked silently at the pitiful woman. She'd slumped to one side, exhausted by the torrent of protest they had paid no heed to. Tears were streaming down her face and splattering upon her sagging bosom. "Your father was right, when he named her timid," Morning Song said. "She is not brave enough to send her husband away, even if she were strong enough to."

She bent and scooped up the crumpled figure, straightened easily, and nodded to her daughter. "Lead the way," she told her.

"We must be far from here before that brute of a trader comes back."

Red Bird was out of the cabin before her mother stopped speaking—and did not shorten her stride until home was in sight.

Morning Song translated the Frenchwoman's words—as many as were coherent—for her astonished family. The woman's terror grew when she found herself in the Turtle longhouse, and Morning Song was hard put to simultaneously soothe her and explain why she'd brought her to the lodge. "She says that her husband will be more furious than he was before, when he finds her gone," she finished finally. "She cannot seem to realize that we will protect her from him."

"She is in a strange place, and sees strange faces wherever she looks," Teller Of Legends said. "Naturally she is confused."

But Marie Briand's fear was not spawned wholly by the firelit longhouse and the copper-skinned women standing around her. What frightened her most was that she risked the wrath not only of Henri, but of her God, by having left her husband's home. "Please," she begged, "I must go back. I must be there to make Henri's dinner."

Morning Song took firm hold of what remained of her patience and squatted beside her. "He has hurt you, and will do so again if you return to him," she said. "Here, you are safe. The matrons of my tribe know how to deal with such a one. We will have him brought here, and when we have had our way with him, Bree-And will be a broken man. No woman need ever fear him again."

Marie Briand's shriek was piercing. "You cannot! You must not. The good God, He shall never forgive me, never, if I permit this." How could she make these people, these kind but godless heathen, comprehend? "When we married," she gasped, "the priest say I must obey Henri. And before God's altar, I promise that I will."

Morning Song stared at her. "You cannot mean," she said slowly, "that you wish to go on being wife to a man who is cruel."

"I do not wish it, no," Marie Briand wailed. "I have the sense enough to know that one day Henri, he will kill me when I have angered him. Yet it is a sin, to deny a vow made in the presence of God." She drew breath sharply as the entrance hide was flipped aside, sighed with relief when it was only another black-haired, ruddy-complexioned woman who entered. "You must see that I cannot stay here," she said then. "You mean to be good to me, I know. But in time Henri will find me. And then . . . !" She shuddered.

Morning Song told her hovering family what the sobbing woman had said.

"It seems to me," Teller Of Legends said, "that a pledge given to a dishonorable man does not require honoring. Even the god she fears would not demand this of her. Still, she is right when she says that Bree-And will find her if she remains here."

"We can protect her from him," Morning Song insisted.

The Matron of the Turtle clan nodded slowly. "Yes. But the trader rules the life of this woman. I think she might suffer more by being separated from him than she has from his abuse of her."

Morning Song started. Had her mother been as thoroughly cowed, as abject, as the Frenchwoman? Was that why she had never fled her own cruel husband, why she had never found the spirit to fight back until her tiny daughter's life was threatened? "We cannot let her return to Bree-And," she said stubbornly.

"No," Teller Of Legends said. "That is not the answer. Yet keeping her here shall serve for a short time only."

When her mother made no reply to this, Red Bird spoke up. "When the other trader comes again, he may be able to help."

"He is another *Onondio*," Morning Song said, "and cares for himself alone. As all of them do!"

"I think we should ask him at least," the girl said quietly.

"I have noticed," Teller Of Legends said while Morning Song was wondering why her daughter was being so uncommonly forward, "that they are as different as corn plant and weed, those two. And Cloud Racer will know whether Lah-Val can be trusted. Until he comes home, we shall keep the woman in our longhouse, and hide her if Bree-And comes looking for her. Tell her this, Morning Song. Do not mention Lah-Val until we have spoken with Cloud Racer, but tell her that we will try to find one of her own people to assist her."

Reluctantly Morning Song went to do as she was bidden. But Marie Briand, weak from the beating her husband's huge hands had delivered and unnerved by this latest turn of events, had slipped into a troubled sleep. Morning Song did not awaken her.

Alarm spurred frantic paddling when the war band's canoes rounded the final bend in the river taking them home. Sentries—drawn from among the old men and the youths—were posted all around the palisade, a palisade whose gate was shut and barred. Had a party of Algonquin traveled this far south after all?

"They are there to watch for Bree-And," Morning Song explained when a worried Cloud Racer confronted her, and told him about the woman the matrons were harboring. "Not a day goes by but she begs to be taken back," she said. "Sometimes I think she is not flesh and blood at all, Cloud Racer, but only a ghost-woman who has put on skin and hair. Her husband has stolen her substance from her."

"Has he come here?"

"Once. Se-A-Wi and Teller Of Legends went to the gate and pretended not to understand him when he demanded to be let in." She grinned. "Well, they did not. But I was standing near them, and I knew what he said." Her eyes flashed. "The fool was not even clever enough to carry a pack as though he'd come to barter."

"He may be a fool in some ways," her husband warned. "In others, he is not. He suspects that his woman is here, and we cannot continue to forbid him entry."

"He should be made to pay for what he did to his wife," Morning Song said hotly.

Cloud Racer nodded. "It is not for me, or for any of us, to claim revenge for what was done to the white woman, however." His jaw clenched briefly as he remembered the vengeance he had claimed for what had been done to Morning Song. That had been both his right and his duty, according to tribal law.

"He speaks truly, Morning Song," Teller Of Legends said. "Which is why we cannot keep her here." She inclined her head toward her granddaughter's husband. More and more, he reminded her of Tall Pine, whose spirit had gone ahead of her into the land of endless sunshine. She thought it would not be long now before she joined him there, so this problem of the trader's woman must be resolved. There were more important matters clamoring for her attention. . . . "What do you think of the trader Lah-Val?" she asked him abruptly. "Your daughter suggests we might entrust Bree-And's wife to him."

Morning Song spoke before Cloud Racer could. "What can Red Bird know of him?" she asked her grandmother. "My children have never been allowed in the compound when the traders come."

Teller Of Legends chuckled. "She is your daughter in truth, my dear. The more you insisted that she avoid the *Onondio*, the more curious she became. Just as you once did, she took to slipping out and watching from a place where she could not be overlooked."

Morning Song was startled into silence. Red Bird's reverence for propriety was extreme. What had moved her to cast it aside? Swift Arrow might do such a thing, but *Red Bird*?

"Lah-Val is an honest man," Cloud Racer was saying. "If he tells us he will care for the woman, I think we may believe him.

Yet he does not have much liking for anyone, that man. He prefers to walk alone. So I am not hopeful that he will help us."

"In any event," Teller Of Legends said, "he must be asked. There is no one else, Cloud Racer."

"On our way home," Cloud Racer said, "we were stopped by a fishing party upriver. When we exchanged news, they told us Lah-Val will be trading at their village two days from now. Whether Bree-And will come too"—he shrugged—"I do not know. But I will go there and speak privately with Lah-Val." He started toward the sweathouse, turned back. "Hawk Hunting has begun to feel," he said casually to his wife, "that marriage to Proud Woman might suit him admirably."

If Teller Of Legends understood the amusement that flared in his eyes when he said this, she was too wise to reveal that she did.

In the end, Cloud Racer brought Gaspard Laval to the Turtle longhouse, and Morning Song was party to another complicated conversation. Her grandmother was ignorant of the sallow-skin's language; the Frenchman's store of Iroquois was limited to phrases used in trading. To be certain they understood one another, Morning Song agreed to translate whatever Teller Of Legends said, and Cloud Racer to repeat the words of Lah-Val. It was as well, Morning Song thought, that they had the lodge to themselves. Day Greeter had herded the children outside, and Pumpkin Blossom had taken Marie Briand to Rain Singing's longhouse.

"He is reluctant," Cloud Racer said quietly while Laval seated himself. "The two of you must convince him. I have done all I could."

"Say to him first," Teller Of Legends said to Morning Song, pausing to bestow a regal smile upon their visitor, "that we consider him a man of honor." She had dressed for the occasion in the elkskin tunic she'd worn at Midsummer, and her hair was freshly braided and fastened with strips of bright red fabric. Strands of beads were draped around her neck, and the moccasins she wore— moccasins suspiciously short for her long feet—were also decorated with beads. She had appealed to Lake On Fire for these adornments, and Morning Song was aware that her grandmother hoped to soften the man sitting across from her by displaying items taken in trade with him.

Lah-Val, Morning Song thought, did not look capable of softening, and his wary eyes confirmed that he meant to resist persuasion. He had arranged himself so that he might sit for hours if need be. And he was, Morning Song concluded as she shifted herself discreetly away from him, as grimy and malodorous as ever. With one knurly hand he combed his filthy beard while she dutifully relayed her grandmother's praise.

She watched Teller Of Legends' face while Cloud Racer passed on Laval's response. It was, of course, highly complimentary to the Matron of the Turtle clan, to her ancestors, and to descendents both born and unborn.

"We do not wish," her grandmother said next, "to grieve you by speaking ill of your friend, so we shall say no more than we must about Bree-And. We are concerned only with his wife."

"Me, I do not count that one as friend," Laval said tersely. "Say what you will of him."

Teller Of Legends turned to her granddaughter. "You will talk to him directly then," she ordered, "and tell him what you found when you went to the home of Bree-And."

Morning Song was not prepared for this, but she made herself recount, in eloquent detail, what had met her eyes that day.

Cloud Racer listened approvingly; surely even this lone wolf of a white man would be moved by the tale?

He was not. "I have no woman of my own," he said bluntly. "Why should I take on one who belongs to another? I say to you, I cannot, and I will not."

"I have heard," Teller Of Legends said placidly, "that you name yourself friend to the Iroquois."

Laval contented himself with an abrupt nod.

"Then would you bring grief to those you call friends? You must know that if we keep the woman here, Bree-And will learn where she is. He is the kind who rejoices to cause trouble, and he does not have the sense that you do; he will not stop to think what effect his actions might have on future trade between Iroquois and *Onondio*." Teller Of Legends, who had leaned forward to signal her earnestness, settled back to give Laval time to consider what she had told him.

He did not ponder long. "Send the woman away," he said immediately. "You Iroquois, you are not responsible for her. As Gaspard Laval is not."

"You would see her return to a man who mistreats her?"

Laval registered his indifference with a hunching of his bony shoulders.

Morning Song had heard enough, and seen enough, of this vulgar creature who pretended to be a man. Without waiting for her grandmother to speak again, to further entreat one who was impervious to entreaty, she sprang to her feet and stood looking down on him.

"My daughter," she said acidly, "has come to feel that you must be possessed of a kind heart. There seemed to me no reason for this, but we trusted that she might see in you something I do not. You have proven to me how much of an innocent she is. I will go to her now and tell her to discard her illusions, tell her that you are in truth like all other white men: You think of no one but yourself, you serve no one but yourself, you care for no one but yourself. And you are as cruel as Bree-And, for it is not necessary to use one's fists against a woman to be that!"

She swung around and began to march toward the entrance.

Laval scrambled to his feet, glanced at Teller Of Legends, at Cloud Racer, then shouted, "Wait!"

Morning Song kept on going and would have passed into the compound if Cloud Racer and her grandmother had not also called to her.

"I do not promise anything," Laval said when she'd stopped and turned around, "but me, I will see the wife of Briand, and talk with her." His glare, as ferocious as the one Morning Song wore, did nothing to moderate her mood. She continued to glower all the way to the Deer lodge and all the way back to her own, so that Marie Briand was cringing with fear once more by the time she was brought before Teller Of Legends and a white man she did not know.

"She must be calmed," Teller Of Legends warned Laval, "before you speak with her."

But the trader's sharp eyes were discovering the discolorations on Marie Briand's forearms, and the purple bruises around her left eye. *"Mon Dieu!"* he muttered.

He thought we were making much of little, Morning Song realized—and did not know if that should fuel her contempt for him or dilute it. "Beneath the dress she wears, it is the same," was all she said.

Laval addressed himself to the frightened woman. "Briand, he did this to you?"

Briand's wife shrank from his inspection, said nothing.

Teller Of Legends signed to her granddaughter. "Answer him," Morning Song said.

Marie Briand cast down her eyes and nodded.

Laval was oblivious to her distress. "He has done this other times also?"

Her silence, the tears that began to trickle over her wasted cheeks, told him that this was so.

The trader cursed again, more softly but with considerably more passion than he'd shown earlier. "It is incredible," he said to Cloud Racer. "Yet my own eyes, they do not lie. You, your woman, the old one"—he bowed clumsily toward Teller Of Legends—"say only what is true: This woman must be kept from that animal Briand!"

For the first time, the fear-ridden woman looked at Laval and spoke to him. "I must go back to him," she whimpered. "Henri is my husband." Her tears flowed more freely, made of the rest of her words a gabble even her countryman could not comprehend.

Apparently he did not want to. He turned his back on her, bobbed his head toward Teller Of Legends, and walked briskly away from the Chief Matron's hearth. "There is a matter I must attend to," he said over his shoulder to Cloud Racer. "When I have seen to it, I shall come back. You and I, we will talk more of this then."

And before anyone had a chance to ask when this would be, the trader was gone.

Morning Song said flatly that they would never see him again. Teller Of Legends and Cloud Racer were more hopeful at first, but when two days passed without his coming they, too, began to doubt. When, on the third day, the shambling, articulated form of Gaspard Laval presented itself at the gate, all three were surprised to see him.

"Make ready the woman," he said after he had greeted them perfunctorily. "She is able to travel, yes?"

It was Morning Song he chose to put the question to and, were not such a thing impossible, she would have named what she saw in his eyes grudging respect. "If you are willing to move slowly, and rest often," she said.

He scowled. "To reach Quebec before the hard-frosts begin," he said, "we must leave at once. But we will stop when the woman needs to, I suppose. Me, I do not wish to deliver a corpse to *Mère* Catherine."

Morning Song looked at her husband, and he at her. Neither knew what Laval meant.

He scowled again, impatient to be gone now that he had decided on this course. "It is to the Mother Superior of an order of holy women that I will take her," he said. "You tell me Madame Briand, she wishes to return to that pig only because she fears to offend God. The good sisters in Quebec, they will bring a priest to hear her confession. Then, she will no longer be afraid."

This made no more sense to Morning Song than the Bree-And woman's earlier attempts to describe the damnation she expected to bring on herself. Yet Lah-Val—whom she would never have judged sensitive—seemed confident that he knew how to deal with the woman's peculiar terror. The *Onondio*, she decided, must surely relish the complicated. "I will bring her to you," she said.

Cloud Racer, having deciphered for Teller Of Legends what had passed between her granddaughter and the trader, turned to Laval. "Our Chief Matron would have me tell you that you are a good man, and shall always be welcome here," he told him. He eyed the disheveled Frenchman speculatively. "You do not worry that Bree-And will track you down and try to take his woman back?"

Laval bared yellowed teeth in a smile that answered Cloud Racer's question before his words did. "That one, he is no threat to anyone now."

'Then I, too, name you good," Cloud Racer said soberly.

Laval made a dismissive gesture, then stood in silence until Morning Song came out of her longhouse with Marie Briand. The woman had been fitted with an assortment of clothing borrowed from various matrons. The fur-lined boots, the hooded cloak she wore over a long-sleeved tunic, and one of Lake On Fire's garish skirts gave her a bulk she had never in her life owned. Only her face identified her, and as usual it was tear-streaked.

The trader sighed again; this was not a trip he was eager to set out on. "We will travel most of the way by canoe," he said to her, and did not marvel to see alarm petrify her features.

"He handles a canoe as deftly as any Iroquois," Cloud Racer put in helpfully.

But his assurance did not cheer her. She could not even make herself smile to show her real appreciation for the basket of food Morning Song pressed into her hands.

Laval said farewell for the both of them and accepted Cloud Racer's offer to accompany them to the river. Then he prodded the still-weeping Marie Briand ahead of him out of the compound and along the path through the fields.

Morning Song stared after them, shook her head bemusedly. "I am astonished to find myself feeling sorry for him," she said to her grandmother.

Teller Of Legends chuckled. "I am sorry for the pair of them. But Lah-Val will survive the mission, if he cannot enjoy it. As for the wife of Bree-And, she shall find peace, if nothing else, when she meets kindness again among her own people." She started for their lodge. "And all of this, I think, has taught a certain granddaughter of mine something I have never succeeded in teaching her. For all that I tried."

Morning Song, falling into step beside her, did not respond until they were seated comfortably by the hearth. "You mean, of course, that Lah-Val—a sallow-skin—has shown himself to be a decent person, and a dependable one."

Her grandmother nodded. "You know now that what I once said to you is true: People are good, or bad, or a mixture of both, depending not upon the color of their skins, but upon the fabric their spirits are made from."

"I cannot deny this any longer," Morning Song said slowly. "But it feels strange to be rid of a belief I've held for so long. Always I credited my Iroquois blood when I did what was right. When I went astray, I blamed my white blood." Her expression was rueful. "I suppose now I must simply charge the whole of Morning Song with both good and bad."

"That is true," Teller Of Legends said, satisfaction larding her voice. "You cannot be other than what you are. Why should you want to be? Yet I worried that you never seemed able to see this. Too often, you were like a leaf blown by the wind, letting yourself be driven by what you thought was expected of you. Our tribal traditions, for instance; you saw them as inflexible rules, and thought you needed to surrender your will to them to prove yourself an Iroquois woman."

"You taught me to respect our traditions," Morning Song pointed out.

"And so you should. But it is senseless to be constantly measuring yourself against them. They are a wonderful history of those who lived before us and we are supposed to learn from them, and to remember that our own lives will be a part of history one day." She studied the rapt oval that was Morning Song's face, smiled. "Whenever you were stubborn enough, or rebellious enough, to go your own way, you always felt—later—that you had done wrong. Yet we Iroquois have as much respect for independence as we do for tradition. We let ourselves be guided by what has been; we should be fools not to. But the Maker Of Life designed each of us to think for himself. We call upon the spirits to lead us; this is one of their reasons for being. But we never permit ourselves to be compelled by them."

Morning Song laughed softly. "Are you saying that, all along, I have been doing no more and no less than I should have been doing?"

Her grandmother echoed the laugh, for it had been pregnant with an emotion she shared. "I will not," she jested, "go so far as to say that. To do battle with your own *orenda*—which you have done on more than one occasion—is to invite defeat. However"—she was serious again—"you have mostly done what is natural to you, and the result is admirable, Morning Song. Your mixed blood cannot subtract from it. For all we know"—she laughed more robustly—"it may have helped make you a woman I am proud to call granddaughter."

Morning Song's smile faded, her brown eyes widened. "You are truly proud of me?"

Teller Of Legends had thought herself ready for this moment. Now she knew that twice the praying and planning could not have prepared her. She lifted one of Morning Song's slim hands and closed it between her broader ones. "I am. And so I shall say to the other Matrons, when I tell them you are to be Matron of the Turtle longhouse when I am gone."

Chapter 31

⬅ ➡

"You cannot mean this!" Morning Song exclaimed.

Teller Of Legends put on a mask of indignation. "Do you think this woman too old for her brain to know what her tongue says?"

"I could never think that," Morning Song said hastily; then managed a smile as she realized her grandmother was teasing her. "But truly, Teller Of Legends, I am not suited to be Matron. Wisdom is a stranger to me. Patience is no friend of mine, either. You know better than most how I speak and act too quickly, how often I scorn to take any time at all to think what is sensible. Only the witless would look to someone like me for counsel."

"Would Lah-Val have agreed to help the Frenchwoman if you had not been moved to accuse him of selfishness and cruelty? My *sensible* words were having no effect on him. He would never have helped us if instinct had not led you to say what you did. Instinct is a gift of the spirits, Morning Song, and it is not bestowed upon everyone."

"It seems unlikely that the spirits would give such a thing to me. Have you forgotten how I quested for a vision and was sent nothing but muddled memories? Or that the only dream ever to visit me was meaningless?"

"It was one you have yet to find the meaning of," Teller Of Legends corrected gently. "Morning Song, you trust me, I think."

Her granddaughter nodded.

"Then have faith in what I say. You will make a fine Matron. The day will come when you shall hear yourself praised not only by our clan but by the whole tribe."

"But what of Pumpkin Blossom?" Morning Song said. "From the moment of her birth, her mother prepared her to be Matron of our longhouse."

"Pumpkin Blossom is worthy of admiration, just as Bountiful Harvest was. Yet she is a follower, Morning Song, not a leader. While her mother lived, she patterned herself after her. When Bountiful Harvest went to dwell among our ancestors, Pumpkin Blossom was as lost as a child who wanders into the forest. Until she found another strong woman to respect and revere."

Morning Song wrinkled her brow. She had not been aware that Pumpkin Blossom admired one matron more than the others.

Teller Of Legends's long mouth quirked. "It is you, Morning Song, that Pumpkin Blossom honors now."

"That is impossible," Morning Song said flatly. "Grandmother, I have never questioned your judgment before, but in this you are mistaken. Pumpkin Blossom knows me—has always known me—for the clumsy person I am. We are good friends at last, and I think we shall continue to be. Yet I do not deserve honor from her, and shall never receive it. Except in the same quiet way that I honor her as both clan-kin and friend."

"Did I say"—a hint of youthful roguishness underscored the words—"that you wholly merit her admiration? She is right to respect you for your strength, however. And Pumpkin Blossom must always have someone to inspire her, Morning Song. My daughter may have been responsible for this need in her; or it may be simply that Pumpkin Blossom was born with it. But hers is a weakness that a Matron must not own."

"Then what of Day Greeter? She is like you in so many ways, Grandmother, and not merely in appearance. She is capable, and kind, and practical, just as you are. And she is no longer so shy as she was. You have seen how easily she talks and laughs with Deer Caller, for instance."

"I agree," Teller Of Legends murmured. "That you see all this proves something else about you, Morning Song. You have learned to peer beneath the surface and discover the person many never recognize. Day Greeter is also perceptive, but her nature is too sympathetic. It would destroy her to make decisions that might

istress others, and Matrons are occasionally called upon to do this.
ou, on the other hand, will be able to accept that compassion,
hile a fine thing in itself, must never corrupt judgment. Be-
des''—her pouched eyes gleamed—''my youngest granddaughter
as already waited overlong to take a husband. Let her concentrate
n him, and on the children she will be mother to.''

''Day Greeter insists she will never marry,'' Morning Song said.
Why do you think otherwise, Grandmother?''

''My own perception has been honed by decades, my dear. De-
ite what she says, Day Greeter will be taking Deer Caller for her
usband. And soon.''

Upon reflection, Morning Song found that the prediction lost its
ower to surprise. ''It is true that they are well matched,'' she said
owly. ''And the twins would rejoice to have Deer Caller return to
ur longhouse. We would all be pleased to have him back, come to
at. And for Day Greeter to have her own children to mother
stead of only nieces and nephews—Why, it would be an excellent
ing, for Deer Caller and Day Greeter to marry!''

''There is love between them already,'' Teller Of Legends said,
''although they do not quite recognize it yet.''

''Otter's spirit,'' Morning Song said softly, ''will approve.''

Teller Of Legends nodded. Then she grunted and shifted position
 ease her cramped legs. ''We are straying from the trail we set
ut on,'' she said. ''Do you see now why it must be you who steps
ito the moccasins I leave behind me?''

Morning Song helped her grandmother to her feet. ''We are
alking this trail prematurely,'' she said. ''It will be a long time
efore your moccasins are empty.''

Teller Of Legends grasped Morning Song's wrist so tightly that
ie younger woman winced. ''Open your eyes!'' she said. ''It is an
d, old woman you stand beside. I have lived a long life. I have
herished every day of it, but it has been a hard life at times. Will
ou condemn a weary old woman to more years than she wants or
eeds, merely to avoid a responsibility that must be yours eventu-
lly? I thought you loved me better than this.''

Sowing the seeds of remorse succeeded where all her methodical
rguments had not. ''My love for you has no limits,'' Morning
ong told her grandmother, meeting her challenging stare. ''When
ie time comes, I will not fail you. I will do all I can to justify your
uith in me. But please let me hope that this will not be soon. I
ave no wish''—her voice broke—''to awake to a world that you
ave gone away from, Teller Of Legends.''

The Matron sighed and embraced her granddaughter. ''I cannot

encourage your hope,'' she said sadly. ''To do so would be to li
to you, and that I have never done. Like Otter Swimming, I as
that you permit the both of us to recognize that I cannot be wit
you much longer. The love we have for each other must not b
strained by pretense, Morning Song.''

Morning Song fought back her tears and returned the embrace
If Teller Of Legends could face her own dying with such compo
sure, then her granddaughter must somehow do the same. As sh
had with Otter. ''No,'' she said steadily. ''Pretense will find n
home with us, Grandmother.'' She smiled. ''You have neve
stopped trying to teach me to accept what must be. In whateve
time may be left to us, I will try to prove that this woman has finally
learned the lesson.''

Morning Song realized she must behave as if each new day wa
no different from the many that had gone before. But she could no
help wondering, when it was her turn to cook, if this might be th
last meal she would prepare for her grandmother. She found ex
cuses to be in the longhouse when Teller Of Legends was there
and felt deprived when old friends visited and captured the whole
of the Matron's attention with gossip and reminiscence. And on a
crisp autumn evening, when she sat in the compound to listen to
one of her grandmother's tales, her heart was heavy in her breast
Would the legend of the healing waters be the last story ever nar
rated by the Matron of the Turtle clan?

Teller Of Legends seemed the same as always. Her strong face
reflecting the dancing flames, was placid. Her smile was indulgen
as she waited for the children to settle. And her voice, when sh
began to speak of the warrior Ne-Ku-Mon-Ta and his adored young
wife Sha-Ne-Wis, had lost none of its power to command and en
thrall.

But Morning Song's melancholy only increased. Surely her face
signaled it—and it would never do to let her grandmother read he
expression. Slowly, carefully, she maneuvered herself back unti
she sat behind the circle of engrossed listeners. Grateful that th
fire's light did not reach this far and that everyone's attention wa
focused on Ne-Ku-Mon-Ta's search for a medicine to cure his dying
wife, she unfolded herself and melted into the dense shadow be
tween the Turtle lodge and its nearest neighbor. She could not bear
this night, to hear how an Iroquois warrior had been led to the
magic waters that saved his woman's life. Not when no stream, no
spring, no river anywhere, could extend Teller Of Legends' ap

ɔinted years. She crept to the rear entrance of the longhouse,
ɪpped inside, and went to her bunk.

What will it be like, she asked herself as she tucked her legs
ɪder her, when Morning Song must move her belongings to the
ɪntral hearth? When those who called this place home looked to
ɪr for guidance, and turned to her in times of trouble? When they
ɪpended upon her to settle differences, lift flagging spirits, and
ɪal capably with any problems that might arise?

She shivered. Better to surrender to the sorrow that had driven
ɪr inside than torment herself with unanswerable questions!

With a barely audible swish of deerhide, a tall figure slid into the
ɪnghouse as silently as Morning Song had done. "I saw you go,"
ɪoud Racer said, sitting down beside her. The face he turned
ɪward her was only a pale blur, but Morning Song was comforted
ɪ it. "I wondered why you left, and why you looked so sad."

To talk with him might help her to cope with her grief and trep-
ɪation. In a voice she struggled to keep even, she told him every-
ɪng, and confessed her fear that she would not be the sort of
ɪatron the Turtle clan was accustomed to.

"My grandmother says I have only been imagining that my white
ɪood constantly battles with my Iroquois blood," she finished,
ɪand I have come to believe her. But I shudder to remember how
ɪpledged to be worthy of her faith in me. I know I never can be.
ɪd I have no wish at all to serve as Matron."

He nodded, stirring the darkness they sat in. "I think we all
ɪmetimes feel torn by warring spirits within us. You know how
ɪuch I long to see the Iroquois live in peace with one another and
ɪth other tribes. And even with the sallow-skins. Every time I lead
ɪarriors into battle I ask myself, How can this promote peace? Yet
ɪwould betray the trust of those who elected me war leader if I
ɪfused to fight. This, I cannot do. Any more than you will betray
ɪe trust Teller Of Legends has in you." His teeth were a flash of
ɪhite as he smiled. "I am a fine war leader, Morning Song, despite
ɪy distaste for war. And you will be an admirable Matron. When
ɪur grandmother dies," he went on more soberly, "you will find
ɪe strength to deal with it. And when you have grieved for her,
ɪat strength will grow as you learn to take her place in this long-
ɪɔuse."

"I wish I could believe you," she sighed.

He reached out and pulled her close to him. "When you had to,
ɪu overcame your fear of the river. You went over the falls, Morn-
ɪg Song, and survived. Be as brave now, and you will be able to
ɪove yourself again."

His hands roamed over her arched back, and she leaned into hi embrace as the strokes lengthened to include the curve of her hip her buttocks. She unfolded her legs, murmured with pleasure a his hands moved down to caress her thighs, moved upwards t explore the moist, warm place that was aching for his touch.

"I feel capable of anything, when we are together like this," sh said against his broad chest as, still embraced, they stretched o on the cornhusk mattress. She let her tongue dart teasingly again the hollow in his throat, slid her own hand between their close clinging bodies until she found the pulsing erection she sough "Promise me you will always banish my doubts this way," sh whispered as she closed her fingers over it.

He moaned softly. "Whatever your needs," he said when he wa able, "I will always be ready to love you, Morning Song." H lowered his head, and his mouth fastened hungrily around on distended nipple. Then Morning Song was moaning, too, and he heart was racing, racing wildly to match the frantic beating of hi

And when his throbbing spear plunged deep into the passion anointed sheath that waited for it, when the joy-filled coupling c war leader and future Matron had brought them to the glory c shared release, they collapsed side by side and drifted together int sleep.

On the following day, a day of lowering skies and wind-lashe rain, a messenger came from the tribe whose position made Keeper of the Iroquois's Eastern Door. Save for building up the fir and pressing food and drink upon him, the women kept their di tance while the man spoke with Se-A-Wi and Cloud Racer. Fis Jumping, a full-fledged warrior now, was invited to sit with them the honor earned him envious glances from the younger boys.

"The French are making war against the Iroquois again," Clou Racer told his wife when their visitor had taken his news to the ne village. "Even though our relations with the *Onondio* have bee uneasy recently, no one expected them to break their treaty wit us. And when they attacked one of our eastern villages, they wer not content with slaying every man and boy who tried to fend the off. When the soldiers had taken the village, they fired the crops i the fields and those the women had already harvested and stored." His black eyes glittered and the angles of his face seemed to hav been given a vigorous honing. "It is one thing when warriors di in battle; it is never dishonorable to slay an enemy, or be slain b him. It is different when old men and women and children are le

die from starvation unless other villages take them in. This calls
r retribution, and I mean to have a part in it.''

Morning Song kept her face impassive. Fleetingly she allowed
rself to be grateful that they had loved so ardently last night; he
uld not be able to share her bed during the preparations for his
aving. ''You will be able to find the sallow-skins that did this?''

He nodded. ''The war leader in a nearby village, when he heard
at had happened, sent out scouts. The French soldiers—and they
re many—went back to a fort near the river that runs along the
rder of Iroquois country.''

Rain drummed on the lodge's roof, wind shrieked around its
rners. Morning Song made no sound at all as she went to the
elf above their bunk and took down Cloud Racer's war hatchet.
When you have flung this into the post, and our warriors gather
hear you speak, you will not lack for volunteers to go with you.''
was the only way she knew to tell him that, much though she
nted him with her, she approved his going.

She did not tell him or anyone that she was visited that night by
dream of the crimson maple leaf. Or how the same dream came
ice more and that, over the three nights, the leaf's five sections
shaped themselves, transformed themselves into a blood-drenched
nd.

With the harvesting over, the women and girls turned to grinding
d sifting the corn that had not been hung to dry. And if Teller Of
egends—who in seasons past had taken pride in her expert wield-
g of the long, double-headed pestle—contented herself with test-
g the fineness of the meal and directing its storage, no one was
oved to jest that she was taking advantage of her status as Chief
atron.

They know, Morning Song told herself as she soused a basket of
iled corn in a tub of river water. The older matrons, at least, are
vare that my grandmother is nearing the end of her life. And she
ondered how such a momentous thing could occur so quietly;
w Lake On Fire could go on prattling about w dress she meant
wear for the Harvest Ceremony; how Rain Singing could whisper
citedly of Proud Woman's plans to take a husband; how Owl
'ying could sit and grumble that the younger maidens must be
osely supervised or they would make a sorry job of stripping the
rs.

She dipped the loop-handled basket one last time to be sure that
stubborn hulls remained, turned to give it to her daughter. But
d Bird's attention had strayed to the far end of the compound,

where the children were engaged in an unruly game of tag. Morni
Song tracked the girl's troubled gaze, saw that it rested on S
Descending. The matron was racing about as enthusiastically as t
youngsters were, and trying just as hard to evade the outstretch
hands of the sturdy little boy who had marked her as his target.

"Why is Sun Descending always with the children now?" R
Bird asked when she realized Morning Song was also watchin
"How is it she does not join the other matrons in their work?"

Her mother set the dripping basket on the ground. "When S
Descending's husband was killed," she said carefully, "her gri
was so great that she tried to hide from it. Only by becoming
child again—in her mind—could she do that." Morning Song we
on to try to explain the unexplainable. "She is able to be hap
again, this way. And her sons—who suffered dreadfully when s
was overcome with sorrowing—can be happy again, too."

"But they will grow up," Red Bird said after a moment, "wh
Sun Descending will not. What happens then, Morning Song?"

"They will accept, as all of us do, that this is how things are w
Sun Descending," Morning Song replied, surprised that an eigh
year-old should think to ask such a question.

"When I am a woman," the girl said, bending to pick up t
hulled corn, "I hope I am like you and not like Sun Descendin
You would know better how to deal with grief."

Her mother stared after her as she trotted away, wondering if s
had heard correctly. She watched as Pumpkin Blossom and R
Bird chatted at length once the girl had handed over the basket, a
her doubts burgeoned. Probably Red Bird had meant only that t
Iroquois woman who lacked the strength to withstand bereaveme
was rare indeed.

Her eyes wandered to where Teller Of Legends sat in front of t
Turtle lodge, her face lifted to receive the caress of the sun; a
she prayed earnestly that Morning Song, when the inevitable ha
pened, would not give her daughter reason to consider her less tha
strong.

The dream returned that night, yet it was not the same as befor
This time, the maple leaf was painted the fresh green of newbo
foliage. Then, with a slowness that commanded Morning Song
attention, it darkened until its five leaflets wore the glossiness
summer green, until she knew that here was a leaf in full an
healthy prime of life. And something in her cried out silently th
it should remain so, that the yellow season which marked the pea

its cycle should be endless, should refuse to make way for the
son that brought both glorification and destruction.

Morning Song stirred restlessly and flung out her arms. The vi-
n shivered, blurred at the edges, resurrected itself. And sound
gan to underscore her dream. Birds chirped; a breeze made sigh-
serenade; the hum and buzz of summer insects praised the
dly sun.

But the enchantment did not last. The murmuring breeze ma-
ed into a whining wind, a chill wind, a wind whose name was
stiny. The leaf's green faded to yellow, became streaked with
nge, then flooded with a brilliant red.

Morning Song, although she did not waken, knew what was
ming now. She thrashed about, muttered, drew her arms and legs
se to her body, and bowed her head over them.

The florid leaflets separated, thickened, rounded, until they were
mistakably the spread fingers of a broad-palmed hand. And from
:h finger globules of crimson slowly began to drip, drip, drip,
til the obscene pendants met and merged and became a sickening
ll of blood.

The awful vision froze, forcing the slumbering woman to ac-
owledge and identify what it was she looked upon. But even
n, Morning Song, huddled against the horror, slept on.

The wind had not ceased its plaint; now it raised its voice to a
eam. The five fingers of that bloodstained hand surrendered sub-
nce, flattened, were once again only parts of an aging maple
f. Yet the horror did not vanish when the hand did, for the sleep-
woman knew that she was witnessing the prelude to death.

The maple leaf, agitating wildly as the wind gusted, deteriorated
she watched. Opaque sunlight pointed up its transparency, and
en the wind rested the leaf drooped dispiritedly. It made no
empt to prepare for a second onslaught; in truth, it seemed to
d itself to the wind's impatient tug. Wrenched free at last, it
fted gracefully to the ground beneath.

The vision shifted, focused on the fallen leaf, treated Morning
ng to the sight and sound of needle-sharp rain. When, abruptly,
rain stopped, the leaf was barely recognizable. It lay amid a
st of others, waiting patiently to be driven into the earth by suc-
eding rains, to decay and become part of the soil which would
rture the leaves that unfolded during the next green season. . . .

Morning Song stretched her cramped limbs and opened her eyes
the grayness of predawn. She put up one hand to push back hair
sted to a cheek that, despite the morning's coolness, was damp
th perspiration.

She grimaced, and wondered why she had ever envied those whom dreams were regularly sent. If this one continued to plag her, if it continued to lengthen and broaden until it had invaded of the hours of her sleeping, she would dread to close her eyes. S dared not do so now, lest it return to repeat a message that, th time, had not been shrouded in mystery. She needed no mc dreams explaining that, in the end, death comes to everything th lives.

She raised her head, shook it vigorously to dispel the remnant of her dream. Why the wind's keening continued to haunt her, s did not know. But she meant to be rid of it!

Suddenly, she realized that the sound came, not from within h head, but from the opposite side of the lodge. From the bed of h grandmother. With a certainty that clutched at her belly and ice her pounding heart, she understood that Teller Of Legends's dea song was weaving itself among the shadows night had not yet r called.

The Matron's anxious family clustered around her. Alone, or twos or threes, they hovered over her bed, listening to the thin wa that pleaded with her ancestors to be ready for her coming. SI took no notice of any of them, paid not the slightest heed to th repeated calling of her name.

"It is as though she walks already in the spirit world," Pumpk Blossom said, and buried her face in her hands.

"The water I tried to give her only dribbled down her chin, Day Greeter said shakily.

Morning Song looked to each of them, looked beyond them where the children stood in a close and silent group. Se-A-Wi alor gave no indication of denial or despair. The Sachem's tired old eye brooded as he gazed at his dying sister, but his shoulders did n sag, his head with its thatch of cloud-gray hair remained resolute erect.

"Are we ignorant children," she said sharply to her cousins, " cower because we are in the presence of death? Teller Of Legen is not afraid, and we dishonor her if we show fear."

Pumpkin Blossom uncovered her face. "It is not death I a afraid of, but losing our grandmother. What will become of th family when she is gone?"

It would not do to admit that this same question echoed in Morning Song's mind. "We will do as she expects us to do," she sai "We shall go on with our lives, and be guided by what she h taught us. We will cherish our memories of her, and invite part ier spirit to remain in this lodge.'' She turned to Day Greeter. 'Teller Of Legends will take no food or drink now,'' she explained, 'even if she is able to. She accepts that her end has come, and has no wish to postpone it.''

"You cannot mean that she *wants* to leave us!'' The choked whisper came from Hidden Moon, and Morning Song waited for Pumpkin Blossom to respond to it.

When she did not, when instead she turned her red-rimmed eyes to her cousin, Morning Song stifled a sigh and thought briefly that, one last time, Teller Of Legends was proven right. "She is ready to die, and willing to die. But this does not mean that she is happy to leave us,'' she said gently. "It means that she is commanded to turn her back on us now in order to follow the path leading into the world of our ancestors. She knows that we shall join her there one day, and she will be the first to greet us when we do.''

"Will Teller Of Legends go to the place where slain warriors go?'' Swift Arrow asked hesitantly.

Morning Song smiled. "Who do you think tends the hearths in that land, and cooks the venison the men bring back from the hunt, if not women?''

Her son turned to the other boys, and the four began to talk excitedly. Morning Song knew they were comparing tales they'd been told of the game-glutted territory that the Maker Of Life had set aside for the spirits of brave warriors. The girls could not help but overhear, and it would comfort them to be reminded that the world Teller Of Legends was going to was filled with wonders.

She wished she herself might be comforted so easily, or might at least confess her need to be. Since neither was possible, she would keep busy instead. And see that the others did also.

"You will make this day's meal,'' she said briskly to Pumpkin Blossom. "Our daughters can help you.''

Pumpkin Blossom opened her mouth to say that surely no one would want to eat. But Morning Song's expression forbade protest, so she called to Hidden Moon and Red Bird and directed Painted Sky to fire up her hearth. Perhaps she could roast the plump goose Fish Jumping had brought home yesterday, and bake a pumpkin to go with it. The girls could make the bread.

Morning Song watched her bustle away, then turned to Day Greeter. "The Matrons must be told what is happening. If you visit the Plover longhouse first, I am sure Tree Reaching Up will go with you to speak with the others.''

"She will probably come here instead,'' Day Greeter said, "to see if she can be of help to you. But Deer Caller will not mind visiting the longhouses with me. He has always been fond of Teller Of Legends. He will want to do what he can for her family.''

"Bring him back here afterward," Morning Song suggested. "I think Se-A-Wi will be glad of his company, and I know the twins will.''

She watched Day Greeter go out and noticed that she looked less mournful than she had—almost certainly because she would soon be seeing Deer Caller. Teller Of Legends had been right about those two, and Morning Song did not begrudge her shy young cousin any consolation Deer Caller brought to her. She only wished Cloud Racer could be home, to console Morning Song.

She walked the perimeter of the lodge, putting to rights the children's bunks, picking up possessions that had strayed from their proper places. She even managed a smile when she came across the bone Swift Arrow was saving as a treat for the floppy-eared brindle pup who had lately taken to following him around. And when a zealous sun poured light upon the compound, she looped back the entrance hide to let in its warmth, its brightness. Her grandmother had always loved the sunshine. . . .

If the Matron of the Turtle clan felt it flooding in, she gave no sign. Morning Song looked upon a face she knew better than her own, upon a woman she came near to worshipping, and warned herself that she must not weep. She seated herself midway between the old woman's bed and her own cold hearth and worked on the winter boots she was sewing for her son. When those were finished, new cloaks must be made for her children. And Cloud Racer's favorite moccasins should have new soles. Morning Song would find excuse enough to sit here, close to the woman who lay so still on the bunk against the wall, for as long as need be.

She rose courteously when Tree Reaching Up came in, and again when the parade of elders and matrons began. She spoke briefly with each one who came to commune silently with an old and well-loved friend. But she never left the spot she had claimed for herself, not even when Pumpkin Blossom—in a hushed and hesitant voice— told her that their meal was ready. She forced herself to eat, of course. If she did not, the others would refuse to fill their bellies and strengthen themselves for the trying time to come.

They were applying their spoons with more diligence than enthusiasm when the rhythmic treble of the death song rose again from Teller Of Legends' bunk. Steadfastly Morning Song continued to eat, to tear at a chunk of perfectly cooked goose. Her mouth was full when the eerie singing stopped, and as she leaped up and ran to her grandmother she was spitting out meat she had known from the start she'd never be able to swallow.

She did not need to look twice to know that the spirit of Teller Of Legends had begun its journey to the place where her husband and her daughters were spreading welcoming arms to receive it. Those who had rushed in Morning Song's wake knew it, too; a chorus of indrawn breaths proved that. Still, the words must be said.

"Teller Of Legends has died," she announced in a voice that sounded not at all like her own.

She straightened and faced the others: Se-A-Wi, whose eyes were fixed on his sister's serene face; Pumpkin Blossom, whose beauty had been savaged by a shock she should have been prepared for; Day Greeter, who groped for Deer Caller's hand; the sons of Otter Swimming, whose identical features displayed an identical grief; Fish Jumping, who tried for stoicism and almost achieved it; and the four children, who huddled together against a chill the weather was not responsible for. She persuaded herself that her own eyes neither stared blindly nor shimmered with unshed tears, that her own mouth had not twisted until it seemed alien to the face it belonged to. But the taste of meat lingered on her tongue, and through all the days of her life she would remember how she had been trying to eat roast goose when her grandmother died.

Chapter 32

◆ ⇒

Morning Song was no stranger to the burden grief lays on the spirit; she had borne it before. What truly weighed her down was awareness of her new responsibilities. A lodge must have a Matron, and everyone in the village looked to Morning Song to take her grandmother's place. All that kept Morning Song from staggering beneath her double load was remembrance of Teller Of Legends' faith in her. Unwarranted though it was, she would not let herself profane it.

Now, as the rites honoring the Chief Matron came to an end, she continued to hold herself tall. Her keening had been done with a dignity that bolstered the rest of her clan, and in a little while she would slip away to the forest and give voice to the anguish she had been repressing. . . .

A discordant murmur issued from the outer edges of the slowly dispersing circle of mourners. When it grew loud enough for Morning Song to distinguish a word here, a word there, her craving for solitude vanished. The warriors' canoes had been sighted! By the time she reached the river, they would have reached the shore. And Cloud Racer's broad shoulder would be there for her to lean against, his strong arms would hold her while she wept, and his love would resurrect the strength she had spent the last of.

Morning Song sped across the compound and into the fields, passing without seeing other matrons hurrying to greet their men. Above her head, an army of storm-dark clouds went into retreat. The sun's jubilant smile was reflected in the river she was approaching, was burnishing the oiled torsos of the men upending the canoes and striding across the stubble to their homecoming.

They saw at once that the wife of their war leader would be the first to bid them welcome, yet they sent no smiles ahead of them. And not even the younger warriors shouted—as they usually did— to ask why they did not smell the meat that should be cooking for their victory feast. Instead, many averted their eyes, or exchanged uneasy glances with their fellows as the distance between themselves and Morning Song narrowed. And several veered away to take a less direct route to the village.

The sun continued to shine, but Morning Song felt suddenly as though winter-cold air had spiraled out of the north and come to eddy around her. She slowed her pace, made herself lift feet that resisted the tensing of her leg muscles, that seemed to understand before the rest of her did that they took her into the gaping jaws of a beast named devastation.

In the end, Hawk Hunting, Bear In The Sky, and Fish Jumping came on the run to support her, for Morning Song began to sway as though that imaginary wind were buffeting her slender body. And when they told her what they must, their voices were tight-woven with their own pain.

"Cloud Racer died bravely," Hawk Hunting said, "as he has always lived. Remember that, while you mourn him. As we shall."

Morning Song stood like a snow sculpture frozen hard. She did not speak; she did not even blink. They called her name, singly and in chorus, but she did not respond. Her involuntary swaying had alarmed the men; her silence terrified them.

"I will fetch my sisters," Fish Jumping said at last. He limped as he moved away; like all the others, he had been wounded during the battle. But Morning Song did not notice; she was blind even to the ugly gash in Hawk Hunting's forearm.

Bear In The Sky and Hawk Hunting put up no argument when Meadow Brook and Proud Woman, coming to meet them, insisted upon relieving them of their vigil. "You will do better to carry Cloud Racer to the village. We shall take care of Morning Song," Meadow Brook told her husband.

When they had gone to where his shrouded body lay, she touched Morning Song's rigid arm. "If you stand here forever, it will not change what is," she said firmly. It was too soon, much too soon, for sympathy.

Proud Woman looked into Morning Song's glazed eyes, then placed a hand on each of her shoulders, and turned her around. Now she faced the village, and not the riverbank over which Hawk Hunting and Bear In The Sky would be bringing their dead comrade. She did not resist when the women flanked her and propelled her forward. But when they had half carried, half dragged her through the outermost field, Meadow Brook gave the arm she gripped a little shake.

"You will walk, Morning Song," she said sharply. "The Matron of the Turtle lodge must not disgrace her clan. She must not bring shame to the spirit of her brave husband by acting the coward."

A shudder, a visible violent shudder, coursed through Morning Song. Her set expression dissolved and she went limp, would have crumpled to the ground if her escorts had not tightened their hold. Then, slowly, she pulled herself erect and took a single plodding step forward.

Together they moved in fits and starts along the path leading home. Before Pumpkin Blossom and Day Greeter had responded to their brother's plea for help, Morning Song was walking on her own.

No one knew what lay at the center of the unnatural calm that was born in Morning Song that afternoon. Pumpkin Blossom praised her remarkable control; the older matrons murmured uneasily among themselves; her grieving children were bewildered by this impassive stranger who wore their mother's face.

She stood with head held high throughout the rites for Cloud Racer, just as she had during the ceremony honoring Teller Of Legends. Neither tear nor tremor betrayed that this woman was not reconciled to her lover's dying. She alone knew that what others viewed as stolid acceptance was merely a mask she had put on. She would wear it until she had earned the right to a measure of genuine peace.

Hawk Hunting had been puzzled when she'd sent for him the day after the warriors returned, and he was reluctant to answer the questions she put to him. "Surely it can only distress you all over again to hear the battle described," he had said.

But Morning Song's quiet tone and steady gaze had reassured him, and he'd told her at last what she needed to know: how the *Onondio* fort had been better defended than they'd expected; how their guns had felled many of the attacking Iroquois even before the combined war parties began to scale the enclosure's walls. "Cloud Racer's shrewdness saved us from being slain at the beginning of the siege," he said. "He told us to go close to the palisade, close enough to hug the walls. 'They will aim outward,' he said; 'no fighter, not even a sallow-skin, will waste time shooting at what he cannot see.' And he was right. But once we were within the gates, we became targets for them."

"You saw Cloud Racer killed?" she asked, and he nodded, his face grim.

"And you saw which soldier slew him?

"Three of them attacked him," he said, "but I saw the face of the one who drove his sword into Cloud Racer's chest."

"What was he like, this sallow-skin who killed my husband?" Her voice was hoarse, but her face remained expressionless. Hawk Hunting eyed her uncertainly, then gave her the information she'd been waiting for.

"I will never forget him. He will be the one I look for when we go back. He was paler than most sallow-skins, and a jagged scar ran from eyebrow to chin on the left side of his face. That scar will guide me to him, and I will give him a twin to the wound that made it before I split his heart with my lance!"

Morning Song had clenched the hands hidden in the folds of her skirt, and managed to smile as she thanked him for coming to talk with her. "When will you go east again?" she asked.

"As soon as our injuries have healed and our weapons have been repaired or replaced," he said harshly. "I will not let someone else get there before me and slay the Frenchman I have marked for myself."

You shall be disappointed, Morning Song said silently to his departing back. *There is one who has more right than you to claim revenge. And nothing and no one will cheat her of it!*

She knew that her son and daughter must be made privy to her plan. After all, they might find themselves motherless as well as fatherless before much longer. Morning Song did not think that would happen; now that she finally understood what her spirit guide expected of her, she trusted him to protect this obedient woman. But she wanted her children to know what their mother intended to do, and why.

She looked into their solemn faces—the huge-eyed oval that was Red Bird's, the youthful cast of his father's features that was Swift Arrow's—and refused to let herself think that she might not see them grow up. "What I am going to tell you, you must speak of to no one else."

The childen looked at each other, looked back to Morning Song, and nodded in unison. They were uncomfortable with the woman their mother had become, but she was their mother still. They would respect her confidence.

"Come and sit by me," she said, patting the ground on either side of her. "There is a story you must hear before I reveal my secret to you. You will not see a reason for it, otherwise."

They hunkered down beside her, and she put an arm around each of them. Only rarely had the three shared such moments of closeness, and she wished she might use this one to speak of ordinary things, pleasant things. But she had no time for that. "My story begins when I was not much older than you are, Swift Arrow," she said. "I went on a Vision Quest then—"

Her son gaped at her, and Red Bird gasped. "It cannot have been a proper Vision Quest you went on," Swift Arrow protested. "Only boys do that, Mother."

She smiled a little. "In many ways, I was not the sort of girl you are accustomed to. For one thing, I had never been visited by a dream when I slept. Which is why I went on my quest, even though I knew that it was something girls were not supposed to do."

"You went alone into the forest?" Red Bird asked. "You stayed four days and nights by yourself?"

"And went the whole time without food?" Swift Arrow put in.

"I did. I even denied myself water during part of my quest. And on the fourth day, a vision was sent to me. It is as clear to me now as it was then. Indeed, it sometimes seems even clearer."

They did not stir while she described the animal faces that had emerged from the river, the crimson sun that was no kin to the one in the sky, her frustration that she could find no meaning in anything she saw. "Not even Hearth Tender, who was a Faithkeeper, could do more than guess what it meant. As for the red maple leaf that I found floating in the river afterward . . . ." She touched the pouch dangling from the thong she wore around her neck. "Whenever I thought I had discovered what it represented, something occurred to prove me wrong."

"A token brought home from a Vision Quest," Swift Arrow said, "must have meaning. Even for a girl."

She nodded. "I know now that mine does. At long last, my spirit guide has been filling my nights with visions, each one about a leaf just like this." She paused. Understanding was flowing sweetly between herself and her children; would she destroy it by what she had to say next?

"In these dreams," she continued presently, "the leaf has been transforming itself into a hand, a hand drenched in blood. Even the vision that foretold Teller Of Legends' dying was ruled by such a hand."

Swift Arrow and his sister traded glances again, troubled ones this time. Was this the secret Morning Song had warned them they must keep silent about?

"When I learned that your father had been . . . slain," their mother said tightly, "I knew what message my spirit guide had been trying to send me." She held up her slim hands, spread the delicate fingers far apart. "I am to avenge Cloud Racer's death," she told her children. "Until these two hands have been stained with the blood of the *Onondio* who slew him, your father's spirit will be unable to rest. And I will not rest, either."

Swift Arrow leaped to his feet. "No!" he shouted. "You may have gone on a Vision Quest, but it is senseless to think this makes you a man! No woman may be a warrior, Morning Song." He threw back his shoulders, flung up his head, tried his best to look as purposeful as the father he had idolized. "It is for Cloud Racer's son to avenge him," he said fiercely. "Not his wife!"

Morning Song was struck dumb. This, she had not anticipated.

Before she could think what to say, Red Bird, too, had jumped up and was glaring at her brother. "You say that our mother lacks sense," she said, "yet you are showing us plain that you have none at all. You have not even begun to train as a warrior. Are you planning to take your child's bow, and the arrows that are good against nothing but small game, and go after the French soldier who killed our father? Besides"—her frown was ferocious, her tilted chin challenging—"Iroquois women are led by the spirits, just as men are. Do you think Morning Song will close her ears to hers just because he has set her a difficult task? Our mother is brave nough to do what she must, Swift Arrow, and we should be glad hat she is.''

No one who saw Morning Song now would have named her calm, or praised her self-discipline. That decorous Red Bird was defending her mother's defiance of tribal custom left her weak with astonishment, and speechless with love and pride.

''I may not be a warrior yet,'' Swift Arrow rejoined, ''but Morning Song has never been one, ever. What can a woman use for a weapon, Red Bird? An awl? A hide-scraper?''

Morning Song did not hear Red Bird's response, but the girl's stance, the look on her face, showed her mother what the older members of the Turtle clan must have seen whenever the child Morning Song made up her mind to resist the pressures of tradition in order to go her own way. ''I have weapons,'' she said quietly, and both of her children fell silent. ''The bow and the lance that hang above my bunk, the ones below your father's, belong to me.'' She tried a small laugh to ease the tension that vibrated between her son and her daughter. ''I shall need to practice with them, of course, before I dare use them again.''

''When you do, I will help you,'' Red Bird told her, turning her back on her brother. ''Cloud Racer said that once you outshot him when both of you were stalking the same stag, so perhaps you will not need a great deal of practice, Morning Song.'' Her voice was nearly as sedate as it ordinarily was, but the gleam that had leaped into her eyes—a gleam her mother had never, ever, expected to see in those eyes—remained undiminished.

''I hope you may be right,'' Morning Song said, ''but I'm afraid I know better. It has been so long since I've even held my weapons that it may take considerable time for me to resharpen my skills. And my practicing,'' she added, focusing anew on the reason the three were having this talk, ''must also be kept secret.''

Swift Arrow looked from his mother to his sister and back again. ''I still feel it is wrong,'' he said gruffly. ''But I can remember a time when Cloud Racer laughed and said that Morning Song would never be swayed from any course she was determined to follow. So''—he swallowed hard—''even though I am against it, I will keep your secret. And I will help you, too.''

It was indeed awkward at first, handling a bow and lance after so many years. But only at first. In a matter of days Morning Song's dexterity was restored to her. Eye and hand began to respond with speed that amazed her children, and only a reluctance to offer explanation in the Turtle lodge and in the village kept her from bringing down more game than could logically be attributed to her son's budding skills. This was merely the start of her training, however. Swift Arrow—if he was a long way from becoming a warrior—had never missed a battle story told by the men whose status he envied. "It is different in war," he told his mother earnestly. "When you hunt animals, you are the only one doing the stalking. This is not so with human prey. The Frenchman will be as ready to kill you as you are to kill him. You will be hunted as well as hunter, so you must learn to be twice as wary."

It was not easy, with only the three of them, to conduct mock battles, but Swift Arrow and Red Bird did not shrink from attacking their mother as she searched among the trees for their tracks. They came at her, separately and in tandem, and if they succeeded in touching any part of her with the long sticks they carried, the exercise must be repeated. Morning Song received scores of painful jabs before she had learned to sense that one or both of them was creeping up on her, before she had trained herself to twist and dodge instinctively even as she loosed an arrow, lunged with her long lance, or thrust with her short-hafted one. But in one way they could not best her at all. Try as they might to distract her from the target of her choice, they never succeeded. Be it tree or boulder or feckless hare, Morning Song superimposed upon each one the figure of a pale-fleshed soldier whose face wore a distinctive scar. She did not know if the man was tall or short, fat or thin, and did not care. It was his face she would be watching for, the face that branded him as Cloud Racer's killer.

Red Bird suggested finally that they ask Bold Leader and Brave Companion to join them on their daily treks into the forest. "They are bigger than we are, and nearer to being warriors than Swift Arrow is. And they can be trusted with your secret."

Yet even when there were four conspirators to contend with, all of whom brought to this sham warfare the single-mindedness only children possess and the deviousness only children are naturally capable of, Morning Song outwitted them right and left. And it was the youngsters who trudged home when the brief autumn twilight signaled the day's ending; Morning Song, buoyed by her sense of mission, strode along with a tirelessness the youngsters marveled at.

To convince Hawk Hunting that the band he was taking east should include Morning Song was a challenge of a different sort.

"If Cloud Racer were here and you asked such an outrageous thing of him, he would refuse," the warrior said sternly. "Knowing that, I would dishonor his memory if I did otherwise. I have heard

your skill with lance and bow, Morning Song; I know that Cloud
cer himself was impressed by it, and he was not easily im-
ssed. But it is not a woman's place to go to war.''

She had been bold enough to approach him at a time when a
mber of villagers had reason to be in the compound. Nor had
kept her voice low; she was indifferent to what others might
ke of the proposal Hawk Hunting named outrageous. "Those
o cared for me,'' she said clearly, "never recoiled from taking
enge for wrongs I had suffered. My mother knifed the man who
s my father when he tried to drown me. My husband tracked
wn and killed the men who had captured and tortured me. Now
s my turn, and I mean to set my feet on the trail my spirit guide
led me to. If you do not permit me to join your war party, then
ill travel to the French fort on my own.''

The newly elected war leader folded his arms and eyed her in-
dulously. "You would not be so foolish,'' he said.

'Do not underestimate her, Hawk Hunting.'' Proud Woman,
led from the Deer longhouse by a stunned Rain Singing, had
led to his side. "No other woman would be likely to do what
threatens to, but I think Morning Song will not belie her words.
d if you name her fool for wanting to take the life of the man
o stole Cloud Racer's, then you must name me fool also. I reed to slay the warrior who struck down my father, and would
e killed more of our attackers if I could.''

Hawk Hunting, by nature and inclination a just man, closed his
s to those who were championing his attempts to thwart Morning
ng. He examined seriously the argument put forth by the woman
meant to marry. Certainly he loved Proud Woman no less be-
se she'd fought fiercely as a wildcat that day. And Cloud Racer
l been openly admiring of her courage. Yet the circumstances
re not the same. The battle had been brought to where Proud
oman lived; her taking part in it had not been planned. To delib-
tely lead Morning Song into war was a different thing altogether,
d it was contrary to everything Hawk Hunting had ever been
ight.

He looked again into the face of the woman who had been Cloud
cer's wife. There was no supplication in her brown eyes; they
rned with a resolution that instinct warned him would not be
mpened. And Fish Jumping, who had shown himself both val-
ous and quick-thinking, was her cousin. Surely he would be will-
g to help shield Morning Song when the fighting began.

It might have been midnight, so great was the hush that lay upon
compound. Whatever decision he made now would become

food for the matrons who fed upon gossip, would be criticized **b**
the elders who still regarded Hawk Hunting and his peers as callo
youths. "You may go," he said at last. "But do not expect, Mor
ing Song, to have things made easy for you because you are
woman. As of now, you must fast, as we do. From the moment **w**
leave this village, you will be considered a warrior like any othe
You will sleep on the hard ground, as we do, and eat trail ration
as we do. And you will not complain of weariness, or of achir
muscles, or of rain or cold should the weather be foul."

Morning Song's gaze did not waver. "I do not look for favor **o**
special consideration," she said. "I would refuse either, were
offered. We are in agreement, Hawk Hunting. And I thank you.**"**

She spun on her heel and walked away. It did not occur to h**e**
until long afterward that her thanks should have gone first to Pro**u**
Woman, a maid she had once loathed for being all that Morni**ng**
Song was not, a woman she had once considered her enemy.

They began their eastward trek in the long canoes, and Morni**ng**
Song stepped unhesitatingly into the one she was assigned to. She
known they would cover most of the distance by water, yet s**he**
remained undaunted. To have been handed a paddle might ha**ve**
dismayed her; compared to the men, she was woefully inept, a**nd**
some would see her clumsiness as proof that Hawk Hunting ha**d**
made a bad decision. But the warriors charged with steering t**he**
elm-bark craft were proud of their skill and never surrendered the**ir**
paddles to anyone. As they moved smoothly and swiftly towa**rd**
their destination, Morning Song ignored the mutters directed in**to**
the air by the disgruntled and spoke only when a brave resigned **to**
her presence spoke first to her. When the canoes were carried ove**r**
land to avoid rapids, or to pass from one river or lake to anothe**r**
she was quick to position herself so that her shoulders bore a sha**re**
of the weight. When her help was not needed with the portagin**g**
she toted one of the huge baskets that would serve more effective**ly**
than litters if there should be wounded to bring home. And whe**n**
they camped, she did not permit herself, even secretly, to rub
muscles that had a tendency to knot after a night spent sleeping **o**
frost-hardened ground. She readily endured all of this, and not ju**st**
to keep her word to Hawk Hunting; her obsession with the ima**ge**
of a scar-faced French soldier inured her to hardship. By the e**nd**
of the journey, she had aroused admiration even in those oppose**d**
to her coming with them. But Morning Song was as deaf to the**ir**
praise as she had been to their grumbling.

Now, as they slipped through the forest bordering the river t**he**

rench fort stood beside, she fumed at the slow pace Hawk Hunting
t. He had conferred the day before with the leaders of two other
ar parties. Cloud Racer had not been the only warrior slain during
e first assault on the fortress, and others besides Morning Song
ere bent upon revenge. The three bands were making this final
pproach separately, to confuse the *Onondio*, but they had agreed
synchronize their movements. Like the men's, all of Morning
ng's exposed flesh was smeared with soot, and she clutched her
w in her left hand, her lance in her right. The flint-toothed war
ub swinging at her waist was balanced by a quiver of arrows. She
as ready, more than ready, to meet the enemy. If only they might
ove along faster than a procession of dull-witted snails!

A pigeon cooed, but no gray-feathered bird had made the sound.
beying Hawk Hunting's signal, Morning Song cautiously lowered
e foot she had raised and squinted through a tangle of bracken to
e if the fort was in sight. Fish Jumping, who walked behind her,
oved forward and stooped until his mouth was close to her ear.
We ford the river here,'' he murmured.

Hawk Hunting had chosen a spot below the fortification, where
bend in the river prevented sentries from sighting them. The
arriors were careful, nonetheless; with bows at the ready, they
aded single file through knee-deep, shockingly cold water. Morn-
g Song gritted her teeth as feeling was leached from feet and
kles and calves. The river's stony bed was treacherous even for
es that recognized obstacles. But she did not fall behind.

Opportunity for concealment was sparse on the far side of the
ver, but the war band made excellent use of what there was. With
e others, Morning Song flitted like a wraith from tree to bush,
d crawled on her belly when the only cover available was rough-
xtured grass or clumps of slow-dying fern.

Hawk Hunting whistled like a grouse, and his followers crept
rward, one by one, until they had aligned themselves with him,
til each warrior was an arm's length from the one on either side.
lorning Song found herself between Hawk Hunting and Fish
mping, but she took no thought for her position. Ahead stretched
space denuded of trees and shrubs, and beyond it rose the palisade
rrounding the *Onondio* fort. This was square-built, and the lodge
at marked its center was uncommonly tall. Although Morning
ng was flat on the ground, its peaked roof was visible to her.

The agile young warrior who was acting as scout slithered sud-
nly between the war leader and Morning Song. His eyes spared, and the grin he wore was jubilant. ''I shinnied up the tree
u told me to climb,'' he reported breathlessly. ''From the top, I

could see into the stockade. I counted the soldiers—and unle
others huddle in the shelters, they number no more than we do.'

Please, Morning Song prayed, let the scar-faced sallow-skin
there. Please.

"No more than this group alone, or no more than the men in
three war parties?" Hawk Hunting asked crisply.

"If there were no more than the score of us," the lad said airi
"I would be volunteering to go alone against them!"

Hawk Hunting shook his head. "You have much to learn. A
if you persist in looking upon war as a game, this day's lesson m
be a bitter one!" He turned his head toward Morning Song. "N
one knows what battle is like until he has survived his first,"
said urgently. "Stay close to me, Cloud Racer's wife. I do not wi
to anger my friend's spirit by failing to protect you."

He did not wait for the protest she was framing, but pursed h
lips and produced the grouse's reedy plaint once more. Three tim
he whistled, and Morning Song obediently raised herself to h
hands and knees at the second signal, sprang erect at the third.

Musket fire broke out before the warriors had sprinted past th
midway point of the clearing. Four men who had kept to the re
snapped up their bows and began launching arrows at the soldie
whose heads appeared along the parapet. At least one arrow four
its mark. As Morning Song put on a burst of speed that broug
her flat against the splintery logs of the palisade, a cry rang out ar
a body hurtled down to land with a thud on the ground behind he

"Keep close to the wall," Hawk Hunting said, "and go to th
corner where the logs meet and jut out."

She bobbed her head, pressed her back tight against the wal
and edged after him. Gray-bottomed clouds were scudding acro
the sky, and her steps took her through a tortoiseshell pattern
alternating shadow and blinding light. But she would not let th
confuse her, or slow her progress to the northwest corner of th
palisade.

She knew what the battle plan was; they all did. A second ban
of warriors would be reaching the palisade's southwestern corn
just about now. The largest of the war parties had split; half wou
be grouping at the stockade's northeastern corner, and half at i
southeastern. "We will not try to storm the gates," Hawk Huntin
had told them earlier. "We Iroquois are kin to raccoons when
comes to climbing, and have no fear of heights. It will be a simp
matter to mount the walls where the logs cross. One after the oth
we will climb up, and if we are quick enough, and silent, th
sallow-skins will not know we are there until we are upon them.

Marksmen had been assigned to draw the enemy's fire. Now a
chorus of caterwauls, followed by a deafening volley of musketry,
advised Morning Song to shoulder her bow and sheathe her short-
handled lance. Both hands would be needed for climbing.

A strangled shout announced that a musket ball had found a
target; but Hawk Hunting's heels were on a level with her eyes, and
she could think of nothing but grasping the protruding ends of the
transverse logs and hauling herself up after him.

Suddenly she realized that the soldiers had been alerted to their
ploy. Already they were training their guns on the corner she must
jump into. There was a confusion of explosive shots, the clash of
metal on metal, an unleashing of battle cries as the first warriors
swooped into the compound. Acrid smoke seeped through chinks
in the logs as a fresh burst of musket fire crackled like a new-lit
hearth.

Fear iced Morning Song's veins—not of being struck by a lethal
musket ball as soon as she'd scaled the wall, but of dying before
she had stalked and slain her prey.

She swallowed hard, and told herself this must not, would not,
happen. Hand over hand, she pulled herself the rest of the way up,
balanced herself atop the palisade, and leaped into chaos. Before
she'd straightened from her instinctive crouch, Fish Jumping landed
beside her. He grabbed her arm and shoved her behind him.

"No!" she screamed. "I have not come this far only to hide
from combat."

But he was drawing his knife from its sheath. With a howl of
fury, he flung it at a soldier who was using his rifle to bludgeon one
of their comrades. The weapon dropped to the ground as Fish
Jumping's blade sank into his back.

Morning Song shrugged off her bow; it was useless here. She
unsheathed her lance with her right hand, snatched up her war club
with her left. When Fish Jumping darted away to retrieve his knife,
she erupted from the corner he'd consigned her to and looked wildly
around her. With no time to reload, the French were being compelled to fight one-on-one with the warriors. Boots beat a thunderous tattoo on rocky ground as the soldiers took up knives and swords
and raced toward the invaders. The Iroquois shrieked their separate
challenges as they met them halfway. Vying with the clang and
scrape of steel were the *Onondio*'s hoarse curses, and brays of pain
punctuated the bleatings of the mortally wounded.

Morning Song was transfixed by a horror no warriors' tales had
prepared her for. Numbly she watched Hawk Hunting elude a lung-
ing sallow-skin, bring up his axe, and cleave the man's skull. As

brains oozed from the bloody split, Morning Song shuddered—an
came out of her involuntary trance.

She looked quickly to be sure the dead man did not wear a sca
on his face. Not far from where he'd fallen, Bear In The Sky, bloo
pouring into his eyes from a gash in his forehead, grappled wit
another soldier. Morning Song raised her lance and raced to hi
rescue, but Fish Jumping was there before her. He dispatched th
soldier with a swipe of his hatchet, then fended off two more unt
Bear In The Sky had wiped away the blood that obscured his visio

The hairs bristled on Morning Song's neck. She spun aroun
with her club already swinging. A blade whistled past her ear an
buried itself in the chest of the soldier who had thought to bury h
sword in Morning Song's back. She looked down at the dying ma
With the tip of her lance, she scraped aside the matted hair th
drooped over his left cheek. No scar. She looked up into the gri
and grimy face of Hawk Hunting. He put one foot on the soldier
neck, bent and pulled out the knife he had thrown. With its poin
he scored the scalp and lifted it with an audible tearing.

"Do not leave my side," he said tightly, trying to keep mingle
anger and puzzlement from his eyes as they raked her face. He ha
felt secure leaving her in Fish Jumping's sole charge while she
seemed firm-rooted by shock. But she had recovered now, and i
her expression there was no hint of fear—not even the healthy fe
that breeds caution. Once more her eyes betrayed only the single
mindedness they had reflected since the day she had attached he
self to his war party. That she did not fear for herself made hi
doubly fearful for her.

"Do not leave my side," he repeated. And to be certain she di
not, he grasped her wrist and pulled her along as he moved farth
into the compound. They dodged pairs of men locked in viciou
embrace, stepped over lifeless bodies—and Morning Song resiste
his tug long enough to inspect the faces of those with pale flesh-
and kicked discarded weapons out of their path. Even sporad
shooting had ceased now, but the smoke-braided air was alive wit
the panting of exhausted men and the groans of the wounded, th
ring of lance and sword, the hollow smack of war club against kne
or elbow or temple. And the stench . . . It seemed to Mornin
Song that the clouds massing overhead put pressure on the earth
squeezed out of it the raw-meat smell of skewered flesh, wrun
from it a sludge compounded of blood and excrement and urin
This made a lavish feast for hordes of buzzing flies, an abominatio
the dead ought to have been spared.

Hawk Hunting peered cautiously around each of the low she

they came to, hurried her past their sagging doors. "What soldiers we have not found are probably in their chief's lodge," he told Morning Song, gesturing to the structure whose roof was higher than the stockade itself, "but it is senseless to take unnecessary risks." He hauled her after him when he responded to the hails of the other war leaders, and she would have screamed her resentment if she had not suddenly spied the youth who had been their scout.

He was sprawled on his back, his eyes dull and unseeing. The mouth that had worn a cocky grin was painfully twisted, as though he still felt the slash that had ripped open his belly. His entrails lay in a glistening heap beside him, and Morning Song came close to gagging before she could make herself turn aside.

"There were too few soldiers here," one of Hawk Hunting's companions was grumbling. "Some of my warriors will have no scalps to take home."

"There was not much opportunity for glory," Hawk Hunting conceded. "But at least our losses were small."

Had he seen what happened to the scout? Morning Song wondered bleakly. Then she hardened her heart against the memory. The boy had been warned that war was no game. And Morning Song could not afford to let her resolution be diluted, not even by pity. . . .

"If we fire the fort," Hawk Hunting said, "the soldiers who are elsewhere will have no place to return to. And any *Onondio* who hid from us there will be sorry they did so."

He had freed Morning Song's wrist at last, and she retreated a pace. Once the fort was aflame, everything would be over. With her mission unaccomplished!

She backed away from the trio of gesticulating men, looking around as she went. The scar-faced soldier might have concealed himself anywhere. And the reek of pitch-soaked wood told her that the warriors were building a pyre and fashioning torches for themselves. How could she find the Frenchman before the fire did?

She wrenched open the door of the shed nearest to her and stuck her head inside. Pallets lined one wall, but there was nobody there. She raced to an adjacent one, clearly a storehouse; she poked among the barrels that were piled one atop the other, but this place, too, was empty of people. She started for the next shed, then recalled what Hawk Hunting had said about the building in the center of the compound. Stumbling in her eagerness, she sped toward it—And was promptly overtaken by warriors whose torches flared against the gloomy sky.

She screeched at them to stop, to wait, but they ignored her.

They were competing to see who would be first to apply hungry flame to dry wood, and had no time to spare for anything else.

Morning Song set her jaw and turned again to the outbuildings. So long as there was the slightest chance she might find the man she'd come to kill, she would go on looking for him. It was at least possible that he was cowering within one of the small buildings that hugged the perimeter of the stockade.

Her head swiveled left, right, left again. Which way to go? What did it matter? She spurted diagonally across the compound, tore the hingeless door from a shed, saw at a glance that nothing but rats had been sheltering there. She streaked away, made for a second hovel, was distracted by the gleeful shouts of the warriors. She looked over her shoulder as she ran; the lodge with the peaked roof had been transformed into an inferno. Any sallow-skin who'd looked for sanctuary there had found death instead. And the torchbearers were turning away from it, were making for the lesser structures on the periphery. She must hurry . . . hurry . . . hurry!

She pelted toward the shed looming ahead of her and felt her foot skid as it came down hard on something soft, squishy, yielding. She teetered, flung out her hands, saved herself from falling by slapping her palms against the rough-hewn doorjamb. Gasping for breath, she looked down. Her foot and ankle were dappled with red. She turned slowly, tracing with her eyes the splotches of crimson that led back to the thing she'd stepped on.

There lay a warrior, his splayed limbs half drowned in a ruddy pool that was darkening around the edges. His head, a hideous fixed grin contorting the face, had been severed from his body. A pulpy mass of blood-soaked tissue and pulverized bone marked the place where his neck should have been. In the middle of it was the blurred but recognizable imprint of Morning Song's foot.

Her stomach heaved. The muscles in her throat spasmed. Her mouth filled with a burning, foul-tasting liquid.

She pushed away from the shed's door and bolted around the side of it, vomit spewing from her mouth as she went. She dropped to her knees, bent double as her belly cramped again, surrendered to the retching until sweat gushed from every pore and tears cascaded down her cheeks.

When the siege was over she spat repeatedly and wiped her mouth, her nose, her streaming eyes on the hem of her tunic. Then she got shakily to her feet and reached down with one trembling hand to pull off her blood-soaked moccasin.

She stayed the movement, came fully erect. No. She had sworn that her *hands* would be red with blood before she left this place.

Should she let revulsion thwart her merely because one foot was stained with the stuff?

She would not. Firming her mouth, she marched back the way she had come. Morning Song would investigate every building in sight, even if she stepped on a score of dead bodies in the process.

But her brief surrender to weakness had cost her dearly. By the time she'd burst into and out of only half a dozen more structures, the rest had been fired by the zealous warriors. She was left with no place else to look.

And they were beginning to move the injured now. Morning Song knew she should be helping. They would expect the lone woman in their ranks to comfort the wounded and make them ready for the journey home, she thought bitterly. She returned her war club to her belt, raised her hand to ram her unblooded lance into its deerhide sheath. Disappointment wrestled with anger because all her planning, all her preparations, had been for naught. And there would be no second chance for Morning Song. Not in this.

A moan, so faint she thought at first she'd imagined it, slid beneath the door of the nearest burning shed. She leaned forward, strained her ears—and heard it again.

She tensed. The spirits, it was said, moved in ways incomprehensible to mortals. Had they been testing Morning Song's loyalty, her perseverance, by waiting until the last possible moment to confront her with her destiny?

She touched her knuckles to the boards of the door. They were hot, but not enough to deter her. Tightening her grip on her lance, she yanked the door open. And saw a rectangle crimsoned with flame where the rear wall should have been. The heat she'd given vent to hurtled forward to steal her breath, to singe her eyebrows, and the hair that framed her face.

She pulled back hastily, and would have rushed away if another deep-throated moan had not held her fast. It came from the right, and from low down.

She filled her lungs with fresh air, with somewhat damp fresh air since drizzle was seeping from the lowering clouds, and stooped low before moving into the flamelit shed. She brushed aside curls of smoke and let her smarting eyes sweep the length of the dirt floor. They came to rest on a pale oval, mouth rounded to cry out again. It was an *Onondio*, and a wounded one. As she watched, he bent his head, hunched his shoulders, tried to haul himself away from the flames lapping at his feet. He could not do it.

He raised his head once more, struggled to put out one hand in a gesture of pleading. A smoldering timber blazed suddenly, and light fell across the left side of the man's face. It threw into sharp relief the scar that extended from eyebrow to chin.

Morning Song's eyes, half closed against the stinging smoke, narrowed further. Her heart began to thump with the passion of a water drum during a Pygmy ceremony. Here indeed was the soldier who had driven the spirit from Cloud Racer's body.

Her right arm lifted, her fingers clenched around the haft of her weapon. Now, *now*, she would do what she had come here to do! Her shout of exultation would split the dreary sky and shred the clouds that masked it. The whole world would know that Morning Song had pierced this man's heart with her lance and watched the life gush out of him in a scarlet flood!

The listless rain had gained both weight and energy while Morning Song gloated; before she could deliver the death thrust she was anticipating, it became a torrent. It washed puddles of new-shed blood into the soil, churned the soil into mud, and threatened the rampaging fires with extinction.

Within the half-destroyed shed, the flames roared a counterchallenge, belched great billows of smoke. Morning Song put up her free hand and rubbed her eyes in an effort to clear them. She looked to where her quarry lay; an undulating gray mantle hid him from her.

The smoke she stared into arched and swirled and burgeoned, its paleness streaked with jet where burning pinewood fed it. Suddenly she tensed. The dark streaks were lengthening, widening, coalescing, arranging themselves—with spellbinding deliberation—into the shape of a lean black wolf!

Morning Song scrubbed at her eyes again; it was illusion, she told herself, and would have disappeared when she looked a second time.

The image did not disappear. It sharpened. It separated itself from the paler smoke until she could identify the animal's long legs and bushy tail, the alert ears that crowned its shaggy head, even the ripple of muscle in its powerful shoulders. Yet it was the creature's eyes that mesmerized her; they were not the mistrustful amber ones of a proper wolf, but eyes black as obsidian, eyes that shone with both intelligence and emotion. Morning Song gazed upon a phantom beast, but the eyes that looked back at her were her husband's.

The rain continued to pour down; the fire, although it squawked peevishly, sustained its rage; the man whose life was owed to her lay groaning nearby. But Morning Song, in thrall to an apparition born of smoke, was cocooned from all else.

When the whisper began—the low-pitched rumble she remembered so well—her eyes went to the wolf's massive jaws. They did not move. But the eyes flickered, and something in their depths commanded her to listen, listen. . . .

"This is not the path Morning Song is meant to take." Each word was distinct, set apart from its fellows. *"It cannot bring peace to those death has taken from her. It will not bring peace to Morning Song."*

The bright-bladed lance slipped from her fingers. She dared not speak; and her own shallow breathing, mandated by the air-eating fire, made a rasp in her ears.

"She knows that a single finger has little strength. But the five leaflets of a maple leaf have shown her how five fingers make a hand, a strong hand. Morning Song's strong hand was designed to heal, not to hurt; to bind, not to sever; to nurture, not to destroy."

The furious rainstorm spent itself, and the fire raised its voice triumphantly. It waved banners of red and yellow in celebration, draped them along the two side walls of the shed, and tossed them into the rafters.

Morning Song saw none of this, and she heard only the quiet voice that was—somehow—Cloud Racer's.

"Words, not weapons, are Morning Song's tools, as they were her grandmother's. And she has the power to wield them as skillfully."

Flames locked elbows to perform a macabre dance. The shape that was wolf-yet-not-wolf wavered, began to disintegrate. And the voice that had been Cloud Racer's-and-yet-not-Cloud Racer's faded into nothingness with it. Morning Song gave a short, keening cry, then gasped as a blast of searing heat warned of the fire that was yearning toward her.

She groped for the shoulders of the man who lay motionless on the cinder-strewn floor. Sweat streamed down her face as she dragged him forward inch by agonizing inch. The timbers that had roofed the shed were crashing around them. Sparks mushroomed from their blazing ends and bit savagely when they met succulent flesh.

Vaguely she heard a shout that might have been her name, but she neither called out nor turned her head. What energy she had left must be directed to reaching the doorway with her burden.

Coughing and sputtering, she tumbled through it. And the momentum of her fall brought the inert soldier with her into the fragrant coolness of rainwashed air. Then Hawk Hunting and Fish

Jumping were helping her to her feet, brushing flecks of persistent incandescence from her clothes, her hair.

It was not until he stirred and loosed another of his piteous moans that the warriors paid any heed to the man Morning Song had rescued. "I have taken a captive," she said when they looked at her for explanation. "He has hurt his legs and will not be able to walk. If our warriors refuse to carry the basket we put him in, then it shall be my back that he rides on. This woman has finished with vengeance."

She managed a smile when Hawk Hunting said that he would carry the *Onondio*, but it was a preoccupied one. She was absorbed still by the vision that had come out of the smoke and flame; but there was no confusion in her. Amazement had drained from her, too, leaving her serenely confident that the words spoken by her husband's spirit were as true as any he had spoken during his lifetime. And Cloud Racer had always scorned to speak other than truth.

Her mind raced ahead of her along the trail that was taking them home. What would happen when they arrived at the village, she could not know. The other Matrons might vote to torture and kill the sallow-skin who was her prisoner; Morning Song would argue for deliverance. A life cannot be paid for with a life—and so she would tell them. Her insistence on joining Hawk Hunting's war party had doubtless cost her the the respect of the other women; but with patience, that could be regained. The suggestions and opinions of the Turtle clan's new Matron need not forever fall on deaf ears.

Meanwhile, she had other matters to attend to. *Words, not weapons, are Morning Song's tools.* Well, she had always enjoyed telling stories, ever since she'd been a girl who described pretend-dreams. Now it would be the legends of the Longhouse People that she told, like her grandmother before her. Through her tales, she would introduce her children and their friends to Hiawatha and Dekana-wida, and to the Tree of Long Leaves planted by those farseeing men. What better way to teach future warriors and matrons about the Confederation of Tribes, about the need for the Five Nations to unite for the good of all? And what better way for Morning Song to achieve harmony with her own *orenda*?

In time, this woman might become as skillful a narrator as Teller Of Legends had been. Then others would gather to listen to her tales. And by keeping alive the ancient dream of peace Cloud Racer had cherished, Morning Song would be walking the trail the Maker Of Life had marked for her feet. The trail it had taken her so long to discover.

She lifted her hands, unknotted her pouch, and tipped into one cupped palm the powdered remains of the maple leaf she had treasured for so many years. Then she spread her fingers wide and smiled to see the stuff caught up and scattered by the wind.

A measure of her grief went with it, which was good. The fabric of legend frays on the loom unless laughter is part of the weave.

About the Author

Kate Cameron is an internationally published author whose fascination with aboriginal cultures gives the ring of truth to her fiction. She builds carefully upon information gleaned from methodical research until she has a solid basis for her historical novels. Lately, she has focused on Native American peoples, and her sensitive interpretation of their world enhances her stories of long-ago events.

She is currently working on another Native American project, this one featuring the tribes who once lived near her present-day home in South Florida.